The FATAL

CROWN

Ellen Jones

Simon & Schuster

New York London Toronto Sydney Tokyo Singapore

SIMON & SCHUSTER
Simon & Schuster Building
Rockefeller Center
1230 Avenue of the Americas
New York, New York 10020

Designed by Caroline Cunningham
Title page and part title illustration by Karin E. Sanborn
Manufactured in the United States of America

1   3   5   7   9   10   8   6   4   2

Library of Congress Cataloging-in-Publication Data
Jones, Ellen.
The fatal crown/Ellen Jones.
p.   cm.
1. Matilda, Empress, consort of Henry V, Holy Roman Emperor, 1102–1167—
Fiction.   2. Great Britain—History—Stephen, 1135–1154—Fiction.   I. Title.
PS3560.04817F38   1991
813'.54—dc20   90-49918
                                                                 CIP

ISBN 0-671-72464-9

Acknowledgments

I WOULD LIKE TO ACKNOWLEDGE WITH GRATITUDE THE MANY CARING friends and excellent research facilities that made possible the writing of this book.

I am indebted to the Research and College Libraries of the University of California, the Los Feliz Branch of the Los Angeles Public Library, the Glendale Library, and the Brand Music and Art Library.

Specifically, I would like to thank: Marjorie Miller, whose inspired advice, unfailing support, and encouragement sustained me through many drafts; the gifted writers who belong to my writing group; Eve Caram, of the Writers Program at UCLA Extension, who went through the manuscript and offered invaluable suggestions and changes; Dr. Marie Ann Mayeski, Professor of Theology at Loyola Marymount College, who read the manuscript, corrected any errors, and patiently answered my innumerable questions.

I am also grateful to my agent, Jean Naggar, for taking a chance on an unknown writer and for all her other valuable assistance, and to my editor, Susanne Jaffe, for her warm validation and expert editing.

Finally, I would like to acknowledge all my caring friends, and, most important, my patient, supportive husband, Mark, who not only made it possible for me to write but believed in me through thick and thin. There are no words to express the depth of my gratitude.

Introduction

IN THE EARLY MIDDLE AGES IN ENGLAND SUCCESSION WAS NOT HERED-
itary. Conquest, descent, and the agreement of the feudal lords all
played their part in determining who gained the royal title; for a
century before the story opens the crown had usually been seized by
armed force.

In 1066 Duke William Bastard sailed from Normandy to England,
defeated the Saxon king, Harold, at the Battle of Hastings, and
claimed the English crown by right of conquest.

In 1087, King William I died, to be succeeded in England by his
second son, William Rufus, and in Normandy by his eldest son,
Robert. His youngest son, Henry, was left silver but no land. Although Robert, Duke of Normandy, fought his brother, William, for
the English crown, he was unsuccessful.

In 1100, King William Rufus was killed in a hunting accident under
questionable circumstances. His elder brother, Robert, was away on
the First Crusade, and the throne was seized without opposition by
his younger brother, Henry. Despite rumors that Henry was an ac-
cessory to his brother's death, had even arranged it, nothing was ever
proved. Nine centuries later historians still debate the issue. As one
noted British historian, Christopher Brooke, summed it up: If Wil-

liam Rufus's death in August 1100 was an accident, Henry I was an exceptionally lucky man.*

In 1106 Henry invaded Normandy, defeated his eldest brother, Robert, then imprisoned him for life, thus becoming Duke of Normandy as well as King of England as his father had been.

Henry married a Scottish princess, Matilda, of the old royal Saxon line, and by her had three children. One died in infancy; the other two, twins, a boy and girl, survived. Henry I begat numerous bastards but the twins, descended through the male line of William the Conqueror, remained his only legitimate children. His son, William, was named heir to the English throne and the Duchy of Normandy. But in the event that anything should happen to him, who then would rule?

* Christopher Brooke, *The Norman and Saxon Kings*.

Author's Note

THIS TALE IS A WORK OF FICTION SET AGAINST THE BACKDROP OF HIS-
tory. The characters, with few exceptions, are real and have their
places in history. Many of the incidents depicted actually occurred;
others, based on rumor and gossip, have no basis in historical fact.
The chronology of events in the twelfth century often varies from
chronicler to chronicler. In order to facilitate the pace of the story, I
have taken my own liberties with dates, locations, and the nature of
the event.

Main Cast of Characters

HOUSE OF NORMANDY
  MAUD, *daughter of Henry I*
  HENRY I, *King of England and Duke of Normandy, youngest son of William the Conqueror*
  ADELICIA OF LOUVAIN, *second wife to Henry I*
  ALDYTH, *Saxon nurse and godmother to Maud*

HOUSE OF GLOUCESTER
  ROBERT, *Earl of Gloucester, bastard son of Henry I*
  MABEL OF GLAMORGAN, *Robert's wife*
  WILLIAM AND PHILLIP, *two of their sons*

HOUSE OF BLOIS
  STEPHEN, *third son of Adela, daughter of William the Conqueror*
  HENRY, *Stephen's younger brother*
  MATILDA OF BOULOGNE, *Stephen's wife*
  EUSTACE, *Stephen's son*

HOUSE OF ANJOU
GEOFFREY, *Count of Anjou and Maine*
HENRY, *his eldest son*

HOUSE OF SCOTLAND
DAVID, *King of Scotland*

HOUSE OF MUELAN
THE DE BEAUMONT TWINS:
WALERAN, *Count of Muelan*
ROBERT "Robin," *Earl of Leicester*

OTHERS
BRIAN FITZCOUNT, *Lord of Wallingford, bastard son of the Count of Brittany*
MILES FITZWALTER, *Sheriff of Gloucester*
RANULF, *Earl of Chester*

PEERS OF THE CHURCH
HENRY OF BLOIS, *Stephen's youngest brother, Abbot of Glastonbury, later Bishop of Winchester and Papal Legate*
ROGER, *Bishop of Salisbury, Chief Administrator to Henry I*
THEOBALD OF BEC, *an Archbishop of Canterbury*
ULGAR, *Bishop of Angers*
WILLIAM OF CORBEIL, *an Archbishop of Canterbury*

Descendants of William I as of 1125

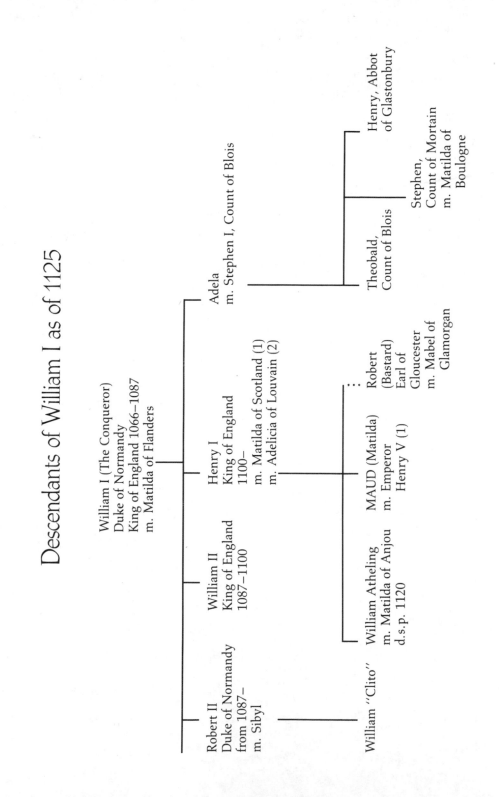

William I (The Conqueror)
Duke of Normandy
King of England 1066–1087
m. Matilda of Flanders

Robert II
Duke of Normandy
from 1087–
m. Sibyl

William II
King of England
1087–1100

Henry I
King of England
1100–
m. Matilda of Scotland (1)
m. Adelicia of Louvain (2)

Adela
m. Stephen I, Count of Blois

William "Clito"

William Atheling
m. Matilda of Anjou
d.s.p. 1120

MAUD (Matilda)
m. Emperor
Henry V (1)

Robert
(Bastard)
Earl of
Gloucester
m. Mabel of
Glamorgan

Theobald,
Count of Blois

Stephen,
Count of Mortain
m. Matilda of
Boulogne

Henry, Abbot
of Glastonbury

THE
FATAL CROWN

Our fatal acts our angels are, or good or ill,
Our fatal shadows that walk by us still.

—Fletcher

The Normans are a turbulent race and, unless restrained by a
firm government, are always ready for mischief. They are eager
for rebellion, ripe for tumults, and alert for every sort of crime.

—Orderic Vitalis,
monk and chronicler

All things to nothingness descend,
Grow old and die and meet their end;
Man dies, iron rusts, wood goes decayed,
Towers fall, walls crumble, roses fade. . . .
Nor long shall any name resound
Beyond the grave, unless 't be found
In some clerk's book; it is the pen
Gives immortality to men.

—Master Wace,
Chronicle of the Norman Dukes

PART ONE

Prologue

Normandy, 1125

AFTER A MONTH'S JOURNEY ACROSS EUROPE THE ROYAL PROCESSION OF litters, sumpter horses, and carts finally arrived at the King's camp in Normandy. Maud stepped from her litter into a lush green meadow and looked curiously about her. From this land, she realized, her grandfather, William, called the Conqueror, had set sail for England fifty-nine years ago. Her eyes passed across a narrow strip of river to the opposite shore. Through the early morning mist she could make out an array of brightly colored pavilions. Surrounded by a profusion of knights, archers, and squires, a scarlet tent, larger than the rest, boasted a red-and-gold banner blowing arrogantly in the autumn wind: the standard of her father, Henry, King of England and Duke of Normandy.

With slender jeweled fingers Maud slipped off the hood of her black mourning cloak. Mingled rage and apprehension coiled like twin snakes in the pit of her belly. She had been sent from her father's court when she was nine years old, to be the bride of the Holy Roman Emperor of Germany. Now, fourteen years later, the Emperor was dead, and she had been summoned by her father, against her will, to return to his domains. As she stared fixedly at the King's pavilion,

Maud knew that the determination of her fate lay behind those scarlet walls.

Startled by the sound of hooves ringing on stone, Maud turned to see a party of richly dressed nobles riding smartly across the arched stone bridge that spanned the river. They must be headed for the King's camp, she thought, to meet her. Assaulted by a terrible sense of futility, the impulse to weep, to succumb to despair, was almost overpowering. No, Maud thought fiercely, she would not, must not, show the slightest sign of weakness. No one must suspect how lost and vulnerable she felt, how much she dreaded this meeting with her father, a virtual stranger, whom she had not seen since she was a child.

The sound of a splash, followed by a sudden movement in the clump of green reeds growing by the river, caught her attention. Her eyes searched the bank but could see nothing. An intimation of danger, a tiny ripple of alarm, passed through her. Was it her imagination or did someone lie hidden in the reeds observing her? She knew she should return to the tent and prepare for the upcoming meeting with her father, but she found herself impelled toward the clump of reeds.

With a half-guilty, half-defiant look over her shoulder, Maud slipped off her cloak and headed for the river. Her shoes sank into the muddy grass, so she stooped to remove them, then her black stockings as well. The feeling of her bare feet against the soft moist ground was delicious. Running lightly over the grass, she stopped just short of the river.

The reeds slowly parted and before Maud's astonished gaze the torso of a naked man rose up from the riverbank. For a moment she had the wild thought that she had come upon a woodland god, the legendary Pan of ancient Greek fable that she had heard about. She caught a quick glimpse of wide shoulders; wet honey-colored hair framed an arresting face with high cheekbones, a curved sensual mouth, and cleft chin. Under tawny brows, arched like the wings of a hawk, green eyes flecked with gold locked with hers. Maud's heart lurched within her breast; danger, fear, excitement—which it was she could not plainly tell. With a sudden surge of recognition, her breath caught in her throat. The moment, reverberating like a cathedral bell, catapulted her back to another time, another place.

Chapter One

England, 1111

MAUD, PRINCESS OF ENGLAND, SHRANK BACK AGAINST THE DAMP stone wall of her father's castle. The fat greyhound puppy, Beau, clutched tightly against her small body, growled softly. Around the corner of the narrow passage she could hear the ominous tread of booted feet coming toward her. It must be one of the guards.

Where could she hide? If no one could find her, she thought, suddenly hopeful, the Imperial escort might leave Windsor without her. Holy Mother, she prayed, do not let them take me away to Germany to be married. Cautiously, she looked down the still deserted passageway and saw the nail-studded oak door of her mother's solar slightly ajar. Running toward it, Maud pushed the door open and slipped inside. Her eyes scanned the open casement window, gold and scarlet tapestries swaying in the April breeze, the royal arms emblazoned on the walls, the prie-dieu and ivory crucifix. The room was empty.

Her disappointment was so intense that her head started throbbing. Yet what else had she expected? When had the Queen of England, her mother, ever been a refuge? But today, of all the days in her nine years of life, today when her need was desperate, she had hoped it would be different.

The sound of heavy footsteps stopped just outside the solar. Maud darted toward the tapestries, sliding quickly behind the soft folds just as someone pushed open the door. Sick with dread, she buried her face in Beau's silken fur.

"Maud! Where are you, child?" She winced at the sound of Aldyth's anxious voice. Distant kinswoman of her Saxon mother, Aldyth had acted as combination nurse and foster mother ever since her birth. "I know you're here, a guard saw you open the door. Maud! Come out at once!"

Maud's heart thumped so loudly she was sure Aldyth must hear it. The puppy, struggling to be free, gave a sharp bark. Footsteps approached the tapestries.

"By the Rood, here you are!" Aldyth's plump arm reached behind the tapestries, jerking her out. "What mischief is this? The Emperor's escort is ready to leave for Germany, and I have run out of excuses to feed your father." She paused. "He's threatening to whip you."

Aldyth scanned Maud's appearance with critical concern. The thick, cinnamon-colored hair, twined with gilt ribbon, fell in two plaits to the tiny waist, framing a creamy oval face. From under dark feathered brows, luminous eyes the color of pewter stared fearfully at Aldyth. The slender body, almost lost in the saffron gown and amber velvet tunic, was stiff with fear. Aldyth's face softened and she made a clucking sound as she straightened the skirt of Maud's gown.

"No tears or tantrums, my child. The King is not to be trifled with this morning. Give me that animal." She pried the puppy loose from Maud's grasp and set it on its feet. "Come." She held out her hand.

Maud shrank back against the tapestries. "I don't want to leave England, Aldyth. Oh, please, can't you find a way for me to stay?"

"What has come over you, child? You've known for months that you must leave in April. The betrothal ceremony is to be held next month."

Maud stared at her in stricken silence. It was true. She had known she was to travel to Germany in order to become the betrothed of the powerful Holy Roman Emperor, a man close to her father's age, ever since his envoys had arrived at the English court to ask for her hand a year ago. The offer had been presented to her as a great honor for the House of Normandy. At the time, the prospect of going to strange places had seemed exciting, an adventure she could lord over her twin brother, William, her father's heir and the focal point of everyone's attention. But now that the moment had actually arrived, she was filled with fear and anguish.

"Come, my poppet," Aldyth continued in a wheedling voice. "Let us find your father and tell him you're ready to go." She held out a plump hand.

Maud's lower lip began to tremble. "Where is Madam, my mother?"

"The Queen is in the chapel, praying you will have a safe journey."

"All she does is pray," Maud murmured with an unaccustomed surge of bitterness, wondering, not for the first time, how her mother had managed to become a queen when she behaved in all aspects like a nun. How could she have believed for a moment that the pious Queen would be able to protect her against her formidable father?

She knew it was wicked to have such thoughts about her devout mother, but at the moment she did not care; her pent-up fears suddenly burst out of control.

"Please, please, please don't make me go," she cried. In despair she threw herself onto the newly spread rushes of the solar floor. The soft grasses mixed with wildflowers felt cool against her burning cheeks.

Suddenly the door of the solar swung open with terrifying force. Henry, King of England and Duke of Normandy, strode into the solar, two greyhound pups snapping at his heels. He was followed by his only legitimate son, Prince William, and the eldest of his bastard sons, Robert. The King's hooded black eyes widened in disapproval when he saw Maud on her knees.

"By God's splendor, Mistress, what wickedness is this? Get up at once!"

Mortified, Maud rose hastily to her feet, brushing bits of grass off her skirts. Her father, his bull-like frame clad in rusty brown tunic and hose, the crown of England planted firmly on his dark head, folded thick muscular arms across a broad chest.

"What is the meaning of this unseemly behavior?" His soft voice held a threatening undertone. "The emperor's ambassador, Graf von Hennstien, grows impatient to leave."

"I don't want to go to Germany to be married, Sire," Maud said in a choked voice.

"Not want to go? Not want to go?" Henry turned to the two boys. "Did you hear that, my sons? I arrange the finest match in Christendom for your sister and the ungrateful creature refuses to go!"

Henry swung round and scowled at Maud. "What in God's name is the difficulty now? Are you squeamish about the marriage itself?

I've already explained that it won't be celebrated until you are thirteen, but the betrothal ceremony has been arranged for May since last year. This was a convenient time for the Emperor and the plans cannot be altered now."

He hooked his thumbs in the wide leather belt encircling his waist and began to pace the solar on legs bowed from many hours in the saddle. He strode to the prie-dieu with its pale blue cushion, wheeled around, and walked back to Maud. The two pups tumbled after him, joined by Maud's puppy, the runt of the litter.

"I just don't want to leave home," Maud whispered. "Please, I beg of you, let me remain in England."

"Where is the Queen?" Henry asked Aldyth, ignoring Maud. "Why isn't she here to deal with this coil? Why are such tasks left always to me?"

"She's in the chapel, Sire," the Saxon nurse replied.

The King glowered at Maud. "I need not have asked. If your mother spent less time on her knees and more time teaching you the rudiments of proper behavior we would all be better served!" He took a menacing step in her direction, as if she were to blame for the Queen's absence.

"Robert—don't let him send me away." In desperation, Maud ran to her half-brother, a sturdy youth of fourteen, with deep-set dark eyes and brown hair, a gentler version of his father. They had developed a deep affection for each other ever since Robert had come to live at court three years earlier.

"Think of all the merry times you will have, Sister," her half-brother said, as he put an arm around her shoulders.

"There's no more time to waste," Henry said. "Robert, fetch me a riding whip from the stables."

Robert's face paled. He tightened his arm protectively around Maud's shoulders. "Let me talk to Maud alone, Sire. I can convince her to be reasonable."

"The time for talk is over. A disobedient child is like an unwilling ass. It must be made to obey. Get me the whip."

"I'll get one for you, Father." Maud's twin brother, William, flaxen-haired and blue-eyed, gave his sister a nasty smile as he ran from the solar.

"Do you think to shame me before the Emperor's escort? To make me the laughingstock of Europe? By God's splendor, I'll teach you a lesson you won't soon forget."

At the ominous tone in her father's voice, Maud's stomach twisted into a coiled knot; terrified, she clung to her brother like a leech.

William ran into the solar waving a short leather whip in one hand. "Here, Sire." He brandished the whip above his head with a triumphant smirk.

As far back as Maud could remember William had hated her. Jealous of her place in the King's affections, which he resented sharing with a girl who was quicker at her lessons and more skilled at games, he lost no opportunity to be cruel, consistently rejecting her clumsy attempts to win his love. Now, enraged and hurt at her twin's gloating expression, Maud suddenly leapt at William, knocking him headlong to the ground. The whip flew from his grasp, and he set up a loud howl as she fell upon him. Clawing, biting, pulling at his flaxen curls, Maud managed to leave several scratches on her brother's pink and white face before Robert succeeded in prying her loose.

King Henry picked up the whip and slapped the leather thongs into his open palm. "Come here, girl, we'll soon exorcise that willful demon."

Maud clutched at Robert with all her strength but Aldyth dragged her rigid body across the rushes to the King. William continued to lie on the ground, sniveling and whimpering.

"Stop bleating like a goat," King Henry growled. "You ought to be ashamed, William, letting a girl get the better of you. If you don't learn to defend yourself more successfully, what kind of a prince will you make, eh?" He gave his son a hard look, before muttering under his breath, "I always said Maud should have been the boy."

William turned crimson. His sobs abated as he rose to his feet and wiped his dripping nose with the sleeve of his grubby tan jerkin. Hatred gleamed in his pale blue eyes as he glanced at his sister.

As the King approached, Maud, her face white and pinched, slowly backed away. His hand shot out and grabbed her shoulder with fingers of steel. She twisted away from his grasp, almost wrenching her arm from its socket, then ran toward the bed, stumbled against an oak table, and fell to her knees. Quicker than the blink of an eye he was beside her. She tried to crawl under the table but his booted black foot barred her way. Maud saw his arm lift in a menacing gesture, heard the sound of the whip whistling through the air as his hand descended. Through her gown and tunic she could feel a stinging pain as the leather thongs bit into her back.

Her body sagged forward against her knees. She made no outcry but bit her lip, drawing blood. Tears welled up in her gray eyes and rolled down her cheeks.

"Stop that weeping at once," Henry commanded sternly as he towered over her. "A granddaughter of the Conqueror does not cry, no matter how great the provocation. Never did I see my mother shed a single tear."

Beau began to howl. Henry reached down to pat the sleek gray head. Straightening, he again lifted his arm.

Maud swallowed convulsively, brushing the tears away with her hand. Tightly screwing her eyes shut, she squared her shoulders, tensing herself for the next blow.

"How stupid Maud is," William said to Robert in a spiteful voice. "Imagine not wanting to be a queen."

Henry glanced swiftly toward William, then down at Maud. After a moment he lowered his arm, slapping the whip thoughtfully against his thigh. Squatting down in front of her, he lifted Maud's chin with his strong fingers.

"Your brother William is wrong, is he not? Surely you wish to be a queen, an empress?"

"Yes," she whispered, with a defiant look at her brother, willing to agree to anything that would make the despicable William wrong.

Tossing aside the whip, Henry slowly lifted the crown from his head, and put it solemnly into her hands. The gold plates studded with sapphires and rubies felt cool and heavy against her fingers.

"Men have fought and died to possess this crown," he said, his eyes fixed upon her in an unblinking stare. "Your grandfather, the great William, took it by conquest amid much bloodshed and suffering. Regard it well." He paused as she looked down. "It represents power, wealth, respect. Everything that matters in this world. When you become an empress such a crown will be yours."

With everyone's eyes on her, Maud turned the glittering gold plates over and over in her hands. Such a small thing, really, to carry so much importance.

"To refuse this opportunity would be considered the deadliest insult imaginable, Daughter." Henry leaned toward her, his voice low and conspiratorial. "After all, you have been promised to the Emperor, agreements have been made. Think of the disgrace. Would you bring his wrath down upon our house because you were too cowardly to leave home?"

"What would he do?" she whispered. Her father's familiar odor of horses, sweat, and damp leather was particularly strong this morning.

"Attack England perhaps. His army is vastly superior to mine. To offend so mighty a prince—would you put us all at risk?"

Fighting back the tears, Maud knew further resistance would be futile. The whipping alone would not have budged her, but now she felt as if the welfare of the realm rested upon her shoulders. What could she do? There was no choice.

"I would not bring disgrace upon our house," she said, feeling more alone than she had ever felt in her life.

"There speaks the true Norman princess! I knew you wouldn't fail me." With a smile of quiet satisfaction, Henry stood up, then reached for the crown.

Reluctantly, for the gold plates had started to have a reassuring pressure against her hands, Maud gave it back to him. Henry placed the crown on his head, then held out his hand to help her up.

By midday, as the church bells tolled for Sext, Maud stood in the courtyard, surrounded by her family and members of the court. The mild April morning had turned chill; the sky, heavy with dark clouds threatening rain, reflected her inner despair. She noticed three new children of noble birth, two of them twins, who had just arrived from Brittany and Muelan to be brought up at the court of the English king. Another boy, Maud's first cousin, Stephen, son of her father's sister, was also due to arrive today from across the channel. The look of abject misery on the faces of the three young strangers as they huddled together filled Maud with compassion. Her heart went out to them but a similar ordeal awaited her in Germany and she could offer no solace.

"It has cost this land dear to dower you properly, Daughter," her father said, weighing the enormous procession of carts, men, and beasts assembled before him.

Maud's eyes followed his. A goodly number of sumpter horses and carts carrying bolts of silk and wool, pelts of fox and ermine, jewels and ivory caskets, stood massed together while Norman and German knights, restive on their huge chargers, paraded up and down the courtyard. An array of waiting litters already held Norman ladies-in-waiting as well as her nurse Aldyth, clergymen, servants, and the Emperor's ambassador, Graf von Hennstien, with his entourage. Two men-at-arms rode in the cart carrying a wooden chest with Maud's dowry of thousands of silver coins.

Suddenly Henry looked round him with a scowl. "Jesu, where is the Queen? Go to the chapel and bring her here at once," he ordered a servant.

A short while later Queen Matilda appeared, out of breath, her face white as alabaster. She was accompanied by her confessor and several priests. Gaunt, almost wasted from long hours of fasting, the Queen was dressed in a plain white wool gown. A simple wooden crucifix adorned her neck and thick flaxen braids formed a coronet around her head. As was usual for her mother during Lent, she had gone to chapel with bare feet, and Maud knew she would be wearing a hair shirt next to her skin.

"Mea culpa," she said, with an apprehensive glance at her husband, as she knelt to take Maud in her arms. "Forgive me. I was in the midst of kissing the feet of the blessed poor and did not realize you were ready to leave."

Having often seen the ulcerous and bleeding feet of the beggars that came to the castle gates, Maud hastily turned her lips away so that her mother's kiss fell on the side of her head.

"May our Blessed Lady send you safe to Germany." She pressed a crude wooden rosary into Maud's damp palm.

"Fare well, Sister," Robert said, holding Maud's puppy in his arms. "I'll miss you." He leaned forward to kiss her hot cheek. "I'll take good care of Beau."

She saw that his eyes were unnaturally bright. Why, he's the only one who really cares that I'm leaving, Maud thought. She cast a longing glance at the small dog, wishing she could take him with her.

William stuck out his tongue, then ran off without a backward look.

"The Graf is ready," King Henry said, as he lifted Maud into the immense gilded litter hitched between two roan mares.

For a moment he stared at her, then reached into the leather purse at his belt. "This was my mother's." He held up a plain silver ring suspended from a finely wrought chain, then slipped the chain around her neck. He patted her cheek with an awkward gesture. "Try to be worthy of your Norman heritage," he added in a gruff voice, then abruptly turned away.

As the long procession wound its way across the outer bailey of Windsor Castle, through the open gates, and started down the road, Maud looked longingly over her shoulder. Numb with suppressed grief, she felt as if she were going into a long exile from which she would never return. The brutal wrench of this parting was unbearable. She reached over to clutch Aldyth's hand. The horses turned a corner; the castle was no longer in sight. Far down the road she could

just make out five riders and a sumpter horse laden with packs approaching the litter.

"That must be Maurice, returning with your cousin, young Stephen of Blois," Aldyth said, giving Maud's hand a reassuring squeeze
as she looked ahead. "I hear the lad has caused so much trouble at
home his mother had to send him away to your father's court. They
say that—"

Maud closed her eyes, unable to listen to her nurse's steady stream
of gossip. Yet something Aldyth said struck a responsive note. Both
she and Stephen of Blois were leaving their native lands at the same
time. It was like a bond between them.

Stephen of Blois saw a cloud of dust ahead that signaled a large
procession. His heart jumped a beat.

"Who is raising all that dust?" he asked the grizzled knight, Maurice, who, along with two men-at-arms, had met Stephen and his
squire, Gervase, at the port of Dover yesterday morning.

"That must be young Princess Maud," the knight replied, a note
of pride in his voice. "Due to leave for Germany today for her betrothal to the Holy Roman Emperor."

Stephen recalled his mother, Countess Adela of Blois, reminding
him of his twin cousins, Maud and William, before he left for England. She had probably mentioned the impending betrothal as well
but he had forgotten it among the host of instructions she had given
him. At the thought of the Countess, Stephen's belly tightened into
a hard knot. His mind returned to that fateful morning, barely a
month ago, when matters had come to a head between his mother
and himself. But for the events of that day, he would not be in
England now.

It had been a cold Sunday in March during the Feast of Annuncia-
tion, which coincided with his younger brother Henry's departure for
the Benedictine monastery at Cluny. Arriving long after the meal
started, Stephen had slipped quietly into a seat at the end of the table,
hoping not to be noticed.

"Where have you been?" his mother asked with an accusing
glance, spotting him immediately. "As your brother leaves for Cluny
tomorrow, you might have had the courtesy to attend the feast on
time."

"I was in the stables," he mumbled, "tending to my stallion. He

—he lost a shoe." Without much hope, for she continued to regard him with suspicion, Stephen prayed his mother would let it go at that.

The Countess, formidable in black and crimson, presided at the high table flanked by her sons Theobald and Henry, her daughter Cicily, and a handful of guests. A tree trunk burned in the vast hearth, filling the cavernous hall with warmth against the chill March wind whistling through the cracks in the tapestry-covered walls.

Ten-year-old Henry repressed a smile as he threw a piece of fish to the hounds sniffing and yelping hungrily in the rushes under the table. Tearing a chunk from the wheaten loaf on the table, Stephen gave his brother a warning look from green-gold eyes.

The Countess, catching the brief exchange, turned on her youngest son with the swiftness of a cat pouncing upon a mouse. "Aha! Why was Stephen late, Henry? What has he been up to?"

Two years younger than his brother, Henry had light brown hair and pale green eyes that carefully avoided his mother's relentless gaze. "Ah, nothing, Madam," he murmured.

Adela, about to attack a boiled carp covered in a thick white sauce, paused to give both boys a speculative look. "I can always tell when you are protecting him, Henry. What has the rascal done now?"

Henry swallowed, a bright flush appearing on his cheeks. "I—that is to say—what has he done?" He stammered, giving his brother a guilty look.

"You heard me. Out with it, my son. No harm will come to you if you speak the truth."

Henry gave a sigh of capitulation. "Stephen was in the stables— playing with the steward's daughter. I saw them. Stephen was—" He glanced at his elder sister, Cicily, who was following his words with breathless interest.

"Traitor!" Stephen's eyes blazed with green fire. "You promised!"

Adela pushed her trencher of bread aside. "What was he doing? Speak up."

"Her skirts were up over her head, his hose was down, and he was —you know—" Henry colored even more deeply. "Touching her here." He touched his chest with a look of disgust. "And down there." He pointed vaguely in the direction of his feet, then turned toward his brother with an air of righteous innocence. "I'm sorry, Stephen, but I cannot lie for you all the time."

His face scarlet, Stephen rose from the table and leapt at his brother, knocking him from the bench into the rushes, disturbing two hounds quarreling over the fish. Cicily began to shriek.

"Telltale!" Stephen began to pummel his brother with clenched fists. "Rotten little piece of horse dung."

"Stephen, I've warned you over and over to stay away from the steward's daughter!" Adela was on her feet now, gray eyes snapping in a face white with anger. "Her father has promised the wench to a knight and if you have tampered with her maidenhead it will be the worse for you! Twelve years of age and lecherous as a stag in rut! Why I haven't cut your stones and member off before now— By God's splendor, Theo, do something!"

Henry, unperturbed despite a bloody nose, was finally extricated from a tangle of snapping dogs and Stephen's blows by his eldest brother, the stolid and dutiful Theobald, newly knighted Count of Blois. Adela, whose temper was on a short rein at the best of times, walked around the table to where Stephen stood brushing wisps of dried grass from his green tunic. She began to cuff him about the head and ears.

"Lustful young hothead," she shouted. "Troublemaker. What is to be done with you? Disobedient, picking quarrels! Is that any way for a grandson of the Conqueror to behave?"

"Then send me away," Stephen shouted back, trying to duck her blows. "You don't want me at Blois. You've always hated me!"

Adela curled her fingers into a fist and hit him with all her strength. Stephen reeled, putting a hand to the livid red welt that marred the high arch of his cheekbone.

"May God strike you dumb for saying such a monstrous thing about your own mother!" Her face purple with rage, Adela drew back her arm for another blow.

"It's true, you know it's true!" Tears of anger and frustration welled up in Stephen's eyes. "Just because I look like my father. Is that my fault?"

The moment the words were out, Stephen was aghast at his folly. What madness had prompted him to remind his mother of her late husband? During the crusade, Count Stephen of Blois, in the midst of a battle with the Turks in the Holy Land, had deserted his men and fled back to his country. Forced by his indomitable countess to return, he had eventually died a respectable death, but it was the earlier cowardice everyone remembered. His name was never mentioned in Adela's presence. Now there was absolute silence in the great hall as the servants, the steward, members of the castle mesnie, the guests, and Stephen's brothers and sister stared at him in horror.

"How dare you remind me of that spineless coward!" Adela screamed, looking wildly about the room. "Someone get me the horsewhip from the stables. At once!"

Half the servants and the steward ran to do her bidding, almost falling over themselves in their haste to get out of the hall.

The Countess glowered at Stephen, her bosom heaving, her eyes reflecting the familiar look of grim hostility that he had come to realize was probably directed at the memory of his weak father, for Stephen closely resembled the Count and bore his name. But whatever its cause, he alone of all her children carried the brunt of his mother's savage antagonism.

Still wiping the blood from his nose and face, Henry approached his mother. "If Stephen wants to leave Blois, then send him away as he asks. Let him go to our uncle in England."

Theo and Cicily turned to stare at their brother. Adela's face slowly returned to its normal color as she looked at her youngest son.

"Why would I wish to inflict this monster upon my brother Henry?"

"As a punishment, Madam, of course," he replied. "He deserves to be banished. Surely our uncle would teach Stephen manners, courtesy, discipline, all those things you so rightly complain about. He would learn respect and obedience at the King of England's court."

Unable to believe his good fortune, Stephen looked from his mother to his brother. "England? You would send me to England?" He could not keep a note of elation from his voice.

"You don't mean to say you want to go?" his mother asked in a steely voice, her eyes narrowing. "In that case—"

"Of course he doesn't want to go, do you, Stephen?" Henry interjected hastily, shooting him a warning look. "He would really hate to leave Blois, wouldn't you?"

"Yes, of course," he mumbled.

His mother's face cleared. "Well, then, I think it an excellent idea. But this will be your last chance, Stephen. If you don't make something of yourself at my brother's court, I wash my hands of you. You won't be welcome in Blois again."

Dismissing him, Adela turned to Henry. "A good thought, my son. Always so clever." She patted him absently on the head. "I shall inform King Henry this very day."

A servant came running into the hall carrying a whip.

"What is that for? Take it back to the stables." She stalked majestically out of the great hall followed by Theo and Cicily.

England, Stephen repeated to himself, I'm to go to England. Infinitely relieved at the prospect of leaving Blois and his violent-tempered mother, who clearly preferred his brothers to himself, he looked wonderingly at Henry, the cause of this unexpected reprieve.

"Thank you, Brother," he said. "You've done me a good service this day."

His brother gave him an affectionate smile. "I hope you'll remember it. When I complete my studies at the monastery I expect to join you in England. By then you must see to it that our uncle has arranged a good position for me in the church."

Stephen nodded. He hadn't the faintest idea how he would accomplish what Henry wanted, but there was time enough to find a way. As always, he found himself impressed—and slightly disquieted—by the artful manner in which Henry so easily manipulated their irascible mother.

Four weeks later Stephen left Blois to set sail for England. Although he was happy to be going, he knew he would never forget that Henry had been sent from home with honor, as a reward, while he was leaving in disgrace, as a punishment.

There was a sudden shout of warning as Maud's litter almost collided with a young boy coming from the other direction. Startled, Maud looked up. Honey-colored waves of hair spilled out from under a scarlet cap perched jauntily on his head. The boy's handsome face, streaked with dust, turned swiftly in her direction. Dazzling green eyes flecked with gold—cat's eyes—met her gray ones in a long curious stare. Just before his horse rounded the corner, a smile touched his lips. He whipped off his cap, bowing his head to her. Then he and the other riders were lost to view.

Maud lay back in the litter. So that was her difficult cousin, Stephen of Blois. For a moment the boy's image, clear as a brush stroke on vellum, stayed in her mind. A wave of emotion she could not identify washed over her, rousing her briefly from the depths of her anguish. She shivered, as if a wolf had walked over her grave, a premonition of trouble, Aldyth would say. Then the feeling passed; the boy's image faded. Misery again settled over her like a shroud. One life was over; a new life not yet born.

Chapter Two

Germany, 1111

Iᴛ ᴡᴀs ᴇᴀʀʟʏ ᴍᴀʏ ʙᴇꜰᴏʀᴇ ᴍᴀᴜᴅ ʀᴇᴀᴄʜᴇᴅ ᴛʜᴇ ɢᴇʀᴍᴀɴ ᴄɪᴛʏ ᴏꜰ ᴍᴀɪɴᴢ where she had been told the emperor would meet her. But when they arrived at the cheerless stone palace at the hour of Vespers he had not yet arrived. Instead, she was greeted by a group of stiff middle-aged men dressed in somber colors of gray and dark brown, and a brittle thin woman with a face like a hatchet and a faint mustache across her upper lip. She wore a dark gray tunic, a white wimple covered her head, and she regarded Maud with a severe expression. Graf von Hennstien, her escort from England, had disappeared along with everyone else in her party, including Aldyth. No one explained anything and when Maud asked a question they replied in German, which she did not understand.

She was given a chunk of black bread dipped in warm milk and put to bed in a huge dank chamber whose walls were covered with dark red and blue tapestries depicting the torments of the holy martyrs. The pictures of burning and other tortures were so vividly represented that Maud pulled the coverlet over her head. Miserable and lonely, she clutched the silver ring her father had given her and cried herself to sleep.

When she woke the next morning there was still no sign of Aldyth.

Sick with fear and uncertainty, badly missing Beau, she huddled under the fur-lined coverlet wishing with all her heart that she was back in England. The same gray-clad woman who had met her yesterday entered her chamber, said something in German, then dressed her in the saffron-colored gown and amber tunic in which she had left England. Around her neck she placed an ornate gold cross set with pearls that Maud had never seen before, and led her down the staircase to the courtyard. Outside, the sky was overcast with gray clouds, the air warm and sluggish. They climbed into a waiting litter and were carried a short distance to where a large church stood in the middle of a cobbled square, just as the bells rang for Prime.

Inside the church, crowded with worshippers, it was cold and dim, penetrated by only a faint ray of light. As Maud was led down the aisle to her pew, she could see people craning their necks to catch a glimpse of her. The odor of incense, the chanting of the choir, the solemn intonation of the office made her head spin. At last the Mass was over and she was carried back to the palace.

When Maud returned to her chamber, she was met by the Graf von Hennstien. Thank the Holy Mother, here was someone who understood Norman French.

"Where is Aldyth?" she asked.

"I regret, Prinzessin, but all your entourage is to be sent back to England on the Emperor's orders."

Stunned, Maud felt an icy chill seep through her body. Send Aldyth away? The Emperor could not be so cruel. Tears welled up in her eyes but she forced them back, remembering her father's injunction that a granddaughter of the Conqueror did not cry.

"Why?" she whispered.

The Graf glanced uneasily around the austere chamber. "The Emperor feels you will learn German more quickly and adjust easily to your new surroundings if you are not constantly reminded of England."

"I want Aldyth back," she said in a choked voice.

"I regret, that is not possible. Come, do you realize what a very fortunate little girl you are? The Emperor is a most powerful monarch, his influence extends south into Italy and as far east as Hungary."

The names meant nothing to her. "I want to go home. At once."

"I regret, that is not possible. All the arrangements for the betrothal ceremony have been made."

"Then I'll return to England afterward."

"But of course you cannot return to England, Prinzessin. Afterward you will live in Germany and learn the language and our customs. By the time you are married, at thirteen, you will be a proper
German, hein?"

Maud did not answer.

"Now eat. You must keep up your strength. The Emperor arrives
this morning, do you wish him to see you in such a sorry state?"

Unable to control her tears, she tried to wipe them away with the
sleeve of her tunic.

The Graf turned to the woman and said something in German. She
nodded, walked toward Maud, took her briskly by the hand, and led
her to a small table set with a bowl of milk, a loaf of bread, and a
plate of something that smelled like salted fish.

"Eat," said the Graf. "You will feel better."

Maud shook her head, unwilling to sit down on the embroidered
stool. The woman took her by the shoulders and forced her onto the
seat. Maud felt a hot surge of rebellion as grief turned unexpectedly
to anger. She bent her head and bit the woman's hand. The woman
shrieked and snatched her hand away.

Leaping up from the table, Maud threw the bowl of milk onto the
tiled floor, overturned the platter of fish, kicked aside the stool, then
ran across the chamber to push open the oak door. She sped along the
passage, half slid down the winding staircase, dashed through a large
hall where startled faces turned to watch her, and out the open front
doors of the palace. The courtyard was filled with servants, grooms,
and palace officials all milling about. The gates stood open to admit a
pair of mounted knights in white surcoats marked with red crosses.
No one seemed to have noticed her. Maud ran across the yard and
darted out through the gates.

She found herself in a narrow street of cobbled stone, and stopped,
uncertain which way to go. Then, at the sound of raised voices coming from the courtyard, went left. Heads turned as she raced past a
cluster of men and women gossiping together and almost stumbled
over two children playing with a cat. The street ended abruptly in a
high stone wall and Maud turned down another street of tall narrow
houses, so close together at the top she could barely see the cloudy
gray sky.

The street seemed to go on forever until finally she was forced to
stop and catch her breath. She had no idea how far she had come, or
where she was going. Her only thought had been to escape from the
palace and find Aldyth. Ahead she could see heavy iron gates and

guards pacing back and forth atop the thick stone walls. This must be
the entrance to the city. While she watched, the gates creaked open;
a troop of mounted knights, similar to the ones she had passed earlier,
trotted through. They were followed by a majestic litter, whose curtains were partially open, drawn by four black stallions. Behind the
litter rode another troop of knights.

The procession turned down the narrow street and Maud tried to
flatten herself against the closed door of one of the houses so she
would not be noticed. The knights trotted by; the litter approached
and passed her. Then she heard a sharp command and the litter
shuddered to a swaying halt. The leather curtains were pushed farther
open, and a figure leaned out and beckoned to her.

Slowly Maud walked over to the litter. She saw an older man of
indeterminate age, younger than her father though, she quickly decided, wrapped in a richly embroidered blue mantle lined with white
fur. Under a velvet cap set with pearls, lank brown hair fell straight
to his shoulders. His face was sallow, its expression austere, like a
cleric's, but his heavy-lidded eyes held a look of amused interest.

He said something to her in German and pointed to the cross she
wore. Maud shook her head and replied in her own language that she
could not understand. He raised his eyebrows and gave her a considering look.

"Well, mein Kind,' he said, in heavily accented Norman French,
"you are far from home, nicht?"

She nodded, her eyes starting to brim with tears when he said the
word *home*. Her lower lip trembled as she fought to hold them back.

"There is no shame in crying," he said, observing her struggle.
"As long as you do not make a habit of it. Such behavior is not
uncommon among little girls, so I'm told."

Maud drew herself up proudly and lifted her head. "I am not just
any little girl. I'm a Norman princess, a granddaughter of William
the Conqueror."

"Ah, well, of course, that is quite another matter." He motioned
her closer. "I think you had better get in, don't you?"

She hesitated, her heart pounding, then got in beside him. He
closed the curtains and examined her with frank curiosity. "Suppose
you tell me what you were doing wandering around Mainz by yourself?"

His voice was unexpectedly gentle and Maud found herself telling
him the whole story from the moment she had arrived at the palace
last night. "And I hoped to find Aldyth," she concluded, "and then

somehow get back to England. I won't stay where everyone treats me so badly. I'm a granddaughter of the—"

"Conqueror. So you have said," he interjected, his lips twitching. "You have an unusual sense of your own value. But then you have an unusual heritage. It's not every upstart Norman adventurer who manages to found a royal dynasty."

Shocked, Maud was about to protest, but he held up a languid hand, ringed on every finger but his thumb.

"No, no, you must not take offense. On the contrary, I highly approve of your attitude. It's entirely fitting for the future consort of an emperor." He gave her a courtly nod.

Maud looked down and saw lying on the man's lap a curious board of inlaid wood covered with squares of silver and gilt. On several of the squares stood heavy ivory figures: a knight on horseback, a bishop with his crozier, a king and queen in ceremonial robes and crowns. They were so lifelike she could not resist touching the queen with a curious finger.

"Are these toys?"

"England is more of a backwater than I thought. No, this is a very special game called chess. It requires great skill."

Maud said nothing but slowly raised her head.

"I bought it for my future bride," he continued, watching her carefully. "Provided, of course, she remains in the Empire and proves intelligent enough to learn the game. As far as her English retinue is concerned, the Graf was right. They must all go." He paused. "With the exception of the woman, what is her name?"

"Aldyth."

"Yes, Aldyth may stay. On condition my bride learns basic German within four months. If not, the nurse must leave as well."

There was a brief pause. Their eyes met. Maud gave a tiny nod. The Emperor, for she had known almost at once who he was, inclined his head in acknowledgment.

"I'm pleased to see you wearing my gift." At her puzzled look he pointed to the cross she wore.

"I'm most grateful—" She paused. What should she call him? Your Grace? She was horrified to realize she did not even know his first name, for he had always been referred to as "the Emperor."

"My name is Heinrich," he said. "A familiar name, so you will feel right at home."

She nodded. "Thank you—Heinrich."

There was a long silence.

"What are your thoughts, mein Kind?"

"I was thinking that it will not take me four months to learn German or chess," Maud replied.

He burst out laughing, and the harsh expression on his face instantly vanished. "Ach, here is material one can work with! Granddaughter of the Conqueror, you and I are going to get along very well. Very well indeed."

Chapter Three

Italy, 1120

NINE YEARS LATER, MAUD, NOW A YOUNG WOMAN OF EIGHTEEN, climbed into a gold-curtained litter drawn by four white palfreys. As she settled back against the cushions of the litter taking her back to the stone palace where she and the Emperor stayed while in Rome, she felt flushed with triumph, having just successfully presided over her second court case. It was a mild afternoon in early December and the litter curtains had been left open to provide a splendid view of deep blue skies, narrow sun-dappled streets, and iron-gated palazzos.

Early this morning the Emperor, who was indisposed, had sent her to the ecclesiastical court to judge a dispute between two priests involving the theft of church property. Maud had often acted as her husband's representative at various social functions concerning the Imperial Empire, but this was only the second time he had given her the authority to try a case all by herself. She was so excited she could hardly wait to reach the palace and tell him how well she had done.

"Bella, bella madonna," called an Italian courtier as the litter passed him. He placed his hand over his heart, rolling his eyes heavenward as if he would expire merely at the sight of her.

Maud blushed furiously, then quickly turned away repressing a smile. She found the Romans so extravagant, so excessive, one could scarcely believe a word they said. She settled the green headdress more firmly over the coils of her russet hair, and looked down at the sleeves of her green gown flowing out of the turned-back cuffs of her gold-embroidered green tunic. Was she truly beautiful? Maud wondered, putting slender ringed fingers to her flushed cheeks. There were times, looking at herself in her silver mirror, when she thought she was not uncomely, with her arched nose, pewter-gray eyes, and creamy skin touched with amber.

Her former nurse, now chief woman attendant, Aldyth, often told her that true beauty came from a gentle demeanor, a modest nature, obedience, and attention to matters of religion. Anything else was vanity. As Maud possessed none of these sterling qualities, Aldyth often reminded her, how could she hope to become beautiful? But for the past two years, Maud had become aware that men's eyes often followed her: at the Imperial court, while she rode in an open litter, even attending holy services. The Emperor did not appear to notice, being far more interested in her varied accomplishments, most of which he had taught her himself.

From the moment Maud arrived in Germany he had taken charge of her education. She had been fearful that after her marriage at thirteen she would be relegated to the company of her women and doomed to a tedious life of weaving tapestries, managing servants, and childbearing. But, to her great relief, life continued as before.

The street suddenly opened onto a large square and the litter was forced to stop while a train of pack mules ambled by. It was market day and in the cobbled square peasants had set up their stalls of fruits, vegetables, nuts, and cheese.

While Maud waited for the mules to pass, she found herself remembering the first time the Emperor had become a husband instead of a beloved mentor. Even before the wedding ceremony at thirteen, she had been well prepared by Aldyth for what was to happen, but the Emperor had not attempted to consummate the marriage until she was sixteen. It had happened one winter night in Speyer. He was dressed in the heavy woolen nightshirt he wore winter and summer, with its carefully placed hole through which his member had attempted to enter her while he avoided any other contact with her flesh. He had extinguished all the candles so that she had not been able to catch even a glimpse of him. There had been a brief spasm of pain and then it was over so swiftly Maud was not entirely sure what had occurred.

From then on he exercised his conjugal rights infrequently. Sometimes Maud wondered if his habits were rather strange, unlike other men, according to the gossip she had picked up from her women, but had finally decided that his role as a religious leader was bound to make him different.

The mule train passed and the litter continued across the square and down another street, so narrow and twisted that a group of black-robed priests and monks had to press themselves against the wall so that the horses could squeeze by.

Maud thought herself quite fortunate to be spared her husband's fumbling nocturnal embraces since he was obviously fond of her, and continued to interest himself in her education. Wherever the Imperial court had traveled, from the towering snowcapped peaks of Bavaria, to the misty castles of the Rhineland, the dark green pines of the Black Forest, the cobbled streets and soaring spires of Paris, or the tranquil waterways of Venice, she had been instructed in those subjects that the Emperor felt a consort should know.

Now Maud had a working knowledge of law, history, mathematics, and philosophy. In addition to Norman French, she could speak Latin, German, and even a little Italian. As the Emperor was the head of Christendom, along with the Pope, with whom he was often in armed conflict, she had also been exposed to a comprehensive study of church affairs, as well as her husband's cynical attitude toward the Holy See.

On her right the litter now passed a crumbling stone church and close beside it the ruins of an ancient marble temple. Amid the fallen scrolled arches stood the gleaming white statue of a young man. One of his arms was missing, the other held a broken urn; his sightless eyes seemed to bore right through her. Maud looked quickly away; she had never seen a man unclothed, and the sight of the naked youth made her uncomfortable.

However, her fleeting glimpse of the statue had been sufficient to inform her that it was probably early Roman in origin. Statuary was one of many unlikely subjects she had learned during her travels with the Emperor. Despite its formal etiquette and stiff atmosphere, the Imperial court was often visited by unusual travelers. There were crusading knights returning after years in the Holy Land, Normans from Sicily, wandering scholars from Paris, troubadours from Provence, and visiting Semites and Moslems, bringing with them translations of classic works from ancient Greece and Rome.

Maud found her encounters with these people of great interest and excitement, affording her a glimpse into unknown worlds. A jongleur had taught her to play a few simple chords on the viol; a physician from Joppa had taught her some rudimentary Arabic; and she was laboriously reading her way through a translation of a Greek tale of a wanderer called Ulysses.

In the distance Maud caught a glimpse of the lichened stone tiers of the Colosseum, and beyond, the soft blue hills of Tuscany. She knew she was most fortunate to be leading such an unusual life, and she never ceased to be grateful to the Emperor.

Of course, there were a few pinpricks. While she was generally respected and liked, Maud was also aware that the Imperial court had more than its share of intrigue and gossip. Not everyone approved of her accomplishments or her education. Behind her back there were those who whispered that such activities were not seemly for a woman, that the elderly Emperor pampered his young Norman bride, whose time would be better spent learning more wifely skills, such as producing sons. A woman's main task in life was raising children, and why were none forthcoming, buzzed malicious tongues.

Maud paid them scant attention. Let people gossip to their heart's content, she thought, so long as the Emperor approved of her.

The litter slowed to a halt in a broad courtyard with a large fig tree in the center surrounded by a wealth of flowers, pale yellow, soft white, and dusky rose. Maud leapt out, dashed past a pink-veined marble fountain spouting water, up crumbling white steps flanked by two stone lions, and into the cool entrance hall with its blue mosaic tile floors.

"Where is His Imperial Highness?" she called to a servitor in white livery.

"In his reception chamber, but he is occupied, Your Grace—"

Maud did not wait to hear the rest but raced down the passage to the reception chamber.

"You will be so proud of me," she cried as she pushed open the door and burst into the dark stone chamber.

She stopped in dismay. She had expected him to be alone, but instead saw that two strangers with somber faces attended him. The Emperor, dressed in gold-encrusted robes of state and covered with a cloak lined in white ermine, was seated in a wooden armchair, his legs propped up on a cushioned stool. Two glowing braziers sat on either side of him, making the chamber stifling. Hazy sunlight, filtered through rose-colored leaded windows, illuminated his long face, creased as old parchment today, and softened the iron-gray strands of his hair and beard. When he was ill he always looked older than his forty-seven years. He exchanged a brief glance with the two strangers, then turned his heavy-lidded eyes toward her.

"In heaven's name, how many times have I told you not to rush into a room like a high wind?" The Emperor put a hand to his heart, then addressed the two visitors who were staring at her. "You must forgive my wife's excessive high spirits. I fear I spoil her, thus her manners often leave something to be desired." He signaled a servant. "Shut the door, I feel a draft."

Maud flushed. "Mea culpa, I will try to remember in future." Contrite, she curtsied to the visitors. "Forgive my intrusion."

As she quickly turned to leave, a smile played at the corners of the Emperor's thin lips. "After such an impetuous entrance, I think you had better remain. Come here, Liebling." He lifted his feet from the stool with a grimace, and patted the cushion. "Sit here by me." When she was seated he chucked her under the chin. "I hear you did very well today, very well indeed."

Maud could not repress jumping to her feet with a little bounce of excitement. "How did you hear? Who told you? What did they say?"

"Benedicte! Such a lot of questions. Can you not be still? Sit down. It makes me dizzy to look at you," grumbled the Emperor, his expression growing sober. "What will our visitors think?"

With a guilty glance at the two strangers, Maud sank back onto the stool. She was bursting with curiosity about these men with their long faces, but knew it would be impolite to ask who they were. She had already committed sufficient discourtesies.

One, a young man with long curling brown hair, was dressed all in black, from his leather boots to his cloak. His brown eyes, which had widened in surprise when she entered the chamber, returned again and again to her face, the slim white column of her neck, her slender waist, and the abundant curve of her breasts thrusting against her tunic.

Under his scrutiny, Maud felt awkward and self-conscious. Sweet Marie, why did he look at her like that! She turned her attention to the other visitor, a Benedictine abbot of middle years, clad in the black habit of his order, with a silver pectoral cross upon his breast.

"We will discuss your affairs later," said the Emperor, in a serious voice. "There are more pressing matters at hand. Let me introduce our visitors, Abbot Peter from the See of London, and Count Auberi of Evreux in Normandy. They have been sent by your father to tell us tragic news: Your twin brother, Prince William, was drowned in the channel last month, only days after his marriage."

Maud's mouth fell open. Stunned, she looked from the Count to the Abbot.

"Yes, Madam, the white ship carrying the wedding party from Normandy to England sank without a trace," confirmed Count Auberi. "It is assumed that not long after embarking, she drifted too near the treacherous rocks that have been the destruction of more than one vessel. With the exception of a citizen of Rouen, everyone on board was lost." He paused. "The King, your father, is inconsolable."

"We're sorry to bring you such sad tidings barely two years after the death of your sainted mother," added the Abbot, signing himself.

Maud could not think of an appropriate response. She had been saddened by her mother's death, but William, who had always treated her with cruelty, had never been her friend. His death had little personal meaning for her.

"May God assoil him," she said at last, signing herself. "My poor father. What will he do? William was his heir."

The two visitors exchanged glances.

"Indeed, Madam, I imagine all Europe is asking that very question," said the Abbot. "Who will wear the crown of England and the ducal coronet of Normandy when your father dies? May that day be far into the future." He signed himself. "Most unfortunate that your brother was King Henry's only remaining legitimate child."

"Except for my wife, of course," interjected the Emperor.

The Abbot and Count Auberi looked at him in mild surprise; clearly, they did not think the matter relevant.

"Who will inherit?" Maud asked. "It cannot be my half-brother, Robert. He is a bastard and Holy Church would never accept him as king."

"Unfortunately that is true, for Earl Robert of Gloucester would be the ideal candidate." The Abbot paused. "It is too soon to say. Much too soon."

"But surely there have been candidates mentioned?" The Emperor looked from one to the other. "Come, do you tell me the matter has not been discussed."

The Abbot cleared his throat. "Of course, one cannot help but speculate."

"And?" persisted the Emperor, narrowing his eyes.

"There's not a very fertile field. Your wife's cousin, Stephen of Blois, Count of Mortain, is the name mentioned most frequently," said the Abbot. "He's the King's nephew, and like a right arm to him.

No child of his body could be more dutiful, more loyal, or more loved by the nobles and commonfolk alike.''

"Stephen stands high in the King's favor," the Count agreed. "Just recently his uncle betrothed him to Matilda, daughter of the Count of Boulogne, a great heiress. With the exception of Madam's half-brother, Robert of Gloucester, no man has been granted greater wealth or honors than Count Stephen."

"Everyone agrees he would be an excellent choice for the throne," offered his companion. "You know, Stephen was actually aboard the doomed vessel, and at the last moment—" He paused uncertainly with an eye on Maud.

The Emperor raised his eyebrows. "Go on. You may speak freely."

The Abbot cleared his throat. "Unfortunately the wedding guests were flown with wine, including Prince William. There was an altercation of some kind and William and his companions threw Stephen overboard."

How like her twin, Maud thought. It was just the sort of vicious behavior one might expect of William.

"One can clearly see God's hand in this matter," concluded the Abbot. "Stephen was meant to survive; William was not."

"And no great loss, from all I've heard," said the Emperor dryly. "If the crew were also in their cups that certainly explains the wreck. This nephew of the King sounds a very paragon, though I must say I never thought too highly of the House of Blois. The stock is weak and unreliable. One of the sons, I heard, has never been sound in his wits, and didn't the father disgrace himself at some battle in the Holy Land? Now I think of it, wasn't there talk—"

"I'm glad my cousin Stephen was spared," Maud interjected quickly, before the Emperor could launch into one of his favorite subjects: scandal. Her husband knew the dark secrets of every ruling house in Europe, and relished discussing them.

As the men continued to talk, a picture sprang into Maud's mind of the smiling youth with the green-gold eyes she had seen but once yet never forgotten.

"Of course, Stephen is only a nephew and I imagine my father would want an heir of his own flesh and blood," she wondered aloud. "Such a coil. What will he do?"

"What would you advise him to do?" asked the Emperor with a sly look at the two visitors.

"Marry again, of course," Maud said promptly. "My father must lose no time in finding another wife so that he can beget an heir before he grows too old." She paused, wishing she had been more tactful, since the Emperor was not that many years younger than her father.

The Abbot nodded. "Exactly what the King's closest adviser, Bishop Roger of Salisbury, has told him."

"You see? My little empress has sound political instincts," the Emperor said, smothering a yawn. "And, if you were to ask, she would be able to tell you the best alliance for her father to make. She knows every important house in Europe. Have I not trained her well?" He sat back with a look of pride on his face but his smile had become fixed, and the lines around his mouth had deepened.

Maud flushed with pleasure. As the visitors seemed to have nothing more to say, and the Emperor was obviously beginning to tire, Maud rose to her feet.

"My husband has not been well, an inflammation of the liver, his physicians say. It's time he rested. If you will excuse us, the steward will show you to your quarters. We look forward to seeing you both at Vespers."

As soon as a servant had escorted the two men out, Maud asked her husband, "Are you feeling any better? Was the interview too much for you?"

He sighed and rubbed his side. "One day better, another worse. What does it matter?" He reached for her hand. "Interesting news, eh?" He regarded her with an enigmatic look.

"Why do you stare at me like that?"

"I was thinking about what I said earlier: At this moment you are the King of England's only legitimate child."

She gave him a puzzled smile. "I can't see why that's important."

"Perhaps it isn't. But your father grows no younger, as you pointed out, and if he ails as much as I do—" The Emperor sighed again. "Neither of us will live forever."

Immediately Maud knelt on the stool beside him and put a hand over his mouth. "Don't speak of such things," she said. "With God's grace you have many more years left, as does my father."

Maud did not understand why her husband talked so often of death when dying was the farthest thing from her thoughts. In truth, men like her father and husband seemed immortal. Both strong, ruthless monarchs, it was impossible to imagine the world without them. She picked up the Emperor's thin veined hand and held it to her cheek. The skin felt dry and fragile as an autumn leaf.

"Would you like to return to England?" he asked.

"Return to England?" She looked at him in shock. "Of course not. I hardly know anyone except my father and Robert. My home is with you, traveling around the Empire. I don't want anything to change."

"All things change, Liebling, that is the way of the world. If your father does not produce an heir, the future of the Norman realm may be of grave concern to you one day in the future."

Sweet Marie, Maud thought. How could the future of England and Normandy be of grave concern to her?

Chapter Four

Germany and Normandy, 1125

Almost five years later Maud was a widow. In May 1125 the Emperor died, and with his passing her glorious years of prestige and authority came to an abrupt end. As Maud had borne no children, the Imperial throne passed to a cousin of the Emperor's house, who, along with many other important German nobles, assured her that everyone would be honored if she continued to make Germany her home.

Stunned by her husband's death, a week after the obsequies were over Maud retired to a remote castle in Bavaria which had been bestowed upon her at the time of her marriage. Here, surrounded by her women and a small household staff, she nursed her grief. Morning after morning Maud would don her gloves, the fingertips removed, and set out her needles and silken thread. Then she would pull up her cushioned stool against the open casement window, take up a square of linen to embroider, and gaze upon the white-tipped peaks sharply outlined against a curve of bright blue sky.

Unable to do more than pick at her food, she soon became listless and pale. She slept poorly, lying awake night after night, unable to think of anything but her wonderful life with Heinrich.

In June Maud was invited to attend the new Emperor's coronation, but she declined. She was surprised at how much she minded being relegated to the background and wondered if she would ever totally adjust to her diminished circumstances. She had always enjoyed being involved in great events, pleased that the mantle of her husband's power had covered her as well. The realization that she was no longer a participant but merely a spectator doubled her sense of loss. At twenty-three her life was virtually over, she told Aldyth.

"I never heard such nonsense. Think of how fortunate you are," Aldyth reminded her. "The Emperor has left you wealth and property in your own right; the Germans honor and respect you. No one pines forever. In time, perhaps, a suitable marriage—"

"Never," Maud stopped her. "Who could I possibly marry after the Emperor?"

"There's finer fish in the sea than have ever been caught," Aldyth replied firmly.

Maud was too melancholy to argue.

A short while later Maud received a formal message of condolence from her father with an unexpected summons to return at once to his domains. Henceforth, he wrote, the Norman realm would be her home; he had always been devoted to her, and now sorely missed the only daughter of his late queen. He longed to have her by his side in his declining years.

"Devoted to me? I never saw any evidence of it," Maud said, surprised. "I wonder what lies behind this offer."

"When the fox preacheth keep an eye on your geese," Aldyth muttered darkly. As a Saxon, she had never entirely trusted the Norman king, all her love and loyalty having been lavished on Maud's mother.

But Maud was inclined to agree with her. She had not seen her father since leaving England fourteen years earlier. Their infrequent letters dealt only with matters of unusual interest: her father's remarriage almost four years ago; her half-brother Robert's accession to the earldom of Gloucester, his marriage and the birth of his sons.

However, despite her pleasant memories of England, the only relative whom she remembered warmly was Robert. Maud had little desire to visit her native land now, much less make it her home.

She thanked her father for his offer, explaining that she did not want to leave Germany, nor could she see any valid reason for doing so. The King quickly replied, insisting that it was imperative she return at once, but refusing to tell her why. As tactfully as possible,

Maud again firmly refused. She wrote that the Germans did not wish her to leave and she was comfortably settled. She assumed that would be the end of it.

A month later, in early August, a troop of Norman knights and archers clanked into the small courtyard of her Bavarian retreat.

"We have come to escort you to Normandy," announced the captain of the escort, handing Maud a roll of parchment.

It was a formal message from her father, reminding her that as a childless widow she now fell under the control of her nearest male relative, in this case, himself. The law was clearly on his side, King Henry went on to say, and no German official, not even the new emperor, would dare to interfere with his orders. She was to leave for Normandy at once.

Completely shocked, Maud let the scroll drop from her hands onto the tiled floor of the courtyard. She was well aware of the law regarding widows. It had simply never crossed her mind that her father would invoke it against her.

"But I'm still in mourning for my dead husband," she protested. "My father has no right to intrude upon my privacy in this unseemly fashion. Suppose I were to refuse?"

Unmoved, the captain said, "I've been instructed to tell you that should you refuse King Henry's summons he has ordered me to remove you by force." He paused. "But I'm sure the situation won't come to that, Madam."

Maud was aghast. Remove her by force? Her head began to throb as she fought to maintain her dignity before her father's minion. But inside she was filled with a helpless rage. It made no difference to the King that her heart lay in Germany, or that if she left she must forfeit all the wealth and property that the Emperor had bestowed on her. The image of herself being trussed up like a goose for market and stuffed into a litter was even worse than the knowledge that she would now be wholly dependent upon her father. As in all her past dealings with King Henry there seemed to be no choice but to obey. By evening her head ached so badly that she could not sleep and had to be dosed with white poppy.

"However you may feel at the moment, this might be the best thing that could happen," said Aldyth the next day, pleased to be returning to her native land. She gave Maud a sly glance as she packed boxes and stuffed saddlebags. "Certainly you've come up out of the doldrums, quick enough!"

Maud glared at her because what Aldyth said was true. Her sense of grief and loss had given way to anger and a resurgence of life as she imagined ways to get back at her father.

In mid-August, accompanied by her father's escort, women attendants, grooms, servants, as well as all her personal possessions, Maud left her adopted country. Surrounded by two score knights and archers, she felt more like a prisoner than a daughter returning to the bosom of her family. As her procession traveled through Germany, people came out in droves to express their affinity and mourn her departure. They would never forget her, they cried, their good and virtuous little empress. Maud was moved to tears. Her bitterness against her father increased.

The journey across Europe took a month. In early September they crossed the Norman border, stopped at an inn with a nearby church in time for Vespers, and started up again when the bells rang for Matins. With any luck they would reach Rouen before the following night, the captain of the escort told Maud. She then fell asleep to the rocking motion of the litter.

Slowly Maud opened her eyes. For some time now she had been trying to ignore the sounds of hammering, carts being unloaded, and horses stamping their hooves against the earth. How could they have arrived in Rouen so quickly? she wondered. Yawning, Maud stretched her arms, arched her spine like a cat, then opened the leather curtains, curious to see Normandy's capital. She gazed out upon a pink September dawn, just visible through a fragile curtain of mist, unprepared for the sight that met her eyes.

The procession of carts, litters, and sumpter horses was scattered over a wild overgrown meadow bordered on one side by an apple orchard. A warm wind swept through the fruit-laden boughs, carpeting the meadow floor with a profusion of apples, some red as blood, others a soft rose color.

As the captain of the escort rode by on a chestnut stallion, she hailed him: "Why have we stopped to set up camp? Surely this cannot be Rouen."

"No, Madam. While you slept a herald met us on the road, turned the procession aside and led us to this village—St. Clair. Your pavilion has just been erected and the women are already unloading your belongings."

A short distance away, surrounded by carts and pack horses, Maud saw a familiar green tent. Two servitors lifted wooden boxes and roped bundles from the carts and carried them into the tent, followed by two others who staggered under the weight of a wooden tub of water. Through the open door of the pavilion, Maud could hear the voices of Aldyth and her German women.

"The King is here?" she asked, incredulous.

"Across the river, Madam," the captain told her.

Maud slowly descended from the litter. Yes, there was the King's camp, a huge cluster of pavilions backed by a squat stone church and a cluster of thatch-roofed huts. Despite the morning's warmth she shivered.

"If you will excuse me, Madam, I have much to attend to," said the captain. He bowed his head and rode off.

She had been expecting a ceremonial entry into Rouen; instead she found herself in the midst of a wilderness. Simply one more humiliation to add to the others she had endured. Bitterness twisted like an adder inside her.

Two grooms passed by leading four horses to the river. One of them gave her a friendly smile. "Welcome to Normandy, Madam," he said in Norman French.

"She cannot understand you, Pierre," said the other. "I imagine she only speaks German."

"Well, she had better learn our language again if she intends to stay," retorted the first groom.

They passed out of earshot. Maud wanted to explain she still spoke their language as well as ever but did not have the heart to call them back. The realization that she was little better than a captive in her father's domains was a heavy weight pressing against her chest.

"Lady?" Aldyth's round face, soft and creased as a dried apple, poked through the door of the tent. "I was about to wake you. Come, the bath is poured. You must be ready when the King sends for you." She withdrew her head.

Maud could not bring herself to go inside the pavilion but continued to loiter outside, wanting to extend these treasured moments of freedom for as long as possible. The reeds that grew beside the river trembled, as if someone moved behind them. She began to walk toward the riverbank.

Stephen of Blois, Count of Mortain, suddenly opened his eyes, awakened by an indefinable sense of danger. He threw off the gray blanket of unwashed wool, then, like a great golden cat, slowly uncoiled his supple limbs and silently rose to his feet. Now, crouched naked on his pallet, he looked carefully around the tent he shared with his two closest friends, Earl Robert of Gloucester, the King's bastard son, and Brian FitzCount, Lord of Wallingford, one of his uncle's trusted advisers.

He could see nothing out of the ordinary in the familiar shambles of crumpled tunics, swords, shields, ivory dice, wooden cups, and an empty henap of wine scattered over the floor. Wrinkling his nose, for the pavilion smelled like a vintner's stall, Stephen stretched his lean body, then ran his fingers through a tangle of honey-brown hair.

Still the sense of danger persisted. It must be coming from outside. Careful not to disturb his sleeping companions, Stephen pulled on a white linen shirt that fell to mid-thigh, unsheathed a knife from the embossed silver scabbard attached to his leather belt lying on the floor, and tiptoed out of the pavilion.

Outside it was still early; over the brow of the hill the King's camp was just beginning to stir. A heavy dew had fallen overnight, drenching the meadow grasses and gnarled apple trees heavy with fruit. Stephen looked to his left but saw only the familiar red-and-gold banners of the King's tent and the outline of village huts and church spire beyond. On his right, wreaths of smoke from the cooking fires rose lazily in the air; a light breeze carried the spicy odor of game roasting over an applewood fire.

There was certainly nothing unusual in this familiar scene, yet the feeling of alarm persisted. Over the years Stephen had learned to trust his instincts, as finely honed, he prided himself, as any forest creature's. From across the river he heard the sound of hammering, and immediately walked through the meadow grasses down to the riverbank. Putting down his knife while he removed his shirt, he waded into the river which swirled in brown circles around the golden pelt of his chest. The shock of the cold water against his skin was invigorating. On the opposite bank he parted the clusters of pale green reeds and climbed soundlessly onto the moist earth. Now, surely, the source of the danger, if such existed, would be revealed.

Through the reeds Stephen could see servitors unloading carts and erecting pavilions. Several grooms were leading pack horses and mules down the riverbank to drink.

The sense of danger abruptly vanished as a woman dressed all in black came into view. Although he could not see her features clearly, Stephen was aware of a graceful neck supporting a flushed ivory face tilted slightly backward, and a luxuriant fall of russet hair that cascaded down her back. She slipped off her black cloak to reveal an elegant carriage, slender body, and swelling bosom.

When she began to walk toward the river, something about the woman's face and the color of her hair seemed vaguely familiar, although he could not place her. Who could she be? he wondered, before suddenly connecting the raised pavilion, the carts, and why he was here. This could only be his cousin Maud, widow of the Imperial Emperor. She had grown into a heart-stopping beauty, more than fulfilling the early promise of the lovely teary-eyed maiden he had seen, and never totally forgotten, the day he arrived at Windsor fourteen years ago.

The sudden sound of hooves pounding across the stone bridge that spanned the river made Stephen sink to his knees in the reeds. A party of nobles trotted past; among them Stephen recognized two of his companions, the de Beaumont twins, riding from Muelan into the tiny village of St. Clair to meet the King's daughter.

The church bells rang for Prime and Stephen turned back to feast his eyes upon Maud once more. Suddenly a voice in his ear startled him.

"What holds you in such thrall? I made enough noise to wake the dead yet you heard nothing."

Caught by surprise, Stephen whipped around to find the saturnine face and ironic blue eyes of Brian FitzCount, who had slipped silently into the water to join him. Brian, bastard son of the Count of Brittany, had arrived in England at about the same time as himself and they had been brought up together at the King's court.

Silently Stephen parted the reeds so that Brian could observe the new arrival.

"Jesu," Brian murmured, "yes, I see. Now I understand the reason for your concentration. Can that breathtaking creature really be the German widow?"

"What did you expect?"

"A dumpy German Frau like as not." Brian paused, a frown creasing his brow. "Still a mystery why the King has summoned her back." He stretched his arms then ducked his head of tight black curls under the water.

"No mystery to me," Stephen said lazily, his eyes riveted to Maud who had suddenly bent to remove her shoes and a pair of black stockings. "The King has a new alliance to be made and his daughter is now an available widow."

"If that was all there was to it why not say so? Why keep the matter secret? Normandy is at peace with both France and Anjou now, pray God it lasts. With whom does the King need an alliance? Much more sensible to have left the lady in Germany where she could be of use to him. No, there's more to this than meets the eye."

Stephen shrugged. "There are always alliances to be made. Perhaps the King wishes to see the only remaining child of his late queen. There could be a hundred reasons."

Brian lay on his back in the water and gently kicked his legs. "In all the years I've lived at court I've never witnessed King Henry take any action that did not first serve the interests of the realm."

"Must there always be a political reason for everything?" Stephen said, impatience in his voice. "You're as bad as my devoted brother, Henry, who scents intrigue as my brachet scents game." He drew his breath in sharply as Maud lifted up the skirts of her black gown and tunic, affording him a tantalizing glimpse of a delicately shaped ankle. She then proceeded to run through the grass directly toward his hiding place.

Brian laughed. "If your brother's keen nose hasn't uncovered the King's secret no one can."

"As far as I'm concerned," Stephen continued, "my cousin is here. Now. And I intend to make the most of it before she is shipped off to another husband."

"God's face, I hope that doesn't mean what it usually does. Such talk from you invariably spells trouble—for the damsel in question. Listen to me, Stephen, it's one thing to pursue a lady of questionable virtue or a tavern wench, but the King's daughter, who is also your own cousin? Remember what happened with that baron's wife last year? You only just escaped her husband's vengeance by fleeing through the kitchens."

Stephen chuckled. "With boots, hose, and cloak left behind as evidence! Will I ever forget? If you hadn't been waiting with the horses—" He gave a mock shudder, his eyes intently watching Maud.

"Exactly. Be warned."

"Don't be tiresome. If I required a sermon, I would go to my brother. Henry's recent appointment as Abbot of Glastonbury has made him more insufferable than ever. You should hear him on the subject of lechery and lust."

Brian laughed. "I can imagine."

Stephen turned to grin at his companion. "My cousin will be

lonely and need consolation after her recent loss. I have a most excellent remedy for pining widows."

"By my faith, now I'm really worried for the lady's safety. You're incorrigible."

Stephen did not reply. For a moment Maud had vanished from his sight and he poked out his head from between the reeds to see where she had gone. Not ten feet from his hiding place a pair of startled smoke-gray eyes met his. For the space of a heartbeat their eyes held. There was an odd, sharp little ache in Stephen's chest, and a sensation in his belly as if he had just fallen from a great height. Before he could speak, Maud's face turned pink, and she quickly ran through the grass back to the camp.

"Look, Stephen, did you ever see such a sorry sight?" Brian asked, laughing.

"What?" Dazed, Stephen tore his gaze away from Maud to see his cousin, Robert of Gloucester, standing across the narrow river, a blanket wrapped around him. Small but strongly built, with a shock of thick brown hair cut straight across his forehead in the Norman fashion, he resembled a hardy pony from the Welsh hills.

"Why do you wear a blanket?" Brian asked, swimming toward Robert. "Come join us."

Robert thrust his foot in the water, then drew back. "By the Mass, the water is cold." A chord of Welsh music ran through his voice, reflecting the heritage of his mother who had been the daughter of a Welsh chieftain when King Henry had captured her during his first campaign in Wales. "Others are abroad and I have no wish to offend by my nakedness."

"Such modesty would do credit to a nun," Brian said, with a wink at Stephen.

Shaking off the effects of his encounter with Maud, Stephen swam through the water after Brian, climbed onto the opposite shore, and before Robert could stop him, pulled off the blanket. Shouting with laughter, Stephen took his arms, Brian his legs, and, ignoring Robert's curses and protests, together they lifted him high then dropped him into the cold water. He emerged, shaking himself like an angry dog, then came after Stephen. Together they wrestled in the water, each trying to throw the other off balance. Stephen was the taller but Robert the more solidly built; neither could best the other.

That had always been the case even as youths, Stephen thought, trying to get a firm grip on his cousin's slippery body. Despite the fact that they were the best of companions, equally favored by the King—he had married them to wealthy heiresses and showered them with land, power, and influence—the two had always been rivals as well. He and Robert competed for the King's affection and attention, for prowess in hunting, skill at arms, and success on the battlefield. But since Robert, as a bastard, could not even be considered to inherit the throne, both he and Stephen knew who would ultimately triumph.

"Ah, now we see what it is that endears him to his wife," Stephen cried. "You shouldn't hide your light under a blanket. Would he not put a stallion to shame, Brian?"

"Indeed, the prowess of the Welsh is well known," Brian replied, "for they breed like hares. Listen, my friend, I have a mare that wants servicing—"

Robert let go of Stephen to leap at Brian and they both disappeared under the water in a flurry of thrashing limbs.

"My lords?"

Stephen turned to see his squire, Gervase, approaching at a rapid pace through the grass.

"The King is calling for you, my lords. His daughter is across the river and he's anxious you attend him before she arrives in his camp."

"We caught a glimpse of her. Tell him we'll dress and be there at once," Stephen said.

"My sister has arrived?" Robert asked, emerging from the water. "Why didn't you tell me?" He hastily climbed onto the bank and wrapped himself in the blanket. "Dearest Maud. Do you realize it's been fourteen years? I cannot wait to see her." He ran up the hill.

Stephen and Brian climbed onto the bank, pulled on their long shirts, and followed at a leisurely pace. The mist was rapidly burning off now, revealing clear blue skies. It promised to be a day of brilliant sunshine, Stephen observed, a day of good omen.

"Tread carefully with your beauteous cousin," Brian advised him in a serious undertone. "You have sufficient conquests to testify to your manliness a hundred times over."

"Now that is arguable." Stephen bent to pick up a grass straw and slipped it between his lips. "Like glory or riches, can one ever have sufficient?"

Brian smiled. "You're beyond redemption, I fear. There will come a day of retribution, mind."

"By God, you can be tedious. I only jest. Do you think me such a fool as to go against my own interests?" Stephen grimaced. "I'll be the very model of chivalry, have no fear. Unfortunately, the lady is as safe with me as in a cloister."

Which was God's own truth, Stephen thought regretfully. He would sooner poke at a wild boar with a short stick than incur his uncle's displeasure. Besides, there was something about that brief, wordless exchange with Maud that did not suggest an easy conquest, a moment's sport easily forgotten. But he had no intention of revealing that to Brian.

Flinging an arm over his friend's shoulders, he gave him a rough squeeze. "I wonder you never took holy orders. You're wasted away from the pulpit."

They reached the pavilion. Before entering Stephen paused, suddenly remembering the sense of danger he had experienced earlier. He had never uncovered the source of that feeling, he realized. Odd, it was the first time he could remember that his instinct in such matters had played him false.

Chapter Five

MAUD RACED THROUGH THE GRASS CARRYING HER SHOES, STOCKINGS and cloak. Still tingling from the impact of her heady encounter in the reeds, she ran full tilt into Aldyth who was waiting for her at the door of the pavilion.

"Where have you been? By the Rood, you have no shoes on and your face is scarlet! If you've caught a fever—" She put an anxious hand on Maud's forehead.

"I'm fine. Don't chastise." It was ridiculous how out of breath she felt.

Aldyth, looking like a suspicious pouter pigeon in her white wimple, rumpled gray gown and tunic, held open the door and Maud, with a quick glance over her shoulder at the riverbank, walked into the tent. Unprepared for the wild disorder confronting her, she looked in dismay at the feather bed lying in a heap on the floor, coverlets and linen sheets spilling out of an open oak chest, stools, a small table, silver basins, ewers, and ivory caskets scattered everywhere. Two female attendants from Germany, Truda and Gisela, were busy shaking out gowns and tunics, then hanging them on wooden hooks fastened to the tent walls. In the middle of the floor stood a large wooden tub half filled with water.

"I don't understand why we couldn't have gone into Rouen as planned," Maud said. "This . . . backwater seems an unlikely place to meet my father." Nor did it bode well for her reception at her father's court, she thought.

After removing her tunic, gown, and shift, and stepping into the tub of water, Maud's attention returned to the man she had seen rise from the reeds like some mythic god. She had almost expected to see nymphs and satyrs prancing about him. But she had immediately recognized her cousin, Stephen of Blois, whom she had not seen for fourteen years. Those unforgettable eyes, deep green flecked with gold, had reminded her of the day she left Windsor. What irony that her cousin was the first person she should encounter on the day of her return.

"The King has his reasons for meeting you here, whatever they may be," Aldyth was saying now, interrupting her reverie. "If you want to get along with him, best not to question what he does."

She began to scrub Maud's body with a damp cloth, then rubbed oil scented with rose petals into the smooth skin of her slender neck, rounded arms, narrow waist, and long straight legs. The soreness and fatigue of the long journey eased under Aldyth's skillful fingers.

"Well, I intend to question everything. After all, I'm no longer a child. The King cannot do merely as he wants with me," Maud said, stepping out of the tub as Aldyth wrapped her in a long, thick towel.

"You're as much a chattel now as you were at nine years of age, make no mistake about that." Aldyth lowered her voice. "As I've told you, King Henry needs you, just as he did when he married you off to the Emperor, just as he needed your Saxon mother, may God rest her soul, to grease his way to the throne." She sighed. "I always said your late husband spoiled you, Lady, in shielding you from the ways of this world. But you'll learn."

Maud, having heard this diatribe many times before on the long journey across Europe, knew there was no point in arguing.

"Mark my words," Aldyth continued, "there's another advantageous marriage to be made, a new alliance—that's the purpose of eligible widows."

"Not this widow." Maud reached for a white silk bandeau that lay across a stool. Despite her defiant words, she could not dismiss Aldyth's warnings. Why else would King Henry have brought her back but to be used again?

"Not the bandeau," Aldyth hissed. "The Bishop of Mainz proclaimed such vanities an abomination, the devil's handiwork!"

Gisela and Truda signed themselves, their round eyes reminding Maud of two fearful sheep.

"What nonsense!" Maud lifted her arms while Aldyth reluctantly wound the white silk bandeau over her full breasts. Uncomfortable with this abundant evidence of her womanhood, the bandeau made Maud feel less conspicuous.

Truda slipped the shift over Maud's head while Gisela held up the black mourning gown and tunic.

"No," Maud said, giving way to a sudden impulse. "I will no longer wear that."

"But you're in mourning," Aldyth said, shocked. "You must dress in black for a year. That is the custom."

"Let me see some other tunics and gowns," Maud said to Truda, ignoring Aldyth.

"Sweet Saint Ethelburga, what has gotten into you?" Aldyth began to wring her hands. "What will people say?"

"They can say what they like," Maud replied.

In truth she did not know why she felt so stubborn, so compelled to flout custom. It would certainly cause a stir, even offense. But at least she would not feel so much the hapless widow, a pawn to be moved about at her father's whim.

She finally decided on an ivory gown and linen tunic with hanging sleeves, circled by a broad girdle of pale gold. Maud sat down on a stool and Truda and Gisela began to rub her cinnamon-colored hair with pumice which would give it greater shine.

"Mulish. Headstrong. No good will come of it," Aldyth muttered, slipping gold leather shoes onto Maud's feet.

There was a noise outside the pavilion. A voice called out in formal tones: "Henry, King of England and Duke of Normandy, awaits the arrival of his daughter, the Princess Maud. The litter is ready."

The four women looked at each other in consternation, their differences forgotten. An air of tension pervaded the tent. Truda's fingers shook as she plaited Maud's long hair, then coiled it around her ears while Gisela placed a purple mantle, embroidered with eagles and vine leaves in gold thread, over her shoulders. Last, Aldyth handed her the silver mirror.

Huge pewter-colored eyes fringed by thick black lashes stared back at Maud from a face the color of ivory. Her earlier flush had vanished. That would never do.

"Get me the crushed pomegranate," Maud said.

"Merciful heavens, you cannot paint your face, it's a sin," Aldyth wailed.

"I won't meet my father looking like a corpse. No one will know it's paint."

"A little pallor becomes a grieving woman," Aldyth continued. "What will people say?"

"Sweet Marie, I've told you I don't care," Maud retorted, with more bravado than she felt.

She took the small stone jar from Truda and rubbed a little of the rosy ointment into her high cheekbones. She glanced again in the mirror. Still not right. Something was lacking. Of course. The Imperial crown. Just what was needed to add the final touch of splendor. To remind the King and everyone else that she was not just her father's daughter, an eligible widow, but a former empress, a person in her own right. Her heart quickened.

"Gisela—the Imperial crown is wrapped in red silk at the bottom of the oak chest. Do you find it for me." The crown, made for her by the Emperor, had been left in her keeping and she had decided that this entitled her to take it with her to England.

Aldyth's face grew ashen. "Child, now you go too far. The bandeau cannot be seen, the paint may go unnoticed, the way you're dressed is inexcusable, but as for the crown—to wear it might be taken as a direct insult to the King and his entire court. Do not tempt fate."

"Don't be foolish. Why would the King object? He sent me to the Empire, remember? Gisela, the crown, if you please." The thought of defying her father was both frightening and exhilarating.

" 'When the old cock crows, the young cock should listen,' " Aldyth said in a resigned voice. "But some people must learn through trial and error. Sound advice is wasted on them."

Gisela looked from Maud to Aldyth, then scurried to the oak chest. She pulled out an object wrapped in red silk and carried it over to Maud. Unwrapping it carefully, Maud held to her breast the gold plates set with pearls and sapphires. Sighing, she remembered the many state occasions when she had worn this emblem of her former power. Truda placed an ivory veil over her head, Maud laid the crown on top of it, then picked up the silver mirror. Yes, just what was needed. The crown lent a regal air to her bearing that was right for the occasion.

She placed a conciliatory kiss on Aldyth's withered cheek. "Don't worry. All will go well." She gave her a half smile. "But your prayers would not come amiss." Instinctively she found herself touching the silver ring through her garments. A reassuring talisman, she was never without it.

Aldyth's eyes became moist. "Remember, 'a silent mouth is sweet to hear.' "

Maud left the pavilion. Outside a groom helped her into a waiting litter led by an escort of knights. She squared her shoulders, lifting her head proudly as the litter started to move toward the river. She had every right to wear the crown, she assured herself, every right to dress as she pleased, to establish herself in front of her father's court.

Yet—she was assailed by doubts, recognizing the paint, the bandeau, her defiant garb, even the crown, for what they were: petty assertions of an independent spirit under siege. The litter crossed the stone bridge. Fear spread like wildfire through her body. Ahead lay the scarlet pavilion and the meeting with her redoubtable father.

Chapter Six

THE PROCESSION CAME TO A HALT IN THE KING'S CAMP JUST AS THE SUN climbed into a cloudless blue sky. Raising her hand to ward off the bright glare, Maud saw a group of horsemen against a background of golden light. Behind them she glimpsed a crowd of people, then the royal tent where the unseen figure of her father waited, his invisible presence casting a giant shadow over the entire area. One of the horsemen, astride a red Flanders mare, detached himself from the others and trotted up to her litter. His honey-brown hair was brushed with fire in the morning sun, a blue silk mantle, fastened at one shoulder with a gold clasp, fluttering gaily behind him in the breeze.

Dazzled, Maud could only stare at him in breathless wonder. Handing the reins to a waiting squire, the rider sprang gracefully from his horse. At first Maud was aware only of a flow of energy emanating from the figure striding toward her. As he came closer she could see a tall, lean man with wide shoulders, dressed in a long blue tunic embroidered in red and gold thread at the hem and cuffs, and wearing tan boots of soft Spanish leather. His face broke into a smile as green-gold eyes stared down at her in a long, searching look of recognition.

"Well met, Cousin," the man said, his voice surprisingly soft, as he half lifted her out of the litter. "I am Stephen of Blois, Count of Mortain, and we first saw each other a long time ago. Do you remember?"

"Indeed." He still resembled the boy in the scarlet cap who had smiled at her in much the same way he was smiling now. "The day I left England is not one I would be likely to forget," she said. "Surely you are the boy with the cat's eyes riding into Windsor as I rode out."

Stephen laughed delightedly. "Cat's eyes! No one has ever compared me to a feline before." His face grew sober. "The day one leaves home marks a turning point, does it not?" He gave her an understanding look. "And the day one returns, another."

Filled with a rush of emotion, Maud looked quickly away, unprepared to find such ready empathy from this unknown cousin. She wondered why neither of them mentioned the incident by the river.

"I thought you the most beautiful maiden I had ever seen," Stephen continued, "but so unhappy. Time has made you even more fair. I hope it brought you happiness as well, before your tragic loss, of course." He signed himself.

Maud felt tongue-tied, ill at ease with the admiration she saw reflected in his eyes, the warmth in his voice. Aware of his large hands still holding hers, Maud tried to pull away, but he held her fast. A spark traveled from his palm to hers; the air seemed to pulse between them. The feeling was so new, so intense, and so unexpected that she felt close to panic.

"You cannot keep her all to yourself, Stephen." A small, stocky man, his brown hair shaved at the back and sides, walked up to them. "Sister!"

As Stephen finally released her hands, the man hugged Maud affectionately, kissing her on both cheeks. "I'm so pleased to see you again. You cannot know how I've missed you all these years."

The Welsh lilt to his voice, the deep-set dark eyes were all familiar. In a wave of relief, Maud threw her arms around her half-brother. Robert was as warm and friendly as she had remembered him. The crown shifted on her veil and she reached up to steady it.

"By Our Lady, you wear a king's ransom on your head, Cousin," Stephen said, apparently noticing her crown for the first time. He could not seem to take his eyes off the gem-encrusted gold plates winking in the morning sun.

"It's the Imperial crown, given to me by the Emperor," Maud said, a hint of pride in her voice.

There was a moment of silence. The two men exchanged quick glances, and Maud sensed their unspoken disapproval.

"Yes, well, you will hardly need it here," said Robert.

"You're in Normandy now where beauty is the only crown a woman wears," Stephen added. "Yours is more dazzling than any diadem."

Light repartee of this kind had not existed at the stiff German court, with its formal etiquette. Maud did not know how to take this unfamiliar banter. Obviously, as Aldyth had warned, it had been a mistake to wear the crown, but she had no intention of removing it now.

They waited a moment as if expecting her to remove it but as she made no move to do so Robert said, "Come, Sister, the others wish to greet you as well."

Robert led Maud to the group of horsemen who had dismounted. One, a hunchback, dressed all in green, had dark brown hair framing a comely, sensitive face.

"Here are the de Beaumont twins." Robert pointed to the hunchback. "Robert, Earl of Leicester in England, whom we call Robin. His twin brother Waleran, Count of Muelan in the Vexin." He nodded at a large man, resplendent in red and black, with a brooding face and a nose beaked like a hawk. He turned toward a third man. "Brian FitzCount, Lord of Wallingford."

This man was almost as tall as Stephen, with a sinewy frame and cropped black curls growing over his head like lamb's wool. Something flickered in his dark blue eyes as they stared straight at Maud.

"Perhaps you will remember they arrived on the day you left for Germany," Robert continued. "Not that you would be expected to recognize them as the sniveling rats they then were."

The men's names were not unknown to her, of course, for the Emperor had insisted she familiarize herself with the most powerful lords at her father's court. The twins were the sons of the late Count of Muelan, King Henry's oldest friend. She gave them a warm smile.

Eyeing her with cool speculation, the three strangers murmured polite greetings. Impossible to believe these grown, self-assured nobles were the frightened children she vaguely recalled meeting so long ago.

"A pleasure to see you again," Maud said.

There was a faint murmured response in return.

"I regret that I do not recall meeting you, Madam," said the Count of Muelan in a blunt, no-nonsense voice. "Do you recall meeting her, Brother?"

"By my faith, I remember nothing of the time I arrived in England," Robin of Leicester replied. "I was miserable and wanted my mother."

Brian laughed. "All I recall is how terrified I was when I met King Henry. A sniveling little rat, just as Robert says."

"And stinking. By God's face, will I ever forget that!" Waleran smote his thigh. "You had pissed in your drawers and when the King came to greet us, he held his nose and said that this one stinks like a dung heap, someone clean him up!"

They began to laugh uproariously, joined by Stephen, each chiming in with his own version of what had happened that day.

It was obvious to Maud they had forgotten her.

And why not? She was the outsider, excluded by experience and gender from their tight little circle. How could she contribute to their memories? Shading her eyes with an unsteady hand, she turned her back on them to gaze at the far horizon. The smudged purple line of hills melted into the deep blue of the sky. Green and yellow fields, cut through by the old Roman road on which she had just traveled, shimmered in the sun. If only she could will herself back on that road heading toward Germany.

"It is the King's pleasure to see the Princess Maud," piped the voice of a page just behind her.

One hand went to her throat and her heart leapt in fear. Then she stiffened, realizing it was the second time she had been called Princess. An oversight, surely, but one she must correct at once.

She smiled at the page. "In Germany I am referred to as Empress," she said.

The page looked puzzled, then bowed and ran off. The men stared at her in surprise. She returned their look in dismay. Had she done something wrong?

"Whoever you may be in Germany, Madam, here you are the King's daughter," said Waleran of Muelan. "And honor enough I would have thought."

The others nodded and murmured assent.

Obviously these men could know nothing of her background, she realized, the respect and importance with which she was regarded in Germany, the decisions the Emperor had entrusted to her care. With a sudden sinking sensation in her stomach, it now dawned on Maud that perhaps no one knew; perhaps this was the response she could expect from everyone. Even worse, her triumphs in the Empire would probably mean nothing to her father's people, even if they did know. England and Normandy comprised the whole world for these Norman barons. How would she ever fit in to their narrow sphere!

"If you want my advice, Madam," Waleran was saying, "do not wear that German bauble before the King lest you offend him. You're a subject of Normandy now."

Stung, Maud gave him a cold look. "Thank you, my lord, but I don't think you fully understand. The crown is not a bauble but an emblem of royalty. I am an empress in my own country and the crown is exactly where it belongs."

She had spoken more forcefully than she had intended and to her dismay saw the Count of Muelan's face turn a dark red. Sweet Marie, had she offended him? He did not speak but the glare of enmity in his black eyes was unmistakable.

In the awkward silence that followed, Maud was uncertain what to do. It was beneath her dignity to ask if she had given offense.

"Come, Cousin."

Stephen stepped smoothly into the breach, offering her his arm to lead her toward the scarlet tent. The others fell in behind.

"Don't let Waleran's manner disturb you," Stephen said under his breath. "He can be prickly as a porcupine if he thinks someone has insulted him. He'll get over it."

Remembering the look in Waleran's eyes Maud was not so sure. She prayed she had not made an enemy her very first day in Normandy. Conscious of the warm pressure of her cousin's arm against her own, Maud approached the King's pavilion.

The entrance was flanked by two poles of long wood, each flying a red-and-gold banner. To one side, standing stiffly at attention, were grouped a score of archers in leather hauberks. Surrounding the tent, knights, squires, ladies-in-waiting, richly dressed nobles, and clergymen whispered among themselves as they examined Maud with frank curiosity. Two bishops in gold-embroidered robes came forward; the sun struck sparks from their miters and crosiers. One Maud recognized as the portly Bishop of Salisbury, the King's chief adviser. Behind them walked an abbot, resplendent in a black silk habit, a gold cross set with pearls lying on his breast. His face looked oddly familiar. Like Stephen's, she thought, startled.

"The Bishops of Salisbury and Rouen, and behind them the Abbot of Glastonbury," Stephen said in her ear.

"The Abbot resembles you," Maud said.

"Not surprising, since he is my younger brother, Henry. He left the Benedictine monastery at Cluny less than a year ago and is already well on his way to becoming a power in the church."

Maud cast Stephen a quick look, curious as to why his voice had developed a marked edge when he talked of his brother. Then she smiled at the prelates, inclining her head.

"Benedicte," the bishops murmured in unison, making the sign of the cross over her head before stepping back.

The Abbot bowed and smiled, a smile, Maud saw, that never reached his pale green eyes. Closer, his resemblance to Stephen was less pronounced.

"Welcome to Normandy, Cousin," he said in a cool voice.

The crowd grew quiet. Maud's throat went dry; her heart beat so heavily she could hardly breathe. She was aware of a solemn hush, the abrupt absence of Stephen's arm.

Suddenly the door opened and a man stepped out. Short, dark, with powerful shoulders, a broad chest, and thick bull neck, his heavy black brows almost met over the dark, piercing eyes Maud had never forgotten. He was dressed in a short black mantle fastened at the right shoulder with a gold brooch, over a plain brown tunic. Cuffed black boots encased his bowed muscular legs. Around his thick waist he wore a heavy leather belt studded with jewels. On the top of his round head rested the golden crown he had once given Maud to hold. Although he had aged since she had last seen him, Henry of England still radiated power, menace, and authority.

Maud opened her mouth to greet him but the words refused to come. Some instinct made her fall to her knees. Fighting back tears, Maud found herself staring at her father's scuffed boots, the gilt spurs secured with brown leather. Iron fingers gripped her shoulders. The King pulled her roughly to her feet.

"Well, well, no need for that. You are a royal princess after all."

Maud detected a note of satisfaction in his voice as he held her at arm's length. Instinct had not led her astray when she knelt.

"You have arrived safely, praise God and all His Saints. There is much to be thankful for."

"An honor to be in your presence, Sire," she managed to say in a strangled voice she barely recognized.

"And you haven't forgotten your Norman tongue, I see. Something else to be thankful for." The King raised an arm high above his head as he shouted: "The Princess Maud speaks the tongue of her

Norman ancestors, the tongue of the great William, her grandfather, as well as ever she did the day she left our court."

Which was not quite true, Maud thought, for now she had a slight accent. Nevertheless, there was a twitter of approval from the waiting crowd. Hooking his thumbs in his belt, Henry slowly walked around her. Finally he nodded his head, apparently satisfied with what he saw.

"Yes, you have become worthy of us, Daughter. Every inch a Norman princess." He paused. "I see you have even put off mourning to signify the importance of this auspicious occasion."

Henry continued to walk round her, reminding Maud of a wild beast circling its prey. Finally he came to an abrupt stop. His jaw thrust out, he pointed a stern finger at the Imperial crown. "Why do you wear the crown of a German empress?"

"The crown?"

"Yes, the crown you wear, what else? I did not refer to mine."

The crowd tittered softly. Maud felt her face turn crimson with shame.

"You are a widow and no longer Empress," Henry continued. "Why do you wear it?"

Maud moistened her dry lips. "To honor my late husband."

"I see. I'm sure that would be much appreciated in Germany."

As Henry fixed her with an unblinking stare Maud wanted to sink into the ground. If only she had listened to Aldyth!

"But you're in Normandy now. The Emperor is dead; that life is finished. Come, take off the crown."

"It is mine," she whispered, her heart hammering.

In desperation, seeking help of any kind, Maud looked around her. All she saw were members of the Norman court, viewing her plight with detached interest.

The King gave her a menacing look. "Take off the crown lest I have someone do it for you."

Squaring her shoulders, Maud lifted her head proudly. She would show him she was no longer a child to be ordered about as he pleased. Her father's eyes, hooded and hard as agates, bored into hers. For a moment she challenged him, her intention battling his own. Every part of her tensed, screaming with the desire to defy him. But she was not strong enough. Not yet. His will was like an iron shield, unassailable, and she knew herself overmatched. Once again the King had backed her into a corner leaving her no choice. He had won—as he always had. But Maud knew she would never forget this moment of humiliation and she wanted him to know it, too.

Her face set, gray eyes blazing, Maud slowly lifted her arms and deliberately removed the crown from her head, resisting an over-powering impulse to smash it into her father's face. As if reading her violent thoughts, he took a backward step. But, to her surprise, he did not look displeased. She turned to give the crown to one of her ladies before she remembered that they had remained in the pavilion across the river. Stephen walked forward.

"Let me help you, Cousin," he said, taking the crown from her.

Not trusting herself to speak, Maud nodded gratefully. The King grimaced in what she took to be a smile, and clasped her in his arms at last. The familiar scent of sweat, damp leather, and stables was overpowering. The waiting crowd let out a long sigh.

"You will not regret the loss of that trinket," Henry said in her ear. "You shall know as much honor in England and Normandy, I promise you, as ever you knew in Germany. More."

He released her so quickly she stumbled backwards, but he caught her arm in a firm grip. "You have much to learn, I think, but you please us well, Daughter."

"Sire." She bowed her head, controlling her rage and shame as the magnates of her father's court came up to greet her.

With a frozen smile on her lips she mouthed polite phrases, her father's words echoing in her head. Honor indeed! Sweet Marie, what honor was there in shaming her before his court? Without her crown, which she knew she could never again wear with impunity, she felt naked, stripped of pride and identity. It was not to be borne! But for the moment, if she meant to survive in this Norman stronghold, she must bear it. And she intended to survive, she told herself fiercely, survive long enough until somehow she became as powerful as her father.

Chapter Seven

THE LITTER CARRYING MAUD BACK TO HER CAMP HAD JUST COME TO THE
bridge, when she heard footsteps running down the hill behind her.
Turning, she saw her cousin Stephen, his blue mantle streaming
behind him. In one hand he held the Imperial crown.

The litter came to a halt as he approached.

"Cousin, here is your crown," he said in a breathless voice. "You
left so quickly I had no time to return it." He handed her the gold
circlet.

"Thank you," Maud replied.

When he made no move to leave she became disconcerted.

"Was there something else?" She knew she sounded ungracious
but at the moment did not care.

"Let me walk you back to your pavilion," he said.

"Walk back?"

"Only a short walk, and it's such a warm day."

It would be pleasant to walk for a change, Maud decided. She was
tired of being carted about in the litter, and missed the daily exercise
of riding her mare which she had done regularly in Germany. Still
she held back, reluctant without knowing why.

"That's settled then," Stephen said, without waiting for an answer. Before she could resist he had taken her hand and the next thing she knew her feet were on the ground.

He waved the litter away; they were alone on the bridge.

"Do you make a habit of enforcing your will on others?" she asked, undecided whether she was offended or amused.

"Never," he said disarmingly. "Persuasion is so much more effective for it brings me whatever I desire."

"Indeed?" Maud struggled to keep her expression serious. "You have a high opinion of yourself."

"I've been assured that it is entirely justified." Stephen's smile was infectious.

He was impossible to resist and she burst out laughing. They began to walk over the bridge. Halfway across, Stephen took her arm and purposefully led her to the stone railing. His smile faded and he looked directly into her eyes.

"Do not be distressed by the incident with your father," he said. "He meant you no harm."

It was the last thing Maud had expected, and she felt her sense of dignity unravel. That he had sensed her distress, that her feelings had been so exposed, was even worse than his having witnessed her humiliation.

She carefully laid the crown on the rail, then forced a laugh. "Why ever should you think I was distressed?"

"There's no need to keep up appearances with me, Cousin," Stephen replied. "At one time or another we have all felt crushed by the King's will and smarted under the lash of his tongue."

Maud hesitated, still feeling the need to shield her vulnerability. But Stephen's voice sounded genuinely concerned, and the need to release her pent-up frustration and bitterness would no longer be denied.

"To disgrace me before all his court—" she began, then stopped, swallowing the flood of impending tears.

"To disgrace you was not his intent," Stephen said.

Maud's hands balled into fists. "Why else would he treat me so? He did not even think me worthy of a proper reception in Rouen."

Stephen looked at her in genuine surprise. "But that is easily explained. St. Clair has great significance for the King, for all Normans." He pointed a finger at the water beneath them. "The banks of the Epte River were the scene of an unprecedented historic event. Over two hundred years ago, on this very ground, the King of France created Rollo the Viking, the first Duke of Normandy. It's my guess your father meant to do you honor!"

"I did not know that," she said slowly, then shook her head. "What you say makes no sense. What possible connection can there be between myself and the first Duke of Normandy? How can he hope to do me honor by forcing me to remove my crown?"

"I think, as well, that perhaps he meant to teach you a lesson. The King will not tolerate defiance." Stephen's green eyes danced. "And it was to defy him that you wore the crown, was it not?"

"And if it was? Why do you defend that tyrant?"

Stephen took a step back and held up his hands in mock protection. "As God is my witness, I do not defend him. But in years of experience with my uncle, I have found that—"

"You do defend him," she interjected, cutting him off. "Sweet Marie, when members of his court came up to greet me none could meet my eye, nor could they escape soon enough. As if the King's displeasure was a catching thing, like a wasting disease."

Stephen was silent. "What can I say to reassure you?" he finally asked. "Whatever the King does, no matter how cruel—and I don't deny that he can be cruel—invariably he has the weal of the realm in mind."

Maud turned away with a despairing gesture. Walking back to the railing, she leaned over the side and stared down into the muddy water of the river. It seemed impossible that this rustic hamlet should ever have been the setting for a great event.

"Oh, what's the use," she said, her back to him. "You, who are so greatly admired by the King, loved and accepted by everyone, how could I ever expect you to understand? After occupying a position of authority and prominence, do you know what it's like to be alone, an outsider, totally at the mercy of a virtual stranger?"

Two strong hands gripped her shoulders and turned her around. There was a look on Stephen's face, a steely glitter to his eyes, that sent a shiver of surprise through her.

"I not understand? By God's birth, matters were not always so favorable for me as they are now, let me tell you. My mother, like your father, is a strong woman with a will of iron. She never had a kind word to say about me, and finally sent me from Blois, not with her blessing but with a warning never to return unless I made something of myself. My father, a deserter and coward, died when I was small, and I have lived with that shame for over twenty years. When

I came to England no one could have been more alone, more miserable for the first year or two. I had to earn my place in the sun."

Maud's rage slowly dissipated, turning to compassion and interest. Miraculously, he did understand. "I had not realized your mother was so like my father."

"Were they not both children of the great William?" Stephen replied, with a bitter edge to his voice. "After all, how far does the apple fall from the tree?"

Maud darted a glance at Stephen's face, which had suddenly become a frozen mask. She let the silence lengthen between them before speaking. "The Emperor always referred to our grandfather as that bastard, upstart Norman adventurer who would not have lasted a day against the Teutonic knights."

After a moment she heard Stephen chuckle. "An upstart Norman adventurer, eh? By God, I would have liked that husband of yours. How you must miss him."

"I do," she whispered, noting that the frozen mask of his face had relaxed.

"Come, I didn't mean to remind you of your loss." He reached out and tilted her face upward. "Smile," he commanded. "You have no idea how fair you are when you smile. Wondrously fair."

Maud blushed and shook her head free. "After a difficult beginning in England you have done well for yourself, Cousin," she said, anxious to change the subject. "Next to my half brother, Robert, I have heard that there is no more powerful lord in all the realm."

Stephen gave her a boyish smile. "Perhaps, with God's grace, to be more powerful still."

"Indeed?" Intrigued, she waited, wondering what he meant. When still he did not speak she prodded him: "Tell me, Cousin. I would know of your impending good fortune."

He took a deep breath. "In Germany you no doubt heard rumors that Queen Adelicia may be barren?"

"Yes, the Emperor mentioned that as a possibility. Do you believe it to be true?"

Stephen leaned over the stone siding and gazed down into the swirling waters below. "After three and one-half years of marriage with no offspring, what else can one think? The King, after all, has twenty bastards hanging about the court so he can hardly be at fault."

"Of course, he's no longer young," Maud pointed out. "But in any case there is still plenty of time, my father doesn't lie at death's door."

Stephen paused. "No. However, he's no longer a well man, I can assure you, though I pray God grant him many more years." He glanced around the deserted bridge. "The point I would make is that if there continues to be no legitimate son, what will happen to the succession when your father dies? If the Queen remains barren . . . there is talk that I am the most likely candidate. Of course, if you had been a boy the question would never have arisen—" He gave her a seductive smile. "But I'm most pleased you're not."

Maud then remembered the two emissaries who, five years earlier, had come to Rome with the news of her brother William's death and that Stephen was the favorite to succeed the King. But her father had married again and she, like everyone else, had assumed another son would be forthcoming. She had wondered if her cousin was still a candidate and now she knew. Under the present circumstances, Stephen might well be the next King of England and Duke of Normandy.

He was regarding her expectantly and Maud gave him a tentative smile, determined not to let him see that she was disquieted by his news. Although why she should be she could not imagine. Perhaps it was only a deep regret that her father's throne must pass to a nephew rather than a child of his own flesh and blood.

Setting aside her reservations, Maud gave him a mock curtsy. "So one day you may become my sovereign! I had better be on my best behavior. I'm glad for you, Cousin. Has the King spoken to you about his plans?"

A slight frown crossed Stephen's face. "Not yet. I imagine he still hopes the Queen will produce a son. But the Bishop of Salisbury assures me, in confidence of course, that in time the King will tell me —and announce the fact to his court as well. After all, who else would he choose?"

"I'm aware of no one but yourself." She sighed. "I only wish that my future was as well assured as yours."

There was a moment of silence before he asked: "You have no idea why the King sent for you? He gave no hint in his messages?"

"None. A new marriage more than likely, what else would he want me for? I cannot bring myself to think about it."

She felt the familiar surge of anger and frustration and her knuckles whitened as her fingers curled over the rail.

A hand grasped her shoulder and lingered there. "Perhaps the new husband will be to your taste," Stephen said in a soft voice. "Young, stalwart, and a very model of chivalry. Try to look on the fair side."

He did not remove his hand and the pressure of his fingers sent her heart fluttering like a captive dove.

"Let us not dwell on the future, either of us," he went on, his eyes sparkling like emeralds. "In the next moment a bolt of lightning may strike us where we stand. We're here now, and I intend to make your stay as pleasant as possible. You have a champion in me, always remember that." His eyes met hers and a shower of sparks flew between them.

Stephen picked up the crown from the railing and handed it to Maud. In silence, they continued across the bridge. Had the sky become a deeper blue? Maud wondered. The sun a brighter hue of gold? Surely the heady scent of the apple trees, warm and sweet on the breeze, had not been there before? She felt vibrantly alive, buoyant, as if she could take wing at any moment. She had not felt like this for—actually she had never felt anything remotely like this. It was intoxicating yet unexpectedly frightening. She glanced at Stephen walking beside her, aware that a bond had been forged between them.

All too soon they reached the pavilion.

Aldyth was standing in the open doorway, a worried look on her face. "Where have you been, Lady? The litter came back quite some time ago." She stopped in surprise when she saw Stephen.

"We walked from the bridge. Here is my cousin, Stephen of Blois, Count of Mortain. My foster mother, Aldyth."

Stephen bowed, gave Aldyth a dazzling smile, and said something to her in Saxon.

Unmoved, Aldyth gave him a brief curtsy. Her eyes were wary; her head lifted like a hound scenting danger. She looked suspiciously from Stephen to Maud.

"Here." Maud handed Aldyth the crown and, before she could protest, walked swiftly around the corner of the pavilion with Stephen.

"You know we leave for England tomorrow. Will you ride with me to the coast?" Stephen asked. "I can arrange for us to board ship together as well."

"You're most kind, but I'm not certain the King—that is to say, he may have made other plans for me," Maud said.

"I will arrange it, Cousin, leave the matter in my hands." Stephen laughed, a light, boyish sound filled with a kind of wild exhilaration. "I would be with you when you set eyes on your native land once again, for it was in England I first saw you."

"Very well," Maud said, her face flushed, her heart racing. It was impossible not to be caught up in Stephen's infectious enthusiasm, his certainty that matters would go the way he intended.

They slowly walked around to the front of the tent, reluctant to part.

"Until tomorrow then," Stephen said, grasping her hands. "I will come to your pavilion in time for morning Mass."

"Until tomorrow," Maud replied, pulling her hands free. She ran, flew, over the grass to the door of the pavilion.

Even after Aldyth had shut the door firmly behind her, Maud could feel Stephen's presence outside. Within a few moments, she heard the sound of his retreating footsteps.

Later, lying in the feather bed, too excited to sleep, Maud realized that she had almost forgotten the humiliating incident with her father. Life seemed filled with promise once again. She even looked forward to returning to England now. Lifting cool fingers to her burning cheeks, she remembered the touch of Stephen's large warm hands on hers. The realization that she would be with him over a period of several days was an unexpected boon.

Her eyelids had begun to close when she became aware of Aldyth standing over her. Maud opened her eyes.

"I was almost asleep," she murmured. "What is it?"

"Something has been nagging at the back of my mind about that strutting coxcomb who thinks so well of himself," she said, hands on hips. "Now I remember what it was."

"You woke me for that?"

"Stephen of Blois is married to your cousin, Matilda of Boulogne," Aldyth told her, with a smile of satisfaction. "Haven't I always warned you? 'Those who have honey in their mouths have stings in their tails.' "

Maud's eyes opened wide and a bolt of disappointment shot through her. Sweet Marie, she had, indeed, totally forgotten.

Chapter Eight

THAT SAME EVENING, JUST AFTER VESPERS, MAUD WAS AGAIN SUM-
moned to her father's camp. Her thoughts were full of Stephen and
his wife, Matilda of Boulogne, daughter of her mother's sister, another cousin whom she had never met.

Maud wondered why her father wanted to see her so soon again.
Her body tired and aching from the rigors of the journey across
Europe, she prayed the meeting would be short and without incident.

A guard admitted her into the dark interior of the tent where her
father sat before a small table, picking at the remains of a dish of
stewed lampreys. A shaggy deerhound lay at his feet, head on its
paws, mournful eyes fixed on its master. The King motioned Maud
to sit opposite him on a small stool.

Warily, Maud obeyed, her senses primed for an unexpected attack.
Looking up, she met the King's hooded gaze.

"You resemble my mother, Queen Matilda," he said suddenly.
"The fairest maid in all Flanders when my father married her." He
reached across the table and touched a tendril of hair that had escaped
Maud's headdress to lay coiled against her cheek. "But your hair is
exactly the color of my father's."

It was the very last thing Maud had expected him to say. Disconcerted, she flushed. "My grandmother—who never cried," she said.

The King poured amber-colored liquid from a leather flagon into a wooden cup and handed it to her. "Just so. You remembered."

Maud took the cup and drank, then almost choked at the bitter taste.

"Norman cider," said the King, amused. "You will get used to it in time." He rose to his feet and opened the tent door, letting in a cool night breeze. "Bring some candles," he called to a page who hovered outside the pavilion.

"We've heard how well you acquitted yourself in the Empire," the King continued, resuming his seat. "The Emperor kept me informed of your progress: your education, most unusual for a woman, the occasions upon which you represented him, the court cases over which you presided—all of it. He was very proud of you."

Tears sprang to Maud's eyes. The King watched her in silence. A page entered, carrying two lit candles set in iron holders which he placed on the small oak table. He then bowed himself out.

"Look here, Daughter," the King said in a gruff voice. "I'm not unmindful of your loss. If there had been any other way I would not have uprooted you as suddenly as I did. But the situation grows desperate and I had to act."

Maud swallowed the tears. "What situation? Why was I not consulted first? Why was I—"

He held up his hands to stop her outburst. "Enough. All in good time." He poured some cider into a wooden cup and sipped it. "In your husband's letters to me there were a few omissions that I found puzzling. For instance, why did he never mention the womanly arts? Surely these were not neglected?"

"Of course not. I can manage a castle, care for minor ailments, brew simples and herbal mixtures. I embroider, and know about the weaving of cloth—" She stopped as a smile crossed the King's face.

"Ah, now that would have pleased your Flemish grandmother. Did you know the weavers of Flanders make the finest tapestries in the world?" He paused and a small frown appeared between his thick brows. "Your accomplishments are most impressive but you've left out the most important one of all: Why are there no children?" He shot the question at her so abruptly, she almost fell off the stool.

"Children?" she repeated, trying to collect her wits.

"Your education, the duties you performed, commendable to be sure, but the main purpose of a woman's existence is the bearing of children. Why do you have none?" He leaned across the narrow table in a manner that was slightly threatening. "Did your husband not honor your bed?"

Maud turned scarlet. Shocked and embarrassed at the brutal frankness of the question, she had no intention of answering him. How dare he question her like some hapless serving maid. The subject of children had never been broached in her presence, except by Aldyth, her confessor, and a humiliating interrogation by the Emperor's physician. It was certainly not a subject she would ever have dared discuss with the Emperor himself, who loftily ignored all matters of the flesh.

"Well? I'm waiting for an explanation." The King's eyes suddenly narrowed. "By God's splendor, you did not refuse him your bed?"

Maud rose to her feet. "I never failed in my duty to my husband, Sire."

"I should hope not, I should hope not. Well?"

"You're not my confessor and have no right to ask me such . . . such immodest questions. I refuse to be insulted further."

His black eyes flashed and he started to raise his arm, then swallowed, obviously trying to keep control. Maud, determined to maintain her dignity, turned and started to leave but the King followed her and grasped her arm.

"Perhaps I put the matter too harshly," he said with an effort. "I have little gift for diplomacy and do not care to mince words. Trust me, the matter is of vital importance or I would not ask." He led her back to the stool. "After all, I am your father. It's safe to reveal the secrets of the bedchamber to me."

Maud sank back down on the stool, and the King patted her hand, the first private gesture of affection he had shown her. Her resistance softened; she had long wanted to tell someone the truth. Before she had fully made up her mind the words were spoken.

"He . . . he honored my bed," said Maud. "On occasion."

"On occasion? How often?"

"Rarely," she whispered.

"Rarely? But why? You're young, beautifully formed—as far as one can tell." He peered at her suspiciously, as though she might be hiding some gross deformity. "Were you unwell in your female parts?" A look of distaste crossed his face. "Your mother, God rest her soul, was frequently unwell."

Maud shook her head, wanting to close her ears to this unforgivable violation of her mother's privacy, but her father seemed to have no sense of decorum.

"You cannot afford to be squeamish with me, Daughter. Modesty must be overcome. The matter is too important. Why didn't he honor your bed?"

"In truth, Sire, I never knew." Now the shameful secret was out. She had never understood the reason for her husband's indifference to her body, but wondered if it might be due, in part, to some fault of her own, some lack of feminine appeal, although she had no way of knowing. "I don't think he was greatly interested in matters of the flesh."

Knowing the King's notorious reputation with women, the numerous bastards he had fathered, Maud could almost have laughed at the look of incredulity on his face.

"Did other women lure him from you?" A prurient gleam appeared in his eyes. "He would not be the first man who took his pleasures where he found them, but that is hardly an excuse for failing in his conjugal duty." He paused, his face suddenly like a thundercloud. "Boys? Was he a sodomite?"

"I'm sure he was not." Maud looked down at her hands laced tightly in her lap. "There was no evidence of such—such leanings. Or of other women."

"I see." Henry looked far from satisfied. "He did break your maidenhead? He wasn't impotent?"

"He broke it, but," she swallowed, forcing out the words, "but he could not always—in fact he was barely able to—"

"Perform his matrimonial duties," he finished for her. "Yes, I begin to understand now. How old were you when he first came to your bed?"

"Sixteen." Maud rose, so she would not have to face him, and began to walk back and forth across the pavilion.

Her father looked dumbfounded. "Sixteen? He did nothing before that? Never fondled you? Looked at you? Nothing?"

As she shook her head, an image of the Emperor, dressed in the familiar nightshirt, appeared in Maud's mind. In all the years of their marriage, following the dictum of Holy Church, he had never seen or touched any part of her body, with the exception of a paternal embrace or affectionate kiss on the cheek. His only contact with her had been through the hole in his nightshirt. Although she was aware that her mind fascinated and challenged him, Maud assumed her physical aspect—perhaps any woman's—left him indifferent.

How much of her husband's ascetic behavior was due to his own bias, and how much to the influence of the church—which proclaimed all desires of the flesh to be sinful, even within marriage—Maud had never been able to determine. Nor had she dared discuss the matter with anyone except Aldyth who, being a virgin, was as mystified as herself.

The one time—prodded by Aldyth—she had tentatively brought the matter up to her confessor, Father Sebastion, he had given her a severe penance for even thinking about fornication. Such thoughts were forbidden, he warned her, while at the same time asking the most intimate questions about what exactly the Emperor did when he came to her bed. Did he touch her body? Her breasts? Her female parts? If so, for how long? Did he kiss her in these places? Did he scrutinize her naked body? What positions did he use to copulate with her? She found herself repelled and shocked by the zeal with which Father Sebastion interrogated her, his voice quite breathless as he asked if the Emperor had ever entered her "more canino." The idea of her austere and aging husband mounting her like a dog was so far-fetched as to be almost laughable.

"So, you have never known love's pleasures." Henry's voice intruded on her thoughts and the Emperor's picture faded.

Pleasures? Remembering her rigid submission to the Emperor's joyless fumblings, Maud could not imagine anything less pleasurable.

"By God's splendor, the Holy Roman Emperor impotent," he continued. "More priest than man, by what you say." He walked over to her, placing his hands on her shoulders. "I understand now that which was not clear to me earlier. God forgive me, Daughter, I did you a great wrong when I married you to this unnatural man, thinking only to bring honor to our house by such an alliance. Who could have known he would disgrace you in this manner."

"Sire, he did not disgrace me," she began hotly, but he silenced her with a look.

"Of course he did, of course he did." His voice was harsh and implacable as he stepped back, his hands falling to his sides. "Did you know that all Europe, ignorant of where the true fault lies, assumes you to be a barren woman? Is that not disgraceful? And what disgraces you, Madam, disgraces the House of Normandy."

Her lack of children had seemed a personal matter, concerning only the Emperor and herself. Was it possible that the world sniggered behind her back, making crude jests at her expense? In despair, Maud watched her father work himself up into a state of righteous indignation. How could she ever explain to this man, who apparently looked upon all her gender as either brood mares, instruments of pleasure, or pawns to be used for political advantage, that she had had great affection for her husband, and he for her. Despite his failure to give her children, the Emperor had opened up her mind, filling it with new ideas, encouraging her to learn and think for herself, giving her opportunities to test her abilities.

"You're upset, I see. Who can blame you? I promise that this insult to our house will be removed; people will soon be singing a different tune." Henry, his good humor restored, smiled at her. "I cannot tell you how relieved I am, Daughter, what a great weight has been taken from my mind." He took her arm and opened the tent door. "I will walk you to your litter." They walked outside into the dusk. "Tomorrow we leave for the coast to set sail for England."

She nodded, and felt emboldened to take advantage of his changed mood. "Have you a new marriage in mind for me, Sire?" she asked. "Is that what all these questions mean? To determine if I would be a suitable breeder? Is this the 'desperate situation' you spoke of earlier?"

To her surprise he did not appear offended. "You'll know soon enough. Soon enough." He patted her hand. "Do not question me further."

"There is something else, Sire," she burst out before she could stop herself. "Why did you force me to take off the Imperial crown? Why did you humiliate me before your entire court?"

"Humiliate you?" He sounded genuinely surprised. "What I did was only for your own good. I have plans for you, Daughter, and to further these plans, the Imperial connection must be broken once and for all. No one must be reminded of that former life." He patted her hand again. "Trust me to act in your best interests."

"And yours," Maud said under her breath.

"Of course mine. Our interests are the same, make no mistake," he said as he helped her into the litter.

"If there are plans being made for me, surely I have the right to know what they are?"

"You have only the rights I allow you," Henry told her. "Remember that." His eyes narrowed. "You must learn to discipline your tongue, Madam, and curb your spleen. If the Emperor taught you the virtues of obedience, patience, and diplomacy I have yet to see evidence of them. A few feminine wiles would not come amiss. Submission, Madam, submission."

Maud bit her underlip and did not answer. Again and again, the Emperor had warned her to curb her impetuous temper or one day it would lead to serious trouble. Still, she could not rid herself of the idea that her father was not really displeased.

The King leaned forward and kissed her on both cheeks. "I said you shall have honor here, Daughter, and so you shall. More than you have ever dreamed. Trust me."

Trust him? What had he ever done to warrant her trust, Maud asked herself, as the litter moved off into the darkness.

As soon as Maud left, King Henry sent for his chief administrator, Roger, Bishop of Salisbury. When the Bishop entered the pavilion, he found the King scanning a parchment map spread out on the oak table.

"The meeting went well, Sire?"

"Remarkably well, Roger, Maud will do splendidly. Better than I had hoped. She made a favorable impression this morning, didn't you think?"

Wheezing slightly, the Bishop eased his fat body slowly onto a stool. "Ah—as far as I could tell she did. A most personable woman. The accent is a little strange, of course."

"People will get used to it, and in time the accent will fade."

"No doubt. What did you discover, Sire?"

"My friend, you will hardly credit the tale I've just been told," Henry said, turning from the table. "I married my daughter to a man unable to honor her bed. Virtually impotent." He dropped his voice. "And worse."

"Worse?"

"A suspected sodomite."

"No!"

"Yes. I could hardly believe it myself."

"Impious," muttered the Bishop, crossing himself. "May God assoil the poor man." He paused. "So one may then assume that the Princess Maud is not barren?"

"Far from from it, far from it." Henry rubbed his hands together. "The lady is basically untouched, innocent as a nun. For all practical purposes, *virgo intacta.*"

"I'm relieved to hear that, Sire. So you mean to go through with your plan then?"

"Of course, of course. Now that I know there is no impediment

I'm determined to see the matter through. My daughter is well educated, intelligent, strong-willed, and no stranger to the responsibilities of a crown. A woman of character and spirit, my mother all over
again. A little too ready with her tongue, but that can be remedied."

Henry began to pace the tent, hands clasped behind him. "Have I
ever told you how well my mother ruled Normandy while my father
was away conquering England?"

"Many times, Sire. Although I never tire of hearing about it,"
Roger added hastily. "A most stirring tale to be sure." Roger followed the King's movements with his eyes. "What will you do in the
event Maud does not wish for the great honor you intend to bestow
on her?"

"Not wish to be queen?" Henry stopped in his tracks, astonished
by the idea. "Of course she will want to be queen. Maud is a daughter
of Normandy, therefore ambitious." He thought for a moment. "Although she may not know it as yet. But I do." He wagged his finger
at Roger. "Do you remember how I always said Maud should have
been the boy? Already she tries to control her fate and take matters
into her own hands."

Roger nodded glumly. "I remember, Sire, but that was a long time
ago. Her lack of knowledge of England will tell against her should she
be called upon to assume the throne at short notice."

"I have many more years of life ahead of me," Henry said with a
dark look at the Bishop. "Time to teach Maud all she needs to know.
And she will be surrounded by able advisors, of course." He strode
restlessly to the table and began drumming his fingers against the
wood.

"There will be problems, naturally," he continued. "She is impetuous, headstrong. The Emperor spoiled her and everything has come
a little too easily for her, but she will have her mettle tested soon
enough, by God's splendor. I shall mold her myself. She will rule in
my image."

Roger gave a discreet cough. "As I have already warned you, Sire,
there will be difficulties with Stephen and his supporters. Not to
mention the other magnates."

Henry began to pace again. "Yes, yes, I know. You remind me
often enough. Well, circumstances change; Stephen must adapt like
everyone else. I've great affection for my nephew, and have always
treated him like my own son. He has never been stinted of wealth,
honors, titles. There is no cause for complaint from that quarter."
He paused. "When we mentioned Stephen as a possible candidate for

the throne, the Emperor was not yet dead, remember. I had no idea Maud would be available. No promises were made, mind. I've never even discussed the issue with him."

"True, but he expects to be the heir should Queen Adelicia not bear you a son. Everyone assumes he will be; everyone wants him to be. Perhaps a word in his ear would not come amiss. To soften the blow."

Henry gave the Bishop a sharp look. "Not one word, do you understand? Not one word. I want no one stirring up trouble before the fact. Stephen will hear the news when everyone else does. When the time is ripe. Meanwhile, God may still answer our prayers: The Queen may still conceive a son." He lifted his wine cup. "Now, are you through playing devil's advocate?"

The Bishop reluctantly nodded.

"I know you're against this, Roger, but you will support me despite your misgivings?" His hooded eyes watched the Bishop's face over the rim of his wooden cup.

"As always, Sire," the Bishop responded with an oily smile that showed his rotting teeth. "But this will be such a violent break with custom. There is simply no precedent for leaving the kingdom to a woman. Even in Saxon times no one would have dared—"

"Enough!" Henry interrupted, banging his cup on the table. "The matter is settled. The magnates will bend to my will." He smiled and pointed a confident finger at Roger. "In truth, Maud will make an admirable queen, eh? Admit it. When have I ever been wrong?"

Chapter Nine

STEPHEN'S BROTHER HENRY, ABBOT OF GLASTONBURY, HAD WITNESSED the encounter between the King and his daughter with intense interest. When the King arranged to see his daughter alone, followed immediately by a visit from the Bishop of Salisbury, he suspected something was afoot. After Vespers, an impromptu visit to Bishop Roger was in order. The Bishop would tell him about the second meeting, and also allay his growing concern about his brother's future as heir apparent, a concern he had not voiced to Stephen. A light wind ruffled the pale brown hair around his tonsure and flattened his black habit against his thin shanks.

As the Abbot bowed his head to enter the cramped interior of the church, the stench of unwashed bodies rose to meet him. He wrinkled his arched nose in distaste. Looking about him with cool green eyes, the Abbot realized that almost no one from the King's camp had attended the service. Not surprising, he thought, in such an ugly, unassuming house of worship. A church should be glorified with beautiful things in tasteful surroundings, not like this filthy place. Impatiently, his eyes sought out the altar. There was no water clock, not even an hourglass. He thought longingly of his own comfortable, well-appointed church in Glastonbury.

Of course Glastonbury was well enough for the moment, he reflected, letting his mind wander. It would serve as a stepping-stone to
greater heights, such as the wealthy and powerful See of Winchester,
recently fallen vacant. He was positive he could persuade his uncle
that, despite his youth, he was the right candidate. Once the King let
it be known that he favored his nephew, the church would appoint
him. It might even be possible to retain his See of Glastonbury as
well.

Yes, Bishop of Winchester was the next rung on the ladder, Henry
thought. But that was not the summit of his ambition. Far from it.
An expectant smile curved his thin lips. When the King died, if all
went as expected, then his brother Stephen would succeed to the
throne. Not long after that, the present Archbishop of Canterbury, a
frail old man, would almost certainly be called to his just reward.
Henry had Stephen's firm promise to then make him Archbishop.
And after that? Archbishop of Canterbury was the highest honor the
English church could offer, the apex of his hopes. Or was it? Half
dozing, the Abbot suddenly saw a picture of himself in a red cardinal's
hat walking up the stone steps of St. Peter's in Rome to a thundering
peal of heavenly bells.

After the service was over, Henry strode quickly through the village until he came to the Bishop of Salisbury's pavilion. Inside, he
found Bishop Roger conferring with the cleric who attended him.

"I would see the Bishop alone," he said to the cleric.

The cleric looked at the Bishop, who nodded his consent. When
they were alone, the Bishop offered Henry a stool.

"I prefer to stand, thank you, after kneeling in that poor excuse
for a church."

"You must be more charitable toward our less fortunate brethren.
I take it this is not a courtesy visit?" The Bishop's shrewd eyes
searched the Abbot's face.

"In truth, I would open my mind to you, Your Grace." He paused.
"You will forgive my bluntness but it has struck me that there's more
to the return of the King's daughter than has been said."

"Are there rumors to that effect?"

"Thick as flies in summer."

The Bishop sighed. "I feared as much. There is a reason the King
has sent for her, but I'm bound by oath not to speak of it."

The Abbot digested this in silence, pleased at his own prescience.
Should he leave it at that or pursue the matter further? He would
pursue it.

"Is there to be an advantageous marriage for her?"

The Bishop examined his pudgy fingers weighted with jeweled rings. No, Henry decided, he was on the wrong path here. Not a marriage. He adroitly switched to another subject.

"Is there any word on when the King will announce Stephen as his heir?"

Roger's face turned the color of suet. "I told you I would let you know," he whispered, his eyes darting around the pavilion in agitation. "We mustn't speak of such matters here."

"It must be spoken of," the Abbot insisted. "Neither Stephen nor I can understand the delay. The King is not in robust health; the Queen remains barren. It's imperative he designate an heir now. You told me so yourself, on numerous occasions—"

The Bishop put a hand up to signal silence. "Never mind what I said in the past." He passed a shaking hand across his forehead. "Listen to me, Henry, I speak as a friend: Stephen will not be designated as the King's heir." Suddenly he compressed his lips, as if fearful he had said too much. "Leave me now for I can tell you no more." Slowly, he raised his vast bulk from the stool.

"Stephen not the heir?" The Abbot stared at him, unable to believe he had heard him aright. An icy chill traveled down his spine. So great was his shock that for the first time in his life he found himself beyond speech. "But—but it must be Stephen," he managed to say at last. "Who else is there, unless—is the Queen with child?"

"Not that I know of. Let us leave the matter now," the Bishop muttered.

"Please—I beg you to tell me who will reign after King Henry. For almost a year now you have fostered our hopes. I thought you supported Stephen."

The Bishop sighed. "Believe me when I tell you I put forward your brother's cause as well as I knew how—to no avail. Stephen will not reign." He lumbered toward the tent door.

"Is the heir to be Robert of Gloucester?" The Abbot drew back his head like a serpent ready to strike. "Is the King so addled in his wits he thinks to foist the by-blow of a Welsh concubine on the realm?" he hissed. "No one will stand for it, I can promise you that."

"No. No. Not Robert."

"Then who? There *is* no one else. You must tell me!" Beside himself with outraged frustration, the Abbot imprudently grabbed the prelate by the shoulders. "Why will Stephen not be king? Why?"

"You dare to lay hands on me? Have you gone mad?" The Bishop struggled in his grasp. "Walter, Walter," he suddenly shouted for his cleric.

The cleric burst in so quickly that Henry knew he had been listening at the door. His arms fell to his sides. It had been an unforgivable breach, totally unlike him to lose control.

"Forgive me, Your Grace, for so forgetting myself. Mea culpa. I accept whatever penance you deem proper for the offense." Hiding his anger and chagrin beneath a frosty smile, he bowed and left.

Shaken, the Abbot walked aimlessly through the camp. God forgive him, but he would have liked to throttle the information out of Roger of Salisbury. He still could not believe what he had heard. It was impossible that Stephen would not be the King's heir.

For more than a year now, ever since he had completed his studies at the monastery school of Cluny and come to England, Henry had expected his brother to eventually reign—should the Queen remain childless. His blood churned; his head felt as if it would burst. His ultimate goal in the church depended on Stephen being crowned, for how else could he make absolutely certain of being appointed Archbishop of Canterbury when the See fell vacant? From that exalted office he would virtually govern the kingdom through his brother, for he had always been able to bend Stephen to his will. Then would the church rule supreme in England. Henry never doubted that his own interests and God's were one and the same. Why else was he put on earth but to honor Our Lord through the rule of the church?

Nothing must come between him and the high purpose he had set himself, he thought savagely. Nothing and no one. The Abbot looked up at the dark sky, suddenly wondering if God had failed him. Impossible. He crushed the treacherous thought before it could take root. Was he not His most worthy servant? Of course. Then matters must fall out as he had envisioned.

As Abbot Henry raged through the night, he knew with every fiber of his being that, somehow, he would see his brother on England's throne, no matter the cost.

Chapter Ten

Later that night the king's bastard son Robert, earl of Gloucester, was awakened from a deep sleep by Brian FitzCount.

"Sorry to wake you, Robert," Brian whispered, "but the King suffers from one of his nightmares. He complains of sharp pains in his belly and is calling for you."

"A moment. I'll meet you outside."

Groggy, Robert rubbed his eyes, rolled his stocky body out of his pallet, fumbled for his tunic and boots, then tiptoed through the pavilion, stepping over the sleeping bodies of his cousin, Stephen, and the de Beaumont twins. Outside, he knelt by a wooden bucket, then splashed his face with water until he was awake. Hastily, he slipped the tunic over his head and pulled on his boots.

"What happened?" Robert asked Brian as they made their way through the quiet camp. Usually, either Brian or himself tended the King when he was ill. Tonight the duty had fallen to Brian.

"I was playing to the King on my lute, soothing him for sleep as I often do. He slept, but then the nightmare started. The usual one."

"Perhaps there was too much excitement today," Robert suggested, "what with the arrival of his daughter and all."

"More likely the stewed lampreys he ate, which his physicians warned him never to touch again. Remember how sick he was the last time he had the dish? But when he wants something, who dares to cross him?"

No one, Robert thought. As they approached the King's tent Robert heard his father groaning, and saw the anxious faces of the guards flanking the entrance. Inside, the King lay tossing on a feather bed, his face beaded with sweat. A squire, crouched by his side, sponged his face with a damp linen cloth. A single candle threw a long shadow across the dim interior.

"Father, Sire, I'm here." Robert knelt beside the bed.

"My son!" Struggling to a sitting position, the King clutched Robert's shoulder with clawlike fingers. "God give me strength, I had that terrible dream again—"

"Prepare a posset of wine mixed with a few drops of poppy," Robert whispered to the squire, who withdrew to a corner of the tent. "Tell me, Sire."

Breathing in labored gasps, the King fell back against the pillows. "Always the same dream. Peasants and knights assault me with lance and billhook." His voice dropped. "They torture me and—" His eyes grew wild, and he touched his groin with a trembling finger.

Robert took his father's hand in both of his. "Calm yourself, Sire."

"Is it God's judgment, Robert?" The voice was barely audible now. "Is it? Is it?"

"No, Father," Robert said soothingly. "Naught but a nightmare. From eating stewed lampreys against your physicians' orders. That's all." He dared say nothing else, although the King suffered similar nightmares so often that, in his heart, Robert concluded it must be a judgment from God.

The squire appeared, holding out a wooden cup. "The posset, my lord."

Robert propped his father up against the pillows, took the cup, and lifted it to the King's lips.

The King turned his head away, wrinkling his nose like a petulant child. "How do I know it's not poisoned," he muttered. "Perhaps you work in league with my enemies, seeking to destroy me before my work is done. Drink it yourself first."

Without hesitation, Robert lifted the cup to his lips and took a small swallow. He handed it to Brian, who did the same. "There. Perfectly safe. Do you drink now."

The King watched them suspiciously for a few moments before

taking a wary sip. Robert watched him carefully as he drank the rest. After a short while the King's eyelids began to droop.

"Robert—" The King's eyes flew open as he clutched Robert's arm. The deep dark eyes, so like his own, fixed him with a compelling intensity. "You must promise me—nay, swear to me upon the soul of your dead mother, whom I loved above all other women—that you'll protect and stand by your half sister under all circumstances."

"Of course, Sire." Such an odd request. Why would the King think Maud needed protection, Robert wondered uneasily; yet there was no denying the urgency behind the plea.

"You too, Brian."

"Of course, Sire," Brian replied.

"Swear now. Wait." Fumbling under the pillow, the King pulled out a crystal vial containing a milky liquid. "On this holy relic—Our Lady's milk. Swear on this."

Concealing his surprise, Robert placed his hand on the vial. "I swear, Sire, on the soul of my dead mother and upon this holy relic, to obey your wishes regarding my half-sister."

Brian also swore.

The King's eyes glazed. "I know I can trust you, my son, and Brian too, not to betray me when I'm gone."

Brian and Robert exchanged startled glances. Betray the King after his death? How would that be possible? It must be the poppy dulling his father's wits, Robert decided.

"I would never betray you," he replied, in the gentle voice he used to allay the unfounded fears of his children.

"You are the child of my heart, Robert," the King whispered, his eyes closing, "and I bitterly regret I cannot make you my heir, for you are the best suited to be king. But the church, the people, the magnates, no one will accept a bastard ruler. Only a child I've begotten on an anointed queen. You understand, my son—" The harsh breathing became regular as the King's head lolled to one side.

Greatly disturbed, Robert rose to his feet. "Let me know if he wakes again," he said to the squire.

Brian picked up his lute and together they left the tent. Outside, they breathed deeply of the cool night air.

"What can he have meant, that the heir must be the offspring of an anointed queen?" Brian asked. "Stephen isn't the son of a queen. He's not even in the direct male line of descent from the Conqueror, yet everyone expects him to be the King's successor—unless the Queen produces a son."

"One can take no notice of what my father says when he's in such a sorry state," Robert said. "His wits are so befuddled that he forgets William is dead. His words make no sense otherwise."

"None whatsoever," Brian agreed. "I wonder where he got that bogus relic."

"Bogus?"

"Come, over the years I've seen enough vials of virgin's milk to have nursed a hundred Christs. I didn't think the King was so gullible."

"What a man believes is his own affair. Who are we to judge?" Robert said, unable to shake off his feeling of distress.

He had long ago accepted the fact that he could never be the King's heir. Yet mention of it stirred up old longings, forgotten dreams once cherished.

"What troubles you?" Brian asked.

"Surely it is a hard lesson God has set me, to know I'm ideally suited for a great task and be denied all opportunity for fulfillment." He had not meant to speak of his feelings; the words had come forth before he could stop them.

Brian reached out and laid an understanding hand on Robert shoulder. "You would make a splendid king, in my opinion, better than Stephen."

"Stephen will do very well," Robert said quickly, not wanting Brian to think him disloyal, although he was inwardly gratified.

"Well enough," said Brian, with an ironic twist to his voice. "He's a great warrior and unsurpassed in the hunt. Well-loved, charming and personable. But there's more to ruling the Norman realm than killing men and beasts."

"He will rise to the task, I've no doubt," Robert stated firmly. Nothing was served by dwelling on what he could never have.

He looked up at the shadowed sky lit by a full moon. With God's grace, he would be home in time to oversee the gathering of the harvest.

"I cannot stop thinking of that oath we swore to protect my half-sister," Robert wondered aloud. "I would stand by her, oath or no, should she need my aid." A warm smile hovered about his lips. "I loved her when we were children. You never saw anyone with so much spirit, far more than William ever had, God rest his soul. She has grown into a lovely, impressive woman, don't you think?'' He yawned.

"Indeed. Go to sleep, I'll join you anon.''

As Robert entered the pavilion his eyes fell on Stephen's sleeping face. A wave of affection rushed through him. Despite their amicable rivalry and his occasional twinges of envy, he and Stephen were part of the same Norman family tree, root and branch, nourished by the same sap. It was unworthy of him to begrudge Stephen the crown. After all, how many bastards were as well-favored as himself? Indeed, how many men could boast of loyal companions, fruitful estates, a castle full of sons, and a devoted wife? Life was good to him; he wanted for nothing, and he owed it all to his father.

Before allowing himself the luxury of sleep, Robert knelt by his straw pallet, closed his eyes, and clasped his hands in prayer. From the fullness of his heart, he offered up his thanks to God for all the blessings showered on him, praying to be kept free of the driving spur of ambition, asking only to be made worthy of his great good fortune.

Outside the pavilion Brian FitzCount, wide awake, gazed up at the harvest moon. He wondered what Robert would say if he told him that he thought Maud the loveliest woman he had ever set eyes on, and that she stirred his blood and piqued his interest as no woman ever had. Cool and detached, Brian was aware that he had rarely given his wholehearted affection to anyone other than the King, Robert, and Stephen, and never his heart.

Unlike Robert, he did not look forward to returning to England, to his dull wife and his childless castle at Wallingford. But his duty lay with the King and where the King went, Brian followed. Brian was a bastard son of the King's old friend, Count Alan of Brittany, and Henry had taken Brian in as a child, educated him, married him to a Saxon heiress, and made him castellan of Wallingford Castle. Brian knew how much he owed his benefactor, and never begrudged the King his years of selfless service.

He sat down on the ground, his back against a tree, his lute propped between his knees. As Brian's fingers idly plucked the strings his thoughts returned to the oath he and Robert had sworn and to the King's strange ramblings. When the most likely explanation finally came to him, he was stunned: Jesu, the King, despairing of ever having a legitimate son, meant to make his daughter his heir! Instantly Brian rejected the thought. It was impossible; without precedent, unheard of. In England no woman had ever inherited the throne, not even in Saxon times. The King could not intend such folly. On the other hand, that would explain the oaths. It would certainly explain why Maud, her husband barely cold in his grave, had been recalled so hastily from Germany. Instinct told Brian that if what he suspected was true, Maud was as ignorant of her father's plans as everyone else.

A guard walked by and raised a hand in greeting. What would the man say, Brian wondered, if he told him his suspicions? Laugh, no doubt, and claim Brian the worse for wine. He could not imagine either the commonfolk or the magnates allowing the King to go through with such a scheme. And yet, in all his years with King Henry, Brian had never seen him fail in his purpose, nor falter in his intent. Whatever the cost, he was relentless in pursuing his goals. Well before Brian's time there were incidents to chill the blood. He let his thoughts rove backwards in time, remembering the tales he had heard, not spoken of openly, but whispered in dark corners.

At the death of William the Conqueror, thirty-eight years ago, Henry's eldest brother, Robert, became Duke of Normandy. His second brother, William Rufus, became King of England. Henry, the youngest, was bequeathed silver but no land. In 1100, thirteen years later, King William Rufus was killed, hit by a chance arrow while hunting in the New Forest. His timely death—then or now no one believed it an accident—had proved most expedient for his younger brother. Whether Henry's hand had drawn the bow or he had arranged for another to do it, the result was the same: King William Rufus was dead; Henry was able to seize the throne without opposition.

Six years later he had crossed the channel, attacked his brother, Duke Robert of Normandy, defeated him in battle, then took the duchy for himself. But he had not killed his eldest brother, choosing instead to imprison the former duke in a Welsh fortress, where the unfortunate wretch remained to this day. Thus both Normandy and England were again united under the control of a single ruler, as they had been in the Conqueror's time.

These were but two in a long life crowded with similar incidents, which made King Henry neither better nor worse than many another monarch in Europe, but gave every indication that, by one means or another, what he wanted he would have.

If the King did indeed mean to force his daughter on an unsuspecting nobility, then he was making a grave error, Brian thought, one that would cost the land dear after his death. However, it would take a braver man than himself to tell that to his sovereign. He wondered what Maud's reaction would be when she found out what lay in store for her, and Stephen's response when he discovered that he would be supplanted by the woman he found so appealing.

Chapter Eleven

England, 1125

A WEEK LATER, SURROUNDED BY A DENSE FOG, MAUD STOOD AT THE ship's rail eagerly awaiting her first glimpse of land. As the ship bobbed in the swells, she suddenly pitched forward, clutching the rail for support. From behind her a hand reached out to grasp her shoulder.

"Careful," said Stephen's voice in her ear, his hand steadying her.

A green wave reared up to shower her with spray and she gave a little shriek, then wiped the fine mist from her face. "Oh, thank you."

"I was hoping to find you alone for a moment," Stephen said. "Do I imagine it or have you been avoiding me since our last discourse on the bridge?"

"My time has really not been my own," Maud said, which was certainly true, as her father and Robert had claimed almost all her attention on the leisurely ride to the coast.

But in truth she had also tried to avoid being alone with her cousin, uncomfortable at her immediate response to his physical presence, as well as distrustful of him since Aldyth's reminder that he was married. She had no intention of being an easy conquest for this man who, Aldyth had warned her, need only crook his little finger for a woman to do his bidding.

"I understand," Stephen replied. "As long as I have done nothing to offend you."

Maud realized that he had not removed his hand from her shoulder and that she had no wish for him to do so.

"On the contrary, you have been most kind and thoughtful." She looked up to see Stephen regarding her with an expression of amusement. So he knew perfectly well that she had been avoiding him.

"It doesn't matter now," he said. "We're together and soon you'll see your first sight of England in fourteen years. The fog should break any moment."

The ship rode the swells like an unbridled colt and Maud was rocked back on her heels. When Stephen caught her in his arms she resisted for a moment, glancing quickly around to see if anyone observed them. But the dawn mist had wrapped them in a soft gray cocoon, and they were isolated from prying eyes. Maud could hear the crew running up and down the deck, their disembodied voices calling to one another, the flap of the ship's sails being furled, and the boom creaking. But she could see nothing.

A brisk wind sprang up. The hood of Maud's brown cloak flew back from her head and russet strands of hair lashed at her cheeks and forehead. Stephen tightened his arms around her and she let herself relax against him. His face touched the side of her head, and Maud could feel his breath warm and quick against her temple. A sweet surge of excitement swept through her body; her eyes dropped to his hands clasped around her waist. They were large, with strong, square fingers, covered with a fine brush of honey-colored hair. She had a sudden shocking impulse to move them up to her breasts, then flushed to the roots of her hair, stunned that she should even think of such a thing, for no one had ever touched her there before. Mortified, she pushed away his hands and leaned against the rail. She would rather be buffeted by the turmoil of wind and wave than by the turmoil of his touch.

"Look," he whispered.

As the wind blew away patches of mist, Maud caught a sudden glimpse of towering white cliffs surmounted by a manned fortress. Within moments she and Stephen were surrounded by members of her party, pointing their fingers and exclaiming at their first sight of England. Aldyth wept unashamedly to see her native land once more.

Maud wished her German ladies could have made the voyage with her, for she had told them so much about her homeland, but the King had insisted they were unsuitable and packed them off to Germany. In England she would be provided with Norman ladies, he assured her, as befitted her new station in life. Intrigued, she had asked her father what that might be and received only an enigmatic smile in return.

The vessel surged forward on an incoming tide and Dover harbor came into view.

"Welcome home, Cousin," Stephen said with a smile.

As her heart leapt in response, Maud realized she was no longer the despondent woman who had resisted coming to England only six weeks ago. Now, despite her uncertainty about the future, she felt poised on the threshold of a new adventure.

After resting in Dover for twenty-four hours, the King's entourage left for Windsor the following morning. Flanked by Stephen on one side and Robert on the other, Maud felt expectant as a child. The royal procession made its way down Watling Street, the old Roman road that ran all the way through Canterbury and London as far north as Chester. The road wound through narrow cobbled streets lined with wooden houses, past fortified walls and well-tended yellow fields where villeins gathered in the harvest. In the distance she could see the green curve of wooden downs.

Everywhere Maud looked there was evidence of peace and prosperity. From time to time they passed other travelers: a group of black-robed clerics on foot making a pilgrimage to Canterbury, a shepherd driving a flock of sheep, a line of carts headed in the direction of the coast carrying a load of wool for export to Flanders. Then a party of women riding alone to market caught her attention. Their pannier baskets were piled high with squawking trussed chickens, bunches of wine-colored beets, balls of pale green lettuce, and stalks of green and white scallions.

The procession came to a halt while the King greeted the women, questioned them in detail about their produce, tested the chickens for plumpness and, with a pinch on the rump of the prettiest girl, sent them giggling on their way.

"These women ride unguarded?" Maud asked in surprise.

"The roads are safe," Robert replied, "since our father enforces the peace with harsh laws. Robbery and violence are punishable by mutilation and blinding. Wait," he cautioned at the look of revulsion on Maud's face. "Do not be so quick to judge. It's the King's boast that in his land a maid carrying a bag of gold can walk the whole day through in perfect safety. How else would that be possible?"

Maud could not think of a suitable rejoinder, though she felt there must be a less cruel way to maintain law and order. In silence she watched Stephen point out castles and great estates held by the King's barons, acres of fertile meadows, well-stocked pastures, and orchards heavy with fruit. Every so often the King would stop and greet a landowner overseeing the work in his fields.

"My father is truly interested in this man's fief?" Maud asked Stephen, watching a burly Norman answering her father's questions.

The King listened attentively, nodded his head, then summoned one of his clerks to note down the man's words on his wax tablet.

"Of course," Stephen replied. "I'll wager my uncle can tell you how many pigs this man has running loose in his fields, if his herd of goats increased since last year, and whether his field of barley failed or prospered."

"I've never seen a ruler behave thus," Maud said, amazed. "The Empire was rarely at peace. The Emperor was either warring with the Pope or putting down one insurrection after another. He never had the time to talk to his subjects in this manner."

"Our father dearly loves order and would rather keep the peace than make war," Robert told her. "That's why his kingdom prospers."

This was a revelation to Maud. She had always, even as a child, considered her father a tyrant, but what she was witnessing this morning hardly fit that image. Apparently there was another side to him. Whatever personal animosity she felt, it was evident she must respect him as a king.

The remainder of the day passed all too swiftly.

Dusk was approaching, the blue sky streaked with rose and purple shadows.

"Our journey's end," Stephen said. "Unfortunately."

He gave her a lingering look that sent a shiver through Maud's entire body. Reluctantly, she forced her eyes away.

A Norman castle, set high on the west bank of the Thames, rose slowly out of the river mist. Windsor. Maud leaned forward in the saddle.

"Does it look familiar?" Robert asked.

Her heart full of memories, Maud nodded. The outer walls were just ahead now and the procession slowed. There was a crowd of well-wishers outside come to greet the King. For one unguarded moment

Maud found herself looking for her mother. Suddenly, without a word, Stephen spurred his horse forward and rode on ahead. A woman in a white tunic and blue mantle, a coronet of flaxen braids crowning her head, appeared out of the crowd. She smiled and waved. Maud caught her breath. Sweet Marie, it was not possible—a scream was torn from her throat, she dropped the reins, and quickly covered her mouth with her hands.

"What in God's name—" Alarmed, Robert's hand gripped the sword swinging by his side. His eyes quickly scanned the crowd.

Maud pointed a trembling finger at the woman. "My mother," she whispered, her face ashen. "It's my mother!"

"Your mother?" Robert stared at her as if she had gone mad. He looked again at the crowd, then laughed in relief. "By the Mass, now I understand. We never thought to tell you how much your Cousin Matilda resembles her aunt, the late queen. That's the Countess of Boulogne and Mortain, Stephen's wife."

The shock of that initial impact stayed with Maud as she made her entry into the courtyard of the castle, teeming with grooms, stewards, and servitors, and through the rushed ablutions of preparing for the evening meal. It was not until she was seated at the high table in the great hall that she had a chance to draw breath and observe Matilda at close quarters. All she knew about Stephen's wife was that she was the only child of her mother's older sister, and heiress to the Count of Boulogne.

Still clad in Our Lady's colors of blue and white, Matilda had undone her hair which now fell in two silver-gilt braids to her waist. Her face was naturally grave, Maud noted, like her own mother's had been, and although she was only two years older than herself, its fragile prettiness had already begun to fade. She had a small rosebud mouth and soft blue eyes which frequently cast adoring glances at her husband. Closer to view, her resemblance to the late queen, thank heaven, was less startling.

Having now recovered from her first reaction, Maud felt an overwhelming relief. Stephen's wife was no beauty and therefore no real threat to her. The treacherous thought shocked her and immediately she felt consumed by guilt. Throughout the evening meal Matilda, obviously delighted to meet her cousin, chatted away like a gentle little wren. Maud barely heard a word as she was desperately trying to avoid Stephen's gaze. The harder she tried the more compelling was the need to look at him. Every time their eyes did meet the air between them crackled like summer lightning, making her blood race even as it increased her sense of guilt. It seemed impossible that Matilda would not notice, but she remained oblivious, which somehow made matters even worse.

Mercifully, the meal was soon over and Maud was able to escape to her own quarters in the castle.

The next morning Aldyth told her Stephen and his wife had gone.

"Gone?" For a moment she could not take it in. "Gone where?"

"To London, where they live," said Aldyth. "Together, if I may remind you. With their children." She raised her brows and gave Maud a pointed what-did-I-tell-you smile.

Maud hoped her disappointment did not show. After all, she had no right to expect her cousin to remain at Windsor. Where Stephen was concerned she had no rights at all, she thought in despair, remembering how Matilda had looked at her husband.

"Why should that be of any concern to me?" she asked, determined to put him out of her mind. The sooner she stopped thinking about a man she could never have, the better off she would be.

"Why indeed. I have eyes in my head, if others do not," Aldyth continued. "Far too intimate, you and the Count of Mortain, and—"

Maud tried to close out the accusing voice as she looked around her chamber, having been too exhausted to do so last night. With a pang she realized she was in her mother's old solar, which the new queen had thoughtfully vacated in honor of her visit. Yes, there were the prie-dieu, the gold and scarlet hangings, worn and threadbare now, but achingly familiar. Even the blue coverlet was the same.

"What a turn the Countess Matilda gave me," Aldyth was saying now. "Not only does she look like your mother, but has a similar nature as well, I'm told. A very saint they say, and devoted to her husband, who is far from being a saint, let me tell you. What I've heard about that one!"

"I'm not interested in servants' gossip," Maud retorted. "We only arrived last night yet already you seem to know all the scandal."

"Naturally, I make it my business to know what goes on. What says the old saw? 'Forewarned is forearmed.' "

Maud made a face. "Well, you can keep your hints and warnings to yourself."

Aldyth, hands on hips, fixed Maud with a stern eye. "Hints and warnings is it? What I'm trying to tell you, plain as plain, is that it would be the height of wickedness to cause the Countess of Boulogne, your own cousin, mind, a moment's unease."

Maud colored as she pulled on her clothes. "Naught has occurred that would cause her a moment's unease." She forced a laugh. "Really, you make too much of—of nothing."

"I'm relieved to hear it." But Aldyth did not sound convinced.

Later, when Maud went down to the great hall, she found that Brian and Robert had also left at daybreak to return to their own lands. She was alone with her father, his queen, and the castle mesnie. She hadn't yet met her new stepmother, a woman some months younger than herself, and was extremely curious to see what she was like.

In the early afternoon, Maud went riding with several grooms, reacquainting herself with the castle grounds and all her old familiar haunts. For the first time in some years she thought of her twin brother, William, remembering how hard she had tried to win his affection, receiving only hatred and envy in return. Though she did not miss him, still it was strange to be at Windsor without him, and she was reminded of the last time she had seen him, the day she left for Germany. Guiltily, Maud recalled how she had knocked her brother to the ground, provoking her father's comment that she should have been the boy, and how he had then given her the crown to hold. What an odd sequence to remember, she thought, shivering, before retreating from the uncomfortable memory.

As she continued to explore the grounds Maud wished Stephen were with her. Yet at the same time she was relieved that he was gone. Without the impact of his physical presence, her cousin seemed much less of a threat to her peace of mind.

When Maud returned to the castle late in the afternoon, a page was waiting on the steps with a message that the King wished to see her. Aldyth and her new attendants, four Norman noblewomen, helped Maud change clothes, replacing her old riding garb for a gown and tunic of dove gray, set off by an ivory-colored headdress. The page led her down the passage and left her at the open door of a large chamber.

"Come in, come in," boomed her father, seated in a wooden armchair, his booted feet stretched out in front of a charcoal brazier.

Inside, the chamber was hung with a huge tapestry in red and blue colors depicting Christ in Majesty surrounded by angels. In the center of the room stood a loom. Two women beat down scarlet wool to a tight warp, while another carded it. Her new stepmother sat on a tapestry-covered bench before the loom; when Maud entered she rose to greet her.

At this, her first sight of Queen Adelicia, Maud was struck dumb, trying to remember what the Emperor had told her about her step-mother: The daughter of the Duke of Louvain, she had wanted to become a nun when King Henry married her four years ago. The Emperor claimed she had the reputation of being the most beautiful woman in Europe. The trouvères vied with each other to sing her praises, declaring that "no fairer maid than she was ever seen on middle earth." They dubbed her Alix La Belle and the name had stuck.

The most significant thing about her father's second wife, of course, was the fact that she had failed to produce an heir. As providing a son was the only reason King Henry had married her, what kind of life must the poor woman lead, Maud wondered, her heart going out in sympathy to the hapless woman who was, easily, the loveliest creature she had ever seen—and the most unhappy looking.

Set in the perfect ivory oval of her face, the Queen's liquid brown eyes, haunting as a doe's, looked as if they would overflow with tears at any moment. Her mouth, the color of a crushed rose, trembled like a child's. She had removed her white headdress and waves of thick hair, the color of yellow buttercups in spring, rippled down her back. She was dressed in a pure white gown and tunic confined at the waist by a girdle of wrought gold. Her only ornament was a jeweled ring and a tiny gold cross descending from a gold chain around her delicate neck. No *joi d'amour*, Maud thought, could do justice to such fragile loveliness. She brought to mind the fragrance of spring flowers, the serenity of a cloudless May sky.

"I wish to thank you, Madam, for letting me stay in your solar," Maud said.

"Not at all, my dear," the Queen said in a soft, slight lisp. "Please call me Alix. You're in a strange land—despite it once having been your home. I felt the solar would be familiar to you, reminding you of your sainted mother—"

"Yes, well, sit down, Daughter," the King interjected, giving his wife an impatient glance. He indicated a cushioned stool.

Alix seemed to shrink into herself. With a fearful look at the King, she resumed her seat at the bench and, picking up a basket of scarlet and blue wools, began to sort through them with trembling white fingers.

She is terrified of him, Maud realized, wanting to rush to the Queen's defense but not quite sure how to do so. Why had her father married this woman? Maud wondered. Alix's passive manner and tranquil air definitely brought to mind the cloister rather than the throne. Strange that the King, a lusty, powerful man, should have married two women destined for the convent, and more suited to such a life. A strained silence fell over the chamber. The King was regarding her with a look of speculation in his eyes, causing Maud to shift uneasily on the stool.

"I have something to tell you both," he said abruptly. "At my Christmas court, three months hence, I shall have a very special announcement to make. All nobles in England and Normandy will be ordered to attend. Even the King of Scotland has been invited." With a smile of satisfaction, his eyes lingered on Maud. "You two are the first to know."

He waited a moment, as if expecting her to ask a question, but she only gave him a cool stare, although she knew instantly that the announcement concerned her. Despite her intense curiosity Maud felt it beneath her dignity to beg for information. She knew she was behaving childishly but every encounter with her father set her teeth on edge, compelling her to behave with an insolent defiance that she made little effort to conceal. The fact that this seemed only to amuse him irritated her the more.

The Vespers bell rang. With a yawn, King Henry rose to his feet. "Let us attend the service."

He left the chamber, followed by the two women. At the door, Maud paused to let Alix precede her. The Queen hesitated for a moment.

"As a former empress you should walk before me," she murmured. "I'm sure your father would wish it."

"I doubt the King cares one way or the other as long as we both dance to his tune," Maud muttered with a dark look at her father's retreating back.

With a little gasp, Alix's eyes widened in shock. Maud seized her soft white hand. "Never mind. We'll walk together as equals, side by side, *contra mundem.*"

Alix gave her a frightened smile but allowed herself to be led along the passage, down the winding staircase to the chapel. I shall have to teach this gentle creature some spirit, Maud decided, lifting her head proudly as she avoided the royal pew and sat by herself. Whatever her father had in store for her, she thought grimly, she would not go to it like a sheep to slaughter but like a knight to battle.

Chapter Twelve

THREE WEEKS LATER STEPHEN'S SQUIRE, GERVASE, RACED INTO THE great hall of the White Tower and up to the high table where Stephen and his friends were just sitting down.

"There is to be a Christmas court," he announced, "and the King will have a very special announcement to make. All nobles in England and Normandy are ordered to attend."

"The King is back at Westminster?" Stephen's heart skipped a beat. If the King were in London surely Maud would be, too. He had not seen her since he left Windsor. "The Queen and his daughter are with him?"

"Yes, they arrived last night," Gervase continued, "and all Westminster is agog with the news. Not only that, my lord, the King of Scotland has been invited to attend the court as well."

In stunned silence, Stephen glanced quickly at Brian FitzCount and Robin of Leicester, who were taking their evening meal with Matilda and himself. By God's birth, this was news indeed.

"Something of great import must be afoot if my Uncle David of Scotland is coming," Matilda said.

She caught her breath, her pale blue eyes suddenly widened, and her hands flew like small white birds to her face. "Stephen—you do not think—can it be—oh, my dearest!"

"My thoughts exactly, Lady Matilda," Robin said softly. "If King David attends the court, it must be the news we have all been waiting to hear."

Stephen's heart began to pound as the meaning of their words became clear. Barely able to conceal his excitement, he looked to the Lord of Wallingford for confirmation. Stephen trusted Brian's judgment above anyone else's. Ambition did not goad him; neither fear nor favor swayed him.

Brian, picking his teeth with the point of his dagger, paused before replying: "Well, certainly that is a possible explanation." There was a slight reservation in his voice.

Stephen frowned. Did Brian have doubts or was he merely being cautious? Impossible to know what the clever Breton was truly thinking.

Robin smiled and rose to his feet. "As always, the Lord of Wallingford is reluctant to commit himself. But I am not. In fact, it's time to do honor to our host—and his lady." He held out his goblet, his eyes radiating goodwill. "My friends, I give you the next King and Queen of England, long may they reign."

Brian lifted his goblet and drank.

The words rang joyously in Stephen's ears. A confluence of emotions—pride, triumph, satisfaction—surged through him. Rising to his feet, he spread his hands in a deprecating gesture.

"My dear companions, perhaps it's premature to speak of such things. After all, my uncle still lives and the Queen may yet conceive—"

Robin interrupted him with an impatient wave of the hand. "And pigs may fly! Now is not the time for false modesty. If the King has at last decided to make a public announcement of what everyone has long since surmised, we will all breathe a sigh of relief."

Matilda gazed lovingly at Stephen. "At last you will be recognized as you deserve, dear husband."

Such a loyal, dutiful wife, Stephen reflected, smiling down at her. What an admirable queen she will make. Yet at the back of his mind, his thoughts were of Maud, wondering if this confirmation of his hopes would impress her. It was absurd, this desire to look well in her eyes, but her approval was important to him.

He grinned at Robin and Brian. "You all know that I hoped my uncle would favor me, and if he has at last decided to bestow this great honor upon the House of Blois—I will spend my life trying to be worthy of his trust." The words had an earnest ring that sounded well in his ears. He must try and remember them.

There was a moment of respectful silence. Then Matilda clapped her hands. "We must invite Cousin Maud to the Tower to celebrate with us. Why, I've hardly set eyes on her and I was devoted to my aunt, her late sainted mother. I so want us to be friends. Do you go to Westminster in the morning, dear heart, and bring her back with you for a few days."

The suggestion caught Stephen by surprise, and he hesitated. He longed to see Maud again, but he would have preferred it be elsewhere. On the other hand, sooner or later Matilda must spend some time with Maud. Such an occasion could not be avoided.

"A good thought, Wife. I will do as you suggest." Stephen, his blood quickening at the thought of seeing Maud so soon, could not now sit still. He rose and strode toward the open doors of the great hall.

"I will join you tomorrow morning," Brian called out.

"Tomorrow is Friday, we are to attend the horse fair," Robin reminded him.

"I'll meet you both at Smithfield," Stephen called over his shoulder, determined to have at least a short while alone with Maud.

Elated at the impending proclamation, he knew he must get word to his brother in Glastonbury at once. Christmas was less than three months away. Only a short time to wait and then the whole of Europe, including his mother retired to a convent now, would know he was to be the King's heir!

It was still dark when Stephen left for Westminster the following morning. He reached the palace about noon only to be told that Maud and Aldyth had gone to the drapers' stalls in Cheapside.

He rode to this section of London with Gervase, left his horse in the care of a groom, and, followed by the squire, wandered through the crowd. Every so often someone hailed him, or stopped to talk. No matter if the person were a great lord or simple yeoman, Stephen always made it a point to inquire about the man's health and family. He had always been popular in London and he knew it was because he had the common touch, readily available to exchange a jest or share a pint of ale at a tavern.

At a goldsmith's stall, Stephen stopped to examine an exquisite enamel box from Limoges. He must buy it for Matilda, he decided. Then a stall selling boots of Spanish leather caught his eye and he ordered two pairs to be made for him. A peddler with a tiny monkey on his shoulder, carrying a large wooden cage of brightly feathered birds, passed him. He must have one for his children. The smell of roasting chestnuts wafted through the air, and Stephen took a paper cone of the hot nuts from a strolling vendor.

Finally he caught sight of Maud, standing alone in front of the stall of a merchant whom he knew specialized in fabrics from the Levant. A bolt of sky blue silk shot with gold thread was draped over one shoulder. Maud saw Stephen at almost the same moment, and his heart leapt at the blaze of joy radiating from her wide gray eyes. With the exception of the Limoges box, which he thrust into the pouch at his belt, Stephen handed all his purchases to Gervase and pushed through the crowd toward her.

"I—well, it's good to see you, Cousin," he said in a husky voice, the urge to take her in his arms almost overpowering. "That blue is a wondrous color, like a midsummer sky at dawn." He could not stop himself from touching her arm, letting his hand linger a little too long for propriety. "It favors your hair and eyes."

She smiled up at him. "I will buy it then. What a happy surprise to see you here." Her body seemed to sway toward him in response to his touch.

"The truth is I've been looking for you," he said, quickly withdrawing, aware they were in a public gathering place. "My lady wife, your Cousin Matilda, invites you to the Tower for a few days."

"Oh. I see." Her voice was heavy with disappointment.

"I also wish it. Very much," he added impulsively at the look of naked hurt in her eyes. She was so open, so obviously vulnerable that Stephen knew an instant of disquiet. Matters were moving too fast, he thought, regretting the easy flow of compliments which came so readily to his lips where women were concerned. This could never be a lighthearted dalliance, he had always known that. It had been a mistake to touch her, he realized. Now was the moment to draw in the reins and curb his growing desire before—he did not allow himself to complete the thought.

Maud said nothing but bent to examine another bolt of silk, this one saffron-colored with silver threads.

"Of course, if you prefer not to come at this time," Stephen said, now hoping she would refuse. He understood her reluctance only too well. If anyone were to perceive what was happening between Maud and himself, it was sure to be Matilda, who would have the opportunity to observe them together over the next few days. Had he not had similar doubts? On the other hand, seeing Maud under the very eye of his wife might be just the damper he needed to bring him to his senses. "Matilda and your mother were very close," he added. "She is eager to see you again."

"Of course," Maud said in a tight voice, her face set. "If I seem hesitant it is only because your wife so resembles my late mother that our first meeting pricked old memories. I will be glad to come."

Aldyth appeared, immediately on guard when she saw Stephen.

"I'm going to see my Cousin Matilda at the Tower, Aldyth, so I won't be returning directly to Westminster," Maud told her, then to Stephen: "Let me complete my purchase and I will join you."

Stephen nodded, aware of an awkwardness that had arisen between them but making no effort to dispel it. Perhaps this sudden coolness was all for the best, he decided in relief. The nature of his feelings for Maud both confused and dismayed him; Stephen preferred everything in his life, including his emotions, to be easy and uncomplicated. With Maud he had been caught off guard, unprepared for the strongly sensuous pull between his cousin and himself, an undercurrent as powerful as the treacherous tides in the channel. She had cast a bewitching spell over him and he knew he must exorcise it before it led to trouble.

He watched Maud smile sweetly at the silk merchant, who returned her look with a bored expression on his swarthy face.

"How much for this bolt?" she asked.

"Ten silver pennies, gracious lady," he said in a thick accent, bowing obsequiously.

After all, Stephen reminded himself, Maud was the King's daughter, his own first cousin, Matilda's first cousin, Robert's half-sister—Jesu, he must have been mad ever to entertain carnal thoughts of Maud considering the intricate coil of family relationships involved. Why, even his future as king might be affected.

"That is outright thievery," Maud cried, her eyes suddenly flashing.

There was such a note of indignity in her voice that Stephen was taken aback and glanced quickly at the merchant. To his astonishment, the man brightened immediately.

"Thievery? Gracious lady, I'm as good as giving this silk away. May God strike me dead if I ask an unreasonable price." His eyes rolled heavenward. "I have a wife, ten children, aged parents, not to mention aunts—"

"You are a liar, the son of a liar, and the grandson of a liar," Maud interrupted, then began to speak haltingly in a tongue Stephen did not recognize.

Clearly delighted, the man, beating his breast, responded with an incomprehensible flow of words and extravagant gestures. After what seemed an eternity to Stephen, Maud and the merchant finally came to some kind of agreement. The man handed her the bolt of silk and they parted with mutual expressions of respect and goodwill.

"I didn't know you spoke a heathen language, Cousin," Stephen said, taking the bolt of silk from her arms. "What did you finally pay him?"

"Five silver pennies. Still too much, but to bargain properly takes a long time. There were many visiting Semites at the Emperor's court, so I was fortunate enough to learn a few words of Arabic," she replied as they strolled through Cheapside, followed by Gervase and Aldyth.

"Where did you learn to bargain like that?"

"At the straw markets in Italy, and from a clever Semite who sometimes advised the Emperor on matters of finance."

Stephen laughed. "There is so much I don't know about you. What other talents lie hidden under that lovely exterior, I wonder." He kept his voice light so she would know he was only teasing, but she did not smile in response.

When they arrived at the place where they had left their horses, Stephen heard himself telling Gervase to accompany Aldyth back to Westminster. "The Lady Maud will ride with me to Smithfield." It was not at all what he had intended to say.

Stephen climbed into the saddle, then reached down to lift Maud up in front of him. Aware of an open-mouthed Aldyth radiating disapproval, Stephen quickly spurred his horse forward before Maud could change her mind. What about his own change of mind? he wondered. What in God's name was the matter with him? His horse's sudden spurt threw Maud against him and his own course, so clear only a moment ago, was once again in doubt.

It was early October, his favorite time of year. The sky was a deep blue, fleeced with white streaks of cloud; the air, crisp and cool, carried a hint of winter in the sudden gusts of wind that blew about them. With the excuse that he wished to show her the sights of London, Stephen rode as slowly as possible through the crowded streets, savoring the feel of Maud's body within the circle of his arms.

He stopped to show her plain wooden houses with tile facings, prosperous dwellings made of stone quartz, public cookshops with their tantalizing aroma of roast meats, and leather craftsmen busy at their benches. A band of students ran by shouting at each other, and Stephen slowed his horse to point out a group of apprentices practicing archery.

"Of course you've heard about the Christmas court," Stephen said.

"Oh yes, some weeks ago. At Windsor various people were speculating that the King has chosen this occasion to name you his successor. I must congratulate you."

"Has your father spoken to you of this matter?"

"As usual, my father says nothing."

Stephen felt her body grow tense. "Not even about his future plans for you?"

"Least of all about that. All in good time, he replies when I ask, like a cat toying with a mouse." She paused. "I cannot help but feel bitter. He brings me back here with the utmost urgency, as if his very life depended on it, and now that I'm here, there appears to be no urgency at all."

Prudently, Stephen decided to say nothing. It was hardly politic to voice a criticism of the King, lest Maud, in all innocence, might repeat it. But he tightened his grip ever so slightly about her waist, hoping she would feel his silent flow of sympathy. He had managed to put all his doubts aside and was now simply enjoying the moment.

Finally they came to Aldersgate. Here they waited to be let through the city gates, double doors of heavy oak reinforced with iron. Atop the massive eighteen-foot walls that surrounded the city of London, guards armed with tall spears carefully watched the throng of people coming and going.

"You will fall victim to this queen of cities," Stephen said in her ear. "London has captured my heart ever since I arrived here from Blois."

"But I have known Rome, Paris, and the great cities of the Empire," she teased. "What is London compared to such as these?"

"What indeed. She will cast her spell over you in time."

They rode through the gates into the open area of Smithfield where the horse fair was already well under way.

"Keep an eye out for my lords of Wallingford and Leicester. We are to meet them here," Stephen told Maud.

They first visited the area where the colts were tethered, then the section where the palfreys were gathered. When they came to the war-horses, Stephen dismounted and helped Maud down.

"I'm in the market for a new destrier. You can help me pick one out."

As they wandered companionably around the compound observing the great stallions, Stephen discovered that Maud not only shared his love of horses but was surprisingly knowledgeable about them. Finally the big event of the day was announced: the horse races. A great crowd began to gather at one end of the field.

"Over here, Stephen," Brian FitzCount called. When they had joined them, he turned to Maud. "A good afternoon to you, Lady. Robin and I have a wager going: I say that the bay colt in the corner will win over all the others."

"A fool and his money are soon parted," Robin said with a grin. "Anyone can see that the bay is too flighty to control. I favor the chestnut over by the fence. What do you think, Stephen?"

Stephen raised his hands in protest. "Oh no, I have learned never to take sides when the two of you wager against each other." He pointed his finger at Maud. "But my cousin is no mean judge of horseflesh. Let us hear what she has to say."

Maud looked carefully over the racing pairs. "I rather fancy the black colt with the white blaze on his forehead."

Robin hooted. "I wager two silver pennies you're wrong. Look at those spindly legs. By my faith, I will be a rich man this day."

Maud gave him a cool smile. "Indeed? That unchivalrous remark will cost you three silver pennies, my Lord of Leicester."

"Done. Three silver pennies it is."

Stable boys, using only a headstall and no other harness or saddle, jumped on their mounts and rode to the starting place. With much shouting from the onlookers, the colts started running across the wide field. The black colt fell back at first, while the bay frolicked ahead of the others.

Maud had an eager look on her face and, to Stephen's amusement, she began to shout words of encouragement to the rider of the black colt. Brian's bay bounded forward, running neck and neck with the chestnut. The colts were about three-quarters of the way across the field now. In her excitement Maud gripped Stephen's arm with tense fingers; he doubted she even noticed. Her face was taut with expectancy, her coral lips parted, and Stephen was surprised to realize that she very badly wanted her colt to win.

Slowly the black colt began to gain speed, finally he shot forward like a dark arrow to overtake the others and reach the end of the field first. The bay colt was half a head behind him.

Flushed with victory, Maud looked up at Stephen. "You see, I was right."

"I never doubted you for a moment," he said, smiling at the sense of triumph in her voice, astonished that only a simple race held by yokels should matter so much to her. Before he realized what he was doing he had reached into the purse at his belt and pulled out the Limoges box he had intended for Matilda. "You must have this as a reward."

"How lovely. But I'm not sure—"

"As a favor to me. I want you to have it." Stephen was absurdly pleased when he saw her fingers curl around the box. Fortunately the others hadn't noticed.

Brian was jubilant. "A fool, eh, Leicester? Where is our money?"

"Well, Lady Maud wins, I agree," Robin said, disgruntled. "But you? The bay did not come in first."

"You're not very sporting, my friend. A close second is almost as good as a first. Surely you can see that."

Stephen and Maud left them arguing while they rode to the White Tower.

The sky had darkened, and London was covered in a swirling fog by the time they reached Stephen's home. Maud knew this fortress had been built by her grandfather, the Conqueror, to keep watch and ward over defeated Saxon London, and that her father had made a gift of it to Stephen when he married Countess Matilda of Boulogne. Built to inspire terror and submission, the Tower's heavy walls, pierced by thin slits, were buttressed from ground to battlements; the massive keep, topped by four turrets, was protected by a wide moat. As they approached, a guard shouted from the gatehouse, the wooden drawbridge thundered down, and Stephen and Maud rode across the causeway into the outer bailey. Huge torches borne by waiting attendants cast an eerie light on the pale stone walls.

Maud did not look forward to this second meeting between herself and Matilda. Her anxiety increased as she followed Stephen into the Tower, past the great hall, the sword room, and the chapel, then on up a winding staircase to Matilda's solar on the third floor. Steeling herself, Maud resolved that neither by word nor gesture would she reveal how she felt toward Stephen.

Seated before a charcoal brazier on a woven wool rug, Matilda, dressed in a soft blue tunic over a white gown, played with her son,

Baldwin. With a welcoming smile, she rose at once when Maud and Stephen entered.

"Cousin, I'm so happy you agreed to come." Matilda held out her arms in a spontaneous gesture. Reluctantly, Maud came forward to receive her cousin's kiss.

"How like my mother you are," Maud said awkwardly.

"Everyone says the same. I'm deeply honored, for my aunt was truly a saint. We must go together to visit her tomb."

"Yes, I would like that." Maud looked down at Baldwin, a large rosy child who, with his green eyes and honey-brown curls, looked just like Stephen. "He is big for his age—three years is it?"

"Just two," Stephen said with pride, sweeping Baldwin up into his arms.

"We have a new daughter," Matilda said. "Perhaps you would like to see her?"

"Why—yes, indeed, that would be very nice." Maud forced herself to smile, growing more ill at ease with every passing moment. She was painfully aware of Stephen's affection for his son.

"Stephen, do you take our cousin to the nursery where the babe is being fed by the wet nurse. Then we will take a light supper. Afterwards I will show Maud the tapestry I'm working on, a scene depicting Our Lord and Our Blessed Lady at the wedding in Cana. By then it will be time to attend Compline in the chapel." Matilda beamed at them.

Silently, Maud followed Stephen out of the solar. There was no mistaking the bond of affinity between Stephen, his wife, and his child. Unprepared for this kind of domestic happiness, which she herself had never experienced, Maud felt like an intruder. She had always known there could never be anything between Stephen and herself, but now, seeing him with his family, that knowledge was confirmed beyond all doubt.

"You will now see the fairest of all maidens," Stephen said, pushing open a sturdy oak door to reveal a small stone chamber warmed by several charcoal braziers.

A large woman, the bodice of her gown open, sat on a stone bench nursing a tiny infant wrapped in a wool shawl. Seeing them enter, she closed her bodice, stood up, and handed Stephen the babe.

"Your daughter thrives, my lord," she said proudly.

Stephen took the child in his arms, cradling her against his chest. "Is she not beautiful?"

"Yes, indeed, most beautiful," Maud said dutifully. In truth, the infant looked like every other she had seen: red, wrinkled, its head covered with flaxen fuzz like a newborn chick.

As Stephen continued to croon over his daughter, Maud found she could not bear to watch. Heartsick, she turned away. Behind her she heard Stephen give the child back to its nurse. He took her arm and quickly led her out of the chamber.

"You have a lovely daughter, Stephen," Maud said in a low voice, knowing she must escape from all this familial contentment. "I—I find myself unwell, very fatigued after the journey from Windsor and the activity today. Is it possible I could return now to Westminster?" She started to walk down the passageway when Stephen caught her arm.

"No, it is not possible. You would not arrive until early morning and Matilda would not understand your urgency to leave."

"But I must go, don't you see—" she said, her voice trembling, and turned to walk quickly down the hall.

Stephen reached out and grasped her arm, pulling her to him in an iron grip. "If you think this is any easier for me—" he began.

Their eyes met, locked, and neither could look away.

Slowly Stephen bent his head, found her lips, and began to kiss her with a fierce hunger that had suddenly, savagely unleashed itself. Instead of pushing him away, Maud found herself yielding to his hunger, and then not just yielding but meeting it with the force of her own need. The warm insistent pressure of his mouth parted her lips, sending currents of fire throughout her body. The urgency of her own response, which shocked and frightened her, seemed to amaze Stephen, whose passion quickened like a bonfire as he crushed her pliant body closer, tasting the sweetness of her mouth as if he could never get enough. His hands slid under her cloak to seek the fullness of her breasts, when the sound of laughter made them jump guiltily apart.

Breathing heavily, her head reeling as if she had drunk too much wine, Maud stood rooted to the stone floor as two guards rounded a corner and walked by them on their way to the battlements.

"Good evening, my lord," they said, nodding to Stephen.

After the guards had passed, Maud and Stephen stared at each other for a moment.

"I will see that you are escorted home at first light," Stephen said in a husky voice.

Deeply shaken, Maud followed Stephen back to the solar. Her body was in turmoil. Nothing in her life had prepared her for the overwhelming feelings Stephen had evoked. It was as if she had been set adrift in a stormy sea with no land in sight. Terrified, she knew that she must never allow herself to lose control again.

Chapter Thirteen

THE NEXT THREE MONTHS PASSED IN A PLEASANT HAZE OF ACTIVITY.
Stephen saw Maud as often as was seemly but, by tacit agreement,
never alone. However, even in the presence of others Stephen worried that he would betray himself by an unguarded word or gesture.
No matter who they were with, if they so much as glanced at each
other, the rest of the world fell away. Stephen feared the pull between
them, as strong as any channel undertow, must be evident to all
around them.

On the night before the King's proclamation, which was to be
announced at a Christmas Eve feast the following day, Stephen and
Matilda were undressing in their chamber. Glowing white tapers illuminated the canopied bed, wooden bench, oak table, and Matilda's
prie-dieu. A charcoal brazier set in a silver basin warmed the room
against the December chill seeping in through the cracks in the massive stone walls.

"What ailed your brother tonight?" Matilda asked, as she turned
down the bed's fur-lined red coverlet. "At supper he was unusually
silent and dour. I would have expected him to be delighted at tomorrow's proclamation. Instead, one would think he attends a funeral."

Shivering in his linen underdrawers, Stephen opened the heavy oak door to ensure the guards were on watch.

"I don't know, dear heart." He had noticed that Henry was troubled about something, had been even before they left Normandy in September. Stephen had no idea what it was.

When his brother arrived in London from his See of Glastonbury, Stephen had also expected him to be jubilant over the news of the special announcement and the King of Scotland's visit. Instead Henry had been reserved, advising Stephen not to get his hopes up too soon, and behaving so strangely that Stephen had become irritated.

Matilda pulled off her linen chemise, and stood naked for a moment, her milky skin in goose bumps from the cold. Aware of Stephen eyeing her slender, childlike body with its narrow hips, small breasts, and rounded buttocks, she climbed quickly into the bed, tucking the fur coverlet up to her chin.

Stephen stepped out of his drawers and slid into bed beside his wife.

Matilda yawned. "Just think, Stephen. On the very eve of Our Lord's birth, you will be announced as heir to the throne." She curled up happily beside him.

Stephen was too excited to sleep, a jumble of thoughts filling his mind: his brother's unexplained attitude; anticipation for tomorrow's events; and, as always, his cousin Maud.

Just the thought of her brought a stir to his loins, and, instinctively, he started to reach for his wife. As his fingers touched Matilda's bare shoulder, he felt her stiffen; the candlelight revealed the look of distaste, quickly repressed, that passed over her face. With a sigh, he patted her shoulder, reached over to the table and blew out the candles, then turned on his back. Beside him he heard Matilda let out a long breath in relief.

"Good night, dear husband," she whispered gratefully.

Stephen closed his eyes, his thoughts traveling to Maud. Try as he would, he could not banish the memory of their encounter in the passage. The warmth of her lips, the feel of her lithe body in his arms, lingered in his mind like the fragrance of summer roses which haunts the air when the blossoms are gone. The situation between them was hopeless, yet, caught in a web of desire that held him in thrall, he could not stop thinking of her.

Turning restlessly in the wide bed, he gave himself up to an impossible fantasy: lying unclothed on a fur-lined coverlet before a roaring hearth, Maud's russet hair flowing loose about her creamy neck and shoulders. Her gray eyes were heavy-lidded with desire, her full lips parted to receive his kiss. The firelight cast shadows on her naked body; warm arms reached out to enfold him.

Maud would be as she had been in the passage: hot-blooded, responsive, her passion matching his own, her body quivering in expectation of being possessed. And his possession of her would be wild and unrestrained. Urgent need meeting urgent need.

Drenched in his own sweat, Stephen suddenly sat up, his heart beating wildly. He looked guiltily at Matilda, breathing evenly in her untroubled sleep. Waking her to ease the ache in his loin would bring only a temporary relief, he knew, for she was unable either to understand or to share the vibrant passion he craved.

As he gazed at his wife's sweet face, desire ebbed. Stephen placed a gentle kiss on her cheek, then lay on his back again, one arm flung over his head. He prayed God that in time his passion for Maud would blow over, a brief, wild storm that vanishes as quickly as it begins. Matilda was his wife, the mother of his children, and soon, with God's grace, she would be his queen as well. Surely that was enough. It would have to be enough.

The next day Maud woke to the sound of the bells of St. Paul chiming throughout the city. Christmas Eve. The big feast and the King's proclamation.

A few hours before the feast, Maud retired to her own apartments to dress. Her father had given her a large Norman retinue of women, servants, grooms, and a chaplain. He had established her in her own quarters at Westminster, and she began to feel that at last he was treating her with the respect due an empress. He encouraged her to explore London and the surrounding countryside, arranged for her to meet the leading citizens of the city and the nobles who came to Westminster. But there was still no mention of her future.

All things considered, Maud felt she would be quite content—if it were not for her longing for Stephen, a longing constantly being stimulated but never fulfilled. They were in each other's company at least two or three times a week, riding through the park between Westminster and Ludgate, climbing the tree-covered slopes of Highgate, or visiting the frozen marsh at Moorfields to watch young men tie the shinbones of animals to their feet and, with the help of iron-spiked sticks, glide over the ice. Together they explored the woods of St. John and hunted with hawk and hound—but these excursions were always undertaken in the company of others.

Wherever they went, Maud was surprised to see the Londoners' warm response to Stephen. Her father might know all the significant landowners in his kingdom, but Stephen belonged to the citizens of London. From prosperous burghers and merchants to humble church-men, weavers, and apprentices, everyone knew Stephen of Blois. And everyone, it seemed to Maud, had fallen under the spell of his easy-going charm. When she was with him their pleasure in seeing Ste-phen was extended to her as well.

Maud finished her toilet just as the Vespers bell rang. When she reached the abbey, the entire court, which by now included nobles from all over the King's realm, was already there to hear the special Christmas Eve Mass. Maud noted that only her father and the newly arrived King of Scotland were absent.

Later everyone assembled in the great hall of Westminster to wait for the King and his royal guest to appear. Yew torches flared brightly around the tapestried walls. Great Yule logs blazed in the central fire; newly spread dried rushes mixed with herbs covered the floor. Scarlet holly, dark green ivy, and white-flowered mistletoe hung from the wooden beams of the ceiling.

"You look beautiful, Sister," said Robert, smiling, his Welsh wife, Mabel, in tow.

Maud returned his smile, but her eyes sought Stephen who pushed through the crowd toward her. With Matilda on his arm, he looked resplendent in crimson tunic and black hose, a black cloak lined with fox fur thrown over his shoulders. The open admiration in his eyes was ample reward for the hours Maud and her ladies had taken with her appearance. Over a gown made of the bolt of sky-blue silk, she wore a tunic of darker blue with long hanging sleeves. A girdle of wrought gold filigree encircled her waist; on her bosom lay a small gold cross set with pearls and rubies, made for her by the finest goldsmith in Italy. About her shoulders hung a midnight blue cloak, lined in ermine. Over her hair lay a gauze veil held in place by a gold circlet set with pearls. Aware of everyone's eyes on her, Maud's cheeks flushed with pleasure and her pewter eyes sparkled.

"Here he is," Robert whispered, making a low bow.

Preceded by his chief steward, King Henry entered the great hall arm in arm with King David of Scotland. He was followed by the

Archbishop of Canterbury, William of Corbeil; the Bishop of Salisbury; and, lastly Queen Adelicia.

The sight of her Uncle David was a shock to Maud, who, knowing he had been partly raised in Norman England, expected him to look and behave like a Norman. Instead, she found herself swept up into the great arms of a sandy-haired giant with a craggy, weatherbeaten face, who kissed her soundly on both cheeks.

"Aye, 'tis a bonnie lass ye have, Henry." David of Scotland held Maud's face in a huge hairy paw, gazing down at her with the trusting blue eyes of her mother. "I canna find a trace o' my poor sister, Matilda," he continued. "Maud do be all Norman."

The chief server blew his ivory horn. Everyone scrambled for seats at the trestle tables laid with trenchers of bread, great pewter salt cellars, and wooden bowls of ale. The King, with his immediate family and chief ecclesiasts, seated themselves at the high table placed on a raised dais. Covered with a snowy linen cloth, the table was decorated with boughs of holly and set with silver goblets. Much to her surprise and confusion, Maud was given a place of honor between the two kings. Surely this place should have been Stephen's?

"I ha' na seen ye since ye were a wee bairn," David of Scotland murmured in Maud's ear.

Before she could reply, the doors at the far end of the hall opened, and a long procession of serving-men emerged, headed by the chief cook who carried a huge platter of boar's head with ivory tusks in its snout and an apple in its mouth, garnished all over with bright red holly berries and leaves of green ivy. The boar was followed by smoking platters of venison, hare, cranes, peacocks in their feathers, a whole roast kid, suckling pig, and a huge goose, its skin brown and crackling. Rabbit in wine, stewed lampreys, a whole carp, and assorted fish pasties came next, until the table creaked with the abundance of food.

Hovering squires carved the meat and served their lords on bended knee. Pages poured wine into silver goblets and raced to and from the kitchen with basins of water and napkins to wash the fingers of the diners.

Maud's Uncle David hovered over her like a doting parent. "Ye must taste this slice o' goose breast, Niece," he insisted. He fed her first, then himself, but saved the choicest morsels, she noticed, for two huge Scottish deerhounds sitting proudly beside him, who had accompanied him from Scotland.

For no reason she could readily determine, Maud could taste nothing of the food her uncle offered her. From time to time she glanced at Stephen, who returned her looks with a brief, conspiratorial smile that filled her with delight. She was aware of tension at the high table, as well as everywhere else in the hall, for everyone's eyes kept turning expectantly to King Henry. Like herself, they were impatiently waiting for the promised proclamation.

The platters of food were removed, replaced by bowls of fruit and nuts, trays of sweetmeats, marchpane, and honey cakes. The steward then carried into the hall a great bowl of "lamb's wool," a highly spiced wine mixed with nutmeg, ginger, honey, toasted crumbs, and roasted crab apples that floated white and fleecy on the surface. The King drank to those attending his Christmas court, and in return the nobles drank to him, crying "Wassail! Wassail! Wassail!"

Maud had never seen this ritual before, but Uncle David explained that it was an old Saxon custom adopted by the King. When the toast was done, Henry's favorite minstrel sang several *chansons de geste*. By the time he was finished, the torches were sputtering, wreaths of smoke swirled round the blackened beams of the ceiling, and the heat in the room was growing uncomfortable. Mantles were opened, booted feet impatiently stirred the rushes, belts were unbuckled, and faces had turned ruddy from the wine; even a few snores were heard.

Finally the tables were cleared, the servitors withdrew, and the steward called for silence.

Rising slowly to his feet, King Henry, hooking his thumbs in his belt, surveyed the great hall in a long sweeping glance that missed nothing and no one. There was not a sound in the room.

"Peers of the church, lords of England and Normandy, I have called you here upon this Christmas Eve to make known my intention for the future of the royal succession."

From the corner of her eye, Maud saw an expectant smile hover about Stephen's lips.

"Let us return for a moment," Henry continued, "to the unhappy blow of fate that took from me my only son, Prince William." He signed himself. "Had he lived, William would have come after me and the problem of the succession would never have arisen." Heads in the room nodded.

"As I was already a widower, following William's death I married the virtuous Adelicia of Louvain, in hopes of begetting more sons.

Unfortunately God has not yet seen fit to answer our prayers." He stopped as all eyes turned to Alix, who sat perfectly still as though carved in white marble.

Maud's heart ached for the humiliation Alix must be suffering at this public reminder of her barrenness.

"Of course, the Queen is young and I hope to live many more years, so we have not yet given up hope." He waited until the murmurs of agreement died down.

"However, in the event that no son is born to me, happily, I repeat, happily, I have a daughter who has returned to England to live amongst her people once again."

Puzzled, everyone's eyes now turned to Maud, who was mystified by her father's words.

"The Princess Maud is the legitimate descendant of rulers: Her grandfather was the great Conqueror, her Uncle William Rufus ruled England before me, and I am sure no one here need be reminded of the great lineage of the Dukes of Normandy."

He walked past Maud until he stood behind the King of Scotland. "On her mother's side, my daughter's forebears are no less illustrious: She is the descendant of fourteen rulers, from the King of the West Saxons, who ruled over two hundred years ago, to the King of Scotland, who sits before you now. In addition, she has the distinction of being the widow of the Holy Roman Emperor, and was bred since childhood to the ways of kingship."

Taking a few steps, Henry placed his hands on Maud's shoulders. "Here is the rightful heir to the throne of England and Normandy, should I lack a legitimate son at my death."

So great was Maud's shock and amazement that she felt as if she had just shot out of her body and was floating some feet above her head. Every action her father had taken, from recalling her to England to insisting she remove the Imperial crown, suddenly became clear; she forgave him everything. Her feeling of joy was intoxicating, overpowering.

Maud drew back her head to look up at her father, her eyes shining with gratitude. She could find no words to express the fullness in her heart. He gave her shoulder a reassuring squeeze.

The silence in the room was like death. The stunned nobles stared at the King in horror. Henry's eyes swept the hall. A frown creased his brow and an implacable expression settled across his features as he spoke.

"In a fortnight's time there will be an homage ceremony, where I will call upon each and every one of you to swear a solemn oath to uphold the Princess Maud as Queen after my death.''

In the glory of the moment Maud had forgotten Stephen and how this news might affect him. Quite suddenly she had become his rival and she knew an instant of fear. Would he change toward her? She quickly looked at her cousin, then drew back with a gasp. His eyes, glittering with overt hostility in a white and frozen mask, were those of a stranger.

Her father's voice forced Maud to turn away from the cold enmity in Stephen's face.

''Should any dissent, speak now or hold your peace hereafter.'' The King's eyes searched the hall once more. No one spoke. ''It is agreed then. I expect to see you all at the homage ceremony.''

When he had finished no one looked at Maud, whose unalloyed happiness was now rapidly fading. In the first shock of exultation she had lost sight of the fact that naming a woman heir to the throne was an unprecedented action. But nothing could have prepared her for the expressions of appalled incredulity, bitter outrage, wild anger, even hatred, she saw reflected in the faces around her.

Her cousin Matilda was openly crying; the de Beaumont twins wore identical expressions of shocked disbelief. Her brother Robert gave her a crooked smile that did not quite conceal the pain shadowed in his eyes. Stephen's brother, the Abbot of Glastonbury, gazed at her with the mournful expression of a man who has feared the worst and seen it come to pass. Maud knew she would never forget that Brian FitzCount was the only noble in the hall to give her an encouraging grin; he alone had rallied to the glory of the occasion.

''Dinna fret at what ye see, lass,'' David of Scotland said in her ear. ''It were a wee shock to the lords. Ye father has broken new ground here and ye must give the seed time to take root.'' He patted her hand. ''Ye father will ha' his way in the end, depend on it.''

Maud wished she could share his certainty. She watched the magnates and their wives, including Stephen and Matilda, hurry out of the hall, pulling their cloaks about them against the winter chill. Not one of them approached either herself or the King to offer congratulations and extend support. Miserable, Maud felt as if she had just committed a heinous crime instead of having received the realm's highest honor. Rising to her feet, she followed her father out of the hall.

''Come to my conference chamber after Sext tomorrow,'' the King, visibly shaken, said to her before he and Alix started for their own quarters.

So he was as surprised by the hostile response as she, Maud reflected. The memory of Stephen's accusing face haunted her. Did he hate her now? Believe that she had known of the announcement from the beginning? She could not bear the thought that he might no longer care for her. Tears pricked behind her eyelids. Yet underneath her concern and shock lay the stunning realization that one day she would be Queen of England and Duchess of Normandy. Never, not in her wildest dreams, had she imagined such an honor. Despite everything, Maud felt a heady surge of triumph that could not be denied.

Chapter Fourteen

In the grip of an icy rage, Stephen pulled Matilda through the throng of nobles, determined to reach the outer doors of Westminster before someone stopped him. He heard the voices of the de Beaumont twins and his brother calling his name, but ignored them. If someone offered him one word of sympathy, he thought savagely, he would fell them with a blow.

Outside, Stephen found Gervase and other members of his mesnie gathered in the courtyard. One look at their stricken faces left no doubt that the shattering news had reached them.

"We are not staying the night at Westminster. Gervase and the others will escort you to the Tower," he told Matilda, helping her into a waiting litter. "You won't arrive till morning but that can't be helped."

Her eyes still wet with tears, Matilda clutched at his arm. "Dear heart, do you come with me?"

"No. I have business to attend to."

"At this hour?"

"At whatever hour I choose." Stephen's face was set in stone, his eyes as frosty as the North Sea.

Frightened, Matilda shrank back into the litter as Stephen slammed the curtains closed. Overhearing their exchange, Gervase approached Stephen with an anxious look.

"My lord—wherever you go, take Arnulf and Gilbert along. I beg you not to travel alone."

Stephen ignored him and jumped onto his mare, Audrade. He spurred the horse forward, and headed toward the river. Some way behind him he heard the sound of horses' hooves. The knights, Arnulf and Gilbert, he assumed, but did not turn back to look.

He was still stunned by the King's proclamation, the crushing, totally unexpected humiliation he had experienced before his peers. It was almost impossible to take in the enormity of his loss. Everyone had assumed he would be named the King's heir. To be deprived of a crown that he had thought virtually within his grasp was an overwhelming disappointment; but to have lost it to a woman—and to Maud in particular, Maud, with whom he had thought himself so hopelessly in love—was devastating. No, he contradicted himself angrily, not love. What a fool he had been to think so. Lust. Yes, he had lusted after her, no more than that. And once he had possessed her, it would have been finished for him, for there was little sport to be had once the game was won.

Approaching the Thames, Stephen looked for the ferry that would take him across to Southwark. The silence of the mild December night was broken only by the water lapping against the riverbank, the sound of horses' hooves smacking against the hard earth. Finally he found the flat-bottomed ferry moored to the quay and, dismounting, led his mare up the gangplank and onto the deck. The two knights followed behind, but he paid them no attention. Perched in the prow, the oarsman pushed off from the bank and rowed the boat silently across the river.

Oblivious to his surroundings, Stephen relived the scene in the great hall over and over. How could he have been so blind, how could they all have been so blind, to the King's intention? Who would have dreamed King Henry capable of such an appalling outrage, such an unprecedented act? For a moment Stephen wondered if the King might not be in his dotage. Irrational behavior was common among men in old age; it seemed the only logical explanation, yet in all other aspects the King appeared as alert as ever.

How much had Maud known? he wondered. Had she been privy to her father's plans from the start, dissembling so adroitly he had never had the slightest suspicion? Stephen writhed with shame to think how deeply he had trusted his cousin, confiding to her his ambitions and hopes for the future. What a fool he had made of himself. Maud. Maud. His heart cried out to her as anguish stabbed through his vitals like a sword thrust. The loss of his dreams, his hopes, stung like a raw open wound.

The ferry bumped the opposite shore. Stephen led Audrade onto solid ground, mounted her, and turned left toward Southwark, galloping recklessly along the riverbank. He had no destination in mind, just an urgent need to give vent to his hurt and rage. Every instinct told him the King had made a fatal mistake. How could his uncle imagine that his subjects would accept such a decision when both magnates and commonfolk had expected he, Stephen, to rule? Had the King forgotten how popular he was? Stephen could not imagine a future in which he would not be king. Something must be done, he vowed; he could not, would not, allow the whole course of his life to be altered. His brother, he thought, a spark of hope penetrating the black rush of his thoughts. His brother Henry would know what to do.

That same night, Brian FitzCount stifled a yawn as he sat across from King Henry in the chamber used to conduct the administrative business of the realm. Beside him, the Bishop of Salisbury, his head fallen over his portly chest, snored softly. The chamber, lit by a score of wax tapers, resembled a monastic scriptorium. In its center stood a long oak table piled high with rolls of parchment and books bound in vellum. Scrolls of parchment and books also filled the iron-bound chests that lined the walls. A black-robed cleric bent over the far end of the table scrutinizing a roll of yellowing parchment, so old it crumbled at the corners. Another cleric, perched atop a high stool, held a wax tablet and stylus in his lap.

The abbey bells rang for Lauds. Three hours after midnight, Brian thought, and they had already been here two hours. King Henry, his chin in his hand, brooded over some inner vision of his own. Suddenly he turned to Brian.

"I still can't believe it," he muttered. "I realized that naming Maud as my heir would take some getting used to, but the hostility I saw, the outrage—" He lapsed again into silence.

So the King was stunned by the unexpected response to the long-awaited proclamation, Brian realized in surprise. He had expected him to be furious. Strange that such a crafty sovereign should be so blind in this instance. But he had also been blind to the despicable character

of his son and heir, William, refusing to see what was obvious to everyone else. Where the succession was concerned, it was now apparent the King saw only that which he wished to see.

"There must be a precedent," Henry said. "There must be."

Brian doubted they would find one. Shortly after Matins he had been awakened from a sound sleep and told to attend the King. When he arrived in the chamber, Bishop Roger was already there. The three men had waited while the clerics conducted a frantic search for any evidence of a woman succeeding when no male of the ruling family was available.

"I have found something, Sire," a cleric finally said, his voice blurry from lack of sleep.

He ran an ink-stained finger over the lines of faded parchment. "A few hundred years ago the King of Wessex passed away and his queen reigned after him for a year." He looked up. "Then she was removed. The writer of this chronicle suggests that perhaps men could no longer stomach taking orders from a woman."

"God forbid the magnates should hear of this. Is that the only example of a female ruler?" the King asked.

"All I can find, Sire."

"Keep looking. Wake up, Roger." He reached over and shook the sleeping bishop. "Listen to this."

Roger started awake. "Yes, Sire." He heard what had been found, then shook his head. "It's as I feared. Nothing in the past will be of any help. but the chronicle brings up a point I've already mentioned to you: Neither noble nor church will accept a woman ruling alone. It goes against the grain and you'll have rebellion on your hands."

Henry snorted. "As I've told you, Roger, there's no question of her ruling alone. Naturally there must be a king-consort. Do I look like a fool? But the first order of importance is that my magnates swear homage to Maud." He rose to his feet and began to pace the chamber.

"You have someone specific in mind? Who is it?" Roger asked.

"Let us say the matter is well in hand. Be patient."

How typical of the secretive king to withhold the vital information of Maud's future husband, Brian thought. Obviously he must be someone the magnates would resist, or why not immediately announce the fact? Brian's heart sank. Every instinct he possessed told him the King was headed for a course that could easily lead the realm to disaster. He must at least make an effort to prevent that.

"Sire, it occurs to me that feelings may run high against this

homage ceremony. There are those who will leave England rather than swear fealty to your daughter. The magnates had their hearts set on Stephen, and Stephen himself expected to be the heir. Perhaps, to give everyone time to adjust—"

Henry held up his hand for silence, slowed his pacing, and came to rest before Brian. "I know all about my nephew's hopes, never fostered by me, I might add. As for the nobles leaving England— I've thought of that and already arranged to have the cinque ports watched. Anyone trying to leave will be stopped. For those who refuse to swear—there's plenty of room in my dungeons."

Brian saw Roger stare at the King in consternation. He gave a sigh of resignation. He had done what he could. So be it. Matters would fall out as God willed.

"The matter is closed," King Henry said, resuming his seat at the table. He pointed to the nodding cleric who held the wax tablet on his lap. "You, what is the order of precedence I gave regarding the ceremony?"

The cleric twitched awake and glanced down at his wax tablet. "Ah, let me see, first to swear will be the Archbishop of Canterbury, then the other peers of the church. The first of the lay peers to swear homage will be the King of Scotland, then the Earl of Gloucester, then the Count of Mortain—"

"What!" Brian and the Bishop rose to their feet in unison.

"A grave mistake, Sire," the Bishop protested, his jowls quivering with outrage. "You cannot allow a bastard, no matter how high his position, regardless of the esteem in which he is held, take precedence before Stephen of Blois. That is truly asking for trouble." He turned to Brian. "My Lord of Wallingford, you'll support me in this?"

"Absolutely, Your Grace. I beg of you, Sire, Stephen and his brother Henry will take this as a mortal insult to the House of Blois, coming as it does on the heels of their earlier . . . disappointment. My Lord of Gloucester must swear after Stephen."

The King was silent. "Robert is the child of my heart. Had it been in my power, I would have made him my heir. You both know he is the best qualified. But fate has determined otherwise. The least I can do to honor him is to have him swear homage to his sister right after the King of Scotland. Surely it is a small thing, but important to me."

His voice had become almost pleading, which fooled no one present, thought Brian. It was not a small thing, and the King knew it well enough. But neither he nor the Bishop voiced further protest.

To continue to oppose Henry of England was the quickest way to the dungeon—or the grave.

Brian knew there was no way he could point out King Henry's mistakes to him, beginning with making Maud his heir, and now letting Robert swear before Stephen, thus adding insult to Stephen's already injured feelings. If the King made enemies of his two nephews there might be far-reaching consequences, consequences that would not be manifest until after his death, when it came time for everyone to fulfill their oath to see Maud crowned. And if, in addition, there was the wrong choice of king-consort. . . . Folly piled upon folly. Where would it end?

Chapter Fifteen

THE FOLLOWING MORNING, ON THE THIRD FLOOR OF THE WHITE Tower, Stephen lay on the wooden frame bed in his chamber, a bruise above his cheekbone, one arm wrapped in a clean white cloth. With his other hand he sipped from a pewter tankard. Beside him, seated on a cushioned stool, his brother Henry fixed him with a stern eye.

"What happened to you last night?" the Abbot asked. "The truth now."

Stephen told him how he had spent half the night riding aimlessly through Southwark, then stopped at a bankside tavern and finally ended up in a drunken brawl. "My head aches and my arm is stiff but I'm none the worse for it."

"Are you able to bear more ill news?" Henry asked.

Stephen gave a bitter laugh. "What could be worse than last night's apocalypse?"

The Abbot moved his stool closer to the bed, and gave a perfunctory glance around the empty chamber. "I have this straight from the Bishop of Salisbury's lips: At the homage ceremony, after the peers of the church have sworn, the first lay peer to swear homage to Maud will be the King of Scotland. By all rights, you should swear next. But Robert is to swear before you."

Stephen stared at his brother, aghast. A cold fury swept through his body. "I take that as a mortal insult to our house and won't attend the ceremony. I'll sail for Boulogne before the week is out."

"The cinque ports are watched by the King's men. Every noble I've spoken with has insisted they won't swear homage to the German empress and threatened to leave England. Empty words. In the end everyone will do the King's bidding. No one wants to see the inside of our uncle's dungeons, have his lands confiscated, or face banishment."

"But we are his nephews!"

"What is that to a man who had one brother killed and another imprisoned for life?"

Stephen stared at his brother, then looked away. "Yes, I see your point. All right, then I'll be too ill to attend. What can he do?" Anger and hurt continued to war within him. "Why has he forsaken us, Henry, why?"

"He hasn't forsaken us." The Abbot rose to his feet. "There was no insult intended, I feel sure of it. The King is of an age when he feels threatened by his own mortality and the judgment of heaven. Robert is his favorite and he hopes to do him this one last honor. He made Maud his heir because the man is obsessed with founding his own dynasty, one sprung from his own loins. How else can he justify the crimes he has committed—and his father before him? His desire to ensure the continuity of the Norman line has clouded his usually sound judgment. Unless steps are taken to remedy the matter we'll all live to regret it."

"It all sounds very complex. The fact remains that he has insulted us and I still refuse to attend."

The Abbot pursed his lips and fingered the jeweled cross on his breast. "Of course, if you're willing to jeopardize your position over a simple matter of wounded pride—"

"What position?"

"I speak of your future, blockhead. Stop feeling sorry for yourself. How can you ever become king if you're in bed nursing your grievances and flaunting the King's will? How can I hope to help you as the brother of a traitor, for that's how the King will view your absence. You must remain our uncle's loyal, devoted servant if you hope to ascend the throne."

Stephen propped himself up on the pillows. "You're as mad as he is. Last night I thought you might be of help, but in the cold light of day I see our cause is lost. The magnates will swear a binding oath to put Maud on the throne. Rome would excommunicate them if they were forsworn."

"Leave Rome to me." The Abbot gave him a conspiratorial smile. "You don't imagine the church or the nobles will actually allow a female to rule England and Normandy, whatever they swear to the King's face." He sat on the bed beside his brother. "Already, we have much support in high places. And low—there's no denying that London loves you."

Stephen studied his brother's face. "What did you mean, exactly, when you said earlier that we must remedy the matter?"

The Abbot smiled. "Come, don't act the innocent."

"Stop playing games with me, Henry. What you imply is not possible!" He dared not let himself hope that his dream might still be fulfilled.

Henry rose to his feet again. "Anything is possible—in the future. While the King lives we can do nothing but comply with his wishes. However, after he dies? Ah, that will be a different matter. Then we'll need powerful friends in the right places, sufficient determination, and the courage to take advantage of the propitious moment. When the time is ripe—*carpe diem*, Brother, *carpe diem*. Trust me. Meanwhile say nothing to anyone. Behave as the King's loyal subject who accepts his will with good grace. Cultivate our friends, make no enemies."

"You're very persuasive, as usual. If I do decide to attend the ceremony—" Stephen sighed and sank back against the pillows, knowing he had already decided. His brother's words had lifted his spirits. Seize the day, Henry had said, and his heart quickened at the prospect. "But the House of Blois takes second place to no one," he continued. "I won't swear after Robert."

"No one has suggested you should, hothead." The Abbot looked again at the closed door. "Now, listen carefully, and I'll tell you exactly what must be done."

A fortnight later the day of the homage ceremony dawned bright and clear. By the time the abbey bells had rung for Sext, all the King's magnates were gathered in the great hall of Westminster.

Stephen watched Robert of Gloucester, resplendent in a dark blue mantle and indigo tunic, stride purposefully toward him. He started to turn away but Robert caught his arm.

"Why have you been avoiding me, Stephen? Do you hold it against me that I will swear before you?"

"Careful, that's my injured arm. Why would I hold it against you?"

"That's not for me to say. But the order of precedence was none of my doing, you must believe me."

Stephen knew that Robert was blameless, but still he resented him. "I understand that and hold nothing against you." He bowed coolly, aware that he had hurt Robert, then walked toward his brother, who had just entered the hall.

The Abbot frowned. "What did Gloucester want?"

"Nothing. A friendly gesture to ensure my nose is not twisted too much out of joint."

The Abbot glanced at Robert. "He may be less friendly after this day's work is done. You're not having second thoughts, I trust."

"And third and fourth thoughts. It's a great risk."

"Naturally, but—ah, there are the heralds. Benedicte, Brother." He touched Stephen lightly on the shoulder with a richly jeweled finger, and joined the procession of clergymen.

Impressive in scarlet-and-gold costume, the heralds blew on their silver trumpets. The peers of the church lined up in order of precedence, followed by the lay peers, magnificent in their fur-lined court robes and glittering jewels. At their head, towering over everyone else, stood the King of Scotland. Robert walked behind him, then Stephen, followed by the Earl of Chester, the de Beaumont twins, and the remainder of the King's most important nobles. Lesser lords like Brian FitzCount brought up the rear.

Inside the great hall, Maud, a regal and imposing presence in a gold-embroidered purple mantle, sat on a magnificent carved chair waiting to receive the oath of loyalty from the magnates of England and Normandy. Jewels blazed at her throat, on her fingers, and winked from the gold chaplet she wore over a purple gauze veil. Beside her stood the King, sumptuous in his royal ceremonial robes.

Stephen could not take his eyes off her. Never had she looked so beautiful; never had she seemed so desirable. But—she was occupying the royal chair, *his* chair.

Since the conversation with his brother the morning after the proclamation, much of Stephen's old confidence had returned. The prospect of action—any kind of action—never failed to revitalize him, and today he would take an action that would do much to establish him as a potential leader of the realm. Prompted by his brother's continual encouragement, Stephen could almost believe he had not, irretrievably, lost the crown. As his self-esteem rose he no longer felt consumed by jealousy and resentment. Although Maud was still a rival, she had become much less threatening to his pride, and his feelings for her had started to return. Of course, the conflict was far from resolved: He wanted Maud and he wanted the throne. She gave him a tentative smile now and Stephen smiled in return. He was rewarded by a look of relief that transformed her face, the warmth that suddenly shone in her sparkling gray eyes melting his heart. Perhaps he could win both.

His eyes fell on the jeweled ivory casket resting beside her. Inside lay the holy relics of saints' bones; it was on this casket that he would be asked to swear homage to Maud. A veil of sweat coated the palms of his hands. Breaking a sworn oath was no light matter, and the thought of it sent ripples of fear coursing through his body. He forced the horrifying thought of excommunication from his mind. His brother had promised to deal with Rome, he reminded himself, and if he could not trust Henry, then whom could he trust?

The ceremony began. The Archbishop of Canterbury swore his homage first, then the bishops and abbots. Just ahead, Stephen saw his brother kneel before Maud; without a tremor he swore homage on the ivory casket. Stephen's heart beat faster. Next the King of Scotland, first of the lay peers, stiffly bent his giant frame and swore to honor his niece as Queen of England and Duchess of Normandy after the King's death, in the event there was no male heir.

Without warning, Stephen was attacked by doubts and reservations and his resolve wavered. By God's birth, he was about to take a fearful hazard. Suppose it did not fall out as his brother had said? Was it worth—the Scottish king was rising; Robert took a step forward. He must make his move or—now!

In one long stride, Stephen pushed ahead of Robert, shouldering him roughly out of the way so that he almost fell. He heard Robert's sharply indrawn breath, and a concerted gasp of surprise from the nobles. Directly in front of him, Maud's eyes widened in shock. The King, his face a black cloud, moved closer to her, fixing Stephen with a menacing look. He raised his hand, pointing a finger at his nephew. A host of guards ringing the hall ran toward Stephen, spears at the ready. From behind, Stephen felt Robert try to push him aside, and for a moment the two of them jockeyed for position in the line. Equally matched in strength, neither could displace the other.

The guards were only a few feet away now. Wrenching himself from Robert's grasp, Stephen, a prayer on his lips, fell to his knees before the King.

"Sire! Sire! Hear me out, I beg of you!"

The King hesitated, then held up his hand. The guards fell back.

"Sire, I deem it a dishonor to the House of Blois, as well as to the House of Normandy, not to swear my oath of loyalty after King David. As God is my witness, and as my peers will testify, I have served you faithfully and well since first I came to your court. Nor am I unmindful of the great affection, wealth, and honors you have bestowed upon me. But even my mother, your beloved sister Adela, daughter of the great Conqueror, would agree that the House of Blois is being slighted. Let me take my rightful position, so that I may be the first among your subjects to honor your daughter as my future liege-lord."

Stephen carefully avoided any mention of Robert or his illegitimacy. His brother had cautioned that this, above all else, would turn the King against him. At his back, he could hear the swelling murmur of approval from the magnates. All of them held Robert of Gloucester in great esteem, but Stephen, scion of a great house, had been denied pride of place and everyone knew it. The expression on the King's face told Stephen that his uncle was in a quandary: He knew his nephew was in the right but his heart lay with his son. He glanced first at Robert, then at Stephen. A shadow passed over his face. Still he did not speak.

Robert of Gloucester, pale as death but composed, approached his father. "Sire, I value your wish to honor me, but it is Stephen of Blois who should take precedence over me in swearing homage. I yield my place."

Father and son gazed at each other for a moment, then the King slowly nodded. The tension in the hall eased. Robert withdrew and Stephen walked up to Maud. It had fallen out exactly as his brother had predicted: The selfless Robert had yielded rather than force the King to choose between them. Stephen felt a stab of pity for Robert, who was dear to him, but he did not regret what he had done.

Triumphant, Stephen knelt before Maud. Placing his hands between hers, he swore his oath of loyalty, sealing it with the ritual kiss upon the mouth. He let his lips linger a second longer than courtesy demanded. Then he laid a hand upon the ivory box of holy relics, noting that his fingers trembled ever so slightly.

In a steady voice that rang throughout the hall, Stephen took his oath: "In the name of the Holy Trinity, and in reverence of these sacred relics, I, Stephen, do swear that I will truly keep the promise which I have taken and will always remain faithful to Maud, my future liege-lord."

He smiled at his cousin, who had a sparkle of tears in her eyes. Exhilaration flowed through him like strong wine. He had taken a hazardous risk and won, upheld the honor of his family, and established himself as a fearless leader among his peers. It was his first concrete step toward the throne.

Chapter Sixteen

Maud, stunned by Stephen's rash assertion of his position, the afterglow of his ritual kiss still warm upon her lips, accepted the homage of her half-brother in a distracted state. She did not fully gather her wits together until Ranulf, Earl of Chester, stood before her and delivered yet another surprise blow.

Maud expected him to kneel but instead he addressed the King: "Sire, before I swear homage to your daughter as my liege-lord, I need assurance that the barons of your council will have a say in her choice of husband. After all, it is he who will rule, and therefore must be acceptable to your magnates."

Ranulf, who ruled the vast palatinate of Chester which bordered both Scotland and Wales, was one of the most powerful and influential magnates in the realm. When he spoke, his peers listened; where he led, others would follow. Now his words swept over the assembled throng like a high wind rustling through a field of grain. After a moment's pause every noble loudly raised their voices in agreement.

Maud froze in her royal chair, far more shocked by Chester's ultimatum than she had been by Stephen's setting aside of her brother. This was an open challenge to the King: Agree to Chester's terms or suffer the consequences. Although her father had made no mention of a future husband except in the vaguest terms, Maud was realistic enough to know there would have to be one. As she would be queen in her own right, however, she did not know exactly what role a king-consort would play under such unusual circumstances. She had resolved to discuss this with her father at the earliest opportunity.

Now her eyes sought King Henry who, stroking his chin, stared at Chester with open enmity. Maud knew he would carefully weigh his options: There was no question of taking hostile action against the Earl, not with all the nobles supporting him, thus he could not openly refuse Ranulf's request. How would he elude the trap?

"Naturally, my Lord of Chester," Henry replied in a soft voice that nonetheless chilled Maud's blood. "If that is the will of my magnates, I can only agree. No marriage will be made for Maud without the consent of my council."

"Will you swear to that, Sire, upon these same holy relics?" Chester pointed to the ivory casket.

The King's face became gorged with blood. Then he forced a smile to his lips and visibly regained control. He snapped his fingers and his steward sprang forward. Henry pointed to the casket of relics; the steward lifted it up and held it before the King. With his hand on the ivory casket, Henry swore his oath not to marry Maud to anyone without the consent of his council.

Maud felt a shiver of apprehension run through her. Every instinct she possessed told her that the King had no intention of consulting his magnates on the subject of her marriage. But the nobles accepted the oath with a murmur of approval. The casket was again laid beside her and Chester bent his knee to swear homage. His face, with its long brown mustache, was flushed with satisfaction.

The rest of the ceremony went smoothly, and there was no overt evidence of the outrage or hostility Maud had glimpsed on Christmas Eve. Perhaps, with God's grace, she would be accepted after all.

The winter of 1126 passed without incident. January turned into February and February into March. Maud was so busy that she hardly had time to notice the change of seasons. Each day since the homage ceremony she had received intensive instruction from her father on the administrative workings of his realm. Her willingness to learn, her ready intelligence, as well as her vast knowledge of European affairs had earned her father's respect and approval. Maud

knew he was pleased—and surprised. As a result the time she spent with him was unusually agreeable.

Even the King's magnates appeared to have developed a grudging tolerance of the situation. Maud was profoundly grateful for the overwhelming change in her fortunes, and if Stephen had been in her company more often she would have been totally content. Since the homage ceremony, however, she had barely glimpsed her cousin. Maud wondered if he still smarted as a result of having his ambitions thwarted, even blamed her in some way, and was thus avoiding her. It was a constant worry to her and she had asked Robert if Stephen held a grudge against her.

"It's not like him to hold on to a grievance," he had replied slowly. "But, of course, losing his hopes for the crown was a heavy blow. In time Stephen will recover, I doubt not. Be patient. His brother, on the other hand, will have taken the loss very much to heart. He was promised the See of Canterbury when Stephen became king, after the present archbishop dies."

"No wonder he's so cool to me," Maud had said. "But the Abbot is less clever than I thought. After all, what is to prevent me from granting him the same prize—if I'm queen at that time. He would do better to woo my favor than shun me."

Robert had laughed. "I imagine that currying favors from a female is anathema to him."

A typical ecclesiastical attitude, she had reflected. Meanwhile, all she could do was wait for Stephen's wounded pride to heal.

One afternoon in early March, Maud walked across the courtyard at Westminster heading for the small chamber located in the southeastern corner of the castle where she met the King for her daily instruction. Overhead, dark clouds scuttled across a gray sky and a raw wind blew from the north. The courtyard bustled with its usual activity: squires polishing hunting horns and spears, huntsmen exercising shaggy deerhounds, falconers airing their hooded birds.

She was halfway up the narrow stone steps leading to the chamber when the sound of hooves made her turn back. Three riders rode into the courtyard. Maud's pulse quickened as she recognized Stephen and the de Beaumont twins. Grooms hurried to tend the horses and the riders dismounted. Stephen's face was flushed from the ride; he threw back his tawny head to laugh at something Robin of Leicester said, then flung a comradely arm over his shoulder. At the sight of his tall, lean body, Maud's heart turned over.

Stephen noticed her on the steps and with a word to the twins went over to where she stood.

"What good fortune," he said. "I came to Westminster especially to see you. Matilda and I have been in our estates at Lancaster for the past month or more, which is why I've been so neglectful."

His eyes met hers, and pulled by an invisible thread, Maud found herself at the bottom of the steps, closer to him.

"I'd prepared a brave speech of apology to you," he said, earnestly, holding out his hands, "but now that I'm here the words are gone from my mind."

"Apology?" She reached out to grasp his hands.

"I didn't respond to the King's news with good grace on Christmas Eve. I should have offered my congratulations on the signal honor the King bestows on you, but the truth is I was heartbroken and angry. You know how much I wanted the crown. Forgive my discourtesy?" He squeezed her hands.

"Surely it is I who should ask your forgiveness for being given what you so badly wanted."

Stephen could not have been more open or disarming, and her fears that he would no longer care for her quickly evaporated. Why, then, remembering his taut face and blazing eyes on Christmas Eve, did his words strike her as somehow too glib, almost rehearsed?

"I'd no idea what my father would say," she continued. "Please believe me, it came as much of a surprise to me as it did to you." She paused and swallowed. "I know how you must feel, having your hopes dashed, and I can't say I blame you, but I hope it won't destroy our friendship."

Something flickered at the back of his eyes, then was gone. "Nothing will ever destroy our friendship, Cousin. Put the matter from your mind. I intend to faithfully serve you as my queen." His eyes danced. "It should prove no great hardship."

Pleased but still faintly troubled, Maud smiled her acknowledgment. She wanted to ask him about the business with Robert at the ceremony but decided to leave well enough alone. She sensed a mystery about Stephen: subtle shifts of mood, something held back, facets of his character that caused a faint doubt in her mind, a cobweb of uneasiness so fragile that it vanished before she could catch hold of it. In truth she was not sure what she sensed.

As he looked at her now, his eyes embracing her, the touch of his fingers intoxicating, Maud's breath caught in her throat; her reservations melted away like wax before a flame.

"I must see my father now," she murmured, releasing her hands.

He stepped back. "Perhaps we'll meet again at supper?"

She nodded and floated up the narrow staircase to the King's chamber.

When she entered the room Maud knew immediately that something of moment had occurred. Attended by the Bishop of Salisbury and one of his physicians, her father's face was pale and his manner agitated.

"Sire, please, take this draught of wine mixed with poppy juice," the gray-bearded physician urged.

"I refuse to have my wits dulled for the remainder of the day. Go, and leave me in peace."

"What's happened?" Maud asked, alarmed.

"The King is upset. He received some bad news from Anjou, my lady. Really, he should be bled—"

"You've said enough. Get out!" The King, suddenly enraged, grabbed the goblet the physician was holding and poured the contents over the dried rushes on the chamber floor. "I would be dead and in my grave if you doomsayers had anything to say about it," he shouted. "Out, out, both of you." He threw the goblet at the man's feet.

Clucking like an old hen, the physician, followed by Bishop Roger, hastily withdrew.

"By God's splendor, what a bunch of old women."

"Of what bad news does he speak, Sire?" Maud ventured. "Has some new trouble arisen between Count Fulk of Anjou and yourself?"

The King looked at her for a moment without speaking, then began to stroke his chin. "Old trouble. Not new." He took a deep breath. "Normandy has had trouble with Anjou for over a century. But ever since your brother William died matters have become even worse."

Maud refrained from saying that it was hardly surprising there continued to be bad blood between Anjou and Normandy. She remembered the Emperor telling her that after William's death her father had shipped his son's thirteen-year-old widow back to Anjou minus her very considerable dowry. When Count Fulk, her father, demanded its return, Henry had delayed, making one excuse after another. When it became evident that he had no intention of returning the dowry, the Count of Anjou had sworn vengeance.

The King walked over to the oak table and looked down at the parchment map of Europe that covered it. "Matters have come to a head with Anjou, far sooner than I'd imagined. It's imperative you fully understand what is at stake, for your support is needful."

Intrigued, Maud joined him at the oak table. "Anything that I can do to help, Sire."

The King stabbed his finger at a large black dot. "Here is Anjou to the south, France to the west, and Normandy to the north, with the Vexin in between. Louis of France has long had his eye on Normandy. In fact, the House of Capet has coveted the duchy since the days of the early Norman dukes."

"I'm familiar with the history of Normandy and France," Maud said.

"Then you'll grasp the situation all the more readily. William Clito, my brother Robert's son, was only a babe when I captured the duchy. Since coming of age, he fancies himself the true Duke of Normandy, and has caused continual unrest in my domains. Caught between these two enemies, France and my nephew, Normandy is in constant danger."

"We heard in Germany that William Clito and Louis of France had made common cause against Normandy," Maud said, her interest quickening as she grasped the full import of his words. "Joined, as I now recall, by Fulk of Anjou."

The King nodded. "Indeed, they formed an alliance with the sole purpose of taking over Normandy."

"But then," she continued, "just after the Emperor died, Anjou suddenly became your ally, and Louis of France backed down. The threat came to naught. That is all I remember."

King Henry tapped his finger against the map. "Anjou and Normandy together would be able to repel successfully any attack from France. Would you agree that such an alliance is vital for our survival?"

"Oh, I heartily agree, Sire." Maud came round the table to stand next to him. "How did you persuade Fulk of Anjou to throw in his lot with Normandy instead of France?"

"I made a bargain with him," the King said in a casual voice, "but if I don't keep my part, he'll withdraw his support."

"What was the bargain, Sire?" She searched her father's face.

With an enigmatic smile, the King hooked his thumbs in his black belt, and began to pace the small chamber. Maud's eyes followed him, more intrigued than ever.

"I regret that you didn't know your grandfather," he said, abruptly changing the subject.

Maud was immediately on guard. When the King talked of his father, she had learned, it usually meant he wanted something. Like a crab, he approached everything sideways.

"The tales he would tell me of our Viking forebears," the King continued. "What a heritage is ours, Daughter, a two-hundred-year-old heritage that began with Rollo, first duke of the Normans, eventually passing on to Duke Richard the Fearless, Duke Robert the Magnificent, Duke William Bastard, the Conqueror, and now myself. After me comes the Duchess Maud, followed by her sons and grandsons."

Distrustful at first, Maud now felt her blood stir at his words. She gazed at her father with a rapt expression on her face.

"We started as savage Norse adventurers, yet the Norman spirit, bold and fearless, has traveled to England, southern Italy, and Sicily." He walked to the window seat and back again. "Queen Maud," he said. "What a noble ring it has."

"Queen Maud," she repeated in hushed reverence, savoring the title in her mind, imagining herself as England's sovereign, beloved as her mother had been, respected as her father was now.

"Nothing must put the realm in jeopardy. Nothing," he stated firmly. "Whatever needs to be done, no sacrifice is too great to ensure the safety of our line, the continuation of our proud dynasty."

Maud nodded vigorously. "Oh, Sire, it is a sacred trust." Tears sparkled in her gray eyes. "Before God and all His Saints, I promise to be worthy."

The King looked deeply into her eyes, reached out to pat her shoulder, then stepped back. "When I tell you of your forthcoming marriage," he said, "I know I can hold you to that promise."

Maud reeled back in stunned disbelief. Her mouth fell open; the blood drained from her face, and her body felt as if it had received an impact of such violence that she could not draw breath.

When there was no answer to his statement, the King said, "You heard me?"

"Yes," she whispered, unable to find her voice. Fool! Fool! With no more caution than an unsuspecting rabbit, she had walked right into the trap he had laid for her. Trembling, Maud sank onto a stool. "To whom will I be married?" But she already knew the answer.

"You're far too clever not to have guessed by now." The King confronted her squarely.

"Count Fulk," she said, in a voice unrecognizable as her own. "So

I'm to be the price of Anjou's support. In return, the Count receives the crown of England and the duchy of Normandy."

Her father nodded. "But it would be more accurate to say Anjou *shares* the crown of England and the dukedom. A fair exchange."

"For whom?" A memory flashed across her mind and she frowned. "Perhaps I'm mistaken, but in Germany we heard that Fulk of Anjou is to marry the King of Jerusalem's daughter. Does he give up the Holy Land for the throne of England?"

The King was silent. He walked back to the table and began to fidget with a corner of the map. "No, you heard correctly. It's not Fulk who will be your husband, but his son. Fulk has abdicated in the boy's favor, and young Geoffrey is now Count of Anjou. The bad news I received was from Fulk, who grows impatient to leave for Jerusalem and his new bride. He demands that our arrangements for the betrothal be completed—or he will withdraw his support of Normandy and again throw in his lot with Louis of France."

"Boy? How young is this Geoffrey?"

"A mature youth of almost fifteen, in possession of a powerful county," the King told her in a calm voice.

"Almost fifteen! You would wed me to a child?" she shrieked.

"Child? Child? It's common to marry at such an age. You were only thirteen when you married the Emperor. Geoffrey is a remarkable youth, I hear, looking far older than his years, and of such an unusual beauty he is called Geoffrey the Handsome. Imagine! Highly intelligent, trained in the arts of war, and a great scholar. With your scholarly background, you'll suit each other well."

Maud heard her father's voice from a long way off but his words had ceased to have any meaning. She felt as if she were in a dream. At any moment she would wake and all would be as it had been a few moments ago. Somewhere in the back of her mind, a great rage simmered, threatening to explode.

Not an hour since, she had been congratulating herself at having won her father's respect and esteem. Now it appeared that he had been toying with her, only pretending to treat her as a person in her own right, beguiling her with a magic rhetoric that would have induced her to agree to anything. She had just begun to trust him, and he had betrayed her. Yet again.

The King poured some wine from the leather flagon on the table into a pewter goblet. "I realize this comes as a shock, but I know you can see what this marriage will mean to Normandy's future—which is to say, your future."

Maud drank the wine in a single gulp, not tasting it but glad of the warmth it bought. Her father stood over her, an expression of concern softening the harsh lines of his face.

He put a tentative hand on her arm. "Daughter—"

She threw off his hand as if it had been a live coal. "I was an empress," she said. "I will be a queen. How can you marry me to a mere count? It's an outrage!"

"I expected that to be your first reaction, but you did agree we need Anjou as an ally."

"Yes, but—"

"Good. Then you'll help to bring that about."

"I'll help you to find another solution."

"There is no other solution," Henry insisted. "The price of Fulk's alliance was your hand in marriage."

"I can't marry a lowly count," she retorted, feeling her initial horror giving way before the force of the King's arguments.

"How many kings or emperors are there available, eh?"

"That's beside the—"

"Didn't think of that, did you?"

Maud fell silent. All that her father said was true: The marriage would ensure the safety of the Norman realm; as Queen of England it would be to her political advantage. But, quite unaccountably, the woman in her rebelled, recoiling in protest and dismay at the unequal, loveless match.

"Geoffrey will not be fourteen forever, Daughter," the King said, sensing a chink in her resistance. "Bear in mind that when you are twenty-nine he will be only twenty. A good age to pleasure an older woman and continue to fill her womb with lusty sons!" He gave her a suggestive wink.

Maud suddenly had an image of her Uncle David of Scotland's thirteen-year-old son whom he had brought to attend the homage ceremony: an ungainly, coltish boy, clumsy and unsure of himself, with a spotty face and fuzzy down on his chin like a newborn chick. Undoubtedly, the young Geoffrey would be like that, regardless of what her father said.

Quite without warning she was assailed by the memory of Stephen's lips on hers, the heat of desire in his eyes, the warmth of his smile, the spell of his vibrant manliness. With every fiber of her being she ached to belong to her cousin, whether or not he ever claimed her. Her heart cried out in protest at the thought of an untried youth touching one hair of her head.

"As far as Geoffrey's status is concerned," the King continued, "for a few years perhaps, you will be a countess. But not for long, Madam, not for long." He rolled his eyes upward. "By God's splendor, I'm not a well man, no, not well at all. In confidence, my physicians have given me only a year or two at the most."

She stared at him suspiciously. She knew that he was not in the best of health, but he would say anything now to persuade her.

"It's true," he insisted. "Soon you will be queen, and Geoffrey will be king. Can it matter then that he was once a count? Of course not." He came to rest beside her stool. "Meanwhile, Anjou marries Normandy, and Maud and Geoffrey make the best of it. Such are empires made. We must all make personal sacrifices."

"We? I notice it is I who makes the sacrifice, not you," she retorted. "As I did when I was nine. Then I had little choice. This time I do."

The King's face grew red. "You have no choice, Madam, none at all. You, like myself, like all rulers, must marry where expediency dictates. Our lives are not our own. Agreement and choice don't enter into it." His voice became confidential. "Geoffrey will have to spend much of his time in Anjou and keep an eye on Normandy. Rarely, if ever, will he have occasion to come to England. After you have given the realm a handful of sons, you can go your separate ways, eh?"

Maud could not bring herself to reply. Every instinct rebelled at this denial of her power of choice.

"As future queen, surely you see where your duty lies," the King said, pressing his advantage. "Private need must give way before the public weal. A ruler is as worthy as he serves the needs of his realm."

Maud stiffened. Duty. Sacrifice. Even thus had the Emperor spoken. She had been serving the needs of the realm, she realized, since she was nine years old, a martyr to duty and sacrifice. Of course she wanted to be queen, but, because of Stephen, she had become fully aware of what that would mean: her private needs never fulfilled; personal happiness forever denied her. Surely there must be a way to escape this trap.

A course of action suddenly presented itself. Did she dare follow it?

"Who knows of this proposed marriage?" she asked.

"Just Fulk, myself, and Geoffrey, I imagine. The Bishop of Salisbury. Why?" The King's eyes narrowed.

"You can't marry me to anyone without your council's knowledge." Her voice was triumphant. "You swore an oath to your barons, remember?"

The shaft had gone home and King Henry's hooded eyes assumed the cruel, predatory aspect of a hawk. "I made my agreement with Fulk first. It precedes any later oath."

"You didn't tell that to your magnates, did you?" she reminded him. "It's no light matter to break an oath of this kind."

"The oath is not binding if I was forced to swear it," he told her. "It was necessary that all swear to honor you as queen. Nothing else mattered then, nothing else matters now."

"Normandy and Anjou have always been enemies, and if the council knew of your intention to marry me to an Angevin, they would forbid it."

"They would try. But all that strife is in the past. Over and done with. I will do what is needful, with or without my barons' agreement. Does the shepherd ask his sheep wither he should lead them?"

It was just as she had suspected. "You don't intend to tell them!"

"When you're safely betrothed—that is time enough for my barons to know. They can do nothing then."

Maud rose from the stool and walked to the turret window, staring down at the Thames flowing darkly under the slate gray sky, the purple shadows gathering over the courtyard. She had the weapon she needed.

"If you insist on going through with this travesty of a marriage— I will be obliged to tell the barons." She held her breath. The fateful words of defiance had been spoken. The world had not tumbled apart.

Then, behind her, she heard a choked gasp. She turned quickly. Her father's face was an alarming shade of purple and he made strangling sounds in his throat. Holy Mother of God, what had she done? Maud ran to the table and poured wine into a goblet. With trembling hands, Henry lifted the goblet to his lips.

"You wouldn't dare," he wheezed, taking short, heavy breaths as he sank onto the stool Maud had just vacated.

"Sire, I would do anything to prevent this marriage," she cried, sinking to her knees in front of him. "Anything. I beg of you, please reconsider. I'm sure we can find an alternative to placate Fulk of Anjou and win his support. There must be someone more suitable I can marry. Even a duke would not be unacceptable."

Rising slowly, Henry grabbed Maud by the shoulders and shook her so roughly she winced with pain. "You shall not defy me, do you hear? A husband has been found for you, the contract has been signed, and you will marry him! Accept it! Damn you, woman, for a wilful, rebellious bitch! If you weren't so vital to my plans, I tell you I would—'' He did not finish his sentence.

Maud tried to tear herself from his grasp but his fingers were like iron hooks digging into her flesh. "You will do it!"

Thoroughly frightened now, Maud stubbornly shook her head.

He threw her away from him with such force, she lost her balance and had to grab the table to keep from falling. For a moment they stood staring at each other, their jaws thrust forward in exactly the same manner. Without a word, she started for the door.

"Wait! Do not leave just yet," the King gasped, as he lumbered after her. "Perhaps, yes, perhaps I've been too hasty. Overzealous."

Surprised, she turned to face him.

"I'm sure we can find a way to resolve our differences, eh?" Henry's face, wiped clean of expression now, was returning to its normal color. "Let me fetch Bishop Roger. We'll all put our heads together and decide what must be done."

"Rest, Sire, let me fetch him for you. And your physician as well." Maud put her hand on the door.

Strong fingers shot out to grip her arm. "No need. The air will clear my head. Wait here."

Alone, Maud walked unsteadily to the window seat and sat down. The waves of resentment and rage that racked her body gradually subsided, to be replaced by a sense of satisfaction. She had held her ground, and, whatever the ultimate outcome, at least bought herself a little time. What an old sorcerer he was, she thought, really outrageous, trying to hoodwink his barons and very nearly succeeding.

Time, Maud realized, was really all she needed. If, somehow, she could stave off this marriage, or any other, then her father might die while she was still free. In that event she could make her own marriage—or, at least, have more of a say in it than she did now. Perhaps she could never wed Stephen but unmarried, at least, she could share part of her life with him. Half a loaf was better than none. A pang of guilt shot through her at the thought of the King's death. How could she contemplate his passing in such a dispassionate way? Yet it would solve so many problems!

After a while, Maud lifted her head and, glancing out the window, saw that dusk had fallen. The courtyard was brightly lit with flaring torches; men-at-arms paced back and forth.

The chamber had grown cold and the coals in the brazier were nearly gone. Where was the King? She had lost track of time, but surely he should have returned by now. And if he did not intend to return, why had no one come for her? She decided to see for herself.

Opening the door, she saw two guards who had not been there before. As she put a foot across the threshold, the guards thrust their spears in front of the open doorway, barring her path.

"The King's order, my lady," one said. "You may not leave."

Chapter Seventeen

FOR A MOMENT MAUD WAS SO STUNNED, SHE COULD NOT BELIEVE WHAT she had heard. Had the guards gone mad?

"Let me through at once," she said, pushing against the crossed spears.

"My lady, I cannot let you pass without the King's permission," one of the guards said respectfully.

"But this is preposterous," she protested. "Did the King say to treat me as a prisoner?"

The guards looked at each other in consternation.

Sensing their uncertainty, she pressed her advantage. "If you don't let me through at once I will scream so loudly that the castle will be set on its ears." She opened her mouth widely.

"Please, my lady, I beg you do nothing until I get further instructions," the guard interjected hastily. "We were only told not to let you leave without further orders." He sprinted down the staircase while the other guard remained outside the door.

Maud slammed the door shut and walked back inside the chamber. Sweet Marie, she understood only too well what had happened. The King, fearing she would tell someone of his scheme to marry her to the Angevin, hoped to guarantee her silence by keeping her under lock and key.

For the moment he had succeeded, she thought bitterly, but if he believed he could bring her to heel in this way, he was very much mistaken. Nothing would induce her to marry the young count. She ran to the turret window and peered out, but it was too dark to see clearly.

How long would she be kept here? She would perish of cold if she stayed in the chamber much longer.

What would the King do? What *could* he do?

Behind her defiance Maud was aware that she was behaving foolishly. In the end she must submit to her fate, as she always had, but this time she stubbornly refused to acknowledge it. When the door opened, she stiffened in sudden fear.

"We are ordered to escort you to the Queen's quarters, my lady," the guard said.

Without a word, Maud followed the guards out of the chamber, down the staircase, and into the courtyard where they were joined by four more men-at-arms. Outside it was bitter cold, with little flurries of snow powdering the ground, and a chill wind that cut right through her fur-lined mantle. As she crossed the courtyard surrounded by even more guards, Maud saw Stephen walking toward his horse.

"I was just now asking what had become of you," Stephen called, catching sight of her.

"Excuse me, my lord," one of the guards said with a deferential bow, "but we're on the King's business and may not be deterred. I must ask you to step aside."

Stephen looked in astonishment at the men-at-arms. "I don't understand."

"Stephen, help me—" Maud began desperately, but two of the guards caught her by each arm, and fairly dragged her across the courtyard. The other four closed ranks behind them.

"I'm sorry, my lady, but you are forbidden to speak to anyone," the guard said, hurrying her along.

The last glimpse she had of Stephen, he was standing in the middle of the courtyard, his hand on the hilt of his sword, his face a study in bewilderment.

The guards took her round the side of the castle into the kitchen courtyard and through a small door that led to the south wing of Westminster. It was a part of the castle Maud had not visited before.

Inside, dominated by an enormous fireplace, was the largest kitchen Maud had ever seen. She caught a glimpse of iron cauldrons set on tripods over the open fire, a haunch of venison turning on the spit, and ropes of onion and garlic hanging from the blackened beams of the ceiling. Scullions were running to and fro with buckets of water. Agitated cooks shouted at one another as they bent over long wooden tables cluttered with basins, knives, platters, and bunches of herbs. No one paid the slightest attention to Maud and her escort.

The irony of the situation was not lost on her: Here was the future Queen of England being led through the kitchens like the meanest prisoner.

From the kitchens she was marched along a narrow passage, past the buttery and butler, up the main staircase, and down another passage on the second floor until they came to the Queen's solar. With impassive faces, the guards waited until she had closed the door behind her.

Alix and her ladies were grouped together over a recently born litter of black-and-white puppies lying beside their proud mother in a wicker basket.

"Alix—" Maud began in a choked voice.

The Queen turned, startled. "Oh my dear, what a fright you gave me." At the look on Maud's face, she gasped, and one soft white hand flew to her mouth. "Leave us," she told her ladies, who retired to a far corner of the chamber.

"Do you know what's happened?" Maud asked in a trembling voice. "My father has made me a prisoner. I'm forbidden to speak to anyone, to go where I will!"

Her face ashen, Alix took Maud firmly by the arm and set her onto a scarlet covered stool. She was garbed in her habitual flowing white gown and tunic, and her eyes were shadowed with fear as she pulled up another stool. Taking Maud's hands in icy fingers, she kept her voice low and composed.

"Listen to me, Maud. You have greatly angered the King over this matter of the Angevin marriage and I must warn you that when he is in this state he's capable of anything. He will almost certainly require bleeding to release the foul humors that torment him. I beg you not to cross him."

"Am I to submit to a hateful marriage so that this tyrant will not have to be bled?"

Alix cast an anxious look at her ladies, whispering together at the far end of the solar. "Oh, my dear, we must all submit to what God sends. And how well I understand what it means to be forced into an unwanted marriage."

"Well, I've no intention of submitting! Not only is it a grave dishonor—he's only a count, after all—but this Geoffrey is a mere child."

"That does seem a bit—excessive, if you'll forgive my saying so. One day you will be queen, surely that is honor enough? Geoffrey of Anjou will not always be a fourteen-year-old count, but your king-consort. And as matters now stand with the King's health, you may not have many years to wait." Alix signed herself.

Maud gave the Queen a suspicious glance. "You sound just like my father! Has he primed you to say these things to me?"

Alix grew even more pale in her distress. "As God is my witness, he did not! I truly believe what I have said. How could you think otherwise?" Her lower lip trembled.

Maud could have bitten her tongue in vexation. How could she have doubted the saintly Queen even for a moment? She caught Alix's hand in her own. "Forgive me, but I'm not myself. The news of the marriage has so upset me that I'm no longer mistress of my tongue."

Alix nodded her understanding. "When you're over the first shock, then you will accept your future with good grace."

"If only I could!" Maud rose to her feet. "The barons will side with me in this matter, you know. The Normans will never stomach an Angevin king."

Alix regarded Maud with a sad expression. "The King will prevail in any dispute with his nobles, surely that is evident to you by now." She walked over to Maud and laid a soft white hand on her arm. "Tell me the truth. Would an older husband, even a reigning king, really make a difference?"

Maud flushed. "What do you mean?" she stammered, surprised to see a glimmer of compassion in Alix's lovely doe eyes. Did she suspect her feelings for Stephen?

How she longed to tell the Queen of her love for her cousin, that the thought of leaving him was unbearable, but she felt too ashamed to admit to anyone that this was the main reason behind her refusal to marry.

Alix sighed, and Maud sensed she chose her words with care. "You must not ask so much of life, Maud. You cannot take the world by storm and force your will upon it. You're far more fortunate than most women. Accept your place in the natural order of things. Yield to your fate. Bloom where you're planted."

"Next you will tell me to be fruitful and multiply. Who can bloom in a wasteland?" Maud shook her head. "I'm not like you, Alix, if only I were! My nature is to fight for what I want until I have it." She took a deep breath. "Had you held firm with your father you would now be serving Our Lord in the convent, not forced to deal with a headstrong stepdaughter."

Alix's eyes filled with tears and she clasped Maud in her arms. "Yes," she whispered, "to seize life by the throat is the Norman way, and perhaps you will prevail in the end. I'm the last person to judge you, my dear. We must each follow our own nature wherever it leads us."

Maud's heart surged with affection for the gentle queen and she warmly returned the embrace. After a moment they broke apart, slightly embarrassed by their mutual display of warmth.

"What is to happen now?" Maud asked.

"You're to remain here in my care until you agree to go to Anjou. There's a small chamber attached to this one being readied for you now." She pointed to a closed door at the far end of the solar. "You may neither leave nor entertain visitors. Food will be brought to you. Each day you are permitted to take the air upon the battlements, accompanied by guards. Aldyth may join you, should you desire her, but if so, she must suffer the same conditions." Alix glanced toward her ladies. "Not even my women may talk to you alone."

Maud clenched her fists. "And if I refuse to abide by these outrageous rules?"

"If you seek to violate them, the King says he will hold me responsible and act accordingly."

A dart of fear shot through Maud. "He wouldn't dare to hurt you." But she was not really sure what her father might do if sufficiently roused.

Her eyes enormous, Alix said: "You threatened to tell the barons of the Angevin marriage, Maud, and when directly opposed the King can be merciless, ruthless!"

"But he breaks his sworn oath if he forces me to wed the young Count," Maud countered.

"Do you imagine he will let that stand in his way? It is madness, madness to defy him!" Alix wrung her hands. "Surely you have heard the tale of how his own grandchildren were blinded?"

"That is a tale I have not heard," Maud said slowly, "nor do I wish to hear it."

"You must hear it, for your own good." She led Maud to a corner of the room where a brazier burned brightly. "The King married Juliana, one of his illegitimate daughters, to the Count of Bretuil in Normandy," Alix began. "After a time the King had reason to suspect that his daughter's husband planned rebellion. The Count denied this and as an act of good faith, your father persuaded him to surrender his two young daughters as hostages. Henry's grandchildren, mind you. In return, the Count was given another child as hostage. In time Juliana's husband rebelled, even as the King had feared, and, as an act of defiance, blinded the child in his care." Alix's voice faltered. "Then—then at the King's instigation, the father of that child blinded Henry's grandchildren in turn."

Maud was speechless with horror. Her father had a notoriously cruel reputation, but this—the bile rose up in her throat, almost choking her.

"What happened to my half sister, to Juliana?" Maud whispered.

"She went totally mad." Her eyes brilliant with tears, Alix's face began to crumple like a piece of old parchment. "Please, Maud, I beg of you, in God's name, do as he wishes." She fell to her knees. "I beg of you!"

Maud quickly pulled her to her feet. "Peace, peace. Do not fret," she said, deeply shaken. "I cannot agree to the marriage, but I'll abide by all the conditions and not cause any trouble."

She held the weeping Queen in her arms, inwardly filled with rage and terror, sickened by the tale she had just heard. What a very devil of cunning was the King to have made Alix her jailer, for he knew full well that Maud would do nothing to put the Queen in jeopardy.

Several hours later, in the comparative safety of her newly readied chamber, Maud told Aldyth what had happened.

"Who would believe the future Queen of England a prisoner in her father's castle?"

Aldyth gave Maud a bewildered glance. "In truth I cannot blame your father. By the Rood, you knew you'd have to marry someone. Now that you're to be queen, what sense is there in resisting him? The Count's only a lad, 'tis true, but you'll have the molding of him this way, and that's all to your advantage, I would have thought." She looked around the cramped chamber, furnished with a large bed, a small trundle bed, an oak chest, and two threadbare stools. "The sooner we're out of this wretched mousehole the better."

Maud set her jaw in the stubborn manner Aldyth knew so well. "I want a grown man, already knowledgeable in the ways of the world! Someone of equal rank."

Aldyth, who had begun to unpack a large box containing Maud's belongings, shut the lid with a bang. "I know very well what you want, but you'll never have him, not in this world, my lady, so make the best of what is offered. You need someone to make a woman and a mother out of you, and the sooner the better."

"Why must you reduce everything to—to matters of midwifery?" Maud walked over to the tiny window and peered out. It was totally black, not a glimmer of moon or stars.

"Because for a woman, of low birth or high, that is all there is!"

"The Emperor never thought so."

. Aldyth planted her forearms on ample hips. "The Emperor was a monk, not a man, and you were his pupil, not his wife. When a woman behaves like a bitch-hound in heat, mooning about with love-sick dreams, then she is ready to be wedded and bedded."

Her face scarlet with embarrassment, Maud turned on Aldyth. "Such talk is unseemly. If I continue to refuse, the King must give in."

Aldyth sniffed. "Indeed? Stubborn he is, just like you." She threw up her hands. "How far does the apple fall from the tree?"

The bells rang for Compline; in stony silence, the two women went to their separate beds.

Sleepless, Maud tossed under the fur coverlet, Aldyth's words repeating over and over in her mind like a trouvère's rondelet. She could not deny their truth. She was ready—more than ready—for love. But only one person could give her what she craved. Impossible to give herself to another. Tears coursed down her face, and she stifled her anguish into the goose-down pillow. It was almost dawn before she finally slept.

Next morning it was still snowing, the ground outside the window a blanket of white. Maud broke her night's fast in the Queen's solar, disappointed that the weather made it impossible to walk upon the battlements. She was already chafing against the unaccustomed inactivity.

"I must leave you again for a while, my dear," Alix said, coming into the chamber from morning Mass. She wore a heavy brown cloak lined with gray fur and her face was pink with cold. "It's the day my women and I go to St. Giles, founded by your sainted mother, to give alms to the good monks who care for the poor lepers." She kissed Maud on both cheeks. "I've left you my tapestry to work upon, should you care to keep occupied. I find such work very soothing in times of inner upheaval."

Maud smiled weakly, and looked with distaste at the tapestry frame set up on the floor.

Alix watched her with worried eyes. "I don't like to leave you alone. Where is Aldyth?"

"She has gone—accompanied by an army of guards—to my old chamber to pack up the remainder of my belongings." Maud paused. "I would see my father, Alix. Can you arrange this?"

"He told me he wouldn't see you until you agree to his wishes."

"I still don't agree," Maud replied, "but I wish further converse upon the matter."

"He was adamant." At the look of defeat on Maud's face, Alix clasped her hands to her bosom. "I shall talk to him for you. Perhaps he will be more accessible today. Of course, I cannot promise—" She smiled bravely, and Maud could see that it would require all Alix's courage to approach her formidable husband.

"Say nothing if it does not seem the right moment," Maud said, noting the look of relief in Alix's eyes.

"You must hear Mass, my dear, and then you will feel better. I will ask the King to send you a priest. Surely he cannot deny you the comfort of confession."

Maud nodded absently, doubting whether a priest would provide any comfort.

Alix and her women left; Maud was alone. She walked from the solar into her own small chamber and back again. Charcoal braziers burned brightly in both rooms. A flagon of wine and a platter of honey cakes stood on the table in the solar. Nothing had been spared for her warmth and comfort, yet she was heartsick and confused. She knew her resolve was weakening, that she could not prevent the inevitable forever. Sooner or later she would be forced to accept her father's command.

She stroked a sleeping puppy and looked at the tapestry: It appeared to be another religious work, the Crucifixion this time, portrayed in bright blue and red and green wools. Near the tapestry lay Alix's psalter. Bound in an ivory and metal cover mounted on wood, the vellum pages were beautifully inscribed with gold and purple ink. Although Alix, like almost all women, was unlettered, her chaplain often read aloud to the Queen and her ladies. Maud, who read Latin fluently, sat down on a stool and picked up the psalter. She had just settled back when a loud knock interrupted her. A guard cautiously opened the door.

"A priest is here, my lady," he said. "Sent by the King."

"Oh, yes." Maud shut the book and stood up.

It must be two hours yet before the noon Mass. Did her father hope to hasten her capitulation by sending the priest earlier so he could reason with her?

A shapeless figure cloaked from head to toe in black entered the solar.

"Come into my chamber," she said over her shoulder, leading the way into her room. "Here we will not be disturbed should Queen Alix return."

The cleric followed her silently. Once inside the chamber, he closed the door behind him and carefully bolted it.

"That is hardly necessary—" Maud began, surprised, then stifled a scream as the cleric threw back his cowl to reveal the green-gold eyes and flushed face of her cousin Stephen.

Chapter Eighteen

Stephen!" MAUD COULD HARDLY BELIEVE IT WAS HER COUSIN. "HOW did you manage to get past the guards?"

Stephen slipped out of the black cloak. "I make a very convincing clergyman. Perhaps I missed my true calling?" He gave her a mischievous smile. "I met Alix as she left Westminster and inquired about you. She mentioned that when she returned from St. Giles she would ask the King to let you see a priest." The smile faded from his face. "When I saw you last night, held captive like a common felon, I was most concerned for your welfare." He scrutinized her face. "What is happening here? No one seems to know and Alix revealed nothing. The King has spread it about that you are unwell and in the care of the Queen until you recover. No one questions it, and if I had not seen you for myself—" As she turned away, he grabbed both her hands. "What is amiss? You must tell me."

Aware of her too ready response to the touch of his hands on hers, Maud wanted to blurt out the whole story but, unaccountably, held back. Stephen dropped her hands, took her firmly by the shoulders, and sat her down on one of the stools.

"Now then," he said, pulling up the other stool to face her, "you must tell me the truth. I will not be put off."

Maud looked anxiously at the door. What if Aldyth should return to find her alone like this with Stephen when she was supposed to be with a priest?

"You're with your confessor, remember?" Stephen said, reading her thoughts. "And the door is bolted. We won't be disturbed."

Maud watched him uneasily. The door bolted made her feel as anxious—in a different way—as the door unbolted. Flushing, she thrust away the thought that for the first time she and Stephen were truly alone with no immediate threat of interruption. Her heart began to beat faster.

"I have displeased the King," she began carefully, "and he has made me a virtual prisoner confined to Alix's care."

Stephen looked at her thoughtfully. "You have told me nothing I did not already know. How have you displeased him?"

Now that the longed-for opportunity to reveal her father's plans had arrived, Maud found herself reluctant to violate the King's intent to keep the matter secret. Aware she had little talent for dissembling, Maud stared at him helplessly.

"Have you promised not to speak of it?" He picked up her hand, lazily stroking her fingers.

She smiled in relief. "Yes, I'm bound to keep silent."

He pressed her hand, but did not release it. "I see. Very well, I will not push you further." His eyes smiled tenderly into hers. "You do know that should you need me—for anything at all, no matter the circumstance—I will always be ready to serve you."

Tears welled in her eyes. Unable to find the words, she nodded, overcome by a rush of gratitude.

Letting go of her hand, Stephen reached out and lifted her to her feet, cradling her body in his arms as if she were a frightened child. Her father, the threat of the Angevin marriage, the fear of losing contact with Stephen, slowly faded from her mind. All that existed was the protective comfort of his embrace, a wall of safety shielding her from the terrors of the outside world.

Maud did not know how long a time had passed before she became aware that the current of feeling between them had changed. One moment she was lapped in a comfortable security, and in the next all her senses began to come alive. A growing warmth slowly pervaded her body. Her pulse leaped; her breath began to quicken.

She knew that Stephen also perceived the change, because he immediately started to withdraw, his arms dropping to his sides. For the space of a heartbeat Maud hesitated; she felt as if she teetered on the edge of a precipice, and one move further would propel her over the edge. As Stephen took a backward step, Maud reached out and clung to him.

Slowly, with obvious reluctance, his arms reached out, tightened, and pressed her body close to his. She could feel the corded muscles of his chest crushing her breasts, the hard sinews of his thighs against her own, smell the pungent male odor of horses, damp woods and leather, hear the sound of his breath, harsh and uneven in her ear. As he drew back his head to look down into her face, she could see the conflict in his eyes, torn between desire and a darker emotion she could not define.

"How fair you are," he whispered, taking her face in his hands.

With unsteady fingers, Stephen unpinned the coils of hair wound about her ears. A russet waterfall tumbled down over her shoulders and back. He ran his fingers through the shining strands, pushing back tendrils from the ivory skin of her temples. Bending, he gently kissed her eyelids and forehead.

"Your hair has the sheen of an October leaf, and you are as vibrant, as alive, as full of color as autumn itself." His eyes searched her face. "I have never cared so about a woman before; it is like a madness in my blood."

"Oh yes," she whispered, her heart pounding, "and for me too. But I would rather be like spring, for autumn turns all too soon to winter."

"True," he agreed, "but how brightly it burns while it lasts."

"In the end the season dies."

"As do all seasons, all things in nature. Does this mean we should not live meanwhile?"

"The risk," she began in a hesitant voice.

"Naught worth doing is without risk," he replied.

Their eyes grappled in an embrace that neither could break. Slowly, Stephen bent his head to find her mouth, savoring its warmth and texture, then parting her lips so that they opened like a flower under the sun. A melting sweetness began to spread through Maud's body and she went limp against him.

Without taking his lips from hers, Stephen moved Maud forward to the bed, kicking the stools aside. He removed her surcoat and then parted from her mouth long enough to lift her tunic and her gown over her head. She felt his fingers slide the linen shift down over her body; his arms lifted her onto the bed. Flushing, Maud crawled beneath the fur coverlet when she heard Stephen's breathing quicken as his eyes eagerly drank in the sight of her naked body.

Reclining against the silken cushions of the bed, she covertly watched Stephen pull off his tunic and shirt, then slip out of his hose and underdrawers. Maud, who had never seen a live naked man before, was awed by the sight of his broad shoulders and chest tapering into a slender waist and narrow hips, the sturdy legs framing the golden plumage of his manhood.

Stephen climbed into the bed beside her, and she heard his sudden intake of breath as he loosed her grip on the coverlet and slowly pushed it back. Through half-closed eyes, Maud saw his gaze linger on the rounded fullness of her breasts. A pulse began to beat heavily in his temple.

"How fair you are," he whispered again, as he slipped under the coverlet and took her in his arms.

As Maud tasted the insistent sweetness of Stephen's mouth, felt the length and breadth of his hard muscular body naked against hers, the warmth and strength of his arms holding her close, she found it impossible to restrain her mounting need of him. When she felt his large warm hand cup the soft peak of her breast, she gasped as if a flash of lightning had shot through her.

"Ma belle, ma belle," he whispered, against her open mouth. Both hands now encircled her breasts, squeezing them gently, his thumbs caressing the swell of her large nipples, while he lifted his head and began to kiss the hollows of her neck. The touch of his hands, the pressure of his body, the feeling of being controlled by him, created in Maud sensations that she had not known existed, and was powerless to deny.

His lips traveled slowly down the creamy column of her neck to kiss the blue-veined mounds of her breasts, his tongue flicking back and forth over each nipple. Maud's arms went round the back of his neck; her fingers twined themselves in the springy thickness of his golden brown hair as she pressed his head deeper into her bosom. When his lips closed over a rosy tip and began to suck, the sensation was exquisite. Swept along by a tide of feeling that threatened to engulf her, Maud begged him to stop, wanting him never to stop.

Stephen finally lifted his head to gaze down at her; his eyes, heavy-lidded with passion, had deepened to emerald. Roughly, he tore the coverlet from her body, and threw one leg across hers, sliding one hand over the smooth skin of her flat belly to stroke the velvet

softness of her hips and thighs with demanding fingers. As she felt
the thrust of his manhood probing her inner thigh like a rock, Maud
stiffened, resisting the flame of desire that burned through her body.

"What is it, dear heart?" Stephen asked, his voice thick with urgency. "I will do nothing against your will. Do you wish me to
stop?"

"No," she murmured.

His lips again found her mouth, drinking deeply of its sweetness
as if he could never have enough.

Stephen lifted his head, his eyes traveling down over the soft
curves of her body, the skin glowing like a pearl, yet warm and
vibrant to his fingers. His hand resumed stroking her hips, then
moved lower to lightly tease the dark red curls between her thighs.
She must stop him, Maud thought wildly, stop him before— Her
legs parted with a will of their own, and when Stephen touched her,
the shock of pleasure was so intense, she wanted to scream. As his
fingers began a lingering exploration, caressing the silken flesh, probing into secret crevices, Maud lay helpless, wave after wave of excitement coursing through her, the juices of her body overflowing. The
need to surrender herself to Stephen had become overwhelming;
every part of her cried out for fulfillment but still she battled against
it, as though fighting for her life.

As Stephen sought to check the force of his own passion, his body
trembled against her own, while his breath came in harsh gasps. His
fingers increased their pressure, more insistent now, leaving a trail of
heat in their wake. She could hear his ragged breath echoing her own.
Without warning she lost control. A blaze of love overran her body
like wildfire, blotting out everything else. A burning cauldron of
pleasure welled up inside her, scorching in its fierce intensity. Her
body took command and she began to arch wildly against his fingers,
until something inside her exploded like a shooting star, and a loud
cry was torn from her throat, quickly stifled by Stephen's hand over
her mouth. Her body writhed, shuddering in a coil of ecstasy that left
her stunned and shaken. Nothing like this had ever before happened
to her.

Restraint gone, Stephen quickly mounted her, when a sudden
pounding on the door froze him in the very act of penetration.

"My lady, is aught amiss?" It was Aldyth's voice, strident with
concern, as she sought to open the door.

"You must answer her," Stephen said urgently in her ear. "Now."
He quickly withdrew.

"Nothing . . . nothing is amiss," Maud called back weakly, terrified of being discovered. "I . . . stumbled and hurt—my toe."

"The priest is with you?"

"The priest? Oh—yes, yes, he is right here."

She sensed a hesitation on the other side of the door, as if Aldyth could see right through the stout wood, and then the sound of reluctant footsteps fading away.

The fear receded and Maud took a deep quivering breath, her eyes wide with wonder. Although the act of love had not been consummated, still, something magical had happened to her body; a barrier long held in place had been removed and she was now aware of a part of herself that had been hidden.

"What happened to me?" she asked in a tremulous voice.

Stephen smiled. "What an innocent you are." He kissed the tip of her nose.

"But you have not been— I don't like to leave you like this, my love."

"Nor do I like being left, let me assure you, but there is no help for it. I must dress and make my way past your watchful dragon." Stephen ran his hands caressingly over her breasts, kissing each tip. "This time it was enough you were pleasured." He sat up, swinging his legs over the side of the bed, and bent to pick up his hose and shirt. "There will be time enough later for both of us," he said, stepping into his hose and pulling the white linen shirt over his head.

Time. The world moved in with a rush, and Maud turned her head away.

Sensitive to her sudden shift in mood, Stephen sat down on the edge of the bed. "What is it?" He took her in his arms.

She buried her face against his chest. "No time," she whispered. "There may be no time at all."

"Why? What do you mean?" He held her at arm's length. "You cannot keep anything from me. Not now."

She pushed him gently away and slid her feet to the floor. He was right; the nature of their relationship had changed forever. Shivering, she picked up her linen shift and gown lying on the dried rushes and quickly slipped them on.

Stephen said nothing but watched her with narrowed green eyes as he pulled on his boots and tunic.

"Indeed," Maud said slowly, looking at him with a troubled expression. "You have lit a flame, Cousin, that will not be so easy to put out; I can deny you nothing now."

Stephen smiled slightly but did not speak.

"The real reason the King keeps me in confinement is because I refuse to marry Fulk of Anjou's young son, Geoffrey." She paused, watched the look of amazement on Stephen's face as he grasped the significance of her words. "But how long can I withstand my father?" she continued, voicing her innermost dread. "In the end, what he wants he will have." Her body gave an involuntary shudder.

He walked over to her and took her in his arms. "By God's birth, the King has sworn an oath not to marry you without the consent of his barons. They will never agree to a marriage with Anjou. Never."

"I threatened to tell them and you see how he ensures my silence: a prisoner until I agree to be wed. Holy Mother, what can I do?"

"My God, my God." Stephen clasped her tightly in his arms and closed his eyes. "We all wed where we must, regardless of inclination, but an Angevin, an untried youth!"

Suddenly he held her away from him. "Perhaps there is something we can do." His voice was vibrant with excitement. "Nothing is to prevent me from telling anyone I choose, starting with the de Beaumont twins, who will raise the whole land they will be so enraged, then my brother, who will surely alert Holy Church."

"But no one must know you've been here. They think I see a priest. You will be questioned as to the source of this knowledge."

Stephen thought for a moment. "I will say that you smuggled out a message through Aldyth who bribed a guard to give it to me. No one will doubt me."

Maud felt a surge of hope. "Is it possible?" she breathed. "If only you could spread the news, the council will force my father to cancel the marriage arrangements. He must let me go free."

A mixture of terror and guilt shot through her when she envisioned the King's rage at having his plans thwarted. Would her reckless words to Stephen doom Normandy to fall to Louis of France? She retreated from the thought. No, no, what Stephen proposed was an excellent solution to her dilemma.

"I had best be gone quickly, Cousin," he said. "The sooner I raise the alarm, the sooner will you be free." He kissed her lips and let her go.

Arranging the black cloak over his head so that the voluminous folds fell forward over his face, Stephen started to open the door. A premonition of disaster seized Maud and she clung to him as if she would never let him go.

"Come, dear heart," he said, gently loosening her arms. "This is unlike you. Never doubt that we shall see each other soon."

"Take this," she whispered, reaching around her neck to lift off the chain with the silver ring she had worn since her father had given it to her on the day she left for Germany. "It belonged to Queen Matilda, wife to the Conqueror. Our grandmother."

"Then it is sure to bring me good fortune. I will treasure it always." He brought the silver circle to his lips, then slipped it over his head, tucking it inside his tunic beneath his shirt. "Trust me to find a way for us to be together again."

Stephen pulled open the door, and quickly strode through the Queen's solar, brushing past Aldyth, who stared after him with open mouth and astonished eyes.

"Good day to you, Father. By the Rood!" Aldyth said indignantly as the cloaked figure hurried out the door before she could catch him.

Muttering under her breath, Aldyth walked into Maud's chamber carrying a large box with her. Taking one look at the rumpled bed and Maud's distraught face, she dropped the box on the floor.

"What is the meaning of this, pray?" she asked in a trembling voice, her face pale as death. "May God forgive you, child, what have you done? That was not a man of God!"

Without answering, Maud ran to the window slit and peered out. The snow had stopped but the ground was still covered with a thick white carpet. After a few moments, a black-cloaked figure could be seen in the courtyard. She almost fainted with relief. Thank the Holy Mother, Stephen had made good his escape. Then, as Maud watched in horror, several guards surrounded Stephen, and marched him back inside the castle.

Chapter Nineteen

WHEN TWO GUARDS ROUGHLY GRABBED STEPHEN BY THE ARMS AND marched him back inside the castle, he did not resist them. Calmly throwing back the cowl of his cloak, he gave them an innocent smile.

"There's no need to treat me like a felon. What do you want?" He hoped his voice did not reveal his inner terror.

Startled, the guards dropped his arms.

"Oh, my lord, we had no idea it was you," one of the guards stammered. "Someone saw a man covered in black running down the passage." He looked anxiously at Stephen. "I hope you won't take it amiss."

"For doing your duty? Heaven forfend."

The guards smiled in relief and stepped back.

Stephen walked unsteadily back into the courtyard where his horse was tethered. His body trembled as he mounted the mare, but whether in relief at his narrow escape or because his loins ached to finish the business he had earlier begun with Maud, he could not tell.

He rode out of Westminster at a fast trot, anxious to reach his brother, who was staying at the Bishop's Palace next to St. Paul's Cathedral. The Abbot would know best how to make full use of the extraordinary news Maud had confided to him. The King's deceit must work to their advantage, Stephen decided. Surely the nobles would raise an outcry. Perhaps they would even go so far as to state that if King Henry did not keep faith with them, why should they keep faith with him?

The mare slowed her pace, picking her way through the snow with care. On Stephen's left rose the dark spires of St. Paul, rearing up like a monolith against the gray afternoon sky. He turned his horse in the direction of the Bishop's Palace.

He found his brother in a small but well-appointed chamber, unpacking a long wooden box. He had intended to pass on to the Abbot the tale of the smuggled message but instead found himself telling him what had actually transpired, omitting any mention of what had occurred between Maud and himself.

"You must have been mad to take such a risk!" Henry's eyes narrowed in suspicion. "What possessed you?"

Stephen avoided his brother's accusing face. "I thought Maud might be in trouble and decided to see for myself." This excuse sounded lame even to his own ears. "Why I took the risk is less important, surely, than the weapon we have been given by this news."

Henry frowned and began to lift handfuls of straw from the wooden box onto the table. "A secret betrothal to an Angevin! I cannot believe the King has made such a foolish mistake. But he has played right into our hands." He turned back to Stephen. "Our wisest course will be to say nothing of this matter."

Stephen looked at him with incredulity. "Say nothing? But if we spread the news the King will be greatly discredited, Maud will not marry a hated Angevin, and the nobles will regard us with favor for having uncovered this plot."

"Really, Brother, sometimes I wonder if you're fit to wear the crown." The Abbot gave an impatient sigh. "Nothing could prove more useful to our cause than for Maud to marry the Angevin. Don't you see?"

"No, I do not see." As usual, his brother appeared to be so many steps ahead of him that Stephen felt confused and resentful.

"The barons will be bitter over the King's duplicity, but they will do nothing about it, for he has too strong a hold upon the kingdom. There will be a few defectors, of course, and demonstrations of protest here and there. Minor disturbances. But most of the magnates will comply and hope for better times. Then, when the King dies—he cannot last more than another few years—the realm will be faced with a woman ruler and a hated Angevin as their king-consort! Nothing could be better for our plans."

Stephen nodded his head slowly as he began to understand. "Then we step into the breach. Yes, I see your point now. But how do we accomplish this?"

"How? How?" The Abbot's lip curled in distaste. "I'm not a crystal gazer, Brother, a reader of palms, God save us." He signed himself. "When the time comes we will know what to do and how to do it. The House of Blois will be welcomed with open arms, I promise you. All we need do is bide our time."

What his brother said made sense; Stephen wondered why he had not seen matters in the same light. He had viewed the marriage as a threat, not an asset. He admitted to himself that he did not want Maud to marry the Count, and had allowed his feelings to overcome his judgment. Yet even now that he had seen how greatly such a marriage would benefit him—he found himself torn, unsure of what he wanted.

"What troubles you now?" Henry asked, watching him.

"I was thinking that all this intrigue is beyond my simple nature. Give me a sword, troops to deploy, an enemy, and a battle, and I know what is required."

The Abbot laughed, and, walking over to Stephen, put his hands on his shoulders and looked deeply into his eyes. "Yes, there you excel. It has been too long between battles, Stephen, that's what has driven you to these hairbreadth deeds of rescue and disguise. What is a warrior without a war? Restless, bored, chafing at inactivity, craving the lure of danger. Go hunting. Take a raiding party across the Welsh border. Test your prowess in a tourney." He leaned forward and kissed Stephen lightly on both cheeks and patted him on the back. "Leave the thinking to me, Brother, and all will be well. Matters will fall out as we envision them."

If only it were that simple, Stephen thought glumly.

Two days later, Maud, still confined to the Queen's solar, had no idea what had happened to Stephen after he had been taken back inside the castle by the guards. Unable to sleep, barely touching her food, she was half mad with worry and fear, torturing herself with all manner of possibilities: Had he been questioned? If so, how much had he revealed? Would she be questioned as well? Suppose their descriptions of events were at odds? Tossing in the carved wooden bed at night, hideous visions passed across her eyes: Stephen confined to a dungeon in chains, beaten, tortured with hot irons, blinded, castrated. Once she bolted up from the bed screaming with terror, to be soothed by an anxious Aldyth.

"The Count will not be harmed. He's far too popular with the nobles and commonfolk alike. What are you afraid of? You told him of the marriage, that's all. What more can the King know?" Her eyes searched Maud's pale face. "What more *is* there to know?"

Maud dropped her eyes. "Nothing. Nothing! I've told you that Stephen was here disguised as a priest and what we discussed. There is no more. Why are you so suspicious?"

"I didn't know I was."

She sank back onto the pillows, wondering if the Saxon nurse believed her. She had debated whether or not to tell Aldyth of Stephen's plan to inform the council about the Angevin marriage but decided against it. This was for Aldyth's own protection, she told herself, in the event the plan miscarried. What Aldyth did not know she could not be made to reveal.

In addition to her fears, unexpected demands of the flesh also plagued her. Her body's needs had never before been awakened, and she ached to fully consummate her love for Stephen. At night she lay fitful, tormented by the memory of his lips and hands worshipping every inch of her body, waking at dawn unsatisfied, yearning for fulfillment.

Neither Aldyth's discreet efforts to solicit information from Alix's women nor Maud's direct questioning of Alix proved fruitful. No one had seen Count Stephen or had news of him.

Finally, on the afternoon of the third day, Aldyth learned from one of the guards who had just come on duty outside the solar that Stephen was in the great hall.

"And in fine fettle, says the guard." Aldyth crossed her arms over her ample chest. "I told you he would come to no harm, my lady. Are you satisfied now? You would do better to worry about your own interests, for Count Stephen can well take care of himself, I warrant."

At first Maud was lightheaded with relief. Stephen must have talked his way out of any difficulty, she decided. Perhaps he had not even been taken to the King, and she had let her imagination run away with her. As the hours of the day wore on, she waited expectantly for some word from Stephen. He had said he would see her again, no matter the circumstance. If no one suspected the previous visit, surely he could arrange another tryst, or get word to her of how their plans fared.

Every few minutes, she ran to peer out of the window slit, praying she would not see Stephen leave. Had he talked to the de Beaumont twins? Members of the council? His brother? Doubts and uncertainties crept over her like a channel fog. The more she thought about their plan the more ill-conceived it became. How could she have been so blind to the risks involved! One of his friends, even a council member, might betray him. When her father discovered who was responsible, he would never forgive Stephen, much less herself. His wrath would be terrible. If only she had taken the time to think the matter through!

By the time the Vespers bell sounded, with still no word, Maud was in such an agony of suspense that she paced her chamber like a penned beast, starting at the sound of every noise.

"Was that the solar door? See who it is."

Aldyth opened the door leading to the solar. "There's no one. The Queen and her women must have just left for Vespers. Jumpy as a scalded cat you are." She looked at Maud with faded blue eyes that missed nothing. "Something is afoot here, my lady, for I've never seen you in such a state."

When Maud turned away, Aldyth waddled after her, grabbing her by the shoulders. "I'm not fool enough to believe you've told me the whole tale, not by half you haven't, but whatever japes you and that slippery cousin of yours have conjured up between you, King Henry will have his way in the end, mark my words."

"Of course I've told you everything," Maud retorted, twisting free from her grasp. Acutely uncomfortable under Aldyth's close scrutiny she said: "Do you go now to the kitchens and bring back my supper."

"What for? You don't eat enough to keep a bird alive," Aldyth grumbled, but left the chamber.

Not long after Aldyth had gone, Maud heard voices and footsteps, then the sound of the bolt being drawn back. At last! She ran into the solar just as the door opened to reveal her father.

"I've come to see how you're faring, Madam," he said with a grim smile.

Her disappointment was so acute she was speechless.

The King stepped across the threshold. "You're not very courteous today."

Maud swallowed. "I am pleased to see you, Sire."

"Have you made up your mind to do your duty?"

"I'm still thinking about it."

The King stood in the middle of the solar, his thumbs hooked in his black belt. "You're taking too long. I can move you to a less—desirable abode that may quicken your willingness to comply."

"You hope to threaten me into submission?" She prayed he would not hear the tremor in her voice.

"Threaten? I do not threaten, Madam, I act." He bowed and walked briskly to the door. "Reflect upon what I've said. I will return tomorrow."

He left the chamber, quietly closing the door behind him.

When King Henry returned to his council chamber he sent a page to find the Bishop of Salisbury. The King seated himself in a wooden chair, the arms and legs of which were carved in ivory to represent the head and feet of a wild boar. Outside the castle a March storm beat heavily against the stone walls. Gusts of wind swept through the window slits, causing the tall white candles to flare in their silver holders.

The Bishop arrived and Henry invited him to sit on a stool near his chair.

"Maud continues to prove intractable," he said. "I'm convinced she will not willingly marry the young count and I dare not set her free for she will go straight to members of my council and tell them what I propose to do. At all costs that must be prevented."

"She was always a headstrong child and maturity has not improved her mettlesome nature," said the Bishop. "Perhaps you should reconsider—" At a look from the King he stopped. "Short of spiriting her away while she sleeps, what can you do?" he asked.

The King's eyes suddenly widened. "Spiriting her away—Roger, you have a mind more devious than my own! Why didn't I think of that?"

The Bishop looked bewildered. "Think of what, Sire?"

"Never mind now. Fetch me a cleric. I must send an urgent message to Fulk of Anjou. He wants a date set for the betrothal ceremony? He shall have one, far sooner than he imagines. A messenger will leave for Anjou this very night." He rubbed his hands together. "Then have the herbalist from St. John's monastery attend me." He thought for a moment, tapping his finger against his chin. "I will also need to see my son, Robert, and, let me see, yes, Brian FitzCount.

They won't like the task I've set them but they are both loyal servants of the crown."

Roger rose to his feet. "I think I understand now, Sire. I will tend to these matters at once."

"Ah, what it is to be a king, Roger, what decisions that weigh upon the soul."

"Shall I hear your confession, Sire?"

King Henry stood up and walked over to the Bishop, placing a hand on his meaty shoulder. "Later, my friend. Until this Angevin business is settled, I can put my attention on nothing else. Even my sins must wait upon the kingdom's weal."

Several days later Maud had heard no word from her father, nor any from Stephen. She had become so disagreeable and on edge that Aldyth finally threatened to dose her with vervain.

One evening, while Alix and her women attended Vespers, and Aldyth had gone to fetch her dinner, she was visited by the Bishop of Salisbury.

"I bring you a gift from the King," he said. "He has received a cask of wine from Gascony and sends you a sample."

"He's relented?" Maud asked, her heart beginning to flutter.

"Alas, no. But be patient. All things in their time." He held up a silver flask, then leaned toward her with an air of false intimacy, nauseating her with the malodorous stink coming from his rotting teeth. "In truth, I believe he may be having second thoughts, Madam. I suspect this wine is intended as a peace offering. Do you try some now."

Listlessly, Maud walked into her chamber and over to the table to pick up a goblet, trying to convince herself this gift was a good omen. "Will you join me, Bishop?"

"No, no," he said hastily, as he followed her inside. Out of the corner of her eye she noted that he closed the door behind him. "I have already had more than my fair share." He smacked his lips. "Ambrosia fit for a king's palate."

Maud brought him the goblet, and he poured a generous amount of the wine into it. "Let us see how you like it," he said, swirling the wine before handing it to her.

As the liquid touched her lips, Maud made a face. The wine had been so heavily spiced with cloves, licorice, and fennel that it was impossible to determine the true taste. Definitely not to her liking, but, dutifully, she downed the contents of the goblet. The Bishop watched her intently.

"Tell the King I'm most grateful for this gift, and convey to him that I—" She heard herself slurring the words. Why did her tongue suddenly feel so thick?

"Do you feel ill, Madam?" he asked.

All she could do was nod. A weakness seemed to assail her limbs and the Bishop's round pudding face had become two faces. Swaying, she walked unsteadily over to the bed.

"Do you wish to lie down? Let me help you."

He helped her onto the bed and as she lay back the chamber spun round and round.

After that, everything passed as if in a dream. It seemed to Maud that she slept, then woke to find herself dressed in a warm cloak, taken from the bed and carried out of the chamber, down the passage and the stairs. She heard familiar voices—they sounded like Brian, Robert, and Aldyth. She was placed in a litter where she was given more wine, then slept again. After what seemed a long journey, during which she was half awake but so fogged she could not comprehend what was happening, the litter stopped. In her dream—for she was sure she must be dreaming—she smelled the brisk salt air of the sea, and a wind whipped her face, briefly rousing her.

"She wakes," Robert's voice said clearly. "Give her more wine before she is put on the ship."

"She will be ill if you give her any more," Aldyth's voice rose on the wind. "Do you want to poison her?"

Poison? What was happening? A goblet was placed against her lips, a trickle of wine slid down her throat, and she slept again, lulled by a gentle rocking motion.

Maud opened her eyes slowly, aware of a throbbing ache in her head. For a moment everything whirled, then her gaze settled on the face of her half-brother, Robert of Gloucester, sitting on the edge of the bed in which she lay.

"Robert?" she whispered, her throat so dry she could barely speak.

The relief on his face was palpable. "Thank the good Lord, I thought you would never wake."

Her mystified gaze took in the unfamiliar surroundings: the red canopy over her head, the sumptuous, well-appointed chamber with its elaborate wall hangings.

"What place is this?" she croaked.

"We are in the ducal palace in Rouen," he said quietly.

The ducal palace in—she was in Normandy? Aghast, Maud struggled to sit up, but her strength seemed to have deserted her and she fell back almost immediately.

"Don't overtax yourself, Sister," Robert said. "Gradually you will begin to feel better as the poppy and mandrake wear off."

Poppy and mandrake. Used to induce deep sleep and subdue pain. How could she—the wine! These herbs had been put into her wine! Suddenly everything became clear. She had been given drugged wine to keep her manageable, then spirited away to Normandy where she could more easily be kept prisoner without awkward questions being asked. Her father's doing, of course. How had she ever dared hope to best Henry of England? A trickle of tears ran down her face.

"Sister," Robert said gently, as he stroked her hand. "Please. Do not weep."

"Where is Aldyth? Was she given the poppy, too?"

"Aldyth is here. There was no need to give her anything. Wild horses would not have prevented her from going with you, you know that."

"I hope you're pleased with yourself, Brother," Maud said. "You and Lord FitzCount—I did hear Brian's voice, did I not?—have much to be proud of aiding my father in this . . . this despicable act."

Robert wore a miserable look on his face.

"And I had thought you both my friends! Would I had never laid eyes on either of you!" She grimaced as a throb of pain lanced through her head.

"We had little choice, Maud," Robert replied. "As you have little choice. One must obey the King and you refused to do so."

"That my father would stoop to such infamy! To spirit away his own daughter."

"If you had agreed willingly to the marriage with Anjou, these measures would not have been necessary."

Again Maud struggled to sit, her heart beating wildly. "How long have I been here?"

"Since yesterday morning. It is just past noon now."

A sudden blast of horns echoed through the chamber. "Who arrives?" she asked, wincing at the sound.

There was a knock on the door and Brian FitzCount entered. "My lady, I'm much relieved to see you're awake," he said, approaching the bed. "How are you feeling?"

"How would you expect me to feel under the circumstances?" she asked accusingly.

Brian met her eyes without flinching. "I deeply regret the manner in which you were brought here. Neither Robert nor I approved of our mission."

"But executed it regardless."

"As loyal servants of the crown, yes."

Maud sighed. "What is happening outside?" she asked.

Robert and Brian exchanged glances. Robert took a deep breath.

"Sister, the horns announce the arrival of—Geoffrey of Anjou."

Sweet Marie, Geoffrey of Anjou! In that moment Maud knew she was lost.

Chapter Twenty

Rouen, 1126

WHEN THE FANFARE TURNED OUT TO BE MERELY AN ADVANCE WARN-ing, a banneret of knights come to announce Geoffrey of Anjou's arrival the following day, Maud was so relieved she immediately began to recover her strength. For the remainder of the day she alternated between fury and self-pity. When she thought about Stephen she wanted to weep; when she thought about her father she was consumed with rage.

Next morning dawned fair. A pale sun shone through a faded blue sky streaked with ragged white clouds. A brisk channel wind blew from the north, and Maud shivered as she huddled deeper into her squirrel-lined cloak. Still somewhat weak from the effects of the wine, she stood with Robert and Brian on the steps of the ducal palace awaiting a glimpse of Count Geoffrey's official entry into Rouen.

"I appreciate your cooperation, Sister," Robert said to Maud. "If you had not been willing to greet the Count, the House of Anjou would have taken it as a mortal insult and our father would have been in a towering rage."

Maud gave him a wan smile. What choice did she have? As her father must have shrewdly guessed, faced with the reality of the situation, she would never disgrace the House of Normandy.

Brian took her arm and gave it a reassuring squeeze.

"Do not pull such a long face, Lady. What we imagine is always worse than what actually exists. With God's grace you may even grow to care for Geoffrey—in time."

With a shake of her head, Maud scanned the spires and turrets of St. Mary of Rouen, the narrow cobbled streets and low wooden houses visible through the open gates of the courtyard. How she longed to say: But my heart is given elsewhere; I will never care for anyone except Stephen.

Horns sounded, then Maud saw a long cavalcade of Angevin soldiers approach the palace.

"We weren't told he would bring an army," Robert said in surprise.

"A most unwelcome sight for the Normans," Maud observed. "What will they think to see Angevin soldiers marching through Rouen like conquerors? One would have thought this paragon might have realized that?"

Robert and Brian exchanged a quick glance.

"I imagine he wants us to know he comes as an equal," Brian said. "After all, he's only a youth. Let us go down to meet him."

The courtyard teemed with servants, seneschals and grooms, all ready to minister to the needs of the Angevin visitors. In preparation for the feast to be held that day, scullions, carrying large buckets of water, ran back and forth from the well to the kitchen; servitors staggered under the weight of huge logs for the palace fires.

Having left his army camped outside the palace walls, Geoffrey, followed by his immediate entourage, rode into the courtyard and drew rein. A score of grooms ran forward to hold his horse as he dismounted.

"By the Mass, I would never have taken him for fourteen," Brian said. "What an engaging youth he is. Geoffrey the Handsome, well named."

Even Maud could not deny the Count's beauty, his graceful elegance, or the pride with which he carried himself. Geoffrey of Anjou was of medium height, with a slender, wiry build, reminding Maud of a sleek greyhound. He had blue eyes fringed by impossibly long lashes. Red-gold curls ringed his face and fell softly onto his neck. His milky skin, covered by a soft peach down over his upper lip, cheeks and chin, was without blemish. Impeccably garbed, he wore a blue linen tunic richly adorned with bands and flowers worked in gold thread. Over this he wore a green silk bliaud also decorated with the same gold bands and flowers. The mantle, fastened on the right shoulder with a jeweled clasp, was lined in squirrel fur; his shoes, dark blue leather over green hose. The blue cap on his head, embossed with a gold lion, passant, was ornamented by a yellow flower.

"Fair indeed, and well he knows it," Maud murmured to Brian. "He preens like a peacock. What is that flower he wears?"

"Ask him."

"What is the flower you wear, my lord?" Maud asked Geoffrey sometime later after they had exchanged stilted greetings and cautiously taken each other's measure.

Eyeing each other warily, the Norman and Angevin entourages milled about the great hall of the ducal palace waiting for more tables to be erected in order to accommodate all of Geoffrey's following. In addition to his soldiers, the Count had brought with him the chief barons of his county and a score of high-born youths.

"The *planta genesta?*" Geoffrey asked in a voice that hovered somewhere between a man's and a boy's. He touched the yellow sprig with tapering fingers that sparkled with rings. "*Grâce à Dieu*, Lady, it is the broom flower that makes the open country of Anjou and Maine a carpet of gold in the spring." He paused to observe the effect of this poetic image on Maud. "I have adapted it as my emblem." He pointed a proud finger at the golden flowers embroidered on his clothing.

"So I see."

"I'd thought of having it emblazoned on my shield when I'm knighted by your father, but decided against it in favor of four gold lions, rampant. After all, everyone knows that the lion is the symbol of Anjou, whereas the significance of the *planta genesta* is not yet known."

"And what does it signify?" Maud asked pointedly.

His eyes suddenly reflected the cold disdain she was to know so well in the months ahead. "As I said, the broom flower is my emblem. In time it will need no other significance."

There was a tense silence as Geoffrey, his nostrils flaring slightly, looked carefully around the great hall. "Where is King Henry? I expected him to greet me when I arrived."

"The King suffers from a minor ailment and sends his deepest regrets," Brian replied. "He hopes to travel within the week."

"That is unfortunate for I expected to be knighted right away, along with my companions. And betrothed directly afterwards." His white skin turned a deep rose as he tried to conceal his annoyance. "My father will be most distressed to hear of this delay."

"It's only a matter of a few days, my lord," Brian said in a soothing voice. "The King hoped you and Maud would get to know each other in the interim."

Geoffrey stole an uncertain glance at Maud. "Oh! Well then, it will be my pleasure to wait." He bowed graciously. "I must inform my companions. You will excuse me?"

"He's not of a meek spirit," Brian remarked, amused, as he watched Geoffrey rejoin his companions. "A true Angevin, if I'm any judge." He smiled at Maud. "The two of you remind me of a pair of wary cats cautiously circling one another, unable to decide whether friend or foe."

Watching the sprig of broom bob up and down on Geoffrey's cap, Maud feared she knew the answer.

As the days passed it became obvious that neither she nor Geoffrey had taken to each other, although even Maud had to admit that Geoffrey tried harder to establish cordial relations between them.

"Would you like to go riding, Madam?" Geoffrey asked one morning a week after he had arrived.

The King was still in England and the Count was growing restive, but doing his best to curb his impatience. He had just presented Maud with a little leather riding crop as his latest gift. Anxious to impress, Geoffrey attempted to surprise Maud every day with a small gift: an exquisitely enameled box from Limoges that reminded her of the one Stephen had given her in London; a leather-bound book of Latin verse by Catullus, very rare and costly; a bolt of precious amber silk, threaded with gold and silver, said to have traveled by caravan from the faraway East.

"I have already ridden this morning," Maud replied. "Perhaps later." She was sitting on a stone bench in the courtyard under the branches of a huge chestnut tree, her face turned to the rays of pale sunlight filtering through the budding green leaves.

"Yes, well—I fear there is not much to do in Rouen."

"No," she murmured, "it's nothing like London."

"Or Anjou," Geoffrey said immediately. "Now, Angers—that is my capital—is a place you will enjoy. In addition to an excellent stable and superb hunting, we have one of the finest libraries in Europe. With your scholarly tastes, I know you will be impressed by it."

"What do you know about my tastes?" she asked, intrigued.

"*Grâce à Dieu*, what do I not know, Madam. For instance: I know you're an excellent horsewoman, competent at chess, and fluent in Latin." He cast his eyes down modestly. "Subjects I've already mastered, of course."

"I'm truly impressed," Maud said sincerely, rewarding him with a benign smile.

In truth, she was awed by Geoffrey's precocious abilities: Highly intelligent, well informed about current affairs in Europe, he had a scholar's interest in literature and history.

From Robert, who shared his tastes, Maud had learned that the young Count was not inexperienced on the battlefield, and had had the running of his father's estates while Fulk was in the Holy Land. She had observed him competing with Robert and Brian at the butts and quintain, noting that he acquitted himself well. Each time the Norman and Angevin parties had gone hunting, he bagged more game than anyone except Robert. Every evening in the great hall Geoffrey played the lute and sang to her in a sweet, true voice, songs of his own composing that would not have shamed the finest minstrels at her father's court.

It was impossible not to respect his prodigious capabilities, but try as she would Maud could not warm up to Geoffrey, much less accept him as her future king-consort and the father of her children. Not with Stephen ever present in her heart.

"When you are Countess of Anjou we will lead a very lively life in Angers," Geoffrey was saying now. He reached over to lay a damp palm on the back of her hand.

"Countess of Anjou," she repeated dully, forcing herself to endure the touch of his fingers. "I hope to retain my title of empress, even after we—after we're married."

He stiffened, withdrawing his hand. "Why? The title of Countess of Anjou is an old and honorable one."

"Of course it is," Maud agreed quickly. "I did not mean to suggest otherwise."

"When I'm King of England I don't ever intend to forget my origins as Count of Anjou. I'm proud to be an Angevin—whatever the upstart Normans may think of us."

As Geoffrey's eyes looked icily into hers, Maud could see the beguiling mask had slipped, briefly revealing another person. But before she could make a judgment, the mask was back in place, and she wondered if she had imagined that fleeting glimpse.

"I will talk to King Henry about the Imperial title," Geoffrey continued, "as it's a matter for men to decide, after all." He smiled, his ease of manner restored. "I understand you are something of an expert at falconry."

"Hardly that," Maud replied, bristling. A matter for men to decide, indeed. She had no doubt as to what her father would say.

"I rather fancy the sport myself, and have something of a reputation in Angers." He rose to his feet, extending his hand to her. "Let us go hawking. Perhaps I can teach you a few fine points. My gyrfalcon, Melusine, is with me, of course."

"You brought your falcon from Anjou?"

"Naturally. I go nowhere without her."

"By all means let's go hawking then," Maud said, giving him her hand. "Directly after we've eaten."

When the mid-morning meal was over, Geoffrey vanished. He reappeared, freshly bathed, in a different set of clothes. Maud had never seen anyone with such a dazzling variety of tunics, bliauds, and jewels.

"But you're wearing the same clothes," he said in astonishment. "Before I go hawking I always bathe and change my garments lest I vex Melusine with an unpleasant odor."

"I only wash my hands," Maud replied, "and ensure that what I've eaten does not exude a strong scent."

"To cleanse the hands is not sufficient," Geoffrey sniffed. "The Norman habits are every bit as barbaric as I had been told. There will be much to teach you in Anjou."

Maud compressed her lips, biting back a quick retort. Really, he was becoming insufferable.

Together, she and Geoffrey visited the grassy courtyard next to the falcon mews, where the castle hawks sat on their wooden blocks enjoying the sun. Preening even more than usual, the Count carried his snow-white gyrfalcon on a black-gauntleted wrist. A high-bred bird from Norway, Melusine's hood was adorned with blue feathers, gold thread, and seed pearls; fine leather jesses trailed from the gold rings encircling her legs. The golden bells attached to her feet were engraved with Geoffrey's name and flower emblem. She was easily the most impressive-looking bird Maud had ever seen.

Accompanied by the falconer, a stooped old man with a brown, seamed face and shaggy white hair, and his two apprentices, Maud walked slowly down the row of hawks looking carefully at each one.

Finally she stopped before a dark gray peregrine with a striped breast and black-tipped wings.

"What a beauty," she said admiringly.

"Aye, she be special," said the falconer, unhooding the hawk. "King Henry sent her to us a year ago. Bred in the cliffs above the south coast of Wales she was, but we had the training of her in Normandy."

The bird had fierce black eyes and a cruel, sharp beak. Plain silver bells engraved with the crest of the Dukes of Normandy ringed her feet. When Maud stroked her, she puffed and swelled her feathers, turning her head in an amiable manner.

"I would like to fly her, with your permission." She gave the falconer a deferential smile. As a very young boy the old man had been apprenticed to the falconer who trained the Conqueror's hawks for him, thus everyone treated him with respect and awe.

"Aye, my lady, as long as I come along to keep an eye on her."

"She's smaller than mine," Geoffrey said, with a proud glance at his bird. "Is this the best you can do in Normandy, import your falcons from Wales? The finest birds come from Iceland and Norway." A condescending smile lingered at the corners of his mouth.

Maud exchanged a look with the falconer, who kept his face impassive as he rehooded the bird before setting it on her wrist. For a moment the hawk perched uneasily on Maud's brown gauntlet, then settled down. Clearly, Geoffrey was not familiar with the falcons bred on the Welsh cliffs, she thought with an inward smile.

Outside the ducal palace they joined Robert, Brian, and several of Geoffrey's companions. In addition to a host of grooms and squires, also present were the head huntsman and the keeper of hounds with the fewterers, who led small black and tan dogs coupled together on long leads. Geoffrey's friends carried tiercels, the male hawks, smaller than the female peregrine. These were to be set against lesser prey, while Maud and Geoffrey hoped to bag bigger game such as a crane or, with luck, a heron.

It was a fine afternoon for hawking; gray clouds now obscured the sun and the wind had died.

They mounted their horses. A groom adjusted the girth on Maud's palfrey, Geoffrey blew the ivory horn that hung from his neck, and the whole gathering trotted toward the city gates.

Outside Rouen, Maud gave the mare her head, letting her race over fences, fields and brooks, through woods, until they came to a marshy meadow. Here the dogs were unleashed and sent into the tall grasses to flush out any birds. Finally a large crane flew out of the underbrush, its wings beating the air as it rose majestically upwind.

"I will enter Melusine against the crane," Geoffrey said, unhooding his falcon. He threw up his arm and the bird flew off. The gyrfalcon was a beautiful sight as she ringed wide circles in the air.

"I fear your Welsh peregrine has no chance against such a large bird," Geoffrey remarked complacently. "Now you will see the art of falconry at its finest."

The last shred of caution frayed and snapped. Maud glanced at the head falconer hovering by her side. He gave an imperceptible nod. Without a word, Maud unhooded her gray falcon and with a flick of the wrist sent her into the air, the mighty talons lifting as her wings spread out like a smoky sail.

Geoffrey frowned, then shrugged. "Melusine is not used to hunting with another bird. No matter. The crane will be dead before your bird comes within striking distance."

"Oh, but the Welsh—" Robert started to say when Maud interrupted him.

"Robert! Geoffrey is not interested in our Welsh birds."

The falconer repressed a smile; Robert colored, biting back his words as he moved his horse closer to Maud's.

"Is this wise, Sister?" he asked in an undertone, watching Geoffrey's bird mount upward.

"Is what wise?" she responded with an air of innocence, her gaze fixed expectantly on the two hawks and the crane.

Accompanied by the chime of her golden bells, Geoffrey's bird soared into the air above the crane. Slower at first, the Welsh falcon hovered above the group, then began to circle higher and higher, until Maud thought she had flown straight into the clouds.

"She stoops," Geoffrey cried, as the white bird reached her pinnacle and began her downward plunge toward the crane.

Maud looked anxiously at her peregrine, who must have reached her full pitch by now. Suddenly the sky was cleaved by a charcoal streak. With a tinkling of bells, Maud's falcon shot straight down like an arrow in flight, overtaking the gyrfalcon, digging her talons into the luckless crane, and bringing it to earth seconds before Melusine had completed her stoop. The hounds raced to the hawk's assistance.

Dumbfounded, Geoffrey stared in disbelief as his gyrfalcon, cheated of its kill and confused, lighted a few feet away from the crane, hissing angrily. Geoffrey blew upon a silver whistle and she sulkily returned to his wrist. He murmured to her, stroked the white breast, then took a dead pigeon from the pouch at his waist and threw it on the ground. The bird flew to its meat, attacking it with a flurry of feathers.

He turned to Maud, his face scarlet. "You have made me look a fool, Madam," he said accusingly. "Why didn't you tell me of the prowess of the Welsh bird?"

"How could I have known it would prove superior to yours, my lord?" Maud said, trying to conceal her intense feeling of satisfaction. "Didn't you say that Norse gyrfalcons are far superior to any other?"

Geoffrey gave her a look of such cold fury she recoiled. He called his bird to him, hooded it, and rode off with his followers without another word.

After Maud's falcon had gorged on her reward—the heart of the crane cut out by the falconer—and the crane had been tied to the back of one of the horses, Maud, Brian, and Robert returned to Rouen.

"That was very wicked, Maud," Robert said, as they rode through the woods on the outskirts of Rouen. "You should have warned Geoffrey of the reputation of our Welsh hawks. No more noble bird exists."

"He is insufferable," Maud said, tossing her head, "and badly needed to be taught a lesson."

"But not by his future wife. That is hardly the way to win his heart," Brian pointed out. "He's still very young, remember, and his pride is easily bruised."

"The Angevins do not take kindly to public humiliation," Robert added, with a reproving glance at Maud. "You behaved like a virago and must apologize to Geoffrey at once."

"Apologize?" she almost choked.

"You heard aright. He was much offended and we must cool the boy's ire before the King arrives tomorrow."

Her heart sank, the minor victory forgotten, at this reminder of her father's imminent arrival and all that would follow: First the King would knight Geoffrey, then the betrothal ceremony would take place. Sometime thereafter the wedding would be held in Anjou. When she thought about her future with Geoffrey, she was filled with despair. Although Maud knew he was as much a victim in this business as she, unreasonably she held him, as well as her father, responsible for the unwelcome marriage.

"For all his youthful posturing, Geoffrey of Anjou has the makings

of a remarkable man," Brian said to her as they approached the gates
of Rouen. "Most women would be delighted with this comely
youth."

Most women had not fallen deeply in love with Stephen of Blois,
she wanted to respond. In truth, she realized, as Alix had already told
her, it would not have mattered much whom she was to marry, for
her heart had been left behind in England, and all that remained was
an empty shell.

How could she tell her half-brother or Brian about the sleepless
nights, the tear-stained pillows, the desire and anguish she was daily
forced to hide? How explain her body's longing, the midnight hours
spent tormenting herself with the memory of Stephen's lips on hers,
the feel of his hands on her breasts, the pressure of his body molded
against her own. The thought of someone else touching her was
unbearable.

That evening after supper she took Geoffrey aside.

"I must apologize for—my jest this afternoon," she said. "I meant
no harm."

He gave her a curt nod. "I do not take kindly to such jests."

"I realize that now. I ask your forgiveness for my thoughtless
frivolity."

"I'm disinclined to give it," he said. "*Grâce à Dieu*, you made me
look a fool. That is not something I intend to forget. When you're
Countess of Anjou, you will never behave in such a disgraceful way
again."

Dumbfounded, Maud watched him walk away. Once again, the
mask had slipped. Beneath the winning exterior and facile charm, she
now detected an overweening pride and humorless nature, a coldness
of heart and lack of feeling that repelled her. Envisioning their life
together, Maud felt an icy chill of foreboding.

Chapter Twenty-one

Le Mans and Angers, 1126

THE FOLLOWING DAY KING HENRY ARRIVED IN ROUEN. THERE IMMEDI-
ately began a stultifying round of ceremonies: Geoffrey's knighting,
the ritual betrothal, and the endless festivities that followed. Through
it all Maud performed her requisite duties as if she were in a dream,
suppressing her desolation beneath an agreeable facade. Her outward
demeanor, courteous and scrupulously polite, could not be faulted,
even toward her father.

In April, Geoffrey and his party left for Anjou to prepare for a
June wedding. Maud was glad to see him go, but when he had gone
she found herself no less gloomy. Her heart ached for Stephen who,
she learned to her intense disappointment, would not be able to attend
the wedding. Someone had to keep an eye on the Welsh who were
causing trouble at the border, explained her father. Stephen alone
would understand her wretchedness; she had counted on his silent
but loving support to get her through the ordeal of the wedding. Each
day she was assailed by memories of her cousin, reliving over and
over again every detail of their brief time together.

In early June the Norman party left for Fulk of Anjou's castle at
Le Mans in Maine where the nuptials were to take place.

. . .

Maud awoke on the day of her wedding with a heavy heart. By contrast, the day itself dawned fair and warm.

"Not a sign of rain, God be praised," said Aldyth, as she opened the narrow casement window to let in a stream of sunlight. "And today is the seventeenth of June, the octave of Pentecost. A good omen for the wedding."

"How I wish that were true," Maud said, as one of her women slipped a tight-fitting violet gown over her head.

"Of course it's true, child," Aldyth replied. "Once you're properly wed, all your doubts will vanish. Remember, one day a son of this marriage will rule England, Normandy, and Anjou. He'll be the most powerful monarch in Europe!"

True enough, Maud realized, but at the moment the thought did not help; there was still the ceremony, the wedding night, and all the months and years ahead to endure.

"You look beautiful, every inch a queen," Aldyth said, taking a skein of gold thread and weaving it through the two russet plaits that hung down over Maud's breasts. "But I have never seen a bride look so unhappy." She placed a violet-colored veil on Maud's head, and over this the gold crown of England, on loan from King Henry for this auspicious occasion.

"You must make an effort, my child," she continued. "The folk of Anjou will think it a funeral you attend, not a wedding. All ready?"

I will never be ready, Maud wanted to say, but she gave Aldyth a brief nod.

As she rode on a snow-white palfrey toward the cathedral church of St. Julian, where, traditionally, the Counts of Anjou were married, Maud did make an effort. Forcing a smile to stiff cold lips, she raised her hand in greeting as the bridal procession passed through the crowded streets of Le Mans.

The sky was a soft blue, the air sweet with the scents of lilies, marigolds, roses and gillyflowers that grew in profusion along the road. Such a glorious day, Maud thought, so at variance with what lay ahead.

When Maud reached St. Julian's and dismounted, she was met by a wave of hostility emanating from the small group of Norman barons and prelates who filled the minster. Maud knew they attended the wedding under protest, making no secret of their outrage at King Henry's treachery for arranging such a marriage without their knowledge. She could almost hear their unspoken condemnation: Bad enough to have a woman ruler, but an Angevin as her king-consort!

She caught a glimpse of the fat Bishop of Salisbury, his face dripping with sweat, and the tall figure of Stephen's brother, the Abbot of Glastonbury.

"The ceremony is about to begin," the King said in her ear.

He took her arm and they walked slowly down the aisle. The great nave burned with hundreds of white candles and the stained-glass windows sparkled like precious gems. The choir sang so loudly it was almost deafening.

Geoffrey, resplendent in the blue-and-green costume he had worn when she first met him, the ever-present golden broom perched on his blue cap, barely looked at her.

All too soon they reached the altar. I cannot go through with the ritual, she thought, panic-stricken, I cannot do it. Stephen, she cried wordlessly, Stephen, help me. She almost turned to run back up the aisle but her father was directly behind her. Still she hesitated, then felt the silent force of her father's will propelling her to do what she must. Aware of every eye upon her, Maud made her body kneel before the candlelit altar. The crown trembled on her head, but the weight of the golden plates steadied her, reminding her of who she was: the future Queen of England. Holding that thought before her as a beacon in the darkness, she endured the solemn mass of the Trinity.

At last the Agnus Dei was chanted; Geoffrey received the kiss of peace from the Bishop. At the foot of the great crucifix, he stiffly embraced Maud, and with icy lips formally transmitted the kiss of peace on her cheek. The ceremony was over. She was now Countess of Anjou and Maine.

The wedding party had barely sat down to the first of a series of banquets held in the great hall of Le Mans Castle when a messenger arrived for King Henry.

"What's happened?" Maud asked Robert.

"I will find out."

He rose, accompanied by Brian FitzCount. When they returned to Maud's side a few moments later their faces were grave.

"The King just received word that a number of Norman barons in both England and Normandy have gone to offer their services to his nephew, William Clito," Robert said.

"Former Duke Robert of Normandy's son?" Geoffrey asked. "He has no valid claim to the duchy."

"Some think a better claim than King Henry," Brian remarked.

Geoffrey looked bewildered. "But why would anyone defect to Clito's cause now?"

Robert shifted uncomfortably in his seat. "The messages from the King's advisers report widespread condemnation of the marriage between Normandy and Anjou. Many nobles openly state that had they known of the King's intention to foist an Angevin upon them, they would never have agreed to accept Maud as their future queen. Thus they turn to his nephew."

"Such statements are treasonous," Geoffrey retorted, his blue eyes smoldering with indignation. "What do they have against the Angevins? We were a civilized tribe when the Normans were mere barbarians raiding the coasts."

That attitude is one reason, Maud barely refrained from saying.

"There's always been bad blood between the Normans and Angevins," Brian said. "The prime cause is no doubt long forgotten."

"Is the King really surprised at his magnates' response?" Maud asked, glancing across the table at King Henry, who was busily conferring with Fulk of Anjou. "Such a result was inevitable when he broke his oath to the nobles."

"I trust that King Henry will put the land to rights before I come to the throne," said Geoffrey. "I've no wish to inherit a realm in turmoil."

Maud, Robert, and Brian looked at him in dismay. That he, personally, should not be troubled was all Geoffrey cared about, Maud realized. The goodwill of the Norman people seemed of no concern to him.

"The Norman party is leaving at once so that the unrest may be quelled before it spreads further," Robert said.

As a result of the King's unexpected departure the wedding festivities were cut short, much to the relief of the Normans, who could now escape Anjou sooner than they had dared hope. To Maud's relief, the traditional blessing of the marriage bed and the undressing of the bride were omitted: The groom and his father left immediately for Angers to prepare for her arrival.

Still unforgiving, Maud parted from her father with cool formality, from Brian and Robert with genuine reluctance.

"When next we meet I look to be an uncle," Robert said, kissing her warmly on both cheeks.

"May I kiss the bride?" Brian asked.

Maud smiled her consent. She was not surprised at the warmth and tenderness with which Brian kissed her, full on the mouth, letting his lips linger far beyond the demands of courtesy. During her time in Rouen she had begun to suspect that underneath his cool exterior, the Lord of Wallingford harbored a growing attachment to her. She responded, clinging to his spare frame as if she were losing her last friend, which, in a sense, she was.

"Don't judge young Geoffrey too harshly," Brian murmured under his breath. "And no more japes with falcons and such. Remember, you catch more flies with honey than vinegar."

She nodded, holding back a sudden urge to weep.

The last to approach her was Abbot Henry, Stephen's brother.

"I'm instructed to give you a wedding present," he said in his clipped, austere voice, putting a small ivory box into her hand. "From my brother, Stephen—and myself, of course—with all good wishes for a happy and fruitful life as Countess of Anjou." He looked at her with frosty eyes.

Maud opened the box with shaking fingers. Inside was a gold ring set with an emerald carved in the shape of a crescent moon.

"I've never seen anything like it," she said, turning it over reverently in her hand. The stone sparkled like green fire, reminding her of Stephen's eyes.

"My father, the Count of Blois, took it off a dead Saracen and brought it back from the Holy Land. It's worth a king's ransom."

Maud could tell that the Abbot disapproved of the present. "Thank you for such a princely gift," she said. "Please tell Stephen that I will treasure this for all time."

She clutched the ring tightly in her palm. Stephen's fingers touched this, her heart sang, something of him lives within this ring.

The Abbot gave her a brief smile, bowed, and left. It was not until he had gone that Maud was struck by his odd choice of words: a happy life as Countess of Anjou? She could easily be queen within a year or two. What did he mean? Shrugging, she dismissed his words, much cheered by the ring. She had given Stephen her grandmother's silver ring, now he returned the gift in kind. The message was unmistakable; she was infused with new courage.

When Maud arrived in Angers several days later, the ring, suspended from a fine gold chain, reposed between her breasts.

There was genuine rejoicing among the folk of Geoffrey's capital when Maud first appeared. They made much of the fact that they had never before welcomed a bride as illustrious as the King of England's daughter. Maud was gratified to see the eager citizens waving banners as they crowded the crooked streets, the white-robed clergy bearing crucifixes and lighted tapers, accompanied by the peal of church bells and the chanting of psalms.

Against a twilight sky, Maud could see Angers Castle set on a high mound overlooking a wide river. The portcullis was up and the drawbridge down when the wedding procession came to the moat. As they rode through the thick stone tunnel into the outer bailey, well lit by flaring torches, Maud noted the mill, well-stocked barns, stables, and huts. She was equally impressed by the large number of grooms, blacksmiths, armorers and fletchers, still at their tasks, waiting, she assumed, to catch a glimpse of the new countess. No one had told her Angers was such a mighty stronghold. Crossing to the inner gate, they rode into the courtyard where the steward and a host of servitors met them at the door of the keep. When she heard the portcullis groaning down, Maud knew in that instant what a prisoner must feel as the iron door of his cell swung shut behind him.

Impatient to be wed to the daughter of the King of Jerusalem, whose crown he would inherit, Fulk of Anjou, who had only been waiting to see Maud ensconced as Countess, departed for the Holy Land at dawn the following day.

Maud and Geoffrey were alone.

As the wedding festivities had been cut short in Le Mans, and Fulk had required his son's presence on his last night in Angers, there had been no opportunity for Geoffrey to assert his conjugal rights. Although they were supposed to share the same room, Geoffrey had retained his old quarters and had given Maud the main bedchamber to share with Aldyth and the small retinue of women she had brought from Normandy. It showed an unexpected sensitivity Maud had not thought him capable of, and she was grateful.

On the night following Fulk's departure a wedding supper was held; the Bishop of Angers blessed their marriage bed, then Maud's women undressed her and put her to bed. She had covered herself with the linen sheet and left her hair unbound to flow down her back and shoulders like a shimmering russet curtain. The bells were ringing for Compline when Geoffrey knocked at her door.

"You're satisfied with your chamber?" he asked, looking around the room with a proprietary air.

Maud nodded, following his glance. The large chamber, like everything else at the castle, reflected the solid tastes of the Counts of Anjou. Tall white tapers in wrought-iron holders cast flickering shadows about the room, throwing into relief the carved wooden bed with its blue-and-crimson coverlet, blue canopy and hangings, the stout chests of golden wood, oak bench, and thick linen tapestries covering the walls.

Dressed in a curious blue silk robe of Eastern design, worked with crescent moons in silver thread, Geoffrey, obviously ill at ease, began to wander about the room. He picked up an ivory casket, where Maud had placed Stephen's ring, examined it, then, to her relief, put it back without opening it.

"Would you like some wine?" she asked, pointing to a jug and two wooden cups standing on one of the chests.

He would need something to calm him, she thought, for he was edgy as a highly bred greyhound on its first hunt. She wondered how much experience—if any—he had had with girls. At his age, it could hardly have been very extensive. Of course, she was little better off than he. The blind leading the blind, as Aldyth might term it. A picture of Stephen's body covering hers swam suddenly before her eyes.

"Wine would be most agreeable," he said gratefully, pouring wine into the cups, and walking over to the bed.

"A delightful wine," she said, taking quick sips.

"From Bordeaux, a wedding gift from the Duke of Aquitaine," Geoffrey replied. He drank, then placed their cups on the floor. Taking a deep breath, he addressed her in solemn tones. "I am aware, Madam, that neither of us favored this match, but we must make the best of it, and put aside our—any other considerations." He took her hand in limp fingers that were clammy with sweat. "Let us get down to the business of producing an heir. Just imagine, Madam, our sons will have the kings of both England and Jerusalem for grandfathers."

"A great heritage," she murmured, not unmoved by his brave little speech, well rehearsed before, she suspected.

Geoffrey leaned forward and pulled down the sheet. He stared round-eyed at this first glimpse of her naked bosom. Moving closer, he gingerly touched a full breast with a tentative finger, as if fearful it might bite him.

Suddenly he rose, blew out the candles, then pulled the blue robe over his head. "I realize you're no stranger to conjugal matters," he said, slipping into bed beside her, "but I want you to know I'm not without experience myself."

Maud smiled to herself in the darkness. "I was sure you would not be."

She forced herself to lie submissively while Geoffrey kissed her with open wet lips, then thrust his tongue into her unresponsive mouth. Meeting no resistance, he began to maul her breasts with both hands, panting heavily through his nose like a dog after game. Drawing the coverlet over his head Geoffrey curled up beside her and, fastening his mouth to her nipple, sucked at it with such relish she felt as if she had a greedy infant at her breast. His body, slender and not yet fully formed, felt like a child's compared to Stephen's muscular frame.

Staring up at the shadowy beams of the ceiling, Maud held herself rigid while Geoffrey poked and nipped at her body. It was all she could do to keep from screaming out loud. Finally he climbed on top of her. At last. Soon it would be over. Dutifully she spread her legs, squeezing her eyes shut. Geoffrey squirmed and wiggled, thrusting and jerking against her. Gradually Maud became aware that she could feel no evidence of his manhood, and had not felt any since they had gotten into bed. After a few more unsuccessful attempts to enter her with a limp member, Geoffrey rolled off her body, got out of bed, and quickly donned his blue robe.

"You were not ready for me tonight, Madam," he said quickly, avoiding her eyes as he wiped rivulets of sweat off his forehead. "You need first to adjust to your new surroundings. I'm sure matters will improve with time."

Dismayed, Maud watched him race out of the chamber before she could speak. She was relieved to have the ordeal over, but concerned that the marriage had not been consummated. With a chill, she remembered the Emperor's infrequent fumbling attempts to bed her, attempts that rarely met with success. Holy Mother of God, would she be subjected to that horror all over again? Like Geoffrey, she prayed that time would take care of the difficulty, for producing a child was the only purpose of the marriage. Otherwise . . . otherwise she could not bring herself to imagine the consequences.

Chapter Twenty-two

Angers, 1126–1127

Two weeks after Maud had arrived in Angers, she approached Geoffrey with several suggestions as to how she might aid him in the running of his affairs. It was a warm afternoon in early July, and Geoffrey had taken Maud on a tour of the lands surrounding the castle. It seemed a propitious moment.

"Besides helping supervise the household staff, I can assist you with both legal and financial matters," Maud began tentatively. "I know something of canon law, and the Emperor always said that I had an excellent head for—"

"As you're no longer in the Imperial Empire your late husband's opinion is hardly relevant," Geoffrey interjected, giving her a cold look. "Nor does the castle steward require assistance in managing the household. He served my father before me and his father served my grandfather and *his* father—you understand?"

"Yes. I only wanted to be of some use—"

"The staff would not welcome the interference of a stranger," Geoffrey continued as if she had not spoken.

"Your wife is hardly a stranger."

"A Norman is bound to engender distrust at first. After several years, of course, when the Angevins get to know you, it may be a different matter." He paused. "I'm quite capable of handling whatever the steward cannot. My mother taught me many things, including details of the kitchen. Canon law is ably dealt with by the Bishop of Angers, who would not welcome your presence in his diocese."

"What am I to do with myself?" she cried, hurt by Geoffrey's attitude. She hardly needed to be reminded that she was in a land that distrusted all things Norman.

Geoffrey scowled. "My mother, God rest her soul, always seemed able to occupy herself. She was an expert needlewoman and her tapestries were the pride of Anjou. Of course, it is to be hoped that you will soon have your hands full raising a brood of sons."

The moment the words were out he looked as if he could have bitten his tongue off.

Maud carefully avoided looking at him, not wishing to be reminded that their attempts to consummate the marriage invariably ended in a frustrating sense of mutual inadequacy. Although neither was willing to discuss the subject of Geoffrey's impotency, Maud knew that Geoffrey blamed her, while she, in turn, believed he was at fault.

There was a strained silence. Geoffrey only sees me as a breeding sow, Maud thought in despair and revulsion, wondering if she would have to wait until she was queen before gaining some measure of control over her life. She recalled Aldyth telling her that Geoffrey's youth was an advantage, for she would be able to mold him. Neither she nor Aldyth had realized that Geoffrey was already a strong character with a mind of his own.

Maud swallowed her pride, determined not to offend him. "Until such time as I . . . find my hands full, or am called upon to ascend the throne, I must have something to occupy my time, something that will help me to prepare for my future as queen. I've worked enough tapestries and embroidered sufficient altar cloths to last a lifetime."

She must have gotten through to him for she saw his face soften. "Very well, that seems sensible enough. Certainly there are duties you could perform." Geoffrey thought for a moment. "If anyone falls ill, naturally you will see to such matters. In addition you may take charge of the reception and entertainment of visitors to the castle. Let us start with that."

Maud gave him a smile of gratitude. It was hardly what she wanted, but something.

The first time they had important guests, two months later, Maud

was going over the seating arrangements with the steward when
Geoffrey walked into the great hall.

"By God's death, you have used the gold saltcellars," he said,
aghast, after one look at the table. "And the jeweled goblets are not
to be drunk from unless royalty arrives!"

"It's an important occasion, I only thought—"

"The gold cellars and goblets are for display only, not to be used."
He turned to the steward. "Take them up at once."

"But—"

"This isn't the Imperial palace, Madam, but simple, down-to-earth
Anjou. Such ostentation is frowned upon. What would people
think?"

Mortified, Maud watched as the steward and several servitors
quickly picked up the gold saltcellars and goblets.

"What dishes have you ordered?" Geoffrey asked.

"Eels in a spicy puree, loach in gold green sauce, a meat tile—"

Geoffrey gave her a suspicious look. "Meat tile?"

"I brought the recipe with me from Germany. It consists of pieces
of chicken or veal simmered, served in a sauce of pounded crayfish
tails, almonds and toasted bread, then garnished—"

"Totally unsuitable. My guests wouldn't like a German dish. Nor
do the eels and the loach complement each other. I'm familiar with
my mother's handling of these matters and I think it best if I consult
with the cooks myself. You need not trouble yourself further."

"If you've never tried these dishes," Maud said, holding on to her
temper, "how can you know if they're unsuitable?"

"They're foreign, what more is there to know?" Geoffrey walked
down the length of the table. "Tell me the seating arrangements."

"I've put the Sire de Faucon next to Lord d'Anduze and—"

"What? They're always quarreling and should be seated as far
apart as possible. Girard knows that." He glanced at the steward, who
paled visibly. "Never mind, I'll rearrange the seating myself."

"If you'll just explain to me—" Maud began.

"In future, I intend taking care of all these arrangements," Geoffrey said, cutting her off. "You cannot be expected to know how
things are done here. No one blames you."

Crimson with humiliation, Maud watched as Geoffrey and the
steward walked out of the hall together, Girard busily explaining why
he had done as the Countess ordered.

From that time forward Maud took no active part in the running of the castle, leaving everything in the hands of Geoffrey and his steward.

Seething and frustrated, she retreated to the well-stocked library and the company of Geoffrey's old tutor, Master Adelhardt, with whom she discussed history, law, and literature. She played chess and backgammon, studied the books in the library, and when she was not daydreaming of Stephen, began to think more and more of what she would do when she was queen, cautiously trying out her theories on the tutor. Each time she received a message from England or Normandy, she found herself wondering if the King was ill and she would be summoned to his bedside. Such thoughts were invariably followed by pangs of guilt and remorse, for on the one hand, despite her annoyance with her father, she did not want him to die. Yet his death would open the doors of her prison, which is how she had come to view Angers.

Once, in a moment of acute loneliness and despair, she wrote a long message to Stephen, pouring out her heart. She had sealed the parchment and actually given it to a messenger, when she suddenly snatched it out of the man's hands. Perhaps Geoffrey had all her messages read. Surrounded by her husband's people, whose first loyalty was to the Count, she did not feel entirely safe in Anjou, she realized.

One winter day she returned to the castle, having spent the afternoon hawking with the head falconer and several grooms.

"Why did Lord Geoffrey not go with you?" asked Aldyth.

"You know Geoffrey only goes riding with me when there are guests and he wishes to present a picture of domestic harmony."

Aldyth gave a glum nod. "I hoped matters were improving."

"Geoffrey has never forgiven me for that incident in Normandy, when his wretched gyrfalcon was outdone by my peregrine," Maud said. "He still refuses to allow a Welsh bird within the borders of Anjou. The Count holds on to a grudge as if it were a priceless jewel."

"A child, my lady, a child is the answer to all your problems," Aldyth told her.

Unfortunately, matters between Geoffrey and herself continued to worsen in this regard. At no time during the past nine months had he been able to consummate their union: He remained as impotent as he had been that very first night.

"I'm at my wits' end," she told Aldyth in despair. "I've tried everything I know, which, admittedly, is not very much. All to no avail."

"You could ask someone who is informed on such matters," Aldyth said cautiously. "A midwife?"

"You cannot expect me to discuss the intimate details of my marriage bed with a stranger," Maud responded. "Suppose she gossiped? Can you imagine the scandal?"

If she had been in England she could have consulted with Alix, Maud thought, although she suspected Alix was even more ignorant than herself. In Angers, there was no one she trusted. Those women she did meet, wives of the neighboring lords, were simple, good-natured creatures, but hardly her equal, and certainly not to be used as confidantes. If matters had only proceeded further with Stephen and herself, she thought, she might be in a position to know what to do.

Aldyth sighed. "I cannot advise you, I fear."

They looked at each other helplessly.

That night, after having drunk several goblets of wine at supper, Maud decided to change her tactics and act as the aggressor for a change. She would go to Geoffrey. It might help—certainly it could not make matters worse. Her women brushed her hair until it shone like polished amber and scented her body with oil mixed with rose petals. She donned a fur pelisse under which she wore nothing at all.

The bells had rung for Compline when she left her chamber, carrying a horn lantern, and walked down the passageway to Geoffrey's quarters. Shivering with cold, she paused before knocking on his door, surprised to hear sounds coming from within: a grunt followed by a squeal. Without thinking, she opened the door, then stopped short, dumbfounded at the sight that met her eyes. Geoffrey lay on his back stark naked, while a young girl rode astride him, and another girl watched. Her presence apparently unnoticed by the absorbed participants, Maud stood rooted to the spot, unable to tear her gaze from the scene before her. Obviously her husband was having no trouble whatsoever with his manhood. Maud did not stay to see the final results of this coupling, but quietly closed the door, trembling with outrage and humiliation.

It was not uncommon for a husband to amuse himself with any number of other women, she knew, and if she were now pregnant, it would not have mattered to her at all. But the dynasty of England and Normandy was at stake. Geoffrey's duty, however distasteful to both of them, was to honor her bed—as her father might have put it —until she was with child, then do as he pleased.

Maud told no one what she had discovered, but her relations with

Geoffrey deteriorated even more rapidly than before. It was all she could do to submit to his vain, frantic attempts to penetrate her, which became more and more infrequent as the months passed. She knew she must do something about the disastrous state of her marriage but found herself powerless to act.

Their unfulfilling encounters at night now turned Maud and Geoffrey into enemies by day. Bickering constantly, they no longer tried to conceal their hostility. Maud again began to think of her father's demise. Racked by guilt, she could not help herself, for his death would solve everything: She could go back to England. Once she was queen, she would find a way to deal with the problem of Geoffrey. It might even be possible to have the marriage annulled since it had never been consummated.

"Your marriage is the scandal of the city," Aldyth told her one morning in October. "You and the Count can be heard all over the castle, screaming at each other like fishwives in the marketplace."

"I don't want to discuss it. Make ready to accompany me to the October fair."

"The fair? Not again!" Aldyth gave her an incredulous look.

"What else is there to do? None of my abilities is being utilized. My womanhood is withering on the vine. I must find some way to pass the time until I become queen. Tell one of the pages to order a litter for me."

When they reached the open marketplace, an hour later, the fair was already well under way. Beneath a crisp blue sky, the open stalls proclaimed their wares in a profusion of color, scent, and sound. There were bolts of gray and blue cloth from Florence, scarlet and azure silks from Lucca, cottons from France and Flanders, wools from England, as well as flax for linen and hemp for nets, ropes, and bowstrings. Sugar from Syria and wax from Morocco ranged side by side with iron and leather from Germany and Spain. One booth specialized in skins from Scandinavia.

Bored and restless in the castle, Maud loved the excitement of the fair, the stirring of life, the new, strange faces, the feeling she was part of a larger world. She enjoyed listening to the babel of voices shouting in French, Arabic, Italian, Spanish, and a few tongues Maud did not recognize. The air was redolent with the pungent smells of mace, ginger, peppercorns, and cinnamon, mingling with the savory odor of hot pork pies and roast chestnuts sold by Angevin vendors.

"Let us stop here first," Maud exclaimed, as she spied the stalls selling luxury goods.

The litter halted and she made her way through the surging crowds. Behaving with unaccustomed extravagance, Maud had been haunting the fair for the past two weeks. She knew she was acting recklessly, but was beyond caring. It was as if she were compelled to fill the emptiness in her heart, the tedium of her days, with an assortment of trinkets and gowns she neither needed nor wanted.

She passed stalls selling camphor, ambergris, musk, and carpets. Finally she stopped by a booth that housed the art of Italian gold- and silversmiths, exquisite work set with lapis lazuli, rubies, and pearls. Prominently displayed was an ebony and silver chess set from the Far East, obviously the work of a master craftsman. I must have it, Maud thought, as her fingers caressed the shiny black figures.

"How much?" she asked haltingly in rusty Italian, addressing the withered Lombard, whose half-closed eyes regarded her with astute cunning.

His lips opened wide at hearing his own tongue, and after cheerfully haggling for a quarter of an hour, she bought the chess set, along with a gold brooch set with rubies and a delicate silver cross ablaze with sapphires and pearls. Our Lady's colors—that would suit Alix, she thought.

A kind of frenzy came over Maud, and she began to indulge herself in an orgy of spending. At another booth, she bought herself three pairs of leather shoes, a pair of boots for her brother Robert, as well as a pair for Brian FitzCount. For Stephen she picked a pair of Spanish-made leather boots, the color of his hair.

Next she purchased six bolts of silk in vermilion, purple and indigo, then selected an ivory carving of the great cathedral of St. Peter's in Rome. By the time she was finished, it took three grooms plus Aldyth and herself to carry all her purchases back to the litter. There was not enough room for everything and a pack mule was pressed into service.

When she returned to the castle and entered the courtyard, she met Geoffrey with a group of his companions getting ready to go hunting.

"Madam, what have you done? Bought out the entire fair?" he cried in a shocked voice as he stared at the array of parcels and bundles.

Ignoring him, Maud walked up the steps and swept through the open doors into the entrance hall. There would probably be an unpleasant confrontation with Geoffrey later tonight, she thought. Not that she cared. Even their scenes of mutual recriminations broke the deadly monotony of her life in Anjou.

Late that afternoon, wearing her new gold brooch pinned to a gray mantle, Maud walked along the ramparts between the red flint towers of Angers Castle. A golden hawk soared above her, then plummeted downward. Pausing, she leaned over the stone parapet but the bird was lost to view beyond the ancient walls of the city. Below, a small party approached the castle, then disappeared as they crossed the drawbridge. In the fading light she saw the deep blue of the merging Loire and Mayenne rivers. A few white sails could still be seen cutting through the water as they headed for the farther shore, beyond which rose the outline of purple vine-clad hills.

The sound of the steward's horn calling the household to its evening meal startled her. Ignoring the summons, Maud leaned her elbows on the parapet and propped her chin in her hands. She sighed, watching the first shadows sweep over the river. A light wind suddenly whipped the water, blowing the edges of her white headdress across her face.

How she longed to share this peaceful beauty with someone she loved. With Stephen. Nineteen months, two weeks, and five days, she counted, since she had last seen her cousin, yet her need of him had not diminished. In truth, the pain of missing him was, if anything, worse now.

Closing her eyes, she allowed herself the luxury of conjuring up his image: tall, tawny-haired, his green eyes dancing, his lips curved into a loving smile. His arms reached out to—

"Madam?"

She turned sharply as the sound of Geoffrey's hostile voice ruptured the evening's tranquility. He had come up silently behind her, his face set in its usual expression of sulky antagonism.

"What do you want?" The animosity in her voice matched his, as she steeled herself for the accusations she expected.

"Didn't you hear the horn?"

"I heard it."

"Well?"

"Well what?"

"Why do you dally? There are guests for supper and we await your arrival."

"Who are they tonight?"

"The only ones of significance are a nobleman from Champagne,

Count Conon and his lady, old friends of my father, and the Bishop of Angers."

"Sweet Marie, I cannot endure another evening of crushing boredom listening to the same dreary talk." Her voice took on a cutting edge. "The condition of the vines in Champagne this year as compared to last; who has been born, died, wedded, and bedded; the latest victory or blunder of Fat Louis of France. Spare me, please."

Geoffrey's face turned a dull rose as he struggled to control his temper. "I regret that you continue to look upon an evening of Angevin hospitality as such an ordeal, Madam."

"I beg to be excused. Say I'm unwell."

"You are not excused. If you were well enough to bleed the treasury dry at the fair, you are well enough to attend the evening meal." His blue eyes looked murderous. "If common courtesy will not move you, let me remind you that when you're Duchess of Normandy, the goodwill of the church—which includes the Bishop of Angers—will be important to you," he hissed, his voice laced with venom. "If you offend the good bishop now, he might prove to have a long memory. It's something your father would take into account—Madam."

"The Bishop of Angers spends more time in the castle than he does tending to his own See," Maud retorted, knowing perfectly well that he was right. "Oh, very well, I'll be down shortly."

"When? The steward cannot serve until you arrive."

"I said shortly," she replied, between clenched teeth.

Geoffrey turned sharply on his heel and strode quickly away, disappearing around one of the towers.

Maud leaned once more on the parapet but the mood had been destroyed. As she gazed out at the darkening rivers and hills, she wondered how she had survived the past sixteen months here in Angers, and how she could endure even one day more. If only her father—she crushed the treacherous thought.

Maud walked along the ramparts, descended the winding staircase to the second floor, and entered the great hall. She seated herself next to her husband in the high-backed carved wooden chair at the high table. The Bishop of Angers said grace, and, at a signal from the Count, the steward blew his horn and the servitors began bringing in the dishes.

"So pleased you could join us, Countess," said Bishop Ulgar of Angers, a powerful prelate with shrewd brown eyes set in a craggy face. He sat at Geoffrey's right hand, in the place of honor.

Despite her earlier complaints to Geoffrey, Maud liked and respected Bishop Ulgar. He was intelligent, charming, and learned; he also seemed well-disposed toward her. Not one of those pious, canting ecclesiasts that the Emperor had never been able to abide. She gave him a friendly smile.

Maud saw the look of relief on the Count's face, as if he feared she might say something out of place.

"The Countess," Geoffrey explained, "regrets her late arrival. She's been out of sorts lately, haven't you, my dear?"

"On the contrary," Maud replied with a bright smile. "In truth I've been feeling particularly well."

There was an awkward silence as the dishes continued to arrive and everyone bent hurriedly to their trenchers. Seated next to the Bishop, the nobleman from Champagne, a grizzled lord with a red nose and a huge paunch, complimented Geoffrey on the quality of the cuisine.

"Thus it was in Angers in your mother's day," he rasped, "and I'm pleased to see the same high standards prevail."

"Delicious! What do you call this dish?" the nobleman's wife asked Maud, as she scooped a dripping handful into her mouth.

"I'm the last person to ask," Maud said, her eyes glinting with mischief.

Geoffrey quickly cut in: "I believe my mother called it porray of leeks, a recipe she brought with her from Maine." He paused. "Let me see now if I can recall what she told me. Yes, a mixture of leeks, onions and minced pork, cooked in milk, and thickened with bread crumbs steeped in broth and drawn up with blood, vinegar, pepper, and cloves."

The Countess turned to Maud with a look of surprise. "How fortunate you are to have a husband who takes such an interest in the preparation of food. I would love to visit your kitchen and learn the secrets of some of your recipes."

"I'm sure the Count will be happy to take you on a tour," Maud replied. "I barely know where the kitchen is located, nor am I familiar with any of the household recipes."

"Oh, yes, I see," the woman babbled, her eyes darting in dismay from Geoffrey to Maud. "I had assumed, of course, that you—that is to say—" Her words trailed off as she looked helplessly at her husband, who was staring at Maud.

"A natural mistake," Maud said sweetly. "One does not expect to find a man so well-versed in those matters which are considered the natural province of women."

There was an appalled silence. Geoffrey turned white before a deep red stained his delicate features. Observing her husband's discomfort, Maud experienced a moment's intense gratification, then immediately regretted her rudeness. But it was too late. The words could not be called back. Frozen with embarrassment, the stunned guests looked everywhere but at their host and hostess. The evening was saved from total disaster by the Bishop of Angers, who stepped skillfully into the breach.

"My lord," he said in a silky voice to the nobleman, as if nothing untoward had occurred, "I understand there's to be an unusually fine grape harvest in Champagne this year, praise God. Will you tell us the yield?"

Somehow the meal continued. Maud did not speak again; Geoffrey finally recovered himself enough to stumble through a stilted conversation with the nobleman and the Bishop. This time, Maud knew, she had gone too far. The repercussions would be formidable. Half fearful, half defiant, she awaited the outcome of her folly.

Aldyth and her women were preparing Maud for bed when Geoffrey stalked into her chamber.

"I must talk to you, Madam," he snapped, ignoring Aldyth and the other ladies.

Maud, clad only in her chemise, quickly pulled on a pelisse. "It will have to wait," she said coldly to hide her inner agitation. "I'm preparing to retire."

"It cannot wait. Your behavior tonight was outrageous. I won't be insulted at my own table in front of my guests. This evening was the last straw. As you have made no secret of your unhappiness here, I give you permission to leave Angers."

Maud looked at him in amazement. "Leave Angers? To go where?"

"Normandy, England, back to Germany, wherever the devil take you, for aught I care, so long as it's well beyond the borders of Maine and Anjou."

"Indeed? When I wish to go you will hear of it."

Geoffrey folded his arms across his chest. "Your wishes no longer concern me. I insist upon your leaving. You have no choice."

"No choice? I wonder what my father will have to say about that! Not that I don't long to go, mind. Sweet Marie, I'm so weary of this paltry backwater I could lose my wits." She paused for breath. "There's nothing I desire more than to be in England, where people are civilized and men behave like men."

Geoffrey reeled back as if she had struck him. Maud advanced relentlessly. "Wait until my father, and yours, hear how you've treated me, a former empress, and the future queen of England!"

From the corner of her eye she saw Aldyth and her women, open-mouthed in horror, scurry to a corner of the room like frightened geese, but she no longer cared what they thought, what anyone thought.

"God's death, Madam, you've been treated like an empress. Every effort has been made to ensure your comfort and pleasure. Have I objected to the gowns and headdresses and jewels you buy daily?" Geoffrey ran to several chests, opened them, and began to pull out armfuls of gowns and tunics. "Just look at these! If you live to be a hundred you could not wear them all."

Running over to a pole stuck in the wall, he tugged at more gowns and mantles, sweeping them to the floor, then tore open several boxes, gleefully spilling boots, shoes, gloves, stockings to the ground.

"You have free run of the castle; the finest horses, falcons, and hounds are at your disposal; the best minstrels sing for you; and my private tutor has quite deserted me to be at your beck and call. You have no cares, no responsibilities for the running of the castle!"

Geoffrey's nostrils distended, his eyes became blazing blue slits; his voice shook with anger. All semblance of control gone, the famous "demon blood" of Anjou raged now in full fury. For one quite terrifying moment Maud thought he might strike her.

"You wouldn't let me take responsibility for the castle or anything else," Maud screamed, taking a step back. "You would never let me do anything of use. How can anyone be happy under such circumstances, particularly when forced to live with an arrogant, spoiled pup of fifteen, who cannot perform man's most basic function!"

"I can perform it well enough with others," he shouted back incautiously.

"So I have observed. Is that something to be proud of?"

His face turned scarlet as his jaw dropped. Swallowing, he quickly recovered. "I was brought to you an innocent victim, Madam, sacrificed for the future of Anjou. Little did I expect a vicious, serpent-tongued woman to be thrust into my bed." He paused for his final blow. "My father was tricked into believing you were not barren and the Emperor was at fault, but I know better! You unmanned him as you do me." He drew a shuddering breath. "If you are not out of this castle by Sext tomorrow, I will have you thrown out."

In a frenzy of rage, Maud picked up the first object that came to hand, a heavy iron candleholder standing on one of the chests. As she ran toward him, Geoffrey turned and fled, Maud hot on his heels. She tried to smash the iron base on his head, and the candle flame actually singed an apricot curl, before Aldyth wrested the candleholder from her and held her, struggling wildly, while Geoffrey made his escape.

After a few moments, breathing heavily, Maud released herself from Aldyth's grip. Her hands were dotted with hot candle grease that burned into her flesh, her hair was disheveled, and her pelisse awry. Collecting her scattered wits, she summoned her frightened women, ordered all her boxes to be brought to the chamber and her belongings packed, ready to leave by noon tomorrow.

"We'll be up all night but there's no help for it," she told them.

"Where will you go?" Aldyth asked, much shaken.

"First to Normandy, then, with my father's agreement, to England."

"But my lady—"

"If you utter so much as one word in Geoffrey's favor, I will leave you behind, do you understand?" She glared at Aldyth before turning to her stricken ladies, who stood paralyzed in the center of the room. "Well, why do you stand there like sheep? Bring the boxes and saddlebags!"

The women fell all over themselves in their haste to leave the chamber.

Despite the humiliation of being thrown out of Anjou, Maud felt curiously relieved. The fact that Geoffrey had thrown her out placed the burden of responsibility on him, although she was too honest with herself to pretend he had not been driven to the deed.

While Maud and her ladies packed boxes and saddlebags, Geoffrey appeared at the door from time to time to ensure, he said, that she took only what belonged to her, for he did not trust her to behave with honor.

Maud ignored him. "Take only what we brought with us," she admonished Aldyth and her women. "Anything acquired in Anjou leave behind. I want nothing that was bought with the Count's money."

Her eyes fell on the leather boots she had bought for Stephen, and the magnificent ebony chess set. For a moment she hesitated. No, she decided firmly, nothing. She would leave exactly as she came.

The bells rang for Sext just as Maud and her exhausted women finished their packing. Geoffrey, having found in his room a carved ivory box, a wedding present to Maud from Matilda of Anjou, now a nun, who had been married to her late twin, William, followed her to the wide door leading to the courtyard. Under the horrified eyes of Bishop Ulgar and the couple from Champagne, he threw the box after her as she walked down the steps of the keep in a pelting rain.

"You've forgotten this, Madam," he called with a sneer.

The box hit her in the small of her back. She staggered on the wet stone step but did not fall. Turning in a fury, she saw Geoffrey standing at the top of the stairs, a hand over his mouth, obviously frightened that he had hurt her. For a moment they stared wordlessly at each other over a gulf as wide as the channel, then she picked up the box, flung it contemptuously aside, and walked proudly down the steps into a waiting litter. With all her heart, Maud hoped that she had seen the last of Angers Castle and the Count of Anjou.

Chapter Twenty-three

England, 1127

ON A COOL MORNING IN EARLY NOVEMBER, KING HENRY WAS AT WIN-chester, in the stone and timber castle that housed the royal treasury.

He was in a particularly mellow frame of mind, having just paid a visit to the vaults with his clerks and the barons of the exchequer. The harvest had been unusually good this year, revenues were up over the last three months, and the treasury bulged with coffers of silver, gold, and jewels. In addition, the rumor that his nephew and rival claimant for Normandy, William Clito, was dead of a wound, had been confirmed. The last remaining element of unrest in the duchy was now fortuitously removed. If Maud would only send word that she was with child, he thought, everything he had set out to accomplish would be fulfilled.

The steward's horn sounded, summoning him to the mid-morning meal. He felt so well today, Henry decided he might even taste a bite or two of stewed lampreys, despite the fact the dish had been forbidden him by his physicians.

"There's a messenger arrived from Normandy, Sire," Brian Fitz-Count said, as the King entered the great hall.

King Henry frowned. "Not trouble, I hope."

"I cannot say as he will speak to no one but you." Brian paused. "I gather, however, that he comes from your daughter."

"From Maud? Then he comes from Angers."

"No, Sire. From Normandy."

Henry's heart thudded, and he felt the familiar pressure beginning to build in his head and chest, the same pressure the physicians had warned him about. Avoid all strain, all undue excitement they were constantly telling him. By God's splendor, how was he supposed to do that and run a kingdom split between two continents? The next thing they would be telling him was to avoid undue breathing.

"I took the liberty of seating the fellow at the lower end of the hall. Whenever you are ready to see him, Sire—"

"I will eat first," the King said, with a sense of foreboding, his pleasant mood dissipating. "Trouble, Brian. Without a doubt, trouble. And trouble always sits better on a full stomach, eh?"

After the King ate, Brian brought in the messenger.

"Why is my daughter in Normandy?" the King asked without preamble.

The messenger swallowed. "The Empress sends you greetings, Sire, and trusts that you are in good health—"

"Never mind the formalities, get to the point," the King interrupted testily.

"The Empress wishes me to inform you that her life with the Count of Anjou has become unbearable; she's been subjected to unspeakable abuse. Matters reached such a pitch that the Count physically threw her out of Angers and forbid her to remain within the borders of Anjou and Maine. She's now in Normandy and seeks permission to return to England. The rest, she says, will wait upon her seeing you, for it is too horrifying to be told in a message. The Empress adds that she feels sure you won't deny her sanctuary."

Half rising, the King's face became gorged with blood, the veins in his neck standing out in thick ridges. "She has abandoned her lawfully wedded husband," he roared, "and dares to seek my aid, my agreement? If there's been any abuse suffered I'll wager I know who caused it!" For a moment his mouth worked but no words came. "Tell that she-wolf that she may rot in Normandy until hell freezes over, or go back to her husband where she belongs. By God's splendor, when I think of the scandal, the shame!" He staggered, holding his heart, and Brian, hovering by his side, threw an arm around him, fearful he might fall.

"That woman will be the death of me," Henry gasped. "How could I have sired such a . . . such a virago!"

Brian gestured to the steward. "Call the physicians. The King will have to be bled. Be quick about it. Bishop Henry, Bishop Roger, do you help me."

The bishops and several barons hurried to the King's aid. Supported on all sides, the stricken king was half carried from the hall.

"For the moment I'd make myself scarce if I were you," Brian said in an aside to the messenger. "Later, I'll give you a private message for your mistress."

When the King had been bled by his physicians and was finally asleep in the royal bedchamber, Stephen's brother Henry, newly appointed to the See of Winchester, took Brian aside in a corner of the great hall. Tall and elegant in his episcopal robes, he wore the silver pectoral cross and ornate ring of his office with undisguised pride.

"What unlikely tale is this?" the Bishop asked Brian with raised brows. "Are we honestly expected to believe the Count of Anjou cast his wife aside and threw away his chance to be king-consort of England? I think it much more likely the Countess left on her own account. For months the court has been rife with unsavory rumors of their marital battles."

Brian shrugged. "You know what gossip is, my lord bishop. Who can know the truth of these matters?"

"Is it not true my cousin Maud was opposed to the match from the start?" the Bishop persisted. "I understand she made no secret of her feelings."

"And if she did oppose the match, who can blame her? The entire realm opposed it. Besides, never were two people more unsuited to each other," Brian said, determined to defend Maud.

"How many who marry are suited, my lord? That is hardly relevant. I'm no supporter of Anjou, but for a woman to desert the marriage bed is a most serious step. It shows dereliction of duty, flouting of custom, an unstable element that does not bode well for one who will be the future Queen of England. Exactly what one may expect of the distaff, people will say. She'll never produce an heir at this rate." He gave Brian a searching look. "Assuming she is even capable of producing one."

Brian kept his face impassive, restraining an impulse to turn his back on the supercilious figure before him. "There's a bright spot in all this, however," he said.

The Bishop glanced at him sharply. "Indeed? I cannot think of one."

"The barons have never reconciled to the marriage," Brian said, as he started to walk across the hall.

"Nor a female ruler," Henry added, keeping pace with him. His eyes continually roved the great hall, noting who came and went. "The marriage merely added insult to injury."

"I was about to say that eventually King Henry will be forced to take her back into his good graces," Brian said, "since public opinion may well be on her side. In fact, leaving Anjou may gain her more popularity with the Norman nobles than she knew before—whatever it does to her reputation across Europe."

"Gain her popularity?" the Bishop repeated with a frown.

Brian stopped at the entrance to the hall and turned to face the Bishop: "The thought dismays you?"

"No, no," the Bishop said hastily. "The possibility is one I hadn't considered."

"Indeed? I had assumed that nothing that has occurred to me would not have occurred to you first."

The Bishop arched his brows, indicating the remark was not worth a reply.

"When do you leave for Rome?" Brian asked, pleased to have put the Bishop off balance.

"Within the week, the King's health permitting."

"A safe journey, Your Grace," Brian said.

They left the palace and stood in the courtyard.

The Bishop gave Brian a frosty smile and left. Brian watched his tall figure disappear. Henry's remarks had struck him as more insidious than a prelate's natural disapproval over a woman's defection from her husband. His words had been designed to discredit Maud as future queen. Obviously the Bishop had not totally abandoned the idea that his brother, Stephen, might still become king. A forlorn hope, yet—he would bear watching, Brian decided.

Bishop Henry of Winchester traveled through Paris on his way to Rome. As in London, the scandal of Maud and Geoffrey was the talk of the city, with much speculation on the possible outcome. The most popular theory was that Geoffrey would try to incarcerate her in a convent to meditate upon the error of her ways and if that came about, King Henry might be forced to put her aside and name another heir. If such an unlikely event came to pass, thought Henry with a sigh, all his difficulties would be solved. Still, it was heartening to know that people in Europe were thinking along such lines.

A month later the Bishop arrived in the Holy City. On this, his first visit to Rome, he found himself impressed. His eyes were full of wonder as he walked through the cobbled streets, marveling at the stately ruins on the seven hills, the churches without number, the ancient catacombs. Reverently, he knelt before the altars dedicated to the Apostles, and made generous offerings at the Stations of the Martyrs. The church of St. Peter left him breathless, and he was equally awed when shown such treasures as Our Lady's shift and Our Lord's swaddling bands.

After a donation of princely gifts and a week of waiting in the papal anterooms, the Bishop was finally granted an audience with Pope Innocent.

"How may I help you, my son?" asked the Pope, clad in shimmering white, and surrounded by several cardinals in glowing scarlet robes.

Henry knelt and kissed the Pope's ring. "Holy Father, as you know, I have just been appointed Bishop of Winchester. My uncle, King Henry, said I might also keep my abbacy in Glastonbury as well, if Your Holiness agrees."

"If that is King Henry's wish," the Pope said with a smile.

"You mean to be bishop and abbot both?" asked a heavyset cardinal whom Henry did not know. "Glastonbury and Winchester are both very wealthy Sees. That would make you the most powerful prelate in England, next to the Archbishop of Canterbury, and almost as affluent as the King himself."

Henry felt his face flush. "I had not viewed it in that light, Your Eminence. I seek nothing for myself, of course, for I'm a devoted son of Holy Church, thinking only to increase its glory."

"You object, Umberto?" the Pope asked with a frown.

"It is not for me to object, Holy Father, but the Bishop is young, only a few years out of the monastery."

"King Henry is the Bishop's uncle, Umberto, after all, and if the King found him worthy to administer two Sees, it behooves us to follow his wishes."

"Of course, Your Holiness."

The Pope gave Henry a benign smile. "You may tell King Henry we have no objection."

"Thank you, Holy Father." Henry paused, then cleared his throat. "You're aware of King Henry's intention to have his daughter crowned after his death?"

"Who is not aware of it?" one cardinal said.

"And now she has left her husband, the Count of Anjou—" Henry began, then stopped as the Pope held up his hand.

"We understand the situation, my lord bishop, but there are some questions better left unasked. You may rest assured that the Holy See follows the events of Normandy and England very closely indeed."

"Believe me, my lord bishop," said another of the cardinals. "We are in full sympathy with your plight. Who would be ruled by a creature subject to the tides of the moon? A woman who abandons her husband and has become the talk of Europe."

"Giovanni!" The Pope wagged a warning finger before turning to Henry. "His Eminence has an impetuous tongue. Forgive him his little outburst. At another time, perhaps, we will speak of these matters. It is a bit premature, yes? After all, what is done today can be undone tomorrow. When the time comes God will show us the way."

Hiding a smile, Henry bowed himself out of the chamber. He had learned what he needed to know: The Holy See was not in favor of Maud succeeding to the throne but preferred to play a waiting game.

"The English bishop labors well in his own vineyards," said Cardinal Umberto in a sardonic voice. "He opposes his uncle's wishes regarding the succession and hopes to see his brother, Stephen, on the throne, if I'm any judge."

"And himself Archbishop of Canterbury," added the Pope.

"He wears ambition like a diadem!"

"Hmm." The Pope reflectively stroked his chin. "They say he leads his elder brother like a shepherd his flock. That would be no bad thing for Rome. When King Henry dies we will be interested to see how the Bishop handles the delicate matter of the Countess of Anjou. Should he be successful we will give him our support. Should he fail—"

The Pope and the cardinals smiled at one another in perfect understanding.

Henry left Rome well satisfied. Beneath the beauty and grandeur of the Holy City, he was aware of the intrigue and corruption, but this did not disturb him. He carried away with him to England not only rare manuscripts, gold plate, marble statuary, and a chest of religious artifacts, but the implicit assurance of the Pope that he would support Stephen's cause, not Maud's. He no longer needed to find ways to discredit his cousin, Henry realized; she was doing a superb job of it all by herself. Should she continue to pursue her present headstrong course, Stephen's accession was all but guaranteed.

Chapter Twenty-four

England, 1129

IN THE SPRING OF 1129, STEPHEN AND THE DE BEAUMONT TWINS WERE outside the King's hunting lodge, preparing to hunt boar in the New Forest, six leagues from Winchester. They were about to mount their horses when, to Stephen's surprise, a herald rode through the gates of the staked wooden enclosure surrounding the lodge.

"My lords," said the herald, as he dismounted. "I've just come from Westminster to advise you that the King will hold a special court at Windsor in two days' time and bids you attend." He looked around him. "Is my Lord of Gloucester not with you?"

"He and the beaters have already gone into the forest, not ten moments ago," Stephen said.

Waleran of Muelan scowled. "We only arrived last night and now we are expected to return? What is the occasion for this special court?"

"The Countess of Anjou's return to England," the herald replied.

Waleran's face flushed red. "By God's wounds, does the King call us back from hunting merely in order—"

"You may tell the King that of course we will attend," Robin interjected smoothly. He turned to his brother. "We will have our day's hunting and leave tomorrow. That should give us plenty of time.'' He dismissed the herald with a smile.

"I cannot believe the King allows that shrew to return,'' Waleran muttered. "She should be escorted back to Anjou under armed guard if she won't comply, horse-whipped by her husband, then retired to a convent to expiate her sins. Her behavior is an insult to the institution of marriage.''

The men mounted their horses and, followed by their squires, trotted out of the palisade.

"Instead he welcomes her like the prodigal daughter,'' Waleran continued.

"That is not entirely fair, Muelan,'' said Stephen, whose heart had skipped a beat when he heard of Maud's return. "The lady has been cooling her heels in Normandy for over a year. Remember how furious the King was at first? He swore she could remain there until her bones rotted. I wonder what has changed his mind.''

"The tide of public opinion flows with her, for a change,'' Robin offered, "and he is wise enough to see that. Everyone knows the King forced her to the Angevin match and by leaving she has gained a measure of esteem with both barons and commonfolk alike.''

Within moments they were so deep into the forest that it was hard for Stephen to believe he was within a spear's throw of the hunting lodge.

Waleran ducked his head to avoid a low-hanging branch. "Never did I think to see the day when a woman abandons her lawfully wedded husband—regardless of the circumstance—and men applaud it!''

"Ah, but she left an *Angevin* husband,'' Stephen pointed out, exchanging an amused glance with Robin.

Stephen and the de Beaumont twins, dressed alike in linen tunics, soft buckskin breeches, and sleeveless jerkins, broke out of the trees and into a small clearing spread with thistles, brambles, wild roses, and foxglove. Here they reined in their horses. Behind them, on foot, came the grooms and huntsmen, followed by the fewterers leading packs of boarhounds and bloodhounds. The hunting dogs yelped and strained at their leashes.

"Have the beaters seen any boar tracks or heard my Lord of Gloucester's horn?'' Stephen asked Gervase, as his squire rode up beside him.

"No tracks as yet, nor signal from the Earl,'' Gervase replied. "Shall I order the dogs unleashed?''

"Not until some scent or trace of this boar can be found," Stephen said. "We will bide here a moment and see if Robert does not sound his horn."

Waleran exchanged a significant look with his brother. "This new-found sympathy for Madam Empress, how deeply can it reach? Not deeply enough to make her acceptable as sovereign."

What intrigue was Waleran up to now, Stephen wondered, keeping his face impassive. "Acceptable or not, the nobles swore an oath to make my cousin queen. I believe you were among them. We are all of us bound by that oath. There the matter rests."

Waleran shot him a speculative glance. "Is a forced oath binding?"

"Some might deny the oath was forced. The matter is open to question, and is for Holy Church to decide. I haven't heard that Rome protests the King's decision. In any case, I refuse to debate theology with you."

"We speak of the future, Stephen," Robin said. "After all, King Henry broke his own oath when he married your cousin to Anjou. Not a very good example to set. When he is dead what is to prevent others from changing matters to suit themselves?"

"As affairs now stand, we will have a female ruler with an estranged husband and no son," Waleran added. "Suppose the King dies tomorrow or next week or even next month?"

"That is the crux of the matter," Robin said. "Maud has had two husbands and no issue!"

"Come, Stephen," Waleran persisted, "do you suggest the Conqueror's great realm be left in the hands of a barren queen?"

The twins looked expectantly at Stephen who remained silent. Such talk bordered on treason, and while Stephen had no mind to rebuke them, it did not seem politic to commit himself, nor did he disagree with a word they said. Indeed, he and his brother had recently had a very similar discussion.

The Bishop believed that years of absolute power had lulled their uncle into complacency, and that he was wrong to assume that through his daughter he would still control his realm from the grave. But Stephen had no intention of repeating this to the twins.

He found he was of two minds about Maud's return to England. When she had first left to marry the Count of Anjou, Stephen had missed her sorely, more than he would have believed possible. Accustomed to taking his pleasures when and where he found them, Stephen knew he was not able to do without women in general, although he had never imagined that he could not do without any one woman in particular. But Maud had captured more of his heart than any woman before her.

Yet during the three years of Maud's absence his desire for her had been overshadowed by thoughts of the crown. His brother had made many friends in the Holy See, and was assured that the Curia had no love for a female ruler. When the time came many would be sympathetic to their cause, as the de Beaumont twins were now.

In truth, the thought of Maud's return was unsettling, Stephen realized. He had no wish to be assailed again by impossible longings, nor to have the even balance of his life disturbed. All memory of their last encounter in her chamber must be ruthlessly crushed. For his peace of mind it would be far, far better if Maud remained safely in Normandy or, better still, return to Anjou.

The piercing sound of a hunting horn reverberated through the forest. Almost in unison the three men lifted their heads, like hounds scenting a quarry.

"Robert," Stephen announced. "He must have picked up the boar's tracks." He lifted an ivory horn chased with gold that swung from his neck on a cord of fine leather, and blew three clear notes.

Gervase reached into two bulging saddlebags at his horse's side, and held up several weapons for his master's inspection: a bowstave and quiver of newly fletched birchwood arrows, a Danish ax, and a boar spear. Stephen immediately reached for the spear.

"Is that all you intend to use?" Waleran asked, taking a Danish ax as well as a spear from his own squire.

"This is all I need," Stephen replied.

"Give me the bow every time." Robin tested a yew bowstave in his powerful arms.

The sound of the horn came again, closer this time. Hearing the call, the hounds began to bay and yelp, eager to begin the chase.

"Where are my hounds?" Stephen called, his voice tense with excitement.

Gervase brought his master's three favorite dogs to him, enormous bloodhounds that always accompanied Stephen on his boar-hunting expeditions. Stephen reached down to pat their heads as they began to bark, showing their pointed white teeth and slavering red tongues.

"Good hunting," Stephen called to the twins, as Gervase unleashed the dogs.

The hounds bounded out of the clearing into the thicket and Stephen rode after them, all thoughts of his cousin banished from his mind, his attention fixed on the sport that lay ahead.

From somewhere behind him, he could hear the twins crashing through the undergrowth, followed by the beaters and baying pack of hounds. The sound of Robert's horn came again, over to the left. Stephen blew upon his own horn and reined in his horse as the hounds stopped for a moment, seeking the boar's tracks. After circling a few times the dogs soon discovered where the boar had dug and rooted for food. They bounded forward once more and Stephen followed.

As he rode deeper into the forest, the sound of the baying packs grew fainter and fainter. Turning his head, he saw neither of the twins behind him nor could he now hear their horses. The echo of a horn sounded faintly from another part of the forest. He had outrun the rest of the hunt, Stephen realized, and, save for his dogs, was alone. Somewhere in front of him, the hounds began to bark furiously, and he spurred his mare onward. Within moments he came upon the boar's lair. Near a spring, in a narrow opening between two uprooted trees, the boar stood erect, ears flattened, enormous feet spread wide, its small bloodshot eyes fixed on the hounds, who looked puny compared to the massive black beast confronting them. One of the dogs, foolishly brave, rushed at the boar who seized it and, shaking the hound furiously in its great jaws, flung it to the ground, its neck broken. Before Stephen could dismount, the boar wheeled around and charged into the thicket where it was lost to view.

Angered now by the death of his hound, Stephen kept up the chase relentlessly, occasionally sounding his horn and hearing a faint echo in reply. Late in the afternoon his dogs finally brought the boar to bay in front of a forest stream. Snorting, the beast bared his huge tusks and dashed toward the two hounds. Stephen jumped from his horse, his supple leather boots landing silently on the moss-green floor of the woods.

"Spawn of the devil, evil seed of a whoreson sow," Stephen shouted, enraged.

The boar paused at the sound of Stephen's voice. Grunting, it suddenly swerved from its attack on the hounds. Straight as an arrow, the great beast leapt over a large bramble bush toward this new threat. Stephen's heart hammered against his ribs. The dry taste of fear clove his tongue to the roof of his mouth. Yet his arms were steady, his mind clear and alert, as he braced himself against a large oak and let the boar come at him head-on. Holding the spear straight before him, his legs slightly bent, Stephen tensed for the impact. Every sinew of his body, every part of him was concentrated on the deadly black shape hurtling toward him. Lifting both arms, he used all his strength to strike at the boar's breast. The point of the spear drove through the black hide, pierced the heart, and came out at the shoulder blade. The weight of the impact almost tore his arms from their sockets. The boar squealed in its death agony, but the momentum of its charge propelled the body forward, straight at Stephen, who let go the spear and quickly pivoted aside. As the animal crashed past him into the oak he could smell its rank odor, see the glaze of death film the vicious eyes. The boar tottered and slowly fell to the ground.

The two hounds rushed in toward the boar while Stephen wiped his sweating brow and flexed his wrenched shoulder muscles. His body felt drained, his hands were trembling slightly as he leaned heavily against the sturdy oak. Alone in the dark woods, with only the dogs and the dead boar, he was able to fully savor the surge of intense fulfillment that always accompanied any victory—whether in battle or the chase. He had bested a worthy opponent in a fair fight, and he was at one with himself and the lush green world surrounding him.

After a few moments, he bent to examine the dead animal. It was an enormous full-grown male, in its prime, with curved tusks as long as his forearm. The two hounds leapt up on him with muddied paws, wagging their tails, their tongues hanging. Stephen patted their heads and necks, their soft jowls, murmuring words of praise. Putting one foot against the beast's side, Stephen pulled out his spear, the point dripping blood. He wiped the spear against his buckskin breeches, then blew several times on his horn to let the hunting party know his whereabouts. Drawing a large hunting knife from his belt, he cut two large chunks of warm meat from the boar's haunch, and flung them to the hounds as their reward.

Whistling a tavern tune as he cut out the boar's tusks, Stephen decided he would hang these trophies of his prowess in the great hall of the Tower.

He also decided to avoid his cousin Maud as much as possible, and not expose himself to any possible recurrence of the incident of three years ago. With each passing year, as the King's health continued to fail, he drew ever nearer his goal. Why take undue risks for a passion that must prove futile as well as transitory? After all, what was a woman to set against a crown?

Chapter Twenty-five

IN MAY OF THAT SAME YEAR, 1129, MAUD SET SAIL FOR ENGLAND, LAND-
ing at Southampton after a rough channel crossing. She was accompanied by Brian, who had been sent by her father to bring her to
London. After more than a year in the ducal palace in Rouen, during
which time her infuriated father had refused to let her come to England and ordered her to return to Geoffrey, Maud had almost de-
spaired. Then, like a miracle, had come the reprieve.

Of course, she had contributed to the miracle, Maud thought with
an inward smile. In a constant barrage of letters written to old friends
in Rome, she had made it a point to ask about the possibility of
obtaining an annulment from the Count of Anjou. She was sure her
father would come to hear of it, and simply to prevent further mischief on her part, if for no other reason, she expected him to relent
and allow her to come to England.

Now, followed by a procession of litters, carts and sumpter horses,
Maud was determined to reach London before Vespers. By the time
she neared the outskirts of the city, she had been riding for almost
twelve hours. Her body ached, but she did not care. She was back in
England at last, and each league brought her closer to Stephen.

Acutely aware of everything around her, Maud eagerly drank in the sights, scents, and sounds of her native land: the shoots of new grass, impossibly green and fresh, a pale blue sky fleeced with puffs of white clouds, a May breeze blowing through the hawthorn carrying the aroma of sweet William, marjoram, and gillyflowers; the gentle chorus of linnet, finch, and lark. For the first time in three years, she experienced a surge of pure joy.

At last they reached Westminster Castle. Maud had just dismounted when the Bishop of Salisbury appeared on the steps of the keep.

"Good evening to you, Madam. God be thanked you've had a safe journey. The King wishes to see you when you've refreshed yourself," he said, then added softly, "I would not keep him waiting if I were you."

Filled with dread, for she knew the King must still be enraged, Maud removed her dust-stained clothes, washed herself in a tub of hot water, then put on a plain gray gown and darker gray tunic, omitting all jewelry.

A page knocked on her chamber door and led Maud to the council room in the southeastern wing of the castle. As she entered, the King looked her over without comment, then motioned to her to sit on a stool opposite him. The Bishop of Salisbury, attended by a cleric on a high stool, stood behind the King.

Maud was shocked to see how greatly her father had aged since she had last seen him. Despite the mildness of the May morning, he was seated near a charcoal brazier, with a fur-lined cloak wrapped about his body. His sallow face was deeply lined, and his black hair heavily streaked with white. A slight tremor rocked the hand that held a pewter goblet of mulled wine.

"Pour the Countess of Anjou some wine, and offer her honey cakes," he said to a hovering servitor. "Then leave us."

Even his voice had changed, his speech slower and more measured. Only the crafty black eyes remained the same.

As she hungrily devoured two of the honey cakes, and sipped the wine, Maud felt the King's gaze boring into her. Ripples of apprehension coursed through her body.

"If you believe that dressing like a penitent will deceive me, you are even more of a fool than I thought," were his first biting words to her.

Maud, attempting to assume a martyred expression, folded her hands in an attitude of prayer, and kept her head down.

"False repentance ill becomes you, Daughter." The King gave her a withering look. "Did you know that the Count and Countess of Anjou are the butt of countless jests in all the courts of Europe? I hear Louis of France has two fighting cocks that he has named Maud and Geoffrey, and it is his great pleasure to set them against each other, placing wagers on who will win. As you are responsible for our good name being dragged through all the filth and muck my enemies can conjure up, what have you to say for yourself?"

With half-closed eyes, the King listened in silence as Maud attempted to paint a grim picture of her sorry life in Anjou. She dwelt heavily on Geoffrey's inability to fully consummate the marriage, and described in detail her humiliating exit from Angers, matters she had already conveyed in her letters.

When she had finished, Henry opened his eyes. "Were you aware that only a fortnight ago, your husband managed to get a child, a son mind, on some kitchen slut in Angers?"

Maud flinched as if she had been struck. "I had not heard that. Naturally the girl would claim Geoffrey is the father," she countered. "Who can attest to the truth?"

The King shrugged. "No one, of course, but rumor has it the babe resembles him. That child," he said in a venomous tone, "should have been your son and my grandson!"

An image of the two young girls in Geoffrey's chamber passed through Maud's mind, and she flushed at the memory.

"Since you left, your husband cavorts all over Anjou, tumbling anything in skirts, telling all who will listen that he is well rid of the Norman shrew!"

"And you allow him to make mock of me?" she asked, her voice trembling with anger.

"Come, Madam, would you have me declare war on Anjou to save your pride? You've brought this disgrace on yourself." He paused. "You don't seem to have much luck with your husbands, neither of whom was either able or willing to honor your bed."

Crimson with mortification, a sudden image of Stephen's manhood, rock-hard against her body, flashed before Maud's eyes. She opened her mouth to hotly contest his words, then bit her lips until she drew blood.

"And another thing, Madam, there will be no further talk of annulment." His hands suddenly clutched his heart.

Both Maud and the Bishop moved to go to him, but he waved them away. "Oh yes, I know of your correspondence with Rome. I know everything that goes on! Now, let me warn you, if the subject of annulment is brought up ever again—to anyone—I swear, before God and all His Saints, that I will shut you up in a convent." He raised his hand. "Roger, you are a witness to this."

A convent! Maud had heard of women who, displeasing their families, were immured in a convent, never to see the light of day again. It must be an empty threat, she thought. He would not permit such disruption of all his plans.

"You would not do it," she relied with more bravado than she felt, "for then I would not be queen."

"There are those among my magnates who would be far from displeased should you be removed as heir," the King said softly, "and greatly relieved to have my nephew, Stephen, rule in your stead. You think yourself indispensable? On the contrary, Madam, on the contrary." He cocked his head to one side. "She doesn't believe me, Roger."

A host of memories rushed into her mind. Alix's story of the blinded grandchildren; the Emperor telling her how her father had arranged for the death of his brother William Rufus and the imprisonment of his oldest brother Robert.

"Oh, I do believe you, Sire, I do," she whispered. How could she have doubted him for a moment?

The King leaned toward her, his eyes cruel and hard as flint. "Very wise. Do you think I will allow you to destroy my efforts to join Normandy and Anjou? Your headstrong behavior is not going to ruin an alliance I have worked so hard to bring about. It's my belief that, in time, Geoffrey will repent of his foolishness, and request your return." He paused for breath. "I have sent messages to King Fulk in Jerusalem asking him to intercede with his son. When Geoffrey comes to his senses, you will go back to Anjou like a dutiful wife. Unless I have your agreement to abide by my wishes I will carry out my threat. Is that clear?"

Maud stared at him as a rabbit might gaze at a stoat. "Yes," she croaked, thoroughly frightened now. "I agree."

"Very well, but I will keep a close watch on you, Madam, make no mistake." He sat back and regarded her. "Now, there must be no more fuel added to an already raging fire. Say nothing of these matters to anyone. You're here for a visit, with your husband's blessing, and anything heard to the contrary is gossip and rumor, put about by our enemies."

"I understand, Sire."

"The only reason I allowed your return is that the barons seem well disposed toward you for leaving Anjou, fools that they are." He reflected for an instant. "It may well be time for them to swear their oath of allegiance to you once again." He gazed at her without expression. "We must do what we can to salvage something from the wreckage you have created."

Maud bowed her head. She had never seen her father so angry and, for the first time, was well and truly afraid that he would carry out his threat.

"You have my leave to go."

Chastened and subdued, Maud walked back to her chamber. She had not expected such a violent reaction. Fortunately, she suspected it was likely to be some time before Geoffrey came to his senses. Eventually, she admitted to herself, unless she wished to spend her years in a convent, she would have to go back to Anjou and fulfill her obligations, no matter how distasteful. In truth, she admitted to herself, losing the crown was even more painful to her than a life with the Count of Anjou. Meanwhile, she would live only in the moment and give no thought to the future.

The king moved back the date of his special court, to be held at Windsor, and there, Maud knew, she would be sure to see Stephen. The day before the court was to be held, Maud, in company with Queen Alix and their respective ladies, rode the ten leagues to Windsor. Stephen, with his wife and children, had already arrived.

The following day dawned fair and clear. After a solemn Mass in the chapel, at which she caught only a brief glimpse of Stephen's back, Maud hurried to her chamber to prepare herself for the feast which was to start just before noon.

As she watched her women sort through her clothes, she half regretted her hasty decision to leave most of her clothes in Anjou. Finally Maud decided on a gown she recently had made in Rouen. The gown was a pale green gossamer silk shot with gold thread. The tunic, made of a darker green, was girdled at the waist with a delicate gold clasp. A narrow collar of gold studded with pearls graced her slender neck. Her pearly-colored gauze veil was held in place by a narrow circlet of gold she had borrowed from Alix.

Maud looked in the mirror held up for her inspection, trying to see herself through Stephen's eyes. The shimmering green brought out the rich cinnamon of her coiled hair, gave a silver sparkle to her eyes and a flush of color to her creamy skin.

Would he still find her fair? she wondered anxiously.

"I assume the Count of Mortain will be at the feast," Aldyth said, eyeing Maud with disapproval.

Maud colored, refusing to meet Aldyth's eye. Throwing a black velvet cloak over her shoulders, she descended to the great hall of Windsor Castle to find the feast already in progress.

Jostled by running pages and servitors, she threaded her way past the trestle tables until she reached the high table. The King and Alix, Robert of Gloucester, his wife, Mabel, and their two eldest sons, Brian and his wife, Stephen and Matilda, the de Beaumont twins and their respective wives, the Bishops of Salisbury and London, as well as other notables sat at the long table.

A place had been kept for her between Robert and her father, and she squeezed between them. The King, stuffing himself with stewed lampreys, and ignoring Alix's admonitions not to eat this favored delicacy, acknowledged her presence with a brief nod. Brian smiled at her, while his wife, plain and dumpy, whom Maud had never met, stared at her with timid curiosity.

"I'm so pleased to see you, Cousin," Matilda called gaily from farther down the table.

Maud smiled weakly, noting how pretty Stephen's wife looked tonight, her gentle face radiating goodwill. Her heart pounding and her throat dry, Maud slowly shifted her gaze to Stephen, certain his eyes would be upon her. To her disappointment, he had his back to her while talking to the twins. She saw Matilda whisper something in his ear. Almost with reluctance, it seemed to Maud, Stephen looked briefly in her direction. His eyes, cool and distant, were those of a stranger. After a perfunctory smile, he immediately resumed his conversation with the twins, his head turned resolutely away from her.

Although no one was looking, Maud felt as if every eye had witnessed her rejection. She had such an intense feeling of anguish that she thought she would suffocate. Her heart was like a stone in her breast and her eyes blurred. Sweet Marie, what had happened? How had she offended him?

"Are you unwell? You're not eating." It was Robert's concerned voice.

Looking down she saw that her trencher had been piled high with food and she had not even noticed. If she took so much as one bite, she thought, she would be sick. Forcing a smile, she pushed the food about. By a supreme effort of will, she managed to get through the feast and the various festivities that followed. As minstrels followed jugglers, she sat like a figure carved in marble, answering questions but originating nothing. Never once in the hours that followed did Stephen glance in her direction or address a single word to her.

Later that night, long after the feast was over, Maud lay sleepless in the chamber she shared with Aldyth and her women. Over and over she asked herself: Why was Stephen treating her with such coldness? Why had he changed? She could not, would not, accept that he no longer cared for her. Until now, Maud had not realized how desperately she needed to be with her cousin again, if only to share a small part of him. What else did she have? Her life lay in ruins: Her marriage was a disaster; her father resented her; and even the prospect of attaining the throne seemed worlds away.

The bells rang for Matins. Midnight already. She had been tossing for hours. Unable to lie in bed a moment longer, Maud rose, pulled on a chemise and tunic against the night chill, and walked over to the narrow casement window that overlooked a section of the courtyard. It was deserted at this hour except for a pair of guards strolling by, and a lone figure walking back and forth. Something about the restless gait, the set of the shoulders, a shaft of moonglow highlighting the tawny head, made Maud catch her breath. Stephen. Without a moment's hesitation, she slipped on shoes, threw a mantle over her tunic, and tiptoed out of the chamber. Whatever the outcome, she had to see him, she had to find out the truth.

Chapter Twenty-six

STEPHEN, PACING BACK AND FORTH ACROSS THE COURTYARD, SALUTED the watch on their rounds of the castle. Unable to sleep, he had left the chamber he shared with Matilda and his children to seek the cool night air, hoping it would clear his head. The hours he had spent at the feast were among the worst he had ever endured, forced to witness Maud's initial shock at his calculated coldness, then the subsequent cloud of misery that settled over her. It had been unnecessarily cruel, he realized, and he owed her an explanation for his behavior. Far better to tell her the truth: It was highly dangerous to pursue a liaison—both of them were married, they could have no future together, the risk was great, and the rewards transistory. Not to mention the fact that she was his first cousin. He could not, of course, tell her of his decision to allow nothing and no one to interfere with his reach for the crown.

Stephen reached the wall and turned, remembering, with a pang, how beautiful she had appeared at the feast. Her gray eyes, almost charcoal against the milky pallor of her face, had been swimming with unshed tears; her coral lips, trembling slightly, had the look of a vulnerable, hurt child. Her bosom, heaving with suppressed emotion, strained against the shimmering green silk of her tunic, and he had wanted to reassure her even as he felt his loins stir with desire.

A faint sound caught his attention. Looking up, he saw a wraith-like form gliding toward him.

"Stephen."

The whispered voice floating eerily across the courtyard was familiar. As the form came closer he recognized Maud, and caught his breath. With her hair flowing down her back, her face silvery in the moonlight, she looked like a ghost.

"What do you here, Cousin?" Stephen asked, glancing anxiously around to see if any of the guards were in sight.

"I saw you from my window," Maud replied, her voice shaking. Distraught, she stopped to collect herself. "I can't understand why you're so cold. What have I done to offend you? I believed—I thought that between us . . . I—" Her voice choked and she could not continue.

Stephen felt as if a dagger had been plunged into his heart. With a supreme effort he stopped himself from taking her into his arms.

"Forgive me, I handled matters very badly, and I do intend to explain," he said, forcing his voice to sound calm and reasonable. "I didn't mean to be so cold, but there was simply no opportunity to tell you how matters now stood."

"And how do they stand?" she asked in a low, intense tone.

"Whatever our feelings for each other may have been," Stephen began tentatively, "it is unthinkable that we should continue—that is to say, there cannot be any repetition of what happened between us. You are also married now, with grave responsibilities. It is too dangerous, and no good can come of it. We must dismiss any thought—"

"But I love you," she interjected fiercely, her eyes enormous. "I thought you loved me."

Stephen did not speak. Love? Yes, in his own way, he loved her. But in truth the concept had little meaning for him. Certainly he found her exciting, responsive, empathetic, and infinitely desirable; he wanted her more than he had ever wanted a woman in his life. But love?

He was spared the necessity of answering by the return of the watch.

"A fine night, my lord," one of the guards called, with a snicker in his voice.

Thank God it was too dark for him to recognize Maud.

"Indeed," he rejoined, quickly pulling her into his arms.

The gesture had been made to conceal her identity, but the moment Maud's body touched his, Stephen knew he had made a fatal mistake. Her response was immediate, like a torch set to dry brush. The dark mantle she wore fell away as her arms suddenly twined round his neck, and he could tell that under the loose tunic she wore no gown. Her breasts felt heavy and firm, the points hardening against his chest; her thighs pressed close to his, and her heart thudded against his ribs. Maud's head fell back, her eyes closed, and her lips parted. Stephen was not prepared for the flame of desire that swept through him, scorching in its intensity; he had forgotten this treacherous tide of feeling that overcame reason, duty, even his own sense of survival.

For a moment he stared transfixed at her upturned face, then hungrily covered the waiting lips with his own. Her mouth was warm and tasted of honey, and as Stephen felt the curves of her body mold to his own the last of his resistance melted like wax before flame. His hands sought the fullness of her breasts and his fingers caressed the hard pointed nipples through the cloth of her garment. When he heard her ragged breath, he pulled up the skirts of her tunic and chemise, slid a hand down the length of her soft belly and found the silky mound of her sex. She was warm, moist, and throbbing with her need of him. Her body trembled when his fingers touched her and a choked gasp escaped her lips. Intoxicated by her response, his senses reeling, it was all he could do not to take her right where they stood.

The sound of footsteps forced them quickly apart. Maud pulled down her garments and turned her back just as two guards passed by on the other side of the courtyard. Deep in conversation they gave Stephen and Maud an incurious glance, and passed on.

"This is madness," Stephen whispered, his heart pounding. "Someone is sure to recognize you. I beg you go inside lest I take you here and now and destroy us all."

Maud, her face radiant in the moonlight, gave him a tremulous smile. In a moment she was gone, gliding away with an easy grace, leaving him alone in the moonlit courtyard with aching loins and the knowledge that he was once again enslaved.

Stephen returned to his chamber, and fell into an uneasy sleep. Next morning he was tense and out of sorts, his desire to possess Maud a raging thirst demanding to be quenched. Unable to decide on a course of action that would ease the conflict, somehow he managed to get through the day. That night, hoping to blot out his cousin's image, he made love to his dutifully submissive wife. But far from satisfying him, the night's work only served to increase his hunger for Maud.

For the next few days reason continued to war against need. When he saw Maud at meals or in company with her father, the connection between them was so strong, he was sure everyone must notice it. What was he to do? If his brother were here, Henry's cold logic might have a dampening effect on his ardor. But the Bishop of Winchester was busy attending to his newly acquired See and had not attended the court. He was alone; only Matilda's continued presence prevented him from committing what instinct told him would be an irreparable folly. In any case there was nowhere to bed his cousin, as the castle afforded no privacy. Day in and day out both he and Maud were surrounded by people.

A week later the festivities were over. Matilda and the children left Windsor in company with Robin of Leicester's wife, Amica. Their departure was followed by that of King Henry and Queen Alix. Maud seemed in no hurry to return to London, and Stephen found himself making excuses not to go. Brian and Robert left for their respective lands, and Waleran of Muelan returned to Normandy. Robin of Leicester stayed on.

The remainder of the barons left and the castle was now virtually empty, with only the castellan and a skeleton staff left to service the needs of the few remaining guests.

The morning after everyone had gone, Stephen, restless and chafing for action, decided to go hawking. He collected Gervase, searched in vain for Robin, then walked down to the falcon mews. After careful deliberation, he decided on a white peregrine from Iceland, similar to one he had at the Tower. Her head was covered in an old leather hood adorned with bright feathers and faded gold thread. The bells attached to her feet were of tarnished silver and inscribed with the insignia of his grandfather, Duke William of Normandy.

The bells had rung for Tierce when Stephen and Gervase rode over the drawbridge and onto a wide road that led to the river. With the falcon perched on his wrist, Stephen was followed on foot by the fewterer who led two hounds: a bercelet who hunted by sight, and a brachet who hunted by scent. They followed a well-worn path along the Thames embankment, then veered away from the river. Soon the castle was lost to view. Presently they came to a large meadow backed by a dark forest.

Unleashed, the hounds bounded out of sight in the green sea of grass. Moments later a flock of squawking partridges flew upwards. Stephen unhooded his falcon and cast her off his wrist. She mounted into the deep blue of the sky, positioning herself above one of the birds. In a flash of white she stooped, digging her talons into the gray partridge. The stricken bird flapped lower and lower, carrying the falcon into the woods flanking the meadow.

"Jesu!" Stephen exclaimed to his squire. "I must go into the woods after her. Wait here in case she flies back. I will take the dogs."

He rode to the edge of the woods, dismounted, and plunged into the trees while Gervase and the fewterer waited in the meadow. A few feet into the forest, Stephen found himself on what had once been a well-marked path, now overgrown with brambles and thick foliage. The dogs raced ahead and were lost to view. Making his way through the thick underbrush, he suddenly found himself in an open clearing. In the center, beside a small cabin made of rough-hewn logs, the falcon, its white head covered in blood, had bought her quarry to ground. The dogs were nowhere in sight. Stephen called softly to the bird, withdrew a dead pigeon from the large purse at his belt and threw it to the ground. Leaving the dead partridge, the falcon flew to her reward.

Curious, Stephen walked up to the cabin, which resembled an old hunting lodge that had seen better days. Suddenly he heard the sound of a groan coming through the partially opened door and froze in his tracks. Careful to make no sound, Stephen withdrew the knife at his belt, crept up to the door and, holding the knife aloft, peered inside. What he saw made him catch his breath. Robin of Leicester lay naked on a wide bedspread with a faded blue coverlet, fondling a slender youth whom Stephen vaguely remembered seeing about the castle. One of the pages or someone's squire, he thought. It was the boy, writhing in the grip of pleasure, who had groaned.

Stephen's foot scraped against the door, and he hastily stepped back, but not before Robin's head had turned sharply. For an instant their eyes met. Without waiting to see more, Stephen sheathed his knife, and closed the door just as the two dogs, barking and wagging their tails, bounded into the clearing. The bercelet ran to the partridge and lifted her gently into his red jaws. Stephen called the falcon to him, hooded her, and went back into the forest, followed by the dogs.

He was surprised by what he had just witnessed, and uncertain

what to make of it. Everyone was aware that men existed who enjoyed the favors of other men as well as women. In fact, he had heard
that on the crusade to the Holy Land, sodomy was not uncommon,
despite the strictures of Holy Church. But that one of these men
should be his close friend, the Earl of Leicester of the powerful House
of Muelan, one of the oldest and proudest families in Normandy—
certainly this would take some getting used to.

"What is that old cabin in the clearing?" he asked the fewterer
when he returned to the meadow.

"A hunting lodge, my lord, built for the old king, William Rufus,
these many years ago. They do say Red Rufus used it for hunting
prey other than game, if you take my meaning." He winked at Stephen. "Not used now, of course."

Stephen whistled softly. So this was where his infamous uncle, the
Red King, had brought his catamites. What irony that it was being
used for the same purpose now.

"You say no one uses this place?" he asked the fewterer as they
rode out of the meadow.

"Not that I know of, my lord. The verderers keep it up in case the
King wants to use it, but he never has done."

Before he left the meadow, Stephen cast a quick glance behind him.
It was not apparent from this vantage point that there was a path
leading into the woods, much less a clearing with a lodge in it.
Thoughtful, he rode back to Windsor.

After Vespers in the chapel, Stephen approached Robin and drew
him aside.

"I'm sorry about this afternoon, Robin," he said. "If I had had any
idea—"

Robin met his gaze with steady blue eyes. "There is naught for
you to be sorry about. Although I would be grateful for your discretion in this matter."

"Naturally, I will say nothing. Does Waleran know—" Stephen
paused. It was an awkward question and he could not think why he
had asked it.

"Of my predilection?" Robin gave him a grim smile. "Naturally
not. Waleran has no tolerance for anyone or anything that differs
even slightly from his view of traditional values and custom. That is
one of the reasons he has taken against Maud so strongly."

Embarrassed, Stephen did not know what to say. "It is none of my
affair, but Holy Church takes a dim view of such . . . practices. I
trust you will be careful."

Robin cocked his head to one side. "I see this matter is more of a trouble to you than to me. Be easy, my friend. I have long come to terms with my inner nature. After all, in the end we can only be what we are, whether for good or ill." He searched Stephen's face. "You must take me as I am, you know."

With a sudden spurt of affection, Stephen grasped Robin's hand. "And so I do, with all my heart. I judge no man because his tastes differ from mine. We need not speak of this again." He took a deep breath. Attempting to keep his voice casual, he asked: "Is the lodge usually empty?"

"I have always found it so on the rare occasions when I make use of it. Why?"

"Well, in truth, there is a tempting wench here in the kitchens that I have long had my eye on—"

Robin held up his hand in silence. "You need not explain. To each his own. I will tell my squire to have the place in readiness. When do you wish to use it?"

Stephen thought for a moment. "Tomorrow, if all goes as planned. One more favor, by your leave. If necessary would you say that we go hunting together?"

Robin looked amused. "Of course. By God's death, you take a lot of trouble for a kitchen wench, my friend. You can just as easily tumble her in the stables."

Stephen grew red but was saved from answering by the steward's horn calling the castle to supper.

When they came into the great hall, Stephen noticed that the castellan of Windsor was being served by a willowy youth with hair the color of ripe corn. Robin's catamite. Stephen sat down next to Maud, who greeted him with a smile.

A dish of stewed hare was set before them. Stephen took a piece in his fingers, and carried it, dripping, to Maud's mouth. She opened her lips and nibbled at the meat, playfully catching one of his fingers in her mouth. Inexplicably, the touch of her wet lips against his finger aroused him to fever pitch.

"Would you care to go hunting with me tomorrow?" he heard himself say.

"Yes," she replied in a breathless voice.

Their eyes locked. Stephen remained on fire for the rest of the meal, barely able to refrain from touching her. He wondered how he would survive until tomorrow, so impatient was he to have his cousin at last.

Directly after breaking his night's fast, Stephen met Robin in the courtyard. The Earl of Leicester and his party of grooms and huntsmen were already mounted.

"We will go on, Stephen, do you join us on the road," Robin said in a loud voice for the benefit of anyone in the courtyard who might be listening. With a wave and a wink he led his party out of the courtyard.

A few moments later Maud appeared with her groom.

"We do not need another groom," Stephen said. "We will join the Earl of Leicester's party."

"Very well," Maud said, her cheeks suddenly flushing. She dismissed her groom and let Stephen help her mount the white palfrey.

She knows, Stephen realized in relief, somehow she knows what will happen and comes willingly. He could already feel her warm and naked in his arms.

In silence they rode across the drawbridge and onto the path along the embankment. Following the road, they veered away from the river and finally came to the meadow. When they reached the edge of the woods, Stephen dismounted, helped Maud down, and tethered their horses to a tree. He took her hand, and for a moment she hesitated, looking up at him with a slight question in her eyes.

"There is no danger," he said. "Trust me."

She nodded, and without a word followed him into the woods and down the tangled path until they came upon the clearing.

"What place is this?" Maud asked, stopping in surprise.

"It belonged to our Uncle William Rufus."

"Indeed?" She ran lightly across the grassy clearing to the door of the lodge. "How did you find it?"

"Stumbled upon it by chance," Stephen said, following her through the door.

Inside, there were fresh rushes on the floor, the room had been aired, and there was a pile of newly cut logs on the hearth as well as water in a large iron cauldron. A flagon of wine and several wooden cups stood on a scarred oak table. Robin had been true to his word. Everything was in readiness.

Pulling off her leather gauntlets, Maud examined the lodge with interest. Suddenly unable to meet her eye, Stephen found himself tongue-tied as an awkward silence settled over them. Now that the long-awaited moment had arrived, Stephen did not know how to proceed. His heart pounded, the blood sang in his ears, but he felt like an untried youth about to bed his first woman and terrified of the outcome. He was so unnerved that when he poured himself a cup of wine, his hand trembled, dashing the cup against the table and spilling half the amber liquid. As he handed her the cup their fingers touched; without a word, Stephen took the cup out of her hand. In one fluid movement they came together.

Within moments their clothes lay heaped in the rushes, their naked bodies straining against each other, starved for one another's touch. Maud's lips were warm and yielding; the feel of her slender, taut body, the silky smoothness of her skin, and the firm peaks of her breasts crushed against him took Stephen's breath away. She was far more beautiful and exciting than in his wildest imaginings.

Unable to restrain himself a moment longer, Stephen lifted her in his arms and carried her over to the bed. His desire fueled to an unbearable pitch, he could not wait, but covered her body with his own. As he entered her she stiffened, as if in pain, and Stephen paused in surprise. By God's birth, she felt almost like a virgin! He proceeded more slowly, thrusting forward in sure, steady strokes until, like a delicate flower unfolding its petals, she opened to receive him.

This coupling had none of the gentleness of their first encounter. Stephen was too greedy, too hot to do anything but assuage the urgency of his own overpowering need. And hers, too, he soon discovered to his amazed delight. Maud blazed with passion, her body arching to meet his, matching his movements with a wild abandon that thrilled him. Together they merged, reaching a pinnacle of joy as one rapturous flesh.

After a time Stephen opened his eyes. He was lying on his side, Maud in his arms, his lips resting on her cheek, one hand curved around her breast. She seemed to be asleep. The arm on which she lay had gone numb but he was reluctant to shift it for fear of waking her. Closing his eyes again, he nestled his face against hers. A delicious contentment filled him, and he felt he could lie here, just as he was, for the rest of his life, no future to strive for, no past to regret. All that mattered was the wonder of this moment. He could give no name to what had happened to him, but never before in his life had he experienced anything remotely like it.

"Stephen."

Maud's voice, soft and languorous, penetrated his thoughts. Opening his eyes, he met her gaze. Her face was luminous, softer than he had ever seen it; a wondering smile played about her lips.

"Yes, ma belle?" he whispered against her mouth.

"I wanted to be sure you were real, not a dream."

"Real enough, I assure you." He laughed, hugging her to his chest.

She sighed luxuriously. "Even in my dreams I could not imagine such happiness." She lay quiet in his arms, running her fingers through the pelt of golden hair covering his chest.

"Nor I," Stephen said, burying his face in the soft valley between her breasts.

She stroked his head and asked, "Have we been here long?"

Time. He sighed. By God's birth, he had forgotten all about the time. They must be back at the same hour as Robin so that it would appear as if they had all gone hunting together. Springing out of bed, he ran to the door, opening it a crack. The clearing was deserted. Pushing the door open more widely, he looked up at the sun. Less than two hours to Vespers, he reckoned. Just barely time to dress and ride back to Windsor.

"We must leave, ma belle," Stephen said, searching in the rushes for his clothes. "We cannot arrive too long after Robin, so let us hurry."

Swinging her legs over the side of the bed, Maud stretched, throwing back her head and raising her arms over her head. She rose from the bed, yawning, and walked naked over to the cauldron of water. Taking a linen cloth from a pile on the floor, she dipped it in the water and began to wash herself, her movements neat and deft as a cat.

Stephen's eyes traveled upward from her arched white feet to the long legs and rounded thighs ending in the apex of the copper-colored triangle, the curve of hip that flowed into a narrow waist and strong rib cage that supported the swell of her generous breasts with their rosy pointed nipples. Then the white arc of her neck, the soft oval of her face framed by a waterfall of gleaming russet hair, the coral lips, slightly parted in a smile, and, finally, the wide gray eyes, radiating love, acknowledging his admiration with pride. She was so lovely that Stephen, stirred to his depths, felt an unbearable ache in his chest.

Maud finished her toilet, dressed quickly, coiled her hair around her ears, and followed Stephen out of the lodge. Outside she stood stock-still gazing in amazement at the scene before them.

"Surely this place was not so lovely when we arrived," she murmured. "Someone has cast a spell of enchantment over it."

Tiny white flowers dotted the mossy earth and tall trees raised green-budded branches toward a deep blue sky. The scent of new grass blew on the breeze, and the sound of birdsong filled the balmy air.

"Perhaps we view the world with new eyes," Stephen said.

Hands intertwined, Maud and Stephen followed the path through the woods. Just before they entered the meadow, Stephen stopped and took her in his arms. Looking down into her eyes, he found them misted with tears. He wiped the crystal drops away with a tender finger, his heart so full he felt it would overflow.

"Somehow we will find a way to be with each other," he whispered.

He bent to kiss her on her softly parted lips, the kiss becoming deeper and deeper until they reeled apart, unsteady on their feet, breathing heavily. As they walked out of the woods and into the sunlit meadow, what came to Stephen's mind were the words Maud had said to him in the chamber at Westminster three years ago: "You have lit a fire, Cousin, that will not be so easy to put out."

The words echoed disturbingly in his ears. Was he to be consumed by that same flame?

Chapter Twenty-seven

A YEAR PASSED AND MAUD WAS STILL IN ENGLAND. AS HER FATHER HAD predicted, Geoffrey of Anjou had reconsidered his hasty decision. He sent several long messages to the King in which he expressed regret for any offense he may have caused his wife or the House of Normandy and begged his father-in-law to send the Countess of Anjou back at once.

King Henry made excuses, promising to bring the matter up before his council, but Maud knew he dared not broach the subject for the barons still resented the marriage and were pleased at the estrangement. However, sooner or later, the King warned her, when the moment was ripe, then she must be prepared to go back to her husband. Meanwhile, Maud lived only for the moment: Her future was uncertain; the past had never existed. Stephen comprised her whole world.

On this eighteenth day of June, in the year 1130, Maud was waiting in her chamber at Westminster for Stephen to arrive to escort her to Winchester.

"The Count of Mortain awaits you in the courtyard with the horses." It was Aldyth's voice, tight with disapproval.

Maud stiffened as her nurse walked into the chamber. Sweet

Marie, not another tirade. She put a white coverchief on her head, threw a dark blue traveling cloak over her shoulders.

"I'm ready. Do you have the herbs?"

"Yes."

"May I please have them?"

"Even with the herbs there is still a risk. Only abstinence is sure."

"As you never tire of reminding me. There has been no difficulty thus far." Maud took several sealed paper cones from Aldyth's reluctant hands, placed them in an ivory box, then slipped the box carefully into a leather saddlebag already packed with clothes and other necessaries for the journey to Winchester.

"There's always a first time," Aldyth said. "You behave as if you are different from other women, proof against the consequences of your actions."

"Not that sermon again—I know what I'm doing."

Aldyth, a suspicion of tears glinting in her faded blue eyes, shook her head. "Do you? Adultery is a mortal sin, as you well know, and with your own cousin to boot! May God and the Holy Virgin forgive you. Should even a whisper of this scandal come to the notice of the King or the barons, your whole future is in jeopardy—"

"Yes, yes, yes. We have been through all this before. Stop worrying." Maud picked up the saddlebag and walked briskly to the door of her chamber.

There was a moment's strained silence. "When do you return?" Aldyth asked.

"Within a week or thereabouts."

"By the Rood, people will gossip if you are gone that long."

"What is there to gossip about?" With a hand on the door, Maud swallowed her ever-growing impatience and turned back to Aldyth. "How many times must I tell you? The King *asked* Stephen to escort me to Winchester to visit the treasury and the mint. It is two days' journey from Westminster, two days back again, and at least two or three days there. How could I be gone for less time?"

Aldyth sighed in resignation. "Always an answer for everything. Be sure to take the herbs regularly; remember the myrrh, rue, and tansy must be placed in a tub of hot water, and you must soak yourself immediately after—after—"

"I remember," Maud interjected. "I will see you in a week or so."

Disquieted by Aldyth's accusing countenance, Maud quickly opened the door, walked down the passage, and descended the winding staircase, hanging onto the thick rope that served as railing.

In the courtyard, Stephen waited on his Flanders mare, Audrade, accompanied by Gervase and several other squires, two members of the King's administrative staff returning to Winchester, grooms, servitors, and an armed guard. Maud greeted her cousin with cool courtesy, only letting her eyes convey her true feelings. A groom helped her mount her white palfrey, then Maud and Stephen led the way out of the courtyard followed by the others, the armed guard bringing up the rear. For a short while they rode along Watling Street, then turned southwest toward Winchester.

"We will find a way to be alone," Stephen said under his breath, as he moved his horse closer to hers. "Although at the moment I cannot tell how. We must see how matters fall out at Winchester." He gave her a conspiratorial smile.

She forced a smile in return, for despite her unfailing delight in Stephen's company, this morning Maud felt unsettled, a prey to guilt and anxiety, as was generally the case after one of her many quarrels with Aldyth.

It was impossible to explain the depth of her feelings to her Saxon foster mother, who saw life only in stark colors of white or black: This was right, that was wrong. I love Stephen, Maud asserted silently, defending herself to a phantom Aldyth, and I am not willing to give up what might be my only chance of happiness. At any moment I may be forced to return to Anjou or called upon to ascend the throne. The remainder of my life will be devoted only to the weal of the kingdom. But now I want to live as I choose. After all, since only Gervase and you know of our liaison, whom are we hurting?

And what of Holy Church, Aldyth would be sure to flash back, do you think nothing of putting your soul in peril? The strictures of Holy Church could always be circumvented, Maud thought with a cynical shrug, so long as one repented in good time. Or so the Emperor had believed.

Contrary to Aldyth's accusations, Maud had barely seen Stephen alone since their initial encounter last May. Due to lack of privacy, as well as their separate obligations, they had been together only four or five times in the past year, never for longer than two hours. Maud lived for these brief joyous encounters. Within moments of their being together time no longer existed, so completely did they create their own world.

Now Maud cast a sidelong glance at Stephen on his roan mare. A shudder of desire ran through her as her eye fell on his hands holding the reins. Large and strong, covered with fine golden hairs, she remembered the touch of those warm, sensitive fingers exploring her body with lingering caresses, arousing such exquisite sensations that she trembled in anticipation.

Maud knew she was helplessly in love, miserable when Stephen was out of her sight, ecstatic when she was with him.

They broke the journey at Guildford. Surrounded by their entire entourage it was impossible for them to be alone for even a moment and they spent the night in separate rooms. They arrived in Winchester the following day as the bells rang for Sext.

Maud looked with interest at this rapidly expanding city which afforded easy access to the coast and was close by the New Forest, which provided the best hunting in England. The town was so ancient that none knew its origins, but fable had it that Winchester had first been settled by the ancient Britons, then the Romans, before the Saxons arrived to make it the capital of West Saxony. Although London was now England's capital, Winchester housed the treasury and the mint, and was the seat of King Henry's administration. One day it would all be hers, she reminded herself.

They rode through the bustling town, past the white stone walls of the great cathedral, across Jewry Street where saffron-robed Semites did a thriving trade, until they came to the River Itchen. Across the narrow water lay Wolvesey Castle, headquarters of the Bishop of Winchester.

"Will your brother be here?" Maud asked.

"I hope not," Stephen replied in a low voice. "Henry has eyes in the back of his head. If we are not on constant guard, he will be sure to guess the truth."

"We must take great care that does not happen," Maud said. Aware of the great influence Henry exercised on his older brother, Maud refrained from telling Stephen she was always on guard in the Bishop of Winchester's presence.

As it turned out, the Bishop was absent, having left the day before for his See of Glastonbury.

"We are in luck," Stephen said, clearly relieved.

That night at the great hall, as they ate freshly caught bream from the river, Stephen said, "I have thought of a plan that will enable us to spend a day or so alone."

"A whole day? How wondrous! Where? How will you manage—" Maud began, unable to conceal her excitement.

"Trust me," Stephen said with a wink. "When the arrangements are complete I will tell you."

For the next two days Maud familiarized herself with the intricacies of the exchequer, and studied firsthand the workings of her father's administration. She attended Mass in the great cathedral, and acquainted herself with the foremost merchants of the town, all the while asking questions and seeking information.

"I'm impressed with the astuteness of your questions, Cousin," Stephen told her as they walked along Jewry Street. "It's rare for a woman to be so knowledgeable in matters of finance and trade."

Maud smiled with pleasure at his praise. "I have the Emperor to thank for that, as well as the many discussions I've had with my father. When I come to the throne I intend to be thoroughly familiar with all aspects of the kingdom. What did the great Alfred say? 'Unlettered king, crowned ass.' "

To her surprise Stephen's face closed in on itself, as if a shutter had been drawn.

"Is something amiss?" she asked.

"What could be amiss?" After a moment his face resumed its usual open expression and she began to wonder if she had imagined the sudden chill.

Looking about to ensure no one was within earshot, Stephen whispered: "The plans are made. I will leave Winchester well before Prime tomorrow with all our retinue and propose a day's hunting at the King's lodge in the New Forest. You must say that you feel unwell, and have decided to remain here for a day or so. Leave the rest to me."

Her heart beating quickly, Maud nodded. "You will come back for me, then?"

"Gervase will return for you and escort you to where I intend to be."

Matters fell out as Stephen arranged, and by late morning the following day, Maud and Gervase rode out the gates of Winchester in the direction of the New Forest, six leagues distant. On the way Gervase explained that while the rest of their party were quartered at the King's hunting lodge deep in the forest, she would be staying at a gamekeeper's cot, located at the edge of the woods.

"They think my lord has returned to Winchester, and will not expect either of you until we join up tomorrow."

"It sounds well in hand," Maud said, uncomfortable at discussing the details with a squire. It was frightening to think that her entire reputation depended upon Gervase's discretion.

It was dusk by the time they reached the isolated cot that stood beside a narrow, rushing stream backed by green woods.

As Maud dismounted, Stephen opened the door, greeting her with a joyous smile. Gervase tethered her horse and brought the saddle-bags inside.

"I will be back for you by mid-afternoon tomorrow, my lord," the squire said, then left them and rode off into the night.

"At last!" Stephen said, taking her hand to lead her inside.

A fire burned in the hearth, an iron kettle bubbled on a blackened trivet, fresh green rushes covered the floor, and several candles set in iron holders cast a welcoming light over the wooden bed and oak chest. A small table was set with wooden bowls, cups, and a tankard of mead. A white cloth half covered a cold roast fowl, round white cheese, and a loaf of dark wheaten bread.

"Are you hungry?" Stephen asked.

"Famished. It's a long journey from Winchester."

"You must wait, I fear," he said with a wicked smile, as he picked her up in his arms and carried her to the bed. "Other hungers must be satisfied first."

He kissed her with warm, lingering lips and Maud instantly responded to his touch. They made love several times during the night, until, satiated, they fell asleep in each other's arms. When they woke to the sound of birdsong outside, Maud and Stephen broke their fast, devouring half of the fowl and most of the bread and cheese. Holding hands, they ventured outside into the warm morning air, radiant with sunshine, and decided to bathe in the rushing stream, alive with darting silver fish, the banks abounding in dark green lady ferns and pale ivory waterlilies.

"It's like ice," she gasped, dipping a foot into the water and hastily withdrawing it.

"It will take only a moment to get used to the cold." Stephen waded in, the water swirling about his knees. He held out his hand. "Bracing!"

As Maud hesitated, he grabbed her foot and pulled her into the water. Gasping at the sudden shock, she righted herself, then threw water in Stephen's face. He ducked her in turn and they began to play and splash and shout like truant children.

"You look like one of those fishtail maids out of the old legends," Stephen teased, his eyes on her breasts bobbing like round fish through the floating curtain of russet hair. "But you do not feel like one." He reached between her thighs.

Maud jumped back, and climbed onto the bank. Stephen followed, grabbing at her wet body, but she twisted away, lithe and slippery as an eel. Finally he wrested her down to the soft earth of the stream bank. Laughing, their bodies streaked with mud, they lay still, catching their breath.

After a moment Stephen rolled over on his back and pulled Maud on top of him so that her breasts rested against his face. Nuzzling between them, he playfully kissed each full globe in turn, then each rosy nipple. A spasm of desire swept over Maud, and she reached down to seek Stephen's manhood, wet and flaccid from the cold stream.

"How forward, Madam," Stephen murmured. "Have you no shame?" His eyes closed as she began to stroke him with loving fingers. "Hmm, do not stop, sweet Jesu, but you are as artful as any strumpet in Southwark. Where did you learn such witchery?"

"From you, my lord," Maud whispered.

Intoxicated by the effect she was creating, Maud continued with her caresses until Stephen began to buck and groan beneath her.

"Hurry, hurry," he gasped, "else I cannot wait for you."

Her own desire having kept pace with his, Maud quickly guided him inside her.

"Dear God, if ever a sheath was forged to fit my sword," Stephen whispered, as they lay still for a moment, savoring anew the exquisite molding of flesh matched to flesh.

Then, almost with reluctance, they began to move slowly in unison, almost as a single body. For as long as possible they tried to postpone the moment of release, but, overcome by ecstasy, they reached fulfillment together, lying on a bed of reeds, their bodies slick with rivulets of water, the sound of the bubbling stream like a choir in their ears.

The rest of the day they spent inside the cot, continuing their exploration of each other. Maud delighted in adventuring with Stephen down any path he led, matching herself against him with the fierce intensity of her own ardor. They constantly astonished themselves by the willingness with which each opened to the other. It was a voyage of discovery for Maud as she found within herself a capacity for giving and receiving love she had not known existed.

"How is it possible that Geoffrey was impotent with you," Stephen remarked lazily as they lay naked on the bed together, "when I am in a constant state of desire? And the more I have of you the more I want."

"He was very young, and much of what went wrong was my own ignorance, I see now," Maud explained. Determined to hold nothing back, she told Stephen the distasteful details of her marriage.

Stephen made a wry face. "Although Geoffrey is hardly a rival, I still cannot bear to think of you in his arms, or in anyone else's for that matter—"

Maud put a loving finger against his lips. He had broken a tacit agreement between them: The future was never to be discussed, neither Geoffrey nor Matilda ever mentioned unless absolutely necessary. Their mutual time was limited and precious, neither knowing if this day might not be their last alone together.

But today Stephen could not seem to stay away from the subject. "Does the King speak of your return to Anjou?" he asked, playing with the gleaming strands of hair that fell over her breasts.

"He speaks of it, of course, but has fixed no time for my return. He prefers to wait until his council agrees to let me go back. At the same time he fobs Geoffrey off with lies and excuses." As it coincided with her own intentions, Maud was able to smile at her father's duplicity. "One day, I know, he must act, but, Sweet Marie, may that day be far into the future."

"Indeed," said Stephen, his fingers trailing idly across the slope of her breasts, circling their rosy peaks.

"Meanwhile," Maud continued with a luxuriant sigh, as a delicious languor consumed her limbs, "in addition to the vast education you are giving me, I'm learning more and more about the realm. When the time comes I shall know how to rule exactly as my father would have wished—with one or two changes, of course. But then every new broom must sweep something away."

The hand cupping her breast was suddenly still. "Being queen—this means much to you?"

She turned her head to look at him in astonishment, then raised herself up on one elbow. "Why, it means everything to me. After all, what happiness I have now will vanish when I return to Anjou. Being queen is my life's work, something that will compensate for being tied to Geoffrey until death do us part." A slight frown creased her brow. "I sometimes forget—the crown must have meant a great deal to you as well, so you, of all people, should understand."

"And I do. Of course, I'm reconciled to the loss of the throne now." Stephen paused. "I wonder, sometimes, what our lives would have been like if we had been able to marry. Do you ever dwell on such matters?"

Maud reached over to touch his face with a tender finger. "Of course. But not often. It's far too painful, dwelling on what I can never have. No purpose is served. These stolen moments are all we will ever have together and I must live out the rest of my life on their memory."

Stephen also propped himself up on one elbow. "How like your father you are sometimes, concerned only with what is real and practical. But then that is the Norman way of things."

"You make it sound as if you're different. Are you not also Norman then?" she asked with a smile.

"Part of me, yes. But I'm also my father's son, and the Count of Blois was everything the Normans are not: a dreamer—a coward, too —but a gentle, kindly man for all that, who wished only to live out his days in peace and tranquility. I have always been ashamed of him." His eyes stared, unseeing, into the distance. "God rest the poor man's soul, he was entirely unsuited to the life my mother forced him to lead."

"But you're not like him, Stephen. How can you compare yourself to such a man?"

"How do you know what I'm really like? How can one ever probe the depths of another's soul?" He was more serious than she had ever seen him, his green eyes intent on hers. "A wise man trusts no one."

"But you have opened your heart to me, as I have opened mine to you. Surely we can trust each other," Maud protested, puzzled at the slightly sinister turn the conversation had taken.

Stephen was silent for a moment, staring at her as if she were a stranger. Then his face cleared. "Of course we can," he said lightly, becoming in the instant his old charming self. "Pay no attention to my meanderings." He bent to brush her lips with his. "Did I tell you what the barons have recently said about you?" he began, abruptly changing the subject.

"No. What do they say?"

"That you've become gentler, more womanly, more approachable. The wild virago has been tamed, they say." His finger slid down her belly and twined themselves in the copper-colored curls covering her sex.

"Wild virago!" she cried. "Tamed! I suppose you're vain enough to think you are the cause of this so-called taming."

He gave her a wolfish grin. "It had crossed my mind."

"Well, you peacock, I'm not tamed, no, nor shall I ever be." She stayed his hand. "Do not think to sway me in this fashion."

"We both know I can." He threw himself upon her and began to kiss her with insistent lips until she lay limp and breathless. "Admit that with me you are as helpless as a haystack in a high wind."

"I admit nothing. My Lord, you are insatiable," she murmured against his warm mouth, "randy as a he-goat."

"As to which of us is the more insatiable, let us not put it to the test," he breathed, his lips trailing down the valley of her breasts, his fingers playing her body like a master troubadour playing his viol, knowing exactly what string to pluck to evoke the most stirring sounds.

His lips scorched a path down her belly and beyond, to explore the warmth of her sex, fueling the fire within her until she almost screamed to have it quenched. She arched back in ecstatic abandon, and in one quick movement he was deep inside her, filling her with intense rapture.

When Maud finally opened her eyes, she felt she could not move so much as a muscle. A deep contentment welled up within her, and she thought she would overflow with love. Stephen stretched and reluctantly left the bed to peer outside.

"It grows late. Gervase will be here at any moment. We must dress," he said.

"I'm so sore I doubt if I can ride back to London," she complained, watching him pull on his underdrawers and hose.

"Indeed? Perhaps it is like the cure for a night's carousing: A hair of the dog that bit you is a wondrous remedy." He walked slowly toward the bed.

"No," she cried, quickly jumping up. "I have had sufficient of your cures—for the moment. Sweet Marie, do you never get enough?"

"Of you? Impossible." He began to imitate the strut of a preening peacock. "In truth, Madam, I confess I have not hit my full stride. This was merely an interlude while I warmed to the task. Had we time enough I would prove it to you." He rolled his eyes as he pulled on his tunic, buckled his belt, and knelt to slip on his boots.

Maud laughed until the tears rolled down her cheeks. "Peacock, indeed! Do you know we have not had our clothes on since yesterday? I barely recognize you." She looked around the room, suddenly aware that there was no tub for her to bathe in. "Is there a wooden tub about?" she asked.

"I have not seen one," he said. "But the water is hot." He pointed to the large kettle that stood on the trivet near the fire. "Will that do?"

She nodded, aware now that she had also forgotten to take the herbs yesterday. Well, there was still time, she reasoned. The kettle was not big enough to sit in, but once she dissolved the herbs in water, she could wash herself off at least. That would have to do.

Outside there was the sound of a horse approaching. Stephen grimaced, ran to the door, and poked his head out.

"Give us a moment," he called, closing the door. "It's Gervase," he told Maud, walking over to her and clasping her in his arms. "Dearest, dearest Maud, what joy you have given me."

She threw her arms around him and tenderly covered his face with kisses. "Sweet love, I cannot let you go."

He laughed, fending her off as he searched for his mantle in the rushes. "Hurry. We are to join up with the others where the road to London forks outside the New Forest, and we must arrive first so it will appear we came from Winchester."

"When will I see you alone again?" She followed him to the door.

"Really, Madam, and you call me insatiable? Soon, I promise you. I had best wait outside lest I be attacked again." Laughing, he slipped out the door.

She emptied half the box of herbs into the kettle, and, singing softly, began to bathe. Totally fulfilled, at peace with herself and the world, Maud felt happier than ever before in her life.

Chapter Twenty-eight

Normandy, 1130

IN EARLY JULY, THREE WEEKS AFTER MAUD AND STEPHEN'S INTERLUDE outside Winchester, the court moved to Normandy where it became almost impossible for them to see each other alone. Much of the time Stephen was gone on the King's business or seeing to his estates at Mortain. Thus he was away when Maud realized that her monthly flux was overdue.

At first she thought she was just late, even though she was as regular in her courses as the bells tolling the eight services of the canonical offices. After nine days had passed, Maud knew she could no longer put off confronting the horrifying possibility that she might be with child.

"What shall I do?" she asked Aldyth, one morning while they were alone in her chamber at the ducal palace in Rouen. She dreaded the reproach she felt sure would be forthcoming.

The Saxon nurse looked at Maud as one who, expecting the worst, is vindicated when it occurs. "When were your courses due exactly?" she asked in a calm voice.

"Eight or nine days ago."

"Let me see now, that would be a fortnight after you returned from Winchester in mid-June. Did you follow my instructions with the herbs?"

Maud thought for a moment. "More or less. I could not follow them exactly. There was no tub to soak in and I did not remember to take the herbs after the first time—that is to say, I only took them later—" She let her words trail off, suddenly sick with fear.

"Very well, let us assume the worst and see about getting rid of the difficulty. A ride in a jolting cart or running up and down stairs is said to be most effective. Wild thyme, I have heard, often works with dispatch, as well as yellow dock or horseradish—why do you look like that?"

Maud had walked to the window slit to look down upon the court-yard where Queen Alix enjoyed the morning air with her women.

"The thought of—I cannot bear to think of getting rid of the babe," she replied with her back to Aldyth.

"Naturally, for it is against Holy Writ." Aldyth signed herself. "But it's a bit late to be concerned about the wages of sin, if I may say so," she added sharply. "Did I not warn you what to expect? 'As you sow thus shall you reap.' But all that is neither here nor there now. You have no other choice but to be rid of this unwanted seed."

"Unwanted? For years everyone thought I was barren, including myself." She turned from the window. "Suppose I were to have the babe?"

Aldyth looked at her in horror. "Have the—are you out of your wits, child? Consider the consequences! Should anyone suspect you carry a bastard seed, your hopes for the crown are gone and your reputation ruined beyond repair. Geoffrey of Anjou would be well within his rights to cast you aside, force you into a convent, or"—her voice dropped to a whisper—"even worse."

"Worse?"

"If a husband learns that his wife is to bear another man's child, who can say to what lengths he may be driven? And what do you think King Henry would do to one who brought such dishonor upon the House of Normandy? Not to mention Holy Church! Branded with the stain of adultery—"

"Stop! Stop! You have made your point. I agree we must terminate this—encumbrance."

But later, as Maud walked down the staircase to the great hall, she was still in turmoil, still undecided. Ridding oneself of an unwanted child certainly occurred, despite the strictures of Holy Church.

Women—especially midwives—often came to the aid of erring females who had nowhere else to turn. In theory Maud did not disagree
with such a practice. The sensible thing to do, of course, was abort
the babe, yet Maud shrank from the thought of destroying this evidence of Stephen's love. How she wished he were here so that she
might discuss the matter with him.

It was too early for the noon meal and the great hall was half
empty but for the servants laying the trestle tables, a few barons
gossiping in one corner, and the steward going over his accounts. On
a raised dais at the far end of the hall stood the ancient seat of the
Dukes of Normandy. Maud walked to the dais and reached up to
touch the carved wooden back of the ducal chair. Richard the Fearless,
Duke Robert the Magnificent, Duke William Bastard—all her illustrious forebears had sat in this chair since time out of mind. One day,
as Duchess of Normandy, she expected to sit here as well, and her
son and grandson after her.

Her son. She touched her belly with hesitant fingers. Could she
really bring herself to abort Stephen's child? Probably all she would
ever have of him for her very own, the only tangible fruit of their
all-consuming passion for each other. To destroy this tiny spark of
life was to destroy the very essence of their love.

The steward blew his horn and the hall began to fill with the King's
mesnie and guests. Waleran of Muelan entered with his wife, whose
face bore a dark bruise on her left cheekbone. One eye was half closed,
she was pale as death, and in obvious distress. No one made mention
of her unsightly condition for it was common knowledge that Waleran abused his wife if she earned his displeasure, and none wished
to interfere in a husband's conjugal rights.

Briefly, Maud forgot her own troubles as she spared the Countess
of Muelan a sympathetic glance, and sent Waleran a hostile glare.
The man was an animal, not fit for human company, yet he was
entitled to do just as he pleased with his wife. As was Geoffrey of
Anjou. During the remainder of the meal, Maud barely listened to
the conversation at the table, totally preoccupied with the dire consequences of her condition and unable to decide which course to
follow.

"Wool-gathering, Cousin?"

Maud looked up to find Stephen smiling down at her.

"I thought you still in Mortain," she said, a wave of joy flooding
through her as she made a place for him.

"I have just this moment returned. All is well with you?"

"I've missed you," Maud said under her breath, avoiding his question. She toyed with a piece of guinea fowl on her trencher.

"If you could manage to be in your chamber directly after the meal, I would speak with you," Stephen whispered. "Only for a moment, so there is no danger I will compromise you."

"I will be there."

Directly the meal was over Maud went to her chamber.

"I expect Count Stephen," she told Aldyth, with a covert glance at her women. "Can you take my ladies outside for a moment?"

"You will see him alone in your chamber?" Aldyth's face was aghast.

"For a moment only. I will leave the door open for propriety's sake."

"Does—he know yet?" Aldyth asked.

"I intend to tell him now."

Aldyth's anxious eyes met hers. "Listen to me, I beg you say nothing. Not to him, not to anyone." She then left the chamber followed by the attendant ladies.

There was a note of urgency in Aldyth's voice that disturbed her, despite Maud's knowledge that the Saxon nurse had taken an unreasoning dislike to Stephen from the very beginning.

Her cousin appeared a few moments later. "I am off for a day's hunting with Robin and Waleran, so there is not much time," he said rapidly. "I've found a place for us, just outside the city gates, the home of a wealthy farmer who travels to Paris sometime tomorrow with all his family. The twins and I will spend the night outside Rouen so I must meet you the day after, about noon. Go to the marketplace—"

"There will be talk if I go alone."

"Then take Aldyth with you. Linger at the silk stall. Gervase will meet you there and bring you to me."

Stephen cast a quick look at the empty passage, then pulled her into his arms. "It's been too long, and I'm on fire." He kissed her hungrily. "Can you arrange it?" he asked against her lips.

"Yes," Maud said, her eyes darting continually to the open door. Her heart began to beat heavily, her throat was so dry she could hardly speak. "Stephen—there is another matter—something I must—" She stopped.

"Yes, my love, must what?" he prompted.

Maud looked deeply into his green eyes, misty with desire. She opened her lips, but the words would not come. Her gaze suddenly dropped, and she moved back from the protective circle of his arms. She never knew what strength of will prevented her from blurting out to Stephen that she carried his child. With every fiber of her being she longed to tell him, but some primeval instinct for survival bade her hold back. A totally wild thought had entered her mind: She must protect the babe at all costs. Even from the one person she loved most in all the world.

"This is very dangerous—you had best go," she stammered finally, as he reached for her again.

Reluctantly, he stepped back with a nod. Then his eyes narrowed and he cocked his head to one side. "I have the feeling you did not tell me what you had intended. Is something amiss, dear love?"

Maud forced a smile as an inspired thought occurred to her. "A female ailment. I am just at the end of my monthly flux, you understand how we women are at such times. I should be quite recovered when next we meet."

Stephen's face cleared. "My sympathies. You must try my wondrous remedy for ailing females, which I will be most happy to show you the day after tomorrow." With a suggestive wink he whipped off his scarlet cap, made her an elaborate bow, then started for the door.

"Stephen!" Maud cried, running after him.

"Yes?"

"I love you," she whispered, clinging to him as if her life depended upon it. "Whatever happens, you must always remember that. Promise me you will never doubt it."

Stephen's face radiated tenderness, and Maud felt her heart dissolve in anguish. "Never. How strange you are today." He gave her fingers a gentle squeeze, walked out the door, and disappeared down the passage.

Holding a hand over her mouth to keep from screaming aloud, Maud ran to the window slit. In the courtyard below, the de Beaumont twins waited on their horses, surrounded by huntsmen and grooms. After a few moments Stephen appeared. Stephen, her heart cried, Stephen, my love. As Maud watched, he mounted his mare and followed the twins out of the courtyard. There was something familiar about his retreating head, and suddenly she remembered that the first time she had seen him as a young boy, passing her on his way to Windsor, he had worn a scarlet cap set at the same jaunty angle.

Tears coursed down her cheeks, her body ached with the pain of her devastating loss. But she had made up her mind: She intended to go back to Anjou and have Stephen's child.

. . .

After a sleepless night, Maud decided on how she might best accomplish her return to Geoffrey. Directly the morning Mass was over, she broke her fast in the great hall, then sought an interview with her father. She found him in his council chamber, crouched, as usual, over a charcoal brazier despite the warmth of the July morning. The Bishop of Salisbury sat across from him, his head nodding. Two old men, she thought, not long for this world, who, between them, held sway over the entire Norman realm. Maud had never liked Bishop Roger, whose loyalty, she felt, could be bought by the highest bidder. Well aware that he had never approved of her as the King's heir, or the Angevin marriage, she was determined he should not be privy to her decision.

"May I see you alone, Sire?" she asked.

The King frowned. "Why? Roger is in our confidence, as you know."

"I do know, Sire. But I would prefer to see you alone, nonetheless. It is of the utmost importance."

He gave a testy sigh. "If you insist. Attend me later, Roger," he told the Bishop, who rose heavily from his chair, and, giving Maud a baleful look, limped out of the chamber.

"Well, Daughter?"

Maud could think of no graceful way to break the news. Better to take the plunge and have the matter over and done with at once.

"I have decided to return to Anjou," she blurted out.

"Return to Anjou? To Geoffrey?" King Henry looked as if she had gone mad. "Surely I did not hear you aright!"

"I feel—yes, I feel that I've been very remiss in my duty—as you pointed out to me when I left my husband." Blessed Lady, how she hated to humble herself before him, Maud thought, writhing inside. She forced herself to continue before she lost courage. "You were right—as usual, Sire. It's time I rectified the matter by returning to him at once."

The King's jaw dropped. "But not a fortnight since, when I informed you I had received yet another message from the Count, as well as Fulk in Jerusalem, *and* the Holy Father in Rome, all begging me to send you back to Anjou, you were adamant. 'I pray for a miracle that I may never have to return' were your very words!" He thrust his jaw forward. "By God's death, I don't understand!"

His reaction was entirely predictable, and Maud did not know how to counter it. Her sudden turnabout *was* incomprehensible.

"Yes, Sire," she stammered, "I realize how it must seem to you, but I have thought deeply on the matter these last two weeks, consulting my confessor and examining my own conscience. God can only look upon me as a faithless wife, and I feel it's time to make amends. Please, Sire, let me go back to Anjou at once."

"Faithless wife? Faithless wife?" He pounced on the words with alacrity. "What do you mean, pray?"

Holy Mother, what had made her choose those words! "I only meant that I should have never left Anjou at all. My place is with my husband."

"Did I not tell you that when you first fled to Normandy? Did I not beseech you to return? God spare me from the vagaries of womankind," the King grumbled. "If this is an example of how you will govern my realm—" He threw up his hands. "Well, your sudden zeal to remedy the marriage is commendable but it won't be possible to send you back to Anjou immediately."

"Why not?" The blood froze in her veins.

"My council now insists they must approve your return to Count Geoffrey, you know that, and they would be quite satisfied never to have an Angevin king." He shrugged. "It will take time to convince them otherwise. Give me another two or three months, and I will have persuaded them. After all, there is no vital need to rush back to Anjou. Why such haste?"

"I feel the need to make amends at once," she cried, frantic.

Henry raised his brows. "What difference will a few months make?"

"It will be too late," she almost screamed.

"Too late for what?" he shot back.

Speechless, numb with terror, Maud stared at him, her face like death, her eyes glazed with unshed tears. She felt like a vixen she had once seen caught in a gamekeeper's trap in the forest. The more the fox struggled to be free, the more securely did the trap tighten its hold.

"You behave as one demented. I don't for the life of me understand this wild urgency—" The King stopped abruptly.

Rising slowly to his feet, his brows met across his forehead; his eyes darkened with menace as he held her gaze for a long moment. He raised one arm in a gesture so threatening that Maud shrank back in terror.

"Have you shamed our house?" he croaked, looking like a black raven about to strike. "By God's splendor, Madam, have you dared to shame our house?"

"No, Sire," she cried, signing herself. "I have not! I swear it."

Her father's face expressed rage and disbelief. His fingers reached for the pommel of his sword as he took a step forward. For the barest instant, Maud saw murder in his eyes. Then, putting himself under restraint, he stepped back, passed a shaking hand over his eyes, and sat down again. Reaching for the tankard of mulled wine on the table, he downed its contents in a single gulp.

"I swear it, Sire," she repeated. "I have brought no shame on our house."

The King made no response, his eyes unreadable. There was nothing for it, she thought in despair; she would have to tell him the complete truth. "Sire—let me explain—"

Before Maud could get the words out the King virtually leapt to his feet—she was amazed he could still move so quickly—and held up both his hands to silence her.

"I don't wish to hear any more. There's nothing to explain," he said with grim finality. "You have seen the error of your ways and duty compels you to return to your husband. That is sufficient." He paused, breathing heavily. "Under the circumstances I see no need for delay. By tomorrow morning you must be ready to leave."

Maud's heart pounded in relief. Thank you, Holy Mother, she prayed, thank you. He is going to let me go.

"You will set out well before Prime, and tell no one of your plans." King Henry gave her a sharp look. "No one."

She felt herself flush. "But the council—"

"Leave the council to me." Holding her arm he walked her to the door. "Take only what you need. The rest can be sent later. Aldyth, of course, must go with you, a few of your most trusted women, and an escort. I will send a messenger to Angers at once so Geoffrey will expect your arrival. Everything must appear—natural and in order." He paused before the oak door of the chamber. "You have thought this matter through, Daughter? It will not be easy to manage and there must be no—mistakes."

"I know," she said, her voice steady. "I'm prepared."

Their eyes met. King Henry thoughtfully stroked his stubbled chin, then opened the oak door. "Well, well, sometimes God works in mysterious ways. We are all in His hand, after all."

. . .

Less than twenty-four hours later, Maud stood shivering in the cold, gray dawn. A heavy mist shrouded the nearly deserted courtyard, almost obscuring the loaded sumpter horses, the armed escort, and the waiting litters carrying Aldyth and three of her women. Beside her, a white palfrey stood saddled, ready to be mounted. In front of her was a man-at-arms dressed in ducal livery.

Maud looked cautiously around, ensuring no one observed her actions, grateful for the swirling channel fog that made visibility difficult.

"You will go to the silk stall in the marketplace just after Sext," she told the man-at-arms, "and give this message into the hands of Gervase, the Count of Mortain's squire. No one else." She handed him a rolled parchment sealed with red wax. "You understand? No one else but Gervase."

The man-at-arms thrust the parchment inside his hauberk. "Yes, my lady. No one but Gervase. I understand the instructions."

Maud pressed some coins into his hand, then stepped back and watched until he disappeared from sight into the mist. How she had agonized over whether or not to send Stephen a message. Her heart was filled with pain at having to leave him so abruptly, yet she must be very careful now, avoiding any shadow of suspicion that might reach Geoffrey's ears. But she could not bring herself to leave him without an explanation. Nothing could prepare him for the shock of her sudden departure, but the message, at least, explained matters so that he would understand.

The King had suddenly ordered her back to Anjou, she had written, without the knowledge of his council, whom he hoped to convince of the wisdom of his decision after she had already gone. There had been no choice, she emphasized, and her father had demanded absolute secrecy. She begged her cousin never to forget her last words to him.

Should anyone else read the message, Maud reasoned, she would not be compromised, yet Stephen would understand.

Grief-stricken, her heart like a stone in her breast, Maud allowed the groom to help her mount her horse.

"Wait!"

She looked up, startled, to see her father emerge from the mist only a few feet away, having been hidden from view by the fog and sumpter horses. How long had he been standing there, she wondered uneasily, hoping he had not seen her exchange with the man-at-arms.

"I didn't expect to see you, Sire," she said, having already said her farewell to him last night.

"I daresay you didn't," he replied with an enigmatic smile. "But it's most fortunate I'm here. Far too hazardous to ride this mare. Anjou is a six-day journey away. The beast could cast a shoe, something might startle her, causing an accident. Anything is possible." He helped Maud dismount and led her to the litter. "You must take better care of her," he admonished Aldyth, who, speechless for once, nodded her agreement.

"You will keep me informed of how . . . matters progress," the King said to Maud, lifting her gently into the litter.

Deeply moved, Maud impulsively pulled the King's head down, kissing his bristly cheek. "Thank you, Father," she whispered in his ear, amazed at her own audacity. She had never made such a gesture to him in her life, nor ever, not even as a child, called him anything but "Sire."

"Well, well," he said in a gruff voice, "there's no need for such an unseemly display." He stepped back from the litter. "Do not concern yourself with anything except reestablishing relations with your husband. The future of our realm depends on it. I will tend to matters here. A safe journey, Maud."

King Henry watched until the procession had disappeared from the courtyard, then strolled back into the ducal palace. Entering the great hall, he stepped carefully over the rows of sleeping bodies until he found the marshal on his straw pallet before the fire. He prodded the man with the toe of his black boot.

The marshal rolled over, looked up into the King's face, then hastily jumped to his feet, rubbing the sleep from his eyes. "Sire?"

"There was a man-at-arms in the courtyard a few moments ago, tall, stoutly built, dark hair, dressed in ducal livery. Find him for me."

The marshal, who was responsible for the men-at-arms, bowed and left the hall, soon returning with the man in question.

"You sent for me, Sire?"

"What is your name?"

"Jean de Guiot, Sire."

"You were given something by the Countess of Anjou?"

The man paled. "Yes, Sire. A roll of parchment."

"Who was the message for?"

Beads of sweat appeared on the man's upper lip. "I don't know for certain. It was to be given to the Count of Mortain's squire, Gervase," he stammered.

"Where?"

"In the marketplace at noon. I was only doing the Countess of Anjou's bidding, Sire," he whined.

"Of course you were." The King pursed his lips. "There is nothing to fear." He held out his hand.

The man reached quickly beneath his hauberk, withdrew the rolled parchment and handed it to the King.

"Speak of this to no one. You may return to your duties."

When he had left the hall, the King called for the marshal. "Send Jean de Guiot out of Rouen at once. Let him see active service on the Vexin border. Put him in the midst of the heaviest skirmishes. Do not let him return in a hurry—if he returns at all."

"I understand, Sire." The marshal withdrew.

The King looked at the crisp parchment and tapped it against his open palm. He started to crack the red seal, then thought better of it. Hesitating for a moment, he held the message over the dying embers, then threw the parchment into the fire, and watched while it vanished in a sudden burst of flame.

Through the rapidly thinning mist, the small procession of horses and litters moved out of the city gates of Rouen to start the long journey to Anjou. Maud did not look back. She spared an anxious thought for the man who would deliver her letter to Stephen, trying to envision her cousin's reaction, anticipating his sense of loss, already sharing his pain. With a sigh she settled back into the litter, realizing she had done all she could; the rest was out of her hands. Forcing the thought of Stephen from her mind, she turned her attention to the vital matter that lay before her, the matter upon which her very survival depended: how to convince the cold and impotent youth she had married that she carried his child.

Chapter Twenty-nine

STEPHEN WAVED FAREWELL TO THE DE BEAUMONT TWINS ON THE EDGE of Lyons-la-Forêt, favorite hunting ground of the Dukes of Normandy, and headed toward Rouen. The air was cool, the sky overcast by a gray channel fog. A perfect day for hunting. Early this morning, after a long and exhausting chase, Stephen had bagged a red buck whose spread of antlers counted ten branches. It had been an exciting chase, one he would long remember, he thought with satisfaction.

As he approached the city the bells began to toll for Sext. Noon already. He must hurry or he would be late. Spurring his horse, he turned left just before the iron gates of Rouen, and rode down a narrow country lane, overgrown with grass, and bordered by hedgerows. There was the sweet scent of apple blossom on the damp wind, and within a few moments Stephen came upon a small wooden house backed by a huge apple orchard.

With the exception of several serfs working in a far corner of the orchard, the place looked deserted. Dismounting, Stephen tied his mare to a gnarled apple tree, and went inside the house. The large room was simply furnished with rough-hewn furniture made of stout oak. On a table stood a pitcher of mead and two wooden cups. In the bedchamber, a wide oak bed spread with a coarse red wool blanket looked inviting.

Tired from the morning's exertions, Stephen lay down, smiling to himself as he stretched his arms above his head. Any moment now he would hear the sound of hooves outside and soon Maud would be lying in his arms. By God's birth, it had been a month since he had seen her alone—except for the few moments day before yesterday—and he was in a fever of impatience.

Yawning, his lids closed, Stephen lost himself in a dream of Maud so sensual that his manhood throbbing painfully against his drawers brought him suddenly awake.

Jesu, he had been so lost in his dream he had lost track of the time. Surely Maud and Gervase should have been here by now. He got up, walked through the house and out the door. Except for his mare, the lane was deserted. Sitting on the stump of an apple tree, Stephen wondered what could have happened. A host of possibilities paraded across his mind: Maud had had an accident on her horse, or been summoned by her father; someone had seen her in the marketplace and she had been forced to avoid meeting Gervase. All highly un-likely, but his thoughts kept turning round and round like a dog chasing its own tail.

From the great cathedral in Rouen square, Stephen heard the bells ring for Nones. Almost three hours since he arrived. There was no question now; something must have happened. He got to his feet just as Gervase galloped down the lane toward the house. Alone.

At his squire's grave expression, Stephen felt the blood drain from his face and a portent of disaster swept through him. "Where is she?" he shouted, rising to his feet. "What has happened to the Countess of Anjou?"

Gervase hastily dismounted. "Gone, my lord."

"Gone?" It was the last thing he had thought to hear, and Stephen could not take it in. "Gone? Gone where?"

"Anjou."

"Anjou!" Stunned, Stephen found himself unable to move; his heart seemed to shrivel within his breast; his legs became like stone. Abruptly he sat down again on the tree trunk. "Gone to Anjou?" he repeated dully. "You had best tell me what happened."

"The Countess of Anjou was not in the marketplace at Sext," Gervase began, "nor was Aldyth or any of her women with a message for me. After an hour's wait, I rode to the ducal palace and made inquiries. It did not take me long to discover that a party—three sumpter horses, two litters, and an armed guard—had left in great haste before Prime this morning, headed, in the opinion of one of the grooms, for Anjou. He says the King was observed up and about the courtyard at that time, but thus far there has been no official announcement concerning the Countess' departure. It appears that the matter is being kept secret."

Stephen stared at Gervase in stupefaction. Maud returned to Anjou? Without telling him? He refused to believe it.

"Did you inquire if there was any message left for me?"

"Oh, indeed, my lord. I did so immediately, that is what took me so long. I could find no one who had received a message for you."

Stephen sprang to his feet. "Impossible! If my cousin did return to Anjou she would have left word with someone!"

Gervase shook his head. "No message was left."

Seizing Gervase by the front of his jerkin, Stephen began to shake him. "You lie," he shouted, his face crimson. "I tell you Maud would never abandon me like this! Without a word! Never!"

"My lord, my lord, you're hurting me—please—" Gervase gasped.

Stephen released him so quickly the squire fell to the ground. Without another word, he strode into the house, poured himself a cup of mead, and downed it. Then another and another until he had emptied the pitcher. How could she do it, he moaned inwardly, how could she leave without a word? Had she never loved him? Had she merely used him, a stud stallion servicing a mare, to satisfy her own lusts? Could he have misjudged her so? Impossible. If she had been forced by her father to return—which was the only sound explanation—surely she would have left a message. Yet Gervase had found none. Feeling as if he would go mad, Stephen sank down onto a wooden stool, propped his elbows on the table, and let his head fall into his hands.

After a time he was aware the room had grown cold; from far off came the toll of the Vespers bell. Stephen heard Gervase walk into the room and stoke up the dying embers of the fire. When he felt something liquid run down his face, and tasted salt on his lips, Stephen did not at first realize they were his own tears.

Six days later, just as a pale sun appeared over the horizon, Maud rode across the drawbridge into Angers Castle. The journey from Rouen had proved unusually long and exhausting, beset as she was by alternate waves of nausea and anxiety. Aldyth assured her this was perfectly natural for someone in her condition, but Maud found this cold comfort. Now every bone in her body ached; she was terrified she would be sick in Geoffrey's presence, and the problem of how to make herself appealing to him was still unresolved. Whenever she thought of Stephen, the sense of loss was so overpowering she did not feel she could bear it.

She glanced apprehensively at her surroundings. Had it really been four years ago that she had first ridden through this stone tunnel and into the outer bailey? The grooms currying their horses, armorers repairing armor, fletchers sharpening arrows—all appeared to be doing exactly what they had been doing when she first saw them. Nothing had changed in Angers. Yet she was not the same woman who had arrived here a bitter and resentful bride. Then she had come as an invader; now she came as a supplicant.

When she caught sight of a man standing by the keep, Maud did not at first recognize Geoffrey. Since they had last seen each other, her husband had been transformed. Instead of the willowy, petulant youth she remembered, here was a young man of nineteen, still slender but with a broader chest and wider shoulders. The youthful face had filled out and was now graced by a reddish-gold beard, the same color as his hair.

"Madam, I hope you had a pleasant journey?" Geoffrey asked, in a voice that had deepened into manhood.

"Yes, my lord. But tiring."

"Of course. You must rest. Your chamber has been prepared."

The Count helped her down from her horse and, taking her arm, led her up the broad steps and into the keep. The disgraceful way in which she had left Angers might never have occurred. She and Geoffrey were behaving like strangers, Maud observed, formal and courteous, but not—thank the Holy Mother—like enemies. She felt a spark of encouragement.

Once in her chamber, Maud allowed Aldyth to put her straight to bed, where she fell immediately into a deep sleep. When she woke in the late afternoon, she felt refreshed and free of any queasiness. A wooden tub of hot water scented with herbs was brought into the room; Maud soaked luxuriously while Aldyth washed the dust of a week's journey from her hair.

"Has my body changed?" Maud asked, rising to let Aldyth rub scented oil into her skin.

"Not to notice."

"Thank Our Lady for that. You know how important it is I please the Count," Maud said, her voice shaking. "I'm lost unless we can fully consummate the marriage."

Aldyth's face softened. "This time you will. I feel it in my bones. After all, though it pains me to say so, you're more experienced in these matters now than you were before. And, as we have heard, the Count has not been idle either."

Aldyth put down the oil and walked over to a pole protruding from the wall. Carefully she took down the green silk tunic and gown Maud had had made in Normandy. "You look wondrous fair in this, my lady. Wear it while you still can."

Several hours later, seated next to Geoffrey at the high table in the great hall, Maud knew Aldyth had been right. Geoffrey's eyes were openly admiring every time he looked at her. With the exception of the Count's mesnie, a few local nobles and their ladies, and the ever-present Bishop of Angers, there were no other guests. The atmosphere was somewhat strained, but not overtly hostile.

"A new dish has been created for you, Madam," Geoffrey announced proudly, as the head cook carried in a great pewter platter in the center of which was a huge molded lion made of pale jelly and minced chicken. "See? It's a replica of the lion of Anjou."

The sight of the quivering mass made Maud want to gag, but both Geoffrey and the cook looked at her so expectantly that she dutifully took a small portion, managing to swallow it down with a great quantity of white wine.

"Delicious," she pronounced with a weak smile, fighting down a surge of nausea. "You have outdone yourself." She paused. "I must say that in neither England or Normandy is the cuisine equal to that found in Anjou. Surely this is one of the most civilized courts in Europe!"

The cook beamed, Geoffrey looked gratified, the Bishop of Angers surreptitiously signed himself, and everyone at the high table relaxed. The slight frosty atmosphere in the hall thawed, and when someone proposed a toast, "to the happy return of the beautiful Countess of Anjou," there was a welcoming chorus of agreement. Looking at the smiling faces around her, Maud knew she was off to a good start. Now, she prayed, let the evening finish as well as it had begun.

Finally, the meal came to an end. Maud excused herself to retire early; her gaze met Geoffrey's for a fleeting second as she got up from the table. The message in his blue eyes was clear: She had acquitted herself favorably, and could expect him to visit her bed that night.

Sitting up in the bed, the coverlet drawn up to her neck, her hair unbound and flowing down her back, Maud waited anxiously for Geoffrey's arrival. Every sound caused her to start. She could not control the trembling of her hands, or still the wild beating of her heart. Nothing will go wrong, she told herself. Nothing. Neither by word nor gesture would she reveal herself to be anything other than a dutiful, submissive wife, grateful to be back in her husband's domains, suitably chastened for her former willful behavior. Her performance must be convincing or she was doomed.

There were footsteps outside the door, and Geoffrey entered alone. Dressed in the same shimmering silk robe of Eastern design that she remembered, he looked calm and certain of himself.

"I'm very glad to have you back, Madam," he said with cautious goodwill. "You appear to have changed and I am well-pleased with what I see."

"Thank you," she replied. "You also have changed."

"Indeed." He smiled complacently. "The boy has become a man."

She took a deep breath and said the words she had so carefully rehearsed. "I wish to apologize for my impetuous behavior before I left Anjou. I intend to be a better wife than I've been in the past."

"Well, well. Both of us were guilty of impetuous behavior, I daresay," Geoffrey replied, pleased by her words. "I trust you will also find me a better husband. Let us say no more about it. _Grâce à Dieu_, here is a new beginning for both of us."

He walked over to the bed, took off his blue garment, then slipped in beside her. As she turned to blow out the candle, standing in its iron holder on the table beside the bed, Geoffrey stayed her hand.

"I had quite forgotten how beautiful you are," Geoffrey said, pushing back the crimson coverlet to let his eyes slowly scan her unclothed flesh.

Encouraged by his approval, Maud gave a tentative smile. If he found her fair, it would make her task that much easier. Suddenly he seized her with such forceful intent, she gasped in surprise. He began to kiss her, his hands roving with expert intimacy over her body, a far cry from the fumbling youth she remembered. As Aldyth had reminded her, Geoffrey had certainly not been idle these past months.

"You have filled out a bit," Geoffrey murmured, his hand sliding up over her belly to squeeze one full breast. "A little fuller here, it seems to me, but it suits you, Madam, it suits you. I prefer women with a little meat on their bones."

Maud began to caress Geoffrey, sliding her fingers over his body, and down his stomach to the patch of hair between his thighs. Caressing him, she anxiously waited for his member to harden, forcing herself to stay calm when it did not. He felt so different from Stephen, his body lacking her cousin's muscular strength and breadth. Even his odor was not the same, she thought, longing for the robust aroma of horses, leather, and woodsmoke she associated with Stephen.

Geoffrey lay quiescent, letting her do what she would. As her seeking fingers stroked his flesh, his breathing quickened, but he remained flaccid. Maud began to panic. What was she doing wrong? Suppose she was unable to rouse him? All the pent-up emotion of the last ten days, the strain of the journey, the painful wrench of her parting from Stephen, suddenly burst forth like a river flooding its banks. Collapsing onto Geoffrey's body, she broke into a torrent of tears, horrifying herself and startling Geoffrey. Her body shook in great heaving sobs, and she could not stop them. To her great surprise, Geoffrey was not ill-pleased, but seemed disposed to comfort her.

"Now then, now then, Wife, this has been a great strain on you. I fully understand that," he murmured in a soothing voice. "But it is over. There's naught to be distressed about." He rocked her gently in his arms until her sobs subsided. "I had not realized how deeply the parting affected you."

Maud choked, forcing down a rising hysteria, but then she felt the miracle of his member growing hard as a stick of applewood, nudging between her legs. The sudden release of anxiety, the tremendous surge of relief was overpowering.

Quickly Geoffrey rolled her over onto her back and covered her body with his own. He moved to enter her, hesitantly at first, but with increasing certainty as she obediently opened her legs and twined her arms around his neck. He could not make much headway at first for she was not ready to receive him. With Stephen she had been more than ready, hot and flowing when he so much as looked at her, catching fire from his slightest touch. In desperation, she wondered how to make this easy for Geoffrey. Closing her eyes, she willed herself to relax, and tried to imagine Stephen making love to her. Maud put Stephen's image into her mind as strongly as she could, substituting his muscular frame for Geoffrey's slenderness, almost hearing the words of love Stephen would murmur into her ear as their pleasure mounted. This is Stephen, she told herself, Stephen.

Geoffrey had fully entered her now, and was moving easily with deep, sure strokes. She could almost believe his newfound confidence was similar to Stephen's absolute mastery over her body. This is Stephen inside me, Stephen's body I hold, Stephen's breath in my ear. Slowly, imperceptibly, Geoffrey merged into Stephen as Maud began to respond to her husband's rhythm. Finally a cry broke from her throat as she felt Geoffrey's body spasm in release and his seed flow into her like a benediction.

Chapter Thirty

THE NEXT MORNING ALDYTH APPEARED WITH A TANKARD OF WARM wine mixed with evil-smelling herbs. A crowd of twittering Angevin women followed on her heels.

"All is well, I hear," she whispered to Maud, who lay in bed propped up against an army of pillows.

"How do you know?" Maud took the tankard and sipped it, wrinkling her nose in disgust.

"Geoffrey's squire told the steward who told the chef who told me that when the Count came into the great hall this morning to break his fast, he was singing! The castle folk have apparently taken this as an excellent omen. You should see them, my lady. Knowing winks, leering smiles, rude jests." She pursed her lips in disapproval, watching the Angevin women unpack boxes and shake out garments.

Maud smiled. "Yes, the night was successful, thank the Holy Mother. Must I drink this witches' brew?"

Aldyth sat down on the bed. "Indeed you must. This posset is very beneficial for women in your condition. By the Rood, I will light a special candle to Our Lady, who clearly has your welfare in mind."

"One hurdle crossed and so many more still to go," Maud whispered, pulling herself upright against the pillows. "The queasiness starting so early; then I will look six months big with child when I am only supposed to be five."She took another sip of the wine. "Then the child will be born four weeks early and yet be of normal weight and appearance!" She clutched Aldyth's hand. "How will I ever manage it?"

"Hush, my poppet," Aldyth crooned, patting her hand. "You mustn't upset yourself. We will trust the Holy Mother to help us, as she already has." She smiled, stroking the damp tendrils of russet hair back from Maud's forehead. "The first and biggest obstacle has been overcome, has it not?"

"Yes," Maud sighed. The events of the previous night passed like a dream before her eyes. The unexpected tears, the impossible moment of madness when she had actually thought Geoffrey was Stephen—yet it had all worked wondrously to her advantage. "Yes," she repeated. "My husband will not be surprised when I tell him I am with child in a month's time." She laid protective hands over her belly. "This will be a splendid son, I feel it in my bones."

"You're so sure it will be a boy?" Aldyth teased.

"Positive," Maud responded, her eyes shining. "Think of it, Aldyth, born of a great love, the grandson of a mighty monarch, a great-grandson of the Conqueror on both sides! Oh, what a magnificent king he will be!"

Seven months later Maud sat in her solar playing a game of chess with Geoffrey, whom she had just backed into a corner. Her Angevin women sat grouped around the charcoal brazier embroidering linen garments for the babe that would be born in two months' time, so they reckoned, and a huge child by the look of Maud's belly at seven months. A trouvère from France gently strummed his lute in one corner of the large chamber as he sang a melodic *joi d'amour*. Outside, a February wind beat against the castle walls.

"You must give me a moment, Wife." Geoffrey, chin in hand, bent his head over the silver and gilt chessboard set up on a low trestle table.

"Of course, my lord," Maud replied, settling back in her chair and closing her eyes. The minstrel's song was a favorite of Stephen's, one he had often sung to her when they were alone.

"Some wine, Countess?" the Bishop of Angers' voice broke into her thoughts.

A page stood in front of her with a silver pitcher of wine and a goblet.

"Not for me, but you have some," she said, noting that the Bishop was staring at the chessboard with a slight frown on his face.

The Bishop shook his head, the frown deepening. Maud knew that His Grace of Angers considered chess both vain and sinful, as reprehensible as gambling. He had even warned both her and Geoffrey that too much chess might prevent them from going to heaven. But Holy Church only forbade clerics to play the game, so he could do no more than voice his disapproval.

"The Holy Roman Emperor actually taught you chess himself?" the Bishop asked Maud—for the third time in as many weeks.

"As I have already told Your Grace," Maud replied, not at all put out, for the Bishop, despite his prejudices, had been a good friend to her. "My late husband was an expert—and he taught me from an early age so that one day I would offer him a real challenge."

"I cannot concentrate, Wife, with all this chitchat," Geoffrey said, his eyes flicking over the gold and ivory chessmen.

"Forgive us, my lord," the Bishop said, bowing his head.

Maud concealed a yawn. A sudden movement inside her belly made her gasp. Smiling, she glanced down at the swollen mound covered by her deep blue gown. Be gentle, my son, she thought, stroking her belly with tender fingers, but she knew already from the abrupt restless stirring within her that he would be a fighter, strong, and impatient of his rights. His father's son. In one month's time, she would give birth, and the long period of waiting would be over. If only Stephen could be here to share the joyous moment with her. Stephen, not Geoffrey.

Not that she had anything to complain of since her return to Anjou. On the contrary, Geoffrey had been delighted to find himself a father so quickly, and, despite their occasional quarrels, had been on his best behavior ever since: attentive, solicitous of her welfare, heaping her with gifts "to sweeten her disposition and her milk." In fact the only thing she really had against him was that he was not Stephen.

For the first three months of her pregnancy Maud had suffered Geoffrey in her bed, although there had never been a repeat of that night when she had imagined he was Stephen. Then she told him that Aldyth had advised against further conjugal relations lest it hurt the unborn child. He had caused no difficulty, and Maud assumed

that he solaced himself elsewhere. She had breathed a sigh of relief
for she had started to find his physical attentions unbearable.

Certainly there were many advantages to being pregnant, Maud
decided. Even her father had become attentive, writing her long mis-
sives with as many admonitions as a midwife on how to care for
herself. The King, troubled by ill health, remained in Normandy, and
every three weeks a herald made the journey from Rouen to Angers
to see for himself the state of the Countess of Anjou's health and
report back to his master.

The castle folk and neighbors petted and praised her, filling her
ears with hours of old midwives' tales: To have a boy she must sleep
only on her right side, for the babe to be healthy she must not bathe
often, eat plenty of white bread, lettuce and almonds, avoid garlic,
onions, and vinegar.

Although she was resigned to life at Angers, enduring the tedious
hours with stoic grace, not a day passed when she did not think of
Stephen with love and longing. Everything reminded her of him: the
trouvère's song, the turn of a man's head in the sunlight, a passing
phrase he had used—

"Check!" With a triumphant look at Maud, Geoffrey sat back. "I
have you mated there, Madam."

Maud looked down at the chessboard, her face impassive. In fact,
there was a move she could make that would win her the game. She
lifted her hand to move the ivory queen, then felt the Bishop of
Angers' eyes on her and thought better of it.

"My Lord, you have won indeed. I concede defeat."

Geoffrey beamed, the Bishop looked relieved, and in the corner the
trouvère began to play a merry air from Aquitaine.

One month passed and February became March. In the lavishly appointed birth chamber in the castle at Le Mans, Maud gasped, bent
double with pain tearing at her body. She bit her lips until they bled
to keep from crying out her agony.

"Not long now, my lady," the midwife reassured her. "Keep walking and you will bear it in no time. The pain must get worse before
it gets better."

Maud straightened up as the spasm passed and Aldyth squeezed
her arm reassuringly. Although Aldyth said she was competent and
could be trusted, the midwife reminded Maud of a witch with her
toothless gums, long nose, and curved back. But she knew that the

midwife's goodwill was essential in order to maintain the illusion that this was an early birth. Despite the fact that the old trot had been heavily bribed to say whatever was necessary to convince Geoffrey she had given birth a month early, it would not do to antagonize her.

Once the baby was in swaddling clothes no one would be able to tell how large he might be, and after the first few weeks it would no longer matter. It was the first moments after birth, as well as the christening, that were vital, especially if the father wished to see the child naked and assure himself that he was not deformed. With that in mind, Maud had decided to have only Aldyth, the midwife, and a stolid, incurious wet nurse—a woman handpicked by Aldyth herself —to attend her. A young servant maid was available outside the chamber to fetch and carry whatever was needed to assist the midwife, but would not be present at the birth. Everyone else was excluded.

Maud's attendant Angevin ladies were mystified by her attitude for it went against all custom and tradition. Men were not permitted in the birth room but most women bore their children surrounded by a roomful of other females. However, the Countess Anjou was known to be different—a Norman, after all—and a law unto herself.

Maud resumed pacing up and down the chamber, which had been carefully prepared for the birth. A cauldron of water sat on a trivet next to the fire. A stack of white linen cloths rested on a small oak table along with jars of oil, a pitcher of wine, goblets, two feathers, a wooden bowl, pots of herbs and butter, a sharp knife, and a stone mortar and pestle.

Maud had wanted to bear the child in the castle in Angers, a town she had grown accustomed to over the last eight months, but Geoffrey would not hear of it. He had been born in his grandfather's castle in Le Mans and that is where his child would be born. When she had been brought to bed three and one half weeks early he had been concerned, but the midwife had reassured him that many eight month babies thrived. Especially as Maud's belly was so large. There need be no cause for alarm.

"Ahhh," Maud gasped as another spasm racked her.

"That's the way, my lady, coming faster now, and regular," the midwife noted with satisfaction. She reached up under Maud's gown and felt her belly with experienced fingers. "Bring me a goblet of wine," she called to the wet nurse, "and the jar of scented oil."

"What is this?" Maud asked, almost swooning as the fumes from the goblet assailed her nose.

"Savin, gladiola, rue, dittany, hyssop, and savory crushed into three ounces of the best white wine. It will speed the birth pangs," the midwife said, rubbing Maud's breasts, abdomen, buttocks, and thighs with warm oil.

As Maud forced herself to down the pungent-smelling liquid, there was a pounding on the door, and Geoffrey's voice came through the heavy oak: "What is happening? Is everything well? Is the babe born yet?"

The midwife left Maud's side to walk to the door. "The fruit will drop when it is ready, my lord," she called out. "Best you leave us to do our business in peace."

Maud could not hear Geoffrey's reply, only the sound of his retreating footsteps. Another spasm gripped her, sharper than the last, and Aldyth had to hold her up with both arms to keep her from falling to the floor.

"The draught is working. Get her onto the birth stool," the midwife told Aldyth, observing Maud with a practiced eye. "It could be any time now." She turned to the wet nurse. "Bring a pitcher of hot water and a pile of linen cloths."

Lifting up Maud's gown, the midwife placed her in the crescent cavity in the middle of the wooden birth stool.

"I need the pot of ointment, butter, and the little knife," the midwife said to Aldyth. "Quickly."

She began to massage Maud from the navel downward with a mixture of butter and ointment of Aragon. The pains eased and the midwife rose to her feet.

"Aldyth?"

Aldyth bent her anxious face over Maud's. "I'm here, my poppet."

"Suppose Geoffrey asks to see the babe without the swaddling bands?" Maud whispered, gripping Aldyth's hand.

"I've told you," Aldyth whispered back. "The midwife will say he had to be wrapped immediately because of his size. Exposure to the elements might cause him a chill or some other foul humor. Do not fret," she soothed, "the matter is well in hand."

"Will it be soon?" Maud asked the midwife, sweat pouring down her face as she let go Aldyth's hand.

"Aye, only a short while now." The midwife again knelt before Maud. "Be sure the cupboard shutters are not closed. The chamber door must be opened a crack," she called to the wet nurse. "Nothing must be shut tight." She turned to Aldyth. "Be sure there are no knots in the room. Untie everything." She pressed a stone into Maud's hand. "This be jasper. It do have powers to assist childbirth."

She held over Maud's abdomen what looked like the foot of a bird caked with dried blood, at the same time muttering a strange gibberish.

"What . . . have you there?" Maud could barely get the words out.

"The right foot of a crane. Very useful in labor." The midwife thrust a small piece of wood into Maud's mouth. "Bite down on this, my lady. And scream if ye need to. There be no airs in the birth chamber."

Maud's proud spirit rebelled against the idea of screaming aloud. She would force herself to endure this wretched ordeal in silence. But nothing had prepared her for the searing agony that now ripped through every muscle and limb, reducing her to an incoherent animal. Holy Mary Virgin, she prayed, let it be over, let my son be born.

"Push down now, my lady. Push," the midwife commanded as she kneaded Maud's abdomen with greased hands.

Maud continued to push as hard as she could, clinging tightly to Aldyth's hand as if it were a spar that would prevent her from drowning in this sea of pain.

"Harder, my lady, harder," urged the midwife.

"I cannot," Maud gasped, bearing down until suddenly a great scream was torn from her throat.

A tremendous, final push, and then—the sound of a slap, a lusty cry of rage, and Aldyth's jubilant voice: "A boy, my lady! A boy!" Followed by the midwife loudly proclaiming: "Small, as one would expect for eight months, but by the Mass, you have delivered a fine, healthy boy!"

While the baby was being washed, his gums and palate cleansed with honey, the tiny body rubbed down with salt before being quickly swaddled in fine linen bands, Aldyth half-carried Maud to the bed where she collapsed against the pillows. Tears of relief and triumph ran down her face. It was over. She had borne the next Duke of Normandy, the future King of England: Stephen's son.

Chapter Thirty-one

England and Normandy, 1131

In mid-march, upon hearing the news that Maud had born a son, King Henry, who had spent the past eight months in Normandy due to ill health, rallied sufficiently to return to England.

"Well, Nephew, you will be pleased to hear that, by God's grace, the Countess of Anjou has been safely delivered of a boy," the King told Stephen the morning he arrived in London.

A hot stab of jealousy knifed through Stephen's vitals but he kept his face impassive. That should have been our child, Maud's and mine, he reflected bitterly.

"Excellent news, Sire," he managed to reply. "A day of rejoicing indeed. I had not realized the babe was due so soon."

The King, looking older and quite frail, Stephen observed, frowned. "Although the child was born a few weeks early he is healthy and well formed. Reports from the midwife are very encouraging; he should most certainly survive."

"I'm pleased to hear it," Stephen said. "Maud—she is also well?"

"Very well. Up and about already." The King fixed Stephen with an unblinking stare. "The child is the very image of Geoffrey, I'm told."

Stephen, growing more and more uncomfortable under his uncle's scrutiny, could not think of an appropriate response.

"As soon as the infant is fit to travel," the King continued, "Maud and Geoffrey will bring him to Rouen. All nobles will attend me there to swear homage to the future Duke of Normandy and King of England."

Stephen forced a smile but his blood chilled. Of course. His attention had been so fixed on Maud that for a moment he had lost sight of the fact that the birth of a son meant the succession was now assured. What this would do to his own hopes, he dared not think. He was spared the necessity of a reply when the King's attention was suddenly claimed by a group of barons crowding around him. As his uncle became engaged in conversation, Stephen took the opportunity to escape.

Walking swiftly to the courtyard, he mounted his horse and, attended by several grooms, made straight for the Tower. As he rode through London, his black mantle streaming out behind him, Stephen's body began to shiver uncontrollably, and his head felt heavy as an iron helmet. Exactly the symptoms he had experienced last summer.

When he had first heard that Maud was pregnant, Stephen refused to believe it. Consumed by anger and jealousy, he had immediately become suspicious.

Was it possible the child was his?

In his mind, he went over and over the last conversation with Maud in her chamber, reading all manner of significance into every word. He recalled her abrupt departure, with no word to him then or since. Everything pointed to an unusual circumstance. Yet it did not seem possible that his cousin could have dissembled so adroitly. It was totally unlike her open, forthright nature. If Maud carried his child she would have told him, Stephen argued with himself. He would swear an oath on it.

Stephen had listened carefully to the King's official explanation of why he had sent his daughter back to Anjou in such haste and secrecy: Geoffrey threatened an annulment if his wife was not returned to him immediately; spies at the French court reported that the Count was in league with Louis of France to attack Normandy; even the Pope himself had intervened on Geoffrey's behalf. As a devoted son of the church, the King insisted, he had been forced to act at Rome's bidding and protect his interests in Normandy as well. The matter had demanded instant action with no time to consult his council.

As usual, King Henry's explanations were both reasonable and compelling. Unpopular as the news had been, no one dared question his decision. No one except Stephen, who felt the King had acted only in order to further his own ends—although in this case it was not clear what these ends were. The idea of King Henry being forced to do anyone's bidding, even the Pope's, was highly suspect.

After speaking with Robert, who had visited Maud in Angers, Stephen learned that the Count of Anjou was overjoyed by his wife's pregnancy. It appeared that Maud, hardly pausing for breath, had gone blithely from his bed to Geoffrey's. Stephen had been devastated; nothing in his life had ever wounded him so deeply. His suspicions that it might be his child seemed groundless. With the King's comment that the babe was the image of Geoffrey, the last vestige of doubt vanished.

He galloped toward the Tower and as the hours passed, Stephen's bitterness cooled and the hurt eased. It was not in his nature to hold a grudge—especially against someone he loved as deeply as he loved Maud. He must accept Maud's departure as unavoidable, prompted by events beyond her control. Undoubtedly she had been reluctant to leave him a message for fear of being discovered.

What remained was a legacy of smoldering resentment against his royal uncle who had sent Maud back to her husband when there was no real need to do so. That same uncle who, but for an obsession with founding his own dynasty, could so easily have made him, Stephen, the heir.

Stephen arrived at the Tower in time for Compline. Inside the chapel he was astounded to see his brother officiating at the service.

"When did he arrive?" Stephen asked Matilda as he knelt beside her.

"Not an hour since. He left Winchester at Matins, and has ridden straight through," she whispered. "The household think it a great honor to hear Mass by the celebrated Bishop of Winchester. I fear they will never again be content with Father Philippe."

Observing his brother, Stephen understood why. Tall, crisply elegant, his jeweled rings catching the light from the burning candles, the Bishop's voice authoritatively resonated throughout the chapel as if God himself inspired him. There was no denying that he cut an impressive figure.

Afterwards, Bishop Henry joined Stephen and Matilda and various other guests for a late supper at the high table in the great hall. The talk was centered on the newly born son of the Countess of Anjou.

"Now that the succession is assured," said a visiting nobleman from Yorkshire, "I wonder if the barons will more readily accept the Countess of Anjou as their future queen. What is your opinion, Your Grace?"

"The problem, my lord, is not only the Countess," the Bishop of Winchester replied. He raised his voice so it could be heard the length and breadth of the great hall. "After all, it is misfortune enough to have a queen forced upon us. But the thought of an Angevin king-consort is enough to strike terror and inspire wrath in the heart of any true Norman."

There was a low murmur of agreement from Stephen's mesnie sitting at the trestle tables. The guests at the high table nodded their heads in guarded approval.

After the meal, Stephen and Bishop Henry sat alone, two goblets and a pitcher of wine between them.

"With the birth of this son our entire cause is in jeopardy," Stephen murmured.

Henry gave a mirthless laugh. "Why do you imagine I rode through a chilly night the moment I heard the news from Anjou?"

"But how could you have known yesterday? The King himself only arrived in London this morning!"

The Bishop allowed himself a complacent smile. "I've told you before, I make it my business to know everything that goes on in the realm. My informants are well placed." The smile left his face. "All that aside, we must now determine who will remain loyal to the King's wishes and who can be persuaded to our cause." He paused. "Not an easy matter while our uncle lives."

"God, if only he would die!" The words were uttered with more vehemence than Stephen had intended. Hastily he signed himself.

"Patience, Brother, patience," Henry said, obviously startled. "What with the King's present state of health it cannot be long now. Leave the matter in God's hands."

"Of course. We agreed to avoid bloodshed. Did I not insist that no harm must come to Maud and the child?"

"The mother and child will be far away in Angers. It is to be hoped that by the time they even hear of the King's death you will already be an anointed king or close enough that nothing can be done to prevent it."

"I wish I shared your certainty." Stephen downed his goblet of wine. "Suppose she *is* in Normandy?"

"Suppose, suppose. God save us, we could both be struck by a bolt

of lightning tomorrow if it comes to that." Henry lowered his voice
still further. "I have a plan which is simplicity itself. Although I will
remain in Winchester, several of my people will stay close to the King
at all times. If he falls critically ill I'll receive word and notify you,
or, should you be with our uncle at the time, you must send word to
me. Wait until he is dead, then join me immediately."

"Simple enough—if he's in Normandy. But should he be in England—"

Henry tapped a ringed finger against his chin. "That would pose a
problem, for the success of my plan depends on the King being in
Normandy. However, I suspect he will remain in Rouen to be nearer
his grandson."

"A good possibility, I agree. Go on."

"Being in Winchester, I'll have access to the treasury. That's how
our uncle seized power, remember, after he arranged his brother
William Rufus's death. He who controls the treasury controls the
realm."

"You anticipate no opposition to our seizing the treasury?"

"It will be a time of crisis. People will be unsettled and confused.
There has never been a time in living memory when the Conqueror
or one of his sons has not reigned. Like scattered sheep, commoners
and nobles alike will be easily led. And not by a woman or an Angevin
shepherd." Henry put his hand on Stephen's shoulder. "You will be
crowned king by popular demand."

"Gloucester will uphold his sister's claim, and FitzCount will remain loyal to the King's orders," Stephen said. "Gloucester is a
powerful magnate, Brother, and Brian is well respected. Others will
follow their lead."

"Robert will be at his father's deathbed and, like everyone else,
will be caught off guard. The element of surprise is vital and no one
suspects our intention." The Bishop looked intently at his brother.
"You must be careful not to arouse anyone's suspicions. Particularly
the Lord of Wallingford. That clever Breton is by far the shrewdest
of your friends."

Stephen nodded.

"Meanwhile," Henry continued, "we make use of our connections.
I will deliver support from the church. You must enlist the aid of the
de Beaumont twins, as well as other powerful allies who would give
much to see you king. Let it be known—discreetly, of course—that
you are not in agreement with the King's choice of successor. The
message will not be lost on those willing to listen."

A shadow crossed Stephen's face. "I confess to feeling uneasy, Brother. Robbing Maud's child of his birthright disturbs me," he said, giving voice to a thought that had begun to trouble him.

The Bishop gave an impatient sigh. "The counties of Anjou and Maine are the child's birthright! An inheritance of immense value and prestige, let me remind you. After all, the boy will not be landless or poverty-stricken. You cannot be squeamish about such minor matters. Keep the weal of the realm in mind."

In the flickering light of the torches, Stephen's eyes were filled with disquiet. "You see nothing . . . treasonous in what we do?"

"Treasonous?" Henry looked shocked. "To save the kingdom from Angevin rule is a test of our loyalty! Really, Stephen, sometimes, it seems to me, you lack a certain ruthless quality necessary for—" He searched his brother's troubled countenance. "What is it that worries you? Do you fear the consequences of breaking your oath to Maud and the King?"

With a shrug and a sigh Stephen turned away without answering.

"Is that all? Benedicte, Brother, I can promise you full absolution. After all, Rome understands these things."

Six months later in mid-September, Stephen stood in the great hall of the ducal palace in Rouen. The court was assembled to await the arrival of the Count and Countess of Anjou and their infant son. The late afternoon sunshine streamed in through the open doors, turning the freshly picked rushes to a carpet of gold.

"God's death, but this sticks in the craw, knowing I must swear homage to an Angevin brat," Waleran of Muelan muttered under his breath.

Robin of Leicester glanced apprehensively toward the King who, clothed in a purple robe, sat in the ducal chair of Normandy mounted on a raised dais. "Hold your tongue, Brother. We have but little choice."

Waleran cast a dark look toward his monarch. "While King Henry lives we are all under the royal thumb. After his death it is another tale."

The twins turned instinctively toward Stephen, who gave a brief shake of his head before leaving them to approach Robert of Gloucester, Brian FitzCount, and the Earl of Chester. Waleran made no secret of his resentment toward the Angevins and Stephen wished he would be more discreet.

"It's time they arrived," the Earl rumbled. "I do not care to wait upon the Angevins much longer." He made no attempt to lower his voice, and thrust out his chin in a defiant manner.

"It cannot be long now," Robert replied with a soothing smile.

The Earl of Gloucester's eldest daughter, Sybil, had recently married the powerful Ranulf, lord of the wealthy and extensive palatinate of Chester, and Robert always behaved with courtly deference toward his formidable son-in-law.

"I think the good Earl feels somewhat eclipsed by the new arrivals," Brian FitzCount whispered to Stephen. "It has been my experience that if Ranulf isn't the center of attention he takes it as a personal affront. Soothe his pride with honeyed words, fawn at his feet, and he will eat out of your hand."

Stephen chuckled, but his eyes turned speculatively toward the barrel-chested Earl, whose drooping chestnut mustache was the butt of many jokes. He wondered how he might use Brian's observation to his own advantage. Never an intimate of Ranulf's, he knew it would be a triumph indeed if he could gain the Earl's future support. Of course, married to Gloucester's daughter made it unlikely. . . .

"The Count and Countess of Anjou," boomed the steward's voice.

The assembled baronage moved toward the entrance, hastily forming themselves into two rows. Ranulf of Chester pushed his father-in-law aside in an attempt to stand at the head of one of the lines. With a deferential bow, Stephen let the Earl step ahead of him. He was rewarded with a grunt of acknowledgment.

Standing behind Ranulf, Stephen's heart quickened; the palms of his hands grew damp with anticipation. It had been fourteen months since he and Maud had last seen each other. He waited expectantly, his body tense as a bowstring.

Maud stood poised in the entranceway, the baby in her arms, then began to walk between the formed lines. As the nobles swarmed forward, she slowed her step to allow them a glimpse of her son. Elegantly arrayed in an apricot gown, with a gold mantle thrown over her shoulders, her dark russet hair bound with a gold fillet, she looked magnificent. Stephen's blood leapt at the sight of her and for a moment he could not draw breath.

"At last! At last!" The King hurried down from the royal chair, almost tripping over his purple robe.

Maud reached him, inclined her knee, and held out the swaddled infant. "Here, Sire, is Henry, your grandson," she announced. Proudly she laid the child in her father's arms.

Stephen pressed forward with the crowd, watching the King's harsh face soften and glow as he gazed raptly at the child. Now Stephen could see the babe clearly. Solidly built, like his Norman forebears, wisps of rust-colored hair framed a rosy face. Large gray-green eyes stared solemnly back at his grandfather. Neither the unfamiliar surroundings nor the fact that he was being held by a stranger seemed to perturb the infant; since entering the hall he had not uttered a sound. An unexpected chill traveled down Stephen's spine. Even at six months of age, Maud's son had unusual presence.

Immaculately dressed in green and scarlet, Geoffrey followed his wife into the hall and now stood beside the King. At first glance Stephen was shocked, for this neatly turned out figure was nothing like the ineffectual youth Maud had described. Of course, that would have been about four years ago. The Count was no longer a stripling. Stephen found himself looking with intense dislike at the handsome, arrogant face, crisp red-gold beard, and the ostentatious sprig of yellow broom perched in his blue cap. If the infant resembled Geoffrey at birth, Stephen reflected, he was nothing like him now. Henry of Anjou was Norman through and through.

A group of richly dressed prelates approached the King, the Bishop of Winchester among them, all eager to catch a glimpse of Maud's child.

"Look, my lords," the King called out, as he held up the infant for all to see. "Look now upon your new prince. Here is Henry, great-grandson of the Conqueror, to whom you must all swear fealty."

Stephen stepped back as the barons came forward to greet Maud. Their manner, reserved but courteous, was not lacking in respect. Toward Geoffrey of Anjou, however, they were covertly hostile. Observing the insolent looks cast in the Count's direction, Stephen knew a moment of grim satisfaction. Among the assembled peers, not one of them treated Geoffrey with the deference that should have been accorded a king-elect. Was his uncle so smitten with his new grandson, Stephen wondered, that he did not notice the snubbing of his son-in-law?

He wandered through the gathered assembly stopping here and there for a smile and a brief word or two, trying to determine who among the nobles present would remain loyal to his sworn oath after the King's death. The new infant would tend to sway matters in the Angevins' favor. Suddenly Stephen's eyes met the icy, calculating gaze of Geoffrey of Anjou. A wave of naked enmity flowed between them. With a start, Stephen realized that the Count was trying to determine the same thing: Now that there was a son to ensure the succession, how many would dispute Maud's right to wear the crown?

"Come greet your new cousin, Nephew," the King called out.

Stephen approached his uncle and held out a finger to the baby, who grasped it in a surprisingly strong fist.

"A mighty grip for one so young," he said, smiling. "Already he shows signs of the warrior to come. A great credit to the House of Normandy, Sire."

"And Anjou, my lord, and Anjou," said Geoffrey in a clipped voice from just behind him.

"Indeed," Stephen replied, but did not look at Geoffrey for Maud had appeared beside her father. "You look well, Cousin," he said, his heart hammering.

Maud gave him a weak smile. There were drops of perspiration on her brow; her gray eyes, enormous in a milk-white face, avoided meeting his but darted continually around the hall; she looked terrified as a cornered doe. It took Stephen a moment to realize that he was the cause of her fear. Why? Stunned and heartsick, he stepped back to let the Earl of Chester exclaim over the infant. Did Maud think he would reveal too much, by look or gesture, in the presence of her husband? Surely she knew him to be more circumspect than that.

Prompted by a sense of urgency, Stephen felt he must see his cousin alone, reassure himself of her love, and tell her what lay in his own heart. Soon she would return to Anjou, and he to England. This might be the last opportunity he would have before events took their course: before . . . he did not let himself finish the thought.

Chapter Thirty-two

Two days later the barons swore another oath of homage to Maud, and an oath of fealty as well. Stephen was the first of the lay peers to swear. When Maud clasped his hands between hers, they were as cold as ice; her face was like marble, but Stephen thought he detected a slight shiver pass through her body.

At a celebratory feast held that night in the ducal palace, Stephen waited until Geoffrey of Anjou had entered the great hall. He caught Maud on the threshold, just as she was about to follow her husband.

"Can you meet me tonight?" he whispered.

"Impossible," Maud said, not looking at him. "Let me pass."

"Please, I beg you not to refuse. It may be the last chance we have to—" He stopped, noting the sudden pallor of her face and the haunted look in her eyes. "Soon I leave for England, and you return to Anjou. It may be years before we see each other again."

She hesitated, then gave a brief nod. "If I can slip away undetected."

"By the falcon mews then, at Matins. It will be deserted at that hour."

The feast, held in honor of young Henry of Anjou, became a long, drawn-out affair. Finally, to Stephen's relief, it was over. Those barons who had not fallen unconscious into the rushes lay sprawled across the trestle tables; the rest stumbled drunkenly to their quarters.

The ducal palace overflowed with guests, and Stephen was packed into a chamber with Brian, Robert, the de Beaumont twins, and Ranulf of Chester. He lay down on a straw pallet, listening to the snores and belches on either side of him, almost choking on the stench of wine and unwashed bodies. The air was stifling, the darkness oppressive. Would Matins never ring?

At last! From Rouen Cathedral came the peal of twelve pure tones that signaled the midnight hour. Stephen rose from his pallet. Groping his way past the prone bodies, he left the chamber and made his way through the sleeping palace and out into the courtyard. The night was cool, filled with the scents of damp earth and summer blossoms; he drank in deep breaths of healing air. Above him, a full moon rode flowing black clouds in a charcoal sky, illuminating the towers and ramparts, touching the shadowed corners of the deserted courtyard with a silver sheen. The window slits of the palace were dark. High on the battlements, a light flickered and was gone: a guard making his rounds. Stephen passed the barracks, blacksmith's forge, and kitchen well. Ahead lay the falcon mews.

"Stephen?" It was Maud's voice, wafting eerily out of the darkness like a disembodied spirit.

He found her standing by one of the wood-screened windows of the mews. She was covered from head to toe in a long black cloak that blended into the night. Her face was in shadow.

"Geoffrey overindulged in wine and lies like one dead," she whispered. "Everyone else sleeps, so I came early."

Gradually, as his eyes adjusted to the half-darkness, Stephen could see her face, a pale oval framed by the hood of the cloak. He reached for her hands under the folds of the mantle and grasped them tightly in his own. To his relief she did not pull away.

"My heart is glad at the sight of you after all this time," he said.

She let out a long sigh. "And mine as well."

"Can this be so?" His grip on her hands tightened. "Truly?"

"I have no reason to speak other than the truth. You knew that once." He heard the slight tremble in her voice and his heart leapt.

"I wasn't certain," Stephen said. "You seemed so fearful when you first saw me in the hall. Did you think I would betray my feelings in front of Geoffrey?"

"That's exactly what I feared. Geoffrey has been much agitated since arriving in Normandy. He is aware of the barons' open hostility to him, and returns it tenfold."

To me most of all, Stephen thought, but refrained from saying so.

"What with showing the babe to the court, Geoffrey's antagonism, the rigors of the journey, and the thought of seeing you again, I've been under great strain," Maud continued. "Especially seeing you again. Forgive me if I seemed distraught."

"I can forgive you anything, sweet Cousin," Stephen replied, with as much gentleness as he could muster, determined not to indulge in recriminations. "Even the manner of your leaving Rouen—abruptly, without so much as a word."

"Without so much as a—what do you mean? Did you not receive my message?"

He shook his head. "No message was left, according to Gervase, and I inquired myself to be sure." He gave a short laugh. "I was like a lovesick swain, demented by your absence, with wild thoughts of following you to Angers."

"I gave a roll of parchment to one of the guards. He promised faithfully to give it to Gervase. I cannot understand what happened."

There was no mistaking the shock in her voice, the troubled look on her face. Stephen's heart lifted. She *had* sent him word!

"Truly, I had little choice," she began. "You see, my father—"

He put a finger over her lips. "I guessed what must have happened. There's no need to explain. It no longer matters." His finger smoothed out the wrinkle of concern on her forehead. "What does matter is that we are here, together, and neither of us has changed. You look even more beautiful than I remembered. Are you happy?"

She took his hand and held it against her cheek. "Happy? True happiness I left behind with you. But my son has brought me much joy. I have accepted my life in Angers, resigned myself to Geoffrey as a husband, and look forward to the day when I will reign as queen."

Stephen held out his arms and she walked into them. Holding her close, he kissed the curve of her temple, held his cheek against hers, and finally found the softness of her lips, warm and responsive against his own. The familiar surge of excitement and desire flooded his body, mingled with an overwhelming tenderness.

As they stood together by the mews, wrapped in each other's arms, Stephen felt himself pass into a dream-like state, quite unlike anything he had ever experienced. The confines of time and location vanished, and within his heart a door magically opened. Words he had never intended to say, never even thought of before, poured out, almost as if someone else were saying them.

"Don't go back to Anjou, dearest love. Stay with me."

"If only I could," Maud said with longing in her voice.

"But you can. There is nothing to prevent it."

"Nothing to prevent it?" Incredulous, she drew back her head to look at him. "You can't be serious."

"I've never been more serious in my life," he said. "Remember our idyll in the lodge outside the New Forest? It was like our own Eden, removed from the vanities of the world while still in the world. That's how we will live."

Speechless, Maud stared at him as if he had lost his wits. He smiled at her, certain she would agree once she fully understood. She would grow to accept the idea of a simple life, a life that flowed with the natural order of things: the forests, the streams, even the animals. Everything had become wondrously clear in Stephen's mind. All he had to do was follow his instinctive nature, that part of him in harmony with all of creation. He would tell his brother that he had forsaken ambition for love. What need was there for crowns, intrigue, power? He and Maud would have each other.

"We can settle on some land in Blois," Stephen said, his heart soaring. "My elder brother, Theobald, is Count of Blois, and he will not turn us away. We can live quietly, raise a handspan of children, and not trouble ourselves with the affairs of the kingdom." It was extraordinary how alive and certain he felt.

"Dearest love," Maud said gently. "You know that's an unreal dream. No one can return to the primitive innocence of the Garden. We would forfeit our children, earn the undying enmity of Anjou, Normandy and England, and be forced to live as adulterous outcasts —if we lived at all. We would be excommunicated, and shunned by all the world. Is this the life you envision for yourself? For me? And what of Matilda? The scandal would be ruinous to her. You must see how impossible—"

"Not impossible," he stopped her, almost resenting her for the harsh note of reality she introduced into his vision.

"What happens to England and Normandy when my father dies?" She stroked his face with loving fingers. "Do you suggest we deny our blood and heritage? How can we ignore the weal of the kingdom? When I'm queen I will be depending on your support and wisdom to guide me. The realm needs us both."

"You now value the crown more than a life with me," he accused.

"You did not use to be the slave of ambition." His dream-like state began to fade.

"That's unfair." Tears glistened in her eyes. "How could I not be ambitious when I've been bred to the responsibilities of royalty since I was a child?" She paused, struggling for control. "But ambition has never been my master, and I pray God it never will be."

"Is that your answer?" he asked, watching the gulf widen between them. "You turn your back on happiness?"

She faltered. "Not willingly! But what choice do we have? The deepest joy I have ever known has been with you. Do you think I haven't thought of the barren years that lie ahead? Of the emptiness in my heart that can never be filled?" She took his face in her hands, looking at him as if she would engrave his image on her soul. "I'm not destined for happiness, only duty."

"Duty," he repeated in a lifeless voice. He had been prepared to give up everything for her, and she had rejected him. The reasons, however valid, did not matter. The door that had opened now closed soundlessly.

Stephen rubbed his eyes and looked around, suddenly wide awake to his surroundings. Everything looked exactly the same, yet different. What was the matter with him? He had come perilously close to —he could give it no name, but the experience had passed and the memory of it was already fading into unreality.

"Of course, you're right, ma belle," he said with a forced smile. "It was madness to even consider such a course." He planted a kiss on her forehead. "Best we return, before someone wakes and misses us."

Her face was a mask of anguish, tears pouring down her cheeks, but he felt helpless to comfort her. She had made the fateful decision and they must both live with it for the rest of their time on earth.

Her words, "when I'm queen I will depend on you," came back to him now. A stab of resentment pierced him. Did Maud honestly think he would be a tame confidant, a safe shoulder to lean on, like Robert of Gloucester? Could she really expect him to be content with that? Stephen's pride rebelled. He had never sought to be her master but he was no woman's slave.

"I must tell you something," she whispered.

"What is it?"

But she did not speak. Curiously detached, he watched the tears running down her cheeks like a misty waterfall.

"Do not weep, sweet Cousin," he said at last. Taking her by the shoulders, Stephen turned her around so she faced the keep, and gave her a gentle shove. "Fare well. Know that my heart goes with you."

He watched as she walked away from him, her shoulders shaking, her head bent like a penitent. Numb with the blow of his great loss, Stephen waited by the mews until she had vanished into the darkness.

"I don't trust the Norman barons," said Geoffrey of Anjou into the shocked silence of the King's chamber. "Particularly the Count of Mortain. If ever a man was capable of treachery, he is that man."

It was early afternoon, several days after the homage ceremony. Maud stared at her husband in disbelief. The Bishop of Salisbury's face twitched with apprehension as he gazed at the Count of Anjou. Brian FitzCount looked thoughtful. Robert of Gloucester let his hand fall to the hilt of his sword. King Henry, sitting in a carved chair, his legs propped up on a stool padded with cushions, put a restraining hand on his son's arm.

"Stephen is our loyal cousin and true friend," Robert said in icy tones. "How dare you accuse him of treachery."

Ignoring him, Geoffrey turned to the King. "I suspect that Stephen of Blois would be the barons' choice to succeed you, Sire. I seriously question whether they will ever accept your daughter as queen or an Angevin husband as her king-consort."

"You have lost all sense of reason," Maud said, the blood rushing into her face. "At one time it was thought that Stephen might succeed my father, but that was before the Emperor died."

"Anyone with eyes in his head can see that the barons still want Stephen of Blois, and well he knows it. It would not surprise me to hear that he and that silver-tongued brother of his have already made plans and wait only upon the King's death before executing them," Geoffrey persisted.

There was a sharp intake of breath and those in the room hastily crossed themselves.

Robert took a menacing step toward Geoffrey. "Only a coward would accuse Stephen and his brother, who have left Rouen this very day, when they are not here to defend themselves."

"It is unthinkable to accuse my cousins of treachery," Maud said, wondering what in the name of heaven Geoffrey was up to.

"Under the right circumstances, who can say what a man might be capable of," the King remarked, observing Geoffrey through narrowed eyes. "If he wants something desperately enough . . ."

Bishop Roger coughed and shifted on his stool.

"But Stephen and Henry are your well-beloved nephews, Sire," protested Robert, aghast. "They owe you everything. You are the father they never knew. As Maud says, it is unthinkable."

The King frowned. "Nothing is unthinkable where power is concerned." He turned to the Bishop of Salisbury. "Well, Roger, your finger is upon the pulse of the kingdom. What do you say to the Count's accusation? Do the barons still want my nephew? I know they did in the past, but now?"

"If that were once the case, Sire, it is so no longer," Bishop Roger said, glaring at Geoffrey. "It has been many years since such a suggestion was made. Of course the barons will abide by your wishes. Have they not sworn a sacred oath?"

Everyone began to talk at once. Maud knew there was more to Geoffrey's accusations, his attack on Stephen, than met the eye, she would swear to it. Did he suspect—no, that was not possible. But the furor her husband was creating hid a purpose, although she could not imagine what it was.

"Geoffrey," she began in a quiet voice, "Stephen and the barons, as well as the Bishop of Winchester and the other prelates, have sworn three oaths to uphold me as future queen. This time they swore fealty to our son as well. We have all heard your suspicions, but where are the facts to support them?"

The King smiled approvingly. "Well said, Daughter. We are waiting for proof, Son-in-law."

Geoffrey flushed, setting his jaw in the stubborn manner Maud knew only too well. "There has not been time to gather any facts. I haven't seen the Norman baronage assembled since my wedding." He looked at the faces surrounding him. "They were not happy about the marriage then, if you will remember, and I find nothing has changed over the years. If I had not seen the hostility with my own eyes, I would not have believed it."

Robert gave him an incredulous look. "You think that sufficient? I don't claim the barons love you, but that is a far cry from dishonoring their oath to the King and my sister."

Geoffrey's lips tightened. Angrily he turned his back on the others and approached King Henry. "It is my opinion, Sire, that the fate of the succession is far from assured. Thus I cannot count on your agreements with me being honored. Therefore—" He paused to take a deep breath. "Therefore I must insist that you grant me the rights agreed to in the marriage contract."

Now we come to the heart of the matter, Maud thought. She was furious with her husband for his high-handed manner, his absurd accusations—and for not consulting her before making such a foolhardy display of greed and temper.

"To what rights do you refer?" the King asked in a deceptively mild voice.

"Those castles and lands that were promised me in the marriage contract. Writ plain for all to see."

"Count Geoffrey must refer to those castles on the Maine border, Sire," said the Bishop of Salisbury.

"Ah! Of course. But they come to you only after my death," the King explained to a scowling Geoffrey. "When you are Duke of Normandy." He smiled unpleasantly. "I am far from dead, however, and one house cannot have two masters."

"If I don't get them now I will never get them at all!" Geoffrey shouted, losing all control. The veins in his neck stood out like iron bars. His face was bright red. "That is what you all refuse to understand. If my wife is not crowned queen I will get nothing!"

"You've gone mad," Maud cried. "Of course I will be crowned queen!"

Ignoring Maud, Geoffrey knelt on one knee before the King. "I ask you for the last time, Sire, will you give me what is rightfully mine?"

King Henry kicked the stool away and rose unsteadily to his feet. "No, I will not. And this unseemly display of the famous Angevin temper leaves me unmoved. Indeed, I had not deemed you so avaricious, Son-in-law. You will come into your possessions soon enough when I'm dead."

"Then I will never get them." Geoffrey stood, his eyes blazing like blue fire. "Unless I take what is mine now." There was no mistaking the menace in his voice. He bowed to the King. "I return to Anjou tomorrow." He surveyed the chamber with a contemptuous glance and strode briskly to the door. "Wife?"

Maud hesitated, uncertain whether to follow Geoffrey's exit or stay and placate her father, who, by the look of him, would need to be bled tonight. Then she heard him say to Robert, "So the Count accuses my nephews to serve his own ends. Fortify the garrisons in our castles on the Maine border without delay."

Robert looked at his father in horror. "You cannot think Geoffrey seriously means to lay siege to your castles?"

The King gave him a grim smile. "Always wiser to take a man at his word. Hope for the best, but prepare for the worst. That is the first law of survival, my son."

Hearing this, Maud quickly left the chamber.

When she returned to her own quarters, Geoffrey was already stuffing his belongings into a leather saddlebag. Maud dismissed the nurses and attendants; she walked over to the carved wooden cradle where Henry lay asleep.

"What was the purpose of that ridiculous scene?" she asked, not bothering to conceal her scorn. "Did you really think my father would give away his possessions? All you have accomplished is to turn him against you."

"Every word I spoke was the truth, only you are all too blind to see it. At the moment nothing is to be gained by further discourse. We leave tomorrow for Anjou."

"You cannot expect me to leave with you," Maud protested. "I must stay and undo the damage you have done here. My father is furious with you and will be with me if I attempt to take his grandson away so soon."

Geoffrey walked over to where she stood by the cradle; his eyes rested on the peaceful countenance of the sleeping baby. The afternoon sun streamed through the window, turning Henry's hair a dark copper hue. Geoffrey slid an arm around Maud's waist and roughly pulled her to him.

"Your father needs many grandsons," he said, his hands roving over her breasts.

Maud stood rigid under his touch, then, as he tried to lift up the skirts of her gray tunic and amber-colored gown, she pulled his hands away. "I agree. But this is not the time."

There was a tense silence. "Very well. But do not remain in Rouen too long, Wife." He gave her breasts a final squeeze but kept his arm about her waist.

Grateful for Geoffrey's grudging acquiescence, Maud forced herself not to recoil from his loveless embrace.

"Thank you. It will mean much to my father to have young Henry about." A sudden suspicion crossed her mind. "You go straight back to Angers?"

"Of course. Where else would I go?"

To attack the Maine border, she barely refrained from saying. Their eyes locked. With a mock bow he walked out of the chamber.

The baby woke. Maud picked up Henry and held him so tightly against her breast that he began to struggle in protest. Soothing him, she walked over to the nurse's chair and sat down, then began to rock him back and forth in her arms.

Alone for the first time, Maud was now able to release the anguish she had been forced to hold back all day. Stephen had left for Mortain at dawn this morning. Her cousin was gone from her life, and although it was entirely her own doing, Maud felt she could never be reconciled to the overwhelming misery of her loss. She wondered, as she had almost constantly ever since she had rejected his wild, unrealistic offer, if she had made the right choice. Reason told her she had, but her heart and body rebelled, and she was assailed by doubts and regrets. Unable to control her grief, she sobbed softly against her baby's fuzzy head. Holding him in her arms was all of Stephen she would ever have. Young Henry must compensate her for all the lonely years that lay ahead.

She wondered why she had not been able to tell Stephen of his paternity. It had been on the tip of her tongue to speak when they were leaving the falcon mews, but an instinctive warning signal rising up from the depths of her being had restrained her. Just as it had when she first discovered she was with child. Now it was too late. The decisive moment had passed and she knew she would never tell him.

At last her tears subsided. Yet still she sat there, Henry in her arms, through the Vespers bell and the steward's horn calling the palace to supper, until twilight shadows covered the chamber.

The following spring Maud was still in Normandy. Each time she made ready to return to Anjou, the King, enraptured with his grandson, prevailed upon her to stay a little longer. Geoffrey had visited her four months ago, reiterating once again his demand for the castles on the Maine border. The King's reply had been the same: While he lived, he would make no one his equal in his own duchy.

As his health continued to deteriorate, King Henry, no longer physically able to make the rough channel crossing, remained in Normandy with his court while his chief administrator, the Bishop of Salisbury, ruled England in his name. Robert and Brian regularly traveled back and forth across the channel, but Stephen remained in England. Maud knew he was deliberately staying away, and was alternately relieved and disappointed. She desperately wanted to see him again, but recognized that for her peace of mind it was far better he did not come to Normandy.

On this morning in early May, Maud, three and a half months pregnant since Geoffrey's last visit, sat in a chair in the solar. Indifferent to his ardor, she had allowed Geoffrey access to her body, hardly noticing his attentions, and had been greatly surprised to find herself with child. Henry played at her feet while her women worked on a tapestry and the chaplain read aloud from a Book of Hours. She was only half aware of horses riding into the courtyard, and consequently was startled, a quarter of an hour later, when Robert burst into the solar.

"Geoffrey has launched an attack on several towns and castles on the Norman-Maine border," he cried. "The King is beside himself with fury."

Maud was instantly alert. "The reckless fool! You are certain?"

"There's no doubt. The King is threatening to send troops to recover his property."

Horrified, she rose to her feet. "Holy Mother! Where is Geoffrey now?"

"Back in Anjou according to our reports, but he has left a garrison behind."

"I must return to him at once." She clapped her hands. "Pack my boxes," she ordered the women. "We leave for Anjou tomorrow."

"Do not count on leaving. The King talks of returning to England and taking you with him."

"Taking me—he knows I'm with child! If I go to England, Geoffrey will indeed launch a full-scale war! Besides, the King would not likely survive the voyage."

Robert nodded morosely. "True, but there's no reasoning with our father at this moment. Led his blood cool. Wait a day or two, then broach returning to Anjou."

"There is no need for you to return, Daughter," the King complained two days later.

He lay in his chamber propped up by many cushions, surrounded by members of the court. Several physicians were in constant attendance; one endeavored to give him a vial of medicine, which he pushed angrily aside.

"It's my duty to go," Maud said. "I will be able to restrain Geoffrey from doing further damage."

The King gave her a skeptical look. "I've not seen any evidence of your influence over him. My troops will be more effective. It's also your duty to remain by my side. How can you be so cruel as to deprive me of my grandson?"

"My son's father has rights as well, Sire. I beg you, do not force me to choose between you and my husband."

"I won't prevent you from returning to Anjou." He gave a long sigh. "To be left alone, ill, nearing death, abandoned in my old age—" He sighed again.

Maud watched him unmoved. Privy to all his little ploys, she knew he might hang on for several years yet. However, she could not deny a guilty pang as she looked at his clammy skin and palsied limbs. It did seem cruel to leave him, to deprive him of his grandson. In truth, she would much prefer to remain in Normandy, where she felt closer to Stephen who, sooner or later, must return to Rouen.

On the other hand, the consequences of not returning to Geoffrey were frightening. Left to his own devices, the impetuous Count might continue to attack her father's possessions and enrage the Norman barons to such a pitch that her future as Duchess of Normandy could be jeopardized. She must protect herself, as well as Henry's inheritance. This was best accomplished by dealing directly with Geoffrey. Despite her father's skepticism, she felt sure she could restrain him, even persuade him to return the castles he had taken. He knew she carried his child, and surely this would dispose him to listen to reason. A wave of anger coursed through her at the thought of her hotheaded husband, who had brought her to this impossible point where she must decide between her duties and responsibilities to him or to her father. Either way she would suffer the consequences of her decision.

"I can do more good in Anjou than here," she said at last. "I leave in the morning—with your blessing, I hope." She gave him a placating smile. "Remember, I'm with child. Geoffrey will expect me to bear it in Le Mans. Then you shall have two grandsons to comfort you."

"I will never see the child you now carry."

She signed herself. "I pray God that is not so."

"You'll regret your hasty departure," the King said in a quavering voice. "You will not see me again in this life."

The scene before her was like a tableau in a religious pageant she had once seen: her father propped up in his bed, surrounded by advisers, courtiers, and physicians all watching her, some with sympathy, others with ill-concealed satisfaction at this sign of estrangement between the King and his heir.

Although he did not cozen her for a moment, crafty old knave that he was, still Maud hesitated. She opened her mouth to explain again, then thought better of it. After all, what was there to say that had not already been said? Sick at heart, Maud left the chamber, the King's words echoing in her ears like a premonition of doom: Would she ever again see her father alive?

Chapter Thirty-three

Normandy, 1135

ON THE 28TH DAY OF NOVEMBER IN THE YEAR 1135, STEPHEN RETURNED to Normandy. After attending to his own affairs in Mortain, he rode to Rouen, arriving at the ducal palace late in the evening.

"How is my uncle?" Stephen asked Robert of Gloucester, who met him in the torch-lit courtyard.

"Still alive, by God's grace, and sleeping peacefully at the moment," Robert said, signing himself. "Fully recovered from a near brush with death not two months past."

"We heard as much," Stephen said. "Gorging himself on stewed lampreys. You'd think he'd have the sense to stay away from the dish, which has always acted as a violent poison in his system."

"Indeed. This time he had to be bled and purged for several days. It was a near miss, let me tell you."

Stephen signed himself. "Had I known it was so serious I would have come over immediately."

"Fortunately he recovered and we thought it best not to alarm the kingdom for naught. In truth, since the birth of his second grandson last month he has been in much better spirits."

"Which will improve still further when he sees his favorite nephew," said Brian FitzCount with a smile, as he ran down the steps of the palace into the courtyard. "The King has planned a great hunt tomorrow, weather and health permitting, and a supper in the hunting lodge." He threw his arms around Stephen. "It will be like old times, eh? By the Mass, I have missed you, my friend." His face grew serious. "I was so sorry to hear of the death of your son, Baldwin. A terrible blow. But our latest news is that Matilda is with child again."

"Yes, she is, thank the Lord. Baldwin's demise was a heavy burden for her to bear." Stephen paused, remembering the anguish of Baldwin's fatal illness. "All is well with her now." He picked up a saddlebag lying on the ground. "I've brought with me some writs from Roger of Salisbury for the King to sign."

"They must wait until tomorrow," Robert said.

As he followed Brian and Robert into the ducal palace, Stephen paused for a moment to look across the courtyard, his eyes coming to rest on the falcon mews where he had last seen Maud alone. Although he still sorely missed her, the initial agony of losing her had eased. But now, once again in the same surroundings, the memory of that fateful encounter brought back more sharply than ever the searing pain of his loss.

"The Countess of Anjou is fully recovered from the birth?" he asked Robert.

"It was a difficult time for Maud, much harder than her first confinement, but yes, both mother and babe now thrive."

"Is the break between Maud and her father now mended?"

Brian exchanged a quick glance with Robert. "Not fully. Not yet."

"Indeed?" Stephen looked from one to the other, his interest quickening.

"You recall the incident last May when Geoffrey of Anjou attacked the King's castles?" Brian asked.

"Only too well. It's still the talk of London."

"I can imagine. Maud returned to Anjou to try to reason with her husband. Thanks to her intervention, Geoffrey agreed to give the castles back, but thus far he has made no move to do so. However, when Maud left Normandy the King was furious. He felt her place was with him, and has still not forgiven her."

"Fortunately, Maud plans to come with both her children to Rouen in time for the New Year," Robert added. "It will surprise the King and do much to heal the breach between them."

"It's late, and Stephen has had a long journey," Brian said. "Let us retire now so we may be fresh for the hunt tomorrow."

As he lay on his pallet, Stephen turned over in his mind the information he had heard concerning Maud and her father. It occurred to him that it would be greatly to his advantage should the King die while still estranged from Maud, but the death would have to take place between now and the New Year, four weeks away, for it to be of any use to him. Regretfully, he dismissed the thought and fell into a dreamless sleep.

Next day the weather brought clear skies and a pale sun. The hunting party left at noon, joined by the de Beaumont twins, who had ridden in from Muelan the day before. By late afternoon the hunters, having brought down two stags, several doe, and a brace of hare, dismounted at the King's lodge on the edge of the forest. One of the stags was skinned, a haunch of venison skewered onto the spit over a roaring applewood fire, and soon the rich aroma of roasting game filled the air.

The evening was mild and King Henry decided to eat outside. Varlets spread a snowy cloth over the mossy forest floor, laid trenchers, and set out dishes of pike pie and stewed lampreys brought from the castle kitchens to accompany the platters of grilled rabbit and smoking slices of venison. The sun sank behind a purple line of hills in the west. The woods darkened to a deep blue-green; the evening air grew chill. Flagons of wine and mead passed round the fire again and again. Hounds snapped and growled; the laughter grew boisterous. King Henry's favorite minstrel tuned his lute and began to sing a popular tavern song.

Across the fire, King Henry, well wrapped in a great black cloak lined with bearskin, sat by himself in the shadow of a great oak. Stephen noted how frail and ill his uncle looked, his skin stretched thinly over bone, a glazed look in his watery eyes. He could not repress a shudder at the thought that this was what lay in wait for him at the end. I would prefer to die in battle, Stephen reflected, rather than grow so old I am always ill and unable to do for myself. By God's birth, the King would be better off dead than to continue in this miserable state.

Out of the corner of his eye, Stephen saw a servitor surreptitiously pick up a wooden bowl of stewed lampreys warming by the fire. With a quick look over his shoulder, the servitor made his way round the fire to where the King sat alone. Everyone's attention was on the minstrel, Stephen noted, and the servitor's action had not been observed. That greedy old man, Stephen thought. Really, the King ought to be ashamed of himself, knowing what effect the dish of lampreys had on his stomach. He rose to his feet and made his way round the fire to where the King sat. The servitor had vanished.

"Ah, Nephew," The King said at his approach. "A most successful day. You knew I killed one of the stags myself?"

Stephen had seen the King aim at the stag, but knew it was Robert's arrow which actually felled the beast.

"A mighty feat, Sire," Stephen said. He pointed to the covered dish. "Is that stewed lampreys I smell?"

The King grunted. "And if it is? I know my physicians particularly forbid it, but what do they know?" He ran a greedy tongue over his bloodless lips, as he lifted off the wooden cover.

Stephen eased himself down beside his uncle. "Come, Sire, you will make yourself ill if you eat the dish. Let me remove temptation."

He reached for the dish but the King stayed his hand.

"Am I master in my own house?"

Firelight rippled across Henry's face like waves on a dark shore. With a deliberate gesture he dipped his fingers into the lampreys and put some into his mouth.

"Ambrosia," he said, licking his fingers. "Those learned men of medicine told me I would be dead and buried well over five years ago. But here I am."

It would be so easy to simply remove the dish, Stephen realized, hesitating. A conflict of emotions began to rage within him: affection and gratitude for the uncle who had showered him with honors and wealth warred with his resentment at being passed over for the crown. He finally reached out to grasp the dish.

"I have cheated death thus far," the King said, chewing the eels with relish, and barring Stephen's hand with a surprisingly strong arm. "Leave me be."

Powerless now to stop him, Stephen watched in horrified fascination as the King plunged his hand again and again into the wooden bowl until it was scraped clean. He washed the last of the lampreys down with a tankard of wine, wiping his mouth with the back of his hand.

"See?" he said with a loud belch. "No ill effects at all."

Stephen gave him a weak smile. The matter was truly in God's hands now, he thought, absolving himself of any wrongdoing. He waited anxiously by the King's side but nothing happened. The eels were not going to affect him after all, Stephen thought, both relieved and disappointed.

After a time, Stephen saw Robert detach himself from the others and thread this way through the seated men.

"Would you like to retire now, Father?" Robert asked as he approached the King.

King Henry yawned. "Yes. The day's outing has done me good. I should sleep well tonight." A sudden spasm crossed his face.

A chill ran down Stephen's spine. "What is it, Sire?"

"I—the—" The King's mouth gaped like a hooked fish but no words came forth. His eyes rolled upward into his head, a white froth bubbled from his lips, and he fell backwards, clutching his bloated stomach.

His uncle had the look of death on his face, Stephen realized, surprised at how numb and frozen he suddenly felt. Then he saw the wooden bowl lying near the King's body. Had Robert noticed it?

"The King has been taken ill," Robert cried, bending over his father's prostrate form. "We must get him into the lodge at once." Everyone ran to the King's side. Robert beckoned to William of Warrenne, Earl of Surrey. "Ride at once to Rouen and bring the physicians back with you. Hurry."

Stephen rose. Without quite knowing why, for he had done nothing to feel guilty about, he attempted to conceal the dish with his body before kicking it backwards into the woods.

Brian and the twins crowded round the King's body and together they carried him into the hunting lodge. Robert and Stephen followed. The rest of the hunting party were made to wait outside.

"By the Mass," Robert said, looking down at his father, "I don't understand it. One moment he is fine and the next he is stricken. Stephen, did you see what happened?"

"No. As far as I could tell, it occurred exactly as you said."

The King began to vomit uncontrollably, gasping for breath, while the distraught nobles hovered over him. As Rouen lay six leagues distant from the woods of Lyons-la-Forêt, it was dawn before the Earl of Surrey finally returned with the physicians. They examined the contents of the King's stomach, then poked and prodded his distended belly. The King moaned and managed to rasp out a few choked words:

"Maud—" he croaked, lifting his head. "Stephen—" His eyes closed and his head fell back.

"There's no mystery here, my lords. The King has been eating stewed lampreys again," said one of the doctors with a severe look at Robert. "He was forbidden the dish, and has not abided by this salutary counsel. I fear there is little we can do now."

"How did he manage to get hold of stewed lampreys?" asked Robert, looking at the shocked group. "Who would be so wicked as to give him any?" His eyes slowly scanned the five nobles present, all of whom vehemently denied knowledge of the act.

Stephen held his breath, waiting for the condemning voice, the accusing finger. But no one paid him the slightest attention. The physicians bled King Henry with leeches, and attempted to pour various potions down his throat, to no avail. Several times he attempted speech but was only able to make rattling sounds in his throat.

At midday one of the doctors turned to Robert. "I fear it is close to the end, my lord, for his heartbeat is so faint I can barely hear it. Send for the Archbishop of Rouen. The King won't last through the night. Nothing can save him. He must confess his sins as best he can and be given the last sacraments."

"I will go myself to fetch the Archbishop," Stephen quickly offered.

He did not wait for agreement but ran from the lodge to where the horses had been tethered. In truth he could no longer bear the sight of the King's contorted face and swollen belly, or the stench of impending death that pervaded the lodge.

The Archbishop was in Rouen Cathedral preparing for Compline when Stephen arrived. He quickly gathered what he would need to give the King his last rites, then, accompanied by several clergymen, hurriedly left for the hunting lodge.

"I will notify the ducal palace," Stephen told him, "then join you later at the lodge."

When Stephen entered the palace, the first person he met was the King's seneschal, Hugh Bigod, on his way to Compline.

"The King lies only hours away from death from a surfeit of stewed lampreys," Stephen said. "The Archbishop has just left to administer the last rites. I pray he is not too late."

Hugh, a small man with sloping shoulders and the narrow face of a weasel, signed himself. "So greed has undone him. May God rest his soul and grant him infinite mercy." He paused. "Did the King make any significant changes in the disposition of his realm?"

"Not while I was there. In truth, he is beyond coherent speech."

"Pity."

Stephen gave Hugh a searching look. "What changes did you hope for?"

Bigod led Stephen down the passage, out of earshot of men entering or leaving the great hall.

"Since the estrangement from his daughter, some among us hoped the King would repent of the oath forced upon his barons, and deny her as his heir."

Stephen's heart began to hammer in his chest. "In favor of?"

Hugh gave him a sly look. "His nephew, Stephen of Blois, naturally."

Their eyes met and held. "He whispered nothing in your ear as you bent to solace him?" Hugh asked with a meaningful smile.

Stephen hesitated. An image of Maud flickered briefly in his mind; her last words of rejection echoed in his ears. Hardening his heart, he made a quick decision.

"If the King had whispered in my ear, I would be the last person to be believed in such a matter, for there is too much I stand to gain."

Hugh stared at him. "What are you suggesting?"

"That, as the King's seneschal, you could easily bear witness to having heard the King's last words. If you left for the lodge at once, you could say in perfect truth that you had been there at the time of his death. He will not last through the night, believe me."

Hugh cast an uneasy glance down the passageway to where a guard yawned. "You must be mad."

"Am I? Who put the idea into my head? Who regretted that the King had not repudiated his daughter in my favor?"

There was a tense silence while Hugh regarded him through half-closed lids. "What persons are present at the lodge now?"

"Two physicians. His son of Gloucester, the Lords of Wallingford, Warrenne, and Perche, and the de Beaumont twins, with the Archbishop on his way."

Hugh licked dry lips and scratched himself under the arm. "What you ask entails great risk. I cannot speak for the others, but Robert and Brian will certainly deny anything I say against the Countess of Anjou. It will be my word against theirs."

"The twins will do whatever I ask, and William of Warrenne has always been favorably disposed toward me. But in truth your word will be the most important."

"Why?"

"Let me explain," Stephen said, trying to banish all thought of Maud and what this would do to her. "I propose to leave for Boulogne tonight, and thence to England."

"Is that wise? Surely your absence will be noted?"

"Not immediately. There will be too much confusion and grief attendant upon the King's death. By the time someone does notice, it will be too late." He could hardly believe the words were coming from his own mouth.

"Too late for what?" Hugh frowned.

"Too late to prevent me from being crowned," Stephen said. Part of him was listening to his words in horror, while another part was oddly elated, justifying his actions by believing that it was all Maud's fault. She could have prevented this.

He heard Hugh's sudden indrawn breath. "By Christ, this is no sudden impulse, but a well thought out plot to take over the realm! That crafty brother of yours is behind this, I'll warrant." His eyes darted up and down the deserted passageway. "Very well, what is it you would have me do?"

"Come at once to Winchester as soon as the King is officially pronounced dead. My brother and I will have all in readiness. All you need do is swear that the King changed his mind at the last and named me heir. The whole realm knows of his estrangement from Maud and Geoffrey. Your word will be sufficient to get me crowned. By then it won't matter who supports your tale." He searched the seneschal's face. "You understand that haste is paramount? The moment the King is dead you must leave for England."

"Indeed, my lord." Hugh gave him a cunning look. "I understand only too well. If at all possible you wish to be crowned before anyone notices anything awry."

Stephen acknowledged Hugh's comments with a curt nod but did not speak. He was already regretting having confided in this man, doubting he could be trusted.

Hugh scratched himself again, his face tense. "You ask me to take an enormous risk. What is my exchange for this act of perjury?"

"Surely it is worth something to be delivered from the Angevins?"

"True enough, but not sufficient to make up for a reputation that will lie in tatters before this business is over. There's my broken oath to consider, losing the goodwill of old colleagues. Not everyone will flock to your side, you know."

Stephen gave him a winning smile. "I know only too well. But there are others who will champion your words and say you acted in a worthy cause, whatever means were used. My brother has promised absolution from the church, so your immortal soul is not in peril." He clasped Hugh's hands in his own. "When I am king I will make it worth your while, I promise you. You only need ask for what you want."

"The earldom of Norfolk. Title and lands."

"Consider it done."

After a long pause, Hugh slowly nodded his head. "Very well, I will do it. And I'll hold you to your promise, my lord. We meet again in England."

The fear of discovery would soon be over, Stephen thought, as he rode through the night to the port of Boulogne to take ship for England. He felt no surge of triumph, only relief that events had at last been set in motion and the prize was almost within his grasp. The meeting with Hugh had been fortuitous, like a godsend. How astounded his brother would be!

Stephen was surprised not to feel any remorse over his uncle. The King had had a prosperous, if uneven reign for thirty-five years. His only regret was Maud. He loved his cousin; he knew he would always love her, and because of the passion they had shared together she would probably never forgive him for taking the throne. Yet was that entirely fair?

He argued with an invisible Maud, reminding her that she had never faced up to the fact that no one wanted to be ruled by a woman, particularly one with an Angevin husband. After all, he thought, stiffening his resolve, she had made her choice; he had made his. So be it.

No sooner had Stephen taken ship from the port of Wissant in Boulogne than a great storm arose. Lightning forked across a black sky, followed by claps of thunder. A torrential rain rocked the ship and the fearful crew wondered what such a sign portended: Was the end of the world come at last?

Undaunted by the storm, Stephen wondered if King Henry had just drawn his last breath, and this was God's way of acknowledging the passing of a mighty monarch. He smiled to himself, knowing the thought would have pleased the king. In fact, the entire venture on which he had embarked was something his uncle would have understood only too well. The great William, his grandfather, had taken England by conquest; his son, King Henry, had taken it by treachery. Was he so very different, then, from his usurping forebears? He must have inherited more Norman blood than he imagined, Stephen thought with a grim smile.

A day later he landed safely at Dover with a force of men he had picked up in Boulogne. First Stephen sent a herald to his brother at

Winchester, informing the Bishop of the events that had taken place in Rouen: the King's death—which surely would have occurred by now—and what he next proposed to do. Then he rode to Dover Castle, held by Robert of Gloucester's men.

"I seek entrance to the castle," Stephen called to the guard in the gatehouse. "King Henry has been mortally stricken in Rouen and is surely in heaven by now."

He waited while the guard fetched the castellan of the castle.

"If the King is dead and the Countess of Anjou is queen, why have we not been informed by Earl Robert?" the castellan called down from the ramparts. "Why do you wish entrance?"

Taken aback, Stephen hesitated, realizing he had not thought this matter through. He had expected the gates to be thrown open immediately and inwardly cursed himself for not having been better prepared for all eventualities. But the hesitation was sufficient to make the already cautious castellan suspicious.

"I'm sorry, my lord, but without orders from the Earl I cannot permit you entrance."

Within moments the battlements bristled with guards.

The castellan was sure to report the incident, which would reveal his intentions to Robert sooner than anticipated, but Stephen did not have sufficient men to lay siege to the castle and time was against him. He decided to make for Canterbury, but as he had not slept in forty-eight hours or eaten since the day before, he stopped at an inn for a quick nap and rushed meal.

When he reached Canterbury he saw what his brief delay had cost him. The castle there, also held by Robert's men, had obviously been warned by the castellan at Dover. The gates of the town were closed against him. Had it all been for naught, Stephen wondered, dismayed at the hostile reception. What did this portend for his future?

When he reached London, however, it was a different story. The leading citizens, with whom Stephen had always been popular, listened to the news of the King's probable demise in respectful silence, shed a few tears, then gave him an enthusiastic welcome. Without any formal right to do so, the most influential of the burghers called for a general assembly at which they declared they would only have Stephen for king. In that instant, all Stephen's doubts vanished.

"I will make a pact with you, good people," he called out to the assembled throng on a frosty morning in December. His tall figure towered above everyone else. A radiant smile illuminated his face;

the winter sun fell upon his bare head like a halo of pale gold. A hush fell upon the crowd. The affection and goodwill flowing between himself and those gathered to hear him were palpable.

Stephen threw out his arms as if to clasp them in his embrace. "I will devote myself with all my might to pacify the kingdom for the benefit of everyone, as did my uncle. Here is my solemn promise, before God and all His Saints."

One of the foremost citizens shouted back: "As long as you shall live, we will uphold you as king with all our resources, and guard your life with all our strength."

There was a thunderous response from the folk of London, who cheered for Stephen, threw their caps in the air, and carried him about on their shoulders. Heady with triumph, Stephen felt he had attained the summit of his ambitions.

Chapter Thirty-four

England, 1135

THE NEXT DAY STEPHEN SENT A FAST COURIER TO TELL THE BISHOP OF Winchester of his acclaim in London. Stressing haste, he urged his brother to gather together all the influential churchmen and nobles who were immediately available, particularly the Archbishop of Canterbury. After spending several days consolidating his position in the capital, Stephen left for Winchester.

As he galloped out of London, Stephen hoped his brother had gained access to the treasury, which, he surmised, must be of huge proportions after his uncle's careful hoarding. Although possession of the treasury, as well as the support of the London citizens and Norman barons, was essential for any claimant to the crown, the recognition of leading churchmen was equally important. Only the Archbishop of Canterbury could crown a king. Stephen knew he must rely heavily on his brother, upon whom the ultimate success of their whole enterprise depended.

He reached Winchester the following day at first light. Bishop Henry, surrounded by a crowd of leading citizens, nobles, and prelates, greeted Stephen with a smile and threw welcoming arms around him. Yet Stephen sensed a tension in his brother's body.

"Oh, well done, Brother," Henry whispered. "You have acted with dispatch and I highly commend you."

Stephen looked quickly over the crowd, noting the presence of the Bishop of Salisbury, the Archbishop of Canterbury, and other leading churchmen, as well as the treasurer. "Will they accept me?" he asked under his breath. "Do you have possession of the treasury?"

"The day is not yet won," Henry murmured, a strained look crossing his face. "The Archbishop is troubled by his oath to the King's daughter; the treasurer is also plagued by an attack of conscience, reluctant to part with the keys to the treasury until he sees which way the wind blows. However, now you're here let us see if we can put the situation to rights."

The Bishop signed himself with an elaborate gesture, then turned to the assembled men and raised his hands for silence. "Benedicte! Worthy citizens, noble lords, men of God. We know King Henry has been called to his just reward." He waited until those present had signed themselves, and murmured a prayer for their dead monarch.

"To follow this mighty sovereign," Henry of Winchester continued, "this very Lion of Justice, who better than his well-beloved nephew, Stephen of Blois, Count of Boulogne and Mortain. A man who has virtually grown up in England—" He paused. "Grown up in England, I say, and familiar with the customs of this land. A man known to each and every one of you, not a stranger reared in foreign parts, but a Norman like yourselves. A grandson of the great Conqueror, my brother is a devoted son of Holy Church, affable, bold and brave, magnificent and unassuming. No finer warrior exists in all the realm! Married to a daughter of Saxon nobility, who can deny that Stephen is the best suited to wear England's crown?"

The crowd solemnly nodded their agreement. The oblique reference to those reared in foreign parts—Maud and Geoffrey—was lost on no one present. His brother's eloquence should convince the devil himself, Stephen thought, with a wary eye on the Archbishop, William of Corbeil, a frail elderly man, who would not meet his glance.

Henry raised his voice. "London has already proclaimed Stephen as the king they desire. Will you now accept him as well?"

There were shouts of approval from members of the crowd. Stephen noticed that the prelates, banded together like a group of black crows, held themselves aloof from the crowd, himself and his brother.

"I doubt if anyone here wishes to be ruled by a female with an Angevin for husband, but what about the oath of allegiance we swore to the King's daughter?" a nobleman from Sussex called out.

Several other voices joined in: "Aye, what about the oath?"

The group of prelates nodded their heads. Stephen started to speak but the Bishop of Winchester signaled him to remain silent. "I believe the Bishop of Salisbury has something to say about that. My lord bishop?"

Roger of Salisbury limped slowly forward and addressed the gathering in his unctuous voice. "The oath of allegiance exacted by our late King was made under duress. Such an oath is not binding."

There were murmurs of agreement from the majority of the crowd. Stephen saw the Archbishop of Canterbury whisper into the ear of his cleric. The cleric stepped forward.

"My lord archbishop recalls no duress, but points out that a sworn oath is binding no matter how it is taken. To break such an oath is to imperil your immortal soul!"

From across the crowd, the Archbishop's eyes seemed to look directly at Stephen.

"Heaven protect us from so-called men of principle," the Bishop of Winchester muttered, his voice tight with vexation. "Surely the Archbishop sees which way the tide runs?"

"He chooses not to. We must convince him," said the Bishop of Salisbury, who again raised his voice. "When I say duress, the threat was implicit. Attendance at the homage ceremony was mandatory. The late King had all the ports closed so no one could leave England. Who would have dared oppose him?"

Henry cleared his throat. "With all due respect, my lord archbishop, there is another reason why such an oath cannot be binding: It was conditional on the King's daughter not being given in marriage to anyone without the consent of the great council."

The crowd now began to talk excitedly among themselves.

"Of course! I had forgotten that. So King Henry has violated our allegiance, and no one is bound by his oath," the nobleman from Sussex called out. "I will have Stephen. Gladly."

There was a roar of approval. "Yes, yes, we will have Stephen," the crowd shouted as one voice.

The treasurer scanned the crowd with a judicious eye. Then he stepped forward and presented Stephen with a ring of heavy iron keys. "A prosperous reign, my lord. I pray you leave this treasury as full as you find it."

The crowd cheered even more loudly at this gesture of confidence. The group of prelates dispersed, the majority of them joining the

Bishops of Salisbury and Winchester. The few that remained looked uncertainly toward the Archbishop of Canterbury.

Henry smiled. "If the sheep desert the fold, can the shepherd be far behind?"

All eyes now turned to the Archbishop. Aided by two clerics, William of Corbeil walked slowly over to Stephen, his gold-encrusted miter sparkling under the morning sun.

"My lord," he said to Stephen in a quavering voice, looking uneasily at the huge crowd. "I am an old man now, and will soon follow my late monarch. The Bishop of Winchester's argument has merit, but not sufficient for me to violate my sworn word. In my heart I share his sentiments, but I dare not crown you king."

Stephen opened his mouth to protest, then thought better of it. Nothing he could say or do would carry as much weight as the arrival of Hugh Bigod, who would surely have left for England by now. With a silent prayer that the shifty seneschal had not changed his mind, Stephen knelt to kiss the prelate's ring.

"Perhaps Your Grace will see fit to change his views," he replied.

The Archbishop inclined his head, then retreated into Winchester Cathedral with his entourage.

Bishop Henry watched him with a sour expression on his face. "How such a timid soul rose so high passes all understanding," he said.

"It should not be long before the See of Canterbury is occupied by one far better suited to its splendor," Bishop Roger said, with a fawning smile that set Stephen's teeth on edge.

It was obvious to him that the Bishop of Salisbury, ever alert to his own survival in the shift of power from one reign to another, had decided to back Henry as the force behind the throne. He needed a new patron, and who better than the future Archbishop of Canterbury? Immediately Stephen felt a stab of resentment toward Roger. If the crafty old prelate thought that the future King of England would become a tool of the church, he was very much mistaken.

Bishop Henry exchanged a look of complicity with Roger of Salisbury. "I fear that day may never come, if my brother is not crowned quickly. For all we know, the Countess of Anjou, my Lord of Gloucester, the entire Angevin contingent in fact, may already be on their way to England."

"There has scarcely been time for news to reach Angers, but in any case Maud will go to Normandy first," Stephen said.

The two prelates looked at him in surprise.

"How can you know that?" Henry asked.

"It would be unlike her to think first of the crown, before paying her filial respects to her dead father, even if they were estranged. She will also want to accompany the King's body to England for burial."

"I believe Stephen is right," said Bishop Roger. "After all, as far as the Countess is concerned there is no urgency to come to England immediately. By the time she learns what has transpired here, it will, with God's grace, all be over. Once Stephen has been anointed as king there will be very little she or anyone else can do."

"Well, that may gain us more time, but no solution. At this moment my brother is no nearer being anointed king than he was when he arrived. Who has any suggestions?"

Stephen held his tongue. Better to wait until Hugh Bigod actually arrived, otherwise he'd look a proper fool if the seneschal failed to turn up.

As he followed the two bishops down the streets of Winchester, heading for Wolvesey Castle, Stephen realized that three of the most powerful persons in the realm, two of them princes of the church, were all at the mercy of one frail, elderly prelate: the Archbishop of Canterbury. The church was far too busy meddling in temporal affairs that were not its province, Stephen decided. How dare the Archbishop go against the will of the people? In truth, if, after Hugh's story, that foolish old man still refused to crown him, he would force him to the act. Stephen knew he was more than willing to be a devoted son of Holy Church, but never its slave.

They walked through the city gates and into the grounds of Wolvesey, covered now with a light frost. Inside his brother's elegantly appointed palace a sumptuous feast awaited them. They had just sat down at the high table in the great hall when the steward announced the arrival from Normandy of Hugh Bigod, the late King's seneschal.

"I've been expecting him," Stephen said to Henry as he rose to his feet. His heart began to thud in anticipation.

All eyes turned to the hall entrance where Hugh Bigod, travel-stained and weary, had just made his appearance.

"My lord bishops," he called out, "I bring important news. With his last breath King Henry released his barons from their oath of allegiance to the Countess of Anjou. Yes, my friends," he continued, raising his voice, "directly after his nephew left Rouen, the King rallied just long enough to renounce his daughter in favor of Stephen of Blois, who is named heir to England and Normandy!"

There was a moment of stunned silence, then everyone began to talk all at once. If he lived to be a hundred, Stephen thought with relish, he would never forget the look of total astonishment on Henry's face. It was the only time in living memory that he had ever caught his brother completely by surprise.

"You have outdone yourself, Brother," Bishop Henry murmured under his breath.

There was no mistaking the new note of respect in his voice. A moment to savor and cherish.

It was well after dark when Stephen, the Bishops of Salisbury and Winchester, and Hugh Bigod arrived at Winchester Cathedral where they confronted the Archbishop of Canterbury with the startling news.

The Archbishop listened carefully. "By the Rood, this is a surprising turn of events," he said, when Hugh had finished. "You have evidence that the King changed his mind? I mean to say, my lord, it is a highly unusual development, is it not?"

"How so?" Roger of Salisbury interjected quickly, before Hugh Bigod could speak. "Indeed, my lord archbishop, it is common knowledge that the late King and his daughter were estranged. Why, Geoffrey of Anjou had as good as declared war on Normandy! This news doesn't surprise me at all."

"Nor any of us," added the Bishop of Winchester.

Obviously uncertain, the Archbishop hesitated. Stephen held his breath.

"I'm sure that Hugh Bigod is prepared to swear a holy oath that the King named Stephen his heir," Henry said, turning to the seneschal with a confident smile.

Slowly, the Archbishop nodded. "Very well. If you are prepared to swear such an oath, my son, I must accept it. And accept it with glad grace," he added timidly, "for as God is my witness, I did not see how we would ever be reconciled to a female sovereign."

Hugh swallowed and glanced at Stephen. "Yes," he said slowly, "I'm prepared to swear such an oath."

Stephen let out his breath in a long sigh of release as he wrung the seneschal's hand. Bishop Roger and Bishop Henry exchanged complacent smiles while Stephen uneasily watched Hugh Bigod glibly perjure himself before the huge gathering. He was unable to quell the feeling that his unholy bargain with Hugh had already diminished some of his power.

After Hugh had sworn, the Archbishop suddenly raised a cautionary hand. "Before I agree to crown you, my lord, there is something I require of you."

Stephen flashed a look at his brother who gave a slight frown as if to say, humor the old fool. He turned back to the Archbishop with a questioning smile.

"You must swear an oath to restore and maintain the liberties of Holy Church," William of Corbeil announced.

"Well said, Your Grace. I am in favor of such an oath," Bishop Roger said promptly.

"And I," echoed the Bishop of Winchester, nodding his approval.

It appeared to Stephen that the three prelates moved imperceptibly closer together, as if aligning themselves against him. Three pairs of eyes, united now in a common purpose, fixed him with a piercing look. He suppressed a strong surge of resentment; the church was forever complaining about its rights. Fortunately, the concept of "restoring and maintaining the liberties of Holy Church" was sufficiently vague that he could not be held to any specific promise.

"I agree, Your Grace. I will swear whatever you like."

Still the Archbishop hesitated, as if not quite certain he could trust Stephen's assurances. The man was less a fool than he seemed, Stephen decided.

The Bishop of Winchester stepped forward and put his hand on Stephen's shoulder. "I will stand surety for my brother's good faith," he said. "Your Grace has my solemn word."

The Archbishop of Canterbury nodded, apparently satisfied. "Then as God is my witness, I promise to crown you King of England."

Henry took Stephen's hands in his and said: "Who would have believed this moment, that fateful day so long ago, when you sailed for England, alone and friendless, one against the world?"

Stephen thought he saw a bead of moisture in Henry's eyes, then decided it must be a trick of the candlelight. On the way back to his brother's castle, Stephen felt bathed in a golden glow of victory; his feet hardly touched the frozen ground and his spirits soared as high as the steeple on the cathedral. Looking up at the dark winter sky he felt he had only to reach out his hand for the heavens to shower him with stars.

Stephen was crowned at Westminster on the twenty-second day of December—St. Stephen's Day; a day of good omen, he was convinced. It was a cold morning, with icy blue skies and an orange sun.

The bells of Westminster Abbey, St. Paul's, St. John's, St. Bride's, and St. Mary-le-Bow rang out in a glorious crescendo of sound to herald the arrival of a splendid new reign. By Stephen's side, Matilda, soon to be brought to bed of her third child, smiled radiantly at the cheering throng. When the Archbishop of Canterbury placed the Conqueror's crown on Stephen's head, he thought his heart would burst. This was the symbol of all his hopes achieved, a golden promise that the peace and plenty of King Henry's reign would continue with King Stephen.

PART TWO

Chapter One

Angers, 1135

On a mild day in late December, Maud stood in the nursery chamber at Angers Castle looking down in dismay at her elder son. Lying on the floor, his fat little legs thrashing wildly, his dimpled fists pounding the dried rushes, Henry bellowed his rage. His nurse, Isabelle, a stout girl from Le Mans, stood over him, plump arms on hips, exasperation written over her face. Next to her, a stolid wet nurse suckled the two-month-old baby, Geoffrey.

"Whatever is amiss with him?" Maud asked, kneeling beside the screaming child, whose eyes were screwed tightly shut in his chubby crimson face. She pushed back wisps of rust-colored hair from his damp forehead. "Henry, my poppet, what is it? Tell Maman."

"There is nothing whatsoever amiss, Madam," Henry's nurse assured her. "Young Master Henry has already gorged himself on six honey cakes and I refused to let him have any more, fearing he would make himself sick. That's what happened the last time, Madam—if you remember?"

"Yes, I remember," Maud replied. Henry had now turned an alarming shade of purple, an uncomfortable reminder of her father in one of his rages.

"Let him have another," she told the nurse with a weary sigh.

Isabelle's face puckered into ridges of disapproval. "A mistake, Madam. Young Master cannot be allowed to think that he will get his own way by tantrums and willful behavior."

"I daresay you're right," Maud said, helpless to deny Henry anything.

Magically the screams stopped as Henry sat up and wiped his nose and round cheeks on the sleeve of his green tunic. Still sniffling, he threw his arms around Maud before reaching for the platter of honey cakes. With a triumphant glare at Isabelle, he stuffed two into his mouth at once.

"Look, Madam." Geoffrey's wet nurse held out the baby for Maud's inspection. "Master Geoffrey has gained nicely. He's quite plump now."

"Splendid," Maud said, trying to muster an interest she did not feel as she gave the baby an absentminded pat on the head.

Little Geoffrey, whose alabaster skin, blue eyes, and red-gold curls proclaimed him a miniature version of his father, continued to suckle while Maud gazed tenderly at her young son. She wiped a dribble of honey from his chin, her heart melting with love and pride.

Already he behaved like a little tyrant, the bane of his nurse, as well as Aldyth, ruling the castle with his whims and rages, his pugnacious, stubborn will. Yet he had the gift of ruling hearts as well. His charm was irresistible—when he chose to exercise it. Young Henry had a precocious intelligence, his strength was that of a child of six, and his desire to learn insatiable. He asked so many questions that he had been given his first tutor a month ago.

"He is unusually clever, advanced for his age, I grant you that, but where do these violent rages come from?" Geoffrey had remarked more than once, looking at Henry with a puzzled frown. "Surely he must be a throwback to his ferocious forebears, those savage Northmen who harried the coast of Europe."

Maud had been tempted to reply that the Angevins were considered a devil's brood, their history peppered with violence, not to mention murder and treachery. She had refrained in the interests of maintaining the uneasy truce existing between Geoffrey and herself.

"Well, that's hardly a heritage to be ashamed of," she had contented herself with saying. "After all, Henry is a great-grandson of the Conqueror, quite an illustrious forebear, I should have thought."

"And what of his illustrious Angevin forebear, now King of Jerusalem," had been Geoffrey's lightning response. Whenever she mentioned "the Conqueror," Geoffrey countered with "King Fulk of Jerusalem."

Maud shuddered at the thought of her husband's reaction should he ever suspect that Henry could claim the Conqueror as great-grandfather on both sides. What a pity it must be kept secret, she thought regretfully, for no other heir in Europe could boast so mighty a lineage. As a child born of so deep a love, Maud had never doubted that her son—hers and Stephen's—was destined for greatness.

The sound of horses galloping into the courtyard and the tone of excited voices caused Maud to walk over to the open casement window. Below she could see her half-brother, Robert of Gloucester, and Brian FitzCount talking to Geoffrey and his steward as their steaming mounts were led away by grooms. She saw Geoffrey say something to the steward, who bowed and disappeared from view.

It must be news of her father, Maud thought, assailed by a premonition of disaster. Dying? Perhaps death had already claimed him. Holy Mary, do not let him be dead, she prayed, not while we are still estranged. I could not bear it.

As she watched, the three men vanished into the keep. Squaring her shoulders, Maud left the nursery and descended the stairs. Inside the great hall the three men, joined now by the Bishop of Angers, had grouped themselves around the open hearth, warming themselves at the fire. Heart pounding, Maud offered her cheek to Robert, and her hand to Brian.

"What do you here?" she asked.

"Wife, there is disastrous news," Geoffrey began, his face deathly pale and his eyes blazing. "You will not believe—"

Brian silenced him with a quick gesture.

"My father is dead," she said, suddenly sure of it.

"More than a fortnight ago, from a surfeit of stewed lampreys," Robert confirmed. His face, drawn and pinched, had aged ten years since she had seen him last. "His body now lies at Caen awaiting burial in England."

Maud signed herself, blinking back tears. Impossible to believe that she would never see that dark, powerful figure again, inconceivable to imagine that iron will extinguished. The conflicts between them faded into nothingness; all she could remember was the time he had helped her return to Anjou, and, more important, when he had broken with precedent and defied popular opinion to make her his heir.

"If God had only called him a month later I would have been with him when he died," Maud said. "I will never forgive myself for not having returned to Normandy earlier. That he should die while we were still estranged—" She choked on her words, remembering the fateful decision of last May, to return to Geoffrey and leave her father.

As she paced back and forth across the hall, there came a sudden realization that now she was Queen of England and Duchess of Normandy. Eventually she would allow herself the luxury of enjoying the excitement and challenge of her new status, but at this moment grief held sway.

Something Robert had said penetrated her thoughts. She stopped in front of her half-brother. "A fortnight? You say he died more than a fortnight ago? Why did no one send word? Had I known immediately, I could have been in Normandy by now." She patted Robert's arm. "Forgive me, Brother, I know you are burdened with much to do." She turned to Geoffrey. "We had best leave at once so that I may accompany my father's body to England. It was always his intention to be buried at Reading Abbey. After the funeral I hope to be crowned—" She stopped, suddenly aware of the tension emanating from the four men.

Something besides the King's death weighed heavily on their hearts.

"Did my father say aught of me before he died?" she asked in some trepidation. Why did they look like that? What were they afraid to tell her?

"He was seized so suddenly there was no time for him to speak of anyone," Robert replied quickly. Too quickly.

"I see." Maud looked at his anguished face. "Tell me what troubles you," she said gently. "Whatever it is, I have the strength to bear it."

Robert and Brian looked helplessly at each other.

"For the love of God, tell her what that conniving thief has done," Geoffrey burst out, his eyes glittering, his mouth working with anger.

"What conniving thief?" Maud's heart skipped a beat; she braced herself for—she knew not what.

"I think it best you sit down, Madam," the Bishop of Angers said.

Bewildered and apprehensive, Maud seated herself in a high-backed chair with carved wooden arms. Geoffrey called for wine.

"I'm listening," she said, after the wine had come, holding the pewter goblet tightly in both hands.

Robert looked down at his booted feet. "Do you tell her, Brian, for I cannot bring myself to do so."

"We had been hunting in the woods outside Rouen and were feasting on the fruits of our labor when the King was stricken," Brian began. "When it became apparent he was at death's door, Stephen volunteered to ride into the city to fetch the Archbishop of Rouen." He took a deep breath. "Stephen didn't return, but the King's seneschal, Hugh Bigod, appeared and stayed until the King died later that night. In all the grief and confusion attendant upon the King's death, none noted that Stephen was still absent, and that Hugh Bigod had also disappeared."

Overcome with fear, Maud felt her heart freeze. "Do you tell me something has happened to Stephen as well?"

"Would that it had, may God forgive me," Robert said, his voice uncharacteristically hard with bitterness. "As it turned out, before our father drew his last breath, Stephen had fled to Boulogne and taken ship for England, followed almost immediately by Hugh Bigod."

Maud felt the blood drain from her face. "Knowing my father was close to death, Stephen sailed for England?" she whispered, her voice unsteady. "But why? Why?"

"To usurp the crown—why else?" Geoffrey shouted, his face contorted with fury. "That vicious wretch and his ambitious brother, lusting after power, have obviously planned this for months, perhaps years! Did I not warn you? Did I not beg King Henry to listen? I knew there was treachery in their hearts!"

The Bishop of Angers laid a restraining hand on Geoffrey's shoulder. Beyond speech, Maud could not take in the sense of what she had just heard; an enormous weight pressed against her head. She signaled Brian to continue.

"As Geoffrey says, we must assume Stephen and Bishop Henry had all their plans in readiness. This was no impulse of the moment." Brian paused. "We heard then that Stephen had arrived in London where he was selected king by popular demand. Thence to Winchester, where his brother had gathered together various nobles and churchmen. The keys of the treasury were turned over to Stephen and he was acclaimed king-elect by all present."

Sudden tears glistened in Robert's dark eyes. "Stephen was like a brother to me. That he should be capable of such treachery passes belief."

"How can you know for certain?" Maud whispered through icy

lips. "Could not this tale be false, a wicked rumor put about by our enemies?" Surely it was not true; Holy Mother, it could not be true! 'That conniving thief has usurped the crown.' The hateful words spun round and round in her mind like a caged animal seeking escape.

"Trusted men, still loyal to the late King's wishes, sent us word of what happened," Brian said in a gentle voice. "At last report the Archbishop of Canterbury himself had agreed to crown Stephen. It was then we left for Angers. We must now assume the coronation has already occurred. Neither Stephen nor Henry of Winchester would delay such an event."

"This is why we dallied so long in Normandy," Robert added. "We wanted to be certain of the facts before informing you."

"How did these treacherous scum buy the consent of the Archbishop of Canterbury?" Geoffrey cried. "When men sworn to serve God make mock of their sacred oath to an anointed king, truly Armageddon has arrived!"

"I refuse to believe the Archbishop was a party to this infamy," the Bishop of Angers cried, shock and horror written over his face. "William of Corbeil would never forswear his oath to the Countess of Anjou!"

"Initially, we heard, he refused to crown Stephen on just such grounds," Robert agreed. "But that was before the arrival of Hugh Bigod who, by perjuring himself, persuaded the Archbishop to change his mind." At Maud's indrawn gasp, Robert nodded. "As God is my witness, it is true: That wretched knave swore a sacred oath that with his last breath the King had disinherited his daughter and named his nephew, Stephen, heir to England and Normandy."

Her face ashen, Maud rose unsteadily to her feet, the goblet of wine falling unheeded to the rushes. "Was Hugh with my father? Could there be any truth in this?" Her hands clutched her throat; a great chasm yawned at her feet threatening to swallow her whole.

"Lies," Robert cried. "All of it lies! Hugh was never alone with the King for a single moment. And even if he had been, the King was beyond speech. We were in the lodge with the King from the moment he was stricken until he died. Hugh only arrived at the end. Bigod has perjured himself for all eternity!"

"Why, then, did no one denounce him?" asked the Bishop of Angers.

"Who in Winchester could have disputed his statement? He and Stephen were the only ones who had been in Rouen," Brian said.

The Bishop of Angers turned to Geoffrey. "I have heard enough, my lord. I leave at once for Rome. Unless Stephen has the Pope's consent, he cannot be legally crowned. When I tell His Holiness the truth, he will see justice done."

"By all means, Your Grace, leave for Rome," said Geoffrey, his voice laced with venom. "But don't be surprised to find that Bishop Henry's minions have been there before you, bringing costly gifts and whispering the right word in a well-placed ear. I doubt not that Winchester and his creatures have been wooing the Holy Father for some time." He paused, looking at Maud's stricken face. "Do you all realize why it has been so easy for the traitors to accomplish their wicked goal? Magnates, commonfolk, churchmen, even the Papal Curia itself—everyone, from the very beginning, has resisted a female ruler."

There was an appalled silence. Geoffrey walked over to Maud and took her hands in his. "I think we must face the bitter truth, Wife." His eyes did not flinch as they gazed steadily into hers. "None would question Hugh Bigod's statement—even had they known for certain he lied—because they didn't want to. The Normans have always wanted Stephen to be king."

Maud experienced a moment's gratitude to Geoffrey for his unsparing look at the truth. "I believe you're right," she managed to say. "We have all been blind."

"What is to be done? We must make plans, Wife."

"At the moment I cannot go on, much less make plans," Maud whispered. "Pray excuse me."

"We will seek vengeance, never fear." Geoffrey's hands gripped hers. "By God, that smiling Judas of Blois will pay for this. Upon the head of my son and heir, I swear to see you upon England's throne!"

"We swear as well," Robert and Brian replied as one voice.

"By your leave then, Count Geoffrey, I will depart for Rome," the Bishop of Angers said. "Regardless of the outcome, I must voice my protest to the Holy Father himself." He turned to Maud with a concerned look. "Is there aught I can do to console you, my lady? Shall we pray together in the chapel?"

Maud forced a grimace that she hoped would be taken for a smile, and shook her head, hoping she would not be sick before she reached the solar. Under the eyes of the concerned men, she walked slowly from the great hall. Once her knees started to buckle, and Robert ran to her aid, but she waved him away. Fearing her emotions would

erupt and she would make a total fool of herself, Maud knew she had
to seek the safety of her chamber at once. No one must suspect the
true nature of the devastating blow she had received.

She half ran up the winding staircase and down the long passage
before flinging open the door to the solar. Inside, her ladies and
Aldyth worked a tapestry together while a minstrel sang a *joi d'amour*
from the Languedoc. Mother of God, she had forgotten they were
there.

"By the Rood, what has happened?" Aldyth asked after one look
at Maud's face.

"Leave me, all of you," Maud choked out. "My Lord of Gloucester
will tell you the news, Aldyth. I cannot . . ."

Twittering like so many sparrows, the ladies left the solar, followed
by Aldyth and the minstrel. At the door, Aldyth started to turn back
but Maud waved her away with a firm hand. The nail-studded door
closed softly behind her.

Alone, Maud bent over a silver basin, swallowing repeatedly until
the wave of sickness passed; then she eased herself down on the
canopied bed. Nothing she had ever experienced could have begun to
prepare her for the crushing anguish now threatening to tear her
apart; her whole being was racked with an agony so intense it seemed
mortal. It was not possible to survive such pain. How could Stephen
do it? How could he have forsworn his oath to her? Betrayed their
love? Dishonored her so completely?

Maud repressed a scream, as images from the past rose unbidden
to torment her: Stephen frolicking with her in the water at Winchester, kissing her with warm, insistent lips, tenderly holding her in his
arms at the lodge near Windsor, taking possession of her body with a
passion that matched her own; Stephen in Rouen, begging her to
abandon responsibility and duty to come away with him.

She called upon God to aid her suffering in this terrible hour, called
upon the Holy Mother to help her withstand the searing, crucifying
pain of loss. Maud could feel no response to her cry for help; no
whisper of comfort penetrated the depths of her wretchedness. Em-
balmed in a shroud of despair, she wept, harsh, wrenching sobs that
tore at her body like a living animal. By his act of betrayal, Stephen
had taken away both the memory of their love, upon which she had
fed for sustenance and support, and her throne, the vital purpose that
motivated her life. Now there was neither love nor purpose. She had
been left with nothing. What was there to live for?

There was an intrusive pounding on the door, and Maud heard Henry's imperious voice calling to her.

"Maman, Maman!"

Numb to the demands of the outside world, Maud did not respond. When there was no reply Henry began to shout, then pushed open the door and ran into the chamber. She saw his gray eyes flash with impatience when he saw her lying on the bed, his expression almost comical in its intense, purposeful masculinity.

"Maman is resting, my poppet," Maud managed to whisper. "Go back to Isabelle."

Always fiercely demanding of his rights, Henry ignored her and climbed up onto the bed, butting his way into her arms like a young kid and nuzzling her neck with his nose.

"Please, my son, let me rest." Maud kissed the top of his little round head.

Henry sat up and gazed silently down at her, seeming instinctively to understand something was truly wrong. He gave her a wet kiss from his rosebud mouth, then scrambled down and ran out of the chamber, closing the door noisily behind him. Henry. Through the searing pain of loss, something stirred at the very core of her being. A reminder that Stephen had left her with something after all, a living legacy of what they had once meant to each other.

A new onslaught of grief threatened to overwhelm her, but this time Maud fought it down as if it were a vicious adversary, burying it deep within her. What good were tears, she thought, remembering her father's words to her so long ago: 'A granddaughter of the Conqueror does not cry.'

I must not succumb, Maud told herself, even if my heart breaks and death would be a welcome release. I owe it to Henry to live. It is his heritage that has been stolen, as well as mine. My father wanted me to be his heir and Henry after me. Then his sons and grandsons to follow. I will not allow Stephen to take what is mine! I will be queen.

The grief froze within her, then encysted into anger; despair hardened into savage determination; agony turned to pride; the wish to die became the need to reclaim her heritage. In a wordless plea from the heart, Maud called upon her blood to help avenge this mortal insult to the House of Normandy. It seemed to her then that a shadowy host of Norman ancestors—the first Duke Rollo, Richard the Fearless, Robert the Magnificent, the great Conqueror and his

proud wife, Matilda, the cunning Lion of Justice, her own father—
rose up to answer her desperate appeal.

She vowed to avenge herself and her blood on this treacherous
cousin of Blois; to pick up the pieces of her shattered life and take
back what was rightfully hers. If love—if even the memory of love
—was to be denied her, then vengeance must suffice. I will not be
beaten, Maud cried. Coldly, she watched the woman she might have
become die unmourned within her, to be replaced by the woman who
would survive.

Chapter Two

England, 1136

STEPHEN'S REIGN BEGAN MOST AUSPICIOUSLY. EARLY IN THE NEW YEAR, still glowing from the success of his recent coronation, he received, via his brother Henry, a message from the Holy See: Pope Innocent cautiously endorsed the fact that Stephen, chosen king by the will of the people, was already crowned and consecrated.

"My informants at the church council debating the Countess of Anjou's claims," the Bishop of Winchester told Stephen, "reported that there was strong opposition among many of the cardinals and a small group of Norman prelates. They called you usurper and Hugh Bigod perjurer."

Stephen, sitting in the great hall at Westminster, was uncomfortably aware of Matilda, big with child, seated next to him, listening with half an ear. He had never discussed with his wife any of the details of the King's death, his agreement with Hugh Bigod, or even how he and his brother had long plotted for the throne.

"The fact that Bigod is now Earl of Norfolk was looked upon with grave suspicion," Henry continued. "The Bishop of Angers, in particular, accused both you and—" At the frown on Stephen's face and his imperceptible nod in Matilda's direction, the Bishop paused, then ran a tongue over his lips. "Ah—not that it's of any importance what false rumors and slanderous innuendo are being spread abroad. What else can one expect from the Angevin contingent? But if the Pope has backed us, the Countess of Anjou's cause is well and truly lost, no matter what venomous accusations are made."

Whatever the circumstances, the Pope *had* accepted him. This put the seal on his triumph, Stephen thought, as he made ready to attend his uncle's funeral at the Abbey of Reading. Maud, he heard, would not be there. Rumor had it that she had threatened never again to set foot in England except to reclaim her throne. Stephen was relieved; he could not have faced her so soon. Instead, Robert of Gloucester had accompanied his father's body across the channel. Stephen hoped for the eventual support of his old friends Robert and Brian. As one of the most powerful magnates in the realm, Robert's endorsement was of particular importance. He knew, however, that such recognition might not be immediately forthcoming and was prepared to wait.

At the moment, Stephen was well pleased with what he had accomplished. Of course, there was always the gnawing guilt over what he had done to Maud, and the fact that he still loved her, but these were more than balanced, he persuaded himself, by the glory of being king.

After his uncle's funeral—where Robert and Brian refused to speak to him and left immediately after it was over—Stephen, accompanied by his brother, rode on to Oxford where a church council had been convened. As many prelates still withheld their approval, the Bishop of Winchester had advised Stephen what subjects he must cover and the promises he should make in order to win them over.

In the great hall of Oxford Castle Stephen addressed the group of black-robed prelates:

"My lord bishops, I give you my solemn promise not to retain vacant Sees in my possession and to allow canonical free election. In addition, I agree to relax the harsher forest laws, and abolish Danegeld."

Danegeld, the tax originally imposed on the Saxons to provide resources to fight Danish invasions and continued as a land tax when Duke William conquered England, was unpopular with the church but a good source of revenue for the crown. Keeping his own counsel, Stephen was deliberately vague as to when he would repeal the tax.

The peers of the church, however, seemed pleased with what he had to say, although, Stephen noticed, they spent more time fawning over the Bishop of Winchester, as if he were the true king, rather than himself. Henry was becoming a little . . . overbearing perhaps? Stephen was extremely grateful to his brother for his help in gaining the crown, but he was also beginning to feel very much like a prize bull, greatly admired while it is being led around by a ring through the nose.

When Stephen returned to London and told Matilda of his promises to the church she was jubilant. "I'm so pleased with the changes you will make," she bubbled. "I always hated those savage hunting laws. And the tax was far too severe for all but the very rich."

Stephen gave her an indulgent smile. "Let us hope that I'll be able to keep my promises."

"Surely you would not promise what you cannot mean to fulfill?" Her voice was aghast.

Stephen sighed. Matilda, bless her, was apt to see all of life in strict terms of black or white.

"How can I explain?" he began carefully. "One always means what one says at the time. But circumstances change. What is politic today might be anathema tomorrow. This is the way of the world."

Her face immediately cleared. "That sounds like your brother talking, not you. You are a man of honor."

"Let us hope so," Stephen replied, not meeting her eyes.

The months went by and Stephen, continuing to ride the crest of the popular wave, felt he could not put a foot wrong. Until one day in late spring when Earl Ranulf of Chester, who, to everyone's surprise, had supported Stephen rather than Maud, sent urgent word to Westminster that King David of Scotland and a troop of Highlanders had marched across the Scottish border and captured Newcastle. Dumbfounded at the news, Stephen dashed up the winding staircase to Matilda's solar.

His wife, the new baby, Eustace, in her lap, looked at him in disbelief when he told her what her uncle had done.

"What can have possessed King David?" Stephen asked.

"Perhaps, unlike others, he takes as a serious obligation his oath to support Maud," she responded, then bit her lip in consternation, obviously fearful she had offended him. "Forgive me," she added quickly. "I meant no reflection on anyone."

Despite his carefully worded explanations to her, Stephen was aware that Matilda had been shocked and dismayed at his usurpation of the throne. Not that she would ever reproach him, of course; she was far too loyal for that. But her unvoiced disapproval made Stephen uncomfortable. Living with a saint, no matter how devoted, had its disadvantages.

"If the people had wanted Maud to rule I wouldn't have been chosen," he retorted now, nettled by her response. "In any case, David of Scotland will rue the day he crossed my borders. I intend to raise the largest army he has ever set eyes on."

Shortly thereafter Stephen marched north to Scotland with a huge force of men, the first true army that had been seen in England in thirty-five years. By the time he reached Durham, however, King David, realizing he could not withstand the English numbers, had already sued for peace.

Accompanied by the Earl of Leicester, Stephen met with the Scottish king in the cathedral at Durham.

"I would not have believed this of you, Kinsman," Stephen said. "Do you forget the Queen of England is your blood niece? You must swear homage to me and promise never in future to take up arms against England."

David regarded him with guileless blue eyes and a grim smile. "Aye, and the rightful queen is my other blood niece. By St. Andrew, my conscience will na permit me to swear homage to ye, Stephen, for I ha' sworn a prior oath of fealty to Maud."

Stephen felt himself flush and could not meet David's unflinching gaze. In the presence of this highly principled monarch, whose integrity was beyond question, he found his confidence ebbing.

"You've been guilty, Sire, of an unlawful aggressive act against England," Robin of Leicester pointed out. "We must exact reprisals and take hostages to ensure your future loyalty."

"Ye think to frighten me?" David retorted. "Stephen of Blois has na right to the throne and well he knows it. My conscience is na up fer sale like some I could mention."

"No need to be hasty, Leicester," Stephen said, as Robin's hand fell to his sword hilt. "There's no cause for talk of hostages and the like. Let us come to terms, Kinsman. I understand your reluctance to forswear your oath and will not press you. What do you require from me in order for us to keep the peace?"

Next to him he heard Robin's sudden indrawn breath. "I strongly protest. Hostages *must* be taken. King David cannot be allowed to think England condones his actions."

In the end Stephen ignored Robin's warning, and the outcome was that David of Scotland reluctantly agreed to keep the peace in return for certain rights in the earldom of Northumbria. In addition, Stephen agreed to give the King a large part of Cumberland and Westmoreland. He could not explain, even to himself, why the Scottish king's goodwill was so important to him.

When he returned to London his brother Henry was waiting for him at Westminster. By the look of exasperation on his face, Stephen realized that the news of what had occurred in Durham had preceded him. Did Henry have spies everywhere, he wondered, even at his brother's court?

"How could you do it?" the Bishop asked in disbelief, following Stephen into Matilda's solar. "How could you show yourself to be so weak a king?"

"Weak? Weak?" Stephen repeated defensively. "Is avoiding a war with Scotland weakness or sense? Why shed blood needlessly?"

"But you had David at your mercy! I cannot understand your reasoning here. A show of strength is what avoids war, not pandering to that old fool's conscience. I never heard the like. The Scottish king should have been forced at sword's point to swear homage; hostages should have been taken, as well as severe reprisals. Instead you have pacified him at your peril."

"At my peril?" Stephen laughed. "Now that I have given him what he wants, what have I to fear?"

Henry threw up his hands in despair. "By the Mass, there are none so blind as those who will not see! You have pacified David at the expense of Ranulf, Earl of Chester. Carlisle is Chester's patrimony and you have given it away to David as part of the agreement concerning Westmoreland."

"What does it matter? Chester is one of my supporters; he will understand."

"Will he? You have made a potential enemy of a powerful earl and shown yourself to be a weak sovereign. Our late uncle would never have behaved thus. In future make no decisions without consulting me first." Bishop Henry flounced out of the room before Stephen could respond.

For a moment Stephen was filled with a murderous rage. How dare Henry treat him as if he were an idiot? While it was true enough that his dealings with the Scottish king had been impulsive, and equally true that he had forgotten that Carlisle was part of Chester's holdings, still, it was inexcusable for Henry to treat him so shabbily. He wanted to follow his brother and smash that supercilious face, then saw Matilda staring at him in consternation, and tried to compose himself.

"One day Henry will go too far," he said to her. "We all make mistakes from time to time, if indeed this was a mistake."

"Calm yourself," Matilda said, laying aside her needlework. "Remember, you are the king, not Henry. It's for you to say what is right and what is wrong in lay matters. The Bishop forgets his place. You must remind him who rules."

Soothed by her words, Stephen sat down beside his wife and accepted a goblet of wine from a hovering servitor. "He seems to think he governs the realm, not I," Stephen reflected aloud. It occurred to him that when his brother became Archbishop of Canterbury he would grow even more powerful and influential. It was certainly something to think about.

Normandy, 1136

ACROSS THE CHANNEL IN NORMANDY, MAUD WAS HAVING HER OWN difficulties. In the town of Argent on the Norman border, Maud listened to Geoffrey's groans in an upper chamber of a drafty, four-square fortress. The chill room, containing only a narrow bed, rickety table, and three-legged stool, was bleak and cheerless in the dim light of an autumn morning. No hangings covered the damp walls, while a brazier of green logs produced more smoke than heat. Glancing out of a narrow slit in the crumbling gray stone, Maud glimpsed a curve of silvery sky under which a squat church nestled among the thatched roofs of a village surrounded by muddy fields.

Geoffrey groaned again. Maud turned from the window slit and walked over to the bed.

"My throat is parched," he croaked.

Silently, Maud poured wine from an earthen pitcher into a wooden cup. Geoffrey hauled himself up on one arm, took the cup, drank thirstily, then made a face. "I would not give my sow this piss."

"That's all there is," Maud replied evenly.

"I must return to Anjou," Geoffrey groaned. "If I'm to die it must be in Anjou."

"You're not dying," Maud said in a weary voice. "You have only a minor wound in the foot."

"It might gather poison at any moment." Geoffrey gave another piteous groan and turned his face to the wall. "Men often die from such wounds."

Stony-faced, Maud watched him. She was not moved to pity for his plight since it had been Geoffrey's behavior that had very nearly brought them to ruin. It had started several months ago when Stephen sent over to Normandy an accomplished lieutenant, the Earl of Mellent, to take command of the duchy. Geoffrey, who had been successful in a few minor skirmishes in Normandy, had boasted that he would do away with Stephen's minion in short order. But he had found the Earl more than a match for him.

The Normans, whom Maud had expected to remain loyal to her, might indeed have done so had Geoffrey not run riot with his Angevin troops. Burning, pillaging, raping, looting, and desecrating churches, the Angevins had turned the Normans against them. Such was the hatred of the Normans that they had chosen to burn the city of Lisieux rather than allow the Angevins to enter it.

Hearing that Geoffrey had been severely wounded while besieging the fortress of Le Sap outside Lisieux, Maud, barely recovered from the birth of her third son, William, had herself raised an army from Anjou and Maine and ridden at their head to her husband's aid. If they were to be successful in regaining the duchy, Maud knew the Angevins and the Normans must make common cause against Stephen's forces. When she arrived two days ago, half fainting from fatigue, her body aching from hours in the saddle, Geoffrey's camp had been in an uproar. To her horror she found that he had ordered an immediate retreat; nothing she said had been able to convince him that he was not dying.

"But I've raised a goodly number of men," she told him in vain. "You must not desert the duchy now. We can defeat this earl if you will only stand firm."

"I wish to die in Angers," Geoffrey had moaned. "Send the troops back to Anjou and Maine."

Now Maud did not know where to turn. Perhaps she should just give up. Nothing had gone well for her since Stephen's betrayal, she thought in despair, tears of self-pity and frustration welling up in her eyes. It seemed as if God's hand were raised against her cause while championing her cousin's. There was a soft knock on the door of the chamber, and Geoffrey's squire entered.

"A courier has arrived from my Lord of Gloucester," he announced. "I left him in the hall with a cup of wine."

"Oh! I will come at once."

"You're not leaving me alone?" Geoffrey whined, raising his head.

"No, my lord," Maud replied. "I am sure Roland will be glad to sit with you until I return."

The squire nodded. "Of course, Madam."

Maud hurried down the twisting staircase, relieved to be out of Geoffrey's presence.

The courier was standing in the hall before a glowing brazier drinking his cup of wine; a brown cloak covered his head and body.

"You've brought me word from my brother?" Maud asked.

The man tilted his head, and the hood of the cloak fell back revealing his features. He put a finger to his lips as Maud stifled a gasp: the man was Robert himself. Fortunately, the hall was empty at this morning hour.

"Robert," Maud whispered. "Why aren't you in England? Is it known you're here?"

"Stephen knows me to be in Normandy, but he believes I'm at Caen. There were rumors that Geoffrey was wounded and lay at death's door. I came to see for myself."

Maud made a face. "He received a wound in his foot. It isn't serious but he's behaving as if he will die at any moment, insisting he be taken back to Angers at once. Nothing will move him. Brother, I am beside myself. Must I lose Normandy too?"

Robert put his hand on Maud's arm. "The duchy cannot be won in a day. Patience."

Maud bit her lip. Patience, as Robert knew, was not her strong point. "How do matters fare in England? Does—does the usurper suspect you?" She could not bring herself to utter her cousin's name aloud.

"I doubt it. As far as Stephen is concerned, both Brian and I are now his supporters. As we arranged, Brian attended his Easter court. I pretended to be reluctant but finally allowed myself to be won over. Stephen also believes the King of Scotland is now on good terms with him, and no doubt envisions only calm seas ahead. Which is what we want him to believe."

Maud nodded. Thus far the first part of the plan formed by herself, Geoffrey, Robert, and Brian—to convince Stephen that Maud's main supporters had gone over to his side—was working well. The second part of the plan—Geoffrey's invasion of Normandy—had suffered a setback.

As if reading her thoughts, Robert gave her a sympathetic glance. "Wait for Geoffrey to recover. He will try for Normandy again and next time be more successful."

"You heard how his troops behaved? Like savages. Against the Normans, their own allies! Sweet Marie, I'm so ashamed."

"Let me talk to him," Robert said gently. "He has more to learn than I had previously thought, but then this is his first large-scale battle. Do not judge your husband too harshly."

"How can I not judge him? We desperately need Geoffrey to win Normandy so we can be free to take England."

Robert gave her a troubled look. "You're still determined to invade England? Knowing that there will be a full-scale civil war if you do?"

"If there is war, whose fault will that be? It is *my* throne that has been stolen. Do you suggest I sit quietly by and let my inheritance, and Henry's, be usurped by the House of Blois?" Maud's body trembled with suppressed rage. "We have all agreed to invade. You can't back out now."

"Peace, peace. No one has suggested otherwise." He took her hands in his. "Brian says the time is not yet ripe for an invasion but if Stephen continues on his present course it shouldn't be too far away. I won't ever desert you, surely you know that by now."

Impulsively, Maud kissed Robert's cheek. "Forgive me for doubting you. What would I do without your support? You're my mainstay, my right arm."

"I have some news for you," Robert continued. "Your stepmother, Queen Adelicia, is to be married again to William de Albini, Lord of Arundel. He's a staunch supporter of Stephen, but Alix still harbors tender feelings for you, I'm sure."

Maud looked surprised. "I would have expected her to enter a convent after my father died, but I wish her well in this new marriage." She paused. "Do you think we may count on Alix's support when we make our bid for England?"

"I think it highly possible she will help you personally," Robert said. "Now, I have very little time left, so take me to Geoffrey."

As they mounted the winding staircase, Maud turned to her halfbrother. "Tell me the truth—do you really believe the time will come when I will be welcome in England? The usurper is popular. Everyone loves him."

"At the moment. As I've said, it won't take the people of England long to discover the true nature of the man they have chosen to rule them,'' Robert said with confidence. ''Their love for the present king will die as his weaknesses become more and more apparent—which is already happening. Stephen is a warrior, not a commander.''

Maud said nothing. Does love ever die, she wondered, even when one knows the weaknesses?

Chapter Three

London, 1137

In the year 1137, Stephen held his second Easter court in London. On Easter day, after Mass in the abbey, the great hall at Westminster was packed with richly dressed Norman lords and their ladies, distinguished prelates, and visiting dignitaries from Europe.

Stephen, seated on the royal throne, caught a glimpse among the guests of his old comrades, Robert of Gloucester and Brian FitzCount, accompanied by Miles FitzWalter, Sheriff of Gloucester. Despite the fact that their personal affection for him had markedly cooled, he was relieved to be on good terms with Brian and Robert, both of whom had paid him a grudging homage.

He was also relieved that so many attended his court. A show of good faith was sorely needed now, Stephen thought with a sigh, reflecting on the series of troublesome incidents afflicting his reign. Beginning with the rebellion of the Scottish king, the difficulties had continued with sporadic bursts of unrest: One high-ranking noble had taken unlawful possession of a castle belonging to the crown while another laid waste the land in his area. In addition, the church kept demanding more and more rights, and the Bishop of Winchester backed them, causing an ever-widening rift between himself and his brother. He had dealt with each incident as it arose, but Stephen could not understand why the moment he handled one problem, another popped up to replace it, each becoming more serious than the last.

Just yesterday, in fact, a most disquieting rumor had reached his ears: Lord Baldwin of Redvers, a crony of the late king and a magnate of high rank and much influence, who had initially sworn homage to him, was now openly declaring himself to be an avowed enemy of the crown. Stephen prayed that the rumor was false, even as his eyes anxiously scanned the hall hoping to catch sight of Baldwin among the crowd. His attention was distracted by his brother Henry, re-splendent in gold-encrusted episcopal robes and miter, pushing his way through the crowd to approach the throne.

"I've looked everywhere but I cannot see Lord Baldwin of Red-vers," Henry said, frowning. "Didn't you tell me that he was ex-pected?"

"I was given to understand he would be here, but I cannot force him to attend my court."

"No one would have dared ignore King Henry's order to attend his court," the Bishop said. "A loyal vassal must comply with his king's wishes or show good cause why not. Baldwin is a man of high rank and powerful connections; he should be here. You're far too reason-able."

Stephen felt his chest tighten. Henry was constantly criticizing him, always exhorting him to do something other than what he was doing. Unwilling to listen to his brother's nagging, he abruptly rose to his feet and began to mingle with his guests.

But Stephen was unable to relax and bask in the warmth and affinity of his subjects. He was always aware of his brother's pene-trating gaze following him through the hall—weighing, judging, con-demning.

A month later, to Stephen's dismay, the rumor concerning Baldwin of Redvers proved to be true: The disaffected magnate seized the royal castle of Exeter and provisioned it as though preparing for a siege. Stephen, after an urgent meeting of his council, sent two hundred mounted men to Exeter.

A week later Stephen received word that his army had failed to seize the royal castle, although they managed to take possession of the city of Exeter. Baldwin himself had escaped from the castle, leaving his wife and children behind. A fortnight later Stephen himself arrived with reinforcements, accompanied by a group of barons.

After their campsite had been established and the pavilions erected, Robin, Waleran, and a score of other nobles accompanied Stephen on a tour of the land surrounding the castle walls. It was a warm day in early June, fragrant with lilac and roses, the meadows filled with soft green grass. Against the far horizon a line of dark blue hills melted into the pale blue arc of the sky.

"Exeter will not be easy to capture," Robin of Leicester said to Stephen. He pointed to the high mound on which the castle stood. "The towers are well fortified and the walls difficult to scale."

"Then we will take it by siege," Stephen said with confidence, elated that so many of the barons who had paid him homage were also willing to do battle for him as loyal vassals should.

Waleran of Muelan suddenly cursed and pointed toward the camp. "The bastard of Gloucester has arrived. Do not trust him, Sire."

"Robert is my oldest friend," Stephen replied. "He has paid homage to me. Why shouldn't I trust him?"

Waleran raised thick black brows. "Baldwin of Redvers also paid homage to you, Sire, so that is hardly a guarantee of loyalty. It's most unlike Robert to desert his precious sister, which is why I'm suspicious. Keep a sharp eye out for treachery is my advice."

As usual, whenever Maud was mentioned, Stephen's heart jumped and all the muscles in his body quivered like a finely drawn bowstring.

"Robert will never betray me," he stated confidently.

After three months the castle still had not surrendered, although the garrison no longer rained arrows on Stephen's army, or attempted furtive sorties in the dead of night.

"The siege is proving successful," Robin said to Stephen. "The summer drought has dried up the springs and I'll wager the castle is out of water. They will be forced to use wine for everything, including washing and making bread."

"Increase the firebrands thrown over the walls," Waleran said. "They must extinguish them with wine and soon there'll be no liquid left of any kind. Then they will surrender on our terms or perish."

Within the week two envoys were sent from the castle to treat with Stephen and ask for concessions.

"Look at them," said Bishop Henry of Winchester, recently arrived, uninvited, at his brother's camp. He pointed to the envoys' dry
skin, cracked lips, and glazed eyes. "They are desperate for water.
There is little need to give concessions. Don't treat with them. They
will surrender everything in a matter of days."

"It seems needlessly cruel," Stephen began, looking in distress at
the two men. "Surely we need not prolong their misery?"

"The Bishop is right," Waleran said, in rare agreement with Henry
of Winchester. Normally the two opposed each other on almost every
issue that arose. "No quarter must be given."

Stephen reluctantly agreed, although such callous behavior went
against the grain.

Two days later Baldwin's wife left the castle and threw herself
down on her knees in front of Stephen. Her feet were bare, ashes
were strewn on her head, and she wept piteously. Shocked at her
wasted appearance and labored breath, Stephen received her cour-
teously.

"Don't listen to her pleas," Henry cautioned.

"But she is blameless," Stephen protested. "I cannot stand by and
let innocent lives be lost. Baldwin's quarrel with me has naught to do
with her."

"Your subjects must understand that they cannot rebel with impunity," Henry urged. "Baldwin has challenged your authority. An
example must be made. The castle must totally surrender or die of
thirst and hunger. Your enemies will learn from this lesson, and men
will fear you."

"Exactly so," Waleran said. "In days to come the barons will think
twice before they rebel."

"Harshness in this instance may prevent much bloodshed in the
future," Robin of Leicester added.

"It's what our uncle would have done," Henry continued, determined to hammer home his point. "How do you think he kept the
peace for so many years? By kindness and mercy?" He turned to
Robert of Gloucester. "Is this not so, Cousin?"

Robert gave Henry an enigmatic smile. "My father kept peace in
this land for thirty-five years, certainly that is so."

Stephen found himself wavering between his instinct to save the
inhabitants of the castle and the brutal advice of his brother and the
de Beaumont twins. "I will think on it," he said at last.

"Good God, man, there is naught to think on!" Henry turned
impatiently away and called to the guards. "Take this woman back to

the castle. It's not enough that she make submission. Every man in
the castle must do the same. The ringleaders will be hanged, the rest
imprisoned for their rebellious behavior. Baldwin's sons will be taken
hostage to ensure his good behavior. Those who do not comply will
be left to starve." He stalked off in the direction of his pavilion.

Brusquely robbed of his authority in front of his magnates, Stephen felt his face burn, aware of the shocked silence around him.
What Henry had done was unforgivable, treating him, the King of
England, like a mere servitor! By God's birth, something would have
to be done about his brother.

The next morning a group of barons approached Stephen as he sat
alone in his azure pavilion, attended only by a squire.

"Sire, we beg for clemency for those trapped in the castle," said
one of the barons. "Many of us here"—he indicated the three barons
who had accompanied him—"are related by blood to Baldwin's men.
They're now all willing to surrender. Why should they be hung or
imprisoned? After all, none of them has ever sworn an oath of homage to you personally, only to Baldwin. How can loyal followers be
condemned for obeying their liege-lord?"

The words made sense to Stephen. It seemed mean-spirited, needlessly cruel, to let these men die. He turned to the squire. "Alex-
ander, do you find my Lord of Gloucester and bring him to me."

When Robert arrived Stephen explained the situation and asked:
"What think you?"

"Your own instincts in this matter will be your best guide, Sire,"
Robert responded.

"That is not my brother's advice, nor the twins either."

"It is for the King to decide. The twins are only advisers; the
Bishop is a man of God, not a military leader." Robert paused. "My
father never permitted the church to interfere in lay matters."

Their eyes met in a long look. Stephen was the first to turn away.

At Robert's words, the leading baron pressed his advantage. "It
will reflect well on you, Sire, if you spare the lives of these men and
let Baldwin's wife and children go free."

"Any seasoned warrior may triumph in a siege, but it takes a noble
and generous heart to deal compassionately with one's enemies,"
Robert added.

"Your pleas have softened my resolve," Stephen said at once. "I
will raise the siege and permit Baldwin's wife and children to depart.

Baldwin's men may make submission to me and go in peace. Inform them at once. Be sure they are then given food and water.''

When Bishop Henry and the twins returned and heard what Stephen had done, they were outraged.

''You have made a fatal mistake,'' Henry hissed, his eyes glittering like green ice. ''Such clemency will be thought of as weakness. Those men who persuaded you to this deed are little better than traitors!''

''That is quite enough, Brother,'' Stephen said, stung. ''Go back to the pulpit if you would preach a sermon. Saving souls is your province; military strategy is mine.''

''But His Grace of Winchester has made a valid point,'' Robin of Leicester ventured. ''Now it will be said that men may flout the King's authority with impunity, for nothing is done to stop them. It's not a question of cruelty, Sire, but of political expediency. None of us enjoys watching others suffer, but that is the price one pays to keep the peace.''

Waleran turned angrily to Robert. ''You were here. Why did you not counsel him against such foolhardiness?''

''I would never be so bold as to question the King's judgment,'' Robert of Gloucester responded.

Waleran smote his thigh with a mailed glove. ''By the Mass, Gloucester, you will never convince me that you have the King's best interests at heart. Sire, take back your agreement with Baldwin's kin. Put them all to death.''

''May God forgive you, Waleran,'' Stephen said, his voice rising in indignation. ''I have given those people my word! The matter is at an end.'' He stormed out of the pavilion followed by Bishop Henry.

''Brother, Brother,'' Robin said under his breath. ''I begin to see a pattern forming here and it disturbs me: No reprisals against the King of Scotland; Baldwin's men freed to return to their lord and stir up trouble! Stephen is too mild. It bodes ill for this land.''

Waleran nodded. ''If this is how his reign begins, how will it end?'' With a scowl at Robert he took his brother's arm and led him out of the pavilion.

Alone, Robert of Gloucester smiled, well pleased with what he had witnessed.

In November of that same year, 1137, Stephen received word of the death of the Archbishop of Canterbury. He attended the funeral in Canterbury, returning to Westminster in early December.

"You discussed the vacant See with the Bishop of Winchester?" Matilda asked Stephen the morning after his return as they sat in her solar. "I imagine he will want to take up his new appointment as soon as may be."

"The monks must hold an election first."

"That's only a formality, as you well know," Matilda said. "Your choice will be their choice."

"As a matter of fact, I didn't discuss the matter with Henry."

"Whyever not?"

"I have grave doubts as to whether my brother is the right person for such a powerful position in the church." Until the words were out of his mouth, Stephen, who had been thinking along such lines for the past several months, had not believed he would really say them aloud.

"But you have promised him the See of Canterbury!" Stephen winced at the shock and horror in Matilda's voice.

"I haven't made a final decision yet," he said hastily, disturbed by her reaction. She would never accuse him of treachery but the expression on her face was accusation enough.

"Why?" she whispered. "Why do you wish to treat him in this manner?"

Stephen swallowed. Why indeed, he thought. Although Matilda was fully aware of the recent conflict between himself and his brother, she knew little of their early history. How could he tell her that ever since childhood he had alternately hated, loved, admired, obeyed, and been driven to challenge Henry. Too often consumed by envy of his brother's superior intelligence, Stephen was convinced that if Henry were in a position of supreme power he would always remain in the Bishop's shadow, a minion of the church, and never become his own man. In the years before Stephen had taken over the throne, he and Henry had worked well together, moving toward a common goal. But since his accession Stephen felt totally oppressed by his brother's attempts to take command.

He had just decided to tell Matilda something of the truth, when, as if reading his thoughts, she spoke first. "I think I understand. Henry behaves as if he were king and you his servant. Like the incident at Exeter you told me about."

"Yes. The twins and others expected me to rebuke Henry, but I felt powerless to stand against him."

Matilda nodded. "What he did was unforgivable, I certainly agree, and, as you know, I have little love for my brother-in-law. He's too worldly for my taste, and lacks a spiritual character, but all that aside, his advice is usually sound." She paused. "Even at Exeter, what he predicted came to pass. Baldwin of Redvers and all his men, the same men you saved from death, instead of being grateful for your clemency, joined the Countess of Anjou's forces."

Stephen was silent. Why must she remind him of the numerous times that Henry had been right and he wrong? At times he did not quite know what to make of Matilda. He had difficulty reconciling the shy little mouse he had married, with hardly two words to say for herself, with this woman of increasing strength and presence, whose instinctual knowledge of current affairs never ceased to amaze him.

"His advice is often sound," Stephen said after a time. "But Henry's interference in the affairs of the realm will only increase when he becomes Archbishop. I cannot rule under such adverse conditions."

Matilda sighed. "You made a bargain with Henry; the two of you are yoked in harness together. You cannot dishonor the crown by going against your given word."

"There's no dishonor involved." Why must she reduce everything to morality, Stephen thought. "I need only withdraw my support. Let it be known I favor another candidate."

"Do not think me foolish, Husband, for I'm ignorant of such matters, but would it not be dangerous to cross the Bishop?"

Stephen frowned. "In what way dangerous?"

"In his rage and disappointment over the loss of Canterbury, Henry may seek vengeance—support the Countess of Anjou's cause, for instance."

If it had been anyone other than Matilda he would have laughed at the absurdity of such a suggestion. She was less astute than he had thought. "Henry would never be so foolish, my dear. Not that Maud would have him, in any case. She will never forgive his betrayal." Nor mine, he almost added, the words echoing in his head so clearly he was surprised Matilda did not hear them.

There was a strained silence. "I'm sure you're right about Henry," Matilda finally said. "I should not have spoken as I did."

"In the event that I do not choose Henry, another candidate has been highly recommended to me, one from Normandy. Theobald, Abbot of Bec."

"An excellent choice," said Matilda, obviously surprised. "He is a saintly prelate, a true man of God. Did Waleran of Muelan make the suggestion? I believe he is a lay patron of the Abbey of Bec."

"Yes, it was Waleran," Stephen said, wondering if there was anything she did not know.

"I'm certain you will make the right decision," Matilda told him.

Stephen walked over to the window slit, wishing he felt as certain. Unaccountably, he suddenly remembered the time he had disguised himself as a priest to visit Maud in secret. His eyes sought the closed door at the end of the solar. In that very room, he thought with an unexpected stab of anguish and remorse.

"I'm told Theobald of Bec is free from ambition, unlikely to meddle in the affairs of the kingdom. An unworldly prelate who would endure the fires of hell rather than dishonor his office." He paused. "But I have not yet decided, you understand. I must think on it," Stephen said, his eye still fixed on the closed door.

Chapter Four

Henry, bishop of winchester, was strolling along the well-kept paths of his garden at Wolvesey Castle, located just outside the walls of Winchester, when a cleric brought him word of the Archbishop of Canterbury's death. As he examined his collection of antique marble statuary set against a background of dark green ivy, he was unable to repress a sense of elation. Now, at last, he would head the church in England, and, through his brother, rule the realm as well. His lifelong ambition was about to be fulfilled.

The Bishop's first action was to write a long missive to the Pope, assuring the pontiff there would be no difficulty in the transition from one See to another; then he left for Canterbury to attend the funeral.

He was surprised, but not concerned, when Stephen said nothing to him about the vacant See, assuming that his brother thought it unseemly to bring the matter up at the late Archbishop's funeral. It was not as if there were any immediate urgency about the matter; everyone expected him to be the next Archbishop, and there were certainly no other candidates to worry about.

After two months passed with no word, Henry sent a courteous dispatch to his brother asking what was being done about the vacant

See of Canterbury. He received a brief reply, pleasant but noncommittal, asking him to be patient. The Bishop began to feel uneasy. Why the delay? When another six weeks passed with no word from Stephen, Henry debated with himself over what course to follow.

It was not until mid-April before Henry was able to pay a visit to London, duties in both Winchester and Glastonbury preventing him from leaving immediately. He found Stephen at Westminster in a small stone chamber that King Henry had used for his administrative duties.

"Have you forgotten our agreement? Why have you not appointed me Archbishop?" he demanded of Stephen without preamble. "You owe your present position to me, don't forget that. Is this how you show your gratitude?"

Stephen flushed, then looked sullen. "I'm sick to death of being perpetually reminded that I'm in your debt. Everyone wants something of me; I'm being pulled in too many directions at once." He paused, avoiding Henry's eye. "The difficulty is Matilda. She thinks you lack . . . spiritual values. 'Too worldly' was the phrase she used."

Henry was nonplussed. "What is that supposed to mean? And what does Matilda's opinion signify? I had not thought you ruled by the distaff!" His eyes narrowed. "You're telling me less than the truth, Brother. If you don't act soon, I will demand the Pope intervene." He left the chamber in a huff.

When no word was forthcoming by May, Henry, swallowing his pride, forced himself to write to the Holy Father demanding that an Archbishop be chosen. Pope Innocent, already upset with Stephen over the delay, agreed, and promised to send over to England a Papal Legate who would convene a council of bishops, abbots, and other leading churchmen to meet no later than the end of the year. By the time the messengers had gone to Rome and came back again it was early September. The Papal Legate arrived in late October. Then it took another month before everyone could be notified and gathered together.

The council was finally held at Westminster in December of the year 1138. During the last week of the month Henry, who had attended, was unexpectedly forced to leave the council for a short time in order to conduct an ordination in Winchester. He was in the midst of the ordination ceremony when he received word that during his brief absence an Archbishop of Canterbury had been elected: Theobald, Abbot of Bec in Normandy.

Almost incoherent with rage, Henry abandoned the ceremony and despite the freezing cold left in the middle of the night for London. I will never forgive Stephen this treachery, he vowed, never in this world or the next.

When he reached Westminster, half frozen, just after Prime, Henry immediately went into the great hall where he found Stephen breaking the night's fast with the de Beaumont twins and his recently appointed commander of mercenaries, the Fleming, William of Ypres. Clad in a peacock blue tunic under a fur-lined mantle, William was small and dapper, with long curling black hair and a trim mustache. He returned Henry's curt greeting with an arrogant stare from his dark eyes.

"I would see you alone, and at once," Henry said to his brother, his voice tight with anger.

"First break your fast," Stephen replied with a forced smile, indicating a round wheaten loaf and a pitcher of ale. His face had paled at Henry's unexpected entrance. "You look chilled to the bone. Why not warm yourself by the fire."

"I'm well enough. I must insist we talk now."

"Speak then, Brother. I'm among loyal friends. We have no secrets from one another." Stephen smiled at William and the twins, but his eyes were wary.

"Friends?" Henry gave an ugly laugh. "You don't know the meaning of friendship, no, or of loyalty either. How you have served me is how you will serve these poor fools."

Stephen's smile vanished. "There's no need to insult me," he said, on a note of defiance.

"A tooth for a tooth, Stephen," Henry hissed. "Have I not just been dealt the greatest of insults at your hand? You promised me the See of Canterbury! How could you prove so faithless?"

Stephen's eyes darted about the hall as if seeking escape. "The council elected Theobald of Bec, the only one upon whom everyone agreed. He . . . has an admirable character, true humility, and is devoted to Holy Church."

"Do you imply that I have none of these qualities?" Henry cried, his face contorted with rage. "That simple-natured old man, who can barely scrawl his own name, what has he ever accomplished? I find it strange indeed that during my absence Theobald of Bec's election is rushed through in the most underhanded manner. Without your connivance he would never have been chosen!"

Stephen's face grew dark red. Waleran of Muelan arched his brows as he exchanged a look of complicity with his brother Robin, adding yet another spark to Henry's fury. The Bishop knew only too well that Waleran had always resented his influence over Stephen; it would not surprise him to discover that Waleran was in part responsible for his downfall. Yes, by God, of course! He had almost forgotten! Waleran was connected with the Abbey of Bec in Normandy, one of their lay patrons, in fact. He would have pushed forward Theobald as a tame Archbishop, a man without ambition and easily controlled.

"You will live to regret what you have done," Henry said in an icy voice. "I would to God I had never helped you to the throne, for I fear the time will come when we shall all rue the day you were crowned king."

Rising, William of Ypres pointed an accusing finger at Henry. "You speak treason, my lord bishop," he said in his heavy Flemish accent.

Henry looked down his long nose as if he smelled something unpleasant. "You dare to accuse me of treason? What are you but a bastard Flemish adventurer, devoted to violence and intrigue, a rogue who sells his services to whoever pays the most gold." He sniffed contemptuously. "What better place to seek employment than at Stephen's court! Two rogues cut from the same pattern!"

William's hand shot to the dagger swinging at his belt. Outraged, the twins jumped to their feet. With a look of disgust, Henry turned on his heel and stalked out of the hall. Stephen suddenly leapt from his chair to run after him.

"Leave the Bishop alone," he called over his shoulder as the three men started to follow. "If you lay a finger on him you will have me to deal with."

Henry was out the door before Stephen caught up with him.

"Wait! Let me explain," Stephen began.

"It's too late for explanations," Henry replied, the bitterness rising in his throat like bile. "Canterbury has always been my dream. You have taken it from me. Do you expect me to forgive you?" How typical of his brother to destroy him with one hand, then try to woo him back with the other. Even when he had done you an ill turn Stephen could not bear that you should hold it against him. Jesu!

"I did what I thought best. You had become—too overbearing, leaving me no voice of my own."

Henry snorted. "Let me remind you of Matthew 7: 'Why do you see the speck that is in your brother's eye, but do not notice the log that is in your own eye?' "

Stephen bit his lip. "I will ask the Pope to appoint you Papal Legate," he said. "You will be Rome's representative in England. Innocent will be happy to comply. That makes the Archbishop of Canterbury subordinate to you." He put a tentative hand on Henry's shoulder.

The Bishop savagely shook off the hand. "Am I to be consoled with that? Theobald will be head of the church in England!" His voice throbbed with mingled anger and hurt.

"Oh God, what have I done," Stephen whispered. "Brother, I—"

"I'm no longer your brother; I am your enemy. Why did you do it to me? What is the true reason?" Before he could stop himself the cry had been torn from Henry's heart, revealing the depths of his anguish.

White-faced, tears welling up in his gold-flecked eyes, Stephen opened his mouth to speak, but no words came forth. Clearly, he did not know why, Henry realized, or could not bring himself to say. For the space of a heartbeat, Henry looked deeply into his brother's eyes and, for the first time, recognized the bitter truth: the years of unexpressed resentment and envy which had begun in Blois when Stephen was a child, despised by his mother, outcast from his family, the black sheep constantly compared to the brilliant younger brother who excelled in all that he did.

Shattered, Henry left the great hall of Westminster. At last he understood, but knowledge did not reconcile him to betrayal. Henceforth, Stephen must rely on the dubious counsel of his Flemish captain and the twins. He would learn soon enough, and to his cost, the consequences of his faithless act.

Chapter Five

EARLY IN THE NEW YEAR, 1139, STEPHEN, STILL TOTALLY ESTRANGED from his brother, underwent a series of major setbacks: Robert of Gloucester, visiting his estates in Normandy, sent him a formal declaration of defiance, naming the King usurper and refusing to honor him any longer as his overlord. As if Robert's defection were the signal for rebellion, various uprisings sprang up all over southwest England. Following this came disquieting rumors that Robert and Geoffrey of Anjou had made common cause and, along with Maud, were secretly plotting to invade England with the help of various nobles who still remained loyal to the late King Henry's wishes.

On the heels of this news, the treasurer, Roger of Salisbury's nephew, informed Stephen that the treasury was so depleted that he would not be able to pay, among others, William of Ypres' Flemish mercenaries. Beset by conflicting advice from the de Beaumont twins, William of Ypres, and the Bishop of Salisbury, Stephen did not know which way to turn.

After much hesitation he finally decided to besiege Robert's stronghold at Bristol as a means of retaliation. No sooner had he arrived than news came that King David of Scotland had again broken the peace, marching across the Scottish border to invade Yorkshire.

Abruptly abandoning Bristol, Stephen made for Yorkshire, but was diverted by an uprising of rebels at Shropshire. In truth, he could have marched in almost any direction and found an insurrection to subdue.

Fortunately, by the time he reached the Midlands the Scottish king was already fleeing back to the border, put to rout by the stouthearted men of Yorkshire. Wearily, Stephen began the long ride back to Westminster, dreading the problems that lay in store for him. He did not know what action to take against Robert, how to prevent more uprisings, or, most urgently, what to do about the dwindling treasury. These were exactly the sort of crisis situations his brother was so adept at handling, he realized with a stab of regret. If he had not acted so precipitously, Henry would still be an ally instead of an enemy.

An icy shiver of apprehension ran through him as he pondered the rumors of a possible invasion. Such an event, while unlikely, could not be discounted. Jesu, all the troubles he had endured up to now would be as nothing if Maud and Robert of Gloucester landed on England's shores.

In September of that same year Stephen was at Oxford Castle for an emergency meeting of his council. After much debate and soul-searching, he and his council decided upon a momentous step: to debase the coinage. He was being forced to it by empty coffers, Stephen argued with himself as he sat alone in the great hall of Oxford Castle staring moodily into a goblet of mullet wine.

After all, was it his fault the treasury was empty? Hadn't he done his best to keep it filled? He was unpleasantly reminded of the incident of last June when William of Ypres and Waleran of Muelan had convinced him that his justiciar, the Bishop of Salisbury, was secretly plotting against the crown with the Countess of Anjou and the Earl of Gloucester. Only the desperateness of the situation had persuaded him to seize Roger's considerable wealth and castles. The elderly prelate and members of his family had been imprisoned and roughly treated—not on his orders, he told himself. By the time he was released Roger had become mortally ill and now lay near death.

Stephen quickly downed the wine. By God's birth, it had never been his intention to *harm* Roger, merely remove him from power and fill the empty treasury. Of course he felt distressed about the poor bishop but, after all, the man was guilty of treason. His advisers had assured him of that.

What he had not expected, Stephen realized with a sigh, was the fact that the church, as well as many barons, were horrified by what he had done. In a humiliating confrontation led by his brother Henry, now Papal Legate, he had been accused of a lamentable crime, an offense unheard of in Christian lands, and severely reminded that he owed obedience to Christ's church. And where was the evidence that Roger had been guilty of treason? Henry had asked. When it came down to it no one could produce any hard facts—only rumors and gossip.

Stephen had attempted to soothe the ruffled feathers of the clergy with promises to make amends to Roger's family. But how was he supposed to do that? The prelate's confiscated wealth had not been sufficient to revive the ailing treasury for long. He could not create bricks out of straw, which was why he was now forced to debase the coinage.

Feeling the need to clear his head, Stephen left the hall and climbed the staircase to the battlements. Two guards stood at attention as he approached. He stood before an embrasure, knowing with a sick heart that the tide was running against him. In a desperate gamble to win the loyalty of all the English barons, now that the church was opposed to him, he had started giving away lands, castles, and titles as if there were no end to them—yet how many true adherents had he won?

The Matins bell began to chime. Stephen, about to seek his bed, thought he saw, far to the south across a range of hills, a flicker of light. He rubbed his eyes. Was he imagining things at this witching hour? No, by God, there it was again. The tip of the range was crowned with a cone of fire.

"Sire, look," said one of the guards. "What can it mean?"

Stephen made no reply, watching in disbelief as the light spread. A beacon suddenly blazed from a tower on the outskirts of Oxford; another appeared behind Reading Abbey. Suddenly his heart began to pound like a drum; his hands gripped the stone merlon. Sweet Jesu! The light was a signal that his worst fears were about to be realized. He knew exactly what path the signal would travel: Abingdon, Faringdon, the Cotswolds, Bristol, Gloucester, and away west to the border of Wales. The burning trail would herald the news to her supporters: Maud had at last come home to claim her crown.

Chapter Six

Sussex, England, 1139

Slowly Maud opened her eyes. Confused, she took in the strange chamber with its blue and gold hangings, carved oak chest, and the dark blue canopy over her head. Where was she? Gradually memory returned: the channel crossing from Normandy, landing yesterday evening at Southampton where she and Robert were met by one hundred and forty knights; the long night ride to west Sussex; the arrival at Arundel Castle and their reluctant reception by Alix's new husband, William de Albini, Earl of Sussex.

Maud yawned and turned over to go back to sleep, when she suddenly remembered that she and Robert were due to leave for Bristol this morning. Forcing herself awake, she slid from the wide bed and quickly dressed in the serviceable brown traveling gown and tunic she had worn yesterday.

Picking up a mirror Maud examined herself, wondering if Alix would think her greatly changed since she had last seen her—sweet Marie, it must be all of six years ago now. This morning she looked absurdly young for a woman of thirty-seven with three sons. Even to her critical eye, the thick plaits of cinnamon-colored hair falling to her waist had lost none of their burnished gleam. Her creamy skin was still smooth and unblemished; her body had remained lithe and slender though perhaps a little fuller in the bosom and rounder in the hips. Only her eyes, yes, something about the smoky-gray eyes reflected an inner turmoil, a reminder of the pain and distress of the last four years.

She put the mirror away. The past was dead, Maud admonished herself, only the future mattered now. Hastily pulling a mantle over her shoulders, she left the chamber for the great hall. The trestle tables were only half filled with the Lord of Arundel's mesnie and a few of Robert's knights who had traveled with her yesterday. Of Robert himself there was no sign. Alix, several of her women, and the chaplain were seated at the high table. On her lap the former queen held a sleeping baby; sitting next to her was a little girl of about eighteen months.

"Alix, what a pleasure to see you!" Maud bent to kiss her stepmother's upturned face. "So these are your children."

Alix gave a proud smile. "And another, three months on the way."

"You're lovelier than ever," Maud said, her eyes admiring Alix's beautiful serene face framed in a white wimple, a tendril of dark gold hair curling on her ivory brow. "This marriage agrees with you, I see."

Alix's face turned pink as she nodded happily. "The years have treated you kindly as well, Maud. In fact, you look very little older than when we first met."

Maud gave her a pleased smile. "Thank you. Ever since last night I've wanted to tell you how grateful I am that you were willing to receive me. It can't have been an easy decision to grant me asylum, for I know your husband supports my cousin."

"He agreed to help you for my sake, despite the risk." Alix paused, a look of concern passing over her face. "I pray Stephen doesn't come to hear of this. He will surely look upon any aid to you as an act of treason."

"I'm well aware of the danger you have risked for my sake," Maud said. "When I've gained the throne I'll find a concrete way of showing my gratitude."

Alix gave her a gentle smile. "I need no reward for following my conscience. Will you break your fast now?" She indicated platters of roast fowl, a haunch of venison, eel pies, baskets of fruit, and freshly baked bread.

Maud made a place for herself at the table; a page poured her a goblet of spiced wine while a servitor topped her trencher with food.

"Is Robert about?" Maud asked.

"He left for Wallingford with half his knights and my husband as escort at least an hour ago. From there he travels to Bristol."

"Left! But I was to have gone with him. How could he leave without me?"

"As you were still asleep, Robert felt you should rest, while you still could, he said. He was also concerned about the dangers of traveling just now. The roads are no longer safe, as they were in your father's day, Maud. When your brother can ensure your safety he will return for you."

"I should be with Robert," Maid said, disheartened. "After all, he goes to raise more men for my cause." She gave an impatient sigh. "If I'd wanted safety I would have stayed in Anjou. I'm of a mind to go after him."

Alix looked horrified. "Oh, my dear, you mustn't think of such an undertaking. If Stephen's army should get their hands on you—"

"We were told we were in no danger from Stephen's forces," Maud interrupted, surprised.

"His troops are rumored to be well away from these parts, true, but I beg you take no risk. As you're a guest in my castle I'm responsible for you now."

Maud knew Alix was right but her place was with her half brother, not cooling her heels in Arundel. It might be weeks before Robert returned. What use would she be to him shut up with the women and children?

"It must have been very painful for you to leave your sons," Alix was saying now.

"Particularly Henry," Maud agreed, aware of an empty ache inside her when she thought of her eldest son. "I do miss him most dreadfully. But he's safe at Angers in Aldyth's care. She wanted to come with me, but she's too old now for such journeys, and ails frequently."

Her glance followed Alix's, whose eyes rested lovingly on the sleeping boy in her arms. If that child had been born to my father, Maud realized with a start, the succession would never have come into dispute. She would still be in Germany, Stephen would not be king, and Henry would never have been born. How different everyone's lives would be now. That matters had fallen out as they did seemed to her a propitious omen for her future.

"For two supposedly barren wives we have done remarkably well for ourselves," Maud said, with a twinkle in her eye.

Alix, who had been gazing raptly at her son's face, turned her soft doe's eyes upon Maud. The two women exchanged a look of perfect understanding, then burst out laughing.

The next two days passed without incident. Then, on her third night in Arundel, Maud was suddenly awakened from a deep sleep by someone shaking her shoulder.

"What is it?" she whispered, as she became aware of Alix standing over her, a lighted candle in one hand. "What is the hour?"

"Just after Lauds. Forgive me for waking you," Alix said in a breathless voice, "but Wulf, captain of the guard, has just informed me of the sound of men and horses outside the castle walls."

Maud's heart jumped a beat. "Robert, back already?" But she knew it could not be Robert.

"The captain fears it may be the King's forces come to besiege the castle." The candlelight flickered on Alix's face, revealing a look of naked fear.

"But how in heaven's name could they know I am here?" She sat up, pulling the coverlet around her to keep warm.

"The captain thinks Arundel may have been watched, Robert and my lord seen leaving, then word sent to Stephen. It's rumored that the King has spies everywhere." The anxiety in Alix's voice was palpable. "Oh Maud, I'm so frightened!"

She has probably never experienced a siege before, Maud realized, and was ill-equipped to do so now. "How many men have been left to guard us?" she asked.

"I—I don't know. All this is new to me. I've never been in any real danger before."

"The captain is sure to know. I'll get dressed and meet you in the great hall." Maud grasped Alix's icy hand and gave it a reassuring squeeze. "I'm so sorry to bring this trouble upon you, but don't worry. Your husband should return any day and Robert within the week. There's no real danger," she added with a confidence she was far from feeling.

Alix gave her a timid smile, lit another candle on the oak table next to the bed, and left. Dressing quickly, Maud was filled with apprehension at the thought of Stephen camped outside the castle walls. If only she had gone with Robert she would be safe in Wallingford or even Bristol now. Well, there was no help for it. Let her treacherous cousin besiege the castle; he would soon know the caliber of the enemy he sought to capture! Lifting her head proudly she marched out of the chamber.

In the great hall, Maud found Wulf, captain of the guard.

"How many men do you have?" she asked him.

"Not enough, Lady, if my men are dealing with the King's forces, particularly those Flemish devils," he told her. "We heard Stephen was at least thirty leagues away in the west country, so my Lord of Arundel took half of the mesnie with him. The Earl of Gloucester left only a few of his knights. And as for supplies—" He shook his head in despair.

Maud's heart sank. "Then the castle is not prepared for a long siege. How long could we hold out if forced to do so?"

"On half rations probably a month, but there's the water to worry about, as we had a dry summer and the well is down."

A servitor offered Maud a pewter tankard of ale. As she sipped the warming brew, she tried to hide her concern.

"It is my belief that if the King is camped outside these walls, he will send a herald to treat with Lady Alix at daybreak," Maud said, determined not to be discouraged.

"I agree, Madam." The captain paused, then lowered his voice. "The Lady of Arundel is with child again, as you must know. But what you may not know, Madam, is that she almost lost the last one, the heir. It is most unfortunate that this . . . this trouble should come upon us just now."

He did not add, "and I hold you responsible," but Maud heard the unspoken condemnation as clearly as if he had shouted it aloud.

At first light, Maud and Alix, accompanied by the captain, climbed to the battlements. In the gray mist of an October dawn, Maud could see an army camped below the outer walls of the castle. Small brushwood fires burned in the meadow; horses whinnied and stamped their hooves while men scurried about erecting pavilions, carrying buckets of water from the nearby river, and unloading carts. As the sun began to burn away the mist there was a sudden flash of arms.

Alix stepped quickly away from the parapet. "I feel a bit queasy," she said in an apologetic voice. "I best go down."

Maud looked at her anxiously, praying she would not miscarry. Reluctantly, she took a last look at the tallest of the pavilions, azure blue, arrogantly flying a silver pennant. It could only belong to the King. A surge of anger almost choked her. Gripping Alix's arm, Maud led her down the stairs, the captain following.

As the bells rang for Tierce, a herald was ushered into the great hall. In the presence of Maud, Alix and her women, the captain and all his men, he relayed the King's message: King Stephen was shocked and dismayed at the behavior of the Earl of Sussex and his lady. The Lord of Arundel had been seen riding from his lands escorting a sworn enemy of the realm, Earl Robert of Gloucester. The Lady of Arundel, whom King Stephen had always held in the highest regard, now harbored within her walls an avowed enemy of the realm who could not be permitted to remain. Unless the Countess of Anjou was immediately delivered up to the King, he would be forced to besiege the castle. King Stephen had with him a large army, as they could see for themselves, and the castle would be cut off from reinforcements or aid of any kind.

Alix's lips trembled. She clutched Maud's hand. "You must give me a moment," she gasped.

The herald bowed and turned away as Alix, leaning heavily on Maud, walked out of earshot.

"I deeply regret having brought this upon you, " Maud said. Two spots of color flamed in her cheeks and she could have screamed with the frustration of her dashed hopes.

To have plotted and planned for four years, waiting for just the right moment to strike. And now, when the land was seething with rebellion and discontent, when Brian's forces were marshaled at Wallingford, Robert's men ready at Bristol, her Uncle David poised on the border of Scotland for his third invasion of England—to be made Stephen's prisoner within days after having landed was simply not to be borne.

Heartsick, Maud was determined not to let Alix see her bitter disappointment. Left to herself, of course, she would have defended Arundel to the death, but she could not put Alix in jeopardy. All she could hope for now was that Stephen would agree to ransom her. A pain shot through the back of her neck and she prayed one of her agonizing headaches was not going to incapacitate her.

"I'll get my things, Alix," she said through icy lips. "Tell the herald you'll give me up to the usurper. Neither you nor your unborn child must be put in any more peril than already exists."

Maud turned on her heel but Alix caught her arm.

"A moment, my dear," she whispered. Clinging to Maud, she walked over to the herald. "I have my answer for your master."

Clasping her hands over her belly, Alix swallowed several times before speaking. Then lifting her wimpled head with great dignity, she looked straight at the herald.

"I'm surprised," she began in a quavering voice, "yes, surprised and shocked, to receive so unchivalrous a demand from the King. To think that such a powerful ruler would so forget his knightly vows as to threaten two weak, helpless, and unprotected ladies is unforgivable."

The herald's eyes grew round; Maud and the captain, indeed the entire array of men and women, gaped at Alix in amazement.

"Return to your master," Alix continued, her voice growing firmer as she disengaged her arm from Maud's support. "Tell him that sooner than give up any guest within my walls to an uncertain fate, I, Adelicia of Louvain, former Queen of England, and now Lady of Sussex, will defend this castle to my last breath, even if it imperil the life of my unborn babe."

Alix's face had turned a deep rose; her bosom heaved with indignation; her eyes flashed defiantly. "It is beneath my dignity to treat with those who make war on women and children!"

The herald stared at her in disbelief, then bowed and left. Maud, somewhere between laughter and tears, was speechless.

"How dare Stephen threaten us," Alix said. She held out a steady hand to Maud. "Come along, my dear, we have not yet eaten a good hot meal this morning. I suddenly find myself quite hungry."

Maud followed her meekly, a lump in her throat and a veil of tears in her eyes.

"Why do you just stand there, Wulf?" Alix said to the captain of the guard who seemed rooted to one spot. "Surely you have many urgent matters to attend to. As of this moment we may consider ourselves under siege."

"Oh my lady," the captain said, flinging himself down on one knee before her.

"Really, there is no need for that," Alix said, her face crimson. "What will the Empress Maud think?"

"She will think what a great lady you are, and how fortunate she is to count you among her friends," Maud responded tearfully, taking Alix in her arms and kissing her warmly on both cheeks.

While the castle inhabitants prepared for the siege, Maud kept watch on the battlements. What would be Stephen's response to Alix's defiance? she wondered. Looking over the parapet into the meadow below she was surprised to find so little war-like activity. Men could be seen polishing their weapons and armor or currying their horses; no attempt was being made to scale the walls with ladders; no timber was being cut to build a palisade; nor were men making trenchbuts or catapults to hurl over the walls. What did this signify?

As Maud watched, a figure emerged from the azure pavilion followed by two others: Stephen, his brother Henry of Winchester, and Waleran of Muelan. Maud's heart stood still as she drank in the sight of her cousin's tall body clad in a hauberk with a black mantle thrown over his shoulders. It was too far to see his features clearly, but almost as if he were aware of her intense gaze, she saw Stephen lift his head and stare straight up in her direction. The effect was as if she had been suddenly hit in the belly with an iron ball and could not catch her breath.

Shaken, Maud drew back, unprepared for the overwhelming conflict of rage, anguish, desire, and love that gripped her vitals. Her head reeled; she clung to the stone parapet while a tumult of feeling rampaged through her body like an invading force. Over the years she had tried to suppress all her emotions concerning Stephen, excepting only the desire for vengeance. But to her horror and shame, Maud knew that at this moment, had Stephen appeared beside her, she would have thrown herself into his arms, and disgraced herself forever.

When the violence of her inner storm had subsided, she hurried to find Alix who, with her women, had gone to the guardhouse.

"Waleran and the Bishop of Winchester are with Stephen," Maud told Alix. "But I see no sign of the Flemings."

"We must thank God for that. So the Bishop is there. It's a mystery why he remains loyal to his brother after the Canterbury affair."

"I've asked myself the same question," Maud said.

With a troubled look, Alix asked, "Do you suppose that if we throw stones, burning pitch hoops, and boiling water from the battlements, that will discourage Stephen's men from trying to scale the walls?"

"We?" Maud repeated.

"Why, all the women, of course. We cannot stand by and do nothing."

At the thought of the gentle Alix and her timid ladies hurling pitch hoops from the ramparts, Maud stifled a desire to laugh out loud. "No, of course you must contribute. Fortunately, I saw no signs of any attempt to scale the walls, but should there be, I'm sure your efforts will discourage them."

Alix remained a constant surprise. Just at the moment one expected her to faint dead away, she drew upon steely reserves of courage Maud had never even suspected.

By mid-afternoon, some six hours later, the herald returned. The entire castle mesnie—knights, men-at-arms, servitors, priests, and women—all gathered together in the great hall to hear the King's reply. The atmosphere was taut with apprehension but the assembled group had acquired a strong sense of purpose since this morning. Of one mind, they were united behind their Lady, determined to prevent the King from taking possession of Arundel.

"The King wishes to apologize to the Lady of Sussex," the herald began, "and truly regrets she found his request unchivalrous. It has never been his intention to persecute pregnant or helpless women. When the Countess of Anjou is delivered into his hands he will send her under safe escort to her brother at Bristol. No harm will come to her, nor will he besiege the castle. King Stephen swears this on his honor as a knight."

Amidst the cheers that rocked the great hall, Maud stood frozen, unable to credit her own ears. Stephen was willing to let her go? Impossible.

"I wonder why he allows you to go to Bristol, Madam," the captain of the guard said, obviously troubled. "It seems foolhardy in the extreme to let you slip through his fingers like this. What does he gain? Is it a trick of some kind?"

"It makes no sense," Maud agreed, "for he gains nothing and loses much."

Alix cleared her throat. "Perhaps Stephen makes this gesture so that he'll not be thought less than knightly. Such considerations are important to him, no matter how ill-judged the action may be."

The captain shook his head. "If he lets the Countess go, he puts his crown in jeopardy and condemns the land to civil war."

"But he has now made a public vow to ensure Maud is taken safely to Bristol," Alix said. "Think of the shame if he broke it."

"We have all seen what his vows have been worth in the past," Maud retorted.

"I would not trust the Countess of Anjou in his care," said the captain.

"I firmly believe that where Maud is concerned, Stephen will behave honorably," Alix insisted.

"In this matter, your good heart may lead you into an error of judgment, my lady. Madam is his enemy. Why should he treat her more honorably than he did his brother, who was not?"

Alix's face turned a deep rose and she avoided looking at Maud. Flustered and ill at ease, she began to wring her hands. "What I meant to say was he is a knight," she stammered. "He has taken vows to protect women and children—"

Sweet Marie, Maud thought, Alix must suspect that she had meant something to Stephen. Surely that was the implication. Was that all she suspected? Anxious that this subject not be pursued, Maud walked quickly over to the herald.

"Who is to be my escort to Bristol?" she asked.

"The Lord of Muelan was mentioned," the herald said.

A chill ran through her. "He is not an acceptable escort. An accident is sure to befall me somewhere between here and Bristol. Tell that to your master."

"Wait," Alix said, taking Maud aside where they would not be overheard. "Do you recall my saying that I did not understand how Bishop Henry remained loyal to Stephen? Well, perhaps his loyalty has never been tested."

Maud's heart began to beat faster as she caught Alix's meaning. "No one has offered him the opportunity to take his revenge, is that what you mean?" She looked at Alix with respect. "Holy Mary Virgin, when I am queen you shall be my chief adviser. Who would have guessed you had such an aptitude for intrigue."

"I was married to your father for many years," Alix said, blushing furiously at the compliment.

Maud smiled. "And the years were not wasted, I see. Now then, suppose I were to request that Bishop Henry escort me to Bristol instead of that ogre of Muelan. It is two days' ride at least. Plenty of time to attempt to suborn my cousin and win him over to my cause."

"That is exactly what I had in mind," Alix said, as she and Maud exchanged a look of affectionate complicity.

Together they approached the waiting herald.

"I wish to send a different message to my cousin of Blois," Maud said. "Tell your master that I'm most grateful for his courtesy to me and the Lady of Arundel, and I'll gladly go to Bristol but only if the escort is my cousin, Bishop Henry of Winchester."

After the herald left, Maud asked Alix, "Will it occur to Stephen that I may try to suborn his brother?"

Alix shook her head with a sad smile. "Unfortunately not. Therein lies his weakness, my dear."

Maud concealed her surprise at Alix's astute perception of this aspect of Stephen's character, an aspect that she herself was only beginning to discover. Whatever his motives in allowing her to leave, Stephen had made a fatal mistake in giving her this freedom. In his place, Maud knew, she would never let an enemy go free. Never. I will win, Maud thought, suddenly buoyant with hope. I will win.

Chapter Seven

THE NEXT MORNING MAUD SET OUT TO JOIN HER HALF-BROTHER, ROBert of Gloucester, at Bristol. Stephen had consented to her request that the Bishop of Winchester escort her, and in return she had reluctantly agreed that Waleran of Muelan might accompany them for the first part of the journey.

"I'm so pleased to have you for company, Your Grace," Maud said to the Bishop riding on her right, having decided to begin her campaign to woo her cousin with a show of flattery. "I hadn't expected such a large escort."

Henry, a hauberk over his cassock and a mace attached to his belt, slid his pale green eyes sideways at her; a brief smile touched his lips, and for a moment she was reminded of Stephen.

"Not safe to travel with less," Waleran said with a short laugh, riding on her left.

"Are the roads dangerous then?" Maud asked, pretending innocence.

"Since Gloucester turned traitor they are," Waleran replied, shooting her a malevolent look from his black eyes.

Maud ignored this, refusing to be baited. "How far do we travel today, Your Grace?"

"I hope to reach Southampton well before Vespers," Henry said, "where we will break our journey for the night. If you tire we can stop sooner."

"How thoughtful." Maud gave him a gracious smile.

"How thoughtful indeed," Waleran repeated mockingly. "Christ! This woman is the King's enemy, my lord bishop! Or had you forgotten she is being escorted to Bristol as a prisoner?"

Maud's fingers tightened on the leather reins as she looked at the Bishop. "Prisoner? That was not how I understood your brother's reply to the Lady of Arundel. Does Stephen of Blois break his sworn word—yet again?"

"Indeed not. We escort you to Bristol for your safety. By no means are you a prisoner," the Bishop said with an angry glance at Waleran. "My Lord of Muelan used a poor choice of words."

"Did I?" Waleran snorted. "In my mind she's a prisoner, an enemy of the realm, and if I had my way, she'd be riding in chains!"

Repressing a shudder of mingled fear and loathing, Maud looked away. With his stubble of black hair and beaked nose, Waleran reminded her of a great bird of prey. As she had already suspected, his intentions toward her were overtly hostile.

"Or better yet, imprisoned in one of the King's castles, where she can do no damage," Waleran continued, obviously warming to his subject. "It's not too late, Henry. Nothing prevents us from taking matters into our own hands and—"

"Enough!" The Bishop's voice sliced through the air like the crack of a whip. "Stephen's intention was for the Countess to go to Bristol and that is where she goes."

"By Christ, Stephen has made the worst decision of his life," Waleran said, his voice rising. "You agreed with me, you know you did. To have your enemy in your grasp and then let her go defies belief. Such an opportunity may not come again and my blood boils every time I look at her!" He gave an exclamation of disgust and spurred his horse forward to the front of the column of armed men.

Maud was shaken by what she had just heard. Her cousin had dared much for her sake. He must still care, her heart sang; despite all that has happened, he still cares.

"I apologize for Muelan," Henry was saying. "Pay no attention to his rantings."

Wrenching her thoughts away from Stephen, Maud wondered if the time was ripe to test the Bishop.

"So you also advised Stephen to imprison me, Cousin," she said, allowing a note of distress to enter her voice.

"I've ceased to give Stephen advice, but it's true I was against sending you to Bristol. I agree with Waleran in principle: Stephen has made a monumental error by letting you go." He paused, then added with a note of venom: "But then who am I to question the King's decision?"

"Only the shrewdest head in the realm, Your Grace, as everyone knows." Maud repressed a smile at the gratified expression that crossed his face. "In Stephen's boots I would have followed your advice."

He gave her a quick glance to see if she mocked him, but when he saw she did not, inclined his head. "You surprise me, Madam," the Bishop said slowly. "I hadn't expected to find a champion in you or have my modest abilities appreciated."

Maud's heart began to beat faster. Was the Bishop sending her a message? It seemed the perfect opening, yet his grave profile revealed nothing. Uncertain of how to proceed, she let the silence lengthen between them.

Maud realized there was little she could offer the Bishop. Canterbury was unavailable and he already occupied a powerful position as Bishop of Winchester as well as Papal Legate. She knew that Henry had pledged his word to the prelates that, if given the crown, his brother would honor the rights of the church and maintain the laws of the land. Thus far Stephen had done neither. Surely, she mused, it was an awkward and humiliating position for the proud Bishop to be in. This, coupled with Stephen's personal betrayal of him, should make Henry more approachable. There was only one way to find out.

Maud took a deep breath. "I was much distressed, Your Grace, to hear of your brother's shameful behavior toward you. It's common knowledge that Stephen could not have been crowned without your help. Of course he treated me in exactly the same manner; thus we are fellow victims, so to speak."

Henry's narrow face turned a deep red and he stared straight ahead with a fixed look. By mentioning Stephen's treachery, Maud knew she had touched an open wound but it also formed a bond between them. She pressed her advantage.

"I've always felt it vital to honor one's promises and obligations to Holy Church, and ensure she maintains all her rights and privileges," Maud continued.

"So say all those who wish to rule and need the church's goodwill to gain the crown," the Bishop said in a cold voice. "Once seated on the throne it seems to become another matter."

"Indeed. But not all who rule need prove faithless," Maud said, with what she hoped was a persuasive smile. "I've had much experience with Holy Church, Cousin. After all, I was married to the Holy Roman Emperor. From him I learned to be steadfast, loyal, and to honor my word."

"Did you indeed?" The Bishop turned his head slowly and their eyes met. "At another time, perhaps, we will speak again of these matters."

"I'm always at your disposal," Maud said softly. She had made a veiled offer. It had not been accepted, but neither had it been refused. A good sign. For the moment she had done all she could.

Pleased with her progress, Maud now looked around the countryside with renewed interest. They were riding past yellow fields ready for harvest but with only a handful of villeins at work. Some fields lay entirely idle. Where were the scores of laborers she was accustomed to seeing? From time to time they passed dead cattle lying across the road, scavenger birds already at work on the bloated carcasses. But where were all the people?

When she had first come to England fourteen years ago, Maud recalled, the roads were clogged with respectable travelers: farmers and their wives jogging to market, bands of pilgrims, young people alone. The few folk they passed today had been vagabonds, men with surly faces and ragged clothing who looked as if they would slit a throat for pleasure.

"Is there famine on the land? Or some disease afflicting the beasts?" Maud asked the Bishop.

"I'm aware of none. Why do you ask?"

"The countryside is so . . . so desolate. No travelers to speak of. Deserted fields. Cattle lying dead. Far different from what it was in my father's day."

"As God is my witness, I can vouch for that," Henry muttered.

They trotted around a sharp bend in the road. Ahead their party slowed as they came in sight of a small village.

"I will tell the Lord of Muelan to stop here so that we may refresh ourselves," the Bishop told her.

The village, backed by a blue-green forest, looked deserted as they rode down the main street. The smell of smoke and burning wood hung like a gray pall in the air. No villagers appeared to watch them ride by; no children played by the side of the road. At the edge of the village a small church surrounded by yew trees stood dark and empty, its door yawning open. Several slaughtered sheep lay scattered nearby, vultures pecking at the bloody entrails.

To the west of the village, Maud could now see sheaves of stacked corn, still smoldering in the ruined stubble of a burned-out field. Beyond the field the sails of a windmill flapped crazily in the wind as smoke poured from a gaping hole in the building's side. There was a sinister air about the place that reminded Maud of Normandy after Geoffrey's men had passed through it.

Up ahead, Maud saw Waleran and his men dismount and begin knocking on the doors of the cots that had not been torched. No one came to greet them. Finally, one of the knights kicked open a door and entered. He returned in a moment and spoke to Waleran.

"Bishop," Waleran called.

Henry rode up to the cot; Maud followed, fearful of what she would find.

"There has been a bloodbath here," Waleran said after Henry and Maud dismounted. "Much of the village appears to have been destroyed."

As Maud watched, several men pushed open the doors of the remaining cots, while others entered the church.

"All dead so far," one of them called.

A penetrating scream came from the interior of the church as a knight half carried, half dragged a young woman with a small child outside and set them down on the grass. The woman's gown was in shreds, her face streaked with blood. She alternately screamed or babbled incoherently. The child, who did not appear to be physically hurt, clung to its mother, struck dumb with terror. Another knight dragged several more bodies from the church.

"These men are also dead—tortured, by the look of them," the knight said, prodding one of the slashed bodies with his booted foot. "There are women in there who have been brutally ravished. Only this one has survived."

Sickened by the sight of the savagely mutilated bodies and the all-pervading smell of death, Maud turned her head away, fighting down a wave of faintness. This was worse than anything she had seen in Normandy.

"Who can have been responsible for this butchery?" Maud asked in an unsteady voice.

Waleran looked at the woman on the ground. Maud could see a

bruised shoulder showing through the tears in her bodice. Her skirts were torn and rumpled, stained with blood.

"There are lawless bands roaming the country. It could have been any one of them," Waleran said.

Sickened by the pitiful sight, Maud flung open the saddlebag tied to her horse and rifled through its contents, her fingers closing round a gray wool shawl. She approached the woman, whose screams had turned to sobs when she realized she would not be harmed.

"This will keep you warm," Maud said gently, wiping the blood from the woman's face, then draping the soft folds over her body.

"Let me see what sense can be gotten from this poor unfortunate," Henry said.

"My lord," one of Waleran's men called out, "what shall we do with these bodies?"

"The dead must be buried and Masses said for their souls," the Bishop ordered.

"If you are going to pray for all of England's dead, my lord bishop, you will have time for naught else," Waleran sneered.

While Waleran's men dug a mass grave, the Bishop questioned the woman.

"She claims that a band of men—rogues and brigands—rode through the village not long ago," Bishop Henry reported to Maud and Waleran. "They were looking for food and hidden wealth, but when the men of the village gave the knaves all their stores and what animals they could spare, insisting they were penniless, they were set upon, tortured, and then killed. Then these marauders burned the fields and some of the cots, set fire to the windmill, and desecrated the church, stealing its few valuables." The Bishop wiped his brow. "This woman confirms that she and others were raped or killed if they resisted. She was left for dead and the boy spared because he hid behind the altar. She thinks the village priest and a few of the villagers may have escaped to the forest with their beasts."

"This looks like the work of the King's Flemish mercenaries," one of Waleran's men said. "They be no better than Godless savages."

"Aye, they even be worse than the Scots," agreed another. "I fought in Cumberland against the clans but saw nothing like this day's work."

"Eh, by God's wounds, this be as bad as the Angevin devils. I were in Normandy a year ago and—" The man was quickly hushed and there was a strained silence.

Pretending not to hear, Maud turned away, her face burning with shame.

A short time later the bodies of the dead were thrown into the mass grave while prayers were said for their souls. The woman and child disappeared into the woods, returning shortly with a few haunted-looking men and ragged women driving a small herd of goats before them. They were accompanied by an old priest who leaned heavily on a wooden staff. Maud listened as the Bishop questioned them.

"Were these landless men, outlaws and the like?" Henry asked.

One of the men shook his head in mute denial and pointed at several of Waleran's knights.

Waleran frowned. "Men like us?"

"Aye," an old man with a gaunt face nodded. "Carrying red and yellow colors. Like this." He sketched circles in the air and two angles.

"Sounds like Gloucester's arms to me," Waleran said, with a sly look at Maud.

"Do you dare imply that Robert or his men were responsible for this massacre?" Maud retorted as a chill ran through her. "Impossible."

"Impossible?" Waleran gave a harsh laugh. "What kind of men do you think flock to the cause of a rebel like Gloucester? Traitors and such scum, those with grievances, men who have forfeited the protection of the law and now have nothing to lose! Such renegades have been roaming the country for a good six months now."

"Because Stephen is incapable of maintaining order in his realm, that is why these atrocities occur," Maud countered scornfully, inwardly trembling with outrage but determined not to let Waleran have the satisfaction of seeing it. To even suggest her half-brother would rape and torture was unthinkable!

"Enough!" The Bishop's voice cut through their hostility. "Nothing will be gained by meaningless accusations!" He looked at Maud with hard green eyes. "Let me remind you, Madam, that your recent arrival in England was the signal for renewed warfare between your supporters and King Stephen's. Whether this butchery is the work of Gloucester's men or the King's, it matters not. To these poor downtrodden souls, there is little to distinguish between you."

"How can you say that!" Maud cried, her control broken at last.

Henry silenced her by pointing at the desecrated church, the open grave of dead bodies, the burned fields and empty cots. His finger lingered on the ashen face of the raped woman, the broken men with their beasts, and the dumb, terrorized child.

"Look well upon this day's work, Cousin, for it is only the beginning."

Maud caught her breath, her eyes riveted to the child.

"What did you think would happen when you landed on these shores? If you have no stomach for this you would do better to return to Anjou," Waleran told her.

"If Stephen had not usurped my throne none of this would have happened," she said between clenched teeth.

"Or if you had stayed in Angers," Waleran retorted, "as any decent wife would have done. It is your return that will lead the realm into disaster! Go back to your devil's brood, woman, no one wants you here!"

"None of you are wanted, if truth be told." It was the quivering voice of the old village priest. "These poor children of God, whose lives are spent working the land and tending their flocks, do not care who sits on the throne as long as they are left in peace."

There was an abashed silence. Maud and Waleran avoided looking at each other.

"I had hoped to make Southampton before dark and we have not yet reached Portchester!" Henry squinted up at the fading afternoon sunlight. "Come, let us be on our way. We can do no more here." He blessed the old priest and the villagers and walked toward his horse.

Maud reached into the leather purse at her belt and pulled out five silver coins which she pressed into the clawed hand of the village priest. Dazed, he looked down at the pile of silver.

"Christ, a few copper pennies would have been ample," Waleran grumbled. "That's more wealth than these folk have seen in the whole of their lives! It does no good to spoil them."

With a defiant look, Maud then added five more coins. From the corner of her eye she saw the suggestion of a smile soften the Bishop of Winchester's ascetic lips, and she knew that her gesture had won from him a degree of approval she would never have gained by words alone. This day she had glimpsed another aspect of the ambitious, cunning prelate whom she had always regarded as her enemy and Stephen's nemesis. Under his cool, disdainful exterior lay a heart touched with compassion for the misfortunes of the oppressed and needy. It made him appear almost human.

Waleran's eyes fairly popped with anger as he leapt onto his horse and rode furiously down the road, waving his knights after him.

Henry helped Maud mount her palfrey; once again the party took to the dusty road. As they trotted westward following the sun, Maud reassured herself that she was not responsible for the destruction of the village. Injustice, cruelty, wanton destruction, wasted lives— these were the unfortunate hazards of war. Just this morning she had thought of Stephen with aching tenderness, but what she had seen reminded her anew that he had stolen what was rightfully hers; *he* had brought about the desecration of the land, not she. When the crown was safely on her head, then she would heal the wounds of the realm, and repair the damage her people had suffered. Order and peace would be restored, as in her father's time; she would be the Lion of Justice come again.

Chapter Eight

Lincoln, 1141

ON THE MORNING OF THE SECOND OF FEBRUARY, STEPHEN OPENED THE door of his azure pavilion and gazed into a misty gray dawn. For the past month he and his forces had been camped within the walled town of Lincoln and today, at last, he would do battle with the enemy. A battle he must win in order to reverse the disastrous decline in his fortunes.

For the last sixteen months—ever since he had so recklessly allowed Maud to leave Arundel—the country had been plunged into a full-scale civil war. From her headquarters at Robert's stronghold in Bristol, Maud had succeeded in rallying to her cause a surprising number of adherents. What had once been sporadic pockets of rebellion was now a unified opposition, far stronger than anything Stephen had imagined. And he had only himself to blame.

"Battle dress today," he told Baldwin FitzGilbert, who attended him. "The cathedral bells will sound morning Mass any moment now."

The mist shifted and Stephen caught sight of the forbidding keep of Lincoln Castle perched on an incline above his camp. Although the castle had been under heavy siege ever since his arrival, the garrison installed by Ranulf of Chester continued to hold fast. At the thought of the treacherous earl, Stephen was filled with a murderous rage. Chester, biding his time, apparently had been plotting vengeance ever since Stephen had given King David the Earl's patrimony of Carlisle. While Stephen's attention was occupied with other matters, Chester had seized the crown's castle of Lincoln. To add insult to injury the Earl had escaped from the castle on the very night Stephen had arrived, leaving his wife and brother behind.

The traitor had then made a pact with his father-in-law, Robert of Gloucester. In return for Ranulf's pledging fealty to Maud, Robert had agreed to help him gather a large army to defeat Stephen's forces at Lincoln and free the hostages in the castle. Gloucester and Chester had marched their host day and night, arriving across the river from Lincoln in the hours before dawn. It had been too dark to estimate the full size of the enemy forces, but Stephen feared the worst.

Tearing his eyes away from the hated castle, Stephen allowed FitzGilbert to dress him for battle: chain-mail hauberk over a padded leather tunic, chain-mail chausses to protect his legs, sleeveless black surcoat over his shoulders, leather baldric to hold his sword, conical helmet with its long nosepiece, triangular shield, and, last, his sword of Damascus steel.

The bells rang for Prime. He was ready, Stephen thought, ready to reap the fruits of victory—or die in battle as a warrior should. He quickly strode out of the pavilion toward the cathedral.

In Lincoln Cathedral, just as the Mass came to an end, the consecrated wax taper that Stephen was holding broke suddenly in his hand and the flame went out. Shortly thereafter the pyx containing the Blessed Sacrament fell upon the altar just as the Bishop of Lincoln was invoking God's blessing upon the forthcoming battle. It was the most sinister of omens. Was God's hand raised against him because he had usurped the throne? Because of his treatment of Holy Church? So great was his fear that he could barely concentrate on the Bishop's final invocation of God's favor on the King's victory and his exhortation to the men to be strong and courageous.

When the ceremonies were over, Stephen left the cathedral and called his leaders together for a final consultation.

"I would seek a temporary truce, Sire," Count Alan of Brittany advised. "The portents are not auspicious."

"I agree," said Waleran of Muelan. "With the unexpected addition of Welshmen to Chester's and Gloucester's armies, the enemy now outnumber us. We must gather more arms and men before risking a pitched battle."

There was a chorus of assent from the rest of the nobles.

Stephen's jaw clenched; his eyes suddenly blazed with resolution. "Is the knight-service of England afraid of a rabble of Welsh tribesmen? Do we turn tail because the odds are against us? We *will* fight this day," he said in a voice of such conviction that none dared gainsay him.

Within the hour Stephen was leading his forces out the west gate of Lincoln and down the road to a meadow at the foot of the hill. Across the marshy terrain, he could see Robert's men already in position.

"Prepare for battle," Stephen said, turning first to William of Ypres. "We fight in three formations as planned: The mounted Flemings will take the left formation; the mounted Bretons and the earls will take the right, led by the Count of Brittany. I'll take the center formation on foot with the soldiers of my army, the unmounted knights, and the men of Lincoln."

The Earl of Gloucester sounded his trumpets for the attack. The men under Earl Robert's command charged the first line of the King's cavalry with such vigor that it was scattered almost immediately. The Welsh attacked the second line of the royal cavalry. The line held and the Welsh were pushed back until Chester's men scattered the Breton knights in turn. As Chester's forces pressed forward, accompanied by a storm of Welsh arrows, the entire body of the King's horsemen fell back and scattered. Alarmed at the enemy's superior strength, they retreated as one body. Stephen was dumbfounded to see his earls and their knights, with his Flemish captain in the lead, take flight.

"Follow us, Sire," William of Ypres cried. "I can take you up behind me."

"I stand firm," Stephen shouted. "Regroup and return!"

Stephen, his foot soldiers, a group of knights, and the men of Lincoln were left alone on the battlefield in the midst of a foe who closed round on all sides, assaulting them with sword, mace, and arrow. A knight astride a black charger, unrecognizable in his helmet, reared suddenly in front of Stephen. A blade flashed. Stephen jumped nimbly aside and holding his shield high, thrust upward with his sword toward the enemy's breast, knocking his opponent's weapon out of his hand. Suddenly, he caught sight of flashing emeralds set into the pommel of the sword falling through the air toward him. Robert!

Just in time he deflected his blade so that it rang harmlessly against Robert's shield.

"You grow clumsy, Gloucester," Stephen cried, as he bent to pick up the sword. He tossed the blade to Robert, who deftly caught the pommel. "Look to yourself, my friend. Next time I may not be so generous."

"I am in your debt, Cousin," Robert said, with a catch in his voice. He turned his charger deliberately away from Stephen and plunged into the battle.

From behind him, through the chorus of screams and curses, Stephen could hear the Norman battle cry: "Dex Ais!" He knew he was losing ground. Vainly he looked to see if the earls and their knights had returned, but could only distinguish his own force of men, now seriously diminished, and the men of Lincoln armed with bills and axes. Sweet Jesu, was it possible that the earls and their men had all deserted?

"To me, to me!" Stephen shouted.

The remaining men formed a living wall behind him. The enemy horsemen dashed against that bulwark, opening a small breach each time but constantly being driven back from the center point where Stephen stood like a lion at bay, cutting down everyone who came within reach of his sword. Soon the hilt and blade were covered in blood, as he slashed and hacked and thrust. Around him the pile of dead bodies and severed limbs grew even larger.

Suddenly a stone hurtled through the air and clanked loudly against his helmet. He staggered, then fell to his knees. An enemy knight jumped from his horse, seized Stephen's nasal, and yanked off the helmet.

"The King, the King, I have the King!"

Stumbling to his feet, his ears ringing from the stone, Stephen seized the knight by the throat and threw him onto the wet, red earth. He looked around him. Only four men remained. All the rest either were slain, had fled, or had been taken prisoner. A ring of hostile faces surrounded him, swords raised, painted shields thrust forward. It was over.

"I will surrender only to the Earl of Gloucester," Stephen said at last.

Robert pushed through the crowd of men and stood before Stephen. He removed his helmet and the two men faced each other.

Ranulf of Chester approached them. He pounded Robert on the back. "Victory, Kinsman," he shouted, his voice jubilant. "Victory is ours!" He turned to a knight standing just behind him. "Bring chains. We will manacle this fallen king and parade him through the streets of Lincoln as an example of our justice."

Robert turned on him in a fury. "For shame that you would think to put this knight in chains! Only by the cowardice of his men has he lost the field to us. Never in all my years of battle have I witnessed greater prowess or courage! We have seen the Conqueror himself this day."

There was a loud murmur of agreement from Chester's and Gloucester's troops as they eyed Stephen with grudging respect and awe. Amidst the shouts of victory and the cries of the wounded, Robert led him off the battlefield.

"We ride to Gloucester, Cousin," he said. "To Maud."

Stephen closed his eyes. Maud. It was the final blow.

Chapter Nine

Gloucester, 1141

Maud PACED HER CHAMBER AT GLOUCESTER CASTLE. ANY MOMENT now Robert would ride into the courtyard with his royal prisoner. She stopped by the window set into the stone wall, removed the heavy wooden shutter, and peered out. A gust of damp February air blew into her face. It was barely mid-afternoon yet the sky was already streaked with dark shadows; a gentle rain fell soundlessly to the earth below.

Maud turned away from the window and walked over to the oak table. There lay the half-written letter to Geoffrey requesting that he send her son Henry to join her in England. She had not seen her son, who would be eight next month, in almost a year and a half. Not a day passed that she did not miss him, wishing with all her heart that he was with her.

She sat down on the stool, picked up the parchment, then put it down again. It was impossible to concentrate. All she could think about was Stephen's imminent arrival. The last time she had been face to face with her cousin was the year before her father died—seven years earlier. A lifetime ago. How would she feel when—

The door opened abruptly and Robert's wife, Mabel, entered the chamber. Her face was flushed, and her black eyes fairly snapped with excitement.

Maud's heart began to pound; she half rose. "Have they arrived?"

"Soon now; they have been sighted a quarter of a league away," Mabel said, giving Maud a brief smile. Her manner was unbending, reflecting the barely suppressed hostility Maud knew her sister-in-law harbored toward all things Angevin.

She had always suspected that Mabel disapproved of her, but it was not until she had joined Robert at Bristol that she realized the full extent of her sister-in-law's resentment. Despite Maud's efforts to win her affection, the Countess of Gloucester remained prickly as a thorn bush. As Mabel's eyes fell on the unfinished parchment, she frowned, her thick black brows making a single hirsute line across her forehead. That a woman was able to read and write, Maud knew, she regarded as the devil's work.

"It's a letter to my husband in Normandy," Maud explained carefully, "telling him about our victory at Lincoln and requesting that he send young Henry to join me."

"I wonder that you did not send for the boy before now."

"I did, many times, but Geoffrey felt England was too dangerous. Henry's safety could not be guaranteed."

"It has been dangerous for all of us, including my own children," Mabel retorted.

"But since that is no longer the case," Maud continued, choosing to ignore the barb, "I can look forward to the joy of having my son and heir stand beside me when I'm crowned."

Mabel's face became impassive. "As well as letting the nobles and commonfolk see for themselves that the dynasty founded by your grandfather will continue into the future. Most politic for your son to be here, Madam."

"Naturally that is true, but it is not why I want him here," Maud began hotly, then stopped herself. There was little point in tilting a lance with her sister-in-law. This was a time to rejoice and she must not allow Mabel's resentment to spoil it.

After a moment's silence the Countess of Gloucester continued with her attack. "I hear that Queen Matilda—the former Queen Matilda, I suppose I must call her—has been dragging her son, Eustace, all over Kent these past few days trying to raise an army on Stephen's behalf. She has been clever enough to ensure the wretched child is visible to everyone, look you, while Henry of Anjou is completely unknown to the English."

At this mention of Stephen's wife, Maud's whole body stiffened. Trust Mabel to remind her that Matilda had stolen a march on her. Only a month ago the former queen had traveled secretly to Paris and persuaded young Louis, the new French king, to betroth his sister to her six-year-old son and recognize Eustace as future Duke of Normandy. When she heard the news Maud had become enraged, for the ducal title belonged by right to Henry. But until Geoffrey attained a clear victory in Normandy there was nothing to be done. Louis of France was the nominal overlord of the duchy and his acknowledgment of Eustace had been a masterstroke on Matilda's part. Overnight, it appeared, her gentle cousin had become a tigress. Of course, now that Stephen was no longer king it would be a different story—

The sound of a horn broke into her thoughts. Walking quickly over to the window, Maud saw a party of mounted men ride into the courtyard. She recognized Robert, and Miles, Sheriff of Gloucester, whose castle this was; then she saw Brian FitzCount. Her heart missed a beat. Where—yes, there was Stephen being helped from his horse by two grooms. Maud had been told her cousin was not seriously injured, yet he walked stiffly, favoring his right leg.

Trembling, Maud clutched the wall for support, unprepared for the treacherous tide of feeling that swept through her. Sweet Marie, was it to be Arundel all over again?

"Have they arrived?" Mabel asked.

Maud nodded, not trusting herself to speak.

"Their baths have been prepared. I will see if everything is readied for the feast," her sister-in-law said.

"I must dress. Tell Robert I will join him at the feast."

Mabel nodded and left.

An hour later Maud was still in her chamber. The Vespers bell had sounded but she could not bring herself to attend. Now a page stood outside her door waiting to escort her down to the great hall. Delay was no longer possible. Slowly she walked down the passage. She had gone over and over what to say to her cousin, preparing one speech, then tossing it aside in favor of another. Right now she could remember none of them.

For six years Maud had suppressed her love for Stephen, nurturing a desire for vengeance, fanning the flames of her hurt and rage until his downfall had become the most important goal in her life. With his defeat she would, at one stroke, not only regain the throne but wound him as deeply as he had her. She longed to pay him back in kind for his betrayal, for the years of anguish she had suffered. At last her moment of triumph was at hand.

Maud descended the staircase, slowing her pace yet further as she approached the great hall. She put her hands to her cheeks; they were burning hot. Adjusting the gold tissue veil covering her hair, she glanced down at the wine-colored gown and tunic, the girdle of fili- greed gold encircling her waist, the gold-and-sapphire brooch at her breast. She had dressed with care, intending to look every inch the queen; she wanted to dazzle Stephen by her elegance, humble him by the majesty of her bearing.

At the entrance to the great hall she paused, suddenly overcome with panic. The page gave her a questioning look. With a forced smile Maud steeled herself and marched inside.

A group of men milled about the central fire while servitors passed around pewter goblets of hot mulled wine.

"Sister," Robert said, detaching himself from the group. He came forward, holding out his arms in greeting.

Maud ran into them. "Dearest, dearest Brother, how can I ever thank you," she breathed into his ear as she hugged him, then kissed him on both cheeks. "I'll never forget what you have done for our cause. How proud our father would be!"

Robert stepped back, his face beaming, his dark eyes bright with the effect of her praise. Overcome with affection and gratitude, Maud seized his hands and held them tightly, determined to be worthy of her brother's loyalty and devotion.

Brian appeared and she kissed him warmly on both cheeks. Then Miles of Gloucester approached her, leading Stephen by the arm. A hulking giant of a man with a shock of corn-colored hair and merry blue eyes, Miles thrust Stephen forward.

"Here is your prize, noble lady," Miles said, forcing Stephen to his knees. "Kneel to your rightful sovereign, knave."

"Miles!" Robert's voice sternly rebuked him. "I've warned you before. Stephen is our prisoner but also our guest. Treat him with the courtesy his former position deserves."

Hardly able to breathe, Maud forced herself to look down at the man kneeling before her. His arms hung limply by his sides; his head was bowed over his breast in the attitude of a penitent. She was shocked to note a number of silver strands in his hair. This was the cousin who had vowed to acclaim her as queen, serve her faithfully, and defend her honor with his life if need be. Instead, he had broken his sworn oath as carelessly as if it had been a piece of applewood to place the crown on his own head.

Here was the father of her eldest son, the passionate lover who had asserted his devotion to her, begging her to desert family and obligations to come away with him, then broken her heart and destroyed her trust. There was every reason in the world to hate him. For a moment Maud allowed herself to dwell on the wrongs he had done her, enjoying his sorry plight. Then the frozen core of bitterness in her heart began to thaw.

For the man on his knees, neatly clothed in blue and freshly barbered, did not resemble the wild and bloody figure she had half expected to see: a raging beast snarling defiance. Only a dark purple bruise near his temple coupled with the pallor of his face bore witness to the ordeal he had recently survived.

Was it possible defeat had broken his bold spirit? Was he truly humbled? Her heart ached in unwitting pity. Appalled and mortified, Maud found that all she really wanted to do was take him into her arms and comfort him like a child.

"Cousin," she said in a faltering voice. "We meet again under most unfortunate circumstances for you." It was not at all what she had intended to say.

When Stephen threw back his head to look her squarely in the eye, Maud saw to her mingled relief and chagrin that he had not changed. The jaunty manner was still evident—if more subdued. Green-gold eyes, gently mocking, certainly unregenerate, challenged her with their old caressing warmth. The blood rushed to her head. The palms of her hands became moist. As his eyes locked with hers, her loins responded instantly. She prayed it was not evident to those present that the captive was at his ease, while the victor was shaken.

"Unfortunate circumstances indeed," Stephen responded. "If it please you, may I rise? Despite the hot bath every muscle is still sore."

She nodded. He rose to his feet with difficulty. Instinctively Maud started to help him but stopped herself in time.

"A far cry from our last meeting in Normandy," he said softly. A crooked smile hinted at old secrets shared between them.

Maud colored deeply, determined to hold firm against his blandishments. "I don't recall our meeting in Normandy, but I well remember catching a glimpse of you at Arundel, though we did not converse directly. I'm glad for the opportunity to thank you for your chivalrous behavior to me on that occasion."

Her words had hit the mark. Maud saw Stephen's lips tighten and knew he did not wish to be reminded of his earlier folly. But for that reckless gesture he would not be standing here now.

"Unfortunately, I'm not of so generous a nature," she continued with satisfaction. "You will be treated with every courtesy, of course, as befits your rank, but I don't mean to let you forget you are my prisoner."

Stephen flushed; he swallowed, as if trying to ingest the unpalatable news that he was truly a prisoner. For a moment something flamed deep within his eyes, then vanished. He gave her a forced smile and took a step toward her.

"I was ever your captive," he said under his breath. "Nothing will have changed."

She was tempted to remind him of Aldyth's favorite warning: Those who have honey in their mouths have stings in their tails. Before she could do so, her nephew Phillip, Robert's youngest son, ran up to them.

"My mother tells me the steward is ready to announce the feast," he said, his eyes looking in awe at Stephen.

A moment later came the sound of the steward's horn summoning the castle mesnie and guests to the feast.

Robert took Maud aside and asked, "Will you permit our cousin to join us at the high table?" When she hesitated, he continued: "Stephen spared my life during the battle when he could easily have killed me." As her eyes widened in shock he pressed his point further: "Remember, he is still loved by the people despite his many drawbacks. Give no one occasion to say he has been treated with less than perfect courtesy by the future queen of the realm."

She did not relish the prospect of having to confront her cousin over a long feast. But, ever the diplomat, Robert was right. "It is our enemy's defeat we celebrate. I would be much honored should he rejoice with us."

She followed Robert and the others up to the high table where Mabel already awaited them. The mesnie of Gloucester Castle seated themselves at the trestle tables below.

Flanked by Robert and Brian, Maud sat in the seat of honor. Stephen had been placed at the far end of the table. Two guards stood behind him. Maud could not keep her eyes from straying in his direction.

"The first step is accomplished," Robert said to Maud following her glance. "Our next opponent to be vanquished is the church. We must gain the support of the leading prelates of the realm."

"I agree. The most important is Henry of Winchester," Maud replied. "His influence can swing the English bishops in our favor, and as Papal Legate he is Rome's representative and has the ear of the Holy See."

"But will he commit to us?" Brian asked.

"When I rode with him to Bristol he did not reject my offer," Maud responded. "On the contrary, I felt he was of a mind to join us but waited only for the politic moment."

"That moment has come," Brian said. "His brother has fallen and England is without a leader. This is the time to renew your offer, Lady, for he is the key to your being crowned."

"Tomorrow I will send to Winchester." Maud turned to Robert. "The Bishop will want to know what arrangements have been made for Stephen."

"He goes to Bristol where he'll be placed in honorable confinement. Well guarded, of course, but treated as befits one of his former station. After you're crowned, when peace is fully restored, we can decide his ultimate fate."

There was a sudden stir as a Welsh bard made his entrance into the great hall. His stocky frame was covered in wolfskins; a thick black beard obscured his face. Walking up to the high table, he bowed before Earl Robert, greeting him first in Welsh, then in Norman French.

The hall quieted; when there was absolute silence the bard began to sing. In a high voice of piercing sweetness, he sang of how the Earl of Gloucester and the Welshmen had won the battle of Lincoln. The words were so stirring, the melody so plaintive, that Maud felt as if she had been there. Tears sprang to her eyes. The bard would go from castle to castle throughout England singing his tale of glory. A hundred years from now men would still be listening in breathless wonder to the battle of Lincoln, as today men listened to the stirring saga of the Battle of Hastings.

Maud's eyes were drawn to Stephen. Listening to the bard could not be easy for him, although his prowess on the battlefield was being described in glowing terms. Thank the Holy Mother he would be leaving soon, she thought. It would be a long while before she need see him again, and when next they met she would be Queen of England.

. . .

When the church bells rang announcing the midnight hour, Maud was still awake. Unable to sleep, she had lain for hours in the canopied bed, an image of Stephen spinning round and round in her mind. She saw him, hurt and vulnerable, kneeling before her, felt again the familiar exchange of excitement pulsing between them. Without warning she was overcome with a desire so piercing she almost cried aloud. Those feelings she had thought successfully buried now rose up like a flooding river threatening to overflow its banks. How she ached to hold Stephen in her arms, to feel again the pressure of his lips against hers, the caress of his warm hands on her breasts. A host of memories ran like wildfire through her body; the touch of his mouth burning a path down to her bosom, kissing her nipples until she began to gasp with pleasure; his fingers sliding between her parted thighs, invoking wave after wave of rising delight. Then the wonder of his body covering her own as their ecstacy was joined.

Trembling, drenched in sweat, Maud sat bolt upright in the bed. Her heart beat wildly and before she was fully aware of what she was doing, she had tumbled from the bed, pulled on a furred robe and leather shoes, picked up the iron candle holder, and run to the door of her chamber. The two women who shared the chamber slept on without waking. She had actually opened the door and started head-long down the passage before a guard came running to inquire if all was well. She stared at him blindly before coming to her senses. With a feeble excuse she returned to the chamber.

Mother of God, what was happening to her? Terrified by her loss of control, Maud removed her robe and shoes with unsteady fingers, then climbed back into the bed. As she huddled under the coverlet she began to weep into the pillow, trying to muffle the sound of her deep wrenching sobs. Exhausted at last, her body stopped trembling; she felt drained and empty but her mind was clearer.

She acknowledged that the flame of her love for Stephen burned as brightly as ever. But no matter the urgency of her need, it was her cross to bear and she must bear it in silence and with fortitude for the remainder of her life. If she had to live with the torment of unsatisfied desire and a lonely heart, she would make power as all-consuming as love. It was the price she must pay in order to be queen.

Chapter Ten

Maud woke early the next morning, attended mass in the chapel, broke the night's fast, then retired to her chamber to write several letters. She was in the midst of a carefully worded letter to Stephen's brother when a knock on the door broke her concentration.

"Good morning," Robert said as he entered the chamber. "Brian, Mabel, and I are ready to leave for Bristol to prepare for our prisoner. We leave Stephen here, in Miles's care, until full security can be established at Bristol Castle. I'll return as soon as possible."

Maud rose to her feet. "That sounds most sensible," she replied, her heart skipping a beat at the thought of spending another few nights under the same roof with Stephen.

She gave her half-brother a farewell kiss, then continued writing her messages until the steward's horn summoned the castle inhabitants to the late-morning meal.

Guards patrolled every floor of the castle and lined the walls of the great hall. When Maud joined Miles and his wife at the high table, she asked how Stephen fared. The former king complained of feeling unwell, Miles told her, and he had sent his own personal physician to examine the prisoner.

"What ails him?" Maud asked.

Miles shrugged. "Nothing worse than a case of resounding defeat would be my guess, but we dare not take a chance. How would it look should he become ill while in our care?" Miles grimaced. "Everyone will assume we have mistreated their beloved Stephen. It passes belief how the people can still care about him, ineffective as he is."

He tore the leg off a roast fowl. "If I had my way, let me tell you, we wouldn't coddle this poor excuse for a monarch but—"

"Perhaps a nourishing broth could be prepared for him," Maud interjected, not wishing to hear what Miles would do to her cousin. "We must take every precaution to maintain his health." Then, lest she sound overly anxious, she added: "It is the politic thing to do, as you have said."

"I will see a broth is prepared, Lady," Miles's wife offered.

The day and night passed without incident. The next morning Miles, ever chafing for action, decided to go hunting.

"I saw Stephen," he told Maud after morning Mass, "and he feels somewhat improved but not fully recovered. As I suspected, the physician can find nothing wrong with him. I'll only be gone for a few hours."

Miles left with a party of his knights, his wife retired to her solar and Maud to her chamber. She found she could put her attention on nothing but Stephen. She felt as if an invisible thread led from his chamber to hers and, slowly, inexorably, she was being pulled toward him. If only Aldyth were here, she mourned, or someone to whom she could unburden her conflicted emotions.

What *was* the matter with her? Here, at last, was the opportunity she had been waiting for: the chance to teach Stephen what it meant to totally abandon hope, to experience firsthand how it felt to have your dreams shattered, the very fabric of your life torn to shreds. She should be jubilant, intoxicated by her victory, which she was, of course she was, but some key ingredient was missing, some—all at once Maud realized what it was: She needed to confront Stephen directly; to accuse him to his face. Why hadn't she recognized it before? She rose from the table, grabbed several rolls of parchment, and resolutely marched out of her chamber.

Her heart pounded like a drum as she approached the chamber where Stephen was confined and saw six guards, armed with lances, standing outside the thick oak door. Assuming a regal air, Maud held up her parchments.

"I'm here to see the prisoner. He must sign some important documents," she said in an authoritative voice, wondering why she felt the need to explain her actions.

The guards bowed and immediately opened the door. Two of them made a move to accompany her inside but she held up her hand.

"That will not be necessary, thank you. If there is need I'll call you."

Maud stepped inside the chamber and the door closed behind her.

Stephen, dressed in a white linen shirt, blue hose, and threadbare tunic that looked like someone's castoffs, was lying on a wooden frame bed, seemingly asleep. He raised his head and opened his eyes, then quickly sat up in astonishment. She was surprised to see that he looked rested and in good health; the purple bruise on his temple was healing nicely.

"Were you asleep? I will return later." Suddenly panicked, Maud turned to open the door.

"No, wait. I was not asleep. Please—don't go."

She paused, forcing herself to remain calm, then turned back to him. "I don't like to disturb your rest when you've been unwell."

He gave her a crooked smile as he swung his long legs off the bed. "Where I am going there will be much opportunity for rest, I doubt not. I would have you stay, though I'm afraid these cheerless surroundings do not offer much inducement."

Maud looked around the sparsely furnished chamber. Besides the bed there was a rickety table holding a basin of water, a pitcher and wooden cup, two threadbare cushioned stools, and an oak chest. Dried rushes covered the floor, and a charcoal brazier burned in one corner.

"Have you sent word to my wife?" Stephen asked, pointing to the scrolls of parchment in her hand.

"Yes, and to your brother as well. A courier leaves this evening for London and another for Winchester." She walked slowly over to one of the stools and sat down.

Stephen's lips tightened. "I see you have wasted no time in contacting Henry." He paused. "You assume now that my fortunes are at their nadir he'll abandon me."

"Why should he remain loyal after the loss of Canterbury? I'm not the only one to suffer from broken promises. Treachery appears to come as naturally to you as breathing."

He had the grace to flush, she noted, pleased that she had discomfited him. After all, this was what she had come for: to hurt, to wound, to taunt. There was a deep sense of satisfaction in venting her spleen to his face, as if, in so doing, she was able to take back what he had stolen from her in terms of pride and esteem.

"I presume you seek Henry's aid in wooing the church?" he asked in a low voice.

"Naturally, I must have the goodwill of the clergy and the Bishop is most influential." Maud paused. "Once I gain ecclesiastical support I shall know how to keep it."

"Even if my brother agrees to help your cause, you will not tread an easy path, Cousin. I do not say this out of spite or vindictiveness."

"Thank you for your concern, but I'm fully aware of the pitfalls ahead."

"I doubt if you are."

"Your mistakes glow like a beacon in the dark," she countered. "All I need do is avoid them."

To her surprise, Stephen suddenly threw back his head and laughed. "By God's birth, when you tilt your lance you draw blood."

"Then we are quits," she said fiercely, determined not to be disarmed by him. "Though the wound you dealt me is far deeper and will not fully heal until I'm on the throne, and you have paid for your crime."

Stephen reeled back as if she had struck him with a spiked mace. How often she had wanted to hurl recriminations, confront him with the enormity of his betrayal, and pierce through the armor of his charm to the vulnerable spirit beneath. By the look on his face, Maud saw that she had succeeded. She should have felt heady with triumph, and she did, of course she did. Yet underneath the triumph her treacherous heart responded to him as it always had.

Unable to meet her gaze, his eyes roamed the chamber like a cornered animal, darting here and there, seeking escape. At last he passed a trembling hand across his ashen face.

"Dear God, you cannot know how I've dreaded this moment," he whispered in a voice hoarse with misery. "In truth there is nothing whatsoever the matter with my health. I simply did not have the courage to face you again, to see the hurt and anguish in your eyes. I would sooner slay myself than cause you pain."

"Liar, liar! Then why did you do it? Why? You swore a sacred oath to serve me. You owed at least that much to my father, who had given you everything. But even more important, I believed there was so great a love between us that I would gladly have lived the rest of my life in the afterglow of such a flame—" Her voice became so choked she could not go on. Tears welled up in her eyes and ran down her cheeks. To her shame she began to cry in deep wrenching sobs.

Stephen slipped from the bed and knelt before her in the rushes. "There *was* so great a love between us. There still is and always will be, I cannot deny it. Please, please do not weep. I am not deserving of your tears." He grasped her ice-cold hands and held them tightly between his own. "I bitterly regret that I hurt you so deeply and forswore my oath, but—but—" He paused as if to marshal his thoughts. "But the unpalatable truth is that my uncle made a fatal mistake when he named you his heir, against all reason and judgment, against time-honored custom, against the will of his subjects and closest advisers. No, let me finish," he said, as she opened her mouth to protest. "The Norman barons will never allow the crown to rest on the head of a woman married to an Angevin who will become their king. Never. What I did, however vile, was done in a just cause."

"This is the first time I've heard treason and ambition called a just cause," Maud managed to say. "You think that exonerates your actions? That you were justified in your act of treachery?"

"I justify nothing," he said softly. "You have every reason to condemn me, to revile me. If I could scourge myself, wear sackcloth and heap ashes on my head, I would gladly do so."

He wiped away her tears with the back of his hand. "Mea culpa. Mea summa culpa. I have no right to ask your forgiveness for I'm not worthy of being forgiven." He sighed. "Console yourself with the fact that your star is in the ascendant now," he continued, "while I will be a captive, denied my friends, my family, even the power of choice." He dropped her hands and rose to his feet. "In truth I dread what lies ahead. I've never been imprisoned before and the prospect is unbearable. I fear nothing in battle, not death or maiming, but to be shut up for months, perhaps years—" His voice broke and he turned away from her.

Her sobs subsided and the tears began to dry on her cheeks as she watched him struggle to gain control. Her heart was moved to unwilling compassion and a sudden impulse took hold of her.

"You need not go to Bristol," she said to his rigid back. "You can be free."

Stephen turned, his eyes blazing with hope.

"All you need do is confess to the world that you committed an act of treason and that Hugh Bigod perjured himself in order for you to gain the throne. State that you recognize me as the rightful heir and relinquish all claim to the crown. I swear that you will be put on a ship for Boulogne where, in time, Matilda and the children will be permitted to join you."

The light died from his eyes. "Is this why you came?" he asked in a harsh voice. "To ask me to betray those who have sworn to serve me in good faith as king?" He drew himself up proudly. "I may be your prisoner but in the hearts of my subjects I am still their sovereign and will remain so until the Archbishop of Canterbury crowns you—if he ever does. You are not wanted, Cousin, that is what you refuse to face."

"You dare to speak of me of betrayal?" she cried. "The people may have welcomed you once, but now? After what you have done to their land? Here is your opportunity to make amends, to undo the damage you have caused. If you are truly sorry you will accept my offer."

"I long to do just that but cannot." His face took on a stubborn look. "I reject your offer. Do not try to overwhelm my intention or bend me to your will."

A hot surge of anger instantly coursed through her. "Bend *you* to *my* will? A poor jest when you know I have always been your vassal, so drunkenly in love I was no longer mistress of my own heart."

"The arrogant, self-willed Empress my vassal?" He laughed shortly. "Obedient? Yielding? Submissive? Now that, like the second coming, I would witness with my own eyes. By God's birth, how little you know yourself! Sick for love of me, were you? But you would not come away with me when I asked, no, the crown was more important! You were not willing to give up anything, if the truth be told. When you have set your heart on something, Cousin, you are like a tempestuous, imperious storm that seeks to flatten all before it."

The last remnant of control snapped; incensed, Maud leapt at him, striking out with her fists, hammering at Stephen's chest and face in a red haze of fury. He caught her wrists and she kicked out savagely with her feet, the toe of one shoe cutting into his ankle.

"Ouch! Vixen! Bitch! Stop this, do you hear? Stop this at once."

He shook her violently, the grip on her wrists tightening. Maud gasped in pain. "You're hurting me."

"I intend to, vixen. Jesu, it is like holding a spitting wild fox—"

Maud bent to sink her teeth into his wrist and with an oath Stephen suddenly lifted her up into his arms and flung her onto the bed with such force that her skirts flew up to her knees and the breath was knocked out of her body. He threw himself over her, pinioning her arms so that she lay spread-eagled beneath him. She struggled and squirmed but to no avail.

"Virago, you badly need to be taught a lesson," he said between clenched teeth, his face white. His green eyes blazed down into hers, then, almost within an instant, anger turned into desire.

For a moment Stephen gazed, transfixed, at her parted lips, then bent to cover her mouth with his own. To Maud's shock, the touch of his lips plunged her into a dizzying whirlpool of feeling and her mouth opened under his. As his kiss grew deeper and deeper, her body, so long thirsting for his touch, began to quiver; she felt her senses drowning in the raging current that flowed between them. He let go of her arms which, with a life of their own, had twined around his neck. Breathing heavily, he continued to kiss her as if he could never have enough of her mouth. His hands sought her breasts, caressing them with a rough urgency until Maud felt her nipples spring to life under his touch. But when he tried to remove her tunic, she found the strength to hold him off.

"No," she whispered, "it is too dangerous. I dare not."

He groaned aloud then, in an agony of impatience, and buried his head between her breasts. He slid his hand down her hips until his fingers met the bare flesh of her thigh above her knee. Afire now, blazing with her own all-consuming need, her body arched upward and her legs parted. Stephen pulled down his drawers and hose and pushed up her skirts.

When he entered her, his whole body shuddered, and Maud heard his labored breath in her ear, his heart pounding against her own.

The feel of him inside her once again was so exquisite she wanted to savor the moment, prolong the enchantment, but her passion was too overpowering, the sense of danger unbearably heightening every sensation. Together she and Stephen swept upward on a rapturous flight, soaring ever higher before exploding into a thousand shooting stars.

When she came back to earth, Stephen was cradling her in his arms.

"Sweet Cousin," he murmured, his eyes dreamy with the aftermath of their lovemaking. "Surely it is a cruel fate that has conspired to make us enemies instead of the true lovers we were meant to be."

"Yes," she whispered, wishing never to leave the safe haven of Stephen's arms, but already anxiously glancing toward the door.

Maud gave Stephen a warm kiss on his forehead, then quickly slipped from the bed, settled her skirts, and smoothed her hair. Stephen pulled up his drawers and hose, and slid off the bed. He stooped to pick up the parchments that had fallen to the floor in their earlier scuffle and handed them to her. Just in time.

There were voices outside the door and Miles of Gloucester strode into the chamber. He looked questioningly from Maud to Stephen, almost as though he could perceive what had passed between them. Terrified, Maud gaped at him in horror. She knew she must explain but she was struck dumb.

"The lady has tried to suborn me, insisting that I sign away my kingdom in her favor and promising me freedom in Boulogne," Stephen said with his usual aplomb. "Naturally, I refused."

Miles's face cleared immediately. "You always were a fool." He turned to Maud. "You should have consulted Robert before making him an offer."

"I did as I thought best. Let me explain," she said, in control now, leading Miles from the chamber. Over her shoulder, she threw Stephen a brief glance of gratitude. He winked at her in such a roguish manner that she had all she could do to keep from laughing aloud.

Maud did not see Stephen alone again and two days later Robert and Brian returned with William, Robert's eldest son, who would escort Stephen to Bristol. The following morning he left to begin his captivity.

Maud joined Brian and Robert in the courtyard where, under a dark sky threatening rain, a banneret of knights and sumpter horses waited. Stephen, clad in a blue mantle and leather gauntlets, was mounted on a black stallion. His face was pale but composed; only his eyes reflected a shadowed sadness. Maud was filled with pity when she thought of the ordeal that lay ahead for him. Not that he would be mistreated or deprived of creature comforts, but for a man of action, confinement was a kind of living death.

Their eyes met and Stephen's face suddenly came alive with warmth. Maud felt as if he had reached out and placed his hand around her heart. He gave her a jaunty smile, pulled the hood of his cloak up over his head, then wheeled his horse around and, surrounded by the knights and sumpter horses, rode out of the courtyard followed by William of Gloucester and a troop of men-at-arms. Softly the rain began to fall.

Chapter Eleven

Two weeks later, on a brisk, cool day in early March, Maud left for Winchester where Bishop Henry had agreed to meet with her outside the city gates. Although she had resolutely tried to push all thoughts of Stephen from her mind, his unseen presence was always with her, a silent witness to all that she said and did. Maud had little time to spare daydreaming about him, however, for an enormous challenge lay ahead: the difficult task of making England accept her as its new ruler. She would need all her wits about her in the stressful days that lay ahead.

Miles, Brian and Robert, as well as her half-brother's army, accompanied her on the road south. Stephen might be a prisoner but a sufficient number of his forces were still at large to indicate the danger was not yet over.

Ten leagues from Gloucester they passed through a small Cotswold town. As Maud and her party rode into the village square, a crowd of eager citizens surrounded her white palfrey and urged her to address a few words to them.

"Good people," Maud began, flattered by their obvious interest, then stopped. She had never before spoken to a large crowd. What would my father say, she wondered, then was suddenly inspired:

"I know what you have suffered under the reign of Stephen of Blois. When I become your queen I promise to bring back the days of King Henry, a time of peace and plenty in the land for men and beasts, a time when no man dared misdo another."

There were shouts of support and agreement. "Aye," a man's voice cried, "bring back the days of the Lion of Justice and we'll bless your reign with all our hearts."

Cheers followed this statement and the crowd surged round her, doffing their caps and smiling. A woman with a little boy clinging to her skirts grabbed Maud's hand and pressed it to her lips. Why, these are my people, Maud realized with a lump in her throat, identifying with them more strongly than she ever had before. Like herself, many were a mixture of Norman and Saxon blood. Despite everyone's warnings they readily appeared to accept her for their queen. Choked with gratitude, she could only give the woman a tremulous smile and pray she would not disgrace herself by becoming tongue-tied.

Suddenly a stone sailed through the air over her head, landing not five feet away. The crowd drew back as a voice from the rear cried: "I hear tell this she-wolf has fettered our gentle King in the dungeons at Bristol like a common felon!"

Maud was aghast. "As God is my witness, that is not true," she cried. "The former king is held in honorable confinement with the free run of Bristol Castle."

Several voices shouted: "Free our true sovereign!"

Robert's soldiers immediately closed in on the crowd; the troublemakers were spotted and hustled away. Maud had a brief glimpse of one dark, malevolent face continuing to hurl insults as he was dragged from the marketplace. She attempted to address the people again, but the damage had been done. The group silently dispersed.

As they continued on their journey to Winchester, Maud put the unpleasant incident behind her. It was an isolated occurrence, she assured herself, and not to be taken seriously. Except for those few malcontents, the people of the village had demonstrated their support. No shadow of doubt must spoil her triumphal march through southwest England. But even as she had the thought, Stephen's words returned to her: "You will not tread an easy path, Cousin."

Two days later she was eagerly awaiting Bishop Henry in her red-and-gold pavilion outside the city of Winchester. When he finally arrived amidst a drenching rainstorm, Maud greeted him with all the warmth she could summon, not trusting the slippery Bishop an inch.

"I've so looked forward to this day," she said, offering him a camp stool and a goblet of wine.

As he seated himself, Henry pulled his cloak more closely about his shoulders, as if withdrawing into himself. Maud could not tell what thoughts passed through his mind but she sensed a resistance within him, one she would have to overcome.

"Move the brazier closer to His Grace," she told Robert, who had joined them. "He looks chilled to the bone."

Although her cousin's aloof manner had always made Maud feel at a disadvantage, this time she would not allow him to intimidate her. Too much was at stake.

"I cannot make you Archbishop of Canterbury while Theobald of Bec lives," she began without preamble, "but when I am queen I'm prepared to appoint you my chief adviser and minister. You will be to me what Roger of Salisbury was to my father. No prelate wielded greater lay power."

Henry raised his brows as a frosty smile played about his bloodless lips. "And what do you demand in return for such a signal honor?"

Maud met his gaze squarely. "The keys to the treasury, the support of the Norman barons and the clergy of England, as well as Rome's blessing."

He gave a mirthless laugh. "Benedicte! You do not want much! I can't work miracles, heaven forfend." His eyes narrowed. "And it will require nothing less than a miracle, Madam, for men to accept a woman with an Angevin husband as heir to the throne of England." He looked down at his hands, the graceful fingers sparkling with rings in the light of the charcoal brazier. "That's always been the difficulty ever since your father made the foolhardy decision to name you his heir."

Although Henry's words were offensive, designed to wound, more terrifying still was the implication that he might not help her. Quelling a surge of panic she wondered in desperation how she might woo him. Flatter him, said Stephen's voice in her head as clearly as if he were standing next to her. Be artful, play the woman, not the queen.

"That is exactly why I'm so dependent upon you, Cousin," she said slowly. "With your wisdom to guide me I hope to convince everyone that my father's decision was not foolhardy." She gave him what she hoped was her most winning smile.

Henry slowly sipped his goblet of wine and she sensed a weakening in his resistance. "You ask me to prevail against centuries of custom and prejudice—"

"What more can I offer you?" she interjected, recalling her days at the Imperial court, watching the crafty Emperor bargain with ambitious princes of the church. "You have only to ask, Your Grace. I'll grant whatever you wish—if it lies within my power to do so."

A fleeting look of satisfaction crossed the Bishop's face. Maud held her breath.

"Should I agree—and I've made no such promise, mind—you must, for a start, be willing to submit to my decision all appointments made to bishoprics and abbeys. In addition, I must have absolute certainty that you will not attempt to interfere in matters pertaining to Holy Church, nor try to make her subservient to the crown in any way."

It was what she had anticipated. "Agreed. I promise to abide by all you have said. On the head of my son and heir, by any holy relic of your choice."

Henry again raised his brows. "Of course you agree now. But why should I accept your word? My brother also made such promises and we all know how he kept them."

"We must trust each other," Maud said simply. "I'm not such a fool as to go against Holy Church when I need her support so badly, when I need *you* so badly. My word is my bond."

He acknowledged this with a slight inclination of the head. "I make no promises," he said after a moment's thought. "Particularly where the barons are concerned. However, I'll admit you into Winchester and summon what clergymen and nobles are willing to come. I'll also invite the Archbishop of Canterbury to attend us. Without him you cannot be crowned." He rose to his feet. "If it appears you may be accepted, then, and only then, I'll arrange for the keys of the treasury to be put into your hands and agree to serve you as my sovereign in the capacity you have suggested."

"Thank you, Cousin," Maud said. "I'm in your hands."

"We are all in God's hands," Henry corrected her as he left.

Robert stood up and wiped his brow. "By the Mass, that was well done, Sister. I would sooner bargain with the devil himself than match wits with the Bishop of Winchester."

"Will he persuade them, Brother? Could I have done more?"

"More?" Robert rolled his eyes. "For a moment I feared you might offer him the crown itself!"

They fell into each other's arms in a sudden fit of laughter.

. . .

Maud waited outside Winchester for over a week, chafing at the
delay. Finally she received word from the Bishop that all was in
readiness and she might enter the city, but he could not predict how
she would be received.

Dressed in cloth-of-gold and purple velvet, her neck, wrists and
fingers glittering with jewels, Maud rode into Winchester at the head
of a magnificent procession. The streets of the city were lined with
people curious to see her. Maud recognized merchants in rich, fur-
trimmed robes, stout yeomen with their wives and children decked
out in their best finery, black-robed priests, threadbare cotters, and
mercenary knights.

No one cheered her as she rode by on her white palfrey but the
faces in the crowd were not unfriendly. Maud smiled at the people
and raised her hand in greeting, drinking in the sights around her.
She had not visited Winchester for ten years yet everything looked
familiar: the numerous monasteries and churches; the gaily decorated booths that gave off the succulent odor of roasted meat and hot
pasties; a brief glimpse at the end of the High Street of the stone-
and-timber castle built by her grandfather. When they passed Jewrey
Street, she was reminded anew of Stephen, and the constant void in
her heart.

When Maud reached the cathedral, undergoing construction, the
bells were pealing the hour of Sext. She was greeted by the Bishop of
Winchester dressed in his ceremonial robes, a gold-encrusted miter
atop his head and a jeweled crosier in his hand.

Off to one side, she saw abbots and bishops clustered together like
black birds of prey. Across the cathedral square hovered a group of
richly dressed barons; Maud recognized many who had first sworn
homage to her and then pledged allegiance to Stephen.

"This was well done, Your Grace," Maud said to Henry as they
entered the cathedral to attend the noon Mass. "I hardly expected so
many to turn out. It is most encouraging."

"So it appears, but remember that none have yet committed themselves."

After the service Maud rode into the marketplace where the Bishop
had arranged for a public meeting to be held. She listened intently as
Henry begin to speak in a strong, melodious voice that carried to the
far reaches of the assembly. Her eyes scanned the faces in the crowd
to catch every response.

"This ship of state, created by my grandfather, Duke William of

Normandy, first Norman King of England, and made even more powerful and strong by my uncle, King Henry, has foundered on the shoals of my brother's disastrous reign." He paused. Two beads of sweat rolled down his temple.

It was so quiet in the square that Maud could hear the thudding of her own heart. She wondered how Henry would explain why he was now deserting the brother he had helped put on the throne six years earlier in favor of herself, whom he had soundly denounced at the time.

"Naturally, I love my brother, as God commands us all to do," the Bishop continued, "but time and again I remonstrated with him to see justice done, to treat Holy Church with the reverence and respect that is her due, to keep peace and order in the land. Yet my words were rebuffed, my efforts scorned." His voice rose on the wind like thunder. "God's judgment has been executed against my brother; he has fallen victim to those who had the greater right to rule than he!" There was a sharp indrawn breath as every eye turned to Maud. "The lesson is plain. We must bow before the wisdom of a higher power and accept the signal God has sent us." He turned to point a finger at Maud. "Here is new hope in the person of Maud, a daughter of England and Normandy, only heir of our late beloved King Henry. A devoted supporter of Holy Church, the mother of three sons, an empress, who ruled with her late husband at the Imperial court, she has all the qualifications to be queen of our realm. Can we do less than promise her our fealty?"

"What a clever rogue," Robert said in Maud's ear. "He tactfully omits all mention of Geoffrey of Anjou, nor does he bring up the uncomfortable matter of previous oaths sworn to Stephen. Impressive."

Maud was equally impressed with the Bishop's crafty eloquence, but had he won her the adherents she so desperately needed?

There was a brief silence while her life seemed to hang in the balance. Then the first murmurs of approval slowly began, building to a modest burst of shouts of support and recognition. Her relief was so intense she could hardly keep from crying it aloud. If this was not the wild, unanimous acclaim Maud longed to hear, that would come, in time. She felt sure of it. A new confidence bubbled up within her and, unable to contain her feeling of buoyancy, she turned to Robert and hugged him so hard he pleaded to be let loose before his ribs cracked.

Maud released him when she saw Henry approaching with a complacent smile on his face. "I flatter myself that we may have made
some slight progress."

Maud clapped her hands together. "You were absolutely magnificent, Cousin. How can I ever thank you?"

Impulsively she tried to throw her arms around his rigid body.

"By heaven, you forget yourself, Madam," he said, his face red as
he quickly took a step backward, well out of her reach. But she could
tell he was not as displeased as he pretended.

The following day in the marketplace Henry announced to the
assembled throng: "We invite you all to swear allegiance to Domina,
Lady of England."

Maud was surprised and elated, for the title Domina was given
only to a queen-elect before she was crowned. She had moved several
paces nearer her goal.

The Bishop continued: "As Domina is the rightful heir, sentence
of excommunication will be passed upon those who oppose her and
absolution given to those who support her."

The barons and clergymen made haste to swear formal allegiance
to her. Directly after the ceremony, her Uncle David, King of Scotland, made an unexpected appearance, marching into the square accompanied by a troop of his Highlanders dressed in animal skins and
grinning savagely.

David lifted her up in his huge arms as if she were a child and
squeezed her until she gasped for breath. Delighted to see him, she
kissed his hairy cheeks.

"I came as soon as I received news of the usurper's defeat, lass,"
he said, his soft blue eyes radiating affection. "To think o' my sister's
wee bairn a queen at last. God be praised." He insisted on swearing
his homage to her at once in a loud voice throbbing with fervor, the
words barely intelligible.

David had just finished when out of the corner of her eye Maud
saw a man dressed in official court robes approach the Bishop of
Winchester. A black-robed cleric walked behind him carrying a carved
ivory box. He was flanked by half a dozen men-at-arms. When the
official reached the Bishop he unlocked the box with a key and opened
the lid. Maud watched the Bishop carefully withdraw an object
wrapped in crumbling red silk. With a solemn look on his face, Henry
walked toward her, the men-at-arms following close behind.

An expectant silence fell upon the marketplace. Maud's heart
pounded as Henry placed the royal crown made for William the Con-

queror into her hands. The last time she had touched these gold plates had been when her father gave her the crown to hold on the day she had left England. His words came back to her as clearly as if she had heard them only yesterday: "Your grandfather won this crown amidst much bloodshed and suffering. It represents power, wealth, and respect." And now it was hers.

As she had done so many years before, Maud reverently turned the glittering jeweled circlet over and over in her hands. She felt alternately humble and proud to be holding within her grasp this symbol of the mighty realm she would soon be ruling. Hovering silently about her, Maud sensed a vast approving presence, the shades of the first three Norman kings: her grandfather, the formidable William; her uncle, the bluff and hearty William Rufus; and her cunning father, Henry. She made them a silent vow: I will be worthy of the heritage you have left me.

As Maud clasped the crown to her breast, she became aware of the Bishop's benevolent gaze, her uncle's freckled paw on her shoulder, the delighted expressions of Miles, Robert, and Brian, the curious faces of the Winchester citizenry, and the tentative smiles of the clergymen and barons.

As she shared with all of them this moment of supreme and unalloyed joy, Maud's heart was so full she felt it would burst. It was the epiphany of her life; a sense of destiny fulfilled at last.

Chapter Twelve

THE FOLLOWING MORNING AFTER TIERCE, HENRY APPEARED AT THE CAS-
tle to conduct Maud to the treasury. As they walked out of the great
hall the Bishop recited a litany of instructions for her:

"You must send a courier to Geoffrey of Anjou requesting that he
send your son to England immediately—although the Count himself
must not be encouraged to come. Whenever possible, Madam, it
would behoove you to appear as a wife and mother—as the former
Queen Matilda has done with so much success. Always bear in mind
that no one wants to see a woman in the guise of a man."

Maud stiffened in protest. Robert gave her arm a warning squeeze.
"I've already sent to Geoffrey with the same request, but there has
been no response," she said, suppressing her irritation. As if she
needed reminding of her womanhood! Sweet Marie, did he imagine
she was going to don hauberk and helmet?

"You need not worry about Geoffrey turning up at the coronation,
Bishop," Robert said. "He still has his hands full subduing Normandy, and there can be no question of a journey to England."

Maud kept silent. As the Normans hated the Angevins, she had no
intention of letting Geoffrey set foot on English soil for a long time
to come—if ever. Not if she had anything to say about it.

"I've also invited a deputation of London citizens to attend us," Henry continued. "Their goodwill is vital for your acceptance in the capital. I understand they have a special request to make—they did not elaborate—but I trust you will be able to grant it."

"Certainly I will do all I can to accommodate them," Maud agreed as they arrived at the entrance to the vaults which housed the treasury.

Four guards with flaring torches led the way down a flight of crumbling stone steps to where the treasurer waited in front of a worn oaken door. At a nod from the Bishop he inserted a scrolled iron key into the ancient lock. With a grating sound the lock turned and the door opened to reveal a large chamber. Mildew stained the lichened stone walls; the air was filled with the odor of damp wood and moldering leather. An oak table, laden with scrolls of parchment, stood against a wall. A massive chequered board marked off in squares, like a chessboard, lay on another table. Clerks perched on wooden stools waited with tablet and pen in hand.

As Maud accustomed herself to the dim light, she heard Robert's sharp intake of breath.

"By God and all His Saints," he cried, "what has happened to my father's treasure?"

In the flickering torchlight Maud could now see the stacks of empty coffers, their lids gaping open like hungry mouths, and the piles of empty leather sacks collapsed upon the floor. The last time she had been here was ten years ago, but she would never forget the awe-inspiring sight of wooden chests, piled one upon the other to the ceiling, brimming with gold and silver, or the row upon row of leather sacks bulging with jewels, silver-gilt goblets, and gold plate. Now there were only a few closed chests and one or two half-filled leather sacks.

Maud's shock was so great that when she tried to speak she found that her voice had failed.

"You must have known the true state of affairs here," Robert said to the Bishop in an accusing tone.

"I was aware of Stephen's mismanagement," he admitted reluctantly, "but not the full extent of the damage." He turned to Maud and signed himself. "As God is my witness, again and again Stephen was warned of the dire consequences of his lavish indulgence, his uncontrolled extravagance. Not only by me but by Matilda and the Bishop of Salisbury as well. But he ignored our advice and listened instead to the evil counsel of Waleran of Muelan and the Fleming, William of Ypres."

"But where has it all gone?" Maud whispered, completely shaken.

The treasurer answered: "Where indeed, Madam. Foreign merce-naries, greedy barons, disastrous campaigns, costly gifts—few who asked went away empty-handed."

"Some of the expenditure was no doubt necessary," Henry said with a defensive look. "The first lesson a sovereign must learn is that the way to keep loyalty in a man's heart is to keep money in his purse or land in his domains. As you shall shortly discover."

Maud barely heard him; she felt as if the bottom had suddenly dropped out of her world. Despite what the treasurer had told her, it did not seem possible that so little remained of her father's vast store, accumulated at such cost, so carefully hoarded all the years of his reign in order to leave his heirs a rich and powerful legacy.

From both the Emperor and her father, Maud had learned that wealth is power. Without it her task would be enormously difficult. At the thought of her treacherous cousin taking his ease at Bristol, while she must rebuild the wreckage he had wrought, something curled and shriveled within her. The glorious taste of victory became like ashes in her mouth.

"Be good enough to have clerks draw up an accounting of what reserves we have left, what reliefs are due, the scutage pending, and what credits are late in arriving," Maud told the treasurer. "In other words, all possible sources of income for the crown. Then draw me a list of absolutely necessary expenditures." She gave him a sharp look. "From this moment on, expenditures will never exceed revenues. Never. You understand?"

Even in the dim light Maud could see the look of amazement on the treasurer's face, a look that was mirrored in Henry's expression. Even Robert was surprised.

The treasurer swallowed. "I understand, Madam."

She saw the three men exchange quick glances and knew she had made her point: Not a farthing would be spent without her knowl-edge.

As she walked up the steps, Maud made a silent but implacable decision: Everything Stephen had done she would undo. Insofar as was possible, she would obliterate all evidence that he had existed as king.

At the door a servitor waited to see her. "The Archbishop of Can-terbury has arrived, Madam," he said.

He was the last person she wanted to see. Her attention was entirely caught up in how she was going to run the kingdom in the light of what she had just discovered. "Have him wait—"

"And say we will see him shortly," the Bishop interjected. "Bring him to an antechamber and see that the steward attends to his wants." The servitor disappeared.

"I can hardly keep my wits about me after this shock," Maud protested. "Is it necessary to see him now?" Inwardly she seethed at Henry's interference.

"I would not delay if I were you. If he's going to cause trouble let us find out immediately."

Maud frowned. "Trouble? Sweet Marie, Theobald is a simple, good-hearted man, without ambition or cunning."

"You may know as much of finance as a moneylender, Madam, but when it comes to Holy Church I flatter myself I have more experience and knowledge than you. That Theobald *is* without ambition is exactly why he may cause trouble."

Sometimes she was unable to follow the tortuous byways of the Bishop's mind, Maud thought, but deferred to his judgment and agreed to see the Archbishop.

She entered the great hall, seated herself in a carved ivory-inlaid chair on a raised dais, and waited for the Archbishop to be brought to her. Leaning on a wooden staff, Theobald of Bec hobbled into the hall dressed in a simple black traveling cloak. Maud stepped down from the dais to kneel and kiss the ring of his office while he blessed her in quavering tones.

"How nice to see you again, Your Grace," Maud said, summoning warmth and enthusiasm into her voice.

"And you, Madam, and you," the Archbishop replied.

"I look forward to a harmonious union between us," Maud said, "just as there was between my father and the late Archbishop." She hoped the meeting would not drag on. The problem of the empty treasury weighed heavily upon her mind and she found it difficult to put her attention on anything else. All that was really required was for Theobald to agree to swear fealty to her.

Despite Henry's warning, she was completely unprepared for his next words.

"But I cannot commit to any union between us, Madam, without the agreement of King Stephen."

Maud could hardly credit what he said and thought she must have misheard him. One look at the Bishop of Winchester's just-as-

I-feared expression told her otherwise. Completely shaken, Maud walked back to the dais and resumed her seat. She gripped the wooden arms so hard her knuckles showed white.

"I don't understand," she said. "Surely Your Grace believes I have a right to the throne? Stephen usurped that right, against the express orders of my late father and his own sworn oath."

"I do not question your right to be sovereign, Madam," Theobald replied. "But that is not the issue here. I never swore an oath to crown you queen. My only oath of fealty is to King Stephen. Unless he releases me from my oath there is naught I can do."

"But that is—ridiculous!" Maud sprang to her feet, two spots of color flaming in her cheeks. "Stephen is my captive, shorn of all power. Why do you not follow the example of the Bishop of Winchester and the other clergymen?"

As she spoke, Stephen's words echoed mockingly in her ears: "I am still sovereign and will remain so until the Archbishop of Canterbury crowns you—if he ever does." And now here was this stubborn old man with the guileless eyes of a saint refusing to do just that!

Theobald looked at her, his innocent round face cracked by deep wrinkles. "My fellow brethren must follow the dictates of their conscience, as I follow mine."

Henry stepped forward. "We understand, Your Grace." He came up to the dais and spoke to Maud in an urgent whisper: "I feared this might happen. You must let him go to Stephen without further argument."

"What! Can you not reason with him?"

"You can see the answer to that for yourself. I know Theobald. For all his mildness he is stiff-necked as a mule. Nothing will change his mind. Do as he wishes or suffer the consequences of having no one to crown you."

As Maud hesitated Henry leaned closer. "In my opinion Stephen will not refuse him." His lip curled. "It would be unchivalrous. In addition, the church will look kindly on your benevolence. Such a generous act will inspire trust and confidence."

Maud nodded reluctantly, recognizing the wisdom of his words. Nonetheless it galled her that acceptance by the Archbishop depended upon Stephen's whim.

"Good, Madam." Henry stepped away from the dais. "You're willing to be guided by me and that is an excellent omen for the future."

"Very well, Your Grace," Maud said to the Archbishop, wishing

Henry would not treat her like a girl fresh from convent school, "you have my leave to go to Bristol."

Theobald rewarded her with a saintly smile.

Next morning the Archbishop of Canterbury started on his journey to Bristol escorted by Robert of Gloucester and a troop of his knights. At the last moment they were joined by a group of bishops who suddenly decided it might behoove them to also be released from their oath to Stephen. Maud graciously granted permission to any who wished to go. When the procession left Winchester, she called her council of advisers to help find a solution to the pressing problem of the empty treasury.

Two and one half days later, Robert of Gloucester came within sight of his castle at Bristol. As he approached the curtain walls, he was amazed to hear the faint echo of cheers and laughter coming from the outer bailey. What in the name of heaven was going on? he wondered.

"Is a tournament being held this afternoon, my lord?" asked the Archbishop.

"Certainly not," Robert said. He looked up and was stunned to find the walls and towers empty of guards and no watch at the gatehouse.

He had left explicit instructions that the castle was to be on full alert at all times while the King was housed there. He had not bothered to notify anyone of his arrival, but that was hardly an excuse for slack discipline and blatant disregard of his orders. Robert blew sharply upon the ivory horn that swung round his neck. Within a few moments he was relieved to see some of the guards peering over the walls, and the watch appear in the gatehouse. When he recognized Robert he quickly lowered the drawbridge.

Someone better have an explanation for this unprecedented behavior, Robert thought grimly, as he and his party rode across the causeway. He trotted into the outer bailey, then suddenly drew rein at the spectacle that met his eyes. A host of squires, knights, and men-at-arms, among them his youngest son, Phillip, had formed two lines opposite each other. Between them raced two horses: Stephen sat astride Robert's favorite bay stallion and Robert's son and heir, William, rode a chestnut horse. The guards who should have been keeping watch were leaning carelessly over the walls and towers, waving their spears and shouting encouragement.

Mabel of Gloucester and her ladies, decked out in gaily colored gowns and headdresses, were among the lustily cheering spectators. Robert was astonished to see his wife tear a bright silken gauge from her long yellow sleeve and toss it to Stephen as he galloped past. He caught it in a deft hand. The former king looked almost like a youth again, Robert thought, his honey-colored hair tousled by the wind, his face flushed with color. A far cry from the downcast gray-faced prisoner who had left Gloucester a month ago.

When Mabel saw Robert and the group of prelates, she turned crimson and her mouth dropped open. As the others caught sight of the Earl, the cheering died and the guards scrambled to resume their positions on the walls; Stephen and William slowed their mounts to a walk.

"My lord, no one had any idea you were expected," Mabel said breathlessly as she ran up to her husband. "Stephen challenged any of our men to ride against him, and William agreed—" Her voice faltered at the look on Robert's face. It was probably the only time in all the years of their marriage that he had ever seen his formidable wife at a loss for words.

"That I wasn't expected is obvious. There is no need to ask how you have all fared here," Robert said with an edge to his voice. "As you can see, we have important guests," he continued in a reproving tone, "who have come upon a matter of some urgency. Inform the steward at once, Wife."

"At once, my lord," Mabel said, scurrying away.

With an apprehensive look on their faces, the knights and squires greeted Robert, then quickly dispersed. William and Stephen hastily dismounted; William approached his father.

"We were practicing our horsemanship, my lord," he said, clearly uneasy. "Stephen has been teaching us some of the skills he learned in tournaments. I didn't think any harm would come of it. He's been most helpful."

"Indeed, but he is our captive, may I remind you."

"My lord, Stephen is also my godfather," William said in a low voice. "It's difficult to think of him as a prisoner."

"And you allowed this bond to influence you? Where is your sense of duty? How can I trust you in the future? Whilst you made merry the castle was left virtually unguarded. Because you disobeyed my orders Stephen would have been easily accessible to an attempt to rescue him."

Robert knew that despite the evidence, neither his wife nor son was totally responsible for the lack of security he had found. He recognized the real culprit. It was so typical of Stephen to charm all and sundry into doing what he wanted.

William looked crestfallen. "I . . . I didn't think of the risk. Forgive me, Father."

Stephen sauntered up to them; behind him tagged Phillip, a youth of fifteen, who gazed up at the former king with worshipful eyes.

"Captivity agrees with you, Cousin," Robert said to Stephen, forcing himself to be civil. "Here are some guests to visit you. After they have rested and eaten I'll bring them to see you upon a matter of some importance."

Stephen smiled at the group of prelates. "An unexpected pleasure, Your Grace, my lord bishops." He knelt and kissed Theobald's episcopal ring. "What is this important matter? I'm greatly curious."

"William, Phillip, take the Archbishop and the others to the keep," Robert ordered before the clergymen could answer. He wanted Theobald's request to catch Stephen by surprise, before he had time to ponder the full consequences of his answer.

William did as he was told. Phillip made no move to leave.

"Run along, my boy," Robert said.

Phillip gave him a defiant look. "I'd prefer to stay with Stephen, Father."

Before Robert could reply Stephen turned to Phillip. "Do as your father says. We'll see each other later."

With a scowl for Robert, Phillip threw Stephen an adoring glance and left.

"I hope you're not offended by our race," Stephen said. "It was only a bit of sport. Certainly the Countess and your sons have made my life far more agreeable than I had any right to expect. I am unused to being sedentary and time hangs heavily on my hands." He gave Robert a smile designed to dazzle and charm.

Robert refused to succumb. It was unworthy of him, but the exchange between Phillip and himself rankled, as had his son's look for Stephen. "That is a prisoner's fate," he said. "You could be fettered and confined to a dungeon, remember. Be warned that I don't intend to let this unseemly behavior continue. You saw for yourself the effect it has already created."

"Don't take Phillip's attitude too seriously, Cousin. The boy misses you, and he is at the age where he needs someone to look up to," Stephen said, with that uncanny ability he often had to see into another's heart. "I worry about my own son, Eustace, with no father to guide him." A shadow flitted across his face, then he smiled. "Well, what is the news? I'm totally isolated in my golden cage. Your sister thrives?"

It was virtually impossible to remain antagonistic toward him, Robert thought in resignation, as he felt his innate love for Stephen returning. He willed himself not to be suborned.

"Indeed she does. Your brother has agreed to be Maud's chief adviser; many barons who swore homage to you have already changed sides. Even London is sending a deputation of citizens to meet with my sister."

"So she is gaining support," Stephen said slowly. The happy flush that had illuminated his face was now replaced by a troubled look. "I confess to being surprised."

"Why? Your reign was hardly a successful one," Robert said, suddenly unable to resist a vengeful thrust. "In fact, what with the state of the treasury and the condition of the land, I can't imagine how you survived as long as you did. It will take years to replace the damage you have done."

Stephen flinched and his eyes darkened, but he made no reply. Robert watched him, filled with a curious mixture of regret and satisfaction. Stephen's confidence was shaken, which was all to the good. The more remorseful he felt the more likely he was to accede to the Archbishop's request. The Vespers bell rang and they walked in silence to the chapel.

After the evening meal, Robert took the Archbishop and the other prelates to see the former king in the chamber Stephen had been given near the solar. A single guard stood watch at the door.

Theobald approached Stephen, who was sitting in one of the very few wooden armchairs in the castle. It had not been in this room before Stephen's arrival, Robert noted. Nor had the red-and-blue coverlet on the bed, nor the silver basin and ewer that rested on the oak table along with a bowl of sweetmeats, a silver-gilt goblet, and a flagon of wine. A golden cage indeed!

"Sire," said the Archbishop, bending his knee, "I have been asked to recognize the Countess of Anjou as Queen of England. I may not do this without your leave. Do you grant me permission to change my loyalties as the times constrain us?"

Stephen blanched; his face worked as he stared at Theobald. Clearly the request had caught him by surprise, Robert thought, not displeased.

Stephen stroked his chin, then tapped one finger against his teeth, weighing the question. Robert held his breath, willing Stephen's generous nature to assert itself and make the chivalrous gesture—albeit not the wise one.

At last Stephen gave a wan smile. "My lord bishops, Your Grace, you must all do as you see fit. I cannot tell you what course to take in this matter. These are trying times and I judge no man for . . . for attempting to survive as he deems best."

It was an equivocal answer but sufficient.

The next day, having issued a stricter set of instructions for the care of the prisoner, Robert and the prelates left for Winchester. The sooner Theobald swore homage to Maud the easier he would feel, Robert thought. Although Stephen had been removed from the throne, he suspected it would be less easy to remove him from the hearts of his subjects.

Chapter Thirteen

THE WEEK FOLLOWING THEOBALD'S SUBMISSION, MAUD SAT ON THE
ivory-inlaid chair in the great hall of Winchester Castle awaiting the
deputation of London citizens, who had arrived the night before.
Directly in front of the dais, Robert, Miles, Bishop Henry, and Brian
stood in a semicircle around her. David of Scotland, flanked by two
Highlanders armed with claymores, sat on the dais with her, as befit-
ting one of his age and rank.

"I have seen the treasurer's report," announced Robert, holding
up a parchment for everyone to see. "It makes grim reading, even
worse than we feared. As the land is in such disorder, it may take
months to collect the revenues due us. Funds are so low we cannot
even hold a proper coronation. If it were not for the generosity of
Miles of Gloucester we would have neither meat nor drink on the
table."

The flaxen-haired giant grinned broadly. "I only wish I had more
to offer."

Maud's eyes rested fondly on Miles, whom she had just created
Earl of Hereford. It was rumored that his great wealth had been
accumulated by years of plunder, but Maud turned a deaf ear to such
tales. All that mattered was his willingness to help her cause.

"Something must be done at once," Robert continued.

"We are all aware of the problem," said the Bishop impatiently. "What remedies do you offer?"

"Ye could borrow from the Semite moneylenders against that which is owed the crown," David of Scotland offered.

Maud sat forward in her chair. "I think that is an excellent idea, Uncle," she said, "but why need we go to moneylenders?"

Robert, Miles, and Henry turned toward her in surprise, as if suddenly reminded of her presence.

"Do not trouble yourself over such matters, Madam," the Bishop said with a dismissive gesture. "Leave us to deal with this coil."

"I'm not merely a figurehead, my lords. I mean to be of use to you. Will you not hear what I have to say?"

They looked at her with polite disinterest, and Maud realized that despite everything said to the contrary, they did view her only as a figurehead, a living symbol of the crown, and if she allowed it, would divest her of all authority. Even Robert and Brian and Uncle David, those who cared for her the most, wanted her to be like wax in their hands, molded to fit a pattern they intended to set for her. She would sit on the throne but they would rule the country. Well, the sooner she disabused them of that idea the better.

"Have the London burghers arrived at the castle for their audience?" she asked.

"Yes," the Bishop replied.

"Send them in."

"Now?" Henry raised his brows. "We're in the midst of a discussion about finances. They can wait."

Without responding, Maud clapped her hands and a servitor came running. "Bring in the deputation of London citizens." She turned to Henry. "I have a plan in mind. Bear with me."

She saw the men look at each other in consternation. Her uncle drew his grizzled sandy brows together in a frown.

"What are ye up to then, Niece?" he asked. "I hope ye won't be headstrong now and take matters into ye own hands."

Henry gave the Scottish king an indulgent smile. "She is wiser than that, Sire. Tell us your plan, Madam."

He made her sound like a child showing off a new trick. Maud's lips tightened.

The servitor entered leading a group of middle-aged men covered in long fur-lined cloaks. Bearded and somber-faced, they reminded Maud of Old Testament patriarchs come to life. She welcomed them pleasantly, offered refreshment, and waited while her advisers greeted them.

Their spokesman came directly up to the dais and bent his knee. "We have a request to make, Lady, and pray you are willing to grant it."

"I will most certainly try. Then I have a request of my own."

Out of the corner of her eye Maud saw the Bishop of Winchester stiffen, his nostrils quivering in alarm. Startled, the spokesman glanced at Henry, then looked quickly away. But not before Maud had seen the brief exchange. She sucked in her breath. Had the Bishop met with the London deputation last night or even earlier? Did he know what they wanted of her? He had told her he did not.

The head of the London citizens was speaking: "We have come to plead for the release of our most beloved King. We beg you to free him from captivity and let him accompany his wife and children to Boulogne."

Maud froze; it was the last thing she had expected to hear. She stole a look at the Bishop but his face was without expression. Had he connived with these people for Stephen's release, she wondered, even put them up to it?

"What you ask is impossible," she told the spokesman, keeping her voice civil. "Stephen usurped my throne, beggared the treasury, failed to exact retribution from those who broke the law, and has made England unfit for human habitation." She almost choked with the effort to control her growing rage. It was past belief that these citizens would seek to free the very person who had brought such misery to their realm.

"I'm sorry," she continued, "but in all conscience I cannot grant your request. It would be far too dangerous to release the former king, who would then become a focal point for my enemies. Surely you can see that?"

"What I see, Lady, is that you refuse to honor our request," the man said in a sullen voice.

The deputation all looked at her as if she were the enemy, not Stephen. He was a Londoner, one of them, while she was the interloper, the stranger from Germany married to a hated Angevin. It was all there in the hostile expressions on their faces. Maud became aware that the din of voices in the hall had grown quieter, everyone listening to the exchange.

"Perhaps you don't realize the disastrous state of the realm," Maud continued softly. Their blank faces infuriated her. Who did they think was responsible for England's terrible condition? "There is so little left in the treasury that I can't put meat on my table without aid, or even hold a proper coronation. The truth, good sirs, is that I desperately need your help. Funds must be raised for me in London at once."

The citizens looked at each other in dismay. Maud could feel them withdraw even further from her. The leader tried to catch the Bishop's eyes. One look at Henry told her he was furious with her for not having first explained what she intended to do.

"It's your duty to support the realm," she persisted. "My eldest son, your future king, will be with me when I come to London, and I must hold a proper coronation."

"We're not prepared to give you an answer now," the spokesman stated. "First we must return to London and consult with our colleagues."

"Nor do we expect an answer now," Henry said with a forced smile as he stepped forward, ready to take charge. "When Domina comes to London for her coronation we'll meet again and hear your decision." He paused. "Meanwhile, the lady will take your request under serious consideration. Serious consideration," he repeated loudly. "Now, I trust you will be my guests at Wolvesey during your stay in Winchester."

Before Maud could stop him, he quickly ushered the men out of the hall, returning a few minutes later.

"God's wounds, what possessed you to ask them for money?" he spat out. "Why didn't you tell me what you intended? You've made me look a proper fool, Madam. And to reject their plea out of hand was the height of folly! Stephen is still very popular in London and Matilda is regarded as a saint! You must learn to be more politic."

Her eyes like storm clouds, Maud regarded him steadily. "Do you suggest that I accede to their request and free your brother?"

"Don't be absurd! But there's no need for these men to know your true intentions. Bargain with them; tell them what they want to hear. If they will raise funds for you then you may seriously consider freeing Stephen. Reveal little, promise much, but commit yourself to nothing."

Maud found herself repelled. "I refuse to make false promises." She appealed to her uncle, Brian, Robert, and Miles. "Haven't we all had sufficient of fair words and deceit?"

Henry raised his voice. "We speak of diplomacy, Madam! London lies in a part of England that remains loyal to Stephen; skirmishes are still being fought in the southeast and Matilda continues to gather an army in Kent. Far better to let me handle all such matters in future."

Robert stepped forward. "Peace!" He looked up at Maud. "The Bishop is right, Sister, our position is far from secure in London. We must give no one cause to turn against us. Perhaps this was not the most auspicious moment to request funds."

Miles and Brian murmured their agreement.

"Listen to the Bishop, Niece," said David. "Henry has ye best interests at heart. Be guided by his judgment."

"I think we're all agreed that until you're crowned, affairs of state would be best left in our hands," Robert added.

The silence in the hall was like a tomb as everyone openly listened to the heated exchange. Maud could feel all eyes upon her, weighing, judging. She saw several of the barons nudge each other while others exchanged significant glances and smug smiles. They were not displeased to see her being put in her place. Maud's cheeks burned with humiliation.

For a moment she hesitated while a parade of images passed before her eyes: All the men who had been important to her had attempted to control her, never letting her fully emerge in her own right. She remembered her father sending the frightened little girl into Germany against her will, then forcing her into a loveless marriage to serve the succession of England and Normandy. She had always seen the Emperor as a benign husband who truly appreciated her. But even he had been continually advising, dominating, steering her in the direction he wanted her to go. Most important of all there was Stephen. Her cousin had captured her heart, enslaved her body, only to betray her love and trust. Now she was left with his bitter legacy: a divided realm that clearly did not want her to rule. Even her own supporters did not trust her enough to make her own decisions.

Thus far she had done what was asked of her, dutifully deferring to the judgment of others. Her mind reeled when she remembered the orders she received on a daily basis: Do this, don't do that, listen to Henry, listen to Robert, heed your Uncle David.

But no more. No, by the Holy Mother of God, no more! She was virtually queen, only weeks away from her coronation; no longer would she be used or treated like a not very intelligent child. From now on she would take matters into her own hands.

Maud rose slowly to her feet. "By God's splendor, if these London citizens do not willingly give me aid then stern measures will be taken against them." She fixed the Bishop with a steely glance. "And against all others who are not fully behind me." She wanted him to know, though she had no proof, that she suspected his underhanded dealings with the Londoners. When all was said and done, Stephen was Henry's brother, a fact she must never forget.

"Stephen has brought disaster to this land. A firm hand on the reins is now needed and that's what England will have, my lords."

Her eyes swept the hall, lingering on the barons, the clergy, and last on her close advisers. "I will be queen in fact, not just in name. I advise you all to remember that."

Chapter Fourteen

In early June Maud and her party rode down Watling Street toward the gates of London. She was far more apprehensive than she had been when she arrived at Winchester three months earlier. This time, against the express counsel of her advisers, who had urged caution and delay, Maud knew she was entering a city overtly hostile to her, and doing so without the protection of her greatest asset: her son Henry.

Geoffrey, continuing to gain ground in Normandy, had refused to send the boy to England claiming that London was still too dangerous and his safety could not be guaranteed. Maud had been furious, but to persuade Geoffrey to change his mind would take precious time. Maud was unable to explain to herself, much less her advisers, why she felt such a compelling urge to be crowned as soon as possible.

Far ahead she could see the walls of the city bristling with guards. Her apprehension increased. Although Robert had bribed the Constable of London—a former supporter of Stephen's known for his dubious loyalties—to ensure their safety, the political climate of the city, a law unto itself, remained unstable. Against her better judgment, Maud had followed the Bishop of Winchester's advice to leave her army quartered at Oxford so as not to offend the London citizens by a show of force. Like everything else the Bishop suggested it made diplomatic sense, and yet, ever since her meeting with the London deputation, she sensed Henry was undermining her authority. He found fault with every move she made, from holding the coronation without her son to revoking Stephen's charters in favor of her own supporters which he knew perfectly well was the time-honored way of establishing the rights of the victor.

The tension between them was growing unbearable and Maud prayed that once she was crowned it would end. If she and her own advisers were not able to work together, how could any of them hope to salvage the kingdom?

The heavy iron gates loomed directly in front of her. For one wild moment Maud wondered if she was riding into a trap. Then, to her immense relief, they swung open. The moment she was inside the city, she was overcome by echoes from the past. The cobbled streets, the vendors' call for ripe cherries, the aroma of hot chestnuts, all carried a bittersweet memory of her carefree days with Stephen.

"Send the she-king back to Anjou," a jeering voice suddenly called out. "We don't want the Angevin bitch." The cry was taken up by other voices, but quickly hushed when the Constable's men rode through the crowd, spears at the ready.

It was an unpleasant reminder that London was still Stephen's stronghold, and the bold appraisal of its citizens let her know they withheld approval. Win us over if you can, their mocking expressions seemed to say. Why was it that these people were so antagonistic to her? I was born in London, she wanted to cry aloud. I am one of you. Accept me.

Maud did not feel easy until they were safely within the walls of Westminster.

The coronation was set for St. John's Day at the end of June. The next week went by in a dizzying round of council meetings, conferences, fittings for the coronation robes, audiences for arriving nobles, and nightly feasts.

One morning, a week before the ceremony, Robert approached her in the gardens of the royal enclosure and handed her a roll of parchment.

"Geoffrey has sent again," he said. "This time he demands money. He has beggared the treasury of Anjou in your cause, he claims, and needs help."

"What cheek!" Maud exclaimed. "However, if he were willing to send over young Henry, I might be persuaded to help him."

"What with? Or have you forgotten that you had to sell off most of the Imperial jewels to provide for your coronation?"

"As if I could forget," she sighed. "Which reminds me—there has been no response from the London burghers concerning my request for money, and that was over two months ago. Have them come to Westminster this afternoon."

"Is that wise?"

"Does it matter? Necessity is stronger than wisdom. Is there anything else that needs my attention?"

"The deputation from the cathedral chapter of Durham has arrived about the vacant See. Have you made a decision yet?"

Maud shook her head. The subject of the vacant See of Durham had put her in an awkward position, which was why she had postponed dealing with it. Two candidates vied for her approval. Her Uncle David recommended his chancellor, as Durham lay close to the Scottish border, while the Bishop of Winchester had put forth his own candidate for the post. Maud had promised Henry that no church appointments would be made without his approval; on the other hand, how could she offend the King of Scotland? What a coil.

"A silversmith has also arrived to see you about the royal seal," Robert continued. "He wants you to examine the rough wax impression before he casts it into silver."

"I'll see him at once. I can do nothing without the official seal."

"You wished me to see the wax impression?" Maud asked the silversmith a few moments later when they entered the great hall.

"Yes indeed, Lady," he replied in a surly voice. "A mistake has obviously been made. The inscription you ordered reads thus: '*Matildis Imperatrix Romanorum et Regina Anglaie.*' "

"Maud, Empress of the Romans and Queen of England," she translated aloud. "Oh!" Her face flushed. "Yes, I see. A mistake indeed. How stupid of me. It should be the other way round."

He stared at her rudely. "To put the Empire on the seal at all is bad enough, Lady, but to place it before England is a mortal insult."

Maud did not know what to say. Amidst the mounting demands made on her time, she had hurriedly scrawled out the inscription to be given to the silversmith, not inspecting it carefully. After all, the last time she had had a seal made for her had been as Empress of the Holy Roman Empire. It was an understandable error, if a foolish one, but she could tell from the man's attitude that her explanation was not satisfactory.

"Forgive me," she said. "Please change it at once; put England first, of course. I'm so grateful that you caught the error."

Maud knew that it would be more politic to omit the Empire from the seal altogether, but vanity would not allow her to give up the most prestigious title she had. It could do no real harm to leave it, she decided.

"Before I cast this into silver I must be paid for my work," the man asserted.

"Surely that's an unusual request? You will be paid in time, of course, but it's urgent that I receive the seal at once."

"Unusual or not, Lady," he insisted, "if you want the seal you must pay me first."

She glanced at the stubborn set of his jaw, and knew it was useless to argue. "Return this evening and I'll see you're paid."

She watched him leave, inwardly berating herself for having made the error. The Londoners already distrusted her, God alone knew what they would make of this latest peccadillo. Why was it she simply could not put a foot right with these people?

Robert frowned. "The man must be aware of the state of the treasury. I've never heard such an outrageous demand before. How will you pay him?"

"With the money I hope to get from the London burghers. Or this if need be," Maud said, pointing to a gold-and-sapphire ring on her middle finger that had belonged to Geoffrey's mother, the Countess of Maine. Geoffrey would be furious, of course, but that could not be helped now. If one more thing went wrong . . .

The bells rang for Tierce and as Maud turned toward the abbey, she was surprised to see the steward running down the passage toward her.

"Lady," he began in a breathless voice. "The Queen is at the gates, requesting an audience with you. The guards would not permit her entrance without my approval. What shall I do?"

Maud froze. "Of whom do you speak? I am the only queen."

The steward turned bright red, then swallowed convulsively. "Forgive me. As God is my judge, the former queen is what I meant to say," he stammered. "The Countess of Boulogne."

The blood drained from Maud's face and her heart missed a beat. Matilda! Holy Mother, what could she want?

"Do not distress yourself," Robert said, giving her an anxious look. "I'll see her for you."

"She will only state her business to the Lady of England," the steward said. "What shall I tell her?"

Maud hesitated. It was foolish to feel so apprehensive. She must get a hold of herself. There was no earthly reason why she need be afraid.

"I will see the Countess in the solar," she told the steward.

"Be careful with Matilda," Robert said unexpectedly. "I don't trust this visit. Perhaps I should stay with you during the meeting."

"Do you have so little confidence in my ability to behave properly?"

Maud turned away and walked down the passageway in the direction of the staircase. Despite the warmth of the day she shivered, as if a wolf had walked over her grave. How she dreaded the coming interview with her cousin.

Maud entered the richly appointed solar that had formerly been occupied by both Queen Alix and Matilda. She dismissed her women, removed her veil, then smoothed back unruly strands of russet hair. Picking up a silver mirror from a small oak table, she spared a quick glance at herself. Would Matilda think she had aged? Her face looked no older, she thought, but there was a sense of strain that had not been there before. And she was far too pale. Matilda would be sure to notice. She pinched her cheeks to give them color.

Should she greet her sitting or standing? Maud sat on the chair, then decided it might be better to remain on her feet. As she was somewhat taller than Matilda, standing would give her an advantage. It was ridiculous how agitated she felt.

There was a sharp knock on the door and Bishop Henry of Winchester entered the room.

"I'm to receive Matilda," Maud said, "I can't see you now."

"I wondered if you might wish me to be present. After all, Matilda is my sister-in-law, and I'm familiar with her ways."

"That is kind of you, but she wishes to see me alone."

The Bishop hesitated, then bowed his head. "Very well. You know the Durham chapter have arrived?"

"Yes."

Before Henry could speak again a shadow fell across the portal. "The Countess of Boulogne is here." One of Maud's women hurriedly announced the deposed queen, then scurried away.

Matilda walked into the room, stopping in surprise when she saw Henry. "Your Grace," she murmured uncertainly.

"Benedicte. You're looking well, Madam," he said, inclining his head, then withdrew from the room, closing the door quietly behind him.

Maud's anxiety increased; she felt flustered and uncertain of herself. "Will you sit?" she asked Matilda, offering her the chair.

"I've always loved this room." Matilda sat down carefully on the chair. In one hand she gripped a roll of parchment.

As she soon felt foolish standing, Maud abruptly seated herself on an embroidered stool across from Matilda, took a deep breath, and folded her hands tightly in front of her to keep them from trembling. Stephen's wife was clad in Our Blessed Lady's colors of white and blue that she had always favored. A white wimple framed her pale face.

Maud could think of nothing to say and the silence, taut as a bowstring, stretched between them. As it lengthened, Maud became impatient.

"What did you wish to say to me?" she finally asked.

Matilda swallowed several times; her fingers, showing white about the knuckles, clutched the silver rosary hanging from her neck. She seemed incapable of speech. Maud's heart went out to her. The poor woman had come to beg a boon from her victorious cousin and it was proving harder than she had thought. As it would be for me, Maud realized.

"Come," she said in an encouraging voice. "I'll not bite your head off. What do you wish of me?"

"Please release my husband from captivity." The words came out in a rush as Matilda held up the roll of parchment. "Here are the signatures of many nobles, as well as the burghers of London, joining their plea to mine."

Maud's lips tightened. She should have known it would be something like this. "You know that's impossible."

"I implore you, Cousin," Matilda whispered. "I beg you to release him."

"If Stephen is now held captive he has only himself to blame. It was his choice to break his oath and usurp my throne. You've always been regarded as an honorable woman, Matilda. Do you tell me what he did was honorable?"

Matilda quickly lowered her gaze. But not before Maud had caught a fleeting look of guilt. Stephen's wife knew full well how treacherously her husband had behaved. Yet blind loyalty forbade her to admit it.

Maud rose from her stool. "I offered Stephen his freedom if he would renounce all claim to the throne, swear that I'm the rightful heir, and admit that what he did was unjust."

Matilda gave a wan smile. "Of course he refused."

"There's no more to say upon the matter. Was that all you wished to ask?"

"No." Matilda lifted her head. "For the sake of my children I beg they be allowed to keep Stephen's possessions: his fief in Lancaster and the estates in Normandy. Your father bestowed these upon Stephen before . . . before he gained the throne."

"Stephen is one of the wealthiest landowners on both sides of the channel. All that he owned is forfeit to the crown and I desperately need his wealth. You must know the deplorable state in which he left the treasury."

She waited for a response. When Matilda remained silent, Maud continued:

"You're still Countess of Boulogne with all the revenues of that busy port at your disposal. It's not as if your children will be reduced to begging in the streets. I regret there is nothing I can do to help you."

"You could, you could," Matilda cried, her voice breaking. "If you had a heart like any normal woman."

Maud felt her body go absolutely rigid; a hot reply was on the tip of her tongue, but she got herself under control before replying. "When Stephen confiscated all of Robert's lands and castles, except for Bristol, did you plead for Robert's sons to keep their patrimony?" she asked. "Did you consider my son's legacy when you bargained with the King of France for Eustace to become Duke of Normandy? Tell me, what would my father do in like circumstances? Or my grandfather?"

Matilda looked at her in piteous mute appeal. Tears glistened in her faded blue eyes. She covered her face with trembling hands. "Will nothing move you to pity?"

"What moves me to pity, dear Cousin, are burnt towns, decaying hamlets, untilled pastures, and the starving populace!" Despite her efforts to remain calm her voice shook with suppressed anger. "What fills me with horror are roads so ravaged none dare venture upon them; innocent men captured and tortured for their gold by scoundrels and rogues who roam unchecked about the land. Does that answer your question?"

"The state of the realm is as much your fault as it is Stephen's," Matilda cried. "It wasn't like this before you landed on England's shores." She clasped her hands in an attitude of prayer. "If you let my husband go free he will become a monk, a pilgrim in the Holy Land, and never return. I swear it!"

Stephen a monk? Matilda could not be serious. But one look at her cousin's face told Maud that indeed she was.

"Stephen has never shown the slightest evidence of a spiritual nature, much less a call to serve God."

"With you that was probably the farthest thought from his mind," Matilda retorted. There was no mistaking the note of bitterness in her voice, and the sudden heat in her eyes. Then, as if aware that she had revealed too much, she hastily rose to her feet. "He'll go mad if he is locked up for the rest of his life." Tears ran freely down her cheeks. "How can you torture him in this way?"

Maud was completely taken aback. Sweet Marie, how long had Matilda suspected what had passed between herself and Stephen? There was no rejoinder she could make without incriminating herself.

Unable to look her cousin in the eye, Maud sat down again on the stool, fighting to keep her head and not let her sense of guilt betray her into folly. In her heart, she did not wish her cousin any ill will. Nor did she intend to keep Stephen prisoner for the rest of his life, as her father had done with his brother. It was on the tip of her tongue to reassure Matilda that she would relax her iron hold when the time was ripe, but then she thought better of it. Matilda might take this as a sign of weakness, or worse, that Maud, as queen-elect, was responding to an implied threat of scandal exposed. Then it would be evident that she had indeed something to hide. At all costs no one must ever suspect the guilty secret of her son's birth. A bastard would never be allowed to inherit the throne.

"Cousin! I beseech you, I humble myself before you, please let my husband go free."

To Maud's horror, Matilda fell on her knees in the dried rushes and clasped Maud around the legs so that she could not move.

"Matilda, get up at once." Maud struggled to free herself but her cousin clung like a leech. "Suppose someone were to see you like this?"

"I care not who sees me. I'm past shame, past pride."

"Come, get hold of yourself." Maud was mortified by this unseemly behavior. Struggling to her feet she gazed down at her cousin's imploring face. Beyond the streaming blue wells of her eyes, Maud sensed the steely quality of Matilda's will, perceived her stubborn singleness of purpose. In that moment she knew Stephen's wife possessed as strong a determination as her own. Matilda would stop at nothing to free her husband and see him on the throne once more. Here indeed was an enemy to be reckoned with.

Her respect for Matilda increased but all trace of sympathy vanished. "Get up," she said sternly. "I will not free Stephen under any circumstances."

Matilda gave a last choking sob, and rose shakily to her feet. Wiping her eyes with the back of her hand, she took a deep shuddering breath.

"Very well," she said, pulling herself together with an obvious effort. "I've tried to appeal to you as a wife and mother, woman to woman, but you're without mercy." Her voice grew cold. "However, I have other weapons at my disposal. My army in Kent grows daily. William of Ypres commands the troops and he will fight on in the King's name. What you refuse to recognize, Lady, is how deeply Stephen is loved, while you . . . you are despised. Never shall you have the goodwill of the English. Never."

The words were hurled at Maud like stones from a catapult, intending to wound, and they did. Each word struck her heart with the force of a heavy blow. She stiffened her back, unwilling to let Matilda see how deeply she was hurt.

"Empty threats. In ten days' time I'll be queen," Maud said, forcing her voice to be steady.

"Will you? I would not count on that, Cousin," Matilda said.

Maud, her face flaming, strode to the door of the chamber and threw it open. "A good journey back to Kent, Madam."

Head bowed, the traces of tears drying on her cheeks, Matilda walked out of the room. Maud watched her until she turned a corner of the passage, then sagged against the door, Matilda's last words echoing ominously in her mind. Was there a scheme afoot to prevent her being crowned? She must tell her half-brother at once.

Chapter Fifteen

WHEN MAUD FOUND ROBERT, SHE TOLD HIM ABOUT MATILDA'S VEILED threats. He immediately arranged for Brian to go to the outskirts of Kent, and Miles of Gloucester to the heart of London, to see what they could discover about the Countess of Boulogne's plans.

While Robert conferred with Brian and Miles, Maud agreed to see the chapter from Durham Cathedral in the council chamber. In the interests of serving justice, she requested that both the Bishop of Winchester and the King of Scotland be present at the interview. The Durham clergymen spoke at length about the respective candidates. It soon became evident they preferred the Bishop's man to fill their vacant See, for the Scots were unpopular in England, particularly along the border, which they frequently crossed to steal cattle and sheep from the Norman barons. Maud knew Henry considered her decision a mere formality, performed out of deference to her royal uncle. Henry's man was the obvious choice; still she hesitated.

She glanced at her uncle, steadfast in his loyalties, who had never deserted her cause despite the expedient truces he had made with Stephen; his chancellor was as well qualified as the Bishop's candidate. Her cousin, Henry, clever and devious, ran with the tide and always would. If he was loyal to anything, other than his own interests, it was to his brother. The issue resolved in her mind and she made her decision.

"I will appoint the King of Scotland's chancellor as bishop to the See of Durham," she announced.

"Thank ye, Niece, ye'll na regret it," said David, with a gratified expression on his face.

The deputation of ecclesiasts, shaken, turned to the Bishop of Winchester, who was so shocked that his eyes almost bulged from his head.

"Return to St. Paul's," he told the clergymen in a strangled voice. "I'll meet you there later."

When they had gone, he marched up to the oak table and unleashed the full force of his outrage. "How dare you humiliate me like that! Church appointments are my province, Madam, mine! Or have you so soon forgotten your promise not to interfere in ecclesiastical matters? You made an agreement with me and you had no right to make such a decision!"

"And I intend to keep that agreement; nothing is forgotten. This was a special case. If it hadn't involved my uncle I would never have interfered. It won't happen again."

"And I'm to be fobbed off with that lame excuse?" The Bishop's body quivered with fury. "You've betrayed me, Madam, and by God, you're right. It will *not* happen again!"

Maud rose to her feet. "I have no need of excuses, nor have I betrayed you. I deeply regret any ill feeling this may have caused."

"You'll have cause to regret more than that before I'm through," the Bishop hissed, with such a look of hatred that she felt a twinge of fear. He turned on his heel and left.

Maud did not see him again until they met with the group of burghers in the council chambers directly after Vespers. The air between them crackled and she knew she must pacify him as soon as the meeting was over.

Maud had given much thought to this second meeting with the London deputation. She did not need Henry to tell her how desperately she needed their support, well aware that these wealthy merchants and magistrates enjoyed an unusual state of independence and authority in London.

When the deputation arrived, Maud, seated behind the oak table, greeted them cordially, then got right to the heart of the matter. "Have you made a decision about the funds I requested?"

The leader of the deputation spoke. "We have, and deeply regret that we can't accede to your wishes. Quite simply, we don't have the resources to do so."

Maud's face paled. "You *know* the treasury is virtually depleted?"

The leader nodded his gray head. "By the same civil war that has crippled us as well. If we hadn't been forced to give our last penny to support King Stephen—"

Maud felt a surge of heat. "How forced! A taste of the lash? Hot irons?"

"After all, he was the king, Madam. And now that the Queen is demanding more money to strengthen her army—" He bit his lip and stopped, as every eye turned toward him in horror.

"The *former* queen has no claim on you, nor any right to ask you for funds," Maud said, her voice dangerously calm. "Your loyalty is to me, no one else." The surge became a hot tide of rage rushing through her.

"So—you refuse aid to your rightful sovereign while behind my back you plot and connive with the wife of the man who has all but destroyed England." She rose to her feet. "The matter is now out of your hands. The London citizens will be taxed. Effective immediately."

"But King Stephen—"

The last vestige of caution snapped like a frayed rope. "You're not to speak that usurper's name in my presence ever again!" Maud shouted, heedless of the effect she created.

The burghers glared at her and she returned their look with equal enmity. Finally the leader bowed his head, and turned. Bishop Henry, with not a look or a word to Maud, followed the deputation out of the chamber.

As Henry and the outraged London burghers walked along the pathway to the abbey, a man approached them through the gathering dusk. He stopped in front of the Bishop holding something wrapped in a linen cloth.

"I beg pardon, Your Grace, but have you seen Domina? She was to meet me here this evening. I be the silversmith who casts the royal seal," he explained.

"Is there some difficulty?" Henry asked.

The silversmith unwrapped the covering from a lump of wax and read aloud the inscription: "*Matildis Imperatrix Romanorum et Regina Anglaie.*"

The London citizens, who had been following the exchange, exclaimed in anger. "By the Rood, that foolish woman has put the Empire first!" said one.

"What kind of queen would forget she was a daughter of the royal Saxon line?" said another.

"Isn't it obvious? Her loyalties are to Anjou and the Empire, not England or Normandy," sneered a third.

"The lady admitted it was a mistake," the silversmith offered grudgingly. "She asked me to change it and put England first. But not till ye pays me, I says. So I've come now for me money."

For a long moment the Bishop stared at the pale oval of the silversmith's face, barely visible in the lengthening shadows. A pulse worked in his jaw, and his hands were suddenly damp. "You know, I do believe Domina mentioned something about the great seal," he said slowly. "Yes, now that I think of it, she said she had decided to let the inscription stand as is. 'Empress' was a more prestigious title."

There was a gasp of disbelief from the silversmith. "God's teeth, she's gone back on her word!"

"Unfortunately that seems to be the case. Oh, yes, and she refused payment until after the coronation. But I'll compensate you out of my own pocket." Henry reached into the scrip at his belt and handed the silversmith a few coins.

"Thank you, Your Grace," the silversmith muttered, surreptitiously biting one of the coins. "Be damned to the lady if this is how she treats us. She be no queen of ours."

"Angevin bitch," said one of the Londoners. "First taxes, now insults to the country she intends to rule! If this is how she begins, where will she end, eh?"

There were angry murmurs of assent.

"Not only that, but the evil woman has chained my brother to a dungeon wall," Henry said, throwing a few more coals onto the fire.

"Shocking, Your Grace, shocking," murmured one of the burghers. "Is there naught we can do?"

"She's not yet your queen," Henry reminded them in a low voice, his eyes sliding up and down the pathway. "If you're of a mind to act, then now's the time to do so."

"How?" the silversmith asked.

"Alone you accomplish nothing, but if you spread the news, tell others what has transpired here this night—the seal, crushing taxes, my brother's cruel confinement—and I'm sure you will find other grievances—the city can be alerted to the lady's intentions. That is," he paused, "if you've decided on what you want to do." There was a tense silence. "For myself, I can no longer submit to the dictates of this unprincipled daughter of Eve."

The men nodded their heads in agreement. What he had said was only the absolute truth, as God was his witness, Henry thought, with a surge of righteousness.

"So you now favor the cause of our good queen Matilda?" the leader asked.

It was an awkward question. Henry had not planned on this turn of events, merely taken advantage of what the moment offered. He did not want to commit himself to an irrevocable course of action. There was always the possibility that something could go wrong, leaving him neither in one camp nor the other. He had not really thought the matter through, but the men were waiting and he had to say something.

"We should consider supporting Queen Matilda and do all we can to free my poor brother, who must be suffering so pitifully chained to his cell."

Henry wondered if he had gone too far but the vehement cries of approval from his audience assured him he had not. He had almost forgotten that anything that threatened their beloved Stephen would move these Londoners to action.

"Our dear king at the mercy of the Angevins!" The leader of the deputation signed himself. "We must do what we can to aid him. At all costs the lady must be prevented from being crowned."

There was a moment of silence while two guards walked by the pathway. A rising moon flickered on their helmets and tall spears.

"Be sure you cast the seal into silver," Henry told the silversmith in an undertone. "Let it bear mute witness against the Countess of Anjou. Now, there's little time and much to accomplish. I leave the matter in your hands."

"You may rely on us. We'll reach the Queen in Kent and join forces with her army," said the leader of the deputation. "The Roman Empress will rue the day she set foot in London. Do you wish to be informed of—"

"Of nothing," Henry interjected firmly. "I return soon to Winchester. We're all in God's hands, my friends."

The Bishop turned on his heel and disappeared into the darkness.

With a twinge of uneasiness, he realized that he had set something in motion whose end even he could not foresee. But should matters go seriously awry, Henry reassured himself, he could always deny all knowledge of what had occurred this night.

Chapter Sixteen

THREE DAYS LATER MAUD ENTERED THE GREAT HALL AT WESTMINSTER with her uncle and Robert in tow. She stopped short in bewilderment: The trestle tables were only a third full, and the high table was empty.

"Why is everyone so late for the evening meal?" Maud asked Robert as she seated herself in the wooden armchair next to her uncle.

"It's very strange," Robert said. "Did you notice there were not many at Vespers this evening? Even Bishop Henry was absent. I like it not."

A procession of serving men entered the hall led by the steward.

"Where is the Bishop of Winchester?" Maud asked him.

The steward looked surprised. "Why, he left early this afternoon, just after Sext it was. Packed up all his belongings and said he was going back to Winchester. Seemed in a great hurry. I assumed he had informed you, Lady."

"Henry is deserting ye," David of Scotland said.

Maud was stunned by the steward's news. "But why? Surely he stands to gain more by remaining loyal to me."

"Ye ha' thwarted him too often, lass," her uncle told her with his usual bluntness.

Maud picked fitfully at the food on her trencher, praying it wasn't true. "If Henry has temporarily deserted," she said at last, surprised at how much she minded, "we must make every effort to get him back. If I have to compromise, I'll do so."

"It looks as though others besides Henry have deserted ye, Niece," the King of Scotland remarked, nodding at the half-empty hall.

"So it seems," she said, with a forced laugh to hide a growing disquiet. "Where is everyone tonight?" she asked the steward.

"Why, most of the nobles have left, Lady, due to the fearful rumors being spread about."

"What rumors?"

"It is said that you have levied a tax that would take a tenth of every man's possessions and refused to maintain the liberties London has always been granted—"

Maud jumped to her feet. "These are monstrous lies! How could anyone believe them?"

"I only repeat what is being said, Lady," the steward replied. "Obviously many nobles believe them."

Robert put a hand on Maud's arm and pulled her back down. "I've heard these rumors too, Sister, but saw no need to burden you with them. Not only do we torture the former king but our army lays waste the countryside, burning villages, raping women—committing all manner of ungodly crimes. This is one of the reasons I sent Brian and Miles into London and Kent."

"My guess be that William of Ypres' Flemings are responsible and our troops blamed," King David told Maud. "I only wish our forces *were* here and na at Oxford. What else have ye heard?" he asked the steward.

"Folk are leaving in droves so they will not have to attend the coronation. London seethes with unrest."

"When Brian and Miles return tonight, we'll soon know the truth of these sorry tales. Meanwhile, the Constable's men—" Suddenly Robert's eyes narrowed. "The Constable of London's troops usually fill up the lower tables—where are they?"

"The Constable himself withdrew them before Vespers, my lord," the steward said, looking fearfully from Robert to Maud. "He said they were being returned to the Tower."

"God's wounds, he has withdrawn all his men?" Robert shouted, jumping to his feet.

Maud felt her stomach lurch. "Brother, what does this mean?"

"It means there are very few guards left to protect us should—"

The sudden ringing of the tocsin interrupted him. Maud's heart leapt and she sprang to her feet.

"The palace is in grave danger, Sister." Robert quickly turned to the two squires who served him. "Oswald, Jehan, go to the gates at once and see what is happening. Hurry." Then, to his small troop of knights: "Arm yourselves and be ready to defend the palace against attack."

The servitors and the steward looked at one another, then almost as one body ran out of the hall.

Panic washed over Maud, yet she could not grasp the full significance of what was happening.

"It sounds like the palace is about to be sacked." David rose from his seat. "But Robert and I will protect ye, lass."

"No, Sire," Robert said. "Our men are too few to withstand an attack. Our best course is to get Maud away from the palace. My advice is that we leave separately and ride in different directions." He paused. "You and your Highlanders make your escape through the front gates, where there'll be much confusion. We'll try to leave through the postern gate."

King David nodded reluctantly. "I'll make for Carlisle." He gave Maud a gentle kiss on her forehead. "May God protect us all," he said, and lumbered out of the hall.

A moment later Jehan appeared. "My lord, there do be a great crowd of men with torches, carrying billhooks and axes, beating at the gates of Westminster. Fires can be seen across the river and all the Constable's troops have vanished. We have only our own men left to fight."

Even as he spoke, Maud could hear a faint angry roar.

"Saddle up the horses," Robert instructed. "We'll meet you at the stables." He grabbed Maud's hand.

"No." Maud stubbornly resisted the pull of his grip. "I'm no coward! I won't let that rabble frighten me out of my own hall!"

"You have no choice!" Robert cried.

The tumult outside increased. The shouts were closer now and there was the sound of hammering. Through the crackle of splintering wood, Maud began to distinguish isolated words and phrases. "Sack the palace—get rid of the she-dragon—we want no foreigners —bring back King Stephen—kill the Angevin bitch—"

For an instant Maud did not know whom they meant. Then, with a sudden blinding awareness that rocked her to the very core of her being, she realized the mob's rage and hatred were directed at her.

Their vicious taunts rained down like barbed shafts piercing her to the marrow. The pain and shock were so great that all the resistance went out of her. Dazed, she let Robert lead her from the hall, down the passage beside the kitchens, through the back courtyard, and into the stables.

They had just mounted their horses when Brian appeared.

"Thank God you're both safe," he said. "The mob smashed the gates with a battering arm and Miles and I managed to ride through by claiming to be Matilda's knights. Her army has entered the city and are stirring up the populace. Londoners are destroying everything in the palace, and it won't take them long to reach the stables. We must try to escape by the postern gate and head for Oxford."

"My uncle—what has happened to my uncle?" Maud asked through numb lips.

"King David is unharmed," Brian told her. "He and his Highlanders raced through the gates just as the rabble poured in. In all the confusion no one recognized him. Our own knights were less fortunate, I fear. They fought on foot and the mob cut them down like sheaves of wheat."

"Brave men," said Robert. "May God give them rest."

"The seal," Maud cried. "The silversmith was to deliver the seal tonight! I can't leave it behind to fall into the mob's hands." She tried to dismount.

Robert gave her mare a sharp rap on the hindquarters. "By God and all His Saints, of what use will the seal be to you now?"

The mare bolted forward and Maud's party raced toward the postern gate and the Oxford road.

Maud's heart kept pace with the steady beat of her mare's hooves as her party galloped toward Oxford. Every few moments she turned her head to see if they were being pursued, but the road was deserted. All that was visible against the night sky was an eerie red glow that grew fainter and fainter as each league took her further away from London—and the throne.

Maud's thoughts were in turmoil. One moment she had been Queen-elect of England, less than a week away from her coronation; now she was shorn of everything, fleeing for her life. The crushing blow to her pride, the pain of loss, mingled with an overwhelming bitterness when she thought of the treacherous Bishop of Winchester, as well as those nobles who had fled Westminster at the first sign of trouble.

How could she have been so blind to the storm brewing around her? Although she had not been popular before she ever set foot in London, what, apart from the vicious rumors spread by others, had she done to precipitate the attack? If her father had taken the same stern measures as herself would he have provoked an uprising? The grim answer stared her in the face.

Uncle David never tired of pointing out to her that what was acceptable in a man, ill became a female. Woman was the weaker vessel. Inferior. Subordinate. Someone who obeyed orders from her male superiors. Maud's spirit had always rebelled against this attitude —despite the fact that everyone shared it.

If matters had progressed normally, peacefully, as her father had intended, she might have succeeded. If Stephen had not stepped in to destroy her chance of success. For a moment she was so choked with hatred and frustration that she wanted to scream at the top of her lungs. But then she began to weep silently as the anguish of love betrayed, suppressed, denied, pierced her body like sword thrusts.

After a time, drained of all feeling, Maud saw the first signs of a pink dawn. As the sun rose, Maud could see the spires and towers of a city emerging from the dawn mist. Ahead lay Oxford—and an uncertain future.

Chapter Seventeen

Oxford, 1141

MAUD HAD BEEN AT OXFORD THREE WEEKS. ONE HOT JULY MORNING A herald arrived from Bristol, sent by Robert's son, William of Gloucester.

"The message is written by the chaplain at William's behest," Robert read aloud, his eyes running down the parchment. "He says there are rumors of Ypres's Flemings in the area, and he fears there may be an attempt to besiege Bristol and free Stephen." He swore under his breath. "William has doubled the guard and taken other precautions, but he remains uneasy and seeks our advice."

"There's little cause for alarm in my opinion," growled Ranulf of Chester who, along with King David of Scotland, had joined Maud at Oxford. "Bristol lies in the west and that part of England has always remained loyal to the Empress and yourself. Stephen's supporters wouldn't dare lay siege to your stronghold."

"After the attack on Westminster anything is possible," Brian FitzCount pointed out. "As a precaution, we must send some of our men to reinforce William."

"If we do, then we'll be short-handed should we need to defend ourselves or mount an attack of our own," Miles replied.

Maud listened carefully as they argued back and forth. At the possibility of enemy troops in the vicinity of Bristol, her heart turned to ice. Stephen was her security; despite the attack on Westminster, and the resulting ebb in her fortunes, Maud was convinced that as long as he was in her power she would still have the upper hand.

"We must spare some of our men," she said. "If there's even the slightest possibility of trouble—"

"By God's face, I've just thought of an even better solution," interjected the Earl of Chester. "If we move Stephen to a safer place, it won't be so easy to free him."

Robert frowned. "There is no safer place than Bristol, Kinsman."

"No need to move him from Bristol," Ranulf explained. "Merely give Stephen a taste of your dungeons, Robert, wrists and ankles fettered." He sat back on his stool with a pleased expression on his face. "Should an enemy succeed in gaining entry to the castle— unlikely as that is to occur—Stephen will be so carefully hidden none could easily find him."

"Why such extreme measures?" Robert asked. "Confine him to a smaller chamber surrounded with guards, by all means, but remember that he's still an anointed king."

"You grow squeamish, Gloucester," Miles said. "It's high time Stephen stopped being cosseted like a pampered child. Let him be treated like the felon he is."

"Stricter measures should be taken since the attack on Westminster," agreed David of Scotland. "It will na hurt Stephen of Blois to get a taste of what he gave poor Roger of Salisbury, and others, may they rest in peace. Ranulf ha made a good suggestion."

The Earl of Chester and the King of Scotland, two of Maud's most powerful supporters, were traditional enemies for their lands marched side by side along the border of England and Scotland, and there were constant skirmishes over disputed territory. Chester's original quarrel with Stephen, whom he had initially supported, had been over land belonging to him that had been granted to the Scottish king. Maud noted that their agreement in the matter of Stephen's confinement was lost on no one present. With the exception of Robert, every man in the hall voiced his support of Chester's plan.

Robert shrugged dismissively. "If that is everyone's wish, so be it. But it remains my sister's decision."

"I doubt she shares your reluctance," Chester said.

Stephen in fetters like a common criminal? Maud felt her heart drop like a stone. But how could she possibly deny the advantages of Ranulf's suggestion? Her spirit cried out in silent protest as she shrank from the horrifying picture in her mind. The men were watching her; Maud knew what she must say if she wanted to keep their respect. The slightest show of reluctance or softening on her part would be taken as a sign of weakness. Just like a woman, would be the verdict.

"An excellent suggestion," she forced herself to say. "Brian, will you journey to Bristol and see these orders carried out?"

"You may leave the matter safely in my hands, Lady," Brian assured her.

"That's settled then. Now," Maud continued, "I've decided how we must deal with the Bishop of Winchester."

"You mean to make peace with that treacherous prelate?" Chester asked. "After the despicable way he abandoned you to that savage mob of Londoners?"

Maud rose from her seat at the table. "How can I afford not to make peace with him? We must not be blind to our own best interests, Ranulf. To regain our lost ground, we need the support of the Bishop. If there were any other course open to me, I would gladly follow it."

There were murmurs of agreement from all present.

"First I'll dispatch Robert to persuade him to return. If he refuses to do so, then we'll march on Winchester as a show of strength."

"Attack Winchester? That would be most unwise," Miles said. "My advice—"

"When I want your advice, Miles, I'll ask for it," Maud stopped him. "I've told you what I intend to do; the matter is not open to discussion." She turned briskly to her half-brother. "Robert, can you arrange to leave for Winchester today?" When he nodded, she smiled. "Excellent. I feel sure you can manage Henry, if anyone can."

The men looked at each other, obviously nettled at her peremptory behavior, and displeased that she had not sought their counsel. Maud watched them, unmoved. Since Westminster, she had wrapped a protective shield of numbness around herself. In truth, she no longer had faith in her supporters who, she had discovered, might be with her today and just as easily gone tomorrow. There had been too many betrayals, too many broken oaths; in the end she had only herself to depend on.

Bristol, 1141

STEPHEN WAS SITTING DOWN TO A SOLITARY MEAL IN HIS CHAMBER AT Bristol when the door burst open and Brian FitzCount entered, accompanied by four guards and Robert's sons, William and Phillip. He stood up, reaching instinctively for his sword, before remembering he had no weapons. At the grim look on Brian's face he backed away in alarm.

"Brian, what do you here?"

"You're going to be taken to the dungeons and held there for your own safety," Brian said.

"Why?" Stephen protested, his throat suddenly dry, and his heart thudding.

"I've just told you. Cause no trouble and you will come to no harm."

The guards pointed their spears at him and marched him down to the bowels of the castle. William unlocked a rusted iron gate and he was led along a chill stone passage. The walls on either side were covered with green slime; the air was fetid and damp with mold. They had passed numerous empty cells when they came to what Stephen thought must be the end of the passage. Then the guards abruptly turned a corner and stopped at a small cell filled with fresh straw. It was separated from the other cells, and anyone looking down the passage would not even suspect its existence.

The cell contained a straw pallet, a coarse gray blanket of unwashed wool, one empty wooden bucket and one filled with water. A chipped earthen cup lay by the water bucket. Age and dampness had mildewed the massive stone walls, and the place stank of old excrement and countless years of unwashed bodies. The stench was so bad Stephen wanted to gag. A narrow shaft set into one wall admitted a ray of smoky light.

"Shall I fetter him, my lord?" asked one of the guards, holding up a pair of iron anklets.

Stephen felt the blood drain from his face as he examined the dismal surroundings, and saw the iron clamps.

"Brian, why is this being done to me?" he whispered.

"Domina's orders," Brian said, without looking at him. "Yes, fetter him," he told the guard, who fastened the heavy iron clamps over

Stephen's ankles. "No, leave his hands free," he added, as the guard started to fasten iron clamps to Stephen's wrists.

"Domina," Stephen repeated. "Then Maud is not yet crowned. Why not?"

"Because the Londoners—" Phillip started to say.

"Hold your tongue, Phillip," Brian cut him off.

Stephen looked from Phillip to Brian. What in heaven's name had happened? Trouble. As he had predicted, Maud had run into serious trouble. "I don't believe these are the lady's orders," he said. "Why is Robert not here? This is his castle, it's for him to say how I'll be treated."

"Believe what you wish. What does it matter who originated the orders? Both Robert and the lady agreed to Chester's—" Brian stopped short, and Stephen knew he had not meant to say so much.

An icy chill ran through him at the mention of the treacherous earl. Jesu! So this was Chester's idea. But why? What had happened to precipitate such harsh treatment?

"There's to be a guard by the cell at all times, and four more outside the gate to the dungeons, William," Brian said to Robert's eldest son. "The prisoner must be treated as befits his rank, and fed in a manner that will not injure his health, but under no circumstances is he to be allowed out of this cell or freed from his chains."

"It's senseless cruelty," cried Phillip, "the kind of vicious behavior one may expect from the Angevins." Tears glistened in his dark eyes. "Stephen is not a common criminal, he's King of England! This is my Aunt Maud's doing, and I hate her for it!"

"If there's one more word out of you, Phillip, I'll take a rod to you this minute, and, by Christ, you won't soon forget the beating you'll get," Brian shouted, raising a menacing arm.

This outburst was so unlike the cool, even-tempered Lord of Wallingford that Stephen did not know what to think. It slowly dawned on him that Brian might not be in full agreement with his orders, and that if Chester himself had come he now would be chained by wrists as well as ankles, perhaps subjected to torture as well. In his own way, without violating his instructions, Brian was attempting to ease the strain of his confinement. Thank you, old friend, Stephen thought, knowing that if he attempted to express his gratitude, Brian would hotly deny any show of compassion.

"You cannot tell me what has prompted this action?" he pleaded.

Brian, still avoiding Stephen's eyes, shook his head. Stephen sighed his frustration. Ever since last spring, when he had given permission for the Archbishop of Canterbury to support Maud, he had been starved for news. No one told him what was happening in the outside world, not even the Countess of Gloucester. At least now he knew Maud had not been crowned and must be having difficulties.

The four guards, Brian, and Robert's two sons left the cell. The door banged shut behind them; the iron key grated in the lock. There was the sound of footsteps retreating down the passage, and a cough as one of the guards took up his position outside the cell.

Stephen had never felt so alone in his life. For the first time since he had left Blois, he could not see a future ahead. What would happen to him? Did his enemies eventually intend to kill him? Was that why he had been put in this dismal place? Maud would never give such an order, but would others do it without her knowledge? It hardly seemed likely, but how could he be sure? Perhaps he would be kept hidden away for the rest of his life? Quite suddenly Stephen remembered that his uncle, King Henry, had kept his older brother, Duke Robert of Normandy, imprisoned in a Welsh fortress for twenty-eight years.

Without warning, his body began to shake as if he had a fever. Twenty-eight years! Merciful God! The thought was unbearable; he would prefer to die. Rather than shame himself in the guard's hearing, Stephen stuffed his fist into his mouth to keep from crying his anguish aloud. Signing himself, he dropped to his knees and prayed.

Eventually Stephen lost all track of time. It might be a week or just a few days that he had been in the cell. He could hardly remember what it had been like to live a normal life. His entire world was defined by the walls of his dungeon, the times he was fed, and whether it was night or day, depending on the degree of light coming from the shaft in the wall. He saw only the guard, changed frequently lest he make one an ally, Stephen suspected. Now and again the guards would engage in a brief conversation with him when he was being fed, but mostly he was left strictly alone.

Stephen's face bristled with the spiked growth of a beard, his body felt stiff and sore, and his knee joints ached like the very devil, as if the dampness had seeped into his bones. The clothes he wore grew filthy and began to smell; there was no part of his flesh that did not itch from lice and vermin. Sometimes he felt he would sell his soul for a hot bath.

One night, awakened by a loud noise, he sat up, half-expecting to see the beady eyes of a large rat that had taken to creeping into his cell after dark. The door to the cell opened, and instead of the guard, Stephen was surprised to see Phillip with a lighted torch in one hand and a jug in the other.

"Sire, are you well? Are you being fed enough food? It's so cold in here, have you sufficient covering?" The sound of Phillip's anxious voice was sweeter than the song of a southern troubadour.

"I'm as well as can be expected, Phillip," Stephen said. "The food is sufficient, but another blanket would be most welcome, and I badly miss my exercise. A change of clothes would also help." He peered past Phillip into the darkness of the passage. "Where is the guard?"

"I bribed him to give me a few moments alone with you. He knows I bring no chisel or hammer to break your chain and help you escape."

Phillip set his torch into an iron sconce fastened to the wall, then knelt in the straw and handed Stephen the jug. "Here is some wine, Sire, it is all I dared bring."

Much moved, Stephen smiled. "You're a brave lad, Phillip, to risk coming to me like this. If it's discovered you'll be soundly punished." He took the jug between his hands and drank thirstily. It was inferior wine, bitter on the tongue, but nothing in his life had ever tasted sweeter. "How long have I been here?"

"Five days, Sire. I would have come before, but my Lord of Wallingford was still here, making sure the castle was secure. He only left yesterday."

"By God's birth, it feels like a lifetime." Only five days, Stephen thought, five paltry days and he did not see how he could endure another hour.

"It's an outrage what they do to you, Sire," Phillip whispered, his voice throbbing with indignation. "I can't bear to see you so demeaned. I'll never forgive my father for this, nor my aunt. I'll never recognize her as queen."

Stephen could not repress a twinge of gratification. Without the slightest effort on his part, he had suborned Robert's son. It was a fitting revenge for the ignoble way he was being treated.

He tousled Phillip's hair. "I'll never forget your kindness, and when I am freed from this prison, I will know how to show my gratitude. Now, tell me the news."

Phillip settled himself in the straw. "Just before the coronation, a London mob sacked the palace of Westminster and the lady barely escaped with her life."

"Jesu," Stephen murmured, signing himself. "Sacked Westminster! I can hardly believe it."

"When the lady fled to Oxford, your queen rode into London with Eustace at her side, and her army behind her. The Lords of Muelan and Leicester and William of Ypres have joined her, as well as others who abandoned you at Lincoln."

"Thank God. Go on."

"New life has been breathed into your cause. That's why you're here, Sire, because it's feared that there will be more uprisings and perhaps an attempt to rescue you."

"By God's birth," Stephen murmured, "I should have known it would be something like that." He was so excited that he threw off the blanket and stood up, cradling the jug in his hands. "So Matilda and Eustace are safe and back in London." His eyes closed as he gave a silent prayer of thanks. "And my brother?"

Phillip also rose. "He deserted the lady's cause shortly before the palace was sacked. Brian says he might even have had something to do with it. My father has gone to Winchester to lure him back."

Knowing Henry, he probably had been involved, Stephen thought, as a great weight lifted from his heart. Now there was reason to hope once more. His brother had the most astute mind in the realm; if there was a way of freeing him, Henry would find it. Tears sprang to his eyes. Should he be released from this foul prison, he vowed, never would he hurt his brother or the church again.

There was a cough, and Stephen looked up to see the guard hovering anxiously in the open doorway. "Now then, Master Phillip, time's up. They'll be changing the guard any moment. Hurry."

"Thank you, Phillip," Stephen said, downing the last of the wine. He watched the torchlight flicker on the boy's adoring young face.

"I'll see that you have another blanket at least, more if I can." Phillip removed the torch, took the jug from Stephen's hands, and left the cell.

As the door closed and the key turned, Stephen sank to his knees in prayer. The news was like a miracle: his throne still vacant; Matilda returned in triumph to London; his brother once more an ally. Or so he hoped.

If God permitted him a second chance, Stephen swore, never again would he allow envy, hostility, rage, and most of all love—blind, unreasoning love—to cloud his judgment, or compel him to act against his own best interests. Look to yourself, sweet Cousin, he thought. Should I ever again have the chance, I will not let you escape.

Chapter Eighteen

Winchester, 1141

In August Robert returned to Oxford from Winchester with the news that Henry was evasive about his future plans and would not commit himself to rejoin their cause.

"We will help him to decide," Maud announced.

True to her earlier word, Maud gathered together her army and, ignoring the protests of her council, set off for Winchester determined to persuade Bishop Henry to return to her camp. Although her cousin was not at his palace of Wolvesey when she arrived, Maud and her forces were admitted into the city without incident. When Henry returned, however, he made one excuse after another to avoid a meeting between them.

Then, without warning, Matilda's troops—greatly outnumbering Maud's—arrived in the dead of night and surrounded the city. Maud knew she had received the Bishop's answer: He had abandoned her cause.

Six weeks later Maud, standing on the battlements of the stone-and-timber castle in the city of Winchester, looked with hatred at the royal standard fluttering from the Bishop's palace that lay just outside the walls. A symbol of defiance, she thought bitterly, proclaiming for all to see that he was once more Stephen's man.

There was a sudden loud hiss. Maud looked up to see a fireball
sailing over the walls of Winchester. It seemed to be headed directly
toward where she stood. Frozen, she could not drag her eyes away
from the flaming orb as it arced across the deep blue of the September
sky, coming closer and closer.

"Maud, get back!"

"In heaven's name, Niece, move!"

Startled, she turned at the sound of Brian FitzCount's voice,
followed by her uncle's. Booted feet raced over stone. Strong arms
wrenched her body forcefully away from the parapet.

"God be thanked, it's missed the castle," Brian said.

The burning sphere fell short of the battlements, then disappeared
from view. Sudden screams rent the air, followed by the sound of a
crackling explosion.

"St. Mary's Abbey has been hit," Brian gasped.

"The nuns will be trapped inside," Maud cried, tearing herself
from his arms.

From below came an anguished cry of pain and terror.

"Mother of God," Brian whispered. "No, no, do not look."

But Maud was already hanging over the embrasure. One of the
nuns who had tried to escape from the burning building was running
around in circles, her black habit on fire. Other nuns were trying to
beat out the flames with their hands. Maud covered her mouth with
her hands as the nun, screaming in agony, became a human torch,
fire engulfing her body. Bile rose in Maud's throat and she gagged
even as she said a prayer.

"How much longer must we endure this," she cried, tears running
down her face. "Today it's that poor sister. Who will it be tomorrow?"

"As God wills, Niece. The good nun will die a martyr's death,"
said David of Scotland, crossing himself.

"As God wills? It is the Bishop of Winchester who sacrifices the
lives of innocent victims." Maud turned and pointed an accusing
finger at the roof of the Bishop's palace. "How can a man of God
destroy his own abbeys?"

"Ach, lass, 'tis the hazards of war. Such devil's work is the Flemish
army's doing, not the Bishop's."

"He allows it, doesn't he? I must go down at once and offer my aid
to the sisters."

The King of Scotland looked at her sharply when, suddenly swaying, Maud grabbed a merlon for support. "When did ye last eat?"

Maud leaned against the stone. "I can't remember, Uncle. I've lost all count of time. Probably after mass this morning." She grimaced. "Stale bread and rancid meat. I remember now I couldn't touch it."

"That's all we have available," Brian said with a sigh, "and we're fortunate to have that. Stores of food are so low some areas of the city are starving." He looked at her in concern. "You must eat something, Lady, no matter how unpalatable. I think you're in no condition to aid anyone at the moment."

"Lack of food and water—" David turned to Brian. "If we do na get provisions soon, my lord, we'll be forced to surrender—or starve to death."

"Surrender? Never," Maud said firmly. "Never will I become Matilda's prisoner, not while I have breath within my body. I'd rather starve!"

"Ach, ye ha' a proud spirit, lass, but ye nay ha' experienced a long siege afore. Nor ha' ye seen men die of starvation."

As Maud watched the citizens of Winchester bring buckets of water to keep the flames from spreading, she wondered, not for the first time, if her uncle and the others blamed her for the disastrous position in which they now found themselves: daily fireballs threatening the city, meager rations, and a growing despair that made life in Winchester a continuing nightmare. The bells tolling for Sext mercifully interrupted her grim thoughts.

After noon Mass when Maud and the others were gathered in the great hall the Scottish king told Robert they could not go on as they were. "A surprise attack, men trying to scale the walls, presents a more immediate threat than starvation. And since ye just lost three hundred men, how will ye resist the Flemish horde?"

Maud sighed, hating to be reminded of their latest failure. Two weeks ago Robert had dispatched three hundred men under cover of darkness to stop their supplies being intercepted and their escorts slain by the enemy before they could reach the city. William of Ypres' Flemings had fallen on the troops in a surprise attack and massacred them to a man.

"Do you say we should surrender, Uncle?" Maud whispered, dreading his reply.

"Nay, lass. But we must retreat, aye, and with no delay, I'm thinking. None of us be safe here."

Robert nodded. "Retreat or be captured."

"The conditions are hazardous for retreat," Miles protested. "We're surrounded by enemy forces."

"We must get Maud to safety," Robert stated, "regardless of the conditions."

"Surely there's something else we can do," Maud cried out in despair. "This is Westminster all over again. We must stand our ground."

"This is far worse than Westminster," Robert said. "There at least we had an army waiting for us at Oxford. Now men are in short supply. No." He shook his head decisively. "We must get you out of Winchester to safety at Bristol."

That night at their meager supper, Robert outlined the scheme for their retreat.

"The escape is planned to coincide with Vespers tomorrow night, a Sunday, which is also the feast of the Holy Cross. It's to be hoped that a greater number of enemy troops will be attending service, leaving fewer to guard the walls."

Using ivory chessmen to demonstrate his strategy, Robert spread out the large pieces on the trestle table.

"An advance bodyguard will be sent on ahead, led by King David and his Highlanders." He slid a few men across the boards, then turned to Maud. "You'll follow on their heels, Sister, attended by guards on either side. Miles and Brian will be right behind you, protecting the rear." He moved another handful of ivory figures.

"And you, Brother? Where will you be?"

"Behind them with my men, overseeing the whole retreat." He swept the rest of the pieces off the table with a flourish.

"Who covers your rear then?" Maud asked.

"None need cover my back," Robert said, tossing his head in a proud gesture. "Come now." He raised dark brows. "Why do you wear such a long face, Sister? I've been fighting battles since I was big enough to wield a sword. Have I ever been captured? Or defeated? The only warrior to match me lies captive at Bristol!"

The next day dragged on endlessly. Would Vespers never come? An hour before the evening service was due to start, Maud sat down to supper with her half-brother, Brian, Miles, her uncle, and the castellan of Oxford Castle, Robert d'Oilli, who had joined her forces when she left Oxford for Winchester.

The Vespers bell sounded at last. It was time to leave. Cloaked and hooded, almost suffocating in the breathless heat of early evening, Maud was hoisted into the saddle of a Flemish bay mare she had never ridden before. She took a last look around the crowded court-yard, shading her eyes from the blood-red rays of the setting sun.

An armed escort rode on either side of her; behind, in the order her half-brother had determined, Brian and Miles waited with their men. At the rear Maud could see Robert astride his horse, with Lord d'Oilli beside him. She knew he was to remain in the town until she had passed safely through the west gate of the city. He raised his lance to her in a huge mailed fist.

Maud wheeled her mare around and trotted out of the courtyard. In the town itself, against a background of wooden houses with tightly closed doors and fettered shutters, the King of Scotland had mustered his Highlanders. Animal skins were thrown over their shoulders; painted blue dragons rippled on muscular arms ringed with metal. Steely eyes confronted her from inscrutable bronzed faces. Even knowing they were her allies, Maud could not control a shiver of apprehension.

"Godspeed, Niece," David said, trotting his horse out from the ranks. He grabbed her mare's bridle. "If we do na see each other again on middle earth, I want ye to know that ye be a true credit to ye Norman kinsmen and ye Saxon forebears."

Fighting a lump in her throat, tears pricking behind her eyes, Maud impulsively reached up, pulled her uncle's head down, and kissed him on his hairy cheek. When you looked at him closely, one saw the face of an old man, she realized, but one still full of determination and spirit. She was so choked with emotion and gratitude that she did not trust herself to speak. David turned his horse and, followed by his Highlanders, trotted down the street toward the west gate. In a moment all she could see was a ray of fading sunlight glancing off his helmet as he became lost to view amid his men.

Guards pressing on either side of her, Maud followed the Highlanders. Her heart beat furiously; the dry taste of fear clogged her throat. Ahead the rusted gates swung slowly open on creaking hinges. From the other side a swarm of men brandishing maces and wooden staves attempted to rush through; they attacked with such violence it seemed her uncle's Scots would be plowed under. But the staunch body of Highlanders, swinging their iron swords and wooden clubs, held firm. Suddenly, as miraculous to Maud as the Red Sea parting, a narrow passage appeared amid the melee of men and horses.

"Ride, Niece, ride fer ye life!" Although she could not see him, David's voice rang out clearly.

Suddenly panicked, Maud found herself unable to move. She had never been so frightened in all her life. Twisting in the saddle, she could see Robert far behind her, his men closely following. There was no sign of either Miles or Brian.

"Go!" Robert's shout echoed faintly above the noise of clashing steel. "For the love of God, go now!"

Spurring her horse forward, Maud plunged into the narrow passage created by her uncle. Hemmed in on either side by the press of the battle, she was aware of the overpowering stench of men's bodies, animal flesh, and rank fear. A shield struck her shoulder, a spur grazed her leg, and she swayed precariously in the saddle. A man's voice cursed, inches from her ear, his foul breath almost choking her. A horse whinnied, thrusting its long head into her lap. Then she was through the gate and outside the city.

Maud galloped a few paces up a small rise before she realized that she had become separated from her guard. She took a last desperate look behind her, searching frantically for some sign of Robert, or her uncle, or Miles, or Brian. She caught a brief glimpse of a gold-and-scarlet plume bobbing on a helmet: Robert's colors.

Then she became aware of knights fleeing in every direction, discarding shields and coats of mail, even helmets, in their flight. Horses galloped riderless, snorting in terror. A group of ragged-looking men ran toward her on foot. Dark, threatening faces surged around her mare. A wooden stave was thrust into her face. Fury drove out fear. With a strength she did not know she possessed, Maud let go the reins, wrenched the stave from a strong grasp, and lifting it with both arms, savagely cracked the wooden club down on a flaxen head. There was a startled grunt; blood dripped from the stave.

The mare snorted in fear and reared up on her forelegs. Maud clenched the reins in one hand and, still holding the stave in the other, tried to soothe the terrified horse. Forcing her way through the angry mob trying to bar her path, she hit out blindly at hands that reached to restrain her. Finally she broke free.

The mare cantered wildly over a ground now scattered with abandoned swords, lances, and spears. Knights and squires, whether friend or foe she could not tell, passed her in headlong flight, some on foot, others on horseback. Maud called out to them but, in their panic to escape, they ignored her. The orderly retreat had disintegrated into total rout. Chaos reigned.

After galloping for what seemed like hours, the mare slowed her breakneck pace, and came to a shuddering stop on the top of a wooded hill, her heaving flanks covered with foamy sweat. The cries of battle could no longer be heard, nor the sound of fleeing men and horses.

Maud looked around, her heart hammering against her ribs, the breath sobbing in her throat. It was now almost dark. There was nothing to be seen but open country. She was alone.

Maud had no idea how far she had come, how long she had been riding, or even where she was. West, she decided, she must have been riding west for she had been headed into the setting sun rather than away from it. She patted the neck of her dripping horse, wondering whether to wait and see if any of her party would catch up with her, or ride on toward what she hoped would be the direction of Bristol.

A noise caught her attention. The mare whinnied softly. Another horse? Yes, she could hear it now, the sound of hooves pounding the ground, heading toward her. Through the gathering darkness she could see a rider—no, a group of riders, galloping in her direction. One of the riders broke out from the rest and rode up the hill. As he came abreast, she raised the stave threateningly.

"Do not dare to come closer," she screamed.

There was a sharp intake of breath. "Maud? Is that you?"

It was Brian FitzCount's voice. "Brian! Oh, Brian."

In a moment Brian had pulled his horse to a stop and leapt from the saddle. He ran over to her, swept Maud off the mare's back and into his arms. She sobbed with relief.

"God be thanked, you're safe, you're safe," he murmured against her cloaked head. "We were so worried about you." He rocked her back and forth in his arms like a child.

Gratefully, she rested against him, laying her head on his muscled chest, feeling the strong beat of his heart through the mantle and mailed shirt. Brian was here and she was safe. Finally she drew back her head.

"Are Robert and Miles with you? My uncle? What of Lord d'Oilli and the others?"

"Miles was with me when we fought our way through the enemy outside the gate. Then we became separated and I lost him. D'Oilli is with me now and some of the others." He paused and Maud felt her heart freeze. "Your uncle and his Scots fought their way through the enemy ranks like lions," he continued. "Never have I seen the like. With God's grace, they should be well on the road to Scotland by now."

"Without them I would never have managed to get through the gate. But Robert? Where is Robert?"

Brian gripped her arms. "You must be brave. We believe Robert has been taken."

"Taken?" Maud repeated, disbelieving. "Taken prisoner?"

"Yes. He fought with great courage, staying in the rear to hold up the enemy until the very last moment. He managed to get out of Winchester, but the enemy caught up with him while he tried to cross the river at Stockbridge."

"Holy Mother, who has taken him?" she whispered.

"Flemish mercenaries. And all his men with him. I was well ahead of him, and had already crossed the river—I saw it happen—he was surrounded—" The anguish in Brian's voice was unbearable. "I was powerless to help him, to save him. We were so few and they so many."

Maud felt as if a violent force had knocked the very life out of her body. Her head reeled. Robert taken! Merciful God, how could she carry on without him? What was she to do now?

Chapter Nineteen

A QUARTER OF AN HOUR AFTER BRIAN HAD FOUND HER, MAUD SAT huddled before a fire while the Lord of Wallingford explained the details of Robert's capture. He broke off as the faint sound of hoof-beats was heard in the distance. Instantly alert, Maud and Brian jumped to their feet.

"My lord, the enemy is sure to be in pursuit," said a knight. "We can do naught for Earl Robert now and in order to save ourselves we should ride at once for Bristol."

"That's exactly what the enemy will expect us to do," said Robert d'Oilli. "May I suggest that we make for Gloucester instead? It will put our foes off the scent and confuse them when they find no trace of us on the road to Bristol."

"A good thought," said Brian. "Are you up to the rigors of a harsh journey, Maud? To evade our pursuers we should travel the back roads and avoid the major towns."

"Of course," she said, praying that she would prove as good as her word. Already exhausted, the news about Robert had so badly shaken her that she could not even think coherently.

Brian, Maud, Lord d'Oilli, and the five knights accompanying them mounted their horses and began the journey to Gloucester. As the night wore on Maud grew more and more tired; her body became chilled, then so hot she felt she was on fire. By sheer effort of will she forced herself to remain upright in the saddle, her eyes fixed on the figure of Brian who rode just in front of her. She was determined not to allow any physical weakness to endanger all their lives.

As a pale gray dawn broke over the west country, they emerged from a thinly wooded forest into open pasture. Here Brian called a halt by the side of a running brook. Lord d'Oilli lifted Maud from the saddle and set her on her feet. No sooner had she touched the ground than she collapsed upon the grass.

"Fetch some water," Brian said to one of the men, as he knelt beside her.

"I don't know what came over me," Maud said in a faint voice. "In a moment I'll be quite recovered."

"Make a litter of branches, place her on the litter, and we'll carry her the rest of the way," Brian instructed the knights.

Mortified at the suggestion of a litter, Maud tried to protest that it was unnecessary, but she did not even have the strength to voice her objection. In a daze she felt herself lifted from the ground and placed on a thick cloak that covered a bed of branches tied together at both ends. Another cloak was gently placed over her, the litter was fixed between two horses, and she felt her body suddenly swing back and forth as the horses started to move. It was a little like being on the deck of a ship in a rolling sea, she thought, then knew no more.

Slowly Maud opened her eyes. Her gaze took in the stone walls of the chamber with their dark blue hangings, the blue canopy above her, and the fur-lined coverlet pulled up to her chin. Was she at Gloucester? Cautiously stretching her arms and legs, she was filled with an overwhelming sense of relief that she had survived the journey with nothing worse than a few sore muscles.

"Thank you, Holy Mother," she murmured aloud. Remembering her captured brother she added: "Please protect Robert from harm."

There was a soft knock on the chamber door.

"Enter," she called weakly.

Robert's wife, Mabel, bustled in, followed by one of her women carrying a wooden tray. "How fare you this morning, Sister-in-law?" she asked, walking over to the bed to peer down at Maud with red-rimmed eyes in a pale face.

"Almost recovered," Maud murmured. She must be at Bristol, she decided, noting that Mabel's thin, brittle body was clothed all in black, as if mourning the dead. "How long have I been at Bristol?"

"This is Gloucester and you've been here two days. I arrived from Bristol yesterday morning, as soon as I heard the news . . . about Robert." Her voice broke as she laid a hand on Maud's forehead. "The fever is gone. To have survived such an ordeal you must have Our Lord's blessing, Madam."

"I only wish Robert were here as well," Maud said in a low voice, steeling herself for an outburst of anguish as a spasm of pain crossed Mabel's face. "I deeply regret Robert's capture and fully share in your loss." Impulsively, she reached out and gently touched Mabel's fingers.

As if a snake had bitten her, the Countess quickly withdrew her hand. She turned to the woman behind her and took a steaming goblet off the tray. "Here is a hot posset I've made with my own hands. Drink this and your strength shall be restored."

Mabel took a wool shawl she had been holding, wrapped it around Maud's shoulders and chest, then helped her prop herself up against the pillows. Gratefully Maud took the goblet in both hands and raised it to her lips. The hot liquid spread through her body, returning warmth and vitality to her sore limbs. She had hoped their mutual loss would create a bond between them, but her sister-in-law remained as prickly as ever.

Much refreshed and alert, Maud drained the posset and handed the goblet back to Mabel. "Thank you. How are Brian and the others?" She paused and dropped her eyes. "Stephen, I trust, is also well?"

Mabel gave her an odd look. "Brian and the others are fully recovered. Stephen is well enough. Oh, Miles arrived last night. Half-naked he was, and like you, raging with fever, his body scratched and bleeding."

"What happened?"

"Apparently Flemish mercenaries pursued him and he had no choice but to throw down his arms and flee for his life." Mabel's lips twitched in resentment. "Perhaps if Robert had behaved in like manner he would be with us today."

Maud made no retort. The Countess is stricken with grief, she reminded herself, do not judge her.

"Speaking of prisoners, Madam," Mabel continued in the same breath, "an envoy has arrived from the Countess of Boulogne not an hour since. Robert is well, unhurt, and being held in honorable confinement at Rochester Castle." The Countess looked away and would not meet Maud's eyes.

"But that is wonderful news! God be thanked he's safe."

"I've sent word to William that Stephen is to be moved from his cell into a comfortable chamber and be treated with all the amenities. The envoy said if this were not done Robert would be chained in a cell as well."

"Of course. We must ensure the best treatment for my half-brother." Maud wondered why Mabel seemed so evasive, why she had not told her this news immediately. Quite suddenly she understood. "Sweet Marie, Matilda sends to offer terms, doesn't she? She will free Robert in exchange for Stephen?"

"Yes, that is her offer. I assume your answer will be affirmative. I told the envoy you would act at once."

Maud had no intention of discussing the matter with the Countess of Gloucester. "You had no right to tell him anything. I'll do what's best for our cause. Be so good as to send Brian FitzCount to see me."

Mabel made no reply, but her eyes burned with resentment; she turned on her heel and stalked out of the chamber, the servant following on her heels.

Maud closed her eyes. She had never felt so weak, so vulnerable. Holy Mother, how could she give up Stephen? On the other hand, she could not let Robert remain a prisoner. The conflict was perfectly balanced, impossible to resolve.

Brian FitzCount soon knocked on the door and entered the chamber. "Mabel tells me the fever has passed, thank the good Lord for that. You look much improved, Lady," he said.

"I feel much improved," Maud said.

Brian perched on the edge of the bed. "You heard about the envoy from Matilda?"

"Yes. Please send him away. I don't agree to Matilda's terms."

Brian was nonplussed. "Don't agree? What choice do you have? I know what a great loss it will be to give up Stephen, but without Robert we can't go on."

"I refuse to even consider such an exchange," Maud said.

"That's a most foolish attitude," Brian countered. "Haven't you yet learned that he is the mainstay of our cause? Half our following will melt away without him."

"I thought I was the mainstay."

"Your ascension to the throne is why we fight, but Robert is the linchpin. You are the end, he is the means. Without him you may as well return to Anjou."

"I know Robert's worth," Maud cried. "But I will never, never, never give Stephen up." She struggled to a sitting position.

"The rigors of the journey have not only left you physically weak but, understandably, affected your wits as well. You're hardly fit, I think, to make such an important decision at this time."

"How dare you. Of course I'm fit." She glared at him.

"Then you will not follow a path that can only lead to disaster. Stephen and Robert *must* be exchanged."

Maud had never seen Brian so obstinate before, so unyielding, and his recalcitrant attitude frightened her. In truth, she realized uneasily, she was trapped inside this chamber, at the mercy of Brian, Mabel, and the others. Too weak to fight them. If they refused to obey her there was no way she could force them to her will. She fought down a surge of panic.

"Brian, as my dear friend and loyal supporter, please hear me out. Safe at Bristol, Stephen acts as a check and balance against our enemies. He is all we have now to bargain with. If we give him up, what is left to us?" She forced a smile, her eyes begging him to see her side of it. "We must find another way to buy Robert's freedom."

"I've always thought you lacked your father's gift for persuasion, but now I wonder." Imperceptibly, Brian's face softened and he rose to his feet. "All right, I'm willing to examine other solutions—for the moment."

"What will you tell Matilda's envoy?"

"That he must return to Rochester. No exchange can be discussed at this time," Brian said, walking to the door. "I leave *you* to deal with Mabel." He gave her an ironic smile, bowed, and left the chamber.

Six weeks after her arrival in Gloucester, Maud still had not come up with a means of freeing Robert. Even after receiving a message from her half-brother urging her to execute the exchange, Maud could not bring herself to take the final step that would allow Stephen to resume the throne once more. What would she have to bargain with then? Her cause would be worse off than before the Battle of Lincoln.

One afternoon toward the end of October she walked with Brian in the courtyard. A brisk wind sent white clouds scudding across the slate blue sky. Soon it would be winter, she thought, her third winter since she had landed on England's shores.

"Mabel is beside herself with rage," Brian told her. "Only yesterday she threatened to find a way to exchange Stephen for Robert whether we agreed or not."

"An idle threat, surely," Maud said.

"The point is that others feel as she does, including her sons. No one understands your reluctance to exchange the two, why you go against your own best interests."

After a quick look, Maud avoided his steady blue gaze. "All is lost if I give him up. We've been over this a hundred times."

Brian shook his head. "All is not lost, Lady, if only you will listen to reason. Now that Geoffrey has successfully recaptured much of Normandy, there is an excellent chance that he will come to England with men and arms." He took her ice-cold hands in his. "When Robert is freed we can, with Geoffrey's help, defeat Stephen's forces. I'm sure of it." He searched her face. "By God's death, Madam," he said in an exasperated voice. "Do you think to fool me? What is the real reason you won't give Stephen up?"

Maud felt her face flush. "I've told you, as well as everyone else, the real reason."

"Have you?" He took her shoulders and gave her body an impatient shake. "Start behaving like a ruler, not a lovesick maid. Where is the Empress of the Holy Roman Empire! Where is the daughter of the formidable Henry, the granddaughter of the great Conqueror?" He moved his face closer to hers. "Where, Madam, is the Queen of England?"

Twisting free, Maud felt as if Brian had struck her a blow in the belly. How dare he talk to her like that—but she could feel the impact of his words penetrating the armor of her resistance. Only Brian would have guessed the basic reason for her stubborn refusal to let Stephen go, a reason she had never fully confronted until this moment. Her love for her cousin, pervading her entire being like a burning fever, had indeed caused her to act against her own best interests. She now realized that hidden in her heart was the wild belief that as long as Stephen remained a prisoner he still belonged to her; this was the only way in which she could possess him. In her unwillingness to face up to the truth, she had lost sight of the larger issue: what Robert's freedom combined with Geoffrey's victory in the duchy could mean in terms of reclaiming England.

Raising her head proudly, Maud squared her shoulders:

"The Queen of England stands before you, my Lord of Walling-ford. Thank you for reminding me that Geoffrey is now in a position to aid us. When Robert is freed, I will send him to Normandy for men and arms."

Brian sighed in relief and kissed her on both cheeks. "Thank God. Shall I send a message to Matilda that we agree, in principle, to the exchange?"

Maud nodded. There was no longer any excuse to hold back Stephen's release, but oh, how bitterly she resented the fact that he would be free—and once again king.

After several weeks of negotiations between Maud's advisers and the Bishop of Winchester and the Earl of Leicester, who represented Matilda, a complicated procedure of hostages left on both sides was worked out; the exchange of prisoners was now ready to take place.

On a gray drizzly morning in November, Maud, who had insisted on riding to Bristol, stood in the courtyard of Robert's castle and watched Stephen mount a chestnut stallion. Although pale and some-what heavier from lack of exercise, he seemed animated and merry, laughing with Brian, Miles, and William of Ypres, who had ridden to Bristol to accompany his sovereign back to Winchester, where Robert was being held by Bishop Henry. It was just like Stephen, Maud thought, to behave as if they were all about to set out on a merry hunt together.

The rain ceased; a flicker of sun burned through the gray clouds, highlighting Stephen's features and brushing his tawny hair with gold. He had grown a beard during his confinement, and it leant his face a becoming air of authority. Maud's heart turned over as she watched him throw back his head and laugh at something said by Miles of Gloucester.

She kept reminding herself how much there was to be gained by Robert's release. Stephen might resume the throne for a time, but with sufficient strength her forces could topple him again, crushing him absolutely. Yet her senses rebelled; her heart cried out against his imminent departure.

Stephen and his escort approached her. Maud had long anticipated this moment, going over and over what she would say to him—scornful words that would leave him in no doubt as to the contempt in which she held him.

"I bid you farewell, Cousin," Stephen said with a formal bow of his head.

Their eyes met and held in a long look that neither could break. "A good journey to Winchester, my lord," Maud stammered, all the accusations she had so carefully rehearsed gone clean out of her mind. Do not leave me, she cried silently, I cannot bear it.

Something flickered deep within Stephen's green eyes, and a look of anguish passed across his face, so fleeting Maud was not even sure she had seen it. His lips opened as if he would speak, he made a sudden gesture toward her, then with an effort brought himself under control. Wheeling his horse around, he headed toward the stone tunnel that led to the outer bailey. In a state of numb despair, Maud watched his escort trot after him. She felt as if a lifetime had passed, but it was only nine months, almost to the day, since Robert had brought him in triumph to Gloucester.

Chapter Twenty

Windsor, 1142

In January of the following year, 1142, three months after Stephen had been freed from captivity, he reluctantly agreed to meet with his brother, the Bishop of Winchester, and leading members of the clergy. The meeting was to take place at Windsor, where Stephen had spent the past twelve weeks slowly resuming his duties as king while he recuperated from his lengthy ordeal in the dungeons of Bristol.

Since his release, he had deliberately avoided a private meeting with Henry, trying to determine how he should best treat his brother: as friend or foe? Well aware that the Bishop had made himself look both a fool and a traitor with his various switches from one side to the other and now back again, Stephen was sure that Henry dreaded the upcoming confrontation with his peers and himself. But there was no way either of them could avoid it.

As Papal Legate, Rome's legal representative in England, it was Henry's duty to officially reconcile the English church to their newly restored king. His task would be made immeasurably easier if Stephen forgave him for deserting the royal cause after the Battle of Lincoln. Despite the fact that Henry had abandoned Maud, organized Matilda's forces at Winchester, and helped negotiate his release, Stephen was not now of a mind to forget his brother's earlier treachery quite as readily as he had been while confined at Bristol.

As he sat in his wooden armchair in the small council chamber, Stephen began to feel apprehensive; beads of sweat formed around his neck and under his armpits, and a peculiar lassitude, a condition that had come upon him since his captivity, held his body in thrall. In addition to the loss of his old vigor, Stephen found he was more cautious in his decisions, less able to fulfill the demands and pressures of kingship. Now, more than ever before, his strength was needed to serve his kingdom, yet he could not propel himself into action. According to Matilda, William of Ypres and Robin of Leicester, the realm was in a disastrous state: Geoffrey of Anjou was rapidly gaining full control of Normandy, and those supporters of Stephen's who had estates in the duchy were rumored to be in contact with the Count, including Waleran of Muelan, who had kept his distance since Stephen's return.

It was inconceivable, thought Stephen. Who would ever have believed that mincing Angevin peacock could be such a successful fighter? His advisers urged him to make an all-out effort against the Angevin forces, pointing out that if the Countess of Anjou were taken captive, there would be a speedy end to the conflict. Stephen knew this advice to be sound, yet he could not bring himself to act. As his physicians had warned him not to plunge into violent activity until he had regained his strength and health, he had used this as an excuse to do nothing.

Whenever he remembered the look on Maud's face as he left Bristol, his heart ached like an open wound. That look of mingled love, agony and loss still haunted him, for those same feelings were mirrored in himself.

The door opened, letting in a draft of cold air.

Preceded by the Archbishop of Canterbury, a group of black-robed prelates and clergymen solemnly filed into the chamber. Behind them came Henry wrapped in a black mantle.

"How pleasant to see you, Sire," the Bishop murmured, stretching his lips into a smile. "Recovering well from your confinement?"

Stephen nodded, unwilling to greet Henry in a friendly manner. Let him stew a little, he thought. His brother cleared his throat, ran his tongue over parched lips, rearranged his parchment scrolls several times, and would not meet Stephen's eyes. He is afraid, Stephen realized with surprise. Fear was not something he had ever associated with Henry, but fear was something he understood only too well, and his heart thawed toward his brother.

The Bishop then began to speak. After a brief preamble, in which he summarized recent events and formally welcomed the King back to his domains, he came to the point.

"Fellow brethren, Sire: You are entitled to an explanation of my conduct during the last year."

Indeed we are, thought Stephen, curious to see how Henry would wriggle out of this coil.

The Bishop continued. "I was forced to support the Countess of Anjou because the King had been defeated at the Battle of Lincoln and his barons had fled to save themselves. The land was in chaos and I found myself trapped in Winchester surrounded by hostile troops. I could hardly allow the city to be put to the torch, and under threat of force of arms—indeed, my very life was at stake—I had little choice but to capitulate and recognize the Countess's claim to the throne."

Henry paused. The chamber was silent as a tomb; Stephen, exactly as if he were in his brother's head, knew the Bishop wondered if he had gone too far.

"As the Countess of Anjou has since broken every pledge she made to maintain the rights of Holy Church," Henry went on to say, "she has forfeited our loyalty and support."

Once again he licked dry lips. "God, in his infinite wisdom, has since guided events so that the Countess's hopes for the throne are dashed. With our Heavenly Lord's continuing aid, and the help of the Holy Father in Rome, we can now support King Stephen, our rightful sovereign, once again."

Oh, well done, Brother, Stephen thought, a masterful performance. Will your fellow churchmen believe you? I don't. But then who will give the lie to this farfetched tale?

There was an uncomfortable silence. A few prelates coughed and shifted in their seats. None met the Bishop's eyes; a few cast covert glances at Stephen to gauge his reaction.

"Will you pass sentence of excommunication on the Countess's supporters as you did on mine?" Stephen asked.

"Naturally," Henry said. "On all of them—excepting only the Countess herself."

Stephen hesitated. Across the length of the table his eyes locked with Henry's. He could sense his brother willing him to forgive and forget the past. You took Canterbury from me, his glance signaled; I deserted you for what I believed to be the winning side. Now we are quits.

"We are prepared to accept the Bishop's explanation in good faith," Stephen said at last. "Are there any amongst us who have not been guilty of an error in judgment? What says Holy Writ? 'Let he who is without sin . . .' I suggest we bury the past and make a fresh start."

There was a stir among the clergymen as a murmur of consent echoed round the chamber. Clearly, Stephen realized, it was what everyone had wanted him to say. In a solemn voice, Henry then passed sentence of excommunication on all enemies of church and King.

As Stephen rose wearily to his feet, he heard the Bishop of Lincoln say in an undertone to the Bishop of York:

"So we're back to where we started three years ago, when the Empress landed: England is still torn by strife, rapine, sacrilege, murder. How much longer must the land suffer for the sake of these ambitious cousins?"

Normandy, 1142

Almost NINE MONTHS LATER ROBERT OF GLOUCESTER AND GEOFFREY of Anjou faced each other in the tilting-yard of the ducal palace of Rouen in Normandy.

"Maud has been under siege at Oxford for almost two months now," said Robert. "How can you continue to refuse aid to your own wife, Geoffrey? Have you no heart?"

Geoffrey raised his hands in a placating gesture. "I don't refuse aid, Kinsman, but surely you can see how hazardous it would be for me to leave Normandy at this time?"

As usual, the Count looked as if he were to going to an audience at the French court: His red-gold curls and beard were neatly barbered; he was immaculately clad in dark green hose and a lighter green tunic bordered in gold thread. The ever-present sprig of golden broom bobbed in the blue cap perched at a rakish angle on his head. His eyes sparkled like ice crystals as he presented Robert with his most charming smile, a smile that Robert had come to distrust as he had come to distrust almost everything about his brother-in-law, except his relentless devotion to his own interests.

"The duchy is barely won," Geoffrey continued in the same soft, reasonable voice that had persuaded Robert to remain in Normandy far longer than he had intended. "Many castles still remain in the hands of the rebels."

"Indeed? I've helped you recapture at least ten castles since I came to Normandy. How many more can there be?" They had had the same discussion, in one form or another, almost daily, but Geoffrey still remained unwilling to commit himself to aiding Maud.

Robert knew his brother-in-law had used him, but he needed Geoffrey's help so desperately that he kept agreeing to his demands in the hope that this would entice the Count to cross the channel.

Geoffrey gave a vague shrug. "Even one rebel stronghold is too many! Don't think I'm ungrateful, Robert. Your aid has been invaluable."

"Then in God's name, man, show your gratitude! I need more than words from you," Robert shouted. "You know how desperate we are in England for men and arms! Maud is trapped in Oxford, surrounded by Stephen's soldiers. Brian sends urgent messages to say his forces are not sufficient to break the siege! This has been going on for two months! Two months! Does it mean nothing to you?"

Beside himself with frustration, Robert felt his face grow hot and his temples swell in helpless fury. If this coxcomb continued to avoid the issue—he withdrew his sword from its scabbard and jabbed it violently into the ground to give vent to his rage. The emerald-studded hilt quivered like a bowstring.

"Of course it means something to me," Geoffrey retorted, his eyes narrowing. "What do you take me for?"

Not trusting himself to answer, Robert pulled his sword from the ground, slipped it back into the scabbard and, turning his back on Geoffrey, walked a short distance away to collect himself.

Ever since he had been exchanged for Stephen last November, Robert had felt helpless and frustrated, as if men and events conspired against him. To begin with, it had taken him almost five months to rally together his party's scattered forces, establish Maud securely at Oxford, and, throughout the west country, garrison a line of castles for her defense. Still he had been reluctant to leave her, trusting no one but himself to be totally responsible for her safety.

Then, last June, Stephen, who had been intermittently ill ever since his release, had taken a sudden turn for the worse. All hostilities had ceased since the two men had been exchanged, as if both sides

needed a breathing space to lick their wounds and recoup their
strength. It seemed unlikely that the civil war would be resumed
during Stephen's illness, so, at Maud's insistence, Robert had reluctantly set sail for Normandy in July, convinced that he would soon
be back with Geoffrey and reinforcements before Stephen recovered.

But the weeks had stretched into months while Geoffrey of Anjou
made one excuse after another to avoid coming to England.

In late August Stephen sufficiently recovered his health and energy
to almost immediately set about attacking the castles Robert had
established for Maud's protection. By October, all Maud's defenses
were destroyed or burnt. Having successfully isolated her, Stephen
then proceeded to lay siege to Oxford itself. Thus far the castle held
firm, but for how long? Robert's blood ran cold when he contemplated
the grim possibilities.

His thoughts were interrupted by the sound of a warning shout
and sudden cry. He reached instinctively for his sword and saw that
Geoffrey had done the same.

"It's only Henry," Geoffrey said, sheathing his sword.

Robert followed his gaze to the far side of the tilting-yard where a
group of men-at-arms, young squires and pages was gathered around
the quintain.

"He's fallen from his horse tilting at the quintain. The third time
in a row."

Robert watched as Count Geoffrey's eldest son, Henry of Anjou,
picked himself up and was lifted back onto his horse by the sergeant-
at-arms for another try at the quintain. The boy, now nine years of
age, was cast in the solid mold of his Norman forebears. Holding his
lance in one grubby fist he galloped furiously at the stand with its
two revolving arms, shield, and sandbag. He struck the shield at full
tilt with his lance but did not turn away quickly enough; the sandbag
swung round, hit him full force, and he tumbled off his mount.

This time, instead of getting up, he lay on the ground screaming
with rage and pounding the earth with his fists. His two younger
brothers, Geoffrey and William, watched him in awe, the sergeant-
at-arms in resignation.

"Henry has the Norman temper, I fear," Geoffrey said, clearly
embarrassed at this unseemly display of personality. "He cannot
accept defeat with good grace, but must give vent to his feelings. I
apologize for his ill manners."

But Robert had little interest for his nephew. "You're not coming to England, are you, Geoffrey?" he said with sudden insight. "You never intended to come."

Geoffrey's alabaster skin turned a faint rose. "How could you think that? But you must see I have my responsibilities here. How can I abandon them?" He brushed a few imaginary crumbs from his spotless tunic. "I've won Normandy for Maud, don't forget that. I can't be expected to be everywhere at once, now, can I?" He sniffed. "Pity that some loyal retainer did not lace Stephen's food with poison while you had the chance."

Robert gave him a look of such disgust that Geoffrey had the grace to lower his eyes just as Henry, slung over the sergeant like a squealing pig, was carried over to his father. His hands beat against the sergeant's stolid back.

"I can do nothing with him, my lord," the sergeant said. "Young Master can't seem to get the hang of tilting at the quintain and refuses to try again."

Robert lifted his nephew from the sergeant's back. "He would get the hang of it if I taught him, I'll wager." Robert smiled down into the pugnacious freckled face streaked with tears. "But I don't teach howling babies, look you."

The noise stopped; Henry's body became still. "Could you teach me, Uncle?" he asked in a choked voice.

"Aye, I could." Robert looked down into his nephew's storm-gray eyes, so like Maud's he felt a chill run down his spine. What a boost to his sister's spirits if she could see her eldest son, he thought. What a boost to their entire cause. An idea flashed across his mind as he set Henry on his feet and tousled the boy's bristly reddish hair.

"Since you won't come yourself, Geoffrey, send the boy back with me, as a token of your good faith," Robert said. "I promise to see he is kept safe. When he returns to Normandy he will have the makings of the finest warrior in Christendom."

Geoffrey frowned. "That's all well and good, Robert, but England is more dangerous now than it ever was. Suppose Oxford surrenders? What then? And what will become of the boy's education?"

"Father, please, I want to go. I want to see my mother." Henry tugged eagerly on his father's tunic.

"Henry will be imbued with letters and instructed in knightly behavior as befits his rank. I swear upon my life that I will keep the boy safe, even as I keep my own sons safe."

"As you did Phillip?" Geoffrey said with a mean smile.

At this cruel reminder of his youngest son Phillip's defection to Stephen's cause last spring, Robert was filled with such a murderous rage that it was all he could do to keep from wringing Geoffrey's elegant neck. He could hardly bear to think about the loss of his son, much less hear him spoken of in such a cavalier manner.

"I shouldn't have spoken as I did. Forgive me," Geoffrey said hastily, as he saw the look on Robert's face. "But to send Henry back with you is a great risk. He is my heir."

"Morale is low in England," Robert replied, bringing himself under control. "He would be a symbol of new hope, of a brighter future, and put heart back into our cause. His presence alone might spur our forces on to vanquish Stephen at Oxford."

Henry threw himself on the ground and began to growl low in his throat. "I will go, I will go." His face started to turn a deep red, then purple.

"Not another tantrum! May God give me patience!" Geoffrey sighed in exasperation. "Oh very well, take him then. At least I'll have peace for a change. My other boys never give me a moment's trouble."

Henry's screams ceased as if by magic; his face resumed its normal color. He jumped up and began to dance wildly in circles.

"Well, well." Geoffrey observed him in obvious bewilderment. "Either rain or shine, feast or famine. There's no middle ground with the boy. As God is my witness, I don't know what to make of him." He gave Henry a stern look. "Don't be any trouble to your Uncle Robert. England is a dangerous place these days. You must take great care to behave properly, and learn your lessons well. Be a credit to your illustrious heritage."

"Of course, Father." Henry gave Geoffrey a withering look as he wiped his nose on his sleeve. "I understand what is required of a Norman king."

Geoffrey raised his brows. "Norman king indeed! That is putting the cart before the horse, my boy, considering your mother is not yet queen. I referred to your illustrious *Angevin* heritage. It seems to me that —"

Before he could continue, Robert grasped Geoffrey roughly by the arm and led him aside.

"Don't meddle with the boy's dreams, Geoffrey," he cautioned. "Henry believes he will rule England one day, and why not?"

"Because the crown still sits on Stephen's head and no one has been able to get it off—and keep it off," Geoffrey replied with a frown. "Not that the boy doesn't already behave as if he were king, a veritable tyrant at nine years!"

"Let Henry's future fall out as God wills it," Robert said. "Whether Count of Anjou, Duke of Normandy, King of England, or all three—no man can escape his destiny."

The two men turned as Henry ran off, shouting excitedly to his younger brothers that he was leaving for England to help their mother regain his throne.

Chapter Twenty-one

Oxford, 1142

IT SEEMED IMPOSSIBLE TO MAUD THAT IT SHOULD BE DECEMBER AL-
ready, and that Oxford Castle had been under siege for almost three
months. From the tower window, she looked down at the scene
below. Snow lay like a heavy white cloud on the ground outside the
castle walls; the river was a block of ice. Only the dark pavilions of
Stephen's army, the guards walking to and fro, and the looming
siege-engines broke the smoothness of the frozen picture before her.

She licked her cracked lips, leaning weakly against the damp stone.
Her body felt numb with cold and ached with hunger, but she was so
used to these sensations by now that she could not remember what it
felt like to be warm and have a full belly.

Maud turned from the window, rubbing her stiff fingers to bring
them back to life, wishing there was some way to revitalize her despairing heart. This time, unlike the siege at Winchester, she was
totally alone. Robert d'Oilli, her last close supporter, had fallen ill
and died two weeks ago. The last word from the outside world had
been from Brian—just before Stephen appeared at Oxford in the fall
—to say that her castles of Wareham, Cirencester, Radcot, and
Brampton had all fallen, and that he had sent a message to Robert in
Normandy, urging him to return.

Since then she had received no news, nor was there any sign of
Robert or his forces. No doubt Geoffrey, whose main concern had
always been Normandy, had refused aid, callously abandoning her to
an uncertain fate.

In the early days of the siege Maud had cherished the vain hope
that Stephen might allow her to leave—as he had at Arundel. But no
trace of that former chivalry was forthcoming. In fact, she had not
caught so much as a glimpse of him. This time, Maud realized, he
was bent on defeating her.

Aware that the castle would soon be starved into submission if help
did not arrive, all Stephen had to do was wait like a giant bird of prey
until the quarry fell helpless into his hands. The war would be over;
she would be his prisoner. He could shut her up for the rest of
her life, in chains if he chose. Had she not done as much to him?
The driving force of her life would be thwarted. Never would she
wear England's crown, never would her son inherit the throne. The
prospect was so horrifying Maud felt she would rather die than endure it.

"Lady?"

Maud turned toward the open door. It was the captain of the
garrison, his arm in a sling from a wound he had received as a result
of a fireball thrown over the walls. She beckoned him inside.

"The cook has just slain the last milk cow," he began. "After we
have eaten her there will be no more fresh meat."

"Is there any salted meat?"

"No. After these two scullions died last week, and a score of other
folk were seized with violent pains and a bloody flux, the cook threw
out all the meat in the barrels. There's too much sickness as it is."

Nodding wearily, Maud shuddered at the dreadful images his
words had evoked. Only chance had prevented her from eating the
tainted meat.

"The larder's now empty, fuel is almost totally gone," the captain
continued, "and there's another problem as well. The cook says the
rats are increasing in number, which means there's so little food they
have emerged from hiding to seek sustenance. I've seen them,
Madam. They're bold creatures, some big as puppies. One bit the
hand of a child, almost severing a finger." He paused, a look of
uncertainty on his face.

Maud knew he held something back. "What else?"

He looked away, unwilling to meet her eyes. "Talk is widespread
that we must surrender lest all the inhabitants perish. The last thing

I want, Lady, is for you to fall into enemy hands, but I have a duty to the folk in the castle as well."

"We both do. The matter weighs heavily on my mind. But I have not given up hope that my half-brother may still arrive to aid us, or my Lord of Wallingford." The words sounded hollow in her own ears.

The captain shifted his weight from one booted foot to another, both wrapped in rags for warmth. "What chance does the Lord of Wallingford stand against a force of one thousand men? If Earl Robert were able to help you surely he would have done so by now. No, Madam, we must face the facts. We cannot depend on outside aid." He paused. "Certain leading citizens who sought refuge in the castle when the town was put to the torch have been stirring up trouble."

"What kind of trouble?"

The captain swallowed. "They blame you for their plight. They claim that King Stephen destroyed their city only to get at you. Why should their lives be further ruined for a woman who has caused nothing but grief and strife from the moment she landed on England's shores."

Maud stared at him, his words like knives tearing into her heart. "They hate me too," she said slowly, "just like the folk in London."

Maud knew time had run out. She could no longer delude herself that help would be forthcoming. Hateful as it was, there was only one step she could take. Drawing a deep breath, she forced herself to say the words she had promised never to utter.

"There must be an end to hardship for these good people. Surrender the castle."

"God save you, Lady." The captain knelt on one knee and bowed his head. "Thank you."

Maud turned her back lest he see what this decision had cost her.

"I ask a day's respite," she said at last, struggling for composure. "Only a day to seek a way out of this coil. With God's help, I may find one."

The captain got to his feet. "Of course. By Sext tomorrow I will send to the King. But it would be politic to tell the folk that you have agreed to surrender."

Maud gave him a bitter smile. "For my own safety you had better tell them."

When he had gone, Maud walked back to the window slit. The frozen world outside was unchanged, in sharp contrast to the upheaval taking place within her. More painful even than her decision to surrender was the realization of how blind she had been to the feelings and needs of the people in the castle. The very people she intended to rule, yet she had no more idea of what went on in their hearts and minds than if she were hundreds of leagues away. She had thought only of her pride and not giving in to her cousin.

As she stared out the window, Maud thought something moved against the vast expanse of whiteness but could not be sure. Were her eyes playing tricks on her? No, something had moved. She could barely make out a vague shape covered in snow making its way across the frozen ground. In a moment it was lost to view. She gazed thoughtfully at the icy expanse outside the walls, at the river frozen fast. The white figure had been hardly visible to the eye. White against white was virtually unnoticeable. The seed of an idea took root in her mind.

An hour later Maud descended to the guard room.

"How many leagues exactly is Wallingford from Oxford?" she asked the captain of the garrison.

"Thirty leagues perhaps," he said. "I'm not sure."

"Is there a village or hamlet in between?" Maud asked, dismayed.

"Not that I know of."

"Begging your pardon, Captain," a young soldier offered, "but I'm from around these parts and there do be a monastery at Abingdon, no more than eighteen leagues away, and a hamlet close by."

"Yes, you're right," the captain confirmed. "I'd quite forgotten about Abingdon."

"Eighteen leagues!" Maud smiled. "That might be just possible. I think I may have found the way out I spoke of earlier, Captain. Not without risk to be sure, but far better than being taken captive! Let me tell you what I have in mind."

That night, shivering in the frosty December air, Maud felt her heart race with anticipation and fear. She looked down at herself, clothed from head to toe in a white sheet that completely covered her fur-lined cloak, then cast a glance at the three soldiers who would accompany her, also draped in white. Once on the ground they would be indistinguishable against the snow—or so she hoped. One-half of Stephen's army occupied Oxford itself. The other half lay camped in the frozen meadows across the ice-bound river. If the enemy did not spot them descending the walls, they had a slim chance of making their way unnoticed through the armed camp. Better to be captured trying to escape than cowering inside the castle.

"The enemy will be changing the guard at Matins and there is always confusion then," the captain said to Maud. "You'll have less chance of being observed. The bells should ring by the time you reach their camp." He looked up just as the clouds passed over the moon. "You must leave now while it's dark. Quickly."

As Maud watched, one of the soldiers, white linen bed sheets knotted strongly around his waist, was lowered slowly from the walls to the riverbank below. He reached the ground in safety, then untied the sheets, which were hoisted up again.

"Are you ready, Lady?" asked one of the soldiers.

When Maud nodded, he tied the sheets securely around her waist.

"May God speed your journey," said the captain. "I pray you reach Abingdon in safety."

"Remember to give me until Sext before surrendering the castle. I shall not forget your loyalty."

"Nor I your courage, Madam." He slipped something hard into Maud's gloved hand. Her fingers closed over the hilt of a slender knife. "Should you need to protect yourself," he whispered.

Grateful, she slipped the knife into the leather bag that swung at her belt under the cloak and sheets.

As two of the soldiers lifted Maud carefully over the wall, her heart leapt. Slowly she sank lower and lower until at last her feet touched the ground. Then the soldier untied the sheets and moments later the two other soldiers joined her. The captain waved his hand in farewell, pulled up the sheets, then disappeared.

Silently the four figures climbed down the bank. They crossed over the frozen river, crouching as low as they dared, slipping and sliding on the ice. The wind rose to an unearthly shriek, stinging Maud's cheeks and freezing her lips. Finally they reached the farther shore on the edge of the enemy camp.

Apart from the campfires gleaming through the darkness there was no sign of a living soul. Maud and her companions moved cautiously toward the enemy tents. Their footsteps fell silently upon the freshly fallen snow; their labored breath rose like puffs of smoke on the frosty air.

They had almost passed through the enemy camp when the bells rang for Matins, followed by a blast of trumpets. Maud stopped motionless in her tracks.

"Changing of the guard," one of her companions reminded her. "It will be over soon."

The four of them waited breathlessly, listening to the sound of voices coming toward them through the snow. One of her companions grabbed Maud's hand, drawing her up against a pavilion. Flattening her body against the tent, she waited, trembling.

"I tell ye I saw something move just a moment ago," a voice said, coming from around the corner of the pavilion.

"You're daft, lad. Ye can't see your hand in front of your face in this snow."

There was a laugh. The voices grew fainter, then vanished.

"Best to move on, Lady," one of the soldiers cautioned.

Heads down against the driving wind, they threaded their way through the remaining tents. They had reached the last line of pavilions when a lone sentry almost ran into them. He stepped back quickly.

"Who goes?" He pointed his long spear at them, then gasped in terror, signing himself. "May God have mercy! Ghosts abroad!"

Maud was rooted to the ground, too frightened to move. The guard approached, took the point of his spear and thrust back the white sheet, then the hood of her cloak.

"Holy Mother, it do be the Countess of Anjou," he breathed, the shock evident in his voice.

Two of the soldiers closed round her protectively, while the third fumbled for something under his white covering. No one spoke. Maud's hand reached under the sheet and cloak for the knife.

"Guard? Is aught amiss?" The familiar voice, heavy with sleep, came from the pavilion just in front of her.

Maud looked up, her heart pounding. Yes, there was the royal standard atop the tent. She had been too preoccupied to notice. It *was* Stephen's voice!

As the stunned sentry finally opened his mouth to raise the alarm, one of the soldiers withdrew his hand from beneath the sheet, lunged forward, a pointed dagger in his clenched fist, then drove it straight into the guard's chest. The spear fell from his hand; he toppled backwards into the snow without a sound.

"All is well, Sire," the soldier called, muffling his voice in a corner of the sheet.

"Get some sleep then, God rest you."

"Let us move on, Lady," whispered one of her companions. "The others will catch us up."

But the sound of Stephen's voice, the prone body of the sentry, whose sightless eyes seemed to be fixed upon her in an accusing stare, had robbed Maud of the ability to act. She could not take her eyes off the lifeless body being dragged out of sight behind a clump of frost-laden bushes. A trail of blood, brilliantly scarlet against the alabaster snow, marked the body's passage over the frozen ground. One of the soldiers brushed snow over the telltale drops with the toe of his boot, while the other heaped armfuls of snow over the guard's body. Within moments there remained no trace of him.

"He won't be discovered till morning, and even then everyone will assume it to be the work of outlaws hiding in the forest." The soldier turned to Maud. "Madam, what ails you? We must move now." And taking her arm, he forcefully led her away.

The remainder of the night, stumbling through deep snowdrifts, sliding across icy streams, and striving to avoid the scourge of wind and frost, became an incoherent blur in Maud's mind. By the time they stumbled through the gates of Abingdon Abbey, a gray dawn was breaking over the horizon. Maud could no longer feel her face, and her hands, even in their fur-lined gauntlets, were numb with cold.

She and her companions stayed only long enough to warm them-selves by a roaring fire and gain strength through a meal of dried pea soup and chunks of black bread. The Abbot agreed to give them the use of four horses so they could speed straight through to Walling-ford, and safety.

They reached the great fortress at Wallingford in time to hear the Compline bell. At first, the watch in the gatehouse refused to lower the drawbridge.

"The Lady of England escaped from Oxford and walked to Abing-don? Through all this snow? Do you take me for a fool?"

"Call for the Lord of Wallingford at once," Maud cried with her last ounce of strength before sliding from her horse into a deep snow-drift.

She could hear voices shouting back and forth. Then one of the soldiers knelt beside her to say that the Lord of Wallingford was being summoned. Barely conscious, Maud heard the creak of the portcullis being drawn up, then the dull thud of the drawbridge as it hit the ground.

Strong arms lifted her from the snow. Incredulous voices mur-mured words of praise and disbelief. She was dimly aware of being carried inside the castle, then placed in a tub of water so scalding she screamed in agony as life gradually returned to her frozen limbs. A burning frothy liquid was poured down her throat; her body was laid in a soft bed heated with hot bricks. Fleece comforters were piled over her. She sank into welcome oblivion.

Gradually Maud became aware of someone sitting on the bed, tickling her face. She felt warm and drowsy, unwilling to open her eyes or move a single muscle. From far off she heard the sound of the Vespers bell. She had slept through the night and an entire day. Perhaps even two days. The tickling continued. Annoyed, she opened her eyes, startled to meet a pair of smoky gray eyes in a freckled face. Chunky arms clasped her none too gently around the neck. Dear God, Holy Mother, it was Henry!

Astonishment turned to joy. The blood began to course through her veins as life returned to her aching body. Weakly she lifted her arms to hug him back. Her tears mingled with his. The ordeal of the siege, the harrowing journey through ice and snow, all of it was as nothing now as she held her son in her arms.

Chapter Twenty-two

Bristol, 1145

"DID YOU SEE THAT, MAMAN?" CALLED HENRY OF ANJOU. "I HAVE HIT the mark every time!"

"Yes, my son, a wondrous achievement," Maud called back.

"Well done, Nephew," Robert of Gloucester shouted.

Henry acknowledged these compliments with an airy wave of his hand.

Maud and Robert, exchanging a look of mingled pride and amusement, stood in the grounds of Bristol Castle on a chilly October morning in the year 1145, watching the young heir of Anjou practice archery at the butts.

Almost three years had passed since Maud's escape from Oxford Castle and during that time Henry had grown into a muscular youth with lively gray eyes and chestnut hair. Exuding raw energy and a winning charm, he was driven to excel at all that he undertook; at twelve he was already expert at the quintain, hunting, falconry, and his lessons, which included a smattering of languages from France to the Holy Land.

"I have arranged for Henry's return to Normandy by the end of the week," Robert told Maud, his face growing solemn. "He will ride under cover of night to Wareham where a ship will be ready to take him across the channel."

Maud frowned. "With a large escort, I assume. Should Stephen's forces get word of his leaving—"

"If there's a large escort it may excite suspicion," Robert interjected. "Trust me to take the necessary precautions."

Maud pressed his hand. "I do, Brother. The constant threat of danger has made me fearful as a skittish filly." She turned her head to cast a loving look at her son. "In truth, I cannot bear to part with him."

Between Maud and her son existed an unbreakable bond, a depth of love and understanding she had never shared with anyone. Every now and then she occasionally caught a glimpse of Stephen in him: a sudden movement, lithe and fluid, a tilt of the head, and a trick of smiling at her in an intimate manner that made her heart stand still and her body grow weak. Once he had grabbed her around the waist and hugged her, as Stephen might have done, and she had almost burst into tears. The prospect of losing him was devastating.

Robert took her arm as they strode up and down the grounds. "Nor can any of us, for he has won all our hearts. But England has become too hazardous for the boy. I promised Geoffrey that when I could no longer guarantee Henry's safety I would send him home. That time has come."

With a sigh Maud sank down onto a stone bench, Robert beside her, and, turning her face up to the weak rays of the autumn sun, reflected on the sequence of events that had prompted Robert's decision to send Henry back to Normandy.

In addition to the sieges, countersieges, rebellions, desertions, and assaults that had become a way of life in England, the last three years had also brought Maud a succession of stunning disasters that had not only hurt her cause, but given her much personal anguish as well. The cycle had started with the death of Aldyth in Anjou. Maud had not seen her for six years but never ceased to miss her. Mother, companion, trusted confidante, no one could take her place in Maud's heart.

Aldyth's death was followed by the inexplicable demise of Miles of Gloucester in a bizarre hunting accident, the Earl of Chester's sudden defection once again to Stephen's side, and, most recently, Robert's unexpected defeat at the castle of Faringdon two months ago, where Stephen had won an overwhelming victory.

Since then her half-brother had sunk into a kind of morose apathy, for in the thick of the battle he had glimpsed his son Phillip fighting savagely against his father's forces. It had broken his heart.

Now, ailing in body, his revenues sorely strained, Robert was forced to husband his resources. He had neither the money nor the men to garrison all his castles against the possibility of attack.

"Truly I sometimes feel as if fate has turned against us," Maud murmured aloud. "As my cause grows weaker, Stephen's fortunes prosper. Yet he is the usurper, not I. Is he never to have his just deserts?"

Westminster, 1145

IT WAS THE WIND THAT SWERVED THE ARROW, SIRE," PRINCE EUSTACE whined. "Didn't you see it?"

"No, I did not," Stephen replied. He glanced up at the gray November sky, then down at the ground where not even a light breeze stirred the dried grass or scattered the piles of red and gold leaves. "In fact, my boy, there is no wind."

"The arrow was not fletched true then." Eustace looked wildly around the grounds of Westminster Castle. "I'll have the fletcher whipped."

"Begging your pardon, Sire, and not to contradict young Prince Eustace, but there be nothing wrong with the arrow," the sergeant-at-arms said to Stephen in a low voice. "The boy just missed the mark."

"I know, I know." Stephen sighed in vexation. "I will deal with it."

He looked despairingly at the petulantly handsome face of his eldest son now arguing with one of his squires. Tall for ten years, slender as a sapling, Eustace had his mother's pink and white complexion, silver-gilt hair, and pale blue eyes. But his nature was vastly different from Matilda's. He was an obnoxious, sulky boy, difficult to control, with a vicious streak that made Stephen uneasy, reminding him of his late cousin, Maud's twin brother, William, who had exhibited many of the same qualities. Exceptionally strong, courageous to the point of being foolhardy, and excelling at arms and the hunt, Eustace promised to be as great a warrior as himself. On the other hand, despite being possessed of a cunning animal intelligence, he was inordinately dull at his lessons, an unforgivable lack in Stephen's eyes.

Unpredictable and dangerous, interested only in activities that involved killing of some kind, Stephen was aware that his son lacked charm, warmth, even common humanity. Those who did not fear him, detested him.

A scream of pain rang through the air. Eustace had knocked his squire down on the ground and now proceeded to jump on him with booted feet. From the far corner of the courtyard, Stephen could see Matilda and his brother, Bishop Henry, turn startled heads in the direction of the screams.

"Eustace," he bellowed, "stop that at once!"

Eustace ignored his father's command and was finally pulled off the squire by two guards. He ran over to Stephen with a smirk of satisfaction on his face. The squire, blood spurting from his nose, was carried out of the courtyard.

"Giles moved the butt just as I drew back to take aim," he said, a yew bow slung over one shoulder and a quiver of arrows over the other.

Stephen regarded his son with an icy glare. "Giles isn't strong enough to move the butt; the fletcher's arrow was true, and there was no wind. Why do you persist in this folly? Where is the shame in a shot gone astray?"

Eustace thrust out his lower lip as he returned Stephen's look with a mutinous expression.

"You simply missed the mark, Eustace, and no one is to blame but you. Behave like a man. Admit it."

Eustace folded his mouth into a stubborn line. He looked down at the ground and rubbed his foot in the grass.

"Admit it, I say," Stephen repeated between clenched teeth. Overcome by a surge of anger, he grabbed the boy by his short brown jerkin, half lifting him off the ground. "Admit it, or by God and all His Saints I'll whip you so hard you won't be able to sit for a week!"

His face ashen, Eustace squirmed in his father's grasp. "I missed the mark," he began sullenly, "because—"

"Because you aren't yet expert enough. There's no other reason."

Eustace's face turned deep red. He gave a tiny nod.

"Now go to your lessons." Stephen let him drop to the ground.

"But I want to—"

"I care not what you want—go to your tutor," Stephen shouted, abandoning all attempt at control. "Learn something for a change. Do you want to be a crowned ass?"

Eustace threw his bow and quiver down on the ground, flashed Stephen a look of murderous hostility, then ran off toward the palace.

"What a look! No matter, that attempt at discipline was sorely needed and long overdue, Brother," commented the Bishop of Winchester who, unnoticed by Stephen, had come up silently behind him. "Tell me, would you really have whipped him?"

"No, God forgive me, probably not." Stephen sighed. "I'm incapable of hurting my children, even for their own benefit. But I would have ordered someone else to punish him."

"Eustace is spoiled and indulged. He needs a stern hand. Do you remember how our mother ruled us all with a rod of iron?"

"Only too well," Stephen replied shortly.

"In my opinion it's the best way to raise a son. What says Holy Writ? 'If you beat your son with the rod, you will save his life from hell.' " Henry picked up Eustace's bow that lay in the grass, tested it in his arms, then bent to select an arrow from the quiver Eustace had dropped. "Touching upon the matter of sons, I've just had confirmed that young Henry of Anjou sailed for Normandy in great secrecy." He frowned. "Pity. If I'd had wind of these plans we might have intercepted him on the way to the coast. That would have been a prize worth taking. Almost as good as having the mother."

"Indeed. I would give half my kingdom to have the boy in our hands," Stephen replied. "He poses a serious threat to Eustace's accession to the throne and the duchy."

"In Normandy young Henry is a threat, certainly, for the Count of Anjou is sure to turn over the duchy to him when the boy comes of age," Henry said.

"Louis of France will never honor him as Duke of Normandy," Stephen argued, a quiver of resentment shooting through him. "Louis has promised me he will only recognize Eustace as the future duke. After all, his sister will be Eustace's wife."

Henry raised his brows. "Louis's promises are not worth that." He snapped his fingers. "Tell me, how will Eustace become Duke while Geoffrey of Anjou controls Normandy?"

Stephen did not reply. Any mention of Henry of Anjou or his father, Geoffrey, filled him with hatred. The Count of Anjou's sweeping conquest of the duchy never ceased to enrage Stephen, who continued to lose supporters willing to forfeit their lands in England in order to keep those in Normandy.

"I didn't recognize at the time how farsighted was our uncle when he forced his daughter to marry the Angevin," Henry reflected. "Normandy and Anjou now form a bulwark so powerful that not even Louis of France dare attack their combined might. It is unlikely that Eustace will ever be Duke of Normandy, make up your mind to it. Best we concentrate on England."

The Bishop notched the arrow to the bow and took aim. An instant later the point quivered in the mark.

"You haven't lost your touch, I see," Stephen remarked. "I could use you on my next campaign."

Henry looked pleased. "With God's grace, there may not be many more campaigns."

"If only that were true."

"My spies tell me Robert is far from well. His defeat at Faringdon was a heavy blow, as was Miles's death, and Phillip's and Chester's defection. I doubt he can muster sufficient resources to do full-scale battle with you. In truth, I would be surprised if he lasts the year. With Robert's death, it should be an easy matter to capture the elusive Countess of Anjou."

Stephen took the bow from his brother, and tested it. He prayed God his brother was right. He no longer had any stomach for the endless fighting that led nowhere, never knowing from day to day when a trusted friend had become an enemy. No matter how many battles he won, he was no nearer to winning the war. His realm continued to seethe with strife and conflict.

Weary and disillusioned, Stephen knew that all he really lived for now was to see the war ended, peace restored, and the succession of Eustace secured. If a son of Blois sat on England's throne, at least some good would have emerged from the wreckage that had become England.

There was only one sure way to forestall Henry of Anjou from becoming a real threat to Eustace in England, and to achieve this end, Stephen had decided upon an unprecedented gesture: He intended to have his son crowned in his own lifetime. Thus far he had mentioned the plan to no one, but this seemed like the appropriate time to confide in his brother.

Stephen took his brother's arm and led him well out of earshot of the guards. "Henry, I want to tell you something. When I visited the monastery at Peterborough last month I went into the scriptorium where I was shown the chronicles the monks have been keeping for the past three hundred years. 'The land is in such a state of misery under King Stephen,' the monks wrote, 'that it is as though Christ and all His Saints slept.' "

Henry looked quickly away. So he had seen that damning entry, Stephen realized. "I told the Abbot it was a harsh judgment, and he replied, looking me straight in the eye, 'As you do, my son, so shall we write of you.' I was too ashamed to argue with him. I left much chastened."

"Well, you know what these unworldly monks are—" Henry began.

"No Henry, do not make less of them," Stephen stopped him. "Before God, did I usurp the throne to leave such a black legacy behind me? A reign of infamy and lawlessness?" He sighed deeply. "I cannot count on Robert's timely death, taking Maud captive or young Henry prisoner. No, I must make plans for the future; I must ensure the succession so that this chaos does not perpetuate itself after my death."

They began to stroll slowly toward the palace. A light wind had sprung up, scattering copper-colored leaves about their feet.

The Bishop said nothing for a moment. "What do you suggest?"

"I want Eustace crowned in my lifetime."

His brother sharply drew in his breath as he came to an abrupt halt. "In your lifetime? Are you mad?"

"Why not? It's a common enough practice in Europe."

"Yes, but not in Normandy or England. Not even the Saxon kings attempted it." Henry shook his head. "Far safer to wait until Maud's forces are defeated and the throne is secure. The war can only have one outcome: We will be victorious. Then Eustace will inherit as a matter of course."

"Isn't that what our uncle assumed, that Maud would be crowned as a matter of course? Look how wrong he turned out to be. Or have you forgotten how we came to power?"

"I remember very well," he hissed, "but the circumstances are not the same."

"No, they were in our favor then, as no one wanted a female on the throne. But this time we deal with Henry of Anjou, a young male, and, like Eustace, in direct line from the Conqueror! Brother, I won't know a moment's peace unless I'm assured that my son will reign after me. If he is crowned while I live, Henry of Anjou will no longer have a valid claim and must take England by conquest alone. Which, as his mother has discovered, will not be so easy to accomplish."

The Bishop looked thoughtful. "I foresee much opposition; it will require the agreement of the Archbishop of Canterbury, who is likely to be against any change in custom." He paused. "I need time to ponder this. Henry is still too young to be a real threat, and Eustace not old enough to be crowned. The matter can be safely left for a while."

"I'll wait until Eustace is knighted, a few years hence. But no longer."

At Henry's nod, Stephen threw an arm around his shoulders and together they resumed walking in the direction of the palace. He felt much relieved. If his brother was behind him in this revolutionary plan, the matter was almost as good as done.

Chapter Twenty-three

Westminster, 1147

THE NEXT TWO YEARS DID NOT SEE AN IMPROVEMENT IN STEPHEN'S fortunes: Geoffrey of Anjou consolidated his control of Normandy and, as many barons owned land on both sides of the channel, Stephen lost those supporters who did not want to give up their Norman holdings—including his old friend and adviser, Waleran of Muelan. It was a bitter blow.

In England he was still having problems with troublesome vassals, most particularly the unpredictable Ranulf of Chester. As the result of an insignificant quarrel between them, about a now-forgotten incident, Stephen had rashly imprisoned the Earl on several trumped-up charges. As Chester was in the King's peace at the time, this caused a hue and cry among the Earl's supporters with accusations that Stephen was attempting to do to Ranulf what he had done to Roger of Salisbury years earlier. Terms were quickly negotiated for Chester's release.

Once freed, the Earl again defected to Maud's side, snarling defiance, and calling the King a treacherous swine. The upshot of this shameful episode, Stephen realized, was that many nobles, no longer trusting him, withdrew support.

One evening in April, Stephen and his entourage were seated in the great hall at Westminster, eating a light supper, when the steward announced the arrival of the Bishop of Winchester.

As the Bishop's figure came up to the high table, Stephen rose to greet him.

"What an unexpected surprise, Henry," he said with a smile. "What brings you to London?"

"A disquieting rumor," said the Bishop. "I hear that Henry of Anjou has landed on the Wareham coast with a force of one thousand men and the promise of support and funds from the Angevin party."

Stephen's face paled. He dropped his goblet of wine into the rushes, spilling half the contents over his green tunic.

"Upstart Angevin pig," Eustace snarled.

"Be quiet, Eustace."

Three young squires attempted to mop Stephen's tunic with a white cloth.

"That seems preposterous," Stephen said, waving the squires away. "You're sure it was Henry of Anjou and not Count Geoffrey who landed?"

"The problem is I can't verify any of this yet, but the report says Henry," the Bishop replied, seating himself at the high table. "Supposedly he's seized one town while putting another to the torch. I agree it seems incredible, but certainly someone has landed at Wareham with a force of men."

Robin of Leicester raised his eyebrows. "When the boy left England two years ago, he was what? Twelve years of age? He can be barely fourteen at the most. Is it possible that the Count of Anjou would be so reckless, so foolish, as to put his son in charge of such an expedition? When was this landing supposed to have taken place?"

"Three days ago now," replied the Bishop. "The word is he heads west, to join forces with his mother and uncle at Bristol."

"Where else would he go?" Stephen retorted.

"Since Count Geoffrey is neither reckless nor a fool we must discover for ourselves whether there is any truth in this wild tale," the Bishop went on. "I propose you send a troop of men to scout the area between Bristol and the coast."

Stephen rose and turned to his Flemish captain. "William, gather together a troop of five hundred men. We'll leave at once for the west country. If we travel by night and split our forces, sending some in the direction of Bristol, others toward Purton or Cricklade, we're sure to intercept the boy somewhere along the way."

"God has not forsaken us," the Bishop said, as he and Stephen left the great hall. "If we capture young Henry of Anjou the war will be as good as over. Without their heir, the Angevins will be done for."

They left the castle and followed the path down to the river.

"Speed is essential here," the Bishop continued. "Sympathy for the boy may lead men to aid him, thus rallying support for his mother's cause. That must not be allowed to happen."

"Have no fear. We will catch him, and once we do—" Stephen smiled grimly.

As they approached the Thames, filled with boats and barges sailing past, Stephen wondered what the young heir of Anjou—Maud's son —would be like. Despite his bitter resentment of this youth who threatened Eustace's inheritance, Stephen could not help but feel a secret spark of admiration for this intrepid stripling who dared cross the channel to defy him.

Worn and bedraggled, Henry of Anjou stood with his men before the gates of Cricklade Castle, shivering in the coolness of the April night.

"I'm sorry, my lord," his sergeant said in a firm voice. "To attempt to take the castle at the odds of one to ten is sheer suicide. Remember what happened at Purton?"

Henry scowled, preferring not to remember his shameful defeat at Purton Castle one week ago. He and his ragged troop of fifteen men had made a halfhearted attack on the castle, barely escaping with their lives, followed by the jeers of the King's garrison. When Henry had started out on this high-spirited adventure, against his father's express wishes, he had had no clear-cut idea of what he would do when he landed in England. Rumors had reached him that the Earl of Chester and Stephen had had a severe falling out, and as a result Ranulf had recently defected back to his mother's side once again. Henry had taken this as an indication that perhaps the time was ripe for his appearance on the English scene to give new heart to his mother's supporters. The men he had persuaded to come with him had agreed to no pay but the promise of future spoils and plunder.

In the back of Henry's mind, he saw himself, backed by a huge following of troops and arms, defeating Stephen and covering himself with glory. But not one of his mother's supporters had rushed to his aid. In order to create a positive effect he had sent out a few scouts to spread rumors that he had landed with a huge force and the promise of funds and support. But, thus far, it had produced nothing. Word must have gotten about that he had arrived with few men and no support—not even from his parents.

"My lord, it grows late," the sergeant said, glancing up at the evening shadows covering the sky. "Best we withdraw into the forest for the night and decide tomorrow what to do."

Henry glared at him. "We could lead a surprise attack when it's fully dark, while the garrison sleeps."

"The men won't risk their lives, my lord. They haven't been paid and now they see there may not be spoils to share. If the men did not admire you, my lord, most would have left by now." The sergeant paused. "Or held you for ransom to the highest bidder."

Henry gave him a fearless look. "Do you threaten me? I'm not afraid of anyone or anything," he challenged.

The sergeant bit back a smile. "No one doubts your courage, my lord, but only a fool is going to pit himself against a well-fortified castle like Cricklade without help."

As Henry and his disgruntled troop trudged listlessly into the nearby woods to spend another uncomfortable night on the damp hard ground, he prayed that his Uncle Robert and his mother would send him money and, hopefully, more men. He was only a day's journey from Bristol, and had sent a messenger yesterday morning. He should hear by tomorrow at the latest. The humiliation of having promised his men spoils which now appeared not to be forthcoming, was eating into his pride like rust into iron.

The following night, while still hanging about the vicinity of Cricklade, Henry received word from his mother and uncle. Their message said that he was risking his life by this hazardous, foolhardy undertaking; money could not be spared for such folly and he must come to Bristol at once. If Henry refused to comply, Robert's soldiers would seek him out and ship him back to Normandy in disgrace.

Henry told the sergeant about the message as they sat on the edge of the woods eating the last of a rabbit grilled on a wood fire. Henry knew there could be no thought of returning to Normandy until he had fulfilled his obligations to his men, but whom could he ask for help?

Suddenly one of his men came up to him, gasping for breath. "My lord," he said, "we are in great danger and must leave at once."

"Danger? Who threatens?" Henry jumped to his feet.

"As I followed the tracks of a stag, my lord, I saw campfires gleaming in the darkness. Curious, I went deeper into the woods to investigate and stumbled upon the King's army, not an hour away, setting up their camp."

"You're sure it was the King's forces?" Henry asked, incredulous.

"I recognized the royal standard, my lord, and the azure pavilion the King carries with him whenever he does battle. It's the enemy, sure enough, and the King himself is with them!"

"Jesu, there is no time to waste," said the sergeant. "We're but a few and no match for the King's forces. I say we head straight for Bristol."

Henry bit his lip. "Let me think."

The sergeant shook his head impatiently. "There's no time, my lord. The Angevin cause is at risk here. If King Stephen's men catch up with us they'll take you prisoner and hold you for ransom. Your father will personally slay me—by the slowest means at his disposal." He signed himself.

"Don't you think I realize all that?" After a few moments' thought, a slow smile crossed Henry's face. "I wish to send a message," he said to the sergeant.

Stephen, his brother Henry, and William of Ypres had just made camp and were now seated around a fire drinking wine when an advance party of scouts returned.

"Sire, the boy and his men are camped not an hour away," said one of the scouts. "The most dispirited, ragtag group of knaves I have ever set eyes upon. I counted fifteen, all told. We could have dispatched them like a warren of hares."

William of Ypres laughed. "One thousand men indeed!"

Stephen frowned. "Fifteen men? I can hardly believe it. I wonder if it's a trap to lure us into thinking their numbers are few. Was the boy with them?"

"Aye, Sire, he sat by the campfire, eating. I doubt it is a trap."

"How did you know it was the Angevin heir?" asked the Bishop of Winchester.

The scout paused, looking perplexed. "I—I'm not sure, my lord bishop, but there was something about the boy, something different. You couldn't miss him."

Stephen exchanged a glance with his brother. So the youth had made an impression. "Very well. I'll take fifty men with me, you keep the rest here, William, in case we are attacked from another quarter. I would see this ragtail group for myself. Brother, do you join me?"

"No, I'll wait until you bring the quarry back to the camp."

Stephen and the Bishop had just gone inside the pavilion when a guard appeared at the tent door.

"A message for you, Sire. Urgent, I'm told."

The Bishop took the wax tablet and handed it to Stephen. "Who brought it?" he asked.

"A stranger left it with the guard posted on the edge of the camp, then disappeared."

Stephen frowned. He lifted a candle in an iron holder and holding the tablet under the flickering light squinted down at the message. Suddenly he gave a shout of laughter.

"By God and all His Saints, never did I see the like!" He laughed until the tears streamed down his face. "Oh, the arrogant young rogue, the knave. By God, what brazen cheek!"

The Bishop looked at his brother in amazement.

"The boy, Henry, would you believe it? He has the gall to ask me for money! Neither his uncle nor his mother will give him any, and he promises to leave at once for Normandy if I'll send him enough money to pay his men. He ends by reminding me of our close relationship as second cousins."

A brief smile crossed the Bishop's face. "He does not lack wit at least, the presumptuous young cockerel."

"Could this be a trap set by Robert, using the boy as bait?" Stephen wondered, more sober now.

The Bishop pursed his lips, took the wax tablet from Stephen, and scanned the contents. "No, it has the ring of truth."

Stephen slipped on his mailed shirt and buckled on his sword.

"To be safe, I'll request the boy meet me alone, and keep my men hidden under cover of tree and brush. When I'm assured that he is indeed alone I'll blow my horn, the men will rush from the forest, and we'll take him prisoner."

"I would not meet young Henry in your own person," the Bishop advised. "He may become suspicious if you claim to be the king. Say you are a lord sent by the King to treat with him. The boy won't know the difference for he has never seen you. Good hunting." He rose to his feet and left the pavilion.

A short time later, a squire poked his head through the tent door. "Your horse is saddled, Sire, and the men waiting."

"Good. I'll join you in a moment."

Stephen saw his ivory horn protruding from a leather saddlebag, and bent to remove it. As his hand reached into the bag it encountered a small leather pouch filled with silver coins. He hesitated, then slowly withdrew the pouch, weighing it in his hand. Without quite knowing why, he stuffed the pouch into the purse fastened to his belt, then slipped the horn's cord around his neck, blew out the candle, and left the pavilion.

It was still dark when Henry felt an arm shaking him awake.

"An emissary from King Stephen," the sergeant whispered in an excited voice.

Henry threw off the cloak that covered him and sat up abruptly, rubbing his eyes. "Did he bring money?"

"I think so," the sergeant replied. "He shook a leather pouch and it sounded like coins."

"Was he alone?"

"I could neither see nor hear anyone else, yet I like it not. It has the smell of a trap. I say we make our escape while we can."

"You worry like an old woman. If he's come with the money then all is well." Henry grinned. "There's nothing to fear."

Hastily he dressed, wishing his garments were cleaner and did not smell so strongly. Through the trees a faint pink glow heralded the break of day. He followed the sergeant deeper within the woods to where a tall man waited beside a horse. Although it was still too dark to see the man's face clearly, Henry could detect an unusual presence about him. Surely this was no common emissary but some highborn lord sent to treat with him. Trying to mask his excitement, he squared his shoulders, lifting his head proudly.

"Henry of Anjou?" the man asked softly. When Henry nodded, he took a few steps toward him. "King Stephen honors his second cousin. He wishes to know what your intentions were when you made this voyage?"

Henry felt himself flush. He cleared his throat. "Well, to be honest, I had hoped to raise support for my mother's cause, but matters didn't fall out that way."

"I see. We heard initially that you landed with a thousand men. Did Count Geoffrey or your mother aid you in this venture?"

"Oh no, my lord. Neither of them knew anything about it until I'd left Normandy. In fact, I have greatly displeased them. I'm commanded to go at once to Bristol and then return home." He paused. "I spread the rumor about the thousand men myself."

There was a faint chuckle from the man. "Did you indeed! Tell me, why do you want the money if you return home?"

Henry hesitated. "Well, in truth, I promised my men—there are only a few—either pay or spoils and I . . . well . . . my uncle and mother would not give me any money—" He was so mortified that he could not continue, but rubbed his booted foot into the mossy forest floor.

"No need to explain further," the man said. "I quite understand. To keep faith with your men is the first sign of a good commander."

To hear himself referred to as a good commander was balm to his wounded pride. Henry's chest swelled and he found himself drawn to this courtly knight. Quite unexpectedly, the man threw him a leather pouch which Henry caught with one hand.

"King Stephen bids you take the money and leave for Wareham immediately. From there you will set sail for Normandy."

Henry hefted the bag. Enough, more than enough it felt like, to pay his men, their passage back to Normandy, and some left over. He could hardly believe it, and found himself much moved by this princely gesture from one who was his avowed enemy.

"I'm most grateful to King Stephen," he stammered, looking up at the man towering over him. "I will never forget his kindness to me this day."

There was a long silence while the two curiously examined each other. In the dawn light, Henry could now see the knight's face clearly: Beneath the hood of his cloak, golden brown hair, streaked with white, curled damply on his brow. A pair of warm green eyes dancing with golden lights illuminated a strongly sculpted face with high cheekbones and mobile lips. The man reached out and gently tilted Henry's face toward the sun.

"Your mother's eyes," he murmured with a catch in his voice.

"You know my mother?" Henry asked, amazed.

"At one time, yes." The man dropped his hand but not before Henry had glimpsed his massive gold ring set with precious stones flashing in the pale sunlight. "The King says that if he finds you or your men in these parts by midday he will take you captive. Be warned and leave now."

"Yes, yes, I leave at once, upon my honor." Henry hesitated. "May one ask your name, my lord?"

"My name is not important. Let us just say one who wishes you

Godspeed." As he spoke, the man mounted his horse. "Fare well, young Henry of Anjou." Turning his mount toward the east, he was soon lost to view.

Thoughtful, Henry walked back through the forest to join his men. He held up the bag of coins and was greeted with cheers. Later, as he told his men of the encounter with the King's emissary, the sergeant asked him to describe the ring again.

"I've seen Stephen of Blois many a time when he was in Normandy, before he assumed the throne, but in the dark I didn't recognize him. That sounds like the ring he always wore, right enough. Green eyes, you say, tall, hair like honey in the comb. God's teeth, that could only be the King himself."

The men spoke among themselves, looking speculatively at Henry.

"A courtly man, is this king," Henry said, wonderingly. "So have I heard men say and now I know it to be true. But in his place I would have withheld assistance and taken me captive for a goodly ransom."

He threw back his head and laughed aloud, a joyous, innocent sound that rang through the stillness of the forest. "Which is why I will win, by God's splendor," he cried, with all the boundless confidence of youth. "Yes, I will win and he will lose."

Chapter Twenty-four

Bristol, 1147

Robert of gloucester lay dying.

In late October, five months after Henry had returned to Normandy, Maud sat by her half-brother's bed in his chamber at Bristol Castle, reading aloud a letter from her son written by one of Geoffrey's clerics.

"Henry claims that next time he will come with enough men to conquer Stephen." She folded the parchment with a sigh. "I could almost envy such confidence."

"Does the young hothead think he can count on the King's chivalry a second time?" Robert mused. "I still cannot imagine what prompted Stephen to give the boy money."

Nor could she, Maud thought, wishing she had been a silent witness to the meeting between them. Despite her sense of relief at Stephen's magnanimous—if incredulous—gesture, she could not help but wonder if Stephen had any inkling that he had come face to face with his own flesh and blood. It seemed impossible, yet there was a faint nagging doubt in her mind. On the other hand, how could he keep such vital knowledge to himself? Just the mere suggestion of her adultery and Henry's bastardy would raise such a hue and outcry she would be forever discredited, Henry would be removed as a threat, and the conflict would be over.

She comforted herself with the thought that Stephen did not know.

"Typical of Stephen, isn't it?" Robert was saying now. "Arundel all over again. Almost as if he *knows* that in the end Henry will be king." Suddenly he moaned, a spasm of pain crossing his face. Alarmed, Maud leaned forward. "What ails you?" She beckoned a servitor who sat in a corner of the chamber. "Shall Garth fetch you something? Wine?"

Robert shook his head and closed his eyes. Helpless to aid him, Maud had watched in fearful concern as her half-brother grew weaker and weaker ever since that fateful morning four months ago when he had quite suddenly become unconscious. When Robert woke two days later he could not move his right arm and the right side of his body was completely paralyzed. His speech had been unintelligible at first but slowly he recovered. He still could not move his right side, however, and the physicians claimed they were unable to help him further. They warned that he was dying. Now his remaining hair was entirely white, his body so frail that he looked almost transparent.

"You know, I've been thinking about Stephen quite a lot lately," Robert said in his slow careful speech. "The past has been on my mind a great deal." He slowly turned his head to look deeply into Maud's eyes. "You know, Sister, I sometimes wonder, if I had it to do over again, would I have counseled you to invade England?"

Maud felt the blood drain from her face. "What . . . what an extraordinary thing to say."

"Pursuit of the crown does not appear to have brought happiness to either you or Stephen, certainly not to the populace of England. Do you ever think of what you have sacrificed for this venture?"

"Never. From the time my father sent me to Germany at nine years of age I knew that I could never lead the life of an ordinary woman. I was bred to regard myself as consort to a great ruler, with equal responsibilities. Surely that is enough."

"Is it? What of love, contentment, raising one's children in peace and plenty? Do you tell me such thoughts have never crossed your mind?"

Maud's heart skipped a beat. Why was Robert questioning her like this? "Perhaps such thoughts have occurred to me," she replied, somewhat unwillingly. "I may even have been tempted to give up the struggle, but in the end I always came back to what is important:

the crown of England and the ducal throne of Normandy. Do you remember what our father always said?"

" 'A great ruler does not lead his own life but the lives of his subjects,' " Robert quoted. " 'Personal happiness must be sacrificed for the public good.' " He paused. "How often did I carry those words enshrined in my heart like a talisman. Now I wonder."

"Wonder what?"

"My life was lived in the service of others and I never questioned it. For you, the struggle and the sacrifices may well have been worth it for you never had a fulfilling marriage. You have never known anything else. But left to myself, I would have enjoyed a quiet life watching my children grow, tending my lands, hunting, and pursuing my own interests."

Maud found her brother's words disturbing. Was he blaming her for a misspent life? Implying that he had had no choice but to serve her?

"I see I've upset you with my fancies. Be at peace for I regret nothing. These are questions that only occur to one at the end."

At his reassuring smile Maud nodded, recognizing that he had come to terms with himself in some way she did not yet fully understand.

The next afternoon Robert died.

Two days later Brian FitzCount arrived to attend the burial services.

"I'm deeply sorry for your great loss," Brian said to Maud as they warmed themselves before a fire in the great hall of Bristol Castle. "For *our* great loss. We will not see Robert's like again." He paused. "You return to Normandy now?"

Lifting the black veil from her face, Maud nodded. "What else can I do? In Normandy, at least, the conflict is over and Geoffrey victorious. My own funds are totally depleted and Geoffrey refuses to send any more. Now that he has firmly secured the duchy he has lost what little interest he ever had in England." She looked at Brian with shadowed eyes. "I would give anything to be able to remain but without funds I'm helpless. And now that Robert is gone, I fear that many of my supporters will go too."

"Don't give up hope. God will not desert us. Whether you're here or in Normandy, those of us who are left will continue to fight on in your name, knowing that one day you must return to us."

"Thank you for that, Brian." Maud paused. "Did you know that at the end Robert said Henry will be king? Not that I will be queen, but that Henry will be king."

"It comes to the same thing in the end."

"Does it?" She sighed. "It feels as if my entire life has been spent in pursuit of the crown. The longer I strive the more it eludes me. I had always intended for Henry to rule after me, of course." She turned on him, tears glistening in her eyes. "After me," she repeated in a choked voice, "not instead."

Brian took her trembling hands in his. "Trust in the natural, right order of things, Maud. Whether you or Henry, in the end justice will be served."

"Justice? Where is the justice?" Maud burst out passionately. "Stephen is the one who has done the vicious deed, taking my throne, forswearing his oath."

Brian regarded her steadily. "And Stephen is not having an easy time of it. Since his patron, Pope Innocent, died, the Bishop of Winchester is no longer Papal Legate and is shorn of power. The current pope is a disciple of Bernard of Clairvaux, who hates the Bishop, as he hates all the Cluniac order. There is now real trouble brewing between Stephen and the church in Rome. In time this will work to our advantage." He paused. "Matilda is seriously ill, an ague in the chest. And Eustace, I understand, is a constant thorn in his father's side. At this moment Stephen is more deserving of your pity than your wrath."

Why should I be merciful? she wanted to ask Brian. That devious weathercock, Bishop Henry, was finally reaping what he had sowed. She could not spare a drop of sympathy for his plight. Yet part of her was filled with genuine regret for Matilda's illness. She could readily understand Stephen's fear of losing his devoted wife, his terrible disappointment over the malevolent Eustace. Her cousin had, indeed, a heavy cross to bear. Maud could only thank the Holy Mother a thousand times over for bestowing upon her a son like Henry.

But as far as her own feelings for Stephen were concerned, Maud knew she dared not crack the shell of anger and bitterness she had erected around her heart. That shell was her only protection; without it the full force of her love would be unleashed to rise up and utterly consume her. The very possibility was so appalling that she crushed it from her consciousness as she might a viper underfoot.

• • •

Her fortunes at their lowest ebb, Maud left Bristol within the week. Upon reaching the Wareham coast she boarded a small vessel that would take her to Normandy. Maud's hands gripped the rail of the deck when the captain swung the ship's prow toward the open, green-waved sea. A biting wind whipped her cloak about her body. As the distance lengthened between the vessel and the shore she wondered what would be the circumstances for her return to England? For return she would; she must never let herself believe otherwise.

Chapter Twenty-five

Essex, 1148

In the autumn of 1148, a year after Maud had left England, Stephen journeyed to Hedingham Castle in Essex where Matilda lay gravely ill. He had been there less than a week when the Earl of Leicester brought him word from Rheims that rumors were afoot that the new pope, as well as the Archbishop of Canterbury, would recognize Henry of Anjou as heir to the English throne.

Ever since Eugenius III had been elected to the Holy See, Stephen and Bishop Henry had been at odds with Rome. The major difficulty, of course, was that this Pope was a disciple of Bernard of Clairvaux, the powerful, charismatic Cistercian monk whose influence extended all across Europe.

To make matters worse, after Stephen had knighted Eustace last winter and ordered the Archbishop of Canterbury to crown the boy king while he still lived, the mild and unassuming Theobald of Bec had proved surprisingly stubborn, refusing to go against custom, tradition, and his own conscience. In a humiliating interview Theobald had accused Stephen of obtaining the throne by perjury. If he had known of this infamy at the time, he said, he never would have agreed to serve the King in any capacity, and he was certainly not going to support Eustace. The new pope had backed the Archbishop's decision.

Angered by Theobald's unwillingness to obey him, Stephen had forbidden him to attend a mandatory church council called for by the Pope in Rheims. To everyone's amazement, Theobald had sailed secretly across the channel in a leaky boat to attend the council. Stephen, thoroughly enraged by this act of defiance, subsequently banished him from the realm. In support of his brother, Bishop Henry committed his own act of defiance by refusing to attend the Pope's council.

The end result was an almost complete break with Rome, the excommunication of the Bishop of Winchester, and the clergy's even deeper distrust of Stephen. England fell under interdict; Eustace was no nearer to being crowned.

"I knew that sanctimonious old fool, Theobald, would somehow betray us," Bishop Henry now said, his voice tight with hostility. "You shouldn't have banished him, Stephen."

Stephen and his brother, accompanied by Robin of Leicester and Eustace, were leaving the chapel after Vespers to return to the great hall. "But you agreed that I should banish him for attending the church council against my orders!"

"It was a mistake to forbid Theobald to attend the council merely because he followed the dictates of his own conscience," Robin commented, watching Henry with cool eyes. "And an even worse mistake for you not to have attended the council, Your Grace. This whole business has been sadly bungled from start to finish."

"So mistakes have been made! Mea culpa! Mea summa culpa!" Henry signed himself. "I don't recall *your* voice raised in protest at the time, Leicester. And as for you, Brother, may I remind you that Henry of Anjou would not now be a threat if you had held him captive instead of sending him home, far richer than when he came, thus making us the laughingstock of Europe!"

Would he ever live down that incredible piece of folly, Stephen wondered, still finding it hard to believe that the seemingly helpless, charming youth who had so moved him in the forest had become such a formidable foe.

"Let us not rake up the past," he said, anxious to retreat from the shameful incident, "but deal with the present. Henry, what do we do with this news from Rheims?"

Henry sniffed. "How can I presume to advise you after my gross errors in judgment."

"You must effect a reconciliation with the Archbishop, Sire, for until you do England will remain under interdict," Robin said as they

paused at the entrance to the hall. "Nor will the Pope lift His Grace
of Winchester's excommunication until Theobald of Bec is returned
to favor and your brother makes amends to Rome."

"My Lord of Leicester is right. How can I be crowned unless you
make peace with the Archbishop?" Eustace asked in his petulant
voice.

Stephen turned wearily to his brother. "Henry, I ask you again for
your counsel."

The Bishop sighed. "We have no choice but to bring Theobald
back. Once he returns, however, tell him he *must* crown Eustace and
you will not take no for an answer. Be firm. Meanwhile, I will try to
make my peace with the Pope and persuade him to lift my excommunication."

"Father!" Stephen's youngest son, William, pale and red-eyed,
was racing across the hall toward them. "Mother has taken a sudden
turn for the worse and the physicians want you to come immediately."

"Dear God, she was better this morning! I'm coming at once."

When, moments later, he burst into the solar, Stephen looked in
horror at Matilda's waxy face, her hands clasped over the silver crucifix on her breast.

"How is she?" Stephen asked the physicians.

"She won't survive the night, Sire," one of them said. "We've
given her a draught of wine and poppy to ease her breathing, but
there's little more we can do. She has been given the last rites and
will die in God's grace."

"But I don't understand," Stephen said, his belly plummeting in
dread. "She seemed so much better this morning. What can have
happened?"

Another of the physicians spread his hands. "Who can question
God's will, Sire?"

"Matilda, beloved," Stephen whispered as he bent over her, aware
of the labored breath wheezing in her throat.

Matilda, drowsy from the effects of the poppy, slowly opened her
eyes. "Stephen," she whispered, "has Theobald returned from the
council yet? Has he agreed to crown Eustace?"

Although she appeared to have forgotten that the Archbishop of
Canterbury had been forbidden to return, it was just like Matilda,
even at the hour of her death, to think first of her son.

"Theobald has returned and agreed to crown Eustace, beloved,"

Stephen replied, smoothing back pale wisps of hair from her damp forehead. "All is in hand." He would make certain that what he told her became the truth.

A wave of relief passed across Matilda's face. "Then my job is done," she whispered. "You must promise me that you will never again offend Holy Church. Our son must be crowned."

"I promise. Rest in peace, for all that you have worked and prayed for has come to pass," Stephen said. He bent to kiss her cheek.

"Stephen—" Matilda's eyes suddenly clouded over in a spasm of pain. "Stephen, there is one last matter—I've never dared to ask you, but now it weighs heavily on my mind. My heart has been so troubled—" She turned her head away.

His body stiffened in protest. Dear God, if it was what he feared . . . He pulled himself together, already knowing how he would respond. "You may ask me anything, dear heart."

"Maud—did you ever truly love her?" Her voice was barely audible. "I . . . would know the truth before I die." Tears trembled in her eyes, and Stephen, wondering how long she had known, could only guess at the agony she must have suffered in silence all these years.

"Never," he lied with complete conviction. "Never. I was possessed by lust that gripped me like a wasted fever. It has long since passed. I've only truly loved one woman: you." He took the silver crucifix from between her hands, pressing it to his lips. "By the body of Our Lord, before God and all His Saints, I swear it." The silver seemed to sear his mouth like a flame. "May I be damned forever if aught but the truth has passed my lips."

At the look of radiant happiness that flooded his wife's face, giving her the illusion of beauty, Stephen knew that if his false oath caused him to suffer the torments of hell for all eternity, it would be well worth it to have given his loyal wife this moment of absolute joy.

Matilda died shortly after Matins. Dry-eyed amid a weeping crowd of mourners, Stephen brushed aside his brother's offer to pray with him in the chapel. He stumbled out of the chamber to walk alone in the grounds.

Outside it was cold, the night sky crowned with a thousand silver stars. How could he go on, Stephen wondered in anguish, how could he live with the immense burden of guilt and shame he carried? Suddenly he threw himself down onto the soft, moist earth sobbing as if his heart would crack in two, his body heaving with the force of his grief. Finally spent, he sat up, wiping his eyes upon the sleeve of his tunic. He took deep breaths until he felt calmer. The intensity of his torment lessened, as if he had purged himself of some poison.

He felt a sudden need to talk to someone, to unburden himself of a lifetime of thoughts and feelings never before revealed. It occurred to him that, except for Henry, he had no one, and, in this instance, his brother would not serve his needs. The companions of his youth —Brian, Robert, the de Beaumont twins—were either dead or estranged from him. Only one person remained to whom he could open his heart and soul, one person who would understand.

Tonight, despite all the enmity that had passed between them, Stephen felt an overpowering need for his cousin. In a silent cry for help, his spirit reached out to touch her. Maud, Maud. A vast silence answered him.

At that moment, he realized that for the remainder of his life he would be alone. His one goal, the only purpose he had left, was to fulfill Matilda's last wish: Eustace must be crowned.

To his surprise, Stephen found he could not wait to relieve himself of that golden symbol of his royal authority. The crown he had so desperately desired, connived and betrayed for, fought for so ruthlessly, had become a crown of thorns. He would be well rid of it. Looking up at the clusters of winking stars, he stretched his arms above his head, remembering that various nobles, Waleran of Muelan among them, had taken the cross and joined a new crusade to free the Holy Land.

I will see Eustace crowned, he decided, ensure the realm is safe from Henry of Anjou, then join a group of knights on crusade. A journey to the Holy Land would be just what he needed to expiate his sins. What better way to seek God's forgiveness? It would be a new beginning. Stephen's heart quickened at the prospect, and he felt Matilda's benign presence gently smiling her approval.

Chapter Twenty-six

Normandy, 1149

In APRIL OF 1149, HENRY OF ANJOU FACED HIS PARENTS IN THE GREAT hall of the ducal palace in Rouen.

"I wish to cross the channel to be knighted by my great-uncle of Scotland," he announced.

It was a request Maud had been expecting—and dreading—ever since word reached Normandy that Earl Ranulf of Chester, once again in Maud's camp, had joined forces with King David of Scotland against Stephen. Maud knew Henry would find some excuse to sail for England, although she was positive his true intention was to stir up trouble against the enemy. The knighting provided a reason with which few could argue.

"You're so young," she reminded him, more for form's sake than anything else.

"Sixteen is not too young to be knighted. I've campaigned with my father all over Normandy and Anjou for the past two years now. I'm a man, and fit to be honored as such."

"Of course you are," Maud said with a sigh. "Very well, if you're determined to go, travel only to Scotland for your knighting, then return at once to Normandy. If you keep to the west country, make no show of arms or let your identity be known, no harm should befall you."

"I understand," Henry replied with an air of compliance that did not fool her for a moment.

"The boy wouldn't be foolish enough to attempt another campaign in England," Geoffrey said. "It's still far too dangerous," he warned Henry, "and your mother's supporters say the time is not yet ripe. In any case a small escort is all I can spare you, which should be sufficient if you go only to be knighted."

"Fair enough, my lord." Henry bowed formally to Count Geoffrey, pristine as always in a new indigo tunic.

When Henry kissed her warmly on each cheek, Maud held back the impulse to cling to him. She knew perfectly well that he would ignore sound advice and, however foolhardy, follow his own bent. After all, he was his father's son as well as hers. For good or ill, both she and Stephen had pursued their own headlong courses regardless of the hazards. She could almost hear Aldyth's words echoing in her head: "How far does the apple fall from the tree?"

"Take care, my son," she whispered. As her eyes followed him out the hall, she prayed that he would not meet up with Stephen's forces. Whenever she imagined her son and his father face to face on a battlefield she felt as if she would drown in a dark pool of anguish. Yet one day it must happen if she were ever to regain the crown.

Retreating from the unbearable thought, Maud closeted herself in the solar to write a long message to Brian FitzCount, still holding his own at Wallingford, asking him to keep an eye on her impetuous son. Beyond that she was powerless to help him.

Six weeks later one of her uncle David's clerics wrote on his master's behalf to inform Maud that on the Mass of the Pentecost, May 22, the King of Scotland had knighted his great-nephew. Misty-eyed, she could imagine Henry in the requisite purple robe and cloth-of-gold tunic, holding his shield engraved with gold lions in one hand, the ash-tipped spear in the other. Surrounded by hairy clansmen and dour Scottish lords she could just see him kneeling reverently before his great-uncle to receive the open-handed sword blow that would dub him Sir Henry Fitz-Empress. Now an invincible knight, Henry probably assumed that Stephen's defeat was a foregone conclusion, and England his for the taking. Maud's heart ached for his courageous innocence.

Not long after this, just as Maud had feared, she heard that Henry had persuaded his great-uncle and Earl Ranulf to ravage the north of England and march as far south as York. Here they were met by Stephen's superior forces and, much against Henry's will, forced to retreat.

In December a message arrived from Brian FitzCount informing Maud that despite being pursued by Prince Eustace, Henry had managed to reach Bristol in safety. Here he had been well received by his cousin, William of Gloucester, whom he had persuaded to ride to the south of England to harry Stephen's supporters there. By this time, Brian went on to say, Henry had picked up quite a following, having had quite a success in Devon and Dorset. At Bridport, he had even forced Stephen's lieutenant to take refuge in his castle.

"Listen to this," Maud told Geoffrey, tears in her eyes as she read from Brian's letter. " 'I've finally persuaded him to return to Normandy and the New Year should see him once more in Rouen. Do not be too harsh on Henry when he returns. Although he cannot as yet hope to defeat Stephen, the boy has acquitted himself with honor. Knighted by a royal monarch, he has successfully won the minor skirmishes he fought, evaded capture, and gained many new adherents to his cause. England will not soon forget this young lion of Anjou.' "

Normandy, 1150

IN JANUARY OF THE NEW YEAR, 1150, MAUD SAT IN THE ANCIENT CHAIR that had belonged to the Dukes of Normandy since time out of mind. Geoffrey stood behind her. Henry, elated as a result of his recent triumphs, marched into the ducal palace and up to the dais.

"Despite the fact that I consider you headstrong and disobedient and foolish," Geoffrey of Anjou said, with a severe look, "one cannot deny that you have proven yourself a leader of men and a courageous soldier." A proud smile briefly warmed his cold, handsome face.

Henry watched his beautiful russet-haired mother echo the smile.

"In consequence," Maud said quietly, "I have agreed to withdraw my official claim to the duchy of Normandy." She paused. "To withdraw my claim in your favor, my son. As soon as you swear homage to your overlord, the King of France, you will become Duke of Normandy." The hint of a tear glistened in the corner of one gray eye.

To Henry's astonishment, Geoffrey, in an unprecedented gesture, briefly touched his wife's shoulder. Henry bowed respectfully to his father, then threw himself on one knee before his mother. Seizing her hand, he brought it to his lips, kissing the slender jeweled fingers with passionate devotion, so choked with emotion he could barely speak.

"I will be worthy of you, Madam my mother. I swear it upon the head of my great-grandfather, the Conqueror, on the head of my grandfather Henry, that I will be worthy of this great honor you bestow upon me."

Henry had always known the depths of his mother's ambition; he understood only too well what this gesture had cost her. Before God, he vowed, he would see to it that she never regretted her decision. But inside he was bubbling over with a wild anticipation: Normandy was his. Next—England.

Chapter Twenty-seven

Normandy, 1151

It was eighteen months before Henry was officially recognized as Duke of Normandy by Louis of France. During that time, to Maud's dismay, the French king, aided by Prince Eustace of England, marched on Normandy's borders. Maud feared a full-scale war was unavoidable, but when Louis suddenly fell ill, hostilities ceased immediately. Peace terms were arranged by Bernard of Clairvaux, who claimed divine intervention had avoided bloodshed. An incensed Eustace, threatening vengeance, was persuaded to return to England.

Accompanied by Geoffrey, Henry left for France to pay homage to King Louis, his nominal overlord. As they were expected to be gone as long as ten days, Maud agreed to stay behind and keep an eye on Normandy. In truth she welcomed the brief respite. Ever since Matilda's death Stephen had been almost constantly on her mind. Now that he was a widower did he ever think of her, she wondered, ashamed of the ridiculous thought. She was still married to Geoffrey and Stephen's avowed enemy. Holy Mother, would this tragic conflict ever end, she thought despairingly, a conflict now continued by Henry and Eustace, who were also half-brothers.

The homage ceremony was held in Paris, and still Geoffrey and

Henry did not return. Disquieting gossip filtered back to Maud that Henry had become enamored of Louis's wife, Eleanor of Aquitaine. A woman of rare beauty and strong will, the French queen held in her own right the wealthiest fief in all France. It had long been rumored that as Eleanor had failed to give France an heir, Louis, with the blessing of Holy Church, was going to have the marriage annulled on the grounds that he and his wife were too closely related—third or fourth cousins.

When Henry did return it was without the Count who, he informed Maud, had decided to visit Anjou and see how his second son, Geoffrey, was managing the Angevin estates in his absence. As he sat in her solar the morning after his return, Maud noted that her son, lolling in a wooden armchair, booted feet stretched out to the charcoal brazier, looked like a self-satisfied tomcat. So the rumors were probably true. She dismissed her women, then resumed work on the square of embroidery in her lap.

"I hear you have become very friendly with Louis's wife," she said, coming right to the point.

"Not Louis's wife for long—but mine."

Maud gasped, pricked herself with the needle and drew blood. "So there *will* be an annulment."

"And a wedding shortly thereafter. Do you disapprove?"

With an effort of will Maud concealed her shock. "Would it matter? It is not for me to approve or disapprove. But I do understand Eleanor's appeal. With Aquitaine added to Normandy and, one day, Anjou, you will rule over more land than the King of France—and become the most powerful prince west of the Rhine." She paused. "Most important, of course, you will have all the resources needed to invade England."

Henry gave her a broad grin. "I knew you would immediately grasp the essential point. Louis will not like my acquisition of Eleanor's duchy, but . . ." He shrugged.

"My son . . ." Maud's voice faltered. Henry had every reason to be jubilant for it was a golden opportunity, yet she could not deny her doubts about this sophisticated woman, eleven years Henry's senior. "Do you love her?"

Henry looked amazed. "What an extraordinary question. Does it matter? We suit each other in every way. She will make a fine consort who will bear *me* sons. In any case there is nothing I would not do to gain England. You of all people should understand that. After what we have been through—the struggles, the battles, the losses—now the crown is almost within reach."

For a moment Maud was silent, remembering that brief period of glory at Winchester when she had believed herself to be invincible, a heartbeat away from the throne, the crown virtually within her grasp. Was everything Henry said true, including the unimportance he gave love? asked a voice in her head. It was a question she could not answer.

Barely a week after Henry had returned from Paris, a herald from Anjou entered the great hall in Rouen Castle where Maud and Henry were seated at supper shortly after Vespers.

"My lord, Countess," the herald gasped. "I bring sad tidings from your sons in Angers. Count Geoffrey is dead."

Maud sat frozen to her seat in shock.

"Dead?" Henry rose to his feet.

"On his way back to Anjou, overheated from the journey, he bathed in the cold waters of the Loire. By dawn he was in a high fever. The next day he died."

Try as she might Maud could not believe he was dead. She had never loved Geoffrey of Anjou, never much liked him in fact. Her heart had been given elsewhere. But she had borne Geoffrey two children, grown to respect his prowess as a cunning campaigner, and admired his unexpected astuteness as a ruler of both Anjou and Normandy. Without him the duchy would not now belong to Henry. For more than twenty years their lives and purposes had been intertwined. She could not weep for him, but she deeply regretted that he had not lived long enough to see Henry become Duke of Aquitaine and herself Queen of England.

Maud and Henry arrived in Le Mans to find plans for an impressive funeral already under way. It was rumored that hundreds from Anjou and Maine would flock to Le Mans to see their popular lord buried. The day after their arrival, Geoffrey's will was read. A surprising clause in the will stipulated that Henry, as eldest son, would inherit Anjou and Maine—unless he became King of England. Then he would forfeit the county, which would pass to the second son, Geoffrey. Furthermore, the Count's body must remain unburied until all three sons swore an oath to fulfill their father's wishes. The funeral was immediately postponed.

The will's contents shocked everyone. Henry, throwing one of his famous temper tantrums, flatly refused to swear the oath, causing immediate trouble between himself and his brother Geoffrey. Maud was forced to watch her sons quarrel violently over their inheritance.

But in the end, at her insistence, Henry grudgingly swore to abide by his father's wishes. Under no illusions about her son, Maud knew that her ambitious Henry would never give up Anjou when he became King of England. In the unprincipled tradition of his Norman forebears, he would seize power whenever and wherever he could, regardless of the cost. He wanted it all: Count of Anjou, Duke of Normandy and Aquitaine, as well as King of England. Would he ever have enough? she wondered.

Geoffrey of Anjou was buried in the church of St. Julien, the same church in which he had been married, on a warm September day, brilliant with sunshine. Inside the church someone had surrounded the bier with armfuls of the golden broom Geoffrey had so loved. Maud noticed tears running down the cheeks of those who passed by his coffin. Despite his years in Normandy, Geoffrey had lived and died a true Angevin and was deeply mourned by his subjects. A black veil concealing her face, Maud gazed down at her husband's body. Geoffrey was dressed in his favorite blue and green, a blue cap with its sprig of broom perched on his head. His love for the bright yellow flower, the *planta-genesta*, had caused him to adopt it as his surname —Plantagenet. The lions upon his mantle, tunic and shield were made of gold. Precious gems adorned his belt and collar. The very picture of elegance, in death Geoffrey the Handsome looked exactly as he would have wished.

Still dry-eyed, Maud wondered why Geoffrey had never discussed his will with her. He must have known the unexpected clause would cause an uproar, setting his sons against each other. What could have possessed him to insert it? It was almost as if—no, impossible, Maud reasoned, yet the niggling thought would not be stilled. Suppose, yes, suppose Geoffrey had always wondered if his eldest son had sprung from his own loins. Had, in fact, half-suspected Stephen of being the father? Then the clause made sense: If Henry attained his own father's throne of England, then Geoffrey wanted his natural son to inherit his own county of Anjou.

Maud would never know; her husband had taken his secret with him. Was it remotely possible he had surmised the truth and kept silent all these years? Never revealing, by word or gesture, what must have been a stunning blow to his pride, always behaving as a devoted and dutiful father to his rival's son? A tear splashed down on Geoffrey of Anjou's comely features, remote and cool in death as in life, as Maud wept, at last, over the dead body of her husband.

Chapter Twenty-eight

Normandy, 1152

MAUD AND HENRY REMAINED IN ANJOU UNTIL THE NEW YEAR, 1152, when they returned to Normandy. In April Henry received word that the marriage of the King and Queen of France had been annulled and Eleanor had returned to her own lands of Aquitaine. Henry immediately made plans to join her.

Maud stood in the courtyard of the ducal palace in Rouen watching Henry's last-minute preparations for his journey to Aquitaine.

"Such haste is unseemly. After all, the annulment is only weeks old," Maud told her son. "Your time would be better spent making plans to invade England."

Henry gave her an exasperated look. "What else am I doing? My marriage to Eleanor gives me unlimited credit to finance the English invasion. Really, Maman, I'm not such a fool as you seem to think."

"Indeed? You know there will be trouble if you marry Eleanor without Louis's consent," Maud continued.

"We have been over this matter countless times," Henry retorted. "The marriage is annulled. It's no affair of Louis's if I marry his former queen."

"Not as Eleanor's ex-husband, no, but as Duchess of Aquitaine, Louis is her overlord, and no heiress can marry without her overlord's consent. You know perfectly well what Louis's reaction will be when he discovers he's about to lose his wealthiest fief to Normandy."

"Well, he mustn't find out until we're already married. I don't want to find the entire French army between me and Aquitaine."

Maud gave him a steely look. "Then why do you take such a retinue of knights, squires, and sumpter horses? Go quietly, make no show, call no attention to yourself in any way. You'll put the wolf off the scent."

"You're right," Henry said. "I should have thought of that." He gave her an impudent grin. "But then I have you to do half my thinking for me, don't I?" He leaned over to kiss her on the cheek. "All of it, if I allowed."

Maud could not help but smile. Henry could be so disarming when he chose—just like his father, she thought. Sometimes, when she least expected it, he reminded her so much of Stephen that she could hardly bear it.

When Henry had gone, Maud's thoughts continued to dwell on Stephen. Eagerly following events in England, Maud knew he was beset by difficulties on all fronts: trouble with the vicious Eustace; his barons, if not in open rebellion against him, went their own way; and the church condemned almost all his actions. Backed by Rome, Theobald of Bec continued to refuse to crown Eustace. Enraged by his refusal, as well as that of the other bishops who supported Canterbury, Stephen had had the bishops locked up in Oxford Castle. Maud's heart ached for his dilemma. Reason told her Stephen was making a disastrous mistake in this harsh treatment of his prelates, yet, she thought with a sigh, what would we not do to see our children crowned?

A fortnight later Maud heard that Henry and Eleanor had been married quietly, and without incident, at Poitiers on the eighteenth of May.

No sooner had Henry returned to Normandy, leaving Eleanor behind to follow at a later date, than all that Maud had feared came to pass. Louis of France, incensed by the marriage, and calling it unholy and unlawful, ordered his vassal, Henry, Duke of Normandy, to appear before his court to answer for his disgraceful conduct.

"By God's splendor, I would be safer in the court of the devil," Henry grumbled.

"I warned you," Maud said, not without a twinge of satisfaction. Perhaps in future he would pay her more heed.

"I'm Duke of Normandy, Count of Anjou, and now Duke of Aquitaine," Henry responded with an arrogant toss of his head. "Strong enough to defy Louis in this matter. Let him rant and rave and threaten. I have no intention of going to France."

"Adding insult to injury," Maud said. "He will be beside himself."

As Maud predicted, Louis of France was furious at Henry's refusal to obey his summons. She knew he would retaliate but even she did not expect him to join forces with Prince Eustace of England and, to her horror, her own son, Geoffrey of Anjou.

"I'm sure they intend to attack your possessions on the continent, with the intention of dividing among themselves whatever they seize," she warned Henry, sick at heart at the thought of her second son turning against his brother.

"That may be their intention," Henry replied grimly, "but it will never come to pass."

While Maud waited anxiously in Rouen, Henry gathered together a huge force of men and arms to march against the French king. She was relieved to hear that after a few brief, indecisive battles, he had forced Louis to retreat across the border back into France. Henry then marched against his brother Geoffrey, who had barricaded himself in a stronghold on the Loire. Maud, determined to avoid bloodshed between her sons, intervened. She rode to where Geoffrey was established, and persuaded him to agree to Henry's terms for peace. Eustace, unexpectedly summoned by his father, sailed hurriedly for England. The immediate danger was over almost as soon as it had begun.

For the moment, at least, Henry had been successful, but Maud knew that precious time had been lost. Time that should have been spent preparing to invade England.

Henry traveled to Anjou to reassert his authority in the county, then on to Aquitaine before returning to Normandy. He brought Eleanor, now six months pregnant, back with him, arriving at Rouen in time for the Christmas festivities.

Within a week after Henry's return to Rouen an urgent message arrived from Brian FitzCount in England: Stephen and Eustace had brought a large force to Wallingford, apparently determined to finally take this stronghold that had stubbornly and successfully resisted the crown for fifteen years. All approaches to Wallingford had been blocked, the supply lines cut off, and Brian feared they could not hold out without help. Henry must come to their aid at once for the whole Angevin cause in England hung in the balance.

"You must go to England, Henry," Maud told her son, seated

across from him in her father's small stone chamber. "We cannot abandon Brian. The moment we have been waiting for is at hand."

"I agree, but Louis still remains a threat not only to Normandy but to Aquitaine as well. If I spread my forces too thin I lose on all fronts. And suppose my brother again decides to stir up trouble in Anjou?"

"Sufficient men must remain here so Normandy can be defended should need arise. Geoffrey you may leave safely to me," Maud said with an iron glint in her eye. "Don't forget that Eleanor will be here to keep an eye on Aquitaine should Louis seek to cross its borders. The duchy will remain loyal to her. It is now or never, Henry."

"It's a risk—"

"The only place without risk is the grave," Maud retorted. "Go now! Victory will be yours. I know it in my heart." She sighed. "If only I could go with you!"

Henry laughed. "There speaks the intrepid warrior who sailed to England thirteen years ago to reclaim my throne for me! A true descendent of our Viking forebears."

For an instant Maud froze. Sudden anger rose like a hot wave within her. "Your throne? *Your* throne?"

For a moment, uncertain, Henry paused. It was clear that her cocky whelp had taken for granted his right to be King of England, assuming she would step down as a matter of course, as she had with Normandy.

"Yes, my throne now," he challenged. "You know perfectly well that you had your chance—and lost it. Threw it away, by all accounts."

His words pierced her like a barbed arrow. How dare he remind her of that painful time in such a cavalier manner! Overwhelmed by a sense of failure, Maud became so choked with rage that her fingers curled into a fist. She half lifted her arm to strike him. Storm-gray eyes met storm-gray eyes in a blistering, headlong confrontation. The air throbbed between them like flashes of summer lightning. She saw Henry's jaw jut out in an arrogant, belligerent manner that was strongly reminiscent of . . . Stephen? Her father?

In an instant Maud realized that it was neither Stephen nor her father Henry reminded her of, but herself. On the heels of that realization came another: Henry was right. By her own doing, she had thrown away her chance to become queen. Stricken with an aching sense of loss, Maud recognized the bitter truth: She would never be Queen of England.

"Very well. Your throne—but only if you can make it yours," she managed.

"Fair enough! Fair enough, Madam." He gave her a long, hard look from beneath unruly brows. "I will go to England, then. All my affairs are in your hands, and I will hold you personally responsible if they do not prosper. In my absence—" He paused, studying her white face and flashing eyes. "In my absence—you will be regent of Normandy."

"Regent? Officially?" She was incredulous.

"Of course! Officially appointed. Writ plain for all to see. Signed with my seal. That is, if you feel up to dealing with such weighty matters."

"If I feel up to—oh Henry, Henry—"

At this unexpected acknowledgment of his trust, this attempt to give her back something of what she had lost, Maud struggled to suppress a rush of tears. It was not the same as being Queen of England, but still, a regent, acting in place of an absent monarch or lord, had all the authority and power of the ruler himself. It was a position of honor and responsibility. Maud remembered her father telling her how her grandmother, Duchess Matilda, had ruled as regent in Normandy while her husband was busy earning his title of Conqueror in England. The past had come full circle.

Despite the winter storms that made the channel almost impossible to cross, early in January of the new year, 1153, Henry made ready to sail for England. It would be the third attempt to claim his inheritance. This time, he announced to his wife and mother, this time, the final outcome would be decided.

Chapter Twenty-nine

Normandy, 1153

INSIDE THE DUCAL PALACE AT ROUEN, MAUD STOOD BY THE OPEN CASE-ment window of her solar; the late afternoon sun bathed the chamber in a golden glow. She closed her eyes for a moment with a silent prayer that when she opened them again a messenger from Henry would be riding into the courtyard. She had heard of his successful march through the Midlands where more and more men had joined him, and enemy castle after enemy castle had surrendered. But since his arrival at Wallingford in August there had been no word. It was now late September and she was sick with worry.

The door opened and one of Eleanor's ladies hurried in with a message that the Duchess sought her mother-in-law's advice: Little William, born six weeks ago, was fretting with colic.

"Tell the Duchess to rub a little warmed wine on his gums." Maud turned away from the window. "Find out if the wet nurse has been eating spiced foods. Give her peas, beans, and gruel to sweeten her milk."

The woman left. Maud walked over to the straight-backed wooden chair, sat down, then beckoned to the chamberlain who was waiting to go over the accounts with her.

"Why were three yards of blue ribbon ordered?" She tapped a finger against the item.

"That was for the Duchess, my lady," the chamberlain replied. "For the baby's christening gown."

Maud's heart warmed at the thought of her young grandson, whose father had not yet seen him. At this reminder of Henry, she immediately became anxious again. Had his forces done battle with Stephen? Was Henry wounded? Or Stephen? The thought of anything happening to either of them was unbearable.

She forced herself to finish the accounts, then dismissed the chamberlain with a word of praise for his accuracy. Next she arranged with the steward to judge a dispute between two landowners the following day, and discussed the birth of four new colts with the marshal. Last, she interviewed the master huntsman, who had this morning caught two young poachers in the forest outside the city walls.

"Give them a stern warning this time and let them go."

The huntsman's face puckered in disapproval. "The usual punishment is blinding them and cutting off their privates."

"I understand this goes against custom," she said, having learned the painful lesson that everything ran more smoothly if people flowed with you rather than against you. "But these lads are so young, not seasoned felons, after all." She gave him a winning smile. "I'm sure you can make them see the seriousness of their offense."

He nodded grudgingly and stumped out of the solar.

Maud leaned back in her chair. She had been regent of Normandy for eight months now and there was always more work to be done than she could easily do. Yet she found herself enjoying life as she had not done in years. Each day brought a new challenge to be met and overcome. She had surprised herself—and others as well, she thought wryly—with an unsuspected gift for organization, sound judgment, and a newfound ability to deal pleasantly but firmly with people under difficult circumstances. She no longer enforced her will as in the old days but won the cooperation of those who served her. Even her father and Aldyth, two of her more outspoken critics from the past, would be impressed with her growing gift for diplomacy.

She drowsed in the warm rays of the sun, reflecting on the beginning of her regency. Shortly after her son had sailed for England, Louis of France, as Henry had predicted, broke his truce with Normandy and marched across the border. Maud promptly raised an army and Louis, unprepared for such immediate retaliation, hastily retreated into France. With the exception of occasional skirmishes, there had been no further trouble from the French king.

Her second son, Geoffrey, although complaining bitterly about his elder brother, maintained—under her watchful eye—the peace in Anjou. All in all Maud was not dissatisfied with the way she had managed Henry's affairs and she hoped he would be pleased with her stewardship. If only she could have word that all was well with him.

The sound of horses in the courtyard startled her. Her heart quickening, she opened her eyes. Perhaps a message from Henry had come at last. She rose and ran to the window. Below she saw the tall figure of Brian FitzCount dismount from his horse. Holy Mother, if Brian had come himself, it must mean—terrified, she would not let herself complete the thought, but turned from the window, flew out the door of the solar, and sped down the winding staircase. Brian was just entering the palace when she reached him.

"Henry is not—Stephen is—nothing has happened . . . ?" Her eyes wide with fright, she clutched at Brian's arms.

"No, Henry is not, nor is Stephen. Calm your fears. When I left England the Duke was in a sour mood but perfectly well. Stephen, I suspect, is in a similar condition."

"God be thanked. I've been beside myself with worry. The last word I had was that he was preparing to do battle with Stephen's forces at Wallingford, and since then nothing."

She looked closely at Brian, whom she had last seen on the Wareham coast six years earlier. He had aged, she realized in dismay, his crisp black curls totally gray, his face gaunt and tired. The years of defending Wallingford had taken their toll. Years spent selflessly in her service.

"Dearest friend, how happy I am to see you." She threw her arms around him. When he smiled down at her she saw that the dark blue eyes, ironic but tranquil, had remained the same.

"There's trouble, isn't there?"

He nodded. Glancing around her, Maud saw that many of the castle mesnie had come into the palace yard and were watching them with anxious expressions.

"The Duke is well," she called out. "Do not worry."

She took Brian's arm and led him outside. They walked the length of the courtyard until they were out of earshot. "Has there been a battle? Has Henry lost Wallingford?"

"No, no. The problem is that there has been no action of any kind.

Henry and Stephen have had their troops lined up on either bank of the river for the past six weeks, ready to fight, but the barons of both sides, influenced by the Bishop of Winchester and the Archbishop of Canterbury, flatly refuse to engage in battle and between themselves have agreed to a truce."

Maud was aghast. "But that is treason! They must fight if their liege-lord demands it. Has Stephen's brother turned on him again?"

"Not this time. The Bishop of Winchester seems to have put aside ambition and honestly sues for peace now. He has proposed a very sound treaty, agreeable to everyone but Stephen and Henry, that would resolve the conflict once and for all: Stephen shall remain king until his death, to be succeeded by Henry, who, everyone now agrees, is the rightful heir."

Maud did not reply as she carefully examined the proposal in her mind. It sounded a very sensible solution, the Bishop of Winchester at his most statesman-like. At last there would be an end to the bloodshed of the last fifteen years. "Why will neither Stephen nor Henry sign?"

"Stephen, stubborn as only he can be when his mind is made up, insists that his flesh and blood must rule after him. Henry, hotheaded and spoiling for a fight, is equally set that the outcome shall be determined by battle. He has hurled angry words at Stephen across the river, calling him usurper and perjurer, taunting him that he would not trust his signature on a piece of parchment. So there you have it. Stalemate."

Maud felt her heart sink. She knew only too well what Henry could be like when thwarted. "Can no one reason with them?"

Brian gave her a weary smile. "The hunger for glory overrules reason, I fear. Henry wants the glory of victory; Stephen wants the glory of founding a dynasty—as a justification for his actions."

"Of course," Maud said slowly. "Such a treaty would disinherit Eustace. Now I understand. What a coil. Can nothing be done?"

"That is why I have come. To see what you might do to break the deadlock." He paused. "You're still so lovely, Maud, almost unchanged since I saw you six years ago."

The Vespers bell rang and they walked through the gate of the courtyard toward the cathedral.

"What can I do?" How could she be expected to resolve the conflict between Stephen and Henry, between her son and his father. "Did Henry send you to me?"

"No. I have left England and its troubles. I'm on my way to the

Holy Land to become a monk or a Templar. I can do no more for your cause, Maud, and in these last remaining years I would follow my own bent. I had hoped for your blessing."

Concealing her shock and dismay, Maud gave him the only possible reply. "Indeed you have it, my friend."

Maud could not imagine her life without Brian FitzCount. Strong and steadfast, duty had been Brian's watchword, as it had been Robert's. But never Stephen's. Nor hers, she realized in stunned surprise. Both ambitious, she and Stephen had attempted to take what they wanted, never really counting the cost. With a start of recognition she saw that they were more alike than she had ever dreamed.

After Vespers, Maud and Brian went into supper at the great hall. "Can't I persuade you to stay with me for a while?" she asked him.

He shook his head. "You no longer need me, Maud. You have found your own voice at last."

"I'm not sure I understand."

"It's hardly a secret that Normandy fares very well these days. Word has trickled back to England that the duchy is in such capable hands, even Louis of France will think twice before crossing the Normandy borders. From the moment I landed at Barfleur yesterday, all the way to Rouen, wherever I stopped I heard your praises sung: The Regent dispenses fair justice, the Regent is wise and strong, and cannot be fooled. She is her father all over again—but with a compassionate heart."

"Brian," she whispered, as a surge of joy swept through her, "do they really say that? Truly?"

"And more besides." He gave her an affectionate smile. "If only you had behaved in the past as you do now, this day would you wear England's crown."

Cautiously, Maud drew aside the curtain of memory, long closed, to face the bitter anguish of those tumultuous seven months when the crown had been within her grasp. What demons had tormented her then, what devils had driven her to behave in so arrogant, ill-tempered, rash, and vengeful a fashion? It seemed incomprehensible now.

"I know," she agreed in a calm voice. "But all that was a long time ago. My time has come and gone and I have accepted this. Now it is Henry's turn." She looked anxiously at Brian as a new thought struck her. "But I fear his stubborn refusal to sign this peace treaty may turn men against him as they turned against me. He must not make the same mistakes."

"My thoughts exactly. That is why I came."

"But how can I stop him?"

"God will show you the way."

Maud made no reply. People were apt to offer that, she thought sourly, when they could think of nothing better to say.

The next morning Brian left Rouen to join a party from Brittany that was traveling to Jerusalem. He took her in his arms before mounting his horse, and gave her a warm hug.

"We've come a long way together and I'll miss you, Maud," he said, his eyes misting as he released her.

"And I you, dear friend," she said, clinging to his tall frame, unwilling to let him go out of her life. "Do you have no last word of advice before you go? No direction that I can follow?"

Brian mounted his horse. "It's my opinion that Henry will not be convinced to alter his course of action. Not even by you." He paused as he wheeled his horse around. "You would do better to appeal to Stephen," he added, almost as an afterthought.

"Stephen?" she asked in astonishment. "How would I appeal to Stephen?"

He smiled, a ghost of a twinkle in his eyes. "It will come to you, I doubt not. Goodbye, dearest Maud."

When he had ridden out of the courtyard, Maud climbed up to the battlements to watch him go, feeling she had lost her last close friend. He dwindled to a tiny speck on the horizon, but still she did not move, her hands grasping the stone embrasure. Why did Brian think she could persuade Stephen to sign the treaty?

Maud began to pace the battlements, then, suddenly, she stopped short. A wave of heat washed through her body, her heart began to pound, and she felt giddy. She let the idea take hold of her, looking at it, considering all the implications. Such a drastic step involved great risk, but it was the only solution that offered itself, and she must act without delay if she were to act at all.

Normandy could safely be left in Eleanor's hands for the short time she would be gone. As soon as possible she would leave for England.

Chapter Thirty

Wallingford, 1153

Henry of Anjou stood on the slippery bank of the river, oblivious to the October rain that had been falling for three days now. Across the Thames he could see Stephen's azure pavilion, the guards walking to and fro, their shoulders hunched against the rain.

Behind him Henry could hear the murmur of voices: the Bishop of Hereford and the Earl of Leicester, who had recently defected from Stephen to join his cause, scheming to get him to sign that damned treaty. The treaty of Winchester everyone was calling it, after the sly serpent, Bishop Henry of Winchester. His jaw jutted out and he gritted his teeth. Well, let them rack their heads and scheme away. He had no intention of signing any treaty. He had come to England to do battle, by God, and battle he would do until the usurper was defeated.

Henry's eyes smoldered. Was the Bishop of Winchester foolish enough to imagine that the volatile Eustace would honor any treaty that cut him out of the succession? His great-grandfather, the mighty William, had not relied on treaties but conquest. His grandfather, Henry, had done away with his enemies: no agreements to be broken, no loose ends left dangling that might rise up in the future and threaten all that had been won. Suddenly his eyes narrowed.

Across the river Stephen appeared out of the mist, accompanied by his brother and William of Ypres. Imposing in a purple mantle, Stephen walked along the riverbank, deep in conversation with the Bishop of Winchester. The Thames narrowed at this juncture and barely sixty yards separated Henry from the King. On impulse he bent to pick up a stone that lay in the mud.

"Is it too wet for you to fight, Sire?" he called out, slicing the stone through the air. As he had intended, the small rock landed well short of Stephen.

Stephen turned, drawing his sword with such speed Henry blinked in surprise. Incredibly fast for a man his age, Henry thought, impressed despite himself. Here was a worthy opponent indeed. Several guards ran to Stephen's side; one raised his spear and took aim. Henry held his ground. For a wild moment he hoped the guard would actually throw the spear; at least that would be an excuse to attack Stephen's forces. His pulse quickened at the thought of plunging into action. But the King restrained the guard's raised arm as he peered through the veil of rain trying to see from where the voice and stone had come. Finally he spotted Henry across the bank and after a moment's hesitation sheathed his sword.

"It's never too wet for me to fight," he called back. "Left to myself I would have done battle long since, and this day would you be resting in my dungeons. But my barons will have peace at any cost."

"Then let us meet in single combat and decide the issue once and for all," Henry shouted.

Stephen pushed back the hood of his cloak. Drops of rain fell onto his beard. "Do you tire of life so soon? I do not challenge untried youths to single combat."

Henry was filled with rage as he heard the mocking laughter of the Flemish captain. He was about to make a hot retort when the Earl of Leicester grabbed him firmly by the arm and steered him down the bank.

"He's baiting you, my lord, come away. Please be more circumspect in future—that guard might have thrown his spear."

"Would that he had. We might have seen some fighting then," Henry snarled. "My destiny is not to die on a muddy riverbank, I assure you."

He stomped into his tent. By God's splendor, how ironic that the only person who felt as he did, who wanted the matter settled by combat rather than treaty, was his greatest enemy.

. . .

Maud landed at Wareham in mid-October accompanied by two knights from Rouen. A party of three was not likely to call attention to itself, and these were men she knew she could trust. After resting the night in an inn, she spent the following day buying three mounts for herself and her companions. To further conceal her identity she intended to ride to Wallingford disguised as a merchant's wife from Normandy traveling to London. Until the conflict between Henry and Stephen was resolved, as far as she was concerned there was still a civil war going on. Should she be stopped she did not want Stephen's forces to discover who she was or where her destination lay.

The next morning, clad in sober gray, Maud began the two day journey to Wallingford. The closer she came to her destination, the more fearful she became of risks that might present themselves. A member of Stephen's forces might find her face familiar and decide to hold her for ransom. She would be a rich prize for anyone. Then there was always the possibility of someone from the stronghold of Wallingford itself recognizing her and informing Henry, who, furious at what he would consider her meddling, was certain to put a stop to her plans. At all costs her son must not find out she was in England. Not now, not ever, if she could prevent it.

Doubts assailed her, and by the following day she was tempted to turn back to the coast. Then, across the wooded downs, she caught a glimpse of the gray walls of Reading Abbey where her father lay buried. The thought of King Henry gave her the strength to go on and accomplish her mission.

It was mid-afternoon when the road suddenly turned and Maud faced a river, swollen from the rains, spanned by a narrow wooden bridge. In the distance she could see the misty towers of Wallingford. A light drizzle began to fall.

"Let us cross the river before the rain becomes heavier, my lady," one of the knights said with an anxious look at the turbulent water. "If the rains continue the water could sweep away the bridge."

"I don't intend to cross the river," Maud said, knowing the time had come to swear the knights to secrecy, trusting them not to betray her destination.

The two knights exchanged startled glances. "But the King holds the right bank and Duke Henry the left bank. In order to get to the left side we must cross the river."

"We remain on the right bank," she said, explaining what she intended to do and making the knights swear never to reveal it.

Ignoring their dumbfounded expressions, Maud turned her palfrey and started down the right bank of the river toward Stephen's camp.

Stephen was dozing inside his pavilion when he became aware of raised voices outside. He had returned from noon Mass and been seized with an attack of queasiness accompanied by the usual feeling of weakness. Such attacks were becoming more frequent of late.

"In God's name, Walter," he finally called to his squire, "what is all that noise about?"

The squire opened the tent flap that served as a door. "Sorry to disturb you, Sire, but there is a woman here who insists on seeing you. We have been trying to escort her out of the camp but she refuses to go."

Stephen sat up with a yawn, relieved that the discomfort had begun to ease off. "Woman? What woman? A camp follower?"

"Oh no, Sire, a very respectable lady, but she won't give her name."

"Is she alone?"

"Yes, Sire."

Intrigued, Stephen rose to his feet. "Show her in, show her in. She sounds harmless enough." He winked at Walter. "After all, if a lady is that eager to see me, how can I disappoint her?"

The squire grinned and left. Stephen looked at the jumble of hauberks, clothes, and weapons scattered across the tent, wondering if the place was fit to receive a female visitor. He set two stools near the charcoal brazier and, finding two wooden cups on the floor, put them on a small oak chest beside a flagon of wine.

Presentable enough, he decided with another yawn, trying to fight off the enervating weakness that was still with him. As he had told his physicians, except for the occasional pain, he did not feel ill so much as apathetic. The forced inactivity of the last two months depressed him; the constant pressure of his brother and barons urging him to sign Bishop Henry's damned treaty infuriated him. In fact, there was nothing wrong with him, he decided, that would not immediately be cured by a resounding battle with Henry of Anjou's forces.

He hoped the meeting with this unknown woman would take his mind off the deadlock with his magnates and the ever-present, gnawing worry about Eustace.

After hearing the details of the treaty that would disinherit him, his son had flown into a violent rage despite Stephen's assurances that he would never sign such a document. He had then stormed out of the camp cursing both his father and his uncle of Winchester, laid waste the estates that supported Henry of Anjou, then senselessly attacked the monastery holdings of Bury St. Edmunds. The alarmed monks had appealed to Stephen for aid, and yesterday he had sent a troop of soldiers to bring back Eustace.

Since then he had received no word. Stephen had worn his knees raw in daily prayer, beseeching Our Lord for a miracle to occur that would transform his evil-tempered son into a man of wisdom and calm disposition. With a sigh he walked toward the door of the pavilion.

As Maud approached the azure pavilion she remembered so well from the sieges at Arundel and Oxford, she was seized by panic. Certain she could not now go through with her plan, she turned to the squire and told him she had changed her mind.

The tent door opened and Stephen, his green eyes disbelieving in a face suddenly drained of color, stood transfixed in the entrance. Maud's breath caught in her throat, her tongue clove to the roof of her mouth, and her heart pounded so heavily she thought it would burst. For what seemed like a small eternity they stared at each other. Stephen recovered first.

"This woman is known to me," he said in a hoarse voice. Then, stepping forward, he grasped Maud firmly by the arm, led her into the tent, and shut the door behind them.

Inside, Stephen indicated one of the stools, then poured wine into two cups, spilling almost half the contents of the flagon. Maud threw back the hood of her cloak, and sat down, her trembling fingers tightly laced together. During the long hours she had spent agonizing over what she would say, she had not imagined that the impact of seeing him would be so overwhelming. It was virtually impossible to take her eyes off him. Despite the fact that he was over fifty years of age, the tall lean body clad in a rumpled blue tunic appeared unchanged. Although the golden-brown hair and beard were heavily speckled with silver, this only lent an air of majesty to his

face, a face furrowed by lines of strain but still arresting, still
comely. She felt the familiar surge of blood race through her
veins, as her body, roused from a long sleep, began to stir with
new life.

What did Stephen see, Maud wondered, fearful of what she might
find in his gaze. After all, she was only a few years his junior. But
the familiar eyes with their golden specks mirrored only her own
admiration, her own realization that neither time nor war, betrayal
nor revenge, had managed to sever the ties between them.

She took a deep breath and collected herself. "Let me explain why
I am here," she began.

At her words a mask shuttered his face and the affinity in his eyes
abruptly cooled. "I know well enough why you are here," he said
with an impatient gesture. "You hope to persuade me to sign my
brother's treaty. Did Duke Henry send you? An odd choice of emissary, I would have thought."

"Henry does not even know I'm in England, much less in your
camp. I left Normandy in great haste and secrecy."

Stephen gave an incredulous laugh. "If not Henry, then Brian
FitzCount sent you. I heard that Brian had left Wallingford. Did he
persuade you to this fruitless errand?"

"He didn't have to persuade me. Once I heard the terms of the
treaty, and that neither you nor Henry would sign it, I knew something had to be done."

Stephen took a swallow of wine. "And you thought me the easier
mark than your flint-hearted son?"

Maud flushed, for he was not far off the truth. "It's a sound treaty
and would put an end to this terrible conflict."

Stephen's whole body grew rigid. "Naturally you would approve
since your son inherits and mine does not."

"You would remain king for the rest of your life with no loss of
honor. The barons want peace, Stephen, they recognize that Henry
is the future. Come, be reasonable."

"What the barons want is no longer important to me," he countered in a bitter voice. "And the rest of my life is not so long as it
once was." He grimaced, as if in pain, and put a hand to his side.

"What does that mean?" she asked, hearing the tremor in her
voice. "Are you unwell?"

"Something I ate. Naught to worry about," he said, brushing off
her concern. "What I meant was that the years of conflict have taken
their toll. I'm sick unto death of the whole sorry business."

"And I. The war has afflicted us all. It killed Robert."

Stephen sighed. "Yes, I was sorry to hear that. There was a time when I claimed no better friend than Robert of Gloucester." His voice softened as he reached down and lifted her chin. "The years have dealt gently with you, Cousin. You are as lovely in maturity as you were in youth. How my eyes have longed for the sight of you all these years. My blood warms just being in your presence." He abruptly removed his hand from her chin. "But this in no way disposes me to sign a treaty that disinherits my son. My mind is made up."

Maud heard the note of finality in his voice. She wondered if she should let the matter rest there; admit she had failed and return to Normandy. The alternative carried tremendous risk: She had trusted Stephen before and he had betrayed her. Why should she imagine he had changed? Reason told her to leave; her heart dictated otherwise.

"There is something I have not told you," she said in a choked voice.

"If it concerns the treaty—"

"Please, hear me out," she interjected.

"Nothing is to be gained by further argument. Never will I disavow my own son."

"You do not have to," she said in a strangled whisper.

With a perplexed look he sat down on the stool opposite her. "How is that possible?"

Abruptly Maud rose to her feet and began to pace the pavilion, agitatedly clasping and unclasping her hands.

"Against all reason, all past experience, I've decided to trust you, for what I'm about to confide can be used to destroy me and everything I've worked for," she began, then stopped.

"Don't trust me, for I promise nothing." His eyes turned a glittering green. "Be warned that if what you tell me aids my cause I will not hesitate to use it. It would hurt me to inflict more pain upon you, but still I would use it." He signed himself. "May God forgive me but that is my nature."

"Yes," she said slowly, recognizing the truth and accepting it. "I know that now." She resumed her seat on the stool. "I don't ask for promises, Stephen, just understanding."

"What is of so powerful a nature that you fear it to be a weapon in my hands?"

Her eyes met his and held them. "You want your son to inherit the throne. Sign the treaty and your son will rule after you, far better than you have done, yes, even better than I could have done had I . . . had I been given the chance. Your son, Stephen—and mine."

His puzzled frown gradually gave way to a look of incredulity as comprehension dawned. "You suggest that Henry is *my* son?" he gasped. "No, it's not possible. You say this merely as a ploy to force me to sign the treaty that will put Henry on the throne." His eyes blazed with hostility. "I would not have believed you capable of such wanton trickery!"

Stephen rose up so abruptly that his stool fell over. "If this outrageous tale were true you would have spoken. How could you keep such a secret from me? No, no, it is too much to expect me to swallow such a blatant falsehood."

Maud also rose, her heart pounding. She had tried to predict Stephen's reaction to her news, never imagining that he would not believe her. What could she say to convince him?

"Listen to me," she said, seizing his hands in hers. "Why would I lie? Think what you can do with such scandalous knowledge: Tell everyone that I am an adulteress, that Henry Plantagenet is not Geoffrey of Anjou's son but a bastard. A bastard cannot inherit. You could spread enough filth to cause the magnates to doubt and question my son's paternity."

"Who would believe me?" He twisted his hands free.

"Some might remember how hurriedly I left England, with no explanation, and without the council's permission, to return to a husband I had said I would never live with again. Others might recall that my son was born a month early yet thrived."

"Jesu! I remember that," Stephen said in a strangled voice. "It was rumored that he was large for such an early birth, and I wondered at the time, was it possible that he was mine—but it was said that he was the image of Geoffrey, so I put it from my mind."

"The image of—who told you that?" she asked.

"Let me see—" Stephen began to walk backwards and forwards, running his hands through his hair. "It was—King Henry. Yes, I'm sure of it."

"My father was an ally in this matter," Maud said. "I never told him I carried your child, but I'm sure he knew. He would have said anything to put you off the scent."

Stephen's shocked eyes intently searched her face, trying to discern the truth. "I still can't believe you could have been so deceitful."

"You accuse *me* of deceit? Have you not just warned me that I cannot trust you? That you would use, for your own ends, whatever I tell you? Can you swear to me, here and now, that had I told you the truth you would not have used it to speed your path to the throne? With such a weapon you would hardly have needed perjury, would you?"

A dark red flush spread over Stephen's face and he lowered his eyes. "How can I be certain now what I would have done then? But no, I cannot swear to you." He took a deep breath. "How could Geoffrey of Anjou allow another man's son to be his heir? Surely a man of his pride would have condemned you the length and breadth of Europe."

Maud kept her voice steady though the blood was drumming in her head. "If ambition and pride war with one another, who can say which will be victorious? Geoffrey may have suspected, but, greedy for Normandy and England, he would never have proclaimed himself a cuckold. We will never know what Geoffrey believed, but while he lived he was a true father to Henry."

Dazed now, Stephen sank back down onto his stool. "I'm unable to accept this," he said brokenly. "The Duke of Normandy—my sworn enemy—is really my son? You, whom I loved above all others, behaving with such guile and deceit? My whole world has tumbled apart." He covered his face with his hands.

With a compassionate sigh Maud sat down. "Can we not have done with mutual recriminations? I would never have told you if there weren't so much at stake. We are both equally culpable, Stephen, for all that has happened. Can we not forgive each other and make a new start?"

He dropped his hands from his face and she could see the bitterness reflected in his eyes. "So now you think you have the means to persuade me to sign the treaty. It is easy for you to talk of forgiveness and a new start, but I swore an oath to Matilda that I would not rest until Eustace's accession was assured. Do I betray my sworn word yet again?"

For a moment Maud let the silence lengthen between them. "We have much to atone for, Stephen. Our ambition, my desire for vengeance—between us we have almost destroyed England. I prayed that if you knew the truth you would help end the conflict and bring about peace. You know Henry will make a far better king than Eustace."

Stephen rose again and, opening the tent a crack, gazed outside.

"Matilda and I were never friends but her character was not unknown to me," Maud continued. "If she knew that your brother's proposed treaty would lead to peace and restore England to what it was in my father's day, how would she counsel you?"

He turned to her. "As usual you are relentless."

Maud could see he was making an effort at banter, but from his drawn face, the haunted look in his eyes, it was evident that he was besieged by a terrible inner conflict.

She held her breath while the battle raged, then his shoulders sagged, his face crumpled, and tears glazed his eyes. Maud rose, held out her arms and he walked into them, dissolving the last barrier between them. He clutched her so tightly she could hardly draw breath; his body trembled violently in her embrace and she realized that he was sobbing.

At last Stephen drew back, took a last shuddering breath, and wiped his eyes with the corner of his sleeve. "So that stubborn, hotheaded young rogue is my son," he said. "Now that I look back, the sequence of events becomes much clearer. To think of you living alone with that fearful secret all these years." He shook his head in wonder.

"Well, Aldyth knew, and my father. Brian must have suspected." She told him what Brian had said to her and he smiled.

"Yes, Brian, bless him, was always the wisest among us. I wish him well in the Holy Land."

He bent and gently kissed her lips, the kiss growing longer and deeper. As always Maud felt an instant response, yet there was a difference. The warm sweetness between them was still there, and the aching tenderness, but the hot obsessive urgency, the agony of being consumed by a passion so intense it must be fulfilled regardless of the cost, no longer held them in thrall. Stephen lifted his head and smiled down into her eyes. A tide of love flowed through Maud, giving her a new, wondrous sense of completion.

"Will you return to Normandy now?" he asked.

"At once. Neither Henry nor anyone else must know I have been here, so I dare not linger. When I left Rouen I let it be thought I was going to Anjou."

Stephen released her and, walking over to the oak table, poured himself another cup of wine. "As soon as you are well on the road, the Duke of Normandy will be sent an unexpected message." He thought for a moment. "King Stephen wishes to meet with the Bishop of Winchester, the Archbishop of Canterbury, and the Duke of Normandy. He agrees to sign the treaty and hopes that Henry of Anjou will do the same."

Tears of joy coursed down Maud's cheeks. "Thank you," she whispered, "thank you, thank you, my dearest love." A sudden thought chilled her. "Eustace? What will you do about him?"

A shadow passed across Stephen's face and he sighed. "At the moment I don't know, but he is my cross to bear and I will deal with him."

From a nearby church came the sound of the Vespers bell tolling the hour of service.

"Do you attend Vespers, Sire?" The squire's voice came from outside the pavilion.

"Do you go," Maud said. "While everyone attends the service I will slip away. My two knights await outside the camp and they will grow anxious if I don't return."

Stephen embraced her for the last time, then walked her to the door.

"In all probability we will never see each other again," he stated.

"No," she agreed. "But our son will sit on England's throne. We must be content with that."

"Our son," he repeated, as if testing the words upon his lips. "Our son."

Maud noted that the lines of strain in his face had eased and he looked much more tranquil. Having come to terms with her, he had also come to terms with himself. For both of them it was a transcendent moment of profound peace.

Fearful she would not have the strength to leave, Maud exchanged with him a silent look of love, pulled up the hood of her cloak, then hurried from the pavilion.

Before a bend in the road took her out of sight of the camp, she turned to see Stephen still standing motionless in the doorway of his pavilion. The path turned and he was gone from view. The past had finally been laid to rest, she thought, tears running down her cheeks. Only the future remained.

Epilogue

England, 1154

On THE NINETEENTH DAY OF DECEMBER, 1154, MAUD, SUMPTUOUSLY dressed in cloth-of-gold and purple silk, her neck, wrists, and fingers sparkling with jewels, stood in a place of honor at Westminster Abbey. A thousand white tapers cast their flickering light across the vaulted roof and leaded windows, over the choir of monks gathered near the high altar. As the Archbishop of Canterbury intoned the solemn Latin words that consecrated a king, Maud found her thoughts turning to the momentous events that had occurred over the last fourteen months.

On the heels of her departure for Normandy, Prince Eustace had suffered a sudden and timely death from natural causes that had been attributed to divine intervention. After the treaty had been signed, Stephen, to Maud's joy, had suggested that Henry spend some time in England learning the workings of his administration so that when the time came there would be a smooth transition from one reign to another. Already there was a vast improvement of conditions in England.

For Maud, of course, the most significant event had been the death of her beloved Stephen, just two months ago in October. Despite his failings as a king, he had managed to retain the affection of his subjects, many of whom mourned his passing even as they looked forward to the new reign. Although Maud knew she would never cease to miss him, her loss was tempered by the knowledge that their love had created a new beginning: Henry.

That thought reminded her why she was here. Maud looked around the abbey, smiled affectionately at Robert of Gloucester's two oldest sons, her nephews, William and Roger. There were the de Beaumont twins, nodding their heads to her in a friendly manner.

The Earl of Leicester had already been appointed co-justiciar of Henry's administration, while the Count of Muelan remained in Normandy.

Maud's eyes rested uneasily on her cousin Henry, Bishop of Winchester, elegant as always in his ceremonial robes, a gold-encrusted miter atop his head, his gold crosier sparkling with jewels. Maud had been told that he had given Stephen the last rites and heard his final confession. Their eyes met warily across the abbey, each taking the other's measure. Let the past rest, Maud thought as she gave him a tentative smile which was instantly returned. There was no mistaking now the warmth in those usually cool green eyes, eyes which achingly brought Stephen to mind. Expecting an enemy she had found a friend.

Maud's gaze passed slowly across the assembled throng, she found herself searching for those who were no longer here, those whose presence should have graced this auspicious day.

Her devoted, selfless Robert; Geoffrey of Anjou, who had fought staunchly in Normandy for Henry's inheritance; and her loyal Uncle David of Scotland, dead these past twelve months. Maud spared a thought for Alix, also deceased; she, too, had played her part in bringing about this momentous occasion.

Her beloved Aldyth, how happy she would have been this day, and her dearest friend of all, the ever-steadfast Brian FitzCount, somewhere in the Holy Land now.

Most of all, apart from Stephen, her father should have been here. He was the forerunner, the first to break with precedent, impose his will on a resisting nobility, to name a daughter heir to the throne.

Her eyes settled on her son, whose square, substantial figure was almost dwarfed in the gold-embroidered coronation robes. Theobald of Bec had finally come to the end of the consecration. After a brief silence, the Archbishop of York stepped forward carrying a white silk cushion. On it rested the golden crown of England, the very same crown that Maud had first held in her hands when she was a child.

Archbishop Theobald lifted the gleaming circlet and walked slowly toward Henry.

Stephen, Maud cried silently, oh my beloved, if only you could stand beside me now. How proud would you be of our son.

At the very instant that the Archbishop reverently placed the crown of England on Henry's head, her son's eyes suddenly swiveled toward her with fierce intent. As his gaze met hers, Maud realized that he was intimately sharing the pomp and glory and majesty directly with her, including her in this moment of their joint triumph. For the space of a heartbeat, Maud stood with him, the crown upon her head.

Then a great cry rose up from within the abbey, to be echoed seconds later by the hordes of folk outside:

"Long live Henry, King of England."

Author's Postscript

FOR THE REMAINING THIRTEEN YEARS OF HER LIFE, MAUD LIVED QUIETLY outside Rouen. While Henry was away consolidating his empire—which stretched from the border of Scotland to the Pyrenees—Maud was virtually Regent of Normandy. Charters were issued in both her and Henry's names, and he relied on her to manage his affairs in his absence.

In the last year of her life, as was not uncommon with great ladies of her time, Maud took the vows of a nun at the abbey of Fontrevaud. Before her death on September 9, 1167, she had lived to see her eight grandchildren, two of whom, Richard the Lionheart and John, would become kings of England. One granddaughter became queen of Sicily, another queen of Castile. Her descendants ruled England until the start of the Tudor dynasty at the end of the fifteenth century. It was not until five hundred and eighty-two years after the death of Henry I that a woman, Mary Tudor, ruled as Queen of England.

While I traveled to Normandy, Angers, Le Mans, and England to research this novel, most of the work was done through the Research Library of UCLA. Of the many books consulted, I would gratefully

like to acknowledge the following historical works as having particularly stimulated my imagination and upon which I relied most heavily. First and foremost is *Empress Matilda*, by Nesta Paine
(Weidenfeld & Nicolson, London, 1978), an excellent and sympathetic biography of Maud. (The chroniclers of the time, as well as
some modern historians, tend to paint a rather unsympathetic por-
trait of her.)

Then there are *Daily Living in the Twelfth Century*, by Urban
Tigner Holmes, Jr. (University of Wisconsin Press, 1952); *England
Under the Angevin Kings*, Vol. I, by Kate Norgate (Macmillan, London, 1887); *Gesta Stephani*, editor and translator K.R. Potter (Nelson
Medieval Texts, London, 1955); *Life in a Medieval City*, by Joseph
and Francis Gies (Thomas Y. Crowell, Apollo Edition, New York,
1973); *Life in a Medieval Castle*, by Joseph and Francis Gies (Harper
& Row, New York, 1974); *The Saxon and Norman Kings*, by Christopher Brooke (B.T. Batsford, Ltd., Great Britain, 1963); and *Sex in
History*, by Gordon Rattray Taylor (Vanguard Press, New York,
1954).

For those who wish to know more about this period of the twelfth
century, there are numerous other books available.